PENGUIN CLASSICS

THE PENGUIN BOOK OF KOREAN SHORT STORIES

Bruce Fulton is Associate Professor and Young-Bin Min Chair in Korean Literature and Literary Translation at the University of British Columbia. With Ju-Chan Fulton he has translated many major works of Korean literature over the past forty years.

THE
PENGUIN BOOK
of

KOREAN SHORT STORIES

Edited and with Notes by
BRUCE FULTON

———

Introduced by
KWON YOUNGMIN

PENGUIN CLASSICS
an imprint of
PENGUIN BOOKS

PENGUIN CLASSICS

UK | USA | Canada | Ireland | Australia
India | New Zealand | South Africa

Penguin Classics is part of the Penguin Random House group of companies
whose addresses can be found at global.penguinrandomhouse.com.

First published 2023
This edition published 2024
002

Editorial material copyright © Bruce Fulton, 2023
Introduction copyright © Kwon Youngmin, 2023
pp. 453–7 constitute an extension of this copyright page

Typeset by Jouve (UK), Milton Keynes
Printed and bound in Great Britain by Clays Ltd, Elcograf S.p.A.

The authorized representative in the EEA is Penguin Random House Ireland,
Morrison Chambers, 32 Nassau Street, Dublin D02 YH68

A CIP catalogue record for this book is available from the British Library

ISBN: 978–0–241–44851–9

www.greenpenguin.co.uk

Contents

Chronology   ix

Introduction by Kwon Youngmin   xi

Editorial Note by Bruce Fulton   xxix

Further Reading   xxxiii

Note on Korean Name Order and Pronunciation   xxxvii

TRADITION

YI HYOSŎK
  When the Buckwheat Blooms   3
  Translated by Kim Chong-un and Bruce Fulton

CH'AE MANSHIK
  A Man Called Hŭngbo   13
  Translated by Ross King and Bruce and Ju-Chan Fulton

CHU YOSŎP
  Mama and the Boarder   40
  Translated by Kim Chong-un and Bruce Fulton

YI MUNYŎL
  The Old Hatter   59
  Translated by Suh Ji-moon

KIM TAEYONG
  Pig on Grass   80
  Translated by Bruce and Ju-Chan Fulton

Contents

WOMEN AND MEN

PAK T'AEWŎN
A Day in the Life of Kubo the Novelist   95
Translated by Sunyoung Park in collaboration
with Jefferson J. A. Gatrall and Kevin O'Rourke

KIM YUJŎNG
Spicebush Blossoms   137
Translated by Bruce and Ju-Chan Fulton

CH'OE YUN
The Last of Hanak'o   143
Translated by Bruce and Ju-Chan Fulton

HONG SŎKCHUNG
A chapter from *Hwang Chini*   166
Translated by Bruce and Ju-Chan Fulton

CH'ŎN UNYŎNG
Needlework   172
Translated by Na-Young Bae and Bruce Fulton

PEACE AND WAR

HWANG SUNWŎN
Time for You and Me   191
Translated by Bruce and Ju-Chan Fulton

PAK WANSŎ
Winter Outing   201
Translated by Marshall R. Pihl

CHO CHŎNGNAE
Land of Exile   215
Translated by Marshall R. Pihl

Contents

HELL CHOSŎN

YI SANG
Wings   263
Translated by Kevin O'Rourke

KIM SŬNGOK
Seoul: Winter 1964   281
Translated by Marshall R. Pihl

O CHŎNGHŬI
Wayfarer   299
Translated by Bruce and Ju-Chan Fulton

KYUNG-SOOK SHIN
House on the Prairie   315
Translated by Bruce and Ju-Chan Fulton

P'YŎN HYEYŎNG
The First Anniversary   321
*Translated by Cindy Chen with Bruce and
Ju-Chan Fulton*

CHOI SUCHOL
River Dark   337
Translated by Bruce and Ju-Chan Fulton

INTO THE NEW WORLD

CH'OE INHO
The Poplar Tree   345
Translated by Bruce and Ju-Chan Fulton

HWANG CHŎNGŬN
The Bone Thief   351
Translated by Bruce and Ju-Chan Fulton

Contents

JUNG YOUNG MOON
    Home on the Range   366
    Translated by Bruce and Ju-Chan Fulton

KIM CHUNGHYŎK
    The Glass Shield   385
    Translated by Kevin O'Rourke

HAN YUJOO
    Black-and-White Photographer   406
    Translated by Janet Hong

KIM AERAN
    The Future of Silence   426
    Translated by Bruce and Ju-Chan Fulton

Glossary   441

Notes   443

Map of the Korean Peninsula   451

Permissions   453

Chronology

1876	Treaty of Kanghwa opens the Chosŏn Kingdom, as Korea was then called, to foreign trade.
1905	Protectorate Treaty gives the Japanese Foreign Office control over Korea's foreign relations.
1910	Korea is annexed by imperial Japan.
1917	Serialization of Yi Kwangsu's *Heartlessness* (*Mujŏng*), regarded by many as the first modern Korean novel.
1919	March 1 Independence Movement, calling for Korea's liberation from Japan, is launched. Its violent suppression leaves tens of thousands dead or wounded.
1926	Publication of Hyŏn Chin'gŏn's *The Faces of Korea* (*Chosŏn ŭi ŏlgul*; story collection).
1933	Proposition for the Unification of Hangŭl Orthography, which standardized the Korean alphabet.
1937	Outbreak of the Sino-Japanese War.
1939–1945	The 'Dark Years' (*amhŭkki*) of Japanese mobilization of Korea for wartime exigencies.
1945	Liberation from Japanese rule.
1948	Founding of the Republic of Korea (ROK; South Korea) and the Democratic People's Republic of Korea (DPRK; North Korea).
1950	25 June: North Korea launches an attack across the 38th parallel, which divides north and south, initiating the Korean War. During the war, the North is supported by the Soviet Union and China, while South Korea is supported by the United Nations, principally the USA. Over the course of three years, the war claims around 3 million lives.
1953	27 July: An armistice is signed, ending the Korean War (though in the absence of a formal peace treaty the two Koreas remain, technically, in a state of war).

Chronology

1960	19 April student revolution forces Syngman Rhee, first president of the ROK, to resign.
1961	Military coup places Park Chung Hee in power in the ROK.
1972	Yushin Constitution enables Park Chung Hee to consolidate power.
1978	Publication of Cho Se-hŭi's *The Dwarf* (*Nanjangi ka ssoaollin chagŭn kong*; a linked-story novel).
1979	Assassination of President Park Chung Hee and seizure of power by Chun Doo Hwan.
1980	18 May Kwangju Democratic Uprising in the ROK.
1987	Resignation of President Chun Doo Hwan and democratization of the ROK political process.
1988	Seoul Olympics.
1994–1998	Widespread famine in the DPRK.
1997–2001	International Monetary Fund-related economic crisis in the ROK.
2021	ROK announces plans to recognize domestic partnerships between opposite-sex couples, but not same-sex couples.

Introduction

I was born and raised in Poryŏng, South Ch'ungch'ŏng Province, at that time a village of fewer than 200 households. My birth took place on Ch'usŏk, the day of the Harvest Moon Festival, 15 August by the lunar calendar, and I arrived around the time the full moon rose, after a morning of ancestral offerings of newly harvested crops and a day of fun activities.

Middle school was the happiest time of my childhood. Despite the two-hour walk to school each way, I was proud to wear my school uniform, the hat at a rakish angle. My favourite subjects were history and Korean, which included literature, and I still remember our Korean teacher reading, a section at a time, 'Mama and the Boarder', the third story in this anthology. I, in turn, used to read it to my elder sister, who wasn't able to attend middle school. Best of all, the nearby American army base had given our school library one thousand books. This was a blessing because in the early 1960s, so soon after the Korean War, it was difficult to buy books of any kind, even our middle-school textbooks. And so I took out one or two books a day. I was obsessed with reading, and by the time I finished school I had read almost all the books in the library. From the beginning I was thrilled by fiction, to the extent that my goal in life changed from ship's captain to author. I never achieved that precious dream, which had taken form as I read in the light of the oil lantern, losing all track of time, but I never abandoned it either.

It was also in middle school that I began to understand the importance of fiction as a form of prose literature. Until then, when my friends and I talked about fiction, we spoke of it as something nonsensical and fabricated – not surprising when you consider that *sosŏl*, the Korean word for fiction, derives from two Chinese characters that literally mean 'small talk', or, more commonly, 'unimportant story'. But, ultimately, I realized that fiction bears a close relationship to everyday life.

Leaving home at the age of twenty, decked out in a sweater and outsized police boots, I arrived in Seoul, the first in my village to enter university.

Four years later, in my senior year at Seoul National University, I made my debut as a writer. In Korea, one of the ways you become an established writer is to win one of the New Year literature competitions sponsored by the daily newspapers in Seoul. You can submit work in one of three categories – poetry, fiction or literary criticism. I submitted a piece of literary criticism, and I won. And so it was that I made my debut as a literary critic, not as a writer of fiction.

It took another four long years in an MA programme to disabuse myself of the notion of being a creative writer. The turning point came one day in our department's graduate student reading room, when a visiting professor from Japan asked our professors how many authors of fiction we had in Korea and how many fictional works had been published since the turn of the century. Despite my limited facility in Japanese, it was clear to me that my professors were faltering in their responses and I had to sneak out of the room in shame, my face burning. I pledged to myself that if I ever encountered that professor again, I would be capable of readily providing him with clear answers, and from that day on I buried myself in our library to research the modern literature of our country. And now, almost fifty years later, as Korean popular culture increasingly drives global cultural production, the time is right to share with readers a collection of stories that affirms Korea's rightful place in world literature.

Tradition

As I have mentioned, fiction bears a close affinity with everyday life. And life for many of us, and certainly for most Koreans, is invested with tradition. Which is why, I suppose, when times are especially difficult – as they were from 1910 to 1945, when Korea was a colony of imperial Japan; or during the Korean War of 1950–1953 that followed the division of the country into north and south; or, more recently, during the almost three decades of military dictatorship – it is from tradition that writers have often drawn comfort. For those of us on the Korean Peninsula, tradition springs from an agrarian lifestyle; from religious faith that draws liberally on native spirituality, Buddhism and more recently Christianity; and from a social system comprising a limited number of venerable clans and governed by neo-Confucian expectations of proper relations between monarch and subject, family members, men and women, and the four classes of scholar, farmer, artisan and merchant (in descending order of status). Koreans in the new millennium might not readily articulate tradition in this way, but you can bet that over the course of generations of family history it has become 'a hitching post' in their psyche, to use the title of a trio of stories by the late Pak Wansŏ, a writer featured in this anthology.

Yi Hyosŏk (1907–1942) was a 'fellow traveller' author in his earlier stories – one who was sympathetic to the working class but did not belong to the short-lived proletarian literature movement in colonial Korea. By the mid-1930s, when fictional works touching on the strictures of colonial society increasingly risked being censored, he had returned from the city to the countryside for inspiration for his stories. Yi was still in his thirties when he was claimed by meningitis in 1942. 'When the Buckwheat Blooms' ('Memilkkot p'il muryŏp') is set in the mountainous P'yŏngch'ang area of Kangwŏn Province that was Yi's home (and the site of the 2018 Winter Olympics). In this story tradition is personified by Hŏ Saengwŏn, an itinerant peddler whose rounds take him to one of the every-fifth-day markets found practically everywhere in the countryside even today. Hŏ happens to be left-handed, making him a rarity in a society that values conformity. Liberated from the daytime bustle of the marketplace, he is bewitched by the play of the full moon on the brilliant white buckwheat blossoms as he yarns to his companion Cho Sŏndal about a night of passion he enjoyed some twenty years earlier. At the end of the story, he notices that Tongi, a young peddler he has befriended, is also left-handed. At the same time, he recalls that his faithful donkey, though getting on in years, has managed to sire a colt. This story contains most of the essential characteristics of Yi's fictional world: a writing style reminiscent of lyric poetry; close harmony of setting, character and event; and meticulous composition.

Ch'ae Manshik (1902–1950) is one of the most distinctive voices of modern Korean fiction. Gifted in description and dialogue, he wrote several memorable plays. By the time he passed away, scant weeks before the outbreak of the Korean War – which he predicted with uncanny prescience in his 1948 novella 'Sunset' ('Nakcho') – he had published enough literary work to constitute a ten-volume edition of his complete works. Ch'ae was

Introduction

fond of retelling tales of old, especially the story of Shim Ch'ŏng, a Korean paragon of filial devotion, as well as works from abroad, such as Ibsen's *A Doll's House*. 'A Man Called Hŭngbo' ('Hŭngbo-sshi') is based on the well-known tale of two brothers, Hŭngbu and Nolbu, the former young, helpless and sweet and the latter older, crooked and powerful. In Ch'ae's retelling, younger brother Hŭngbu is recast as 'good ol' Hyŏn', a well-meaning but incapable fellow who is kind to all but struggles to fulfil even the simple promise of bringing a bento box to his disabled daughter. In the original tale, a good heart begets good fortune. But Ch'ae rejects such traditional values. Good ol' Hyŏn is weak and thwarted at every turn. Life under colonial rule has become so desperate that kindness by itself no longer suffices.

Like Yi Hyosŏk, Chu Yosŏp (1902–1972) wrote stories early in his career that realistically depict the miserable life of the lower class. But in his stories from the 1930s onwards he examines the inner life of women bound by traditional gender expectations. The narrator of 'Mama and the Boarder' ('Sarang sonnim kwa ŏmŏni') is six-year-old Okhŭi, who describes what happens between her young, widowed mother and a young man who rents the study in their home. Okhŭi is an unwitting mediator between the two adults, conveying the boarder's love letters to her mother, even though she cannot comprehend their contents or the inner conflicts of the adult world. Despite Okhŭi's desire for the boarder to become her father, her mother restrains her feelings and ultimately rejects his love because of the convention that a widow should not remarry. But rather than emphasizing issues of societal ethics and morality, author Chu has the mother reaffirm herself by pledging to her young daughter that the girl will always be her first priority.

Yi Munyŏl (b. 1948) is a politically conservative author who uses myth and history to create contemporary fables. His richly textured classical writing style has marked out new territory for prose writing in Korean, in works that variously problematize the territorial, ideological and psychic division of the Korean Peninsula and the violence permeating South Korean politics. His father went to North Korea during the Korean War, never to return, an event that has shaped much of his fiction. Yi's columns have appeared in the *New York Times*, and he runs a creative writing centre in his ancestral home that nurtures aspiring authors. His linked-story novel *You Can't Go Home Again* (*Kŭdae tashi nŭn kohyang e kaji mot'ari*) deplores lost tradition, as seen in the story included here, 'The Old Hatter' ('Sarajin kŏt tŭl ŭl wihayŏ'). Old Top'yŏng has spent his life weaving trad-itional Korean hats in his ancestral village for men to wear over their topknots, which were a symbol of male adulthood in the Chosŏn period (1392–1910). Times have changed, however, and the village has been sub-jected to billowing modernization. The old man tries hard to pass on his skills, but young people wishing to inherit the artisanship of a bygone era are hard to find. His efforts to train a successor in hat-making having failed, the old man visits the grave of a low-born friend who kept his topknot until his death, and offers him a lifetime's masterpiece of a hat, before burning it. Top'yŏng's unfortunate life story, related with wry irony by the narrator in the form of flashbacks to his childhood, honours trad-itions deemed trivial and consigned to oblivion amid the currents of modernization.

We could say that for Kim Taeyong (b. 1974), literature was salvation. While completing his compulsory military duty as a medic, he was hit by an explosion that left him with burns over 80 per cent of his body. Confined indoors for a year in order to avoid sunlight, and unable to sleep, he attempted suicide, and only then did a desire to express himself in writing restore in him a strong desire to live. Like many of the younger writers represented in this volume, he studied creative writing at university level.

He has described the writing experience of 'Pig on Grass' ('P'ulbat wi ŭi twaeji') as one of the smoothest of his life – perhaps because the father–son relationship looms so large in Korean tradition? It is an impressive story, clever, playful and witty, while also serious and poignant. The author's humorous treatment of weighty subject matter may appeal to readers who consider modern Korean fiction overly gloomy. The author invites us inside the mind of a man suffering from dementia, his dead wife and their pig still a living presence in his life. Not until the end of the story, when the man's son visits to remind him that he is soon going abroad and cannot leave him alone to fend for himself, do we learn that his wife is deceased. The implication of this – that the father may end up in a nursing home – would not so long ago have been an outrage in a society in which parents traditionally lived under the same roof as their eldest son and his family until death.

Women and Men

The authors of the stories in this section are divided between men and women, but only one-third of the stories in the volume overall are written by women. Does this mean that in modern Korea women are less accomplished than men as writers of fiction? No, it is a reminder, rather, that until the modern period, female writers were discouraged from displaying their literary works in public, which was viewed as the sphere of upper-class men. Today women are perhaps more visible than men, whether they write literary fiction or genre fiction. But traditional gender-role expectations remain in play, as we shall see in the following stories.

Pak T'aewŏn (1910–1986) was born and educated in Seoul and published poetry in his teens before making a transition to fiction. Later in life he wrote historical fiction. He disappeared from Seoul in 1950, only to re-emerge after the Korean War in North Korea, where he continued to write until his death in 1986. Over thirty years later, his grandson Bong Junho (Pong Chunho) would achieve international fame when his Korean-language film *Parasite* won four Academy Awards, including Best Picture and Best Director. 'A Day in the Life of Kubo the Novelist' ('Sosŏlga Kubo-sshi ŭi iril') is one of the seminal works of literary modernism of 1930s Korea. Kubo is modelled on Pak T'aewŏn himself – Kubo was one of his pen names – and his story begins and ends with the most important woman in his life, his mother. It follows him from morning to night as he saunters about Kyŏngsŏng, as Seoul was known during the era of Japanese occupation. His aimless wanderings recall the French poet Baudelaire, whose verse was inspired by his walks in Paris, as well as the so-called 'modern boys' of 1930s Japan, who moseyed about Tokyo's glitzy Ginza neighbourhood. What does Kubo see as he roams the colonial capital, notebook in hand, recording the changes in daily life that he encounters? Streets for vehicles where the city walls once were; a tram line; Kyŏngsŏng Station, hub of a Peninsula-wide rail network; a zoo and playground replacing a 500-year-old palace; the new Japanese Government-General building blocking the view of Kyŏngbok Palace; the wall of Tŏksu Palace and, close by, the Bank of Chosen (the Japanese name for its Korean colony); Japanese residential neighbourhoods and commercial districts with department stores, pharmacies, coffee shops and cafés; entertainment districts – all of it emblematic of colonial modernity. The only unchanged place is the start and end point, his home, where we are presented with the humble image of his fretful mother doing her household chores and sewing. The stream-of-consciousness narrative is complemented by original illustrations by Pak's friend and fellow writer Yi Sang.

Kim Yujŏng (1908–1937) published only twenty-eight stories and one short-story collection in his short life. And yet his stories continue to be enjoyed today for their command of native Korean vocabulary, to such an extent that high-school students writing their all-important university entrance exam will find his works cited in the set of questions testing their proficiency in Korean. 'Spicebush Blossoms' ('Tongbaek kkot') tells of a budding relationship between a boy and girl in the countryside. The boy, our first-person narrator, and the girl, Chŏmsun, are from different social classes: he is the son of a tenant farmer and she is the daughter of the overseer who collects the farmers' rent. But instead of focusing on class issues, the story portrays the awakening feelings of the girl and boy, the latter too naive and insensitive to recognize that the girl's antagonistic behaviour disguises her attraction to him. Notably, all the action in the story is initiated by Chŏmsun. Only towards the end does the boy exhibit his own aggressive behaviour, which ironically leads to his submission to her. In the homespun setting, their courting is like a landscape painting brought to life by Kim's signature brand of humour.

Ch'oe Yun (b. 1953) is a rare combination of creative writer, professor (of French literature) at an elite university and literary translator. Her first published work of fiction, the novella 'There a Petal Silently Falls' ('Chŏgi sori ŏpshi han chŏm kkonip i chigo'), uses three narrative voices to describe the trauma of a girl whose mother has been shot dead in the May 1980 government massacre of citizens in the city of Kwangju. Since then, she has continued to experiment with narrative method and style. 'The Last of Hanak'o' ('Hanak'o nŭn ŏpta') is masterful in its restraint and irony as it exposes the prejudices against women that men collectively exhibit in their daily lives. While in college a group of young men, including the story's narrator, diminish the eponymous Hanak'o with a nickname focusing on a single facial feature – her nose – and repeatedly reveal their self-interest and immaturity in their dealings with her. As the years pass, they find in her a uniquely comfortable presence, but fail to appreciate her sincerity or to recognize her for who she is, an accomplished young woman in a same-sex relationship. Not until the end of the story are she and her partner revealed as an internationally known design team. The title of the story (a literal translation of which would be 'There Is No Hanak'o') is in my view a manifesto of female identity, suggesting that reductive images of womanhood no longer have meaning in a society working towards gender equality.

Hong Sŏkchung (b. 1941) is a native of Seoul, but in 1950 went to North Korea with his father, a Korean-language scholar, and his grandfather, author of *Im Kkŏkchŏng*, a multi-volume novel about a historical bandit. Hong has stated in an interview that he wanted to be a scientist but was encouraged by Kim Jong-il, former Supreme Leader of North Korea, to write historical fiction. *Hwang Chini* was born of a desire to restore the richness of the Korean language and traditional Korean culture. The novel was published in Pyongyang in 2002 and was awarded the prestigious Manhae Literature Prize in South Korea in 2004. Responding to Supreme Leader Kim Jong-il's suggestion to break the cookie-cutter mould of socialist realist fiction that had dominated the North Korean literary landscape, Hong produced a novel that displays a lively historical imagination, creative use of the dialects of the two Koreas, and a literary style replete with proverbs, metaphor, folksy slang, monologue and elegant poetic expression. The eponymous protagonist is born to a *kisaeng*, a profession that denies her and her offspring a place in the traditional class structure. Chini is trapped in the contradiction of her status as the daughter of a patrician man and an outcaste mother. In forming a relationship with Nomi, a commoner, she breaks free from a class structure that oppresses women, an effort that begins in the excerpt here, in which Chini publicly renders herself accountable for the death of a young man who was infatuated with her. In doing so, she rejects the life of a parasitic being in the shadow of men, and stands proudly as an independent agent of her life.

In the fiction of Ch'ŏn Unyŏng (Ch'ŏn Un-yŏng, b. 1971) women relate to men in unusual ways. In her 2011 novel *The Catcher in the Loft* (*Saeng-gang*), a young woman shelters her fugitive father, a torture operative serving the military dictatorship of 1980s South Korea, from the authorities. 'Needlework' ('Panŭl'), her debut story, features a daughter and mother who both use needles (tattooing needles and *hanbok*-stitching needles, respectively) to take control of the male body. Needles are tools that cause pain and are capable of evoking a sadistic impulse. The daughter prefers hand-tattooing to machine-tattooing because it gives her more agency over her male clientele. In taking control of male bodies as she tattoos them, she is also serving the needs of men who compensate for their feelings of inferiority and even emasculization by wanting to look dominant. In this way, the story is a chillingly sharp depiction of the tensions between conflicting desires, and the shifting power dynamics between the genders.

Peace and War

This section is titled 'Peace and War' rather than 'War and Peace', a reminder that the two Koreas – the Democratic People's Republic of Korea (North Korea) and the Republic of Korea (South Korea) – remain, technically, in a state of war, there being no formal treaty to conclude the 1950–1953 Korean War. The division of the Korean Peninsula into two separate countries, at the conclusion of the Second World War in August 1945, followed by the establishment of a US military government in what is now South Korea and the presence of Soviet military advisors in the North, continues to loom large in the psyche of the Korean people, many of whom have family on opposite sides of the DMZ (the ironically named demilitarized zone), which separates South from North.

Hwang Sunwŏn (1915–2000) had direct experience of the division of Korea and of the civil war that followed. Born near Pyongyang in present-day North Korea, he migrated with his family in 1946 to Seoul, now in South Korea. During the war he and his family, along with countless other Koreans, were displaced to refugee communities, first in the city of Taegu and then in the city of Pusan on the southeast coast of the peninsula. Originally a poet, Hwang soon turned to fiction and became arguably the most accomplished writer of short fiction in modern Korea. He wrote over 100 short stories, including the coming-of-age classic 'The Cloudburst' ('Sonagi'), which is read in Korean schools. He is also one of very few Korean writers to write directly of the battlefield experience. (More commonly, writers of his generation focused on the after-effects of the war.) His war stories and novels embody not only the civil strife of the late 1940s and early 1950s but also the equally important conflicts taking place within individual souls struggling to survive on the battlefield. In delineating the spiritual chaos experienced by the young generation who survived the spectre of death in battle, these works question the meaning of life and the potential for human salvation. 'Time for You and Me' ('Nŏ wa na na man ŭi shigan') features a wounded captain, a lieutenant and a private first-class trying to break through an enemy siege. The question soon arises – are the men better off looking out only for themselves, or should they stick together? Hwang was introduced to Freudian thought during his years at Waseda University in Tokyo, and his capacity for understanding basic instinct and the operation of the human psyche in the most desperate of circumstances is showcased in this story. The translators of the story once asked the author how he was able to depict battlefield survival stories so realistically – was he himself a veteran of the war? No, he answered, but he had sought out the stories of battlefield survivors – a testament to the foundations of his masterful storytelling skill.

I must confess that Pak Wansŏ (1931–2011) is my favourite writer. For forty years she bestowed on her readers sharp critiques leavened with gentle satire on how the ethics, values and norms of the Korean family have been overturned by the experiences of the colonial period, the division of the nation and war. What distinguishes her narratives above all else is her colloquial style, which imbues her fiction with an almost palpable empathy that earned for her the affectionate nickname 'the auntie next door'. 'Winter Outing' ('Kyŏul nadŭri') is a story-within-a-story. The narrator is a devoted mother and wife, but is increasingly discontented with her husband. Seeking a respite, she travels to a hot spring, and at the inn where she spends the night she encounters an elderly woman with a peculiar habit of shaking her head. It is revealed that this is the result of trauma from the war, when the old woman inadvertently revealed her son's hideout to enemy soldiers and he was executed before her eyes. Thus do the wounds from the civil war continue to fester decades later. Through a deep sympathy for the elderly woman and her family, the narrator is able to free herself from her own internal conflicts.

Much of the fictional work of Cho Chŏngnae (b. 1943) narrates how the sufferings of the colonial period and the tragedy of the Korean War have influenced the lives of Koreans. Intertwined with this is the theme of resentment, caused by the conflict between rich and poor. 'Land of Exile' ('Yuhyŏng ŭi ttang') analyses the damage from the war sharply. The protagonist loses everything: his ancestral village, to which he can never return after shedding blood there; and his family – both the wife he slaughters, along with the People's Army commander who seduced her, and the son he must give up for adoption at an orphanage. As vice-chairman of the North Korean People's Army unit occupying the village where he was born, Mansŏk takes the helm in massacring the reactionary clan that previously controlled it. But after killing the People's Army commander he must escape, erasing his identity, and begin a new life of constant wandering, a kind of self-exile. Few writers have proved more adept than Cho at exploring how individual enmity stemming from social inequality and prejudice expanded into ideological conflict before, during and after the Korean War. His ten-volume novel *T'aebaek sanmaek* (*The T'aebaek Mountains*, 1989) is the summit of his career and a sterling achievement of literature focusing on the nation's division.

Hell Chosŏn

Hell Chosŏn is a term that has only recently come into popular usage in South Korea, but its roots go all the way back to the Chosŏn Kingdom (1392–1910), when the attainment of rank consequent to passing the government civil service exam was the aim of every young man in any self-respecting clan. Today the term reflects the discontent of a generation of young people who have dutifully obtained a university education (and in many cases studied abroad) only to find a paucity of jobs commensurate with their education. More generally the term reflects disappointment with a lifestyle marked by economic inequality, crony capitalism, excessive work hours and inadequate salary, and the societal manifestations of this malaise, such as the highest suicide rate among the OECD nations, a negative birthrate and a divorce rate that hovers around 30 per cent. More recently you will find on social media the term *t'alcho*, the *t'al* meaning 'escape' and the *cho* referring to Chosŏn – in short, 'leave Chosŏn'.

The desire to escape Chosŏn is made clear at the end of Yi Sang (1910–1937)'s classic story 'Wings' ('Nalgae'). Yi Sang is the pen name of Kim Haegyŏng; he adopted it as a wry commentary on the Japanese convention of addressing an individual by his or her family name followed by the title *san* – in his case, he was mistakenly called Yi, a family name almost as common as Kim in Korea. He is a writer who has always interested me, to the point that I compiled a five-volume collection of his writings, *Collected Writings of Yi Sang* (Yi Sang chŏnjip, 2009). In the 1930s he caused a sensation with his imaginative stories and experimental poetry. 'Wings' is one of the highlights of Korean modernist literature. The narrator is an incapable intellectual, a self-described 'stuffed genius'. He lives a bizarre life with his wife, a prostitute, who represents the pathology of the city. He desires to break the bounds of his meaningless existence in 'my room', a dark, cramped space partitioned off from the lighter and airier space where his wife receives her clients. To reach the outside world he must pass through his wife's space. His frustrated desire to escape culminates with him perched on the roof of the Mitsukoshi Department Store wanting to cry out, *Sprout again, wings! Let me fly, fly, fly; one more time let me fly.* Will he jump? And if so, will he do so out of a desire for transcendence, out of naked anger at his inability to escape, or in symbolic defiance of imperial Japan's occupation of his homeland?

In the 1960s we saw the emergence of the first generation of Korean writers to be educated in their own language (during the colonial period, the language of instruction was Japanese, and before then, boys fortunate enough to attend one of the village 'academies' were taught Chinese characters), and by virtue of this they are called the Hangŭl Generation, Hangŭl referring to the Korean alphabet. Coming of age during the first two decades of the Republic of Korea and experiencing both the triumph of the 19 April 1960 Student Revolution, which resulted in the resignation of heavy-handed President Yi Sŭngman (Syngman Rhee), and the oppressiveness of military dictatorship following the May 1961 coup led by young officers loyal to Park Chung Hee, these writers combined mordant critiques of a society in rapid transition with an imaginative world-view.

We might think of writer and visual artist Kim Sŭngok (b. 1941) as the genius of this generation. When the Yi Sang Literature Prize, the most prestigious award for literary short fiction in South Korea, was launched in 1977, it was Kim who was the first recipient. But he was unable to make a living from fiction and ultimately turned to writing screenplays. He was born in Osaka, Japan, but returned to Korea with his family in 1945. The protagonists of 'Seoul: Winter 1964' ('Sŏul, 1964nyŏn kyŏul') are a young public servant, a university student and a man in his mid-thirties who has just sold his wife's corpse to a university hospital, where it will be dissected by medical students. These three lead different lives but share the experience of alienation from the massive metropolis and the despair and boredom that this engenders. This sense of alienation reaches a climax in the story with the not entirely unexpected suicide of the third man.

O Chŏnghŭi (Oh Jung-hee, b. 1947) was once asked in an interview to explain what she considers to be good writing. She responded that she admires writing that feels truthful but leaves her ill at ease, head aching and mind swirling with thoughts. She likes stories that must be read slowly because of the pointed questions they raise. And she likes works that leave ample space for the reader, while, as far as possible, concealing the writer's voice. She is by now admired almost universally by critics but has yet to attract a wide readership. Perhaps this is because her early stories are populated by characters with destructive impulses expressed through motifs such as physical deformity, kleptomania, infertility and pyromania. The narratives in her subsequent story collections focus more on coming of age and trauma. Absence figures prominently in several of her stories, including 'Wayfarer' ('Sullyeja ŭi norae'). The protagonist of this story is a middle-class housewife who is also a talented puppet-maker. She has recently been discharged from a psychiatric hospital, following an incident in which she stabbed a burglar. Abandoned by her family, she returns to an empty house and the start of a lonely journey to liberate herself from a world in which human relationships are destroyed by prejudice and misunderstanding.

Kyung-sook Shin (Shin Kyung-sook, b. 1963) is from a village in North Chŏlla Province. She was the first South Korean and first woman to win the Man Asia Literature Prize (2012), for *Please Look After Mother* (*Ŏmma rŭl put'ak hae*). Better known as a novelist, she is especially adept at a type of fable-like short story that often explores family dynamics. 'House on the Prairie' ('Pŏlp'an wi ŭi chip') is a ghost story about trauma and memory, in which reincarnation links happiness and misfortune. The author is perhaps playing the role of *mudang*, the practitioner (by definition female) of native Korean spirituality, who in the performance of her rituals often channels the voices of those who have died a premature and/or unnatural death ('Then why did you push me, Mummy?').

P'yŏn Hyeyŏng (Pyun Hye-young, b. 1972) began publishing in 2000. She writes about the duality of human nature, which hides anxiety and subversive urges within the comfort and tranquillity promised by civilization. One of her novels was inspired by the 2011 earthquake, tsunami and nuclear meltdown in Japan, many of the casualties of which resulted from panic. 'The First Anniversary' ('Ch'ŏtpŏntchae ki'nyŏmil') depicts the repetitive but stressful life of a delivery person – a worker seen everywhere in Korea today. The protagonist's regular route involves making deliveries to a woman on an upper floor of an apartment building mostly vacated due to an urban renewal project. The woman is rarely at home and the delivery man takes her items home with him instead of leaving them to pile up at her apartment door. He eventually locates her at a nearby amusement park and they go on a Ferris wheel ride together. He tries to suppress his fantasy that he is on a date with her by sharing his résumé with her, but she responds with a list of all the items that remain undelivered to her; they are unable to make a connection with each other. Whether viewed from the Ferris wheel gondola or the window of the woman's apartment, the landscape is populated by dour multi-family residential construction, much of it the half-basement apartments that symbolize the ambiguities of life in Hell Chosŏn.

Choi Suchol (b. 1958) is a native of the city of Ch'unch'ŏn and made his debut in 1981, influenced by his father, a Korean-language schoolteacher and himself an aspiring writer. His fiction tends to be impressionistic and abstruse, but his thematic interests have expanded steadily, and his unconventional writing style is distinctive. No other fiction writer has been nominated more times for the Tongin Literature Prize, the oldest Korean award for literary fiction. Recently he has focused on the legacy of the Korean War, as in his linked-story novel *The Dance of the POWs* (*P'oro tŭl ŭi ch'um*). The novel was inspired by his discovery of Magnum photos taken at a prisoner-of-war camp off the south coast of Korea in which the inmates, shrouded by hoods to protect their anonymity, are seen dancing with each other. 'River Dark' ('Kŏmŭn kang'), written in 2001, foretells an ecological malaise that would be revealed in real life a decade later. The World Wetland Network recognizes countries for their efforts in wetland management, with Grey Globe awards drawing attention to poor practices. In 2012 South Korea received a Grey Globe for a river project implemented without a proper environmental assessment. Ground water was found to be polluted, and the newly dammed rivers exhibited 'rotten water mass'. The story, in which the protagonist reminisces fondly about his visits to a neighbourhood stream while on a remote island, foreshadows this debacle. It is an all-too-rare example of fiction tackling the theme of environmental degradation in Korea.

Into the New World

The title of this section originated in the last chapter of *What Is Korean Literature?* a book that I authored with the editor of this anthology. It draws on an iconic song of that name by the K-pop idol group Girls' Generation, reflecting the increasing prominence of women writers in Korean fiction at the dawn of the new millennium. Six of these writers are represented in this anthology, including Kyung-sook Shin, Ch'ŏn Unyŏng, P'yŏn Hyeyŏng, Hwang Chŏngŭn, Kim Aeran and Han Yujoo. Among these writers from the new millennium, we also see a movement away from traditional realist narratives and towards more metafictional stories about language and the process of writing itself.

If Kim Sŭngok is the presiding genius of the Hangŭl Generation, then Ch'oe Inho (1945–2012) was its child prodigy. There is a well-known story about the small, second-year high-school boy who arrived to accept a new writers' award wearing his black student uniform only to have the master of ceremonies, who mistook him for a stand-in, bark at him, 'Where's your big brother?!' Ch'oe was the youngest writer ever to have a novel serialized in a newspaper, the first writer to be photographed for a book jacket, the first creative writer to make a living from his work, and the author with the most film versions of his works (some twenty of them, the scripts for some of which he wrote himself). His novel *Homeland of the Stars* (*Pyŏl tŭl ŭi kohyang*) was an instant million-volume bestseller that earned him a month-long world tour and prompted a host of bar girls to change their work name to Kyŏng'a, after the heroine of the novel. In earning a popular readership Ch'oe broadened the appeal of Korean literary fiction in general. Unsurprisingly, considering that he was a native of Seoul, much of his fiction foregrounds the urban landscape that was the central space of Korean life during industrialization from the 1960s on. Often deploying a playful, speculative style, his works convey the shock of new living patterns, such as the shift from the multi-generation family in the ancestral village to the impersonality of the metropolitan apartment building. 'The Poplar Tree', one of three linked stories constituting the series titled 'Strange People' ('Yisanghan saram tŭl'), is a fable and a coming-of-age story with elements of magical realism.

Hwang Chŏngŭn (Hwang Jung Eun, b. 1976) is also a native of Seoul and for a time played the hourglass drum in a Korean traditional percussion band. Her works depict the marginal figures who live a shadowy existence in a traditional class- and status-based society. Hwang gives voice to these individuals, to victims of violence and to those who are homeless and abandoned. In 'The Bone Thief' ('Ppyŏ toduk'), a man initiates a journey in the dead of winter to raid the funerary urn of his male lover, who has been killed in an accident. The story shows how the suppression of homosexuality, via which conventional gender norms forbid mourning for a deceased lover, generates hatred and 'ethical violence'.

Jung Young Moon (b. 1965) taught himself English as a *Katusa* (a Korean soldier attached to the US Army) during his mandatory military service. To make a living he has translated more than 50 books from English to Korean. His writing is characterized by a sardonic sense of humour, beguiling dialogue and a linguistic rhythm in even the longest of sentences. He is more interested in human nature and its cross-sections than in plot-driven works. His fiction tends to have no story line but instead takes readers along for the ride, following the narrative wherever it may go. 'Home on the Range' ('Yangtte mokchang') is a whimsical story in which the narrator, who is working at a friend's sheep farm, visits a local market and nearby temple, his conversations with a monk and two elderly women providing comic relief from his constant daydreaming.

Kim Chunghyŏk (b. 1971) has a diverse résumé – web designer, illustrator, webtoon artist, book and film reviewer, music columnist, restaurant industry writer and, of course, author. 'Glass Shield' ('Yuri pangp'ae') is a wry take on a central aspect of Hell Chosŏn – unemployment among those fresh out of university. The two friends transform the all-important first-job interview into performance art and thereby become celebrities. But in spite of their efforts, they do not find meaningful work, and seem ultimately bound to part ways forever, like the two young men in 'Seoul: 1964, Winter'.

Han Yujoo (b. 1982) made her debut as a writer at the age of twenty-two and has since produced a significant body of recursive, metatextual narratives. She utilizes a playful, almost magical sense of wordplay and has an unsettling tendency to establish a situation and then negate it. She encourages readers to approach her stories as they see fit, professing to write intuitively and saying that there is no right way to read and enjoy her work. 'Black-and-White Photographer' ('Hŭkpaek sajinsa') presents us with a black image and a white image. Both are of a primary-school boy kidnapped with a demand for an outrageous ransom. In the black image he is strangled; in the white image he is released. Either way, ambiguity remains. The story eschews a linear plotline – an intentional disturbance that renders the boy's narrative unreliable. This style of writing reminds us that what we are reading is fictional – an important realization, given that some Korean netizens have suggested that this story was the model for a 2018 kidnapping of an eight-year-old girl that ended in tragedy.

Kim Aeran (b. 1980) displays a precocious gift for storytelling. 'The Future of Silence' ('Ch'immuk ŭi mirae') is a dazzling tale, partly inspired by Nicholas D. Evans's non-fiction work *Dying Words: Endangered Languages and What They Have to Tell Us.* According to this book, the next century will see more than half of the world's 6,000 languages become extinct, and most will disappear without being adequately recorded. In Kim's story, the Museum of Moribund Languages is devoted to housing and recording the sole surviving speakers of minor tongues. The story is a fable that explores how the languages that sustain civilization are born and die. By using the spirit of the last speaker of a dead language as her narrator, Kim is in effect reanimating human destiny. Underpinning the story is a profound sorrow, the residents of the museum knowing they will never again enjoy a genuine conversation in their mother tongue. With their death, the language dies too. And with the death of a language, an anthology such as this one becomes impossible.

Kwon Youngmin

Editorial Note

The emergence of the short story is one of the great ironies of modern Korean literature. In the beginning there was only *sosŏl*, literally 'small talk', as Kwon Youngmin mentions in his Introduction to this anthology, but generally understood today as 'fiction'. There was no generic distinction based on the length of the narrative. Not until the early 1900s, when the Enlightenment movement swept East Asia, did the Western-style short story arrive on Korean shores, typically by way of Japan. Though considered something of a Western import, the genre quickly assumed elite status, and today the most prestigious Korean awards for domestic fiction go primarily to the short story.

The reader will note, in the Further Reading section, a variety of anthologies of short fiction. One might legitimately ask, Why another one? For the late Kevin O'Rourke and myself, the answer was simple: we wanted a collection of stories that have engaged us over the decades – indeed in several cases compelled us to translate them – and we wanted stories that come alive as works of English-language literature.

I have forsaken the common practice of arranging the contents of an anthology in chronological order, preferring instead to highlight several recurring themes to be found in Korean stories. Korean fiction has earned a reputation, to an extent deserved, of being gloomy and depressing, but the reader will see in the Tradition, Women and Men and Into the New World sections glimpses of humour, albeit often sardonic, that offer insight into the lives of the inhabitants of the Korean Peninsula past and present. And lest readers be intimidated by the Peace and War and Hell Chosŏn designations, a reminder that a dash of empathy may leaven a disturbing narrative with a modicum of hope, healing and closure.

For readers desiring to read the stories in chronological order:

1. Pak T'aewŏn, 'A Day in the Life of Kubo the Novelist' (1934)
2. Chu Yosŏp, 'Mama and the Boarder' (1935)

3. Kim Yujŏng, 'Spicebush Blossoms' (1936)
4. Yi Hyosŏk, 'When the Buckwheat Blooms' (1936)
5. Yi Sang, 'Wings' (1936)
6. Ch'ae Manshik, 'A Man Called Hŭngbo' (1939)
7. Hwang Sunwŏn, 'Time for You and Me' (1958)
8. Kim Sŭngok, 'Seoul: Winter 1964' (1965)
9. Pak Wansŏ, 'Winter Outing' (1975)
10. Yi Munyŏl, 'The Old Hatter' (1979)
11. Cho Chŏngnae, 'Land of Exile' (1981)
12. Ch'oe Inho, 'The Poplar Tree' (1981)
13. O Chŏnghŭi, 'Wayfarer' (1983)
14. Ch'oe Yun, 'The Last of Hanak'o' (1994)
15. Kyung-sook Shin, 'House on the Prairie' (1996)
16. Choi Suchol, 'River Dark' (2001)
17. Ch'ŏn Unyŏng, 'Needlework' (2001)
18. Hong Sŏkchung, a chapter from *Hwang Chini* (2002)
19. Jung Young Moon, 'Home on the Range' (2003)
20. Kim Chunghyŏk, 'The Glass Shield' (2006)
21. Kim Taeyong, 'Pig on Grass' (2006)
22. P'yŏn Hyeyŏng, 'The First Anniversary' (2006)
23. Han Yujoo, 'Black-and-White Photographer' (2007)
24. Hwang Chŏngŭn, 'The Bone Thief' (2011)
25. Kim Aeran, 'The Future of Silence' (2013)

With the exception of the excerpt from Hong Sŏkchung's novel *Hwang Chini*, each of these is a discrete work of fiction.

Many of the stories herein appeared previously in periodicals or anthologies, the editors and publishers of whom are gratefully acknowledged here; facts of publication are cited in the Permissions.

Compiling an anthology is necessarily a team effort, and I have several individuals to thank. The immediate inspiration for this collection was a presentation at the University of Washington by Jay Rubin on his *Penguin Book of Japanese Short Stories*. Jay was kind enough to connect me with his Penguin editor, Simon Winder, who in turn put me in touch with Jessica Harrison, an editor with heart, vision and endless patience. I am grateful as well to the other members of the Penguin team: Louisa Watson for her sensitive and gracious copy-editing of the manuscript; Rebecca Lee for coordinating editorial-production in a timely manner; and Edward Kirke for the thankless job of copyright clearance. Thanks are due to the translators, among whom I wish to single out two who are no longer with us, Kim Chong-un and Marshall R. Pihl. Both were mentors I revered, and I shall forever remember the translations I did with the former as a master class in Korean-to-English literary translation. I also wish to mention that several of the stories were translated or co-translated by former students of mine at the University of British Columbia. Primary thanks are reserved for three individuals. Kwon Youngmin, a professor at Seoul National University and the University of California, Berkeley, has been a mentor, colleague, co-editor, co-author and friend for forty years; I can think of no one more capable of introducing this anthology. Kevin O'Rourke was a respected friend and colleague attuned like perhaps no other to the heart and soul of the Korean literary tradition. He played a strong role in text selection, contributed two translations to the volume and assisted on a third, and should be regarded as the spiritual co-editor of this volume. Finally, Ju-Chan Fulton, life partner and co-translator, contributed materially to the volume and remains a source of unflagging energy at a time when life seems increasingly to be having its way with the denizens of the globe.

Further Reading

Korean names appear as spelled and ordered in the published volume.

Short-Story Collections by Writers in This Volume

Ch'ae Man-shik. *My Innocent Uncle*. Ed. Ross King and Bruce Fulton. Trans. Bruce and Ju-Chan Fulton, Kim Chong-un and Bruce Fulton, and Robert Armstrong. Seoul: Jimoondang, 2003. (Includes the stories 'My Innocent Uncle,' 'A Ready-Made Life,' and 'Once Upon a Paddy.')

Ch'ae Manshik. *Sunset: A Ch'ae Manshik Reader*. Ed. and trans. Bruce and Ju-Chan Fulton. New York: Columbia University Press, 2017.

Choe In-ho. *Deep Blue Night*. Trans. Bruce and Ju-Chan Fulton. Bloomfield, N.J.: Jimoondang, 2002. (Comprises the title story and 'The Poplar Tree.')

Ch'oe Yun. *There a Petal Silently Falls: Three Stories by Ch'oe Yun*. Trans. Bruce and Ju-Chan Fulton. New York: Columbia University Press, 2009.

Hwang Sun-won. *The Book of Masks*. Ed. Martin Holman. London: Readers International, 1989. (Stories from his last collection of short fiction.)

Hwang Sunwŏn. *Lost Souls: Stories*. Trans. Bruce and Ju-Chan Fulton. New York: Columbia University Press, 2010. (Contains the story collections *The Pond*, *The Dog of Crossover Village*, and *Lost Souls*.)

Hwang Sun-won, *Shadows of a Sound*. Ed. Martin Holman. San Francisco: Mercury House, 1990. (Stories covering his entire career.)

Hwang Sun-won. *The Stars and Other Korean Short Stories*. Trans. Edward W. Poitras. Hong Kong: Heinemann Asia, 1980.

O Chŏnghŭi. *River of Fire and Other Stories*. Trans. Bruce and Ju-Chan Fulton. New York: Columbia University Press, 2012.

Pak Wansŏ. *My Very Last Possession*. Ed. Chun Kyung-Ja. Armonk, N.Y.: M. E. Sharpe, 1999.

Short Stories by Other Writers

Cho Se-hŭi. *The Dwarf.* Trans. Bruce and Ju-Chan Fulton. Honolulu: University of Hawai'i Press, 2006. (A linked-story novel, each story of which may be read independently.)

Kim Tong-in. *Sweet Potato.* Trans. Grace Jung. Croydon, UK: Honford Star, 2017.

Lee Ho-Chul (Yi Hoch'ŏl). *Panmunjom and Other Stories.* Trans. Theodore Hughes. Norwalk, CT: EastBridge, 2005.

Oh Yong-su (O Yŏngsu). *The Good People: Korean Stories by Oh Yong-su.* Trans. Marshall R. Pihl. Singapore: Heinemann Asia, 1985.

Yang Kwija. *A Distant and Beautiful Place.* Trans. Kim So-Young and Julie Pickering. Honolulu: University of Hawai'i Press, 2003. (A translation of the linked-story novel *Wŏnmi-dong saram tŭl.* Each of the stories may be read independently.)

Yi Cheong-jun (Yi Ch'ŏngjun). *Two Stories from Korea.* Portland, ME: MerwinAsia, 2016. (Contains 'The Wounded', trans. Jennifer Lee, and 'The Abject', trans. Grace Jung.)

Yi Ch'ŏng-jun (Yi Ch'ŏngjun). *The Prophet and Other Stories.* Trans. Julie Pickering. Ithaca, NY: Cornell East Asia Series, 1999.

Yi T'aejun. *Dust and Other Stories.* Trans. Janet Poole. New York: Columbia University Press, 2018.

Kim Young-ha. *Photo Shop Murder.* Trans. Jason Rhodes. Seoul: Jimoon-dang, 2003. (Contains the title story and 'Whatever Happened to the Guy Stuck in the Elevator?')

Anthologies

Chun Kyung-Ja, trans. *The Voice of the Governor General and Other Stories of Modern Korea.* Norwalk, CT: EastBridge, 2002.

Fulton, Bruce, ed. *Waxen Wings: The* Acta Koreana *Anthology of Short Fiction from Korea.* St Paul, MN: Koryo Press, 2011.

Fulton, Bruce and Ju-Chan, trans. *The Future of Silence: Fiction by Korean Women*. Brookline, MA: Zephyr Press, 2016.

——*The Red Room: Stories of Trauma in Contemporary Korea*. Honolulu: University of Hawai'i Press, 2009. (Stories by Pak Wansŏ, O Chŏnghŭi and Im Ch'ŏru.)

——*Words of Farewell: Stories by Korean Women Writers*. Seattle: Seal Press, 1987. (Stories by O Chŏnghŭi, Kang Sŏkkyŏng and Kim Chiwŏn.)

Holstein, John, trans. *A Moment's Grace: Stories from Korea in Transition*. Ithaca, NY: Cornell East Asia Series, 2009.

Hughes, Theodore, Jae-Yong Kim, Jin-kyung Lee and Sang-Kyung Lee, eds. *Rat Fire: Korean Stories from the Japanese Empire*. Ithaca, NY: Cornell East Asia Series, 2013.

Kim, Chong-un, trans. *Postwar Korean Short Stories*. 2nd edn. Seoul: Seoul National University Press, 1983.

——, and Bruce Fulton, trans. *A Ready-Made Life: Early Masters of Modern Korean Fiction*. Honolulu: University of Hawai'i Press, 1998.

Lee, Peter H., ed. *Flowers of Fire: Twentieth-Century Korean Stories*, rev. edn. Honolulu: University of Hawai'i Press, 1986.

O'Rourke, Kevin, trans. *Ten Korean Short Stories*. Seoul: Yonsei University Press, 1971. (Also published as *A Washed-Out Dream*. Seoul: Korean Literature Foundation, 1980.)

Park, Sunyoung, trans. in collaboration with Jefferson J. A. Gatrall. *On the Eve of the Uprising and Other Stories from Colonial Korea*. Ithaca, NY: Cornell East Asia Series, 2010.

Pihl, Marshall R., ed. and trans. *Listening to Korea*. New York: Praeger, 1973. (A collection of stories and essays.)

Pihl, Marshall R., and Bruce and Ju-Chan Fulton, trans. *Land of Exile: Contemporary Korean Fiction*, expanded edn. Armonk, NY: M. E. Sharpe, 2007.

Reunion So Far Away: A Collection of Contemporary Korean Fiction. Seoul: Korean National Commission for Unesco, 1994.

Periodicals

Seeing the Invisible (Korea-themed issue of *Manoa*, 8, no. 2 [1996]). Five stories from South Korea's post-democratization period by women writers.

The Wounded Season (Korea-themed issue of *Manoa*, 11, no. 2 [1999]). Five stories relating to the Korean War and the May 1980 Kwangju Uprising.

Azalea: Journal of Korean Literature and Culture.

Note on Korean Name Order and Pronunciation

By convention, Korean names are cited with the family (clan) name first, followed by the given name, the former consisting usually of one syllable and the latter consisting usually of two syllables, which may be separated by a hyphen or (as in this anthology) spelled as one word. Thus the family name of the author of the Introduction is Kwon and the given name consists of the elements Young and Min. (The spelling preferred by the author is Kwon Youngmin.)

Romanized Korean vowels are pronounced somewhat as follows: *u* as in t*u*ne; *o* as in p*o*pe; *a* as in f*a*ther; *i* as in l*ea*p; *e* as in sk*a*te; and *ae* as in s*e*t. Two other vowels are distinguished by a breve (˘): *ŏ* is pronounced like the *u* in r*u*n, and *ŭ* is pronounced like the *oo* in b*oo*k. An apostrophe distinguishes aspirated consonants (those pronounced with a strong puff of air). Thus, for example, the *Ch'* in the family name Ch'oe is pronounced like the *ch* in *ch*alk. In the absence of an apostrophe, *ch* is also pronounced as in *ch*alk but with a weaker puff of air.

Certain well-known place names, such as Seoul, the capital of the Republic of Korea (South Korea), and Pyongyang, capital of the Democratic People's Republic of Korea (North Korea), are by convention spelled without the breve and/or apostrophe.

Authors' names are often spelled idiosyncratically by commercial publishers in the West. Authors in this volume who are known by variant spellings are identified as such in the Introduction.

TRADITION

YI HYOSŎK

When the Buckwheat Blooms

Translated by Kim Chong-un and Bruce Fulton

Every peddler who made the rounds of the countryside markets knew that business was never any good in the summer. And on this particular day, the marketplace in Pongp'yŏng was already deserted, though the sun was still high in the sky; its heat, seeping under the awnings of the peddlers' stalls, was enough to sear your spine. Most of the villagers had gone home, and you couldn't stay open for ever just to do business with the farmhands who would have been happy to swap a bundle of firewood for a bottle of kerosene or some fish. The swarms of flies had become a nuisance, and the local boys were as pesky as gnats.

'Shall we call it a day?' ventured Hŏ Saengwŏn, a left-handed man with a pock-marked face, to his fellow dry-goods peddler Cho Sŏndal.

'Sounds good to me. We've never done well here in Pongp'yŏng. We'll have to make a bundle tomorrow in Taehwa.'

'And walk all night to get there,' said Hŏ.

'I don't mind – we'll have the moon to light the way.'

Cho counted the day's proceeds, letting the coins clink together. Hŏ watched for a moment, then began to roll up their awning and put away the goods he had displayed. The bolts of cotton cloth and the bundles of silk fabrics filled his two wicker hampers to the brim. Bits of cloth littered the straw mat on the ground.

The stalls of other peddlers were almost down, and some groups had got a jump on the rest and left town. The fishmongers, tinkers, taffy-men and ginger sellers – all were gone. Tomorrow would be market day in Chinbu and Taehwa, and whichever way you went, you would have to trudge 15 to 20 miles through the night to get there. But here in Pongp'yŏng the marketplace had the untidy sprawl of a courtyard after a family gathering, and you could hear quarrels breaking out in the drinking houses. Drunken curses together with the shrill voices of women rent the air. The evening of a market day invariably began with the screeching of women.

A woman's shout seemed to remind Cho of something.

'Now don't play innocent, Saengwŏn – I know all about you and the Ch'ungju woman,' he said with a wry grin.

'Fat chance I have with her. I'm no match for those kids.'

'Don't be so sure,' said Cho. 'It's true that the young fellows all lose their heads over her. But you know, something tells me that Tongi, on the other hand, has her wrapped right around his finger.'

'That newbie? He must be bribing her with his goods. And I thought he was a model youngster.'

'When it comes to women, you can never be sure ... Come on now, stop your moping and let's go have a drink. It's on me.'

Hŏ didn't think much of this idea, but he followed Cho nonetheless. Hŏ was a hapless sort when it came to women. With his pock-marked mug, he hesitated to look a woman in the eye, and for their part women wouldn't warm to him. Midway through life by now, he had led a forlorn, warped existence. Just thinking of the Ch'ungju woman would bring to his face a blush unbefitting a man of his age. His legs would turn to rubber, and he would lose his composure.

The two men entered the Ch'ungju woman's tavern, and sure enough, there was Tongi. For some reason Hŏ himself couldn't have explained, his temper flared up. The sight of Tongi flirting with the woman, his face red with drink, was something Hŏ could not bear. Quite the ladies' man, isn't he, thought Hŏ. What a disgraceful spectacle!

'Still wet behind the ears, and here you are swilling a brew and flirting with women in broad daylight,' he said, walking right up to Tongi. 'You go around giving us vendors a bad name, but you still want a share of our trade, it seems.'

Tongi looked Hŏ straight in the eye. Mind your own business, he seemed to be saying.

When the young man's animated eyes met his, on impulse Hŏ lashed Tongi across the cheek. Flaring up in anger, Tongi shot to his feet. But Hŏ, not about to compromise, let fly with all he had to say.

'I don't know what kind of family you come from, you young pup, but if your mum and dad could see this disgraceful behaviour, how pleased would they be! Being a vendor is a full-time job – there's no time for women. Now get lost, right this minute!'

But when Tongi disappeared without a word of rejoinder, Hŏ suddenly felt compassion for him. He had overreacted, he told himself uneasily; that wasn't how you treated a man who was only a nodding acquaintance.

'You've gone too far,' said the Ch'ungju woman. 'Where do you get the right to slap him and dress him down like that? To me you're both customers. And besides, you may think he's young, but he's old enough to produce children.' Her lips were pinched together, and she poured their drinks more roughly now.

'Young people need a dose of that now and then,' said Cho in an attempt to smooth over the situation.

'You've fallen for the young fellow, haven't you?' Hŏ asked the woman. 'Don't you know it's a sin to take advantage of a boy?'

The fuss died down. Hŏ, already emboldened, now felt like getting good and drunk. Every bowl of *makkŏlli* he was given he tossed off almost at a gulp. As he began to mellow, his thoughts of the Ch'ungju woman were overshadowed by concern for Tongi. What was a guy in his position going to do after coming between them? What a foolish spectacle he had made of himself!

And for this reason, when Tongi rushed back a short time later, calling Hŏ frantically, Hŏ put down his bowl and ran outside in a flurry without thinking twice about it.

'Saengwŏn, your donkey's running wild – it broke its tether.'

'Those little bastards must be teasing it,' muttered Hŏ.

Hŏ was of course concerned about his donkey, but he was moved even more by Tongi's thoughtfulness. As he ran after Tongi across the marketplace, his eyes became hot and moist.

'The little devils – there was nothing we could do,' said Tongi.

'Tormenting a donkey – they're going to catch hell from me.'

Hŏ had spent half his life with that animal, sleeping at the same country inns and walking from one market town to the next along roads awash with moonlight. And those twenty years had aged man and beast together. The animal's cropped mane bristled like his master's hair, and discharge ran from his sleepy eyes, just as it did from Hŏ's. He would try as best he could to swish the flies away with his stumpy tail, now too short to reach even his legs. Time and again Hŏ had filed down the donkey's worn hooves and fitted him with new shoes. Eventually the hooves had stopped growing back, and it became useless trying to file them down. Blood now oozed between the hooves and the worn shoes. The donkey recognized his master's smell, and would greet Hŏ's arrival with a bray of delight and supplication.

Hŏ stroked the donkey's neck as if he were soothing a child. The animal's nostrils twitched, and then he whickered, sending spray from his nose in every direction. How Hŏ had suffered on account of this creature. It wouldn't be easy calming the sweaty, trembling donkey; those boys must have teased it without mercy. The animal's bridle had come loose, and his saddle had fallen off.

'Good-for-nothing little rascals!' Hŏ yelled. But most of the boys had run away. The remaining few had slunk off to a distance at Hŏ's shouting.

'We weren't teasing him,' cried one of them, a boy with a runny nose. 'He got an eyeful of Kim Chŏmji's mare and went crazy!'

'Will you listen to the way that little guy talks,' said Hŏ.

'When Kim Chŏmji took his mare away, this one went wild – kicking up dirt, foam all around his mouth, bucking like a crazy bull. He looked so funny – all we did was watch. Look at him down there and see for yourself,' shouted the boy, pointing to the underside of Hŏ's donkey and breaking into laughter.

Before Hŏ knew it, he was blushing. Feeling compelled to screen the donkey from view, he stepped in front of the animal's belly.

'Confounded animal! Still rutting at his age,' he muttered.

The derisive laughter flustered Hŏ for a moment, but then he gave chase to the boys, brandishing his whip.

'Catch us if you can! Hey, everybody, Lefty's gonna whip us!'

But when it came to running, Hŏ was no match for the young troublemakers. That's right, old Lefty can't even catch a boy, thought Hŏ as he tossed the whip aside. Besides, the rice brew was working on him again, and he felt unusually hot inside.

'Let's get out of here,' said Cho. 'Once you start squabbling with these market pests there's no end to it. They're worse than some of the adults.'

Cho and Tongi each saddled and began loading his animal. The sun had angled far towards the horizon.

In the two decades that Hŏ had been peddling dry goods at the rural markets, he had rarely skipped Pongp'yŏng in his rounds. He sometimes went to Ch'ungju, Chech'ŏn and neighbouring counties, and occasionally roamed farther afield to the Kyŏngsang region. Otherwise, unless he went to a place such as Kangnŭng to stock up on goods, he confined his rounds to P'yŏngch'ang County. More regular than the moon, he tramped from one town to the next. He took pride in telling others that Ch'ŏngju was his hometown, but he never seemed to go there. To Hŏ, home sweet home was the beautiful landscape along the roads that led him from one market town to the next. When he finally approached one of these towns after trudging half a day, the restive donkey would let out a resounding hee-haw. In particular, when they arrived around dusk, the flickering lights in the town – though a familiar scene by now – never failed to make Hŏ's heart quicken.

Hŏ had been a thrifty youth and had put away a bit of money. But then one year during the All Souls' Festival he had squandered and gambled, and in three days he had blown all of his savings. Only his extreme fondness for the donkey had restrained him from selling the animal as well. In the end, he had had no choice but to return to square one and begin making the rounds of the market towns all over again. 'It's a good thing I didn't sell you,' he had said with tears in his eyes, stroking the donkey's back as they fled the town. He had gone into debt, and saving money was now out of the question. And thus began a hand-to-mouth existence as he journeyed from one market to the next.

In the course of all his squandering, Hŏ had never managed to conquer a woman. The cold, heartless creatures – they have no use for me, he would think dejectedly. His only constant friend was the donkey.

Be that as it may, there had been one affair, and he would never forget it. His first and last – it was a most mysterious liaison. It had happened when he was young, when he had begun stopping at the Pongp'yŏng market, and whenever he recalled it, he felt that his life had been worth living.

'For the life of me, I still can't figure it out,' Hŏ said to no one in particular. 'It was a moonlit night . . .'

This was the signal that Hŏ would begin yarning again that night. Being Hŏ's friend, Cho had long since had an earful of what was to come. But he couldn't exactly tell Hŏ he was sick of the story, and so Hŏ innocently started anew and rambled on as he pleased.

'A story like this goes well with a moonlit night,' said Hŏ with a glance towards Cho. Not that he felt apologetic towards his friend; rather, the moonlight had made him feel expansive.

The moon was a day or two past being full, and its light was soft and pleasant. Twenty miles of moonlit walking lay before them to Taehwa – two mountain passes, a stream crossing, hilly paths along endless fields. They were traversing a hillside. It was probably after midnight by now, and it was so deathly still the moon seemed to come alive right there in front of you, its breath almost palpable. Awash with moonlight, the bean plants and the drooping corn stalks were a shade greener. The hillside was covered with buckwheat coming into flower, and the sprinkling of white in the gentle moonlight was almost enough to take your breath away. The red stalks seemed delicate as a fragrance, and the donkeys appeared to have more life in their step.

The road narrowed, forcing the men to mount their animals and ride single file. The refreshing tinkle of the bells hanging from the donkeys' necks flowed towards the buckwheat. Hŏ's voice, coming from the front, wasn't clearly audible to Tongi at the tail end, but Tongi had some pleasant memories of his own to keep him company.

'It was market day in Pongp'yŏng, and the moon was out, just like tonight. I'd taken this tiny little room with a dirt floor, and it was so muggy I couldn't get to sleep. So I decided to go down and cool off in the stream. Pongp'yŏng then was just like it is now – buckwheat everywhere you looked, and the white flowers coming right down to the stream. I could have stripped right there on the gravel, but the moon was so bright, I decided to use the watermill shed instead. Well, I want to tell you, strange things happen in this world. Suddenly, there I was in the shed, face to face with old man Song's daughter – the town beauty. Was it fate that brought us together? You bet it was.'

8

Hŏ puffed on a cigarette, as if savouring his own words. The rich aroma of the purple smoke suffused the night air.

'Of course she wasn't waiting for me, but for that matter she didn't have a boyfriend waiting for her, either. Actually, she was crying. And I had a hunch as to why. Old man Song was having a terrible time making ends meet, and the family was on the verge of selling out. Being a family matter, it was cause enough for her to worry too. They wanted to find a good husband for her, but she told me she would have died first. Now you tell me – is there anything that can get to a fellow more than the sight of a girl in tears? I sensed she was startled at first. But you know, girls tend to warm to you more easily when they're worried, and it wasn't long until – well, you know the rest. Thinking back now, it scares me how incredible that night was.'

'And the next day she took off for Chech'ŏn or thereabouts – right?' Cho prompted him.

'By the next market day, the whole family had vanished. You should have heard the gossip in the market. Rumours were flying: the family's best bet was to sell the girl off to a tavern, they were saying. God knows how many times I searched the Chech'ŏn marketplace for her. But there was no more sign of her than a chicken after dinner. My first night with her was my last. And that's why I have a soft spot in my heart for Pongp'yŏng, and why I've spent half my life visiting the place. I'll never forget it.'

'You were a lucky man, Saengwŏn. Something like that doesn't happen every day. You know, a lot of fellows get stuck with an ugly wife, they have kids, and the worries begin to pile up – you get sick of that after a while. On the other hand, being an itinerant peddler to the end of your days isn't my idea of an easy life. So I'm going to call it quits after autumn. Thought I'd open up a little shop in a place like Taehwa and then have the family join me. Being on the road all the time wears a man out.'

'Not me – unless I meet her again. I'll be walking this here road, watching that moon, till the day I croak.'

The mountain path opened onto a wide road. Tongi came up from the rear, and the three donkeys walked abreast.

'But look at you, Tongi,' said Hŏ. 'You're still young – you're in the prime of life. It was stupid of me to act that way at the Ch'ungju woman's place. Don't hold it against me.'

'Don't mention it. I'm the one who feels silly. At this stage of my life, I shouldn't be worrying about girls. Night and day, it's my mother I think about.'

Downhearted because of Hŏ's story, Tongi spoke in a tone that was a shade subdued.

'When you mentioned my parents at the tavern, it made my heart ache. You see, I don't have a father. My mother's my only blood relation.'

'Did your father die?'

'I never had one.'

'Well, that's a new one.'

Hŏ and Cho burst into laughter.

'I'm ashamed to say it,' said Tongi with a serious expression, forced to explain himself, 'but it's the truth. My mother gave birth to me prematurely when they were in a village near Chech'ŏn, and then her family kicked her out. I know it sounds strange, but that's why I've never seen my father's face, and I have no idea where he is.'

The men dismounted as they approached a pass, and fell silent while climbing the rough road. The donkeys frequently slipped. Hŏ was soon short of breath, and had to pause time and again to rest his legs. He felt his age every time he had to cross a pass. How he envied the young fellows like Tongi. Sweat began to stream down his back.

Just the other side of the pass, the road crossed a stream. The plank bridge had been washed out during the monsoon rains, so they would have to wade across. The men removed their loose summer trousers and tied them around their backs with their belts. Half naked, they presented a comical sight as they stepped briskly into the stream. They had been sweating a moment ago, but it was night-time and the water chilled them to the bone.

'Who the devil brought you up, then?' Hŏ asked Tongi.

'My mother did. She had no choice but to remarry, and she opened up a drinking house. But my stepfather was a hopeless drunk – a complete good-for-nothing. Ever since I was old enough to know what's what, he beat me. We didn't have a day's peace. And if Mother tried to stop him, she'd get kicked, hit, threatened with a knife. Our family was one big mess. And so I left home at eighteen, and I've been peddling ever since.'

'I always thought you were quite a lad for your age, but to hear all this, it sounds like you *really* had a hard time.'

The water had risen to their waists. The current was quite strong, the pebbles underfoot slippery. The men felt as if they would be swept from their feet at any moment. Cho and the donkeys had made quick progress and were almost across. Tongi and Hŏ, the younger man supporting the older, were far behind.

'Was your mother's family originally from Chech'ŏn?' asked Hŏ.

'I don't think so. I never could get a straight answer out of her, but I've heard say they lived in Pongp'yŏng.'

'Pongp'yŏng . . . What was your dad's name, anyway?'

'Beats me. I never heard it mentioned.'

'I suppose not,' mumbled Hŏ as he blinked his bleary eyes. And then, distracted, he lost his footing. His body pitched forward, plunging him deep into the stream. He flailed about, unable to right himself, and by the time Tongi had called out to Cho and caught up with Hŏ, the older man had been washed some distance away. With the sodden clothes on his back, Hŏ looked more miserable than a wet dog. Tongi lifted him easily from the water and carried him piggyback. Soaked though he was, Hŏ was a slender man, and he rested lightly on Tongi's sturdy back.

'Sorry to put you to this trouble,' said Hŏ. 'I guess my mind's been wandering today.'

'It's nothing to worry about.'

'So, didn't it ever seem to you that your mother was looking for your dad?'

'Well, she's always saying she'd like to see him.'

'And where is she now?'

'In Chech'ŏn – she went there after she split up with my stepfather. I'm thinking of moving her up to Pongp'yŏng this autumn. If I put my mind to it, we'll make out somehow.'

'Sure, why not? That's a swell idea. Did you say this autumn?'

Tongi's broad, agreeable back spread its warmth into Hŏ's bones. And then they were across. Hŏ plaintively wished Tongi might have carried him a bit farther.

Cho could no longer suppress a laugh.

'Saengwŏn, this just isn't your day.'

'It was that donkey colt – I got to thinking about it and lost my balance. Didn't I tell you? You wouldn't think this old fellow had it in him, but by God if he didn't sire a colt with the Kangnŭng woman's mare in Pongp'yŏng. The way it pricks up its ears and prances about – is there anything as cute as a donkey colt? There are times I've stopped at Pongp'yŏng just to see it.'

'Must be some colt to make a man take a spill like that.'

Hŏ wrung a fair amount of water out of his sodden clothes. His teeth chattered, he shivered, he was cold all over. But for some unaccountable reason he felt buoyant.

'Let's hurry to the inn, fellows,' said Hŏ. 'We'll build a fire in the yard and get nice and cosy. I'll heat up some water for the donkeys, and tomorrow I'll stop at Taehwa, and then head on to Chech'ŏn.'

'You're going to Chech'ŏn, too?' asked Tongi, his voice trailing off in surprise.

'Thought I'd pay a visit – haven't been there in a while. How about it, Tongi – you and me?'

As the donkeys set off again, Tongi was holding his whip in his left hand. This time Hŏ, whose eyes had long been weak and dim, couldn't fail to notice Tongi was left-handed.

As Hŏ ambled along, the tinkle of the donkeys' bells, more lucid now, carried over the dusky expanse. The moon had arched far across the heavens.

CH'AE MANSHIK

A Man Called Hŭngbo

Translated by Ross King and Bruce and Ju-Chan Fulton

I

A Japanese lunchbox in one hand and a pint bottle of *chŏngjong* in the other ... betcha you're thinking this story's about the gentleman in the bowler hat and morning coat – or is it a frock coat? – with the artificial flower pinned to his lapel, his face bearing a healthy sheen and a ruddy glow, a toothpick in his mouth, a man on his way home from some commemorative event, a public servant of note or the local Lord Muck, but actually we'll be concerned instead with the doings of good ol' Mister Hyŏn, the odd-jobs man at a primary school.

The esteemed principal had arrived at school that morning in his *hurok kotto*, which is Japanese for 'frock coat,' which led me to believe he had a function to attend, and sure enough he had stepped out briefly after the lunch hour and was now returning with the lunchbox and *chŏngjong*, but this man, a confirmed teetotaller, had left the bottle capped and taken only a couple of nibbles from the fixings in the bento lunch.

'You come, Hen' – this was how he pronounced Hyŏn's name – 'this sea bass good,' he says, offering the lunchbox and *chŏngjong*.

The steamed rice was prepared with polished grain, white as jade and glossy like oil, with thick, tender grains, but it was the *fixings:* so savoury, so precious, they'd make good snacks for children, and Hyŏn couldn't help thinking of his little girl Sundong.

Day in and day out, Hyŏn returned home around dusk, stepped inside the roofed, pillar-flanked gate, and *ahem*ed to announce his arrival, but before he could call out 'Sundong-*a*!' she had recognized his footsteps, hobbled out to the threshold as fast as her gimpy little legs would take her, called out 'Daddy!' and latched onto him. So pathetic and yet so lovable, she was his little Sundong, always happy to see him at the end of the day. So imagine her delight and excitement if he arrived unannounced, sneaking into the yard with these precious, tasty snacks in hand! Oh, how she would savour them!

As luck would have it, an opportunity had come up for him to hurry to the post office and post a document.

It was not far from Chae-dong, where the school was located, to the six-way intersection in An-dong, so all he had to do was stop by the house on his way back to school.

Parents as a rule try to be fair to all their children, and so his thoughts turned belatedly to his boy Sunsŏk, at which point thoughts of his wife crept in as well (she *loved* fishcakes).

But if it had been his intention to do something special just for young Sunsŏk or his wife rather than his little girl, he wouldn't have gone to the trouble of squeezing in this side trip and making extra legwork for himself, and besides, since today was the twenty-first, the monthly payday, he could bide his time and before long he would have his pay envelope and make the customary evening return home from his 'day at the office.'

(Come to think of it, parents *are* fair to their children, but ultimately it seems difficult to get around the fact that it's a matter of degree. Just like fingers both long and short can come out of the same mother's belly at the same hour on the same day.)

In any event, although it contained someone else's leftovers, and notwithstanding its origins in Hyŏn's poverty, this was now a good, solid bento lunchbox jam-packed with love and affection.

So at this very moment good ol' Hyŏn was on his way to the Chae-dong intersection, walking briskly along the avenue that led past Unhyŏn Palace, the lunchbox in one hand, the bottle of *chŏngjong* in the other.

It was already the twenty-first of May, the breeze was past being pleasantly warm, and he was downright hot in his black Western suit (imagine that, a suit!) of heavy cotton.

And the sky: the quintessential May sky, as clear and blue as you could want.

Outside the gate and within the walls of the palace there was the

14

dazzling green of new growth everywhere – the grass, the sculpted pines, the willows, everything!

This was the scenery good ol' Hyŏn saw during his daily comings and goings, but now, as he bustled along, it caught his attention and he couldn't help turning his gaze to the verdure that graced the old palace so conspicuously.

This first greenery, ringing in summer and seeing off spring, was as ripe as a pert young Buddhist nun, and as he passed by, good ol' Hyŏn thought he felt the vague stirrings of his own youth, which had passed so suddenly and so long ago.

As he gazed up at the immaculate sky he fancied himself back in those youthful days, and the thought excited him almost enough to make him forget for the moment that his hair was flecked with grey and that he was long past forty.

It didn't take long for good ol' Hyŏn's presence to botch this splendid scene and aggravate everything in sight. His forty-odd years of exposure to the sun, wind and rain had left him with a leathery, ashen-coloured face blotched with liver spots, and on this foundation were sleepy, shifty eyes that eluded contact; a feeble attempt at facial hair, consisting of a few faded whiskers that would barely have distinguished him from a eunuch; meagre lips; a deflated nose resembling a starving bedbug – all of which combined to lend him a wistful air – ears so grandly huge (read *deformed*) they seemed bound and determined, if only out of spite, to compensate for the insufficiency in every other area; and too much white hair to hide: how pathetic to think that with these hoary, grotesque features, which must have generated many a complaint from the fine surroundings silently suffering this considerable indignity, he could feel his bygone youth as his heart thrilled to the May sky and the emerald colours. But this wasn't the half of it . . .

His jet-black suit with its shiny splotches of starch, plus the pockets, like ox testicles drooping in the heat of the season, positively bulging with what he'd squirrelled away, were almost so heavy as to bow him over. His manner of walking, bent over and knees flexed, was one thing, but the way the soles of his olive-coloured plimsolls dragged along so that his heels kicked up twin trails of dust and made a cloud even worse than an aerial smokescreen could not help but mar the crystal sky of May.

Good ol' Hyŏn himself was well aware that it was a very bad habit, this heel dragging.

And come to think of it, it amounted to a considerable waste of money when the heels wore down to the soles even though the shoes were otherwise quite serviceable, and scuffing his heels wasn't the best way to make a good impression – what self-respecting person would do this in public? – and so when he walked down the street he would hear insults from time to time – 'Look at that poor dimwit' – but what could he say, since he's the one kicking up all that dust . . . The list goes on and on.

As long as we're on the subject of insults: people on the street were the least of his worries, for once his own wife (née Kang) lit into him she would always start by heaving a sigh and saying, '*Ayu!* Just look at these heels – can't you pick up your feet when you walk!' and then it was on to his eyes, nose, mouth, whiskers, ears, waistline, legs, even his belly button – well, there was plenty more where that came from.

Insofar as good ol' Hyŏn was sufficiently aware of this bad habit, it was not as if he was never mindful of the need to desist. But (and of course this might have been a question of his fate) ever since he was old enough to know better, and in spite of a good thirty years of constant reminders to himself, he just couldn't kick the habit, and apart from those sporadic occasions when he felt compelled to pay attention to the way he walked, he would be going along with something else on his mind only to realize in a rare moment of clarity that there it was again, that same old bad habit.

And sure enough, right this moment, a pair of nice, puffy billows of dust were rising from good ol' Hyŏn's feet every time his heels scuffed along the dirt road – and wouldn't you know it, they were coming off a long drought and the road was bone-dry, and there was a soft breeze in the air – and the result was a sight to behold.

'What's with the dust storm!' someone barked.

Starting at this sudden assault on his ears, good ol' Hyŏn whipped around and found himself looking at the Chae-dong police substation square in the façade, and there sat Constable Kim grinning at him.

'Heh-heh . . . I was wondering whose dulcet tones I was hearing, sir . . .'

Good ol' Hyŏn lifted one hand to remove his hat, realized it held the lunchbox, then lifted the other hand only to realize it held the bottle of *chŏngjong*, and finally he settled on bowing from the waist.

'How are you, Kim Chusa?'

'How in hell can you walk around like that? Look at yourself!'

'Heh-heh . . . Now mind that sun, sir, don't want it blinding you in the performance of your duties!'

Good ol' Hyŏn and Constable Kim were on such an equal footing that they could talk with each other in this completely unaffected way. Goodness knows, the one was a lowly gofer at a primary school while the other was a provincial constable for the Government-General who at least occupied the lowest rungs of Japanese officialdom, but even if you want to ignore lineage and status, there *is* such a thing as social standing, and people are going to raise an eyebrow, or maybe get downright indignant, at the notion that lack of ceremony translates into equality, and yet on the other hand, while we grant you that lineage and status are a fact of life and there are inevitable distinctions between high and low, is it not the case that every so often humanity prevails in a relationship?

Now if that notion rankles you, then picture this:

Good ol' Hyŏn and Constable Kim were neighbours, their front gates opening onto each other across a slender alley, and the year before last, when Constable Kim had moved in, Hyŏn's daughter Sundong, despite her gammy leg, had become fast friends with Kim's daughter Chŏngja, who like Sundong was five years old, and within half a year the womenfolk had struck up a friendship, and through this agency the two men's nodding acquaintance had grown chummier.

And then this past March, when Constable Kim was attempting to enrol Chŏngja at good ol' Hyŏn's primary school and everyone was having a devil of a time getting even their seven- and eight-year-olds registered because of the usual enrolment squeeze, good ol' Hyŏn had done some fast footwork, thanks to which Chŏngja was admitted without incident.

'This here girl's the daughter of a cousin on my mother's side, so you've got to find a place for her even if that means turning away ten other children.'

Of course he told the principal and vice-principal this, and he even went out of the way to make several appearances before the school board because he happened to know one of the clerks there. And even if the constable wasn't actually a cousin, a good neighbour is worth his weight in cousins, as the saying goes, and so it's not as if good ol' Hyŏn was a pathological liar.

Be that as it may, liar or not, after all this fuss and bother the constable's darling little girl was admitted. And so the family was grateful to good ol' Hyŏn, and this gratitude could only mean a closer connection between the two men.

To make a long story short, it would not be out of line for me to say that this lowly gofer and a certain constable were on the freest of terms (with due allowance for their different pedigrees), and enjoyed a relationship free of pretension.

2

The constable gave the bottle of *chŏngjong* a meaningful look and with a twinkle in his eye teased good ol' Hyŏn: 'Lucky you. Later today, eh?'

It would be unseemly of me to say that he was salivating as he said this, but the constable was a drinking kind of man, and although he would be above blatant ogling of the vulnerable vessel in good ol' Hyŏn's hand, the mere sight of the bottle triggered his drinker's hankering, and this hankering couldn't help but play across his face.

They say good ol' Hyŏn's a little slow on the uptake, but insofar as he had served a considerable apprenticeship in the ways of drinking ever since he was a wee lad, he could not possibly misread such a telling hint from a fellow tippler.

'Heavens! You didn't think I was planning to drink this by myself, did you? Where's the fun in that? Eh, Constable Kim?'

So saying, good ol' Hyŏn flashed the constable another look-see at the bottle, along with a wink and a grin.

'Are you out of your mind? On duty?' His words sounded solemn enough, but the attendant snicker suggested that the constable was only too happy to be tempted. He continued, upping the ante: 'We can do better than that lunchbox, though . . . What a bottle like that needs is for your wife to whip us up a pound of sukiyaki, which we wash down with a drink while we watch the sun set.'

Needless to say, these instructions to good ol' Hyŏn were seasoned advice from a fellow boozer.

But good ol' Hyŏn didn't dare.

'Then why don't I drop the bottle off at your place, Constable Kim?'

'No no no. No need for that.'

'Come on, you're just saying that . . . Tell you what, you get home for supper and have yourself a drink, how's that?'

'Oh, fine, then. I'll buy some meat and after it's cooked and we sit down to supper I'll give you a shout, all right?'

Now it was good ol' Hyŏn who felt a powerful temptation. Even so, he said, 'Who me!? You know damn well I can't drink.'

'You mean you're not *allowed* to drink . . . You want to, but your old lady's got you spooked. You just get yourself over when I holler. Leave your wife to me – I'll make something up.'

'Heavens, no!' Good ol' Hyŏn chuckled sheepishly. 'How could I? How about I just take this bottle over right now?'

Thus was good ol' Hyŏn saved the trouble of disposing of the offending pint bottle of *chŏngjong*.

The principal had made a point of giving him the bottle as a sign of gratitude (he knew that although good ol' Hyŏn rarely drank, he appreciated a brew). Granted, it was just a small bottle, but for good ol' Hyŏn it was precious indeed. On the other hand, as Constable Kim was always joking, good old Hyŏn's wife, née Kang, was such a terror when it came to alcohol, he could not bring himself to partake; instead, even a fleeting glimpse of it, or its momentary possession, was a source of pleasure and excitement. And this was why good ol' Hyŏn had felt so uneasy just then while reverently escorting the cursed bottle and attendant lunchbox to his home.

Anything involving booze, even the mere sight of it, triggered antipathy in his wife, along with the anxious thought that her husband might up and drink the stuff, and so she felt compelled to let loose with a double-whammy two-for-one barrage of squawking about the here-and-now bottle and any yet-to-come partaking thereof.

He'd taken nary a whiff from the bottle, but it was enough for him to realize what a precious windfall it was. The notion itself worked him into a tizzy, but if he took it all the way home there would be hell to pay for his transgression, and therein lay the problem. And he mustn't forget his esteemed principal. Half-eaten bento or not, food it was, and one just doesn't go and throw it in the ditch. That was no way to thank the principal, besides which it might incur the wrath of heaven; it was simply beyond the pale.

That being the case, to be on the safe side, both business-wise and personally, what if he ran into an acquaintance and simply handed over the bottle? That way you keep up appearances and come off looking like a great guy. Now *there* was a capital plan. Such was good ol' Hyŏn's intention when he happened upon Constable Kim (I clean forgot to mention this earlier, but he held the constable in great esteem), and when shortly after the fact he reflected on how the two of them had settled the fate of the bottle he decided all in all that the outcome couldn't have been better.

And so it was, with the delight of being relieved of a major headache, together with the satisfaction of finally being able to do something for Constable Kim in the way of a little neighbourly assistance, that with a bounce in his step – alas, preoccupied as he was, he had once again lapsed into dragging his heels – good ol' Hyŏn was hustling towards the main intersection of An-dong.

He had picked up his pace with the intention of making up for the time he had lost dallying with the constable at the police box, when he found himself sidetracked yet again. A couple of girls were coming his way, book bags strapped to their backs, arms around each other's shoulders, swaying back and forth, tittering and chattering and generally carrying on. These two were third-year students at the primary school. They didn't recognize good ol' Hyŏn until they were practically upon him, whereupon one of them giggled, 'Eek, it's the vice-principal!'

'The vice-principal!' said the other. 'Salute!' And just like schoolboys would have done, they both held their little hands to their short, bobbed hair in a salute.

Good ol' Hyŏn came quickly (if somewhat clumsily) to attention and returned their salute, bringing the bottle up to his visor in the process. Then followed an amused chuckle.

It's late in the game to be mentioning this, but at school good ol' Hyŏn was known as 'good ol' Hyŏn,' as 'the odd-jobs man,' 'the gofer' and – get this – the 'Vice-Principal'!

There comes a time when an odd-jobs man who has worked long enough at a company will be nicknamed 'Vice-President.' Or if he works long enough at a police station, 'Deputy.' It's the same at a school: a long-serving odd-jobs man just ends up with the moniker 'Vice-Principal' one day.

This is good ol' Hyŏn's nineteenth year running as the odd-jobs man at the primary school. Those years have seen the principal replaced six times and the school building renovated three times, and good ol' Hyŏn has received medals for ten years' consecutive service, and then fifteen, to be followed in turn next year by the medal for twenty years.

Given all those years, good ol' Hyŏn is thoroughly versed in the ins and outs of the history of the school. He knows Principal Joe was appointed at such-and-such a time of year, that Principal Shmoe was transferred to such-and-such a place and at what time of year, and that's just for starters. He has the lowdown on all the various teachers, from date of hire to date of retire, he knows the number of graduates, he knows about the renovations to the school building, the results of sports events – you name it.

And the power of recall he has over all that goes in those two ears of his is simply phenomenal. This powerful memory not only helps him remember past events, but comes in even handier in the present, such that he can recite the name of every single student from the third year on up. On the street, or wherever, no sooner does he see you then he'll let you know who you are, without a moment's hesitation: 'Yep, Year such-and-such, So-and-so's classroom,' and any other pertinent details.

And that ain't the half of it: he knows where practically every one of them lives, too.

Which brings us back to the two girls. Well, they're both third years, both in Pine classroom, the one with the big eyes is Yun Sunae, the one with the mare's face is Ch'oe Pokhŭi, and they live across from Hwimun Academy, in Wŏnkkol to be precise, and they're neighbours . . .

Like I told you, this guy knows his stuff.

That alone qualifies him for 'Vice-Principal,' but hell, for my money you can get rid of the 'Vice.'

There should be no doubt, of course, that 'Vice-President,' 'Assistant Chief,' or 'Vice-Principal,' spoken in reference to a gofer who's seen better years is a jocular yet not altogether kind appellation tempered with a mixture of pity and contempt, the type of thing one's betters might say of a mere underling whose fate it is never to ascend to such a position. For good ol' Hyŏn, though, just as for the great majority of the boys and girls at the school, calling or being called 'Vice-Principal' held no subtle or underhand meaning, but in truth was a term of endearment infused with the innocent purity and artlessness of these young children. In other words, this was all because good ol' Hyŏn loved these children to pieces.

3

Good ol' Hyŏn shook with laughter as the two girls flanking him, each clutching one of his thighs, giggled hysterically . . . And then, as good ol' Hyŏn looked down solicitously at the two little dears looking up at him with their adoring, fawn-like eyes and their grinning faces, he was struck by a thought. These third-year girls from the Pine classroom had been dismissed from school way back when, at two o'clock, and here it was just shy of four and all this time these girls had been out and about on the streets – boy, were they in for it!

'Now – now just a minute here, you two,' good ol' Hyŏn said with concern, bending over and peering into the two faces. 'Where've you girls been – you ought to be home by now.'

Sunae, the one with the large eyes, was the first to answer: 'Playing . . .'

Followed by Pokhŭi: 'At our friend's house.'

'At your friend's house? Playing?'

'Mm-hmm.'

'Mm-hmm.'

The two of them nodded furiously.

'Heyyyy! That's no good.'

'How come?' each girl asked in turn.

'How come? Well . . . you're supposed to play with your friends at school . . . And when school gets out you scoot home!'

'But we got out early today.'

'And Okcha said we could play at her house, so we went to Okcha's.'

'Heyyyy! That's still no good! . . . What if Mummy, Daddy and Grandma are waiting for you? What if they're all worried, saying, "Oh, what's happened to our little Sunae?" "Why isn't our little Pokhŭi back from school yet? Did she get hit by a bike? Did she get a scolding from her teacher and have to stay behind after school?" Look – those big, huge buses, those cars charging along, those bicycles whizzing by, those pony carts – see 'em all? What if you get hit? And here you are playing in the street . . .'

'No problem here,' Sunae giggled, shaking her head and indicating the street surface with her foot.

'Yeah!' said Pokhŭi. 'This street's only for people. No cars allowed, not even cats! . . . Long as we walk here we won't get hit – our teacher said so!'

This brought a laugh from good ol' Hyŏn. 'Well, aren't you two remarkable!' Good ol' Hyŏn had an urge to pat the girls on their bobbed heads, but with the lunchbox in one hand and the bottle of *chŏngjong* in the other, the backs of his hands had to stand in for the palms. 'The things you two know already – that's just remarkable.'

'What does "remarkable" mean, Vice-Principal?'

'Vice-Principal, where did you get that bento?'

'Huh? Oh! . . . Oh yeah, "remarkable." Well, that means you're good girls, and bright too –'

'Ooh, alcohol!'

'Ah, this? The principal brought it back for me from some function.'

'For *you* to drink, Vice-Principal?'

'Vice-Principal, you *drink*?'

'Drink? Not me!'

'It's bitter, isn't it?'

'Yes, very bitter – nasty stuff!'

'So why do you have alcohol?'

'Well, ah . . . I've got somebody in mind for it –'

'But the bento's good, right, Vice-Principal?'

'It's *really* good, Pokhŭi – isn't it, Vice-Principal?'

'You bet it is! Pokhŭi, you've never had a bento lunch?'

'Nope.'

'But you have, Sunae?'

'Yep . . . When Father takes me down-country . . . to Grandfather's place . . . on the train.'

'Well . . . you don't say! But this here bento is tastier than any bento they sell on any train . . . Want a taste? I'll give you some if you want.'

You can tell the girls want to, but they don't immediately respond. Instead, they eye each other, all the while grinning sheepishly at good ol' Hyŏn.

'There, have some, mmm? . . . Maybe just a smidgeon of the fixin's, mmm?'

Good ol' Hyŏn sets his bottle on the ground and begins to unwrap the lunchbox.

'My mum'll give me an earful . . . Eating on the street, and all.'

'My mum too . . . She says only beggars eat on the street.'

'Well, I'll – gosh, hadn't thought of that!' Good ol' Hyŏn can barely control the emotions accompanying this revelation. 'Why, yes indeedy . . . I clean forgot . . . Yes, yes! No eating on the street, no sirree! Only tramps do that!'

Good ol' Hyŏn chuckles, but what a shame not to share. And the girls, in spite of what they've said, struggle to keep their composure, eyeing that scrumptious bento lunch all the while – if only they could have a taste of it!

How could good ol' Hyŏn, seeing those expectant faces, just turn and walk away? But as the girls said, to pick at morsels from the bento on this busy street – why, that's like taking these precious kids and making urchins out of them . . . *Plus, what would people think of me?*

Might be better to send Pokhŭi off home with a bit of the fixin's, since she's never tried one of these lunchboxes, but that obviously wouldn't sit well with her parents either, seeing as how it's not fresh out of the box – another awkward situation . . . But he wasn't about to dwell on it because it had been his intention all along to take the lunchbox home to his own little Sundong.

Wish I hadn't met the girls in the first place . . . shouldn't have opened my big mouth either. Good ol' Hyŏn was about to scratch his head in bewilderment when an idea occurred to him. A quick gander around revealed a baker's shop nearby. Sad to say, good ol' Hyŏn didn't have so much as a copper in hand (it's not like he ever wandered around with spare change in his pocket anyway).

Oh yeah, that's right! . . . payday's comin' up – darned if isn't today – I'll just tuck away twenty chŏn *before handing over the rest to the old lady, and tomorrow or the day after, I'll buy each of the girls one of them ten-*chŏn *cookies . . . yeah, that's what I'll do . . .* Once this decision was firm in his mind, his otherwise uncooperative feet turned towards home.

He takes a few steps before looking back and offering one last reminder: 'You girls run on home now, you hear?'

'Yes, Vice-Principal, *gut-bye*.'

'*Gut-bye*, Vice-Principal.'

'Yes, *gut-bye*, and we should go straight home, right?'

'Yes indeedy.'

'That's right, we'll both go straight home.'

'Of course! And every time we cross the street we'll be extra careful and look both ways for cars, buses, bikes and pony carts.'

'That's my girl!'

'Vice-Principal, you be careful crossing the street too, all right?'

'You betcha,' good ol' Hyŏn chuckled.

4

Down his alley he goes, and at the gate to his house good ol' Hyŏn hesitates – go on in, or pop over to Constable Kim's first? Needless to say, he is itching to hurry on in to his little Sundong and everything else he holds dear. But that pesky bottle in his hand – you just can't keep a good bottle down. Since he was going to give it to the constable anyway, no point in catching hell at home first. The old lady has an uncanny knack for ferreting out contraband, and the moment she caught sight of him coming in, devil's brew in hand, he'd catch hell from the old bag before he even had a chance to come clean.

Without further ado, good ol' Hyŏn eases open the inner gate to Constable Kim's house and announces himself with a shallow cough.

'Pongja, anybody home?' So saying, he ventures into the courtyard.

The sliding doors to the family room are wide open, revealing Constable Kim's wife dozing inelegantly on the warm part of the floor, her upper torso clad in an *appappa*. She must have heard good ol' Hyŏn enter, for she sits up, woozy, passes one hand over her bulky bun and rubs the cotton-seed-sized sleep from her eyes with the other, then lumbers out on elephantine legs to the edge of the veranda before letting loose a couple of healthy yawns that would have done a hippopotamus proud.

'Good afternoon to you, Mrs Kim!'

'Who's that? Oh, it's you. I must have dropped off.'

'Uh, actually I, uh, thought Constable Kim might like . . .' He offers up the bottle, and wouldn't you know it, she stretches out not only one hand for the bottle but the other hand for the bento. Evidently it wasn't unknown for the man of the house to return home bearing a bottle in one hand and a bento in the other, which would explain her presumption that her husband has flagged down good ol' Hyŏn passing by the station and said, 'Be a good fellow, will you, and take these home for me, if you're going that way anyway.'

Once good ol' Hyŏn has unravelled her thoughts thus far, a sinking feeling hits him in the stomach – *Oh no!*

Sure enough, she blurts out, 'So nice of you to run this errand!' and opens her palms wide.

A fine pickle good ol' Hyŏn finds himself in now. Good ol' Hyŏn that he is, he can't for the life of him muster the nerve to pull the hand holding the lunchbox behind his back and say, 'No ma'am, it's just the bottle I'm delivering.' When good ol' Hyŏn realizes he is nigh on losing the both of them he feels like plopping himself down and bawling. All the pains he has taken, all the hustling he's done just to be able to enjoy the sight of little Sundong eating the bento – the prospect of having it taken away from him was already a crying shame, and in light of the situation with the girls just now, it was adding insult to injury.

So there you have it: on the one hand, since good ol' Hyŏn has got the lunchbox as sloppy seconds from the principal, if Constable Kim's wife were to open it now it would be clear in an instant that someone has already partaken of it . . . On the other hand, she may think nothing of it and assume that her husband has taken a few nibbles before sending it along, but when the constable comes home it'll be only a matter of time before they suspect good ol' Hyŏn himself of having had his hand in the cookie jar. At some point she'll almost certainly say to her husband, 'Wait a minute, I thought *you* had taken a few bites before sending it along with Hyŏn.' And then the constable will say, 'What! You mean someone's already been eating it? Of

26

all the lowdown . . . So he's giving me bento leftovers that he's already been rooting around in. That weasel Hyŏn!'

Annoyed they would be, but it wasn't the possibility of verbal abuse that worried him, rather the prospect of a sound spanking on his bare behind.

The more he thinks about it, the more helpless he feels, the more hopeless he becomes.

For the life of him, good ol' Hyŏn can't fathom how a lunchbox can rear its measly head and from the first moment on the street with the girls till now cause him so much grief and trouble.

'Your wife's not home? I haven't seen her . . .' As if good ol' Hyŏn weren't feeling sorry enough for himself already, these parting words from the wife of Constable Kim (polite chit-chat though they were) ushered him out the gate. 'Looks like little Sundong is all alone at home. Shouldn't you go check on her first before you go about your business?'

'Yes, ma'am, for sure.'

'I sure do wish that husband of mine wouldn't go sending you on errands like this all the time.'

'Don't you mention it! At your service. Say, is Pongja back yet?'

'Mm-hmm, school got out just before lunchtime. She's probably out playing somewhere.'

5

Sundong, knowing as she does from the sound of his footsteps that her father is home, and given the proximity of the two houses – how could she not know that her daddy is home? And so just as good ol' Hyŏn is pulling shut the gate to Constable Kim's house, little Sundong, hobbled by her crippled leg, is flinging open their outer gate to meet him, taking dainty little hops on her good leg.

Father's 'Sundong!' is met with Sundong's 'Daddy!'

Good ol' Hyŏn sweeps his daughter up and gives her cheek an affectionate rub. He manages to say 'I'm going to buy my little girl a bento' before he gets choked up – he *has* to do something about this wretched lunchbox business and that's when this idea strikes him.

Sure enough, good ol' Hyŏn has stumbled upon a wish fulfilled, and the dark cloud lifts from his face in an instant and a bright smile fills it instead. It was this revelation that had choked him up, not sadness.

But it's all a mystery to Sundong – what's this about a bento? Usually, the best he could do was a cookie. And for Sundong, 'bento' could only mean the tin container with the measly portion of rice with black beans cooked in soy sauce that her father and her brother took to school every day for lunch.

'A bento? You're buying me a bento?'

'Yes, indeedy, just you wait.'

'Yippee! So you can buy bento too?'

'Yes siree.'

'Where?'

'Uh, for starters, at the train station.'

'Yippee! Are they good?'

'As tasty as can be!'

'Oh goodie – I can't wait to try one!' And she isn't just playing cute either – that she really wants to try one is written all over her face.

Atrophy from the waist down, the overall wasted appearance, the bulging eyes, her long skinny neck, the narrow, bowed shoulders – scrofulosis, is that what they call it?

Good ol' Hyŏn really ought to be feeding her cod liver oil or calcium supplements, but even if we were to allow that he lacks the means, this much he surely could have afforded, so it was due to his ignorance that the girl was left untreated, with the result that she looked like a plucked bean sprout and suffered from perpetual hankerings. Besides which, because of her deformed leg, even though she's turned seven this year she can't run around outside and take in the sun, let alone attend school, so all she does is sit cooped up at home day and night, with the result that she doesn't grow properly.

As far as good ol' Hyŏn was concerned, disabled though she may be (and this is precisely why her future is so bleak), it's not that he doesn't want to send her to school – which, if she finishes, would mean becoming more than a glorified factotum like her father. But thus far, say what he might, and because she was still too immature, at the mere mention of the word *school* she would complain that people were mean to her and kids made fun of her, and she couldn't bear the thought of it. What could he do – you can't force these things.

Good ol' Hyŏn was so wrapped up in little Sundong and the bento that he was oblivious to the fact that little Spotty had followed the girl out the gate. A speckled terrier cross with black spots on a white background, Spotty is his second most favourite thing in the world after little Sundong. When little Spotty, wagging his tail in greeting, goes unnoticed, in a bid for attention he begins humping good ol' Hyŏn's leg. This catches his master's attention:

'Oh Spotty, didn't see you.' Good ol' Hyŏn lowers little Sundong to the ground and strokes Spotty's head. Spotty lies down on his back, ears perked up, and wags his tail like he can't get enough of it.

'All righty, then, let's all go inside.'

Supporting little Sundong with one hand and guiding Spotty, he leads them both through the gate.

'Where's Mummy?'

'She went out to pray!'

'To pray? Is somebody else sick now?'

'Yeah, somebody or other.'

'Your brother home yet?'

'Nyuh-uh.'

'Really. Weren't you bored all by yourself?'

'Yeah . . . But me and Nabi and Spotty – the three of us – were playing. Nabi was playing with the marbles, and me and Spotty were watching.'

As if on cue, a black cat with a white mouth, underbelly and legs comes to attention at the edge of the veranda and produces a cute meow.

'You don't say.' And then good ol' Hyŏn addresses the cat: 'Hello there – did you have fun playing with my baby?' He strokes the cat's back. Nabi was his third most favourite thing in the world.

Seeing little Sundong all alone and bored like this, good ol' Hyŏn can't help feeling exasperated: *If only I didn't have that pesky bento taken away, I could have given it to her. And if only I could have given little Spotty and little Nabi a morsel or two each, boy, would they have lit up!*

Good ol' Hyŏn is momentarily lost in thought when little Sundong calls out, 'Daddy, Daddy!'

'Yes, dear, what?'

'The swallows . . .'

'Oh right, I almost forgot,' says good ol' Hyŏn, looking up at the swallows' nest under the eaves of the room across the way.

These first nestlings were almost ready to fly and that morning had been bunched up at the edge of the nest, taking turns trying out their wings, when one of them had misjudged and fallen to the ground below. Good ol' Hyŏn had rushed over in alarm, scooped up the fledgling in his hands and placed it back in the nest. When the mother swallow came back with food in her beak, she unceremoniously evicted the poor thing. Thinking this strange, good ol' Hyŏn picked it up and replaced it, and once again the mother swallow pushed it out. This sequence was repeated several times.

Good ol' Hyŏn wasn't aware that swallows have the peculiar habit of never returning to a nest that comes into contact with a human, and always pushing out of the nest and refusing to rear any chick that smells of a human touch.

'So what happened?' Good ol' Hyŏn looked hopefully up at the nest and counted the chicks.

'She pushed it out again!'

'Again? So then what?'

'I made a nest for it out of cotton and brought it inside.'

'Really. Good for you . . . And then?'

'I gave it a teeny bit of rice but it won't eat.'

'It won't? . . . It must be awful hungry. What should we do?'

Good ol' Hyŏn looks around for a fly, but not finding one, heads into the kitchen, emerging some moments later with an offering. In the meantime, little Sundong fetches the swallow chick, still swaddled in cotton, and father and daughter join forces to pry open its beak and feed it (the wretched thing struggling all the while). Whether from hunger or confusion, swallow the fly the swallow does.

Good ol' Hyŏn is so taken with the little chick he forgets he has to go back to school, and so engrossed is he with fly-hunting and swallow-feeding that he's having the time of his life. But wouldn't you know it, here comes the mother swallow, who, seeing her chick in human clutches, flies into a rage, chirping and flapping like you've never seen.

'Oh, jealous, are we. Here, be my guest. And next time, don't go pushing it out of your nest,' says good ol' Hyŏn, as if admonishing a person, and then places the chick back in the nest.

But damn it if in the next breath that mean old mother swallow, in cahoots with the male who has just flown back to the nest, doesn't push the little fellow right back out again.

'Of all the miserable creatures!' Utterly perplexed and exasperated though he was, there was nothing much that good ol' Hyŏn could do about it; on the one hand he felt sorry, and on the other hand it drove him nuts.

6

Once your day decides it's got it in for you, it's just one nasty surprise after another. For starters, at the crack of dawn this swallow chick goes and falls out of its nest, and there's been no end of trouble ever since. *And then for the life of me why does this darned lunchbox and bottle of* chŏngjong *show up in the middle of the street, and lead to more grief at the hands of those two kids, and the next thing I know I'm giving sloppy seconds to my neighbour, which means I'm in for it now with Constable Kim's finicky old lady (which also means I've got a lot of fence mending to do)* . . . Not to mention all the hassle involved in going out to the South Gate to buy a bento, because he feels so badly for little Sundong . . .

And that was the easy part.

Of all the people, who should he run into on his way back from buying the bento, but that no-good Yunbo; there's no escaping his clutches without first downing at least three drinks apiece – and so, in goes good ol' Hyŏn behind him, and there they are polishing off drink number one, when who should go marching by but his good wife, who must have had some informants in the spirit world, and good ol' Hyŏn is caught in the act. No doubt if he had consulted a fortune-teller, he would have learned that spiteful ghosts and mortal danger awaited him in the southeast quadrant[1] – it doesn't get much worse than that.

Just a little while before, he had gone back to school to pick up his pay envelope, and after giving a lick and a promise to a couple of errands he scurried off to the South Gate, asked around in the market area outside, and managing to find a stall still selling bentos, and after buying one, he huffed and he puffed his way back to the intersection at An-dong, by which time it's well past seven in the evening. In late spring the days are long, and it hadn't even thought about getting dark yet, but good ol' Hyŏn had eaten breakfast at 7 a.m., and had a poor excuse for lunch and for the next seven hours he's been on his feet, constantly on the go – this was one hungry man. Seeing as how he was no stranger to the bottle, even though he had suffered a decree of prohibition, he had never sworn off the stuff, and so how could the effervescent jolt of downing a drink on an empty stomach not tickle his fancy?

In fact good ol' Hyŏn had been quite the drinker until something like early in his thirties, when his wife, née Kang, had found Jesus and demanded that he become a good God-fearing Christian and swear off tobacco and drink. (At least those were the orders she handed down.) Even if we grant that from where good ol' Hyŏn sat, his wife's dictatorial demands carried the force of law, they constituted an emasculating act of violence that took no consideration of the humanity of the oppressed – i.e., the husband.

The way good ol' Hyŏn saw it, believing in Jesus was about the same as hiking up to the shrine at the top of Samch'ŏng-dong and watching a *mudang* do her song and dance; it was so repugnant to him, he couldn't bring himself to do it. Think about it – all a *mudang* does is deck out one corner of her shaman shrine all colourful-like and install the titular spirit and worship her – bow to her, pray to her, give her a song and a dance and supposedly if you're sick you get better, your luck improves and your path to the next world is free and clear. Now think about this – in Christianity, instead of a shrine you've got a big brick house where you install some naked guy on a couple of crossed logs in the shape of the Chinese number ten and instead of bowing you get down on your knees in front of him, and instead of banging a drum and chanting they sing things called hymns to the tune of a harmonium ... The purpose is the same: if you're ill you get better, your luck improves, the path to heaven is free and clear. The only difference is that you make a big deal out of going around asking for forgiveness (by saying 'I repent!'), and speaking just of this sinning and forgiveness bit, good ol' Hyŏn through firsthand observation had developed a pretty good idea of how it worked: the Kang woman, his wife, would sin up a storm and then head off to the chapel, where she would get down on

32

her knees and bawl and wail and swear up and down, 'Lordy, Lordy, I have sinned; I promise I won't do it again; please forgive me,' and then come home all smiles and titters. The next time it would be the same all over again, and again and again ... If she took out her frustrations on Spotty by pouring steaming water over him, she would run off to chapel to wail and pray and collect her forgiveness; if she swore at little Sundong and smacked her, saying 'You little bitch, you deserve the leg screws, better still, why don't you go get yourself run over by a tram,' she would run off to chapel to wail and pray and collect her forgiveness.

But once you've done that a couple of times, once you've gone and committed your sin and wailed and prayed and collected your forgiveness, you need to stop committing those sins. She can smack little Spotty ten times in a month, and wail and pray and collect her forgiveness every time, and swear at and spank little Sundong fifteen times, and wail and collect her forgiveness every time. So in the end, as long as you cry and pray you can collect your forgiveness, so basically you can sin as much as you like. It didn't take long for good ol' Hyŏn to realize what a sweet deal that was. *Sin as much as you like, 'cause as long as you pray you'll be forgiven.*

Good ol' Hyŏn had got so fed up observing all this that once upon a time he had even torn into his wife: 'Quite generous this God of yours, eh? Different from the old God of Chosŏn times, who would strike a man dead with a lightning bolt if he sinned. For all I know, a disgusting crook like Chŏn Yonghae could set up his White-White Bright-Light Cult and commit his sins and collect his forgiveness and go to heaven and all he has to do is believe in Jesus.'

In any case, it was only natural that good ol' Hyŏn, with his limited wisdom, and knowing only what he saw in terms of spiritual practice among his wife and her small circle of co-religionists, would be unable to distinguish between religion and superstition, and therefore it should be no less surprising that for him, believing in religion was no different from a bunch of womenfolk with a mean streak finding solace and future happiness in visits to the local shrine to take in a *mudang* song and dance.

For good ol' Hyŏn shamanism was as appealing as insects crawling along his inner thigh, and understandably enough he couldn't bring himself to believe in Christianity, which he found just as distasteful. For a good year and more the climate on the home front was stormy practically day in and day out, but finally husband and wife came to an understanding. Good ol' Hyŏn was damned if he would believe in Jesus Christ, but he would quit drinking and smoking. And there you have it: booze was forbidden. And somehow he'd been dry for a decade now.

And so good ol' Hyŏn had avoided the fate of becoming a lush. His salary wasn't much at barely forty *wŏn* a month, but he was still able to send his boy Sunsŏk to a commercial high school, he was able to keep his family of four in food and clothing without being a skinflint, and he could keep making the two-*wŏn* and one-*wŏn*-fifty-*chŏn* payments on two insurance policies for little Sundong.

At the odd times when he considered how his fate had taken a turn for the better, he felt a profound upwelling of gratitude for his wife's tough love – even though at first he had had to be dragged kicking and screaming into abstinence. And since it was only ever a case of prohibition rather than going on the water wagon for all time, and seeing as how his wife couldn't very well follow him around all the livelong day to keep him honest, on a day like today when he was feeling hungry and hankering for a drink and happened to meet an old drinking buddy, good ol' Hyŏn just didn't have it in him to fend off the temptation of a nightcap.

7

It was a delightful place – up past the six-way An-dong intersection, find the alley on your left that skirts the palace wall and half a dozen steps in, just before the pawnshop on your right, is a sorry excuse for a building cobbled together from dilapidated tin and wooden siding and straw matting – and you'll find the tastiest soybean mash and *makkŏlli* in town.

And here comes good ol' Hyŏn looking resolutely to the south and doing his damnedest to avoid the sight of this peerless drinking hole and skedaddle on by, the heels of his tired legs dragging along the pavement and the arm holding the bento torquing him along.

As good ol' Hyŏn fled this otherwise dearest of places, as if it were an arch-enemy, his head spun from the dizzying battle of wits.

And suddenly, 'Ah, Brother!'

Good ol' Hyŏn didn't have to look up at the pock-marked mug of the

giant towering before him to know that the husky, cheerful voice belonged
to Yunbo, already pickled on rotgut, and none too displeased to see him.

'Ah, Yunbo!' For his part good ol' Hyŏn was as pleased as punch to meet
a comrade in arms.

'Fancy meeting you here – what's up?'

'Oh, nothing in particular . . . How about your good self?'

'You know me, always on the move.'

'And how's the missus and the little ones?'

'Eating me out of house and home . . . And how's your good wife?'

'Oh, just . . .'

'And, your little girl, Sun . . . Sundongi?'

'Sundongi? Well, all things considered, what's a fella to do?'

'I hear you,' Yunbo tsk-tsked. 'Say, instead of standing out here in the
street, what say we . . . ?' Scanning the surroundings, Yunbo grabbed good
ol' Hyŏn by the arm and led him off in the direction of said drinking
establishment.

'Come on, brother, in we go!'

'Oh, this place – I really shouldn't . . .'

'Speak no more, brother, I know your troubles . . . But jeez, we only
meet once in a dog's age – what kind of pal would you be not to let me
stand your good self to a bowl?'

And with that, good ol' Hyŏn's urge to backpedal dissipated on the spot.

'Cheers, brother, bottoms up!'

'You bet – here's looking up your old address.'

They had just raised their bowls of *makkŏlli*, the beverage refreshing at
room temperature (most like it warmed, some like it chilled), and were
glug-glugging it down when . . .

At the best of times her protuberant eyes were like all-seeing search-
lights, so you can well imagine how fearsome she looked with those orbs
half-rolled back in fury. With those same eyes good ol' Hyŏn's wife, née
Kang, flanked by the reverend and two Bible women, stopped short for
four or five seconds and glared at good ol' Hyŏn as he imbibed the devil's
brew. And not just the eyes, but her lips, thick as a newlywed's quilt, and
indeed her limbs and all of her, trembled like a *mudang* possessed.

Needless to say, if she had been by her lonesome, unaccompanied by a
respected reverend and the Bible women, a battle scene worthy of *The*

Romance of the Three Kingdoms[2] would have ensued. Such being the case, she martialled superhuman forbearance, suppressed her awful ire and discreetly rejoined her entourage.

8

Here we are back at good ol' Hyŏn's sweet home.

It's getting on towards eight in the evening but still bright as day.

Little Sundong sits expectantly on the yard side of the veranda, and parked in the yard Spotty gazes up at her as if she were the empress of all canines in this world. Both are hungry, and so little Sundong waits ardently for her father.

When Mother is late coming home it's Father who gets the rice going, but now Father too is late, and little Sundong's face droops lower and lower. He said he would buy her a bento, but there's no bento and on top of that no father – what a mean father! To make things worse her big brother is sprawled out in the family room swearing up a storm – he's so annoying!

'Ya little bitch, you're seven years old, make me something to eat.'

'Why can't you do it yourself, Brother?'

'Men don't cook!'

The way little Sundong snorts at him would have done her mother proud. 'Worthless layabout!'

'Who you calling a layabout – you little bitch!' He jerks himself to a sitting position and glares at her. It's normal in this world of ours for the son to resemble the mother, but heaven help us if this young man isn't the spitting image of her: protuberant eyes, a disappearing forehead, bulbous nose and a pair of fleshy lips that must have weighed a pound if they weighed an ounce. The face of this eighteen-year-old boy is plastered with pimples, and the collar of his black school uniform bears the two horizontal strokes of the Chinese character for two, indicating he's in the second year at the commercial high school. It's taking him two years to get through each of the grades (such is life when you want to master the course material!), and if he keeps up the good work he just might make it all the way through a commercial college.

'How come Father's not back!' After spouting off, Sunsŏk plops down on his back again.

Sundong pouts, then says, 'Should I tell Father to make dinner?'

'Yeah, why not?'

'But you said men don't cook.'

'Father's not a man, he's a devil!'

'What do you mean? Why do you talk like that? Why is Father a devil?'

'Think, ya little bitch – since he doesn't believe in Jesus, he's a devil!'

'Why does he have to be a devil if he doesn't believe in Jesus? . . . I'm gonna tell on you.'

'Go ahead, ya little bitch, I'm not afraid o' him.'

'I'll tell him to give you a spanking.'

'Huh – *Father* spank *me*? Do you know how strong I am, ya little bitch!'

'Huh yourself – just because you're strong, doesn't mean you're number one!'

'You know how good I am at boxing, ya little bitch! . . . Oh, shit.' He jerks himself back up, and the next moment he's like a different person. 'Did Father get paid?'

'Who knows, brown-nose!'

'Hmm, today's gotta be payday. Hmm, I gotta tell him to buy me a pair o' boxing gloves, hmm.'

'Huh, even after I tell him you called him nasty names?'

'No way! I was just pretending – can't a guy have some fun? . . . So come on, no tattlin', huh?'

'I can't hear you, did you say something?'

'Cut it out! I'm serious! . . . Father's a good dad, all right!'

And that's when all hell broke loose. *Thunk thunk thunk* came the sound of hurried footsteps and with no preliminaries, '*Aiguuuu!*' followed by the *crash!* of the gate being kicked open, then, '*Aiguuu!* Lord save me!'

Son and daughter flinch, and then Sunsŏk scuttles for the yard, little Sundong crawls, trembling, to the corner of the veranda, Spotty hides beneath the veranda, tail between his legs, from the threshold of the family room Nabi looks out with eyes wide as saucers, and the entire neighbourhood is up in arms.

'*Aiguuuu!* Lord save me!'

'Mother! Mother!'

'*Aiguuuu!*'

Getting a helping hand from Sunsŏk and staggering into the yard, yelling all the while, their mother, her bun coming apart and her hair trailing every which way, her jacket ties undone and a goodly amount of her cargo exposed, one of her rubber shoes still on its foot and the other in her hand – you get the idea (and did we mention her period started yesterday?). Helped up onto the veranda, the moment she's laid down, she stretches out arms and legs and with fists and heels begins pounding on the floor – *bang bang . . . !*

'*Aiguuuu!* That no-good – what am I to do with him? Tell me! That no-good!'

If you, dear readers, had just moved into the neighbourhood you'd have to assume that the no-good in question had just taken a concubine, and the poor wife, née Kang, had flipped. Needless to say, if you'd heard the first verses of this lament, you'd look at each other and say, 'Now *that's* a laughing matter.'

The yelling was if anything more energetic, while for his part Sunsŏk had parked himself in the far corner of the veranda, and from there he shot a sharp retort to his sister.

'Sundong!'

No response.

'Go fetch the Pak woman, the Ch'oe woman, Sŏpsŏp's mother, tell them to get over here – now, ya little bitch!'

Silence.

'If I get my hands on you I'm gonna wring your neck!'

Still no answer from Sundong.

'You little bitch, move! Or I'll put the leg screws to ya!'

9

It's May, but when it's the middle of the night and you're out in the open it can get a bit nippy.

And here was good ol' Hyŏn, squatting with his back against the gate, the precious bento tucked against his side, Spotty clutched to his chest, nodding off and waking up the whole night through.

Since he wasn't going inside, why you might ask couldn't he sleep in the night-duty room at his school? The answer was, not that he preferred spending the night all by his lonesome, but when he thought of his little Sundong crying herself to exhaustion waiting for her father, then curling up and falling asleep, he felt much more comfortable seeing out the night crouched outside the gate with his worries keeping him company, shivering though he was.

And lucky man that he was, he'd been sniffed out by Spotty, who had come outside to huddle in his bosom, and oh did that leave good ol' Hyŏn feeling safe and sound.

The moon had passed over the horizon and the stars were once again free to twinkle.

Ttaeng, ttaeng. Inside the house the clock strikes two. It's quite chilly now, and good ol' Hyŏn keeps hunching his shoulders to conserve body heat. It's another couple of hours before the sky will begin to brighten, but when it does, he'll be sure to call softly for his little Sundong and give her the bento. And when he thinks of the happy look on her face, he rubs his cheek against Spotty's head with a beaming grin of his own.

The night is dead still, and a shooting star streaks far across the heavens.

Once again good ol' Hyŏn nods off.

CHU YOSŎP

Mama and the Boarder

Translated by Kim Chong-un and Bruce Fulton

I

My name is Pak Okhŭi, and this year I'll be six years old. There's just two of us in my family – me and my mother, who's the prettiest woman in the whole wide world. Whoops – I almost left out my uncle.

He's in middle school, and always running around, so he's hardly ever here except for meals. A lot of the time we won't even see his shadow for days on end. So can you blame me if I forgot him for a second?

My mother is so beautiful, there's really no one else like her in the world. She'll be twenty-three this year, and she's a widow. I'm not sure what a widow is, but since the neighbours call me the 'widow's girl,' I figure she must be a widow. The other kids all have fathers, but not me. Maybe that has something to do with it.

2

According to Grandma, my father passed away a month before I came along. He and my mother had only been married for a year. My father was from somewhere far off, and he came here to teach school. So when they were married my mother stayed here and they bought this house (it's the one next to Grandma's). They weren't here even a year when my father suddenly died. Because he passed away before I was born, I never saw him in person. And I can't picture him no matter how hard I try. A couple of times I've seen what's supposed to be his picture, and he was really good-looking. If he was still alive, he'd definitely be the most handsome father in the whole world. It's just not fair that I never got a chance to see him. It's been quite a while since I've seen his picture. My mother used to keep it on her desk, but every time Grandma came she'd tell her to put it away. So now it's gone and I don't know where. Once I came home and saw my mother sneaking a look at something from the chest. When she heard me she hid it in the chest really quickly. Maybe that was his picture?

My father left us something to live on before he passed away. One day last summer – actually I guess it was almost autumn – Mother took me to a little mountain a few miles away to see it. At the bottom of the mountain was a house with a straw roof. We scooped up some chestnuts, then went inside and had some chicken soup. She said this was our land. We get enough rice and such from it, so we don't have to go hungry. But there's no money for meat and vegetables or goodies. So Mother takes in sewing. That's where she gets the money to buy herring and eggs, and sweets for me.

So there was really only my mother and me. But since Father's study was now empty, my mother decided to get some use out of it and at the same time have someone to run errands for her. And that's how Little Uncle came to live with us.

3

One day Mother said she was going to send me to nursery school in the spring. You should have seen how proud I was with my playmates. But as soon as I came home from playing, I saw Big Uncle (I mean the big brother of Little Uncle who lived in my father's room) sitting there talking with someone I'd never seen before.

'Okhŭi,' Big Uncle called me. 'Okhŭi, come here and say hello to this man.'

I felt bashful and just stayed where I was.

This man I'd never seen before said to Big Uncle, 'What a lovely girl – is she your niece?'

'Yes, she's my sister's daughter . . . She wasn't born yet when Kyŏngsŏn died. She's his only child.'

'Okhŭi, come here, hmm?' said the stranger. 'Those eyes are just like your father's.'

'Okhŭi, you're a big girl now – why so shy? Come here and say hi. This man's an old friend of your father. He's moving into your father's room here, so you'd better say hi and get to know each other.'

The stranger was moving into my father's room? That made me very happy. So I went up to the man, gave him my best bow, then ran out to the inner courtyard. I could hear Big Uncle and the man laughing.

I went into Mother's room, and right off, I tugged on her sleeve.

'Mother!' I said. I was all excited. 'Big Uncle brought a man here! He's moving into the guest room!'

'That's right.'

I guess she already knew about it.

'When's he moving in?'

'Today.'

'Yippee!'

I started clapping my hands, but Mother grabbed them.

'Now what's all this fuss?'

'But what about Little Uncle?'

'He'll stay there too.'

'You mean the two of them together?'

'Umm-hmm.'

'In the same room?'

'Why not? They can close the sliding partition, and then they'll each have a space.'

I didn't know who this new uncle was. But he treated me nicely, and right away I took a shine to him. Later I heard the grown-ups say he had been a friend of my father ever since they were little. He went off somewhere to study, and just came back, and he got assigned to teach at the school here. He's also a friend of Big Uncle, and since the boarding-house rooms in our neighbourhood aren't all that clean, they arranged for him to stay in our guest room. Best of all, the money he paid us for his board would give us some of the extras we wanted so much.

This new uncle had a whole bunch of picture books. Whenever I went in his room, he sat me in his lap and showed them to me. Every once in a while, he gave me a sweet. Once I sneaked into his room after my lunch. He was just starting his meal. I sat down without a peep to watch him eat.

'Now what kind of side dish does Okhŭi like best?' he asked me.

Boiled eggs, I told him. Well, wouldn't you know it, he had some on his meal tray. He gave me one and told me to help myself. I peeled it and started eating.

'Uncle, which side dish do *you* like most?'

He smiled for a moment.

'Boiled eggs.'

I was so happy I clapped my hands.

'Gee, just like me. I'm going to tell Mother.'

I got up to go, but the uncle grabbed me.

'Oh, don't do that.'

But once I make my mind up there's no stopping me. So I ran out to the inner courtyard.

'Mother! Mother!' I yelled. 'The new uncle's favourite side dish is boiled eggs, just like me!'

'Now don't make such a fuss,' Mother said. And she gave me her Please-don't-do-that look.

But the fact that the new uncle liked eggs turned out to be quite nice for me. Because Mother started buying eggs in bunches from then on. When the old woman with the eggs came around, Mother bought ten or twenty at a time. She boiled them up and put two of them at the uncle's place at mealtime, and then she almost always gave me one. And that wasn't all. Sometimes when I visited the uncle, he'd get an egg or two from his drawer for me to eat. After that I ate eggs to my heart's content. I really liked the uncle. But Little Uncle grumbled sometimes. I guess he didn't take to the new uncle too well. And he didn't like the way he had to run errands for him – that was probably the real reason. Once I saw Little Uncle arguing with Mother.

'Now look,' said Mother, 'don't you be running off again. Why can't you wait in his room? You'll have to take him his dinner tray when he comes back.'

Little Uncle made a face.

'Aw shit, whenever yours truly has something to do, it seems like he's always late for his meal.'

'Well, what can I do? I need *somebody* to take him his meal.'

'Can't you do it yourself, Sister? Times have changed. Why do you have to be so old-fashioned when it comes to men?'

Suddenly Mother's face was all red. She didn't say anything, but you should have seen the look she gave Little Uncle.

Little Uncle gave a laugh to lighten the mood, and went out to the guest room.

4

I started nursery school, and our teacher taught us songs. She also taught us dancing. She was really good at the pedal organ. The organ was a little thing compared with the one at the Protestant church we went to, but it still made a nice sound. Then I remembered seeing something that looked just like our nursery school organ sitting at the far end of our room at home. So as soon as I got back that day I pulled Mother over to it and asked:

'Mama, this is an organ, isn't it?'

Mother smiled.

'That's right. How did you know?'

'It's just like the one at nursery school. Can you play it too, Mother?'

I had to ask, because I'd never seen her playing it. But she didn't say a word.

'Try it, Mother – please?'

Her face got kind of cloudy.

'Your father bought this organ for me. I haven't even raised the lid since he passed on ...'

She looked like she was about to burst into tears at any second, so I changed the subject.

'Can I have a sweet, Mama?'

And then I led her back to the near end of our room, where it was warmer.

Before I knew it, a month had passed since the uncle moved in. I stopped by his room almost every day. Once in a while Mother would tell me it was no good pestering him like that. But if you want to know the truth, I didn't pester him one little bit. It was the uncle who pestered *me*.

'Okhŭi, those eyes of yours look just like your father's. But maybe that cute little nose came from your mother. And that little mouth, too. Am I right? Is your mother pretty like you?'

'Uncle, you're silly! Haven't you seen her face?'

But when I answered him that way, he didn't say a word.

'Shall we go in and see Mother?' I asked, taking the uncle by the sleeve. You should have seen how strongly he reacted.

'No, we'd better not – I'm busy now,' he said, pulling me back the other way. But he really didn't seem all that busy, because he didn't ask me to leave. Instead, he patted my head and gave me a kiss on the cheek – he wouldn't let me go. And he kept asking me such funny questions: 'Who made you this pretty jacket? . . . Do you sleep with your mama at night?' He made me feel like I was something special to him. But when Little Uncle came back, the new uncle's attitude changed all of a sudden. He stopped asking me about those kinds of things, and he wouldn't hug me tight. Instead, he got all proper and showed me a picture book. Maybe he was afraid of Little Uncle.

Whatever the reason, Mother scolded me for pestering the uncle. And every once in a while she kept me in our room after dinner. But pretty soon she'd get caught up in her sewing, and I'd try to sneak out. When she heard the door slide open she'd pop up and catch me. But she never got annoyed with me. 'Come here so I can fix your hair,' she'd say. And then she'd pull me inside and make my braids nice and pretty again. 'We want your hair to look nice. What's the uncle going to think if you go around just the way you are?' Or she'd braid my hair and say, 'Now, what did you do to your jacket?' and make me change into a new one.

5

One Saturday the new uncle asked me if I wanted to go for a little walk. I was so happy I said yes right away.

'Go inside and ask your mother first,' he said.

Wow, he's right, I thought.

Mother said it was okay. But before she let me go she scrubbed my face and did my braids again. Then she hugged me really tight.

'Now don't be too late,' she said in a loud voice. I bet the uncle heard it too.

We climbed to the top of a hill and looked down at the train station for a while, but no trains were running. I had fun pulling at the long blades of grass and pinching the uncle while he was lying on the ground. Later, when we were on our way down the hill, the uncle was holding my hand and we ran into some of the kids from my nursery school.

'Look, Okhǔi went somewhere with her dad,' one of them said. This girl didn't know my father had passed away. My face got hot, maybe because I was thinking just then how nice it would be if the uncle really was my father. I wanted so much to be able to call him 'Papa,' even if it was just once. You don't know how much I enjoyed walking home through the alleyways with the uncle holding my hand.

We arrived at the front gate.

'Uncle, I wish you were my papa,' I blurted out.

The uncle turned red as a tomato and gently prodded me.

'You shouldn't say things like that,' he said, almost in a whisper. His voice was shaking an awful lot. The only thing I could think of was that he must be angry. So I went inside without saying anything more.

Mother gave me a hug and said, 'Where did you go?'

But instead of answering I started to sniffle.

'Okhǔi, what happened? What's wrong, honey?'

All I could do was cry.

6

The next day was Sunday, and Mother and I got ready for church. While she was changing, I poked my head inside the guest room to see if the uncle was still in a bad mood. He was sitting at his desk writing something. I tiptoed in, and when he looked up he had a big grin on his face. That smile made me feel easy again. Now I knew he wasn't angry any more. The uncle looked at me from head to toe.

'Okhǔi, where are you going all prettied up like that?'

'I'm going to church with Mama.'

'Is that so?' said the uncle. For a moment he looked like he was thinking about something. 'Which church?'

'The one right over there.'

'Oh? Over where?'

Just then I heard Mother's soft voice calling me. I hurried back to our room, but on the way, I turned around to look at the uncle. His face was red and angry again. I couldn't figure out why he was getting cross so easily these days.

We took our seats in the church and sang a hymn, and then there was a prayer. During the prayer I started wondering if maybe the uncle was there too. So I sat up and looked over at the men's side of the aisle. And what do you know – there he was. But he wasn't praying with his eyes closed, like the other grown-ups. His eyes were open, just like us kids, and he was looking around every which way. I recognized the uncle right away, but I guess he didn't recognize me. Because even when I gave him a big smile, he didn't smile back; instead he had a faraway look in his eyes. So I waved at him. But the uncle ducked his head down quickly. Mother finally saw me waving, and pulled me back with both hands. I put my mouth to her ear.

'The uncle's here,' I whispered.

When Mother heard this, she gave a little jump and put her hand over my mouth. Then she sat me in front of her and pushed my head down. This time, I noticed it was Mother who was red as a tomato.

Well, church that day was a big flop. Mother was angry till the end of the service. All she did was look straight ahead at the pulpit. She didn't look down and give me a smile once in a while like she usually did. When I looked over at the men's side to see the uncle, he didn't once look back at me but just sat there looking angry. Mother didn't look at me either but just kept grabbing me and pulling me down – it was too much. Why was everyone cross with me? It reached the point where I felt like crying out loud. But then I noticed our nursery teacher not too far away, and I managed to keep myself from crying, though it wasn't easy.

7

When I started going to nursery school, Little Uncle walked me there and back. But after a few days I could do it all by myself. When I got back home Mother was always waiting for me at the side gate. (Our house has two gates – the side gate and the gate to the uncle's room, and Mother only used the side gate.) When Mother saw me, she'd run over and hug me and we'd go inside.

But one day, Mother wasn't there, and I didn't know why. I thought she'd probably gone to see Grandmother, but still, here I was back home with no one waiting for me. I thought it was awful of her to leave the house like that. Well, I decided I'd give Mother a hard time. Just then I heard her voice outside the gate.

'Goodness, I wonder if she's home already.'

I ran inside, taking my shoes with me so she wouldn't know I was there. Then I hid in the storage loft. I could hear Mother's voice just outside in the yard.

'Okhŭi – Okhŭi, aren't you home yet?. . . Hmm, I guess not.'

And then it sounded like she had gone out again. I thought this was fun, and started giggling.

But then a little later the whole house suddenly became noisy. First I heard Mother, then Grandmother, then Little Uncle.

'Well, I was home all day, Mother, until I realized I didn't have any cookies for Okhŭi, and that's when I visited you. And now something's happened.' That was Mother speaking.

'And at the nursery school they said she'd left a good twenty minutes ago. Gracious, do you suppose on the way home. . . ?' That was Grandmother.

'I'll go out and look for her. Little troublemaker must have gone somewhere.' That was Little Uncle.

Then Mother started crying, and Grandmother said something I couldn't make out. I told myself it was time to stop the game, but then I thought, 'I've got to get even with her for getting angry with me at church last Sunday,' and I lay down. The loft was stuffy and hot, and before I knew it, I had drifted off to sleep.

I have no idea how long I slept. But when I woke up, I'd completely forgotten about going into the loft. What was I doing lying in such a strange place? It was kind of dark, it was cramped, it was hot . . . Suddenly I was scared, and I started crying. And just as suddenly I heard Mother scream close by, and the door to the loft was yanked open. Mother rushed inside, took me in her arms, and lifted me down.

'You little devil!'

She spanked me several times, and that made me cry even louder. Mother pulled me close, and then she started crying too.

'Okhŭi, Okhŭi, it's all right now, Mama's here. Don't cry, Okhŭi. You're all there is, the only thing Mama lives for. I don't need anything else. You're my only hope. Don't cry, Okhŭi, don't cry, hmm?'

While she kept telling me this, she couldn't stop crying herself.

'Little brat – the devil must have got into her,' said Grandmother. 'What made her hide in the loft?'

'What a lousy day,' said Little Uncle. He got up and went out.

8

On my way home from nursery school the next day I started thinking about how I had made Mother cry so much when I hid in the loft. I felt so ashamed. I want to make her happy today, I thought. Now what could I bring her? Then I remembered the vase on our teacher's desk. It had some beautiful red flowers, though I didn't know their name. They weren't forsythias and they weren't azaleas. I could recognize those flowers, and I knew they'd already bloomed and gone by. The ones in the vase must have come from across the ocean. I knew my mother adored flowers. How happy she would be if I brought her some of those red ones.

And so I went back to my classroom. Goodie! No one was there. Teacher must have gone somewhere, because she wasn't around either. I snitched a couple of the flowers and ran out.

Mother was waiting near the gate, and she took me in her arms.

'Where did you get those lovely flowers?' she asked, taking the flowers and smelling them.

I didn't know what to say. I was too ashamed to tell her I'd brought them from nursery school. What could I tell her? Somehow, I thought of a little fib.

'The uncle in the guest room told me to give them to you,' I blurted out.

Mother was all flustered. I guess my words had startled her. And then all at once her face turned redder than the flowers. Her fingers holding the flowers began to tremble. She looked around like she was thinking of something scary.

'Okhŭi, you shouldn't have taken them.' Her voice was shaking so much. Mother loved flowers, and so for her to get so angry over these flowers was the last thing I expected. I told myself it was a good thing I'd fibbed about the uncle and not told her I'd brought the flowers myself. I didn't know why she was angry, but as long as she was going to be angry at someone, I was glad it was the uncle and not me. A little while later Mother led me inside.

'Okhŭi, I don't want you to tell a soul about these flowers, hmm?'

'All right.'

I thought Mother would throw the flowers away, but instead she put them in a vase and kept them on top of the organ. There they slept night after night, and finally they withered. Mother then cut off the stems and saved the flowers between the pages of her hymnbook.

That night I was back in the uncle's lap reading a picture book. Suddenly I could feel the uncle tense up. He was trying to hear something. I tried too.

It was an organ!

Surely the sound was floating out from our room. It must be Mama, I thought. I jumped up and ran into our room.

It was dark there, but it was around the time of the full moon, and silvery light filled half the room, making it light as day. There was Mother, all dressed in white and very calm, playing the organ.

I was six years old, but this was the first time I had seen Mother play the organ. She played better than our nursery teacher. I went up beside her, but she didn't budge and kept on playing. I guess she didn't know I was there. A little later Mother began singing to the music. I didn't know she had such a beautiful voice. Her voice was much lovelier than our teacher's, and she sang better too. I stood there quietly listening to

Mother sing. It was a beautiful song. I felt it was coming down to me on a silver thread from Starland.

But then Mother's voice got a tiny bit shaky. The sound of the organ got shaky too. The song grew softer and softer, and finally it was gone. And then the organ stopped too. Mother stood up, still calm, and gave me a pat on the head. The next instant, she took me in her arms and we went out on the veranda. Mother gave me a big hug, not saying anything. In the full moonlight her face was pure white. She's a real angel, I told myself.

Two streams of tears were running down Mother's white cheeks. The sight of those tears made me want to cry myself.

'Mother, why are you crying?' Now I was sniffling too.

'Okhŭi.'

'Hmm?'

She didn't say anything for a minute. And then, 'Okhŭi, having you is enough.'

'Yes, Mama.'

But that's all she said.

9

The next evening I was playing in the uncle's room when I began to feel sleepy. As I was about to leave, the uncle took a white envelope from his drawer and gave it to me.

'Okhŭi, would you take this to your mama? It's last month's room and board.'

I took the envelope to Mother. But when I handed it to her, she turned pale. She looked even whiter than the night before, when we were sitting on the veranda in the moonlight. She looked anxious, like she didn't know what to do with the envelope.

'He said it's for last month's room and board.'

'Oh.' When Mother heard this she looked startled, as if she had just woken up. The next instant, her face wasn't white as a sheet of paper any longer; now it was red. Her trembling fingers reached inside the envelope and pulled out several paper bills. A tiny little smile formed on her lips, and she breathed a sigh. But then something else must have surprised her, because she tensed up, and the next minute her face was white again and her lips were trembling. I looked at what Mother was holding, and beside the paper money there was a piece of white paper folded into a square.

Mother looked like she didn't know what to do. But then she seemed to make up her mind. She bit her lip, unfolded the paper really carefully, and read it. Of course, I didn't know what was written there, but I could see Mother's face turn red right away and then back to pale again. Her hands weren't just trembling, they were positively shaking, enough to make the paper rustle.

A good while later Mother folded the paper back into a square and put it in the envelope along with the money. She dropped the envelope into her sewing basket. And then she sat down and just stared at the lightbulb like someone who had lost her senses. I could see her chest heaving. I thought maybe she was ill or something, so I ran over and snuggled into her lap.

'Mama, can we go to sleep?'

Mama kissed me on the cheek. But her lips were so hot. They felt just like a stone that's been warmed up in a fire.

We went to sleep, and after a while I half woke up and reached out for Mother. I was in the habit of doing this from time to time. I'd reach out, half-asleep, and feel her soft skin. Then I'd go back to sleep. But this time she wasn't there.

Mama wasn't there! Suddenly I was afraid. I opened my eyes wide and looked all around. The light was off, but the moon shone full in the yard, and enough of its light came into the room so I could see things just a little. At the far end of the room was the small chest with Father's clothes. Sometimes Mother took them out and felt them. Now the chest was open, and the white clothing was piled on the floor. Next to it was Mother in her night clothes, half sitting and half leaning against the chest. Her head was up but her eyes were closed. I could see her lips move. She looked like she was praying. I sat up and crawled over and wormed myself into her lap.

'Mama, what are you doing?'

She stopped whispering, opened her eyes, and looked at me for the longest time.

'Okhŭi.'

'Hmm?'

'Let's go back to bed.'

'All right. But you too, Mama.'

'Yes. Mama too.'

Somehow her voice gave me a chill.

One at a time Mother picked up Father's clothes, gently smoothed them with the palm of her hand, and returned them to the chest. When the last one was in, she shut the chest and locked it. Then she gathered me up and back we went to bed.

'Mama, aren't we going to pray first?'

Mother didn't let a night go by without praying when she put me to bed. The only prayer I knew was the Lord's Prayer. I had no idea what the words meant, but from following along with Mother, I knew it by heart. But then I remembered that for some reason Mother had forgotten to pray the night before. I felt like reminding her then, but she looked so sad that I kept quiet and ended up falling asleep without saying anything.

'All right, let's say our prayer,' Mother said in her calm voice.

All of a sudden, I wanted to hear the gentle voice Mother used when she prayed.

'Mother, you pray.'

'Our Father who art in heaven,' she began, 'hallowed be thy name. Thy kingdom come, thy will be done, on earth as it is in heaven. Give us this day our daily bread; and forgive us our trespasses, as we forgive those who trespass against us; and lead us not into temptation . . . and lead us not into temptation . . . lead us not into temptation . . . lead us not . . . lead us not . . .'

I couldn't believe it – Mother had lost her place! It was so funny. Even I can say the prayer without losing my place.

'. . . lead us not . . . lead us not . . .'

Mother kept saying those words over and over, and when I couldn't wait any longer, I said, 'Mama, I'll do the rest: "But deliver us from evil. For thine is the kingdom and the power and the glory for ever and ever."'

After a long while Mother finally whispered, 'Amen.'

10

It was all I could do to figure out Mother. Sometimes she was quite cheerful. In the evening she might play the organ or sing a hymn. I liked that so much that I just sat quietly next to her and listened. But once in a while, what started out as her singing would end up as tears. When that happened, I would be in tears too. Then Mother would give me more kisses than I could count, and say, 'Okhŭi, you're the only one I need, yes you are.' And she kept crying, on and on.

One Sunday Mother got a headache and decided not to go to church. (It was the day after nursery school closed for the summer.) The uncle in the guest room was out somewhere, and Little Uncle was out somewhere, so it was just Mother and me at home. Mother was lying down because of her headache. Out of the blue I heard her call my name.

'Okhŭi, do you miss having a papa?'

'Yes, Mama, I want to have a papa too.' I put on my baby act and whined a bit.

Mother didn't say anything for a while. She just stared at the ceiling.

'Okhŭi. You know your father passed away before you were born. So it's not that you don't have a papa; it's just that he passed on early. If you had a new father now, everyone would call you names. You don't know any better, but the whole world would call you names, everyone in the world. "Okhŭi's mother is a loose woman" – that's what they would say. "Okhŭi's father died, but now she has another father; what will they do next!" – that's what everyone would say. Everyone would point their finger at you. And when you grew up, we wouldn't be able to find you a good husband. Even if you studied hard and became successful, other people would say you're just the daughter of a loose woman.'

She said this in fits and starts, like she was talking to herself. After a few minutes she talked to me some more.

'Okhŭi?'

'Hmm?'

'Okhŭi, I don't want you to ever leave my side. For ever and always I want you to live with Mama. I want you to live with Mama even when she's old and shrivelled up. After nursery school, after primary school, after all your schooling, even if you're the finest woman in all the land, I want you to live with Mama. Hmm? Okhŭi, tell me how much you love Mama.'

'This much.' I opened my arms wide.

'How much? That much! Okhŭi, I want you to love me always and for ever. I want you to study hard and be a fine woman . . .'

I got scared when I heard Mother's voice trembling, because I thought she was going to cry again. So I opened my arms as wide as I could and said, 'This much, Mama, this much.'

Mother didn't cry.

'Okhŭi, you're everything to Mama. I don't need anything else. I'm happy just with Okhŭi. Yes I am.'

She pulled me close and held me tight. She kept hugging me until she had squeezed all my breath out.

After dinner that day, Mother called me, sat me down, and combed my hair. She made a new braid for me and then dressed me in new bloomers, jacket and skirt.

I asked where we were going.

Mother smiled. 'We aren't going anywhere.' Then she took down a freshly ironed white handkerchief from beside the organ and put it in my hand.

'This handkerchief belongs to the uncle in the guest room. Could you take it to him? Now don't stay long – just give it to him and come right back, hmm?'

I thought I could feel something tucked in between the folds of the handkerchief, but I didn't open it to look.

I stopped at the uncle's door. He was lying down, but he sat right up when he saw the handkerchief. For some reason he didn't give me a smile, like before. Instead his face turned awfully white. He started chewing on his lip as he took the handkerchief. He didn't say a word.

Somehow something wasn't right. So instead of going into the uncle's room I turned around and went back. Mother was at the organ. She must have been doing some hard thinking, because she was just sitting there. I sat down beside the organ and didn't say anything. And then Mother started playing, soft as could be. I didn't know the tune, but it was kind of sad and lonely.

Mother played the organ till late that night. Over and over again she played that sad and lonely tune.

II

Several days went by, and then one afternoon I finally paid another visit to the uncle. He was busy packing his things. Ever since the day I gave him the handkerchief, the uncle always looked sad, like someone with worries on his mind, even when he saw me. He wouldn't say anything, but just stared at me. And so I didn't go to his room to play very often.

I was surprised to see him packing all of a sudden.

'Uncle, are you going somewhere?'

'Uh-huh – far, far away.'

'When?'

'Today.'

'On the train?'

'Uh-huh.'

'When are you coming back?'

Instead of answering, the uncle took a cute doll from his drawer and handed it to me.

'You keep this, hmm? Okhŭi, you're going to forget Uncle soon after he leaves, aren't you?'

'Uh-uh.' Suddenly I felt very sad.

I went back to our room with the doll.

'Mama, look! The uncle gave it to me. He says he's going far away on the train today.'

Mother didn't say anything.

'Mama, why is the uncle going away?'

'Because the school is on holiday.'

'Where is he going?'

'He's going to his home – where else?'

'Is the uncle going to come back?'

Mother didn't answer.

'I don't want the uncle to leave,' I pouted.

But Mother changed the subject: 'Okhŭi, go to the closet and see how many eggs there are.'

I trotted inside the closet. There were six eggs left.

'Six,' I called out.

'Bring all of them here.'

Mother proceeded to boil the eggs. Next she wrapped them in a handkerchief. Then she put a pinch of salt in a piece of writing paper and tucked it inside the handkerchief.

'Okhŭi, take these to the uncle and tell him to have them on the train, hmm?'

12

That afternoon, after the uncle left, I played with the doll he gave me. I carried it around on my back singing it a lullaby. Mother came in from the kitchen.

'Okhŭi, how would you like to go up the hill and get some fresh air?'

'Goodie, let's go!' I practically jumped for joy.

Mother told Little Uncle to mind the house while we went out for a while. Then she took my hand.

'Mama, can I take the uncle's doll?'

'Why not?'

I held the doll close, took Mother's hand, and we climbed up the hill behind our house. From the top we could see the train station clear as could be.

'Mama, look, there's the train station. The train isn't here yet.'

Mother didn't say anything. The hem of her ramie skirt fluttered in the soft breeze. Standing quietly on top of the hill, Mother looked even prettier than she did other times.

And then I saw the train coming around a faraway hill.

'Mama, here comes the train!' I shouted in delight.

The train stopped at the station, and practically the next minute it gave a whistle and started moving again.

'There it goes!' I clapped my hands.

Mother watched till the train had disappeared around a hill in the other direction. And then she watched till all the smoke from the chimney had scattered into the sky above.

We went down the hill, and when we were in our room again Mother put the lid back on the organ. It had been left open all these days. Then she locked it and put the sewing basket on top, the way it was before. She picked up the hymnbook as if it was something heavy and flipped through the pages until she found the dried-up flowers.

'Okhŭi, take these and throw them away.' She handed me the flowers, and I remembered they were the ones I had brought her from nursery school.

Just then the side gate creaked open.

'Get your eggs!'

It was the old woman who came every day carrying her basket of eggs on her head.

'We won't be buying them from now on,' said Mother. 'There's nobody here who eats them.' Her voice didn't have an ounce of life to it.

This took me by surprise. I wanted to pester Mother to buy some eggs, but when I saw her face lit up by the setting sun I lost heart. Instead I put my mouth to the ear of the uncle's doll and whispered to her.

'Did you hear that! Mama's a pretty good fibber too. She knows I like eggs, but she said there's nobody here who eats them. I'd sure like to pester her. But look at Mama's face. Look how white it is! I don't think Mama feels very good.'

YI MUNYŎL

The Old Hatter

Translated by Suh Ji-moon

I

The first encounter between our clan's urchins and the horsehair-hat maker, Top'yŏng, took place one summer on a market day towards the end of my childhood. To be sure, his modest hat shop had stood there for as long as we could remember, but we no more noticed it than the pebbles on the shores of our creek or the grass in the shade of our valley. However, we happened to discover that horsehair, being strong and nearly transparent, made excellent string for hanging bait in a squirrel trap or cicada nets. After this momentous discovery, we would go to his shop almost every market day to get horsehair. For children without money like us – it was before Korean parents gave their children regular allowances – the only way to get what we needed was to steal. In the childish parlance of the day, we 'snatched' it.

Of course, old man Top'yŏng didn't just put himself at our mercy. But we were indefatigable, and we needed horsehair badly, having neither toys nor recreational facilities. Old man Top'yŏng was bound to be defeated by our brilliant tactics.

On days when the old man tried to drive us away, believing he had safely hidden his horsehair, we took more of it than was necessary. Our tactic was to start a conversation with him on topics such as 'the day Elder Hahoe came back without his topknot.'[1] He was sure to get excited and hotly denounce the impious act of the late clan elder, failing to notice what was going on around him. Meanwhile, our commandos circled around to the back of the shop and snatched some horsehair. It took us a decade to understand why the anecdote so excited and infuriated the old man, but we were clever enough to use the circumstance to our advantage.

Even on days when the old man generously handed each of us horsehair not good enough for him but quite usable for us, he would still lose good horsehair, though in somewhat smaller quantity. On such days we would effusively express our gratitude and insist on helping him, blowing on the glue stove until the shop floor was covered with white ash or embellishing with our crayons his small and humble signboard, which said 'Horsehair hats and headbands for sale. Repairs also undertaken,' to make it still more ridiculous. He would then scowl at us and tsk-tsk in disapproval, but always ended up handing out superior-grade hair.

Sometimes we distracted him. For example, some of us would throw sand or fiercely knock on the door of his bedroom, which adjoined the shop. That was sure to send him rushing to his apartment. Then those of us who lay in wait would dash into the shop and carry off as much horsehair as we could grab. We only used this tactic when we were desperate, however, because we not only took as much as we wanted, but the remaining horsehair also often got so messed up that it was rendered useless, creating a heavy loss for the old man.

But the Goddess of Fortune didn't always favour us. The practical jokes we played on each other even into adulthood derived from her frequent neglect of us. The joke we called 'hatband' consisted of drawing a line across someone's forehead with the hard knuckle of a tightly clenched fist. It sometimes hurt so much that it brought tears to our eyes, but none of us could get angry, because it was the punishment we used to get from the old hat maker if he caught us. Grinning to himself, he would repeatedly draw hatbands on our foreheads. We, his helpless captives, could only smile (with tearful eyes) in a feigned display of good sportsmanship. Those of our gang who eluded the old man's grasp were sure to observe the punishment from a distance, taunting and provoking the old hatter:

Old man, old man, foolish old man,
Old man, old man, fallen into a piss jar,
Old man, old man, fished up with a tobacco pipe,
Old man, old man, washed with dishwater,
Old man, old man, dried on a stove rack,
Old man, old man, how much does horsehair cost?
Old man, old man, you'll never be rich however much you grudge us.

To tell the truth, not one of us escaped getting a hatband at old man Top'yŏng's hands. Huni – one of our gang in those days and now a respectable municipal office clerk in the provincial capital – once received such a harsh one that he couldn't wash his face for a whole week.

But the 'hatband' notwithstanding, we raided the old hat maker's shop for three summers and caused constant trouble in our own houses with the horsehair. When a family member had a sudden stomach ache or if one of our cows got bloated, it was always attributed to the inadvertent swallowing of horsehair. So our mothers wouldn't allow us within ten feet of the kitchen, and the house servants wouldn't let us near the cowshed. In addition, dead cicadas tied to strings dangled from pillars and door handles, and squirrels sprang out of empty jars, frightening the wits out of the women who opened the lids. Such troubles would have gone on for at least a couple more years had it not been for the incident we called 'the hat disaster.'

This catastrophic event occurred in the third year of our gang's warfare with the old man. It started when a member of our commando team snatched a hatbox from the old man's shop instead of a handful of horsehair. At first we were all shocked by his audacity. But when the boy removed from the box a smooth, shiny new horsehair hat, we were overcome by curiosity and the desire to imitate grown-ups. A horsehair hat was an emblem of adulthood and authority.[2] The boy who had dared to steal the hatbox became our hero, and we spent one of the most pleasant afternoons of our childhood trying the hat on under the flattering illusion that we were fearless adventurers.

But what made the afternoon unforgettable for decades afterwards took place that night. Having reduced the delicate new hat to a rag by wresting it out of one another's hands and trying it on, we hid it between two big rocks on a distant hill and parted, agreeing to meet for another adventure on the next day. But we were to meet again that night – as criminals awaiting justice. When we returned home, the lights were already on in our houses, and a summons awaited us from Elder Yean, who was then the most revered clansman. Our parents dragged us to this living law of the clan, who thundered at us:

'A gentleman's hat and robes are more important than his body. Zilu[3] gave up his life pausing to straighten his hat while fleeing from his pursuers. You little devils, how dare you steal the august hat that has covered scholars' heads since the time of the Three Han Kingdoms!'[4]

The elder was so furious he could not continue. On his face there was no trace of the benevolent and gratified approval he would bestow on us when we brought him the biggest fish we'd caught by spreading pounded poison weeds in the pool or the most succulent fruit of the year as a token of our families' respect and solicitude. Sitting behind him was a row of elders who also regarded us with grave disapproval. In the next room a young uncle was whittling a bunch of bush-clover switches.

To us it was a totally incomprehensible fury and an unjustly severe punishment. Only his lament as he regarded us, wailing and writhing with pain – 'Alas, are these the future heirs of our noble ancestors?' – and his sad eyes made some impression on us.

That night, back in our homes, we heard how the old hatter had turned the town upside down with his complaints and his search, and what a colossal recompense he'd demanded for the stolen hat. That washed away any sense of guilt we may have felt and made us regard the old man as the cause of all our unjust sufferings. When he could find neither the hat nor any of us till nightfall, he'd demanded a payment equivalent to half a bag of rice from each of our parents, insisting that the missing hat was his father's masterpiece.

That night, as they spread ointment on our calves, our mothers told us for the first time that, from the very beginning, the old man had collected payment each autumn for the horsehair we'd stolen from him. Although land reform and then the war had drastically reduced our clan's wealth, most families still harvested more than 200 bags of rice each year at that time; our parents therefore paid him liberally for the horsehair because they didn't want to break our spirits.[5] Thus, we discovered that our frequent victories in the war with the old man were not entirely due to superior strategy; nor was the old man's relatively light punishment due to generosity. Not knowing that, we had spent many a summer's day exulting in our victory and lamenting our defeat! 'Oh, sly old fox! You won't pull such tricks on us again!' we vowed.

Over a period of many months, we carried out our crude vengeance. If on market days the old man left his shop, even for a few minutes, some calamity was bound to occur. Sand would show up in his boiling black lacquer, the bamboo-splitting knife got chipped, or the smoothing iron was stuck in the stove, handle first. Someone smashed his signboard, and on the plank door was a crude drawing of a ridiculous male figure with horrendously large private parts and the caption 'Old Man Top'yŏng's something-something.' In addition, his carefully selected and stored best-quality bamboo, which was to be split thin and woven into hat frames, got sprayed with urine. Sometimes even his rice pot and soup bowl stank of the same. After we had satisfied our thirst for revenge in that way, we stopped even going near his shop.

2

Years have gone by since then and my hometown has changed as much as we have. Just as the scampering urchins in black cotton outfits and straw or rubber shoes grew into pimply adolescents in neat school uniforms, so our village underwent drastic changes. From a rustic village dominated by an old clan, it became a new town trying to catch up with modern times. The cheap rent for newly cleared land and the fertile soil, so favourable for the cultivation of tobacco, attracted many immigrants, while the rich forest and newly discovered deposits of copper lured greedy city folk and their capital.

Thus, many time-honoured traditions disappeared and were supplanted by new things. On the empty grounds where ash battles and tug-of-war games took place stand a colossal tobacco warehouse and mushroom culture house; around the clear pond where my ancestors held poetry competitions there sits a lumber factory powered by a huge electric motor. The copper mining office appropriated the site of the Ŭnhyŏndong Sŏwŏn, the Wise Hermits' Academy, and on the site of the old horse station, long-distance buses daily disgorge hundreds of passengers.

Changes were especially rapid in and around the marketplace, where the inhabitants were mostly descendants of our clan's bond servants and hired hands and therefore had little reason to cherish the old and every reason to welcome the new. The roads and alleys, which ended up as so many puddles on rainy days, were solidly paved, and the vendors who used to sell their wares displayed on low food tables have built neat shops with shiny showcase windows. On the fairgrounds, where unlicensed peddlers used to spread out their goods for sale on pieces of cloth, now stand a row of booths run by tradesmen belonging to a cooperative. In one corner of the square, where roving clowns and itinerant actors used to set up their portable stage, a modern cinema house now attracts film-goers. Other unheard-of amenities have sprung up: a coffee house, a billiard room, a shoe shop, a dry cleaner's, an audio shop and a clock and watch shop.

The proprietors are no longer commoners, as they used to be, but petty bourgeois, sure to be the future lords of the town and far more powerful and prosperous than their erstwhile masters, the descendants of the former nobility.

Not only have the vendors changed, but the merchandise and the buyers are different, too. In the old days the women of my clan would cross the marketplace rapidly, their faces hidden behind headcloths.[6] As recently as during my childhood, the customers of fairs were almost all women and servants, and the merchandise used to consist mostly of farm produce, fabric and artisans' wares. But now, in this age of equality, the market teems with people of both sexes from all walks of life who loudly haggle over the price of a wide variety of mass-produced goods.

Once you pass the marketplace, however, the rest of the town is totally different, especially the section inhabited by my clan, which is sinking deeper and deeper into the abyss of history and whose disintegration is almost palpable.

Oh, the glory of a past whose sun has sunk without even a magnificent final glow!

The power and wealth our clan enjoyed for many centuries came to an end in my father's generation. We had failed to adapt ourselves to the new system, and in the whirlwind of social change could not even preserve our inherited wealth. With the single exception of a cabinet minister in the caretaker government after the fall of Syngman Rhee, our clan produced not a single high-ranking official, and the vast land estate once owned by its various families passed bit by bit into other hands.

The clan itself, which at one time comprised more than 300 families, also dispersed. The many grandfathers, once so numerous that they filled the spacious head house's study to overflowing; the many uncles and aunts who dotted the hill on picnic days; the many cousins who half-filled the primary school classrooms – most of them have disappeared into old people's homes, or dark, cramped offices, or shabby, low-roofed houses in back alleys of the city. Only those major families[7] that had an obligation to remain with the clan and those clansmen who returned to their home-town after failing to obtain footholds in the cities were permanent residents. But those who adhered to the old scholarly tradition, rejecting both the costly modern education and physical labour, were sinking into destitution. And the old mansions on the hills were decaying and crumbling, their gates warped by the storms of many decades, their plaster walls soot-stained, their roofs overgrown with grass and their servants' quarters caved in from long disuse and disrepair. Sometimes unfamiliar faces replaced those of the old occupants of these houses and made our home-comings even more gloomy.

The mountains and rivers, which over the centuries were the clan's unofficial domain, became depleted and disfigured once they fell into the hands of new inhabitants. The forest that used to be a quiet retreat for my ancestors and supplied us with many necessities of life; the fertile land that enabled my ancestors to live the life of true scholars, unham-pered by the need to earn livelihoods and spending their days in philosophical speculation; the clear, deep pond that taught them the wisdom of the sages and provided a haven for many varieties of fish – these have all been depleted, and we are left with a mountain denuded by reckless logging, fields acidized by chemical fertilizers and ravaged by flood and a polluted pond. But saddest of all is the complete disappear-ance of the spiritual heritage that for generations inspired and sustained my ancestors.

What declined first was the old learning that for centuries upon cen-turies had nurtured my ancestors' minds. It had given my ancestors everything but can give us nothing now. The books, which every house is said to have had at least five cartloads of, were scattered and discarded by their owners' descendants, and the fragrance of Chinese ink has long departed from the men's quarters. The village *sŏdang*, which used to resound with the voices of children reciting passages from the elementary classics, is now piled high with dust. Its last teacher, a renowned master of both Confucian and Buddhist teachings and one who shone at scholarly gatherings with his superb wit and erudition, moved to the city with his son's family without as much as composing an ode of parting.

Our old morality went the way of the old learning. The pious man who cooked his son to feed his old father; the filial daughter-in-law who cut off her finger to bring her mother-in-law back to life by feeding her drops of blood; the faithful wife who took her own life after her husband's death – we have totally forgotten these virtuous people, whose memory once shone brighter than any monument of gold. The world now belongs to those sons whose filial piety amounts to not striking their aged fathers, daughters-in-law who can earn praise by not throwing out their old fathers-in-law, and wives whose loyalty simply meant not having children by other men.

Concepts such as loyalty to one's country or friend are trampled down by colossal selfishness, and decorum between the sexes is nonexistent. Lovers carry on openly, not hesitating to hold hands in public or walk entwined in each other's arms. Girls no longer bind up their chests to avert male gazes and expose their legs without any sense of shame. And none of them hesitates to laugh or giggle in public places.

Codes governing the relationship among clansmen are also forgotten. Clansmen are now divided into common-interest groups; loyalty to the clan and solidarity among its members, which used to be so precious to us, have crumbled before trifling self-interest. Reverence for ancestors has also disappeared, so that permanent tablets are now discarded and even the neglect of commemorative ceremonies goes unreproved. What gods would protect and take care of us with so much tender concern and loving care as the spirits of our ancestors?

The legends and tales of our people, the creations of childlike imaginations and naive explanations of natural wonders, are now smothered by scientific theory. The ancient kings who were born from eggs; the hero who married the female dragon; the embittered ghost that punished her children's evil stepmother; the monk who could make icicles form on his beard in the summer; the Chinese general who drove ceramic stakes[8] into every auspicious spot of the country to prevent the land from producing great warriors; the goblin residing in the old pond; the dragon, foremost of the four auspicious animals; the phoenix that nests only in paulownia trees, eats only bamboo fruits and drinks only from the divine fountain; the holy giraffe that neither treads on living grass nor consumes living creatures; the thousand-year-old snake; the cunning fox with nine tails and various other legendary animals; the spirits of the fields, the mountain, the kitchen, the pond ... All these myths and legends made us cling to our grandmothers' knees and cherish in our memory our grandmothers' scent long into adulthood. At one time they prompted tingling fear, but now they are the stuff of delicious memory. And our grandmothers were the last transmitters of those wondrous tales.

The old religion has also disappeared. How profound and firm was our ancestors' religion! None of them thought that the will and the acts of heaven could be explained in a few volumes of scripture. None of them sought to ascribe a name or a personality to the divine creator, and it never occurred to any of them that God could be partial or selective in his love and protective care. Instead, our ancestors saw wind as the breath of the mother goddess, and the net of heaven as vast and loose but tight enough to catch all human guilt. They believed heaven was silent but responsive to the prayers of honest men. To them not a meteor fell, not a mountain heaved, without the distinct will of heaven, or without presaging some major cataclysmic event. Our ancestors, therefore, strove to obey the will of heaven and to live in accordance with the laws of Nature. But this religion of our male ancestors has disappeared, together with the many guardian deities worshipped by our female ancestors.

The guardians of the land, of the pillars, the beams, the kitchen, the gate and the toilet, together with the guardians of crops and property and the various figures represented on talismans, have vanished. The blind fortune-teller, whose shop is just outside the town, has few customers, and the mortuary plank[9] of the neighbourhood geomancer is coated with dust. People step on the charcoal dropped on the kitchen floor without fear, and let rice grains fall into water jars. Children paint each other's sleeping faces for fun.[10] An imposing church was built in the centre of my hometown. On Sunday evenings its vesper bells sound like a death knell to all that profound and subtle heritage that has passed away for good.

3

One thing in the marketplace remained unchanged despite the rapid transformations going on all around. It was old man Top'yŏng's hat shop. Already quite advanced in age, the old hatter opened his shop every market day for an ever-dwindling number of customers, his appearance as unchanging as his shop.

His constancy at first struck us as ridiculous, accustomed as we were to change. His shop was the only remaining thatched-roof one, and the only shop without a signboard and a window display. And there was something comic about an old man who clung to his old trade despite constant losses. But, as we approached adulthood, we began to have different thoughts about such stubbornness. In the course of our painful encounter with the new ways and mores, we had learned to see the old and the new from a different perspective. And in the shabby old hatter and his shabby hat shop we began to see the fate of our clan as it was sinking into the bottomless abyss of history.

The history of the old man himself, which we learned at about the time we came of age, also made a strong impression on us. His grandfather had been a master hatter who had made no less than four hats for the kings; his father had also owned the most famous hat shop in T'ongyŏng, the foremost city for traditional headwear. But the 1895 ordinance prohibiting topknots[11] deprived his family of half their customers, and the subsequent loss of sovereignty to Japan and abolition of the hat makers' association hastened the hat makers' ruin by creating reckless competition among them. Old man Top'yŏng's father moved to our hometown as a final haven. Once every three years my clan used to invite a master hatter to our town and have him make new hats and mend old ones for all its members. Old man Top'yŏng's father, who had been to our town once before on such an invitation, remembered our clan's munificence and moved here as a last resort.

The route the hatter's family traversed – 140 miles – was a bitterly painful one. When at last they arrived in our hometown two months after leaving T'ongyŏng, the nine-member family had been reduced to just three. At the outset the old man's grandmother died of heartbreak; his mother died of fatigue from their journey; and his two older brothers left the group with their wives. When they arrived in our hometown the family consisted only of old man Top'yŏng, who was then a child, his father and his grandfather.

Our clan, an island of conservatism in the sea of rapid change, gave them a warm welcome. They were given an empty hut and the farmland normally given to grave keepers, as well as a year's sustenance. Thus began the nine-year-old Top'yŏng's bond with our clan. Though he moved later on to the marketplace, in his heart he surely must have considered himself an inhabitant of our clan's hill.

So, at about the time we came of age, the bitterness occasioned by the 'hat disaster' was forgotten, and reconciliation was effected between us and our old adversary. It became a custom among us to pay the old man a visit when we came home on vacations. Most of the time we brought him spirits and snacks, drank with him, and reminisced about the incidents of our younger days. On such occasions, the old man became for us a living monument to all that has disappeared. His utterances were like an epitaph in a dead language remaining on the ruins of a dead city.

It was during one such visit that we learned the real meaning of the episode we had, as children, made use of to infuriate and distract the old man, the episode about 'when Elder Hahoe came back without his top-knot.' The incident took place the year after the old man's family came to live in our town. A young man of the clan who had gone to Seoul on some errand came back 'enlightened' – that is, without his topknot and in a Western suit. This was Elder Hahoe, who later became the first in our clan to acquire a college education. In any event, the entire clan was beside itself with horror and fury. At the time our clan stuck so adamantly to the old ways that it hadn't even complied with the royal ordinance to free the bond servants; to cut off one's topknot, therefore, was an unthinkable sacrilege. Elder Hahoe's tribulations began at the entrance of our town. Before he could get very far, he was splashed with excrement. Then the clan installed a thorn fence around the house of this irreverent rogue who had defied the teachings of all the holy sages, this renegade who had profaned the sacred hair inherited from his parents. Even after the thorn bush was removed, clan members continued to avert their faces when they saw him in the street. He had to undergo a week's penance to obtain his parents' forgiveness, kneeling on a rush mat in the yard, and his wife wore mourning robes and stopped grooming her hair or wearing make-up until pardon was granted.

Each time this story was retold, Elder Hahoe became more and more degraded and his tribulations more and more severe, but none of us blamed the old man for that. It was his justifiable fury towards a traitor. Even supposing Elder Hahoe was a pioneer, what could the Western civilization he and men like him had imported offer our old friend but insult and indignity?

4

About a dozen years ago the shocking rumour that old Top'yŏng was a changed man created a stir in the marketplace. One autumn morning people stared in disbelief at the old man's shop, where renovation had begun on a grand scale. The beholders looked as if they were witnessing a terrible outrage. An unknown carpenter was renovating the old man's shop, and a familiar cabinet maker from a nearby town and his assistant were making a modern display case. In a matter of days the shop took on a refreshingly modern look.

Everybody assumed that with the refurbishing of the shop the merchandise would change also. In truth, people had long harboured many questions about the old man. For whom did he open his shop every market day, when no one wore horsehair hats any longer, and whose orders was he filling by working so hard and so constantly? What did he live on? It had been a long time since he'd sold his last hat, and even the repair work he was given occasionally had stopped coming in altogether some time ago. People made guesses. But the best they could come up with was the supposition of a well-known gossip. Citing her nine-year-old grandson as an eyewitness, the woman said that the old man only pretended to make hats but never completed any, that he wove a crown or a brim on market days and unwove them in the intervals. As to what he lived on, she repeated, without conviction, that the old man was seen bringing rice husks from the grain mill and carrying away a piglet that had died from eating poison. Sometimes, getting excited, she said that he ate frogs and mice, but if anyone asked for further details, she would immediately back off, saying that it was just what she had heard from other people.

When her words reached his ears, the old man became furious. He rushed to her at once and gave her a violent tongue-lashing. Together with the famous incident of a hen-pecked husband knocking his wife senseless in a moment of reckless fury and a *kisaeng* biting a philandering town mayor's nose, their battle has become one of the 'three major brawls' of the marketplace. Since the shop's renovation was undertaken shortly after the momentous incident with the town gossip, people expected a drastic change in the old man's way of life. The most prevalent assumption was that he would switch to some other trade.

But that assumption soon proved wrong. What the old hatter placed in his new display cabinet were several horsehair hats and various headgear accessories. And on the varnished floor were laid out the same old iron stove and hat-making instruments. A few days later a large new signboard went up; on it was written the shop's name, Shinhŭng Ipchabang, New Sensation Hat Shop, and in flourishing strokes such fashionable phrases as 'most elegant' and 'time-tested skill.'

At first people were simply astonished. By and by there were other reactions. Some people laughed themselves hoarse at the incongruity. However, a few gazed at the shop and the old man with mixed emotions and turned away with downcast eyes. But most felt, in an undefinable way, snubbed and cheated and were angry with the old man. They began to laugh at his impracticality and scoffed at his perverse stubbornness.

The old gossip he had shouted down was the most elated. Till then, she'd been intimidated by his fury and her own lack of hard evidence, but this time she thought he'd supplied visible proof of his madness. She rushed about, asserting that the old man was both senile and demented.

The old man repaid the hostility of others with his own. He had changed as drastically as his shop. From having been a talkative and gregarious man, he was now taciturn and belligerent. He drank without restraint, and when drunk he quarrelled with anyone who offended him in the least. Within a few months he had quarrelled with just about everyone in and around the marketplace.

Once, more than half my childhood buddies and I happened to be visiting our hometown at the same time, after having completed our compulsory military duty. It was shortly after the old man had created a stir with his harsh treatment of the barber and his younger brother. The barber's shop stood facing the old man's shop. It seems that the barber's kid brother had stolen some horsehair from the old man's shop, just as we had years before. However, instead of letting him off with a 'hatband' as he'd done with us, the old man gave him a heavy thrashing. When the boy's older brother, the barber, came to protest at such excessive severity, the old man repulsed him with a bamboo-splitting knife.

We did not blame the old man. Rather, we felt profound pity for what resembled the last defiant fury of a cornered beast. This sentiment led us to renew our acquaintance with the old man, which had been interrupted by our military service. We called on him several times while waiting to return to our jobs or for the new school term to begin. Even though our motive for visiting him had changed, we took the usual gifts of spirits and snacks. But his blind hostility extended to us too. Sometimes he would petulantly stare at us, as if mocking our goodwill; at other times, he embarrassed us with a determined silence. Sometimes, he would feel insulted by our trifling jokes and become infuriated. He might have become just an unpleasant memory if it hadn't been for the deep impression his words made on us the final time we visited him.

That visit took place the night before most of us were to depart. We went to say goodbye but also to make an important proposition. One of our clansmen, who had long had his eye on the prime location of the hat shop, had asked us to persuade the old man to sell or rent it to him. This kinsman, like most people in my hometown, knew of our special friendship with the old man, so he called on us to be his emissary. But our mission was a failure. The old man not only refused the offer but also became enraged when we gently recommended that he combine his hat trade with some other business.

After gazing at our dismayed faces for a long time, he said quietly, 'Don't you understand? I'm not doing this for my livelihood any more. That's why I'm so hard on little boys who steal horsehair. I'm waging a war now, and horsehair is my weapon. The people who once splashed a young man with faeces for abandoning his hat laugh at me now for sticking to this trade. To wage war against such thoughtless people and against these barbarous times I need more and more horsehair to make more and more hats. And this shabby shop is my fortress. If I give it up, where can I fire my guns from? And how can I face my father and my ancestors when in a short while from now I encounter them in the next world?'

His gleaming, tearful eyes exuded maniacal fury. His hands shook with drunken infirmity. He went on:

'I know I'm at the end of a blind alley. In the old days we were able to move here from T'ongyŏng, but there's no further retreat. Even if there were, I couldn't undertake such a journey a second time. Even now I dream of that long and bitter journey and wake to find my pillow soaked with tears. I will keep up my battle here as long as I can, and when I can't endure any more I'll just die. That's why I sold off all but one last piece of land to improve the shop. My father had seen hard times, so he saved up and bought land for security. I sold it off bit by bit, almost to the last. But I don't regret it. I sold my last major parcel of land to keep this shop, and most of the money is still here, transformed into the showcase and the signboard and these hats. Hats enabled my father to buy the land. So how can I not sell the land when the hats need it? As long as there is one man in this country who still wears horsehair hats, I'll continue to make them.'

5

'Wouldn't it be better to go back home and marry old man Top'yŏng's daughter?' That was the joke that circulated among us shortly after, a roundabout way of conceding that we were depressed and our prospects dim. Then others would catch our meaning, recall our unfortunate old friend and gloomily tilt their glasses in acknowledgement.

Old man Top'yŏng had a daughter, left behind by his late wife after an otherwise long, childless marriage. The girl grew up to be a sultry beauty. To tell the truth, there was a time when she made our hearts beat wildly. But the joke, with its allusion to her seductive good looks, was not just sexual. The girl embodied the old man's sad wish. Determined not only to preserve his craft until the end of his own life but to prolong its life for one more generation, he had long been looking for a successor. But it was hard to find an apprentice, and harder to keep one. All traditional Korean crafts are intricate and require a long, difficult apprenticeship; making horsehair hats is perhaps the most intricate and complicated craft of all. Moreover, the old man was a master of not just one kind of traditional hat, as with most hat makers, but of several, from the royal hat to hats worn by ministers and officials of various ranks, down to those donned by ordinary scholars. He had also taught himself the skills for making numerous accessories for hats, when their supply became scarce. Each required several years of devoted study. Realizing he didn't have long to live, the old man was in a hurry to pass on his various skills. He consequently exhausted one apprentice after another. Moreover, traditional hat making had no future. So the apprentices ran away after just a few weeks. Nor were their parents especially eager to have their children master such a difficult and moribund craft.

So, under these circumstances, the old man hit upon the idea of acquiring an apprentice son-in-law. After his fourth apprentice had run away, he dropped hints that horsehair hat making had a bright future as a protected traditional craft and let it be known that if he saw promise in his next apprentice he would make him his son-in-law. That brought in applicants. Although she was thought to have a roving eye, his daughter was a buxom beauty, and the hat shop was located in a very advantageous part of the marketplace. But this time, too, in spite of the alluring prospect of marriage and heirship, successive apprentices still took to their heels and departed. The intricacy of the craft and the discipline it required were simply too demanding.

At last the old man came by a patient and devoted apprentice, but was not able to make good on his promise. A widower brassware artisan, whose trade had been swallowed up by mass-produced stainless steel and plastic wares, became his next apprentice and devoted himself to acquiring the complicated set of skills. But one night the enticing girl eloped with the assistant manager of an insolvent cinema company. Despondent, the widower then departed as well.

The old hatter returned to his lonely battle. Most of us were then living the life of college drop-outs or were low-salaried clerks in industry or government offices, and would jokingly mutter when we got together, 'Oh, wouldn't it be better to marry old man Top'yŏng's daughter and be his heir?' Which was a way of saying that we were tired of the race for survival in the city and weary of being tiny cogs in the gigantic wheel of our industrialized society.

6

We next heard that the old man had sold off his last remaining plot of land and left on some kind of quest. People assumed that he had left in search of some place new to settle, but a friend of mine who was staying in our hometown at the time told us that in fact the old man had left in search of the 'blue bamboo.' Like the legendary bamboo that supposedly grew on the shores of Lake Xiaoxiang, the 'blue bamboo' was a divine plant whose roots were said to penetrate boulders and whose new shoots could sprout through marble. It was a tree so rare that only one of its kind could be found in the country in a decade.

'I've been living like a fool all this time. My grandfather told me that the king, the monk and the butcher each has his own perfection. But instead of devoting myself to perfecting my skill and creating great masterpieces, I've let myself be distracted by anger and have waged a stupid war against the times. Now I'm returning to my true way. I care no more about what other people might think or do. I'll concentrate solely on producing a work worthy of the great master I hope to become, if only once, in the last days of my life.'

He aimed to produce a hat woven with 500 bamboo strands that the 'blue bamboo' was intended to supply. As he left on his journey early one drizzly winter day, the old hatter reportedly muttered that, like Ju Zhizi of old, who boiled his wife to get the perfect liquid to smelt a pair of divine swords, his own devotion was sure to move heaven, which would direct him to a blue bamboo growing somewhere. My friend said that he didn't dare try to dissuade the old man, who seemed to be setting out on the journey ordained by Fate.

It took a long time. During a blizzard towards the end of that winter, the old man returned. His clothes were ragged and he limped, but as he pulled a few stalks of bamboo from his backpack his eyes shone with a strange gleam. He told my friend, 'I realize that there's no such thing as the blue bamboo. But I also realize that what makes a bamboo divine is not the plant itself but the artisan who uses it. Look at this. This is just an ordinary bamboo, but in my hands, it's going to be as good as a blue bamboo.'

Our old friend's last battle began about a fortnight after his return home. It took him about that long to work the bamboo until it became pliant. But even during that fortnight he was not idle. He washed and cleaned all his tools and whetted all the steel implements. And each morning at dawn he washed himself clean. My friend said that the process resembled an ancient priest's preparations for a solemn tribal ritual, and the people of the marketplace no longer denigrated or ridiculed him.

At last the real work began. After making a simple but solemn ritual offering to the guardian spirits, he commenced his work by skinning the bamboo. The thin skin was split into strands as fine as hair. Throughout the process beads of perspiration stood on the old man's aged forehead. But as he examined the gossamer-like strands one by one, his eyes seemed to burn with a thousand flames.

He made another small offering to the spirits on the morning he wove the hat's crown. Once he began the delicate work, he kept at it without eating or sleeping. Once – probably on the day he was to complete the hooks that secure the hat's ribbon – a neighbour, taking pity, made a fire in the stove to heat the cold floor[12] on which the old man worked and slept.

But the old man rebuffed him with, 'Don't do me any unwanted favours. Warmth is no good for an artisan. Warmth just makes a man dull and lazy.'

The old man was strict with himself. In the extremely intricate process of weaving the fine bamboo strands with the most delicate silk threads, he undid his work many times on account of a tiny mistake not perceptible to ordinary eyes.

The work showed steady progress. While weaving the hat's outer silk lining, the old man told my friend, 'Today, I've decided to make this hat a gift to any man who still wears horsehair hats. You can't set a price on it. Even if you could, no one could afford it. Now, after the ribbon hooks are wrapped with red silk thread and if I can give the brim the right curve, it will be worthy to grace the head of a king. If only these were my grandfather's times ... But I won't begrudge it. Any man who has to this day loyally adhered to the ways of his forefathers has ample right to this priceless creation.'

My friend told me that the old man sounded utterly forlorn as he spoke.

There were four in my hometown who still wore horsehair hats until the early 1970s. There were even more if you included those who wore them without topknots, but the old man heartily despised such boors. So, in his view, there were only four who wore them properly. But one of these had moved away to Kangwŏn Province with his children the previous year, and another, a clan elder and revered patriot, had died the year before that. And that very night, old man Kim Ch'ilbok, a commoner who had been wearing horsehair hats ever since commoners were first allowed to, passed away. He had been a most faithful customer and friend of the old hatter. That left only one candidate for the gift of the priceless hat – Kyoch'ŏn, an elder of my clan.

Hearing of his friend's death, the old hatter sank into thought, but before long he took up his work again with a stony face. Only his hands seemed to shake a little. He sped up his work. When people asked him why he hurried, he explained that he had to finish the hat and give it to its rightful owner as soon as possible. But it was obvious that he was spurred on by some ominous presentiment.

The hat was completed without further mishap or delay. The brim traced a beautiful curve, and the hat looked so light and elegant, you thought it might float up and dance in the air any minute. Its smooth silken surface gleamed with high-quality lacquer paint, and the amber buttons on its headband gave it ineffable dignity. Even to an ignorant layman it looked like a work of art, the creation of a great master craftsman. Our worthy old friend had at last made the incomparable, true silk hat, woven with 500 bamboo strands. It was a glorious day.

7

When the old man hurried with his priceless hat to Kyoch'ŏn's house, the elder was not home. He had gone to Seoul to attend his grandson's wedding, and his return was delayed by bad weather. The old hatter became restive. For days on end he hovered around Elder Kyoch'ŏn's house and kept asking his family when they expected him back.

Then, one day, the clan was surprised by a noisy quarrel from the direction of the entrance to the village. Elder Kyoch'ŏn was walking towards the hill, supported by his grandchildren. The old hatter followed, shaking his fist at the clan elder, from whose head the accustomed horsehair hat was conspicuously missing.

'How could you do this? How could you cut off your topknot and expose your bare head to the sun? Aren't you ashamed in front of the spirits of your ancestors who protested to the king that they'd rather have their heads cut off than get rid of their topknots? Tell me, how could you do this? Tell me, if you're not utterly dumb!'

The elder tried his best to appease the infuriated hatter. He explained that a horsehair hat was too inconvenient in the busy metropolis and that he'd had his hair cut because he couldn't go around with a bare topknot. He kept repeating to the hatter, 'Please understand.'

But the old hatter's fury was unabated. He kept repeating the phrase 'as a *yangban*,' and 'your hat that's more precious than your head,' and went on to accuse Elder Kyoch'ŏn of deceiving and betraying him.

Elder Kyoch'ŏn was at last driven to anger. 'Are you crazy? When did I deceive you and how did I betray you? If you made this hat for me, why don't you just give it to me? Did you make the hat to insult and harass me?'

The hat maker followed Elder Kyoch'ŏn to the gate of his house. 'Pay me for all the hats I gave you for free over the last seven years. You accepted my gifts without any qualms and now you give up your hat because of a small inconvenience. Isn't that deception? Isn't that betrayal?'

The clan elder disappeared into his house in embarrassment and anger. His entire family came out and tried to appease the hatter, but it was no use. The other townspeople looked on with heavy hearts. Tears ran down the old hatter's cheeks. Nobody could think of anything to say. Then somebody said quietly, 'Let's go back. The hat doesn't belong to Kyoch'ŏn.'

What that person probably meant was that the old hatter should wear the hat himself. But, wildly sobbing, the old man said, 'You're right. This hat belongs to Ch'ilbok. Yes. Ch'ilbok's the rightful owner. Let's go to Ch'ilbok, quickly.' Then he led the way, keening loudly and muttering, 'This town's come to an end. It's a town without shame.'

He walked the mile to Kim Ch'ilbok's grave, weeping, and wept even more bitterly when he stood before the grave. He addressed it, 'Are you having a good rest, Ch'ilbok? Why did you leave in such a hurry? I'm sure you're resting peacefully in heaven. You never did anyone any harm and were always kind to everyone. You were the only true man in these evil times.'

Then he gathered the fallen leaves and dry straw scattered about the grave into a heap and, putting the hat on it, lit the pile before anyone could stop him. The hat burned up with a loud crackling noise.

'Ch'ilbok, I send you this precious hat. It's yours. You won't be ashamed to wear it where you are. It's the last great work of my life. Do you hear me, Ch'ilbok? Please accept it and wear it in your eternal home!'

Long after the hat turned to ash and the ash grew cold, the old man continued weeping. Only after nightfall did he come down the hill, his steps uncertain.

After that, he didn't open his shop on market days and never came out of his house. Even when his signboard dangled precariously over the shop's entrance from a broken wire, he did nothing about it. Out of pity, his neighbours brought him food, but he just turned towards the wall, lying on the floor under his quilt. He died one April day, before it was fully spring. Somehow the news must have reached his daughter, for one day she appeared in town, colourfully attired and accompanied by a new husband. She sold the shop to the first bidder, then went away, never to appear again.

KIM TAEYONG

Pig on Grass

Translated by Bruce and Ju-Chan Fulton

She kicked the pig in the balls, and off flew her purple sandal. Her foot was so dirty – bony and withered like an old tree that no amount of sunlight and water can resurrect. I've been thinking I ought to wash those feet, but so much for good intentions. With a squeal the pig took cover in the sty. There's an empty *soju* bottle lying on the ground, courtesy of yours truly, who admittedly was under the influence. Landed square on the pig's snout, and he squealed then too. As I recall, I did some squealing of my own and had myself a good laugh. The pig used to play with that bottle – licked the spout, tried to chew off the label, sent it rolling with its snout, gave it a head-butt for good measure, but when the bottle didn't fight back, he'd lose interest.

The pig started rooting around, its butt facing me – not a happy camper. Below its haunches hung its dark, filthy balls.

She located the sandal and put it back on, managed a few steps, then stopped to pound the kinks out of the small of her back while glancing up at the sky. She repeated the process, her rickety steps more laborious, the sandals scuffing behind her. She reached the grass, heaved a great sigh and sprawled out – or rather plopped down *splat* on her back.

We have a patch of grass. It's just grass, a couple of hundred square feet of it, and once upon a time it was dear to our hearts. In fact, it was the clincher in our decision to purchase. When we first saw the property, we could tell the grass used to be a garden. It must have been a tidy little affair, designed by the man who built the house, but when we saw it then, it was like a neglected grave, overgrown with weeds. I decided I had to tend to that grass. She wasn't crazy about the notion, but she humoured me with one of her far-be-it-for-me-to-tame-your-stubborn-hide looks.

So we moved in, and one day I said, 'How about we call that grass our little cemetery?' and she responded with her what-are-you-asking-me-for-you've-already-decided pout. But I've never actually called it a cemetery. I mean it's stupid to bestow a name on something like grass. And to my wife, being the wife she is, grass is simply grass. I got off to a good start, weeding and mowing, but then benign neglect set in. The previous owner had no doubt gone through the same process, ultimately leaving the grass in a state of nature – he who tends least tends best. Watching me fall out of love with my grass, my wife was kind enough not to remind me that that was my style with everything. But if she had, I was ready to say that he who loves least loves best. Too bad I never had a chance to say that. So we began neglecting the grass and the grass began beckoning us. And when the grass beckoned us, we vouchsafed body and soul expressing our true love for it. Before we knew it we'd developed a routine – one of us would lie down on the grass and the other would follow suit. How it happened was, one day I was feeding the pig and I saw my wife sprawl out on the grass; I tossed the feed bowl aside and ran over and lay down beside her. It took only a few repeats to turn into a game. But it's more than just fun – it's my wife's way of telling me she *really* wants to take a rest and *really* wants me watching over her.

I lay down at an angle next to her. She was gaping at the sky, where a mass of dark clouds was billowing like a swelling echelon of dark birds. She turned and looked at me. I saw moisture pool in her eyes and then disappear – bored to tears. She reached over and felt my ankle. The one with the scar. She likes to feel that scar. I got it a long time ago. Our boy had just started walking. I saw him reach for a kettle of water boiling on the stove. I grabbed him just in time but in the process knocked the kettle over and scalded my ankle. The boy saw my ankle all swollen and angry red, and he started squalling. My wife came to the rescue, making a dressing out of grated potato, cucumber and watermelon peels and securing it with a cloth nappy. The pain went away and I was left with a puckered scar. Irked by the sight, she fetched my socks and covered it up. 'Godawful flower.'

One night in bed, when I'd practically forgotten about the scar, she made a confession: she got hot whenever she felt it – strange, wasn't it? And then she caressed it, licked it even. It was just before her period and her lips were dark red like a pomegranate. From then on, whenever she felt my ankle we were off and running. I got to thinking, *What if I'd scalded my crotch?* Long after menopause, she still fondled that scar. And as often as not that brought a little dribble from my manhood – I could feel the moisture in my drawers.

Yesterday we were lying on the grass head to foot. She felt my ankle and I tickled the sole of her foot. She didn't react to my tickling. Over time layers of dead skin have built up like strata of earth and now her sole is one big callus. Gradually she nodded off – for her the tickling is more like a languid caress – and before I knew it, she was asleep. Her legs were visible among the folds of her dirty skirt with its red flower pattern. There are little crevices in the skin, like a paddy gone dry in a drought. I found an ant in the grass and placed it on her calf. It climbed her leg – maybe it was drawn by the odour of her privates. Once it had disappeared inside her skirt I sat up. For all I knew, it was burrowing into those folds and wrinkles, but she was snoring away, dead to the world, a trace of spittle at the corner of her mouth. I counted the wrinkles in her face. It's those two dozen wrinkles that make her face hers.

My grandson once took a pen to my face. I was taking a nap and I heard someone count *One, two, three, four*, but I thought it was all in my dream. Then I woke up, and saw the boy counting my wrinkles and numbering them. I lurched up, grabbed the pen and snapped it, then pulled down his trousers and spanked him until my daughter-in-law intervened.

I oinked like a pig – I felt an urge to number my wife's wrinkles, just like my grandson did then. The pig gave me a blank look – *What's up with this fool?* I gave him the finger, the way kids do. The pig's head went back and forth – *That's pathetic.*

Do pigs have their own language? I asked her this once when we were lying on the grass, and got her *You're silly* snort in response. For the fun of it I tried imitating a pig. *Oinkoinkoink oinkoink.* She picked up right away – *oinkoinkoinkoink.* We had a conversation: *Oinkoink. Oink. Oinkoinkoinkoinkoink. Oinkoinkoink oinkoink. Oinkoinkoinkoink. Oink. Oinkoinkoink oinkoink oink. Oinkoinkoink. Oink oinkoinkoinkoink oink. Oinkoink. Oink. Oooiiink.* The last thing I said was, *Oinkoink oinkoink oinkoinkoink oinkoinkoink oinkoinkoinkoink.* Meaning, *See – if I die first, you can talk to the pig.* I think she understood – *Oink*, she said.

And then I wondered if by understanding the pig's language we could understand the pig. But maybe the pig wouldn't want to talk to us. If I died first, maybe my wife would scream *Oinkoinkoink oink oinkoinkoinkoink!* at the pig (meaning, *Get over there, you damned pig!*), but maybe the pig would respond in a different language – *K'yŏlk'yŏlk'yŏl*.

And maybe, after I died, the pig would break out of his sty one night and go inside. He'd sneak into bed with my wife and root around in her crotch, sniffing and saying, *Oinkoink*. My wife would feel his jet-black balls and say, *Oinkoinkoink oinkoink* (meaning 'Aigu,' *good boy*). And after that hot night the pig would be the man of the house. And on any old lazy day my wife might plop down on her back in the grass and the pig would trot over, balls swaying in the breeze, and sprawl out beside her. And they'd have this sort of conversation – *Where do the clouds come from? Where do the clouds go?* My god, I couldn't stand it any more. I felt a jealous rage. The more I think of the impossible, the more the impossible becomes possible. So here we are – the pig and my wife are having an affair.

Shuddering with anger I went up to the pig and pissed on him, one hand aiming my equipment down, the other holding my trousers up. The pig opened his mouth wide and let it slop in, the sweetest of rain. When the stream stopped, I shook my cock to get the last drops out. The pig regarded my balls and licked his chops. I felt an irresistible anger towards the way it was acting. *Oinkoink – That's pathetic*, his eyes were telling me, *a shrivelled-up cucumber*. I wanted to kick the pig's balls. *You big rascal – stop acting like a pig!* My foot swung out, my trousers fell down, and my skinny arse landed in the dirt. And there I sat, naked butt on the bare ground. The ground was chilly and I felt like I was turning into a cold hard rock. What if I ended up dying like this? Like in that game my grandson used to play where everyone dances like crazy and someone shouts *Freeze!* What a disgrace, losing out to the pig. I searched for a comforting thought.

Instead I came up with the story my grandfather told me about how *his* grandfather had died. The maid was delivering his breakfast tray-table and when she slid open the door to his room, there he was sitting like a *kisaeng*, legs bent and gathered modestly to the side – it was really weird. A thin strand of saliva clung precariously to his half-open mouth, as if trying desperately not to be dislodged, and moisture had gathered in his eyes. If there had been cameras back then, the scene could have been captured for posterity, 'My grandfather the *kisaeng*,' worthy of inclusion in *Tales of Mystery from Around the World* – my grandfather got worked up when he related this old family story that I found so difficult to believe. Ei, *you expect me to believe that?* I had said, and then my grandfather said, *Mark my word, boy, I'll die the same way – it skipped my father's generation, and now it's my turn, and if I die like that, who knows, maybe you'll suffer the same fate.* His belief soon materialized: when his body began to break down he would spend time out in the yard, contorting himself in peculiar ways in preparation for his death. But instead of a charming young *kisaeng* he became a crouching cat, a spread-eagled frog, a rooster with its head poking into the ground, a snake slithering along the wall of the yard. The neighbours hush-hushed to one another that the old man was senile, but I tried out those various poses for myself and ended up believing him. Now that's *style*, I told myself – movement suddenly frozen, breathing stopped. I remember a vague feeling of lonely pathos, a person helpless in the face of imminent death.

But there was nothing stylish about my grandfather's death. It was disgraceful, wretchedness itself. He took a shit wherever the spirit moved him and smeared the faeces all about. He called the maid to his room, buried his face in her skirt, and whimpered, *Mummy, I don't want to die – help me, Mummy.* He left one last mound of shit in his bedding before closing his eyes for the last time. He was full of bravado at the end: *Look at me, I'm shitting, look* – did he mean these his last words to be a capsule of his life? The watery faeces spread, staining the white quilt. With a grimace everyone clapped a hand over mouth and nose. I'd never smelled anything so vile. But I didn't cover my mouth or hold my breath. Or cry either. I wanted to take it all in, my grandfather's death. The shit smell went right through me – I could almost feel it in my anus and I kept wiggling my bottom where I sat. More than sorrow, I felt a kind of betrayal at his death. A scary thought occurred to me: perhaps my grandfather's grandfather had died in this manner. And if so, what would prevent me from proclaiming my own death with a pile of shit? Sucked into the vortex of a fate no man could oppose, I couldn't take a crap for a while and eventually my face got jaundiced. My mother got fed up and cooked a pot of kelp porridge and stuffed me with it. I had the cold sweats that night and finally a greenish, watery poop came pouring out of me.

And now the pig was making fun of me by pooping in the corner of his sty. I could hear the turds plop to the ground. They were as dark as his balls and looked just as mushy. I brushed off my bottom as I got up, then pulled up my trousers. I rejoined my wife on the grass and gazed at the sky, hunched up like a woman abandoned by her husband. Gazing at the inky clouds arriving from the far reaches of the sky, their changing aspect an attempt to convince us the atmosphere was unsettled. These days I often feel under pressure because natural phenomena are changing by the minute. When I look in awe at such displays of irresistible nature, I feel shattered at the thought that perhaps my life until now has been one failure after another. And it doesn't stop there – for some time now I've been thinking deeply about thought. But my thoughts are only thoughts that lead to other thoughts. There's no substance to them, only the ridiculous traces of one thought leading to another. I can't stand being absorbed in trying to think just for the sake of thinking. It takes energy to make myself think and it takes energy not to absorb myself in thinking – but isn't there some other energy I need besides those two? I've lived my entire life without thinking. There's the fact that I've always been a mere salesman, but also, I just don't like to think, and when I do think of something, I pretend I'm too busy to think. If I'm in a whirl of activity there's no room for thoughts. And now that I'm getting old, all those thoughts that I nudged aside are nudging back at me as sweet as a nap. But those thoughts are tough to swallow, like the barley we used to eat to tide us over during the hungry times before the autumn harvest. If I were fated from now till my death to do nothing but think, perhaps I would barely be hanging on to life, accepting my fate and at the same time resisting it. I'm not saying that thought alone can alter my present unpleasant state; more precisely, I know of no other way. I don't long to change anything through thought. It's just that now I have time to think. And I want to accept, to push, the me that's loyal to the notion of being in time with time. I often ask myself, *Hey, what have you been thinking?* But I never get an answer. Well, actually, the answer is contained in the question *What have you been thinking?* It's natural for the conclusion to one thought to be postponed by another thought. All my present actions are simply grist for further thought. I'm thinking constantly as I rush towards death determined to die.

I rolled her sleeping form one complete revolution. She was back on her back. I rolled her again, this time more forcefully. Back on her back. I rolled her to the edge of the yard, then back the other way. Normally this would have awakened her, but she was sleeping the sleep of the dead. Just as the two legs of a rocking chair bestow order on meaningless motion, I rolled her back and forth across the grass. If there's a rule to this activity, it's that I have to roll her back the other way when she reaches the edge of the grass. The rolling reminded me of a winter night long ago.

The two of us and our five-year-old boy were bundled in a quilt sharing a bowl of thin noodles in radish kimchi broth. The boy was complaining – why were we eating cold food on a cold winter day? It made his teeth sting. She tried patiently to explain to him using the old saying 'Treat cold with cold.' The look on his face told us it still didn't make sense. She realized she needed to explain further but had done all she could, so she looked to me instead. *Stop your fussing and eat up*, I told the boy. *It's winter food, and it's best eaten cold*, I added. *It's not as good if you don't eat it right away*. They both looked disappointed at my explanation but went back to work with their chopsticks. After we finished, the boy didn't seem in any hurry to go to bed. Instead he rolled back and forth on the quilt, trying to get our attention. When he rolled my way, I took both corners of the quilt and lifted, sending him rolling back towards my wife. The boy burst out giggling and my wife lifted her end of the quilt and sent the boy rolling back towards me. The boy laughed himself breathless – he looked like he was having the time of his life. I told my wife to hold on to the quilt and get up, figuring I really would give him the time of his life. She said it was too much, her arms were sore. *No excuses*, I told her. *Come on, get up*. And I made her stand up, asking if she meant to neglect her motherly duty to keep her boy happy, and reminding her I myself was tired when I came home from work but still tried to have fun with him. *So what do I do?* she asked. *Like this*, I said, jerking the quilt up so that the boy flew into the air before dropping back onto the quilt. I wish I could describe how much fun it was for him – his expression, his squealing in delight, said it all. After we'd launched him several times, she asked if we could stop, it was too much work. *One last time*, I said, and then I yanked the quilt as hard as I could. This time the boy almost reached the ceiling. I let go of the quilt. The boy came down and slid off the quilt, landing with a thump on the floor.

He looked stunned, and the next moment he was howling. Startled, my wife gathered the boy up and rubbed his head. *Oh, I didn't mean it,* I muttered, but the fact was, I'd decided to let go of the quilt, and that's what I did. The boy had a huge lump on the back of his head. My wife brought an egg and tried to smooth the lump with it, then bared her bosom and offered the boy her breast. Only then did the boy stop crying. I protested, he was a big boy by now, but she didn't look at me, merely smoothed the boy's hair. There was no longer milk to be had, but he sucked away on her nipple until he fell asleep. Later that night she asked me why I had let go of the quilt. I told her my arms were worn out – it was a half-arsed explanation and we both knew it. She didn't say anything and after a time began to stroke me. She lowered my pyjama bottoms, reached into my briefs and after fondling my balls she put them in her mouth. She rolled them around, and suddenly bit down. *Ouch!* She'd done it on purpose, but I gritted my teeth and didn't make a peep.

I heard the patter of rain. After pacing restlessly, the pig disappeared inside his sty – maybe he wanted to bed down. Hoisting her by the armpits in her half-asleep trancelike state, I dragged her inside and lay her down in the bed. Her eyelids were trembling even while she slept, and I imagined her eyeballs moving inside them. That delicate trembling felt like the appeal of someone at death's doorstep, and I had to look away.

I felt hungry. For breakfast I'd eaten some pine mushrooms she had grilled for me. I checked the refrigerator – nothing but fruit and vegetables. She's obeying to the letter her doctor's dictum that if she wants to live longer she mustn't eat meat. I myself have always preferred vegetables, but now that we're meatless, meat is what I'm craving. Keeping a pig is a reflection of this craving.

So I make a hole in a box and put the pig inside with its snout sticking out through the hole. I take a slice of the pig's snout, fry it up in a greased pan and eat it. In a few days the pig's snout grows back and once again appears through the hole. I slice off another piece and fry and eat it. I often imagine myself going through the slice-fry-eat routine. Through imagination alone I satisfy my craving for meat. The pig's snout sticks out and it's flat – perfect for slicing and frying.

I sit in the rocking chair eating a raw sweet potato, skin and all. The rocking chair squeaks when it rocks, just as a good rocking chair should.

My son bought it for me. I've got my sweet potato in one hand, my book in the other. The book is also a gift from my son. He wrote it. I sit in the rocking chair my son bought for me and read the book my son wrote. It's pretty dreadful stuff. Day in and day out I open this dreadful book my son wrote and think to myself, *Let's see how much more dreadful it's going to get.* My son is a philosophy professor at the local university. Once I tried to get an explanation out of him – didn't he have better things to do than study philosophy? I wanted to say to him that a person like me who doesn't know squat about philosophy, *I* should be the one studying it, but a nincompoop like him doing philosophy has nothing to offer the philosophy field. He took the wretched money I earned over a lifetime of people calling me a peddler, and he squandered it for his PhD. Not once has the kid given me a proper thank you. He doesn't understand all the thought that's gone into my life and instead goes around with an anguished expression consistent with the title Philosophy Professor that others have graced him with. What a damnable little wretch. On the first page of the book is printed 'For my mother.' Well of course – he didn't give the book to me, he gave it to her. Contained in the preface to the book is the following:

> *My first philosophical problem occurred when I was five. It was a cold winter night and my parents and I were bundled up in a quilt eating thin noodles in radish kimchi broth, and I asked why we were eating cold food on such a cold winter night. My mother tried to explain with the saying 'Treat cold with cold' but for me it wasn't much of an explanation. It was kind of like restating my original question, the same meaning with only the words changed. I learned from this that when adults don't understand phenomena and words, they run from their ignorance by concealing it with other words. It occurred to me that perhaps language did not reveal the meaning of phenomena or the truth of events but was merely a tool for covering over meaning and truth. This was my first philosophical question, my incentive, and it still occupies me.*

That's my son for you – puffing up his philosophical authority with words that don't make sense. And then he added the following:

> *That night I was playing on the quilt and I banged my head on the floor. I was crying and my mother rubbed my head with an egg. I had a lump on*

*my head, and to this day it feels like I can still feel it. That lump was my first
separation point from the world, and it wrapped me up in the question of
why I couldn't help but be me. Ever since then, I've had a habit of rubbing
the site of that lump whenever I'm confronted with a philosophical problem.
I call it the existential lump.*

Existential lump, my arse. Just like my wife tried to hide her ignorance
with 'Treat cold with cold,' my son tries to camouflage his philosophical
limitations with smoky words. As far as I'm concerned, he's the existential
lump in *my* existence.

Beneath a cherry tree with a messy scattering of blossoms, she beseeched
me to marry her because I'd made her pregnant. I demanded proof that
what was in her belly was mine. *You want to see me kill myself?* she said,
clutching at my trouser legs and pleading tearfully. So I married her – what
else could I do? It's not that I never wanted to get married, but the fact
that she brought it up first somehow pissed me off. And then the boy was
born and everyone made a big deal of what a chip off the old block he
was. I had to admit it, he did resemble me. But for some reason I didn't
take to the boy. And I couldn't help feeling more and more upset listening
to her say how much he resembled me in everything he did as he grew
up. But who knows, if he hadn't resembled me, maybe I would have spent
the rest of my life suspecting my wife of being unchaste and maybe I would
have made a point of showering the little guy with love. And with time
came a confession: she was not in fact pregnant when we got married. She
was afraid that if she hadn't told me she was pregnant, I wouldn't have
gone ahead with it – but wasn't I happy that we had ended up married,
that our boy was so clever, that we were living a happy life? Which made
me feel all the more that the boy was not my own. And even though he
was blameless, I considered it all his fault. I kept putting off the day when
I would tell him I wasn't his father, and look at me now.

My son's book is dreadful, and it's tedious to boot. Philosophy – what
a useless discipline, spieling on to no good end. And on the heels of this
realization comes an annoying thought – the boy probably chose philosophy with an eye to tormenting me. I'm capable of philosophical thought
without having read a single philosophy book. In contrast, my son writes
like a guy who wants everyone to know he's read dozens of such books.

Just like yesterday, I can't get through the first page; I'm only barely able to restrain myself from throwing the book. Instead I toss the sweet potato and rock my rocking chair and close my eyes.

I kick the pig in the balls, and off flies my purple sandal – my foot is so dirty. The pig knows the routine by now – a kick in the balls, a new day – and he retreats with an oink. I hear a vehicle trundling towards me from the distance. The trundling gets louder and finally the vehicle comes into view. A jeep. Trailing a plume of dust, it comes to a stop in front of the house. The door opens and a man climbs out. His hair is streaked with grey – why doesn't the kid dye his hair, for God's sake? My son must think grey hair symbolizes the notion that he's a big-shot philosopher. He approaches me.

'The pig's a lot bigger. But it's really gross.'

'What are you doing here at this time of day? What about your classes?' I ask without looking at him.

'I told you I'd drop by, didn't I? And today's Sunday. She and the boy were going to visit, but something came up.'

A pretty flimsy excuse, I told myself. My daughter-in-law and grandson have always been leery about visiting me. Why can't the kid be more upfront about things?

'Father, did you think it over?'

'Think over what?'

'We won't have another opportunity like this any time soon. How can you live alone like this?'

'Damned if I know what you're talking about.'

'I won't have any choice if you keep persisting in your stubbornness.'

'Damned if I know what you're talking about.'

'How many times do I have to explain?'

'Then explain.'

'I'm going overseas on an exchange and I don't have anyone to look after you.'

Since when have you ever looked after me? I want to ask him, but I hold my tongue. He plops himself onto the grass – he looks pretty frustrated. I feel like telling him he'll feel better if he kicks the pig in the balls. He grabs a handful of grass. Those hands, so plump and glossy, have never done a rough day's work in their life.

'There's only two months left. You should have made a decision by now – then we could take care of things and leave.'

Here comes the tantrum. He'll flop down on the grass and start kicking for attention like on that winter night back then. I feel like feeling the back of his head. To see if that existential lump is still there.

'All right, all right.'

I want to tell him I'll go along with it as long as I can take the pig and the grass along. My son gets up, his face lit up with joy. He takes my hand, tells me he can take it from here, house and all, and says he'll drop by again in a few days. The warmth of the kid's hand holding mine gives me an unpleasant feeling. I try to free my hand but he's not about to let go.

'Are you feeling all right?'

'I'm feeling good enough to give the pig a kick in the balls.'

'All right, then, now that I have your answer, I'll be on my way. If she were here, I could stay longer. But I'm so busy, you know, there's so much to take care of. So I'll be back with her in a few days.'

My son has already decided, he's proceeding according to plan, and consulting with me is just a formality. I could have answered him differently but it wouldn't have changed his mind. He passes a hand through his greying hair as he retreats. I figured that I'd shoo him home if he said he wanted to stay longer, but he beat me to the punch and that hurt my feelings. He's leery in the extreme about being alone with me, just like I am with him. The kid is exactly like me, down to the last ugly detail, and that's something I still can't abide.

'Aren't you going to say hello to your mum?' I ask as he's about to climb into the jeep.

'Father, what do you mean?'

'Your mum thinks about you day in and day out, she reads that book of yours even though she doesn't understand it, and you're going to take off like this? Have a heart, boy.'

'I have no idea what you're talking about, Father.'

'I was playing with her right there on that grass yesterday.'

'Father, stop it. You're going too far. I'm not going to play your games any more.'

And then my son tells me that she died last year. I listen carefully to what he has to say and think maybe he's right, but I tell him I don't think so. I'm about to say something else, but then he makes a call somewhere and starts telling someone about me. I'll bet it's his friend who happens to be my doctor. Now he's listening, and at the same time examining me, and finally he says 'All right, all right' and ends the call. He looks annoyed.

'So I'll be back with her in a few days.' He's like a broken record.

He climbs in and starts the jeep. Then yanks the steering wheel around and takes off as if he's running away from something. He disappears, leaving a cloud of dust behind. Once the dust settles, a stillness even more desolate than before envelops the surroundings.

Once again I couldn't say it – couldn't tell my son I'm not his father. As I look at his tyre tracks I wish with all my heart he'll leave me here all by myself and sneak off overseas with his family. If the kid leaves without advance notice, I can spend the rest of my days trying to understand him, sympathize with him, long for him even. I feel like my strength is draining out of me. I lie down on the grass and let go. The pig is pacing back and forth oinking – probably angry that it's past feeding time and I haven't fed him yet.

I look up at the sky. The white clouds break up the way they always do and then come together again. Time and again they disperse and rejoin, disperse and rejoin. The process speeds up. Those clouds are going to fall to earth and shatter and scatter. I feel like I'm about to have a convulsion. I don't feel any pain, but I'm trembling like a living creature that's watching itself suffer.

I roll once on the grass. I'm back on my back. I roll again, this time more forcefully. Back on my back. Before I know it, I've rolled across the grass and back. It's time to stop, but I'm not stopping. Someone is rolling me. I want to get off the grass but someone is blocking me. *What in heaven's name is it?* The more I think about it, the more amorphous it becomes. There's only a force that no man can oppose. To resist this strange force that's rolling me, I gather my energy, shuddering. And then my sphincter tightens and releases and a liquid mess pours out.

I'm lying on the grass. The muddy mess sets my body contracting, then seeps back inside me. Lying soiled on this filthy grass, I feel the scar on my ankle. I hear oinking from far off and then close by, far off and close by, far and close.

WOMEN AND MEN

PAK T'AEWŎN

A Day in the Life of Kubo the Novelist

Translated by Sunyoung Park in collaboration with
Jefferson J. A. Gatrall and Kevin O'Rourke

The Mother

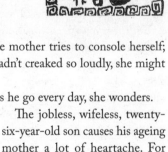

heard the son leave his room and put on his
shoes at the edge of the veranda. He's taking
his walking stick off the nail on the rack and
walking towards the inner gate.

'Are you going out?' No answer.

The son is already at the gate; he may not
have heard. Or his reply may not have reached
her ear. The mother figures it's one or the other
and raises her voice so as to be heard from
beyond the gate.

'Come back early!'

Again, no response.

The gate creaks open and closes. The mother tries to console herself;
she's a bit frustrated. If only the gate hadn't creaked so loudly, she might
have heard her son's 'Yes!'

She resumes her sewing. Where does he go every day, she wonders.

The jobless, wifeless, twenty-
six-year-old son causes his ageing
mother a lot of heartache. For
instance, if he goes out in the
afternoon, he doesn't return until
very late at night.

The frail old mother lies down
on the bare floor and rests her

95

head on her arm, waiting for her son. Soon she's dozing. And just as soon she's awake again – it's uncomfortable sleeping like that, and she never lasts more than two or three hours at a stretch. She glances at her son's room then checks the clock on the wall.

Midnight – not too late. He'll be back soon. Praying that he actually does come back soon, she nods off again.

This time she's out for the better part of two hours. When she wakes up she notices the light is on in her son's room.

He always turns off the light when he goes to bed. Maybe he's already home; maybe he's reading in bed? That would be just like him.

The mother tiptoes to the son's room, puts her ear to the door, then eases it open. No one there. What's keeping him? Her face forlorn, she is about to close the door but changes her mind and goes in.

Sad the way her grown-up son's room lacks any hint of perfume or fragrant oil. She fixes his pillow and bedding – they're just as they were earlier in the evening – and sits down beside them. She has raised him all these twenty-six years, but you never stop worrying about your own child. Even if those twenty-six years were doubled, her heart would always be burdened. If only she could marry him off, she wouldn't have to suffer this late-night anguish.

Why doesn't he want to get married?

Whenever she talks about marriage, the son says, 'I'm penniless. How can I support a wife?'

But there must be a way. Surely whatever job he eventually gets will support a family of two.

The mother is heavy at heart, feeling sorry for her son. He has no intention of looking for a regular job. All he does is read, write and wander aimlessly through the night.

He'll change once he's married, she thinks. If he loves his wife he'll think about making money, it's only natural.

Last summer he was introduced to a nice girl. Surely he won't turn her down. I'll have a good talk with him when he comes home, she thinks. And before long she's imagining a grandson.

The Son

eventually got home, but before his mother could say, 'You're still up? Good night now,' he changed into his pyjamas, sat down at his desk and opened his writing pad.

The son would assume an offended air if she were to speak her mind now. That always hurt. And so she left after barely managing to say, 'All right, it's late, get to bed, you can write tomorrow.' The talk could wait till morning.

Next day, the son got up at eleven – or maybe it was noon. He ate without a word and was off again.

To make money he sometimes sells what he writes.

'Is there anything special you'd like to eat?' he asked her once.

She was amazed and delighted that her jobless son could earn a little money with which to buy her something.

'Don't worry about me,' she said. 'Buy yourself some socks.'

The son, as usual, was stubborn. Normally she didn't like his obstinacy, but on this occasion, the more stubbornly he insisted, the more satisfied she felt. A mother's love seeks no reward, but a child's display of love gladdens her heart.

'So what will you buy me?'

'Whatever you wish.'

'Something other than food?'

'Certainly.'

So the mother ventured to say what she really wanted.

'Could you buy me a skirt?'

When the son readily agreed, she added, 'And your sister-in-law, too?'

His face clouded over and he asked how much two skirts would cost.

Maybe he hadn't earned so much after all those sleepless nights.

'It's all right,' the mother said. 'Just buy one for your sister-in-law.'

'No, I have enough,' he said. 'Here – would you buy them?'

And he held out the money.

The mother hesitated, then accepted the money. How proud of him she was. She surprised her daughter-in-law at the sewing machine in the next room. 'Let's go and buy some fabric. Look, your brother-in-law gave me money for skirts.'

When her skirt was finished, the mother put it on and went out.

She visited a relative's and waited like a child for a chance to show off the new garment. When the woman of the house unwittingly said, 'Oh, that's such a nice skirt,' the mother was quick to answer, 'It's a present from my second son – he bought one for his sister-in-law too.' She took such pride in her son, lost all inhibition when boasting of him.

Such scenes are rare. The mother believes a regular job would be much better than writing and concludes that her gifted son will prosper in whatever he does. Her son talks about how difficult it is to get a job these days. Yet she's seen others doing just fine at companies or in government jobs, even though they only made it through primary school. She can't for the life of her understand why her son can't find a job – he graduated from high school after all, he even studied in Japan.

Kubo

is out of the house now, walking along the stream-side street towards Kwanggyo. He regrets not replying with a simple 'Yes' to his mother. The word had been on the tip of his tongue, but the distance between him at the outer-quarters' gate and his mother inside required a voice loud enough to be heard above the laughing and chattering of the three schoolgirls who happened to be passing by at that moment.

Still, he should have answered. Kubo imagines the lonely look on his mother's face. The girls have drifted out of sight.

At last he reaches the bridge. Ostensibly he's been walking with a purpose, but he stops. Where to? He can go anywhere, but there's nowhere to go.

On the sunlit street, Kubo suddenly feels the onset of a headache – it's going to be a bad one. Though he has a good appetite and sleeps well, he figures he must be having a nervous breakdown.

He looks glum.

KBr 4.0
NaBr 2.0
NH4Br 2.0
MgI2 4.0
Water 200. 0
2 days, 3 times a day, before meals

The medicine – the young nurse
at the hospital pronounces it *ppisu* – has no effect on him.

Kubo jumps aside. A bicycle whizzes past, narrowly missing him. The young man riding it throws back a contemptuous look – he must have been ringing his bell from a considerable distance. That was a close call, and you might think Kubo was distracted by the prescription for B*su*.[1] But that's not the whole story.

Kubo wonders about the hearing in his left ear. The young medical assistant who examined him was not very skilful but dared declare there was nothing wrong with the ear except it was filthy inside. How humiliating! Better to have a four-week treatment for an ear infection than a lump of earwax. Still, Kubo managed to clean out the ear every day, nerve-racking though it was.

Fortunately he did seem to have an infection. Browsing through a medical dictionary, he decided for no particular reason that he had *otitis media catarrh*. According to the dictionary, *otitis media catarrh* can be acute or chronic, the chronic type having two subtypes, one wet and one dry. Kubo concluded that his complaint must be the chronic wet type.

Of course, the problem wasn't just Kubo's left ear. He hadn't much confidence in his right ear either. He had neglected his hearing for a year now, always thinking he would see a specialist soon. Some day in the not-so-distant future he might have to wear a Dunkel ear trumpet or an electronic hearing aid as a result of overusing the comparatively sound right ear to compensate for the dysfunctional left.

Kubo

starts off, aware of the senselessness of lingering idly by the bridge. He walks towards Chongno. He has no business there, but his right foot – randomly extended – veers left.

A man appears from nowhere and crosses his path. Kubo imagines a collision and staggers to a halt.

Damned eyesight! He can't even see straight in broad daylight. The 24° glasses perched on his nose mitigate his short-sightedness but have no effect on all his retinal scotomas. He wonders if his vision-test chart from the Government-General Hospital is still lying in his gloomy drawer. The chart is titled *Ophthalmologist Follow-up Visit. R, 4 L, 3.*

Kubo recalls the optical perimeter – he saw it on a small table at the ophthalmologist's during his first visit. After two weeks of fever he had gone there to complain about his weakened eyesight. The doctor, himself sporting glasses with thick lenses, marked all the scotomas with chalk.

In spite of his visual handicap Kubo strides across two sets of railroad tracks and marches towards the Hwashin[2] Department Store. Before he knows it, he's inside.

A young married couple with a boy of four or five wait for the lift. They'll want to enjoy a nice lunch in one of the restaurants. The couple's eyes gleam with a desire to show off their happiness, or so it seems to Kubo. For a second he considers cursing them, but the next moment changes his mind and instead gives them his blessing. Who knows, perhaps he envies the couple – they're enjoying a day out together, renewing their sense of happiness despite several years of married life. It's obvious they have a happy home.

The lift descends and the door opens and closes, the young couple disappearing from Kubo's sight, along with their boy Lucky or Rich.

On his way out, Kubo wonders where he can find happiness. He follows his feet to the tram stop and stands with others at a safe distance from the tracks. He looks at his hands. A walking stick in one hand and a notebook in the other – needless to say, there's no happiness to be found there.

To the other people waiting for the tram, happiness is an unknown. But at least they have a place to go.

The tram arrives. People get off and people get on. Kubo remains where he is. But when he sees the people standing with him get on board the tram, he feels sad and lonely at the thought of being left behind. He jumps onto the moving carriage.

On the Tram

Kubo couldn't find a seat at first. The last seat was taken by a young woman who had got on board just before him. He stands near the conductor's seat and wonders where to go. The tram is heading in the direction of the East Gate. At which stop might happiness await him?

Before long the tram will skirt the East Gate and then Kyŏngsŏng Stadium.[3] Kubo looks at the blue flannelette-lined window. The Train Bureau posts news there. Recently people don't seem to be playing football or baseball.

To Changch'ungdan, to Ch'ŏngnyangni, to Sŏngbuk-dong . . . Kubo doesn't like the suburbs any more. Nature and leisure are there for the taking . . . it's true. Even solitude . . . is all prepared for him. But nowadays he fears solitude.

He loved it once. But to say he once loved solitude may not be an accurate description of his previous state of mind. Perhaps he never really loved it. Maybe he always dreaded it. No matter how often he wrestled with solitude, he could never conquer it. At times maybe he just let himself get lost in it and pretended to love it.

Tickets, please – the conductor approaches. Kubo rests his walking stick on his left arm and thrusts his hand into his trouser pocket. He sorts out five coins; the tram stops at Chongmyo and the conductor returns to his seat.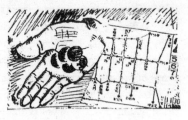

Kubo lowers his eyes and looks at the five coins in his hand. They are all tails. Taishō[4] twelfth year, eleventh year, eighteenth year . . . Kubo tries to find meaning in the figures. This proves fruitless. Even if he could make sense of them, it would still not be *happiness*.

The conductor approaches again. 'Sir, where are you going?' Kubo looks where the tram is headed and wonders if he should say Ch'anggyŏng Park, but he doesn't answer. A man on a tram with no destination has nowhere to get off.

The tram stops, then starts again. Looking out the window, Kubo wonders if he should have dropped by the university hospital. He has a friend who studies mental illness in the lab there. Visiting him – seeing a different world – might not bring happiness, but at least it would count as doing something.

Kubo turns back to the tram and, lo and behold, a woman he recognizes – she must have just got on. If when he goes home he says he met *her*, his mother's face will light up and she'll keep pressing him: 'And then? . . . And then?' If he says that's all, his mother will be disappointed and accuse him of tactlessness. But if someone else hears about it and talks of her son's timidity, she'll make an excuse, saying, 'My son is always so shy . . .'

Kubo looks nowhere in particular, afraid of meeting her eye. Did she see me standing here? he wonders.

The Woman

saw him – or did she? By now there are only a few passengers, and a man standing in the corner, ignoring the empty seats, is readily visible. She would have certainly seen him. But did she recognize him? That's uncertain. It wouldn't have been that easy to recognize a man she met only once last summer, and has never met since, not even on the street. It is a lonely and disconsolate experience for a man to reflect that a woman he remembers has lost all memory of him. His bold or rather insolent attitude at the time, he thinks, must have made quite an impression. Kubo wants to believe that she, too, sometimes thinks of him.

She must have seen me; she must know who I am. In which case, what are her feelings now? Kubo's curiosity is piqued.

He glances timidly at her profile – she's sitting diagonally across from him, about ten feet away – and instantly looks away, afraid of eye contact, thinking she may also have glanced his way and noticed him stealing a look at her. She may know him to be the man, and she may also know that he knows she's the woman. *So what should I do?* Kubo racks his brain. *Maybe I should say hello. But then maybe it's more polite to pretend not to have noticed her. I wish I knew what she wants.* Suddenly he feels funny about being nervous. *How can I be so worked up about a trifle? Maybe I really had a secret longing for her.* Then again, he hasn't seen her in his dreams since their meeting last year, and it dawns on him that he was probably never really in love with her.

And if not, his mind-reading and flights of fancy are – to say the least – an emotional violation, a sin of sorts.

But what if she did long for him?

Just as he turns her way for another look, she stands, picks up her umbrella, and gets off at the East Gate. Heartsore at the sight of her waiting for a Ch'ŏngnyangni-bound tram, Kubo wishes he'd got off. But if she were to spot him on  a second tram and discover that he'd got on for no other reason than to try his luck with her, how crass she would find him. While he wavers, the tram moves on; the two grow farther apart. Finally, she is out of sight. *Damn!* Kubo thinks with a surge of regret.

Happiness

– the happiness for which he so yearns – perhaps departed for ever with her. As the bearer of his happiness, she may have longed for him to open his heart. *Why can't I be more daring?* Kubo lists her merits one by one. Will there be someone else to offer me the promise of happiness?

With the destination board changed to Han River Bridge, the tram passes the Training Centre. Kubo sits down and sorts the five-*chŏn* coins in his pocket, wondering whether she might after all be the only woman for him, even if she never appeared in his dreams.

His belief that he didn't think about her much may be a kind of self-deception. When he returned home to his anxiously waiting mother after the first meeting, he certainly expressed his opinion, a sort of 'she-might-do' endorsement. All the same, Kubo forbade his mother from making a proposal to her family. He did so not simply from vanity. He didn't want to cause her unwarranted distress in case she wasn't interested in him. Kubo wanted to respect her feelings.

Of course, nothing was heard from her. From time to time, Kubo wondered whether she might be secretly waiting to hear from him. Yet to entertain such an idea was ridiculously self-conceited. Meanwhile, time passed, and he began to lose interest. Perhaps, if her parents had made contact first, Kubo would have been able to rouse his interest again. At one point, an old lady who was somehow related to the girl's family hinted that they were observing the moves on his side. Kubo smiled wryly. If this were true, he thought, it's not so much a comedy as a tragedy. Still, he was unwilling to take any action to save them both from tragedy.

The tram passes Yakch'ojŏng. Kubo is distracted from his absorbing line of thought by a young woman sitting in front of him with an umbrella between her knees. He grins slyly. He learned from a maga- zine that this suggests the  woman is not a virgin. But a woman of her age would naturally have a husband. Maybe that's why she wore her hair up. *She*, where did she put her umbrella? Kubo toys with this wayward idea. He considers whether someone making such an observation isn't bound to make the woman he marries unhappy. Will a woman be able to make him happy? He considers his female acquaintances one after another and he sighs softly.

Once

Kubo had an unrequited love for a friend's sister. On summer evenings when he visited his friend, this sister came to the door to meet him. She seemed beautiful and pure, sufficiently so for young Kubo to admire her. The fifteen-year-old bookish boy thought he wanted to love her, thought he would certainly be happy if he could marry her some day. He visited his friend frequently in the hope of meeting her, blushed at chance encounters, and upon returning home drafted many a late-night love poem. But the knowledge that she was three years older made him feel insecure. By the time he reaches the age when confessions of love to a woman are no longer awkward, she will already have embraced another, an older man.

She ended up in an older man's arms before Kubo could devise a solu- tion to his problem. Seventeen-year-old Kubo liked to think that his heart was filled with sorrow, and yet he tried to wish for their happiness, especially the man's. A great deal had been written about such sentiments in the books he had read. Three thousand *wŏn* to cover the wedding expenses. A honeymoon in Tokyo. A house in Kwansu-dong, recently renovated. This seemed to guarantee their happiness.

This past spring Kubo and his friend visited the couple. Without blushing Kubo could carry on an ordinary conversation with the wife, who was already a mother of two. When he complimented her clever seven-year-old boy, the young mother complained that the boy was the youngest in the neighbourhood, and that the older children were nasty towards the smaller ones. She proudly told him how she once marked each of her son's picture cards[5] with a pencil, since she pitied him for always coming home after losing his cards to the other children. When he returned that day with all his cards gone, she summoned the children of the neighbourhood and recovered the cards by picking out 'her child's' from the ones they had ...

Kubo sighs gently. It's no loss that he couldn't marry her after all. With that kind of woman, he would probably never have had the chance to know what happiness is.

He gets off the tram at Chosŏn Bank and heads for Changgok ch'ŏnjŏng. He's tired of thinking; he feels like stopping at a teahouse to enjoy a cup of tea.

What time is it? He has no watch. If he had a watch, it would be an elegant pocket watch. A wristwatch – that suits a young girl. Kubo recalls a girl who wanted a wristwatch. She wanted an 18-carat gold watch in the local pawnshop. It  had a price tag of four *wŏn*, eighty *chŏn*. And if she could also buy a new skirt, she thought she would reach the pinnacle of happiness. A voile Bemberg silk skirt. Three *wŏn*, sixty *chŏn*. In all, eight *wŏn*, forty *chŏn* would complete her happiness. Kubo has not heard whether her modest wish was ever granted.

Kubo wonders just how much he would need to be happy.

In the Teahouse

it's about two in the afternoon. Jobless types are sitting around on cane chairs, talking, drinking tea, smoking cigarettes and listening to records. They are mostly young, but despite their youth, they look world-weary already. In the dark, partially lit teahouse, their eyes broadcast a litany of trials and tribulations. Occasionally, a buoyant footstep glides into the teahouse, or a bright laugh fills the room, but such exuberance feels out of place here. The teahouse regulars disdain them above all else. Kubo orders coffee and cigarettes from a young waiter and heads for a cane table in the corner. Just how much would I need? A poster hangs over his head, a painter's 'Farewell Exhibition upon Leaving for Europe.' Kubo imagines that if he had money to go abroad, he would be almost completely happy, at least for a time. Even to Tokyo. Tokyo would be good. Kubo thinks he'd like to see how Tokyo has changed since he left. Or even somewhere closer to home. Somewhere nearby would do. Kubo believes that he would certainly feel happy were he to find himself at Kyŏngsŏng Station with his small suitcase, even if his destination were only 12 miles away. That is a happiness only time and money can offer. He is prepared to go on a trip at any moment …

Sipping his coffee, he counts all the types of happiness a little money can buy. Even with eight *wŏn*, forty *chŏn*, he would be able to acquire, for a time, some small happiness, or even more. Kubo doesn't want to mock himself for that thought. Doesn't a heart that can be consoled for a while with a little money deserve sympathy, love even?

What is my greatest wish? Kubo lights a cigarette. While cleaning his pipe at the hearth, Ishikawa Takuboku[6] once asked, What is my real desire? Kubo felt he ought to have such desire, but he found he hadn't. Probably true. But if you try, you can put anything into words. Tzu Lu[7] wanted to go for a carriage ride with a friend, wearing light clothes and enjoying himself to his heart's content, while Kong Jung[8] wished for a room full of guests and a cup of spirits that never ran dry. Kubo wishes that he, too, could find pleasure among good friends.

Suddenly Kubo yearns for a friend. He wishes he had a friend here to chat with over coffee, to share the same thoughts.

Footsteps stop on the pavement in front of the teahouse; the door silently opens. The man is not one of Kubo's friends. When their eyes meet, the two almost simultaneously turn their heads away. Melancholy settles on Kubo's quiet heart.

The Man

and Kubo once exchanged greetings. On a dark street. A friend introduced them. 'I've heard a lot about you,' the man said. He must have known Kubo's name and face. But Kubo didn't know him. The meeting in the dark ended without Kubo seeing the stranger very clearly, and when he came across him afterwards, he failed to recognize him. The stranger must have felt insulted when Kubo passed without acknowledging him. If he thought that Kubo recognized him but pretended not to, naturally he would take offence. But Kubo didn't know this, and he was at ease in his ignorance. He just found the man odd because whenever they bumped into each other, the man averted his eyes, looking embarrassed and upset. As long as Kubo merely found him odd, he felt fine. But when he finally recollected who the man was, a shadow was cast over his heart. Ever since then, Kubo has been turning away involuntarily when he spots him, equally embarrassed and confused. Kubo, trying now to block a corner of the teahouse from view, feels the complexity of human relationships anew.

Kubo leaves a couple of coins on the table and exits the teahouse with notebook in hand. Where to now? He walks towards the Prefecture Hall. One way or another, I'd like to see a friend. In Kubo's mind the faces of his friends parade before him in the order of their streets. No one was likely to be home at this time of day. Where to now? In the middle of the street, he looks past the spacious yard at Taehan Gate. *Try the swing in the children's park?* The shabbiness of the old palace[9] weighs on his heart.

Kubo throws his cigarette butt on the street. He notices a boy standing beside him. The boy has the walking stick Kubo left behind in the tea-house. 'Thanks.' Kubo chuckles at his absentmindedness, gazes for a while at the boy running back to the teahouse, and follows him.

A young painter runs an antique shop in the alley next to the teahouse. Kubo knows nothing about painting, but he has an artistic temperament, and given the chance, he would like to hear a few stories about that profession. A writer requires all kinds of knowledge.

Kubo's friend is not in. 'Master just went out.' The clerk looks at the clock on the wall. 'About ten minutes ago,' he adds.

Kubo wonders what effect those ten minutes will have on him as he walks down the alley towards the tram tracks.

People come and go in the street, in a hurry, at work. Kubo comes to a stop on the pavement. I should go somewhere, he thinks suddenly, maybe to the Sŏsomun area . . . for the sake of my writing. For a long time he's been lazy about his *modernology*.[10] That thought gives Kubo an acute headache and a sense of general fatigue. He can't take another step; he stands there in a stupor.

After a While

Kubo decided to walk on. The scorching midsummer sun on his bare head makes him dizzy. He can't stand here like this. Neurasthenia. Of course, it's not just his nerves. With this head, with this body, what will I ever accomplish? Kubo feels somewhat threatened by the energetic body and resilient gait of a virile man just passing. Suddenly he regrets having read *The Tale of Ch'unhyang*[11] at the age of nine – he had to hide from the watch-ful eyes of the adults in the family. After visiting some relatives with his mother Kubo decided that he too, like them, wanted to read story books. But it was forbidden at home. Kubo consulted a housemaid. She told him about a rental agency that had all kinds of books and lent them for one

wŏn a volume, no more. 'But you'll get a scolding . . .' And then she muttered to herself, 'For sheer fun nothing beats *The Tale of Ch'unhyang*.' A coin and the lid of a copper bowl were the price of his first story

book seventeen years ago, which was perhaps the beginning of everything that followed, as well as all that is to come. The storybooks he read! The fictional works he spent his nights with! Kubo's health must have suffered irreparable damage in his boyhood . . .

Constipation. Irregular urination. Fatigue. Ennui. Headache. Heavy-headedness. Syncope. Dr Morida Masao's training therapy . . . Whatever his illness is, T'aep'yŏngt'ong Street, humble, no, but barren and cluttered, darkens Kubo's mind. While thinking about how to drive those dirty rag-and-bone men off the streets, he suddenly remembers how Sŏhae papered his ceiling to hide its loud patterns. Another unmistakable case of nervous exhaustion. A grin forms on Kubo's lips. He recalls Sŏhae's horse laugh. Come to think of it, that, too, was a hollow, lonely sound.

Kubo remembers he hasn't read a single page of *Scarlet Flames*,[12] his late friend's story collection, and he feels pangs of regret. It's not just Sŏhae's work that he hasn't read. Already he's three years behind in his reading. When Kubo became aware of the dearth of his knowledge, he was dumbfounded.

A young man suddenly appears in Kubo's line of sight. He has come from the direction in which Kubo is walking. He looks familiar. Someone Kubo should definitely recognize. Finally, the distance between the two is reduced to less than six feet. Kubo sees one of his old childhood buddies in the man's face. The good old days. A good old friend. They haven't seen each other since primary school. Kubo even manages to extract the name of his friend from memory.

His old friend had a hard life. He looks so shabby in his ramie overcoat, white rubber shoes and straw hat – the hat is the only new thing on him. Kubo hesitates. *Should I pass without noticing him?* The old friend seems to have clearly recognized him, and he seems to be afraid of Kubo noticing him. At the last moment, just as the two are passing each other, Kubo musters his courage.

'Long time no see, Mr Yu.'

His friend blushes.

'Yeah, it's been a while.'

'Have you been in Seoul all this time?'

'Yes.'

'Where have you been hiding?'

Kubo manages to say no more than this. He feels depressed and wishes he could add something more. 'Excuse me,' his friend says and goes on his way.

Kubo remains a little longer, then resumes his walk, head low, hopelessly fending off tears.

A Little

joy is what Kubo decides to look for. For this purpose he decides to stroll through Namdaemun Market. All he finds are a few baggage carriers squatting listlessly on both sides of the path, no wind blowing in.

Kubo feels lonely. He wants to go where there are people, where the crowds are lively. He sees Kyŏngsŏng Station ahead. There's certainly life there. The scent and feel of the ancient capital city. It's only proper that an urban writer should be well acquainted with the gates of the city. But of course such professional conscientiousness isn't what's important. Kubo would be satisfied if he could escape his loneliness among the crowd in the third-class waiting room.

Yet that is just where loneliness dwells. The place is so packed with people that Kubo can't even find a seat to squeeze into, and yet there's no human warmth. These people are preoccupied with their own affairs. They do not exchange a word with those sitting next to them, and should they happen to say something to each other, it's only to check the train schedule or something similar. They never ask anyone other than their travelling companions to watch their luggage while they run to the toilets. Their distrustful eyes look weary and pathetic.

Establishing himself in a corner, Kubo looks at an old granny in front of him. Maybe she was the hired help in somebody's house. Now she's dragging her frail, aged body on a visit to her daughter who lives in an impoverished rural area. The palsied muscles of her face will never be smoothed out, not by any stroke of luck, and her cloudy eyes may never move again, not even if her daughter takes the best possible care of her. The middle-aged country gentleman next to her probably runs a small general shop in his village. His shop probably carries silk fabrics, everyday goods and everyday medicines. Soon he'll pick up the parcels next to him and proudly get on board. Kubo notices how the man is trying to keep his distance from the old woman. Kubo despises him. With an ounce each of intelligence and courage, this man of overflowing arrogance would have taken a seat in the first- or second-class waiting room, his third-class ticket tucked safely away in his pocket.

Suddenly Kubo realizes that the man's face is swollen. He walks away from him. Nephritis. In addition, the man's face stirs up the unpleasant memory of Kubo's own chronic gastrectasia. He walks to a kiosk only to find himself once again face-to-face with a sick man. A forty-year-old labourer, goitre on his neck, protruding eyeballs, trembling hand – evidently he has Graves' disease. Doesn't seem very conscious of hygiene. The seats on either side of him are empty, but people are not willing to occupy them. About ten feet away from the man, a young wife with a child on her back drops a peach while taking it from her basket. She sees it rolling towards the feet of the invalid but decides not to recover it.

Drawn to this small incident, Kubo opens his notebook. He notices a man in a linen suit with a turned-up collar standing by the door. The man is watching him suspiciously. Kubo is gloomy again; he leaves hurriedly.

Two Men Are Standing

in front of the ticket barrier. From their worn panama hats, ramie over-coats, yellow shoes and empty hands, Kubo confidently judges them to be unemployed. Nowadays these jobless types are mostly gold-mine brokers. He looks around the waiting room again. People like them could be seen here and there. The Age of Gold Mines.

Kubo emits a deep sigh. To search for gold, to search for gold . . . this, too, is clearly an honest way of life. Their lives might be more sincere than his, which he spends wandering the streets aimlessly with a walking stick in one hand and a notebook in the other. Those countless mining offices scattered throughout the downtown area. Stamp duty, a hundred *wŏn*. Admission fee, five *wŏn*. Service fee, ten *wŏn*. Guidance fee, eighteen *wŏn* . . . Registered mining claims are 70 percent of Korea's land. Day after day people get rich in an instant and subsequently lose everything. The Age of Gold Mines. Men of letters – critics and poets included – are among the gold seekers. At one time Kubo thought of visiting his friend's mine and recording details for his own writing. Speculative minds, the dreadful power of gold – he wanted to see and feel such things. Yet the most severe cases of gold fever were to be found in the Government-General Building, in the highest offices of the Oriental Development Company, and in the library of the Mining Bureau . . .

Suddenly, a man with a smile on his round, vulgar face extends a shapeless hand to Kubo. He, too, could be called a friend. A slow-witted classmate from middle school. Kubo almost smiles as he extends his hand awkwardly, walking stick still in it. How long has it been? Are you going somewhere? Yes, I am. And *chane*? he asks.

Kubo always feels irritated when a mere acquaintance addresses him as *chane*. An imperative verb is more tolerable than the condescending second-person pronoun. The man takes a gold watch from his pocket. He considers Kubo. 'Why don't we have tea?' But Kubo has no intention of drinking tea with such a man, the second son of a pawnshop owner. Yet, he lacks the nerve to make up an excuse to turn down the invitation. The man takes the lead. 'Well then – let's go over there!' But he is not just addressing Kubo.

Kubo turns to see a woman coming up behind him. One glance tells him she is the man's lover. Since when does this kind of man care about love? Kubo notices his vulgar face again. But then this is an age when even sentimental poets are becoming gold maniacs.

The man sits down casually. 'Calpis for me,' he says to the waitress. 'You too?' he asks Kubo. Kubo hurries to shake his head. 'Tea or coffee for me.' Kubo is not fond of Calpis. The milky drink has an obscene colour. Also, the taste doesn't agree with him. Sipping his

tea, Kubo suddenly wonders, wouldn't it be possible to figure out a person's character, taste and educational level from what he orders in a teahouse? Drinks can also express passing moods.

Kubo plans to conduct research on this subject some day as he responds casually to the coarse stories of the man sitting across from him.

To Wŏlmi Island

they seemed to be going on a picnic. Kubo exits the station. If they leave at this hour, he thinks, they'll stay overnight at least. He imagines the man's face as even uglier now. He imagines him grinning lewdly and wantonly caressing the woman's naked body. Kubo feels nauseous.

The woman was certainly pretty. More attractive perhaps than the women Kubo has so far found beautiful. Furthermore, she was sensible enough to turn down the man's recommendation of Calpis and order a bowl of ice cream instead.

Kubo wonders why such a woman would want to love such a man, or why she allows him to love her. It must be the gold. Women easily find happiness in gold. Pitying her and resenting her, Kubo is seized with envy of the man's wealth. Money, in fact, would be wasted on such a man. He would stuff himself with rich delicacies, enjoy plump whores and proudly show off his gold watch to everybody.

Kubo smacks his lips, imagining for a brief moment that the money the man throws about is actually his. He rebukes himself immediately. Since when have I been so obsessed with money? He knocks the toes of his shoes with his walking stick, crosses the railway tracks quickly, and is soon striding along the pavement.

The woman was certainly pretty and . . . Kubo wonders if she gave herself to the man a long time ago. The mere thought upsets him. Ultimately, she is far from being sensible. On second thought, something in her reeks of indecency. Her figure has no grace. She is only somewhat pretty.

However, her easy smiles for the man need not cause Kubo to underestimate her. The man enjoys her body, the woman consumes his gold; they may both be happy enough. Happiness is very subjective . . .

Kubo arrives at the Chosŏn Bank. Feeling as he does now, he doesn't want to go home. So where to now? He is beset again by loneliness and fatigue. 'Shine your shoes!' Kubo gazes at the cobbler in astonishment. The cobbler apparently scrutinizes people's shoes and invariably finds fault with them, however minor the fault. Kubo walks on. Has the cobbler any right to criticize someone's shoes? Kubo curses all kinds of street irritations. Suddenly he senses the danger of being out alone at a time like this. Anyone will do. A friend might cheer him up a bit. Or at least make him pretend to be cheerful.

At last, a friend comes to mind, and Kubo phones him from a tailor's shop. Fortunately, the friend is still at his office. Just about to leave, he says.

Kubo begs him to come to the teahouse, fumbling a moment for something to say, then growing anxious lest the other hang up. He falters momentarily.

'Please, come right away,' he adds.

Fortunately

the teahouse is not too crowded when he gets back. And when he looks around – self-consciously – he realizes that the friend who is not a friend has already gone. Kubo sits close to the counter. He is developing a fondness for this teahouse, which is now playing Schipa's 'Ahi Ahi Ahi.'[13] If it were allowed, he would swap his cane chair for an armchair and take a sweet nap. Were he to see the cobbler he saw earlier, he would be able to tolerate him without getting irritated.

In a far corner of the teahouse, a small puppy is licking the insipid shoe tips of a man who is munching toast. The man withdraws his foot – *shoo shoo* – driving the puppy away. The dog wags its tail for a while, looks at the man's face, then turns and goes to the next table. The young lady there is obviously afraid of the dog. Legs curled up and the colour draining from her face, she follows the dog's movements wide-eyed. The dog, still wagging its tail, seems to recognize those who like him. He does not stay long but moves on to the next table. From where Kubo is sitting, it's hard to see this new table. He can't tell what kind of treatment the poor puppy is getting. The dog doesn't appear to achieve a satisfactory result. It moves away and rolls over on its side, its legs stretched out about six feet from Kubo, as if renouncing once and for all its search for man's love.

Loneliness seems to lurk in the pup's half-closed eyes, and with it, a renunciation of the world. The poor puppy! Kubo wants to let it know that at least one man in this place cares. It occurs to him that he has not yet expressed his love for the dog by stroking its head, or by letting it lick his hand, and so he holds out his hand to get its attention. It's normal to whistle in such cases, but Kubo doesn't know how to whistle. After a moment of reflection, he whispers *Come here*, just loud enough to be heard by the puppy.

Maybe it doesn't understand English.

The dog lifts its head, looks at Kubo, then drops its head again, as if not at all interested. Kubo leans forward once more, says *Come here* a bit louder this time, but in as coaxing a voice as possible, and follows up with the equivalent Korean, *Iri on!*

All the puppy does is repeat its previous motions, opening its mouth this time in what appears to be a yawn and then closing its eyes.

Kubo grows anxious, angry even, but he suppresses his feelings. This time, he goes so far as to leave his chair to caress the puppy's head. The startled puppy jumps up before he can touch it, confronts him in a hostile pose, barks – *ruff ruff* – and, scared by its own barking, dashes off behind the counter.

Kubo blushes despite himself. Cursing the dog's fickleness, he wipes his face with a handkerchief, although he is not sweating. He feels slightly angry at his friend who has not shown up yet despite all his pleading.

At Length

the friend arrived. Earlier Kubo contemplated accusing him of being late, but now his face beams a welcome. In fact, he now feels happy to have a friend.

The friend is a poet, one with quite a robust physique who works as a journalist at the local-news desk of a newspaper. There were times when this saddened Kubo. Still, sitting with him makes Kubo feel somewhat lighter at heart.

'Soda for me, please.'

The friend likes to order soda. Kubo always finds this funny. But of course there's nothing offensive about this.

Like a schoolgirl the friend may always order soda in a teahouse, but he has a great passion for the development of Korean literature. That twice a day a man like him has to visit Chongno Police Station, the provincial government and the post office is perhaps a tragedy of the times. With a pen meant for poetry, he has to write run-of-the-mill articles on murderers, robbers and pyromaniacs. So when he has free time, he pours out his repressed passion for literature.

Today's talk is mostly about Kubo's latest story. He is one of Kubo's regular readers. And one of his fans, too, someone who enjoys commenting on Kubo's works. Despite the friend's goodwill, Kubo does not trust his opinion much. Once, after reading what was only a mediocre piece, the friend presumed that he knew everything about Kubo.

Today, however, Kubo has no choice but to listen. The friend points out that in the latest story, the writer appears much older than Kubo. That's not all. The friend judges that the writer is not really old but just pretends to be. That's possible. Kubo may have this tendency. On second thought, Kubo should be pleased that the friend found the inflated age merely a disguise, not a sign of actual senility.

Maybe Kubo is unable to be youthful in his fiction. If he tried to be young, his friend would say he is assuming an unnatural pose. And that would certainly hurt Kubo's feelings. Kubo finds the topic boring. Without realizing it, he turns the conversation to the question of 'the five apples.' Say we have five apples – in what order should we eat them? Three strategies immediately present themselves. Start with the most delicious. That would give us the satisfaction of thinking we are always eating the tastiest of the bunch. But ultimately wouldn't that land us in misery? Better start with the least delicious. A gradually improving taste. But that means we are always eating the worst of the bunch. The third option is to forget strategy; choose indiscriminately.

By introducing this irrelevant, playful question, Kubo baffles the friend sitting across from him, who busily quotes André Gide to back up his ideas on literature. The friend wonders what possible connection the five apples could have with literature. He says he never thought of such a problem before.

'So . . . what about it?'

'Nothing comes to mind.'

And for the first time today Kubo laughs a lively, or at least an apparently lively, laugh.

Suddenly

a child is heard crying in the street outside the window. It's a child all right, but the voice is more animal than human. Kubo pays no attention to his friend's oration on *Ulysses*. Someone has given birth to yet another child of sin, he thinks.

Kubo once had a poor friend. The friend had many childhood misfortunes, suffered all kinds of hardships, experiences that made him exceptionally generous. He was more or less Kubo's friend, but he had one most unfortunate human failing. Were Kubo with him now, Kubo would proffer an aphorism such as 'Love much, regret much.' But this was merely rhetoric, for his friend's uncontrolled sexual urges seemed pathetic to everyone. From time to time Kubo even doubted his friend's taste in women. Things were all right for a while. Then tragedy struck. The friend took to a woman neither beautiful nor intelligent, and the woman thought of him as her one true love. And so the seeds of misfortune were sown. One evening, as the woman was sitting beside him, blushing considerably, she confessed that now she had more than herself to think of. By then, though, he had lost almost all affection for her. She had wanted to know the joys of motherhood and foolishly believed she could secure his love through a child. But he only resented this, and maybe even hated her, already a mother, because now he had to take responsibility for her.

The woman seemed not to have noticed his change of heart. Besides, even if she had taken it into account, at this stage she probably didn't have a choice. With a one-year-old baby in her arms, she travelled

to Seoul, looking for him. But there was no happy ending awaiting mother and child. The friend had a wife, to whom he had been married a long time, and compared with her, the newcomer was a distant second in everything. A quick comparison between the children made this especially poignant. This poor bastard had a huge body, quite disproportionate to its age, and an idiotic face too.

All this might have been tolerable. But when people heard the baby crying, they couldn't help feeling a strange revulsion. The cry was inhuman. It sounded as if a god, furious with their (particularly his) sin, were condemning their (particularly his) sin through the child's eerie voice, casting an eternal curse . . .

Kubo's attention wanders back to his friend's discussion of *Ulysses*. One should of course admire this new experiment by James Joyce. Still, novelty alone is not a just cause for praise. Just as the friend is about to mount a protest, Kubo rises from his chair, touches his friend's shoulder, and says, 'Let's go.'

When they step outside, the sun is setting. Kubo takes in the serenity of the street at this hour and turns to the friend.

'Where should we go?'

'Home,' the friend answers without a moment's hesitation. Kubo feels at a loss. Who should he spend the rest of the evening with?

By Tram

the friend was already on his way home. Not home. An inn. Did he have to leave now to make it back in time for dinner, to an inn where nobody's waiting except the innkeeper's family? If it's just a matter of not missing dinner . . .

'What are you going to do at home?'

That, of course, was a silly question. A man with a 'life' should naturally dine at home. Compared with Kubo, the friend really did have a life.

After being tied up all day with the affairs of the world, he could now enjoy some quiet hours alone after dinner, reading and writing. Kubo can't share in this pleasure.

Shortly thereafter, Kubo stands at the main intersection of Chongno, gazing at the twilight, as well as at the loose women who usually appear on the streets at this hour. They are out in force again today, with all their usual indiscretion. Night is falling fast, and night belongs to them. Kubo looks down at the pavement and steals glances at a variety of splendid and not so splendid legs. How peril-

ously they walk! Not all of them are new to high heels, and yet they all walk in the most clumsy and unnatural fashion. One is certainly justified in calling them 'the precarious.'

But, of course, they aren't aware of this. They're not aware of how unsteady their footsteps are in the world. Not one has a firm goal in life; ignorance blinds them to their common instability.

But what resounds on the pavement is not just the rickety heels of their shoes. The toes of all who have a life are heading home. Home, home, they are so happily walking in search of supper and family faces. Some rest after the daily grind. Takuboku's haiku flows from Kubo's lips.

> The sorrow of everyone with a home –
> like entering a grave
> they return home to sleep

Not that such a sentiment really applies to Kubo on the twilit street. He doesn't have to go home yet. And small as Seoul is, there are still streets for him to roam till late, still places to visit.

Twilight . . . with whom . . . Kubo is walking, almost confident now. He has a friend. A friend with whom to spend the rest of the evening. He passes Chongno Police Station and enters a small, white teahouse.

The owner is out. Kubo turns around; he is filled with regret. Why didn't I make an appointment? Just then the young clerk says, as if it has just dawned on him, 'Oh, the master said he'd be back soon, he said a visitor could wait for him.' 'A visitor' might refer to a specific person. Maybe this friend won't be able to keep Kubo company. Still, one must have hope, and Kubo, who has no other friend to call on, has no choice but to sit there and wait for his friend's return.

A Young Man Is Sitting

with a woman, close to the music box. He seems to be very proud and happy to be sipping tea with a girl who is not a prostitute. His body is healthy, his suit elegant, and his woman is smiling so readily at him that Kubo can't help but feel slightly jealous. There's more. The young man seems to be shamelessly proud of his *ŭndan* pillbox and Roto eyewash.[14] Kubo genuinely envies his superficiality.

A twilight melancholy loneliness may be mixed in with these sentiments. Kubo is aware that his facial expression must be far too gloomy. It is fortunate, he thinks, that the place has no mirror. A poet once referred to Kubo's current state of mind as 'bachelor's blues.' Though at first glance this seems right, it's not quite that simple. For a long time now, Kubo has been unwilling to seek new love and has depended on the goodwill of friends.

Without Kubo noticing, the woman and the lucky guy have disappeared. The night air wafts in and out of the teahouse. *Now where should I go?* Kubo realizes he has forgotten the friend he's waiting for. He smiles wryly. This slip-up is definitely more pathetic than when he felt weary and lonely with the woman he loved sitting in front of him.

A new thought lights up Kubo's eyes. What ever became of her? Memory, good or bad, calms the heart, inspires joy.

It happened one autumn in Tokyo. After buying new nail clippers in a hardware shop in Kanda, Kubo visited his favourite teahouse at Jimbōchō. This time he definitely had not stopped for tea or relaxation. He stopped for the sole purpose of trying out the nail clippers. A table in the farthest corner, a chair in the farthest corner. The setting of all those romances by popular writers. In this ill-lit place, Kubo stumbled upon a college notebook, on which was written 'Ethics' and the family name 'Im.'

Picking it up was probably a sin of sorts. But that amount of curiosity is permissible to young men. Kubo, sitting where he couldn't be easily seen, opened the notebook and forgot all about clipping his nails.

Chap I, Introduction. 1, The Definition of Ethics. 2, Normative Science. Chap II, Principal Argument. Object of Ethical Judgement. C, Motivism and Consequentialism. Example 1, The Son of a Poor Family Steals to Support His Parents. 2, Charity to Gratify One's Vanity. Second Semester. 3, Elements of Personality Formation. 1. The Will to Believe . . .

And the following was written in pencil in the margins: 'But a sense of shame heightens a lover's ability to imagine.' 'Shame gives life over to love.' The first section of Stendhal's *De l'amour . . .*' – and then, without connection – '*All Quiet on the Western Front.* Yoshiya Nobuko, Akutagawa Ryunosuke.'[15] 'Where did you go yesterday?' 'Did you see *A Love Parade*?'[16]

The owner of the teahouse has returned. 'Ah, when did you get here? Have you been waiting long? Any good news?' Kubo gets up without answering, picks up his notebook and walking stick. 'Let's go for dinner,' he says, and he tries to resume his reverie on his little romance from the distant past.

Outside the Teahouse

as he walks with his friend towards the Taech'angok Restaurant, Kubo recalls the postcard between the leaves of the notebook. He had hesitated at first, but couldn't pass up the opportunity; he knew he could find out where she lived. First of all, he was young, and the mystery was intriguing. That night Kubo had immersed himself in all kinds of fantasies. Next morning he tracked her down. Yarai-cho, Ushigome-ku. Her boarding house was near Shinchōsha, the publishing company where he worked. A kind-hearted landlady appeared and then disappeared; the owner of the notebook came to the door, and she was certainly . . . A beauty approaches from the direction Kubo and his friend are walking in. She smiles at them and passes. A barmaid from the café next door to his friend's teahouse. The friend turns and asks Kubo's opinion. 'Isn't she pretty?' The girl has a beauty rare in women of her class. But *she* must have been more beautiful than this barmaid.

'Come on in.'

'*Sŏllŏngt'ang* for two!'

The woman had blushed when Kubo took out the notebook and apologized for seeking her out. There seemed to be something more in that blush than a courtesy from a strange man. *Where did you go yesterday?* Kubo remembered her scribblings and smiled to himself. Across the table, his friend's hand with the soup-spoon stops in mid-air. He stares at Kubo. His eyes seem to ask Kubo what he's thinking about. To guard his secret, Kubo replies with a meaningless smile. 'Why don't you come in?' she had said.

Her tone was calm, but her cheeks blushed in maidenly fashion. Kubo, about to accept her offer, instead blurted out, 'Would you like to go for a walk . . . that is, if you're free?' It was Sunday, and she had her Sunday dress on, apparently about to go somewhere. A popular work of fiction should have a quick tempo. The previous day, when Kubo picked up the ethics notebook, he had already become the hero – as well as the writer – of a work of popular fiction. He even thought that, should she turn out to be Christian, he'd be willing to go and listen to a minister's boring sermon. She blushed again, but when Kubo said . . . 'If you have other business?' she replied in haste – 'No, just wait a second, please,' and she came out with a handbag. Encouraged by her apparent trust in him, Kubo said, 'Well, have you been to the Musashino Theatre this weekend?' He worried that, walking around with her like this, he must look like a good-for-nothing jobless type, and that if she were to succumb so easily to his seduction, it wouldn't be credible, not even in a work of popular fiction. Kubo sniggered to himself. But even if she followed him readily, Kubo didn't want to think her frivolous. It can't be frivolousness. Kubo's self-esteem demanded that she be wise enough to find him trustworthy, even in their first encounter.

And so she was. As they were getting off the tram in front of the theatre, Kubo had to pause for a moment, not to wait for her to step down first, but to accommodate a grinning foreign lady who was standing in front of him. His English teacher looked alternately at him and the girl and smiled knowingly. 'Hope you're having a nice day,' she said and went on her way. A thirty-year-old spinster's sarcasm towards a young couple may have been insinuated here. Kubo is aware that he's sweating copiously, like a schoolboy, both on his forehead and along the bridge of his nose. He pulls out a handkerchief from his trouser pocket to wipe himself off. The bowl of *sŏllŏngt'ang* is too hot on this summer evening.

Outside

they stand motionless on the street. After all, Seoul is small. If it were Tokyo, Kubo would head for the Ginza.[17] In fact, he had wanted to ask the girl if she would like to go to the Ginza for tea. A scene from a film he had recently seen flashed through his mind. Perhaps this was the reason Kubo lost confidence. A rogue tempts a respectable girl to the opera, and on the way back, late that night, he drives to his villa. In this fleeting image, the rogue's profile seemed to bear some resemblance to Kubo's. Kubo smiles grimly but dismisses the memory. Even if it's not the Ginza, I'd like to take her somewhere nice for tea, he had thought.

'Ah, how forgetful I am,' the friend suddenly exclaims. 'I have to meet someone now.'

He makes an apologetic face, knowing that Kubo will be lonely when left on his own. The girl must have worn such an expression when she had glanced at Kubo, hesitated and said, 'I should be going home now.'

'Let's meet at the teahouse around ten o'clock.'

'Ten o'clock?'

'Yes, half past ten at the latest.'

The friend walks towards the tram stop.

Gazing at his friend crossing the tracks and vanishing into the crowd on the other side of the street, Kubo – for no clear reason – remembers the sad girl in front of Hibiya Park on a drizzly evening.

Ah, Kubo jerks his head up, looks aimlessly around, and then mechanically takes a few steps forward. *Ah, I remember . . . Oh, why do I fumble through memories to the one incident I hoped to forget forever?* A sad and bitter memory is the last thing to help keep one's heart calm and cheerful.

She had a fiancé when she met Kubo, and she had pleaded for Kubo's advice. Unfortunately, Kubo knew the man. A classmate from middle school. The man's face was distinct in Kubo's mind though more than five years had elapsed since they had heard from each other. An honest, ordinary face. The thought of his gentle eyes stung Kubo to the quick. They wandered in the rain-drenched park, deep in thought, in tears, oblivious of the setting sun.

Kubo is restless. He sets off. *Maybe I acted like a coward. Maybe I should have felt more elated to have her love all to myself. When she blamed me through her sobs, saying that my sense of loyalty and fear of reproach derived from a lack of love and passion, she was evidently right . . . right.*

Kubo had offered to walk her home. 'No,' she said, 'leave me alone, I'll go by myself.' Her back wet from the rain, and her cheeks wet with tears, she walked down the street in the dusk, on and on, not taking the tram. She didn't marry her fiancé. If she were unhappy, it was the result of one man's indecisiveness. At times Kubo wanted to believe that she lived happily in some other, more fortunate place, but the thought rang hollow.

Kubo finds himself at the Hwangt'o Ridge crossroads. On an impulse he stops and emits a tortured sigh. *Ah, I miss her. I want to know where she is.* In the seven hours since he had left home that afternoon, this perhaps was his only goal. *Ah, I miss her. If only I knew how she's doing!*

Kwanghwamun Avenue

Kubo wondered if he was a hypocrite as he walked randomly along this deserted and inelegantly broad street. That would be a consequence of his irresolute personality. *Ah, all the evils caused by human frailty, all the misfortunes!*

Once again he sees the pitiful sight of her receding figure. Water running down her raincoat, and her hair, with no hat or umbrella, drips with sorrow. Shoulders drooping, losing heart, no heart left to be lost. Hands in her pockets, head hanging low,  she takes one step forward, then another; her small, frail feet are not at all sturdy. I should have run after her. I should have seized her slender shoulders, I should have confessed that all my words till now have been lies, that I could never forgo our love, that we must fight for our love against all obstacles. On that rainy street in Tokyo I should have cried a heart-wrenching lament with her.

Kubo kicks a pebble as hard as he can. Maybe he wanted to derive some worthless pride from his ability to restrain his ardour, his true desire, wanted to think that tragedy was the natural finale to their love. Wanted to believe – again remembering his friend's gentle eyes – that his well-rounded personality and wealth would make her happy. In the end, this misguided sentiment had obscured the true voice of his heart. And that's not as it should be. What right had he to toy with her feelings, or his own? He would never be able to make her happy, despite his love for her – hadn't that sense of his own imperfection driven everyone, especially her, his poor love, to misery? Kicking myriad pebbles across the street, Kubo thinks to himself, *Oh, I was wrong, so wrong!*

A child of about ten passes, humming a springtime song. The child has no worries. Two drunkards, their arms around each other's shoulders, slur the 'Song of Sorrow.'[18] They're feeling happy now. Kubo is struck by a bright idea; he stops in his tracks on the dark street. *If I were to meet her again, I wouldn't be weak. I wouldn't make the same mistake. We would never be apart again . . .*

But where can I find her? My god, how empty and blind an idea can be. How can a man's heart feel so lonely and wretched on the broad, open streets of Kwanghwamun.

A student in a college cap passes by, walking shoulder to shoulder with a young woman. Their steps bounce, their voices whisper. Dear lovers, may the light of your love always shine. Like an old benevolent father, his heart full of generosity and love, Kubo bestows his wholehearted blessing on the couple.

Now

seemingly having forgotten where he was going, and seemingly no longer needing to go anywhere, Kubo comes to a stop. Poor love. Is the ending to the story good enough as it stands? Are they fated now and in the future to remain sad and lonely? Never to meet again, both nurturing their wounds? Yet, at the same time, *ah . . . let's leave this thought alone.* Kubo self-consciously shakes his head and hastens to retrace his steps. Pain lingers in his heart. As he walks the street, head hanging low, pebbles roll around his feet, countless fragments of memory. Again Kubo shakes his head. *Let's . . . let's forget this . . .*

He should go back to the teahouse, rejoin his friend there, and find a way to alleviate the night's anxiety. But before he can cross the railway tracks, someone calls out to him, 'Uncle Eye –' and when he stops to look around, his hands, still holding his walking stick and notebook, are seized by the little hands of two children. 'Where have you been?' Kubo showers them with smiles. Nephews of a friend. The children call him Uncle Eye because of his glasses. 'We were at the night market. Why don't you come by any more, Uncle Eye?' 'Oh, I've been busy . . .' But that's a lie. Kubo realizes he has completely forgotten the guileless boys for over a month, and he feels truly sorry.

Poor children. They have hardly known a father's love. Their father started another family in the countryside five years ago and they have been brought up almost exclusively by their mother. The mother was not to blame. The father, then? The father, too, was, generally speaking, a good man. Yet he certainly had a streak of libertinism when it came to women. Despite severe hardships, the mother sends the boys to school. A sixteen-year-old daughter and three younger brothers. The youngest will reach school age next year.

When the mother – even as she complained about her difficulties – spoke joyfully about sending the youngest to primary school, Kubo felt like bowing to her to show his respect.

Kubo loves children. Likes to be loved by children. Sometimes he even tries to ingratiate himself with children. What if the children he loves don't like him? – the very idea makes him sad and lonely. Children are so simple. They are always drawn to those who care for them.

'Uncle Eye, have you seen our new place? It's there in that alley. Come with us, won't you?' He half wants to go, but considering the time, and afraid of missing his friend, he has to abandon the idea. What to do? Kubo spots a cart piled high with watermelons on the other side of the street. 'You're not having stomach problems, are you?' 'No, why?' He buys two watermelons, one for each to carry. 'Here, take them to your mother and ask her to slice them up for you. Same size portion for each of  you, no fighting.' The older boy says, 'The last time Uncle P'irun brought bananas, our sister was ill and couldn't eat, so we teased her a lot.' Kubo grins at the image of the tomboy's face on the brink of tears. A passing woman throws a sharp look at him. She is far from pretty. Plus, she has dozens of patches – for whatever reason – all over her face. Naturally, she must have felt insulted by his grin. Without intending to, Kubo bursts into laughter. Maybe, now, he'll be cheerful.

Still

the children wanted him to visit their house. After sending them away, Kubo heads for the teahouse. At night this area generally has few pedestrians, and the tram crawls along the middle of the thoroughfare. A couple of women are standing on this poorly lit street, and a couple of others are sitting under a tree. They, most likely, are not *belles de jour*. Still, their figures cut an alluring, if sombre, presence against the forlorn darkness. All of a sudden, a debauched sexual desire takes hold of him.

A telegram boy rides past on a bicycle, as lithe as a swallow. What kinds of lives are compressed into the small bag tied around his waist? Uncertainty, anxiety, expectation . . . Words on a small piece of paper exercise such effective sway over one's emotions. When a man receives a telegram addressed to him, his hand trembles before he realizes it. Kubo has a sudden craving for the experience of holding an unopened telegram. If not a telegram, an ordinary letter would do. At this point, even a postcard would impress him.

Hah! Kubo scoffs. That craving must be another manifestation of sexual desire. But of course he has no intention of simply dismissing this not-so-unnatural, almost physical craving. In fact, he keeps forgetting to write to his friends who live outside Seoul, and they haven't contacted him for a long time either. What are they all doing now? He feels a spontaneous rush of sweet nostalgia, even for that friend who only sends him a New Year's card. Soon, Kubo has thousands of blank postcards on the table in the corner of the teahouse, and he finds himself writing to his friends with unchecked abandon. He doesn't notice his burnt-out cigarette in the ashtray as he scribbles the names and addresses of all the friends he can remember on one postcard after another. He smiles contentedly. This is not so bad an ending for a short story. But what kind of short story? Kubo, of course, has not thought up the plot yet.

Literary concerns aside, he really wants to receive letters from his friends. *Won't somebody permit me this joy?* Suddenly, Kubo slackens his pace. *Maybe there's a letter waiting for me at home, impassioned words from the least expected of old friends . . .* Though he knows this fantasy is utterly groundless, Kubo does not want his melancholy reverie to be so mercilessly dispelled. The letter at home need not have been sent by a friend. A newspaper company maybe, or a magazine publisher . . . His mother, hopeful and expectant before the printed envelope, holds it up and down against the light bulb as if it carries within it a grand future for her son, even worrying about the possibility that her son, who does not return despite all her waiting, might read the letter too late and hence miss an opportunity. But the letter upon which the poor mother piles so much hope, once opened, will likely turn out to be just a request for an essay, a one-off article for a newspaper or a magazine. Kubo smiles wryly, then goes into the teahouse. He finds a large crowd there, but no friend. He has to wait for him.

The Teahouse

patrons, for whatever good reason, favour seats in the corner. Kubo has to take the one remaining table in the middle of the room. Still, he can enjoy Elman's *Valse Sentimentale*, his mind calm, at ease. But before the melody plays itself out, a rude voice calls, 'Aren't you Mr Kup'o?' Sensing that all eyes are on him, Kubo looks to where the voice came from. Someone who finished middle school two or three years before him. Said to have become a salesman for a life insurance company. His red drunken face might account for his pretension of familiarity, for there had been no previous correspondence between them. Kubo

gives a slight nod, his face expressionless, and promptly turns away. But when the man says again just as loudly, 'Won't you join us?' Kubo has no choice but to get up, albeit sluggishly, and switch tables. 'Sit here. Mr Ch'oe, this is Mr Kup'o, the novelist.'

For some reason he pronounces Kubo's name Kup'o. He waves his empty beer bottle, shouts at the boy for more, and turns to Kubo again. 'So are you still writing a lot?' the man asks. 'I must *confess* that I haven't written much,' Kubo answers. Kubo, finding it quite unpalatable having to associate with such a man, decides to keep his distance by uttering polite trivialities. But this clueless man seems rather flattered by Kubo's honorific tone. Furthermore, by ordering beer, the man may have developed a sense of superiority over those who are sipping tea (which costs a measly ten *chŏn* a cup) and thus may now be savouring an even higher level of happiness.

He offers a glass to Kubo, saying 'I'm a fan of Mr Kup'o's works.' He notices that Kubo shows no sign of being impressed by such a comment and adds, 'In fact, I talk about Mr Kup'o with everyone I meet.'

Then he roars himself hoarse with laughter. Kubo, an ambiguous smile on his face, has a fleeting thought. What if he were to hire this presumptuous ignoramus to sell his books? He might get tens, even hundreds of new readers. Kubo chuckles to himself. 'Mr Kup'o!' The man called Ch'oe intervenes, seeking Kubo's agreement that Tokkyŏn's *Tragic Melody of a Buddhist Temple* and Yun Paengnam's *Tale of a Great Robber*[19] are masterpieces. And this man, who may well be a salesman for some fire insurance company, deftly adds, 'Of course, aside from your works ...' Kubo, with considerable effort, brings himself to say they are good books. Whereupon Ch'oe launches another question: what is the rate of pay for Korean writers? Thank heavens he said *wŏngoryo*, thinks Kubo, instead of mispronouncing it *wŏnhoryo*, the word for relief payments, but he feels no obligation to discuss the financial status of Korean writers with this kind of man.

So Kubo, knowing full well that he may be humiliating the other, says curtly that he knows nothing about pay rates, since he's paid. Right then, he sees the friend he's been waiting for. 'Excuse me now.' Before the two can say anything, Kubo returns to his seat, picks up his notebook and walking stick, and says to his friend, who is just about to sit down, 'Let's get out of here. Let's go somewhere else.'

Outside, summer night, and a cool, pleasant breeze.

The Chosŏn Hotel

comes up alongside them, as they silently walk down the night-darkened street. Even during the day this street is not very busy. 'Any good news these days?' Kubo asks casually, looking at the three-storey Kyŏngsŏng Post Office. 'Good news?' The friend's eyes turn towards him, revealing signs of fatigue. They continue their walk towards Hwanggŭmjŏng. 'Have you ever had, for example, a small joy, a modest joy, such as a surprise postcard from a friend?'

'Sure,' the friend replies readily. 'The kind of letter a good-for-nothing like you will never receive in your lifetime.' And he sniggers. Yet his laughter rings hollow. Certified mail, most likely. In times like these, even running a small teahouse isn't easy. Three months' unpaid rent. The sky has become overcast, the shimmering stars disappearing from sight. The friend suddenly whistles. A poor writer, and a poor poet . . . Kubo's thoughts drift to his country, so poor, and his mind clouds over.

'Don't you want someone new to love?'

The friend stops whistling and throws a playful glance at Kubo. Kubo smiles. A lover, good. A girl who's not a lover, that would still be fine. What Kubo wants right now is any girl at all. Or maybe a wise, caring wife . . . A bold idea crosses his mind – I wish I could adopt a daughter, instead of a wife or lover, a seventeen- or eighteen-year-old, if possible. The girl must be pretty, cheerful and bright also. He would be a benevolent, devoted father and take her on trips.

Kubo laughs in spite of himself. Have I grown that old already? Still, he can't dismiss his fantasy so quickly. Keeping in check the urge to share it with his friend, he indulges this line of thought privately. Three choices. With only one, he might easily reach happiness. But then maybe even with all three choices fulfilled, he still wouldn't find peace for his weary heart.

No doubt this is an idea inspired by 'loneliness.'

Even the Round Moon Does Not Know What I Want
Kubo recited Satō Haruo's one-line poem. The sky is dark, threatening a downpour. Kubo does not know what he wants. Soon they are back on Chongno, and Kubo, feeling the weight of the walking stick and notebook in his hand, turns to his friend. 'Can you buy me a drink tonight?' The

friend nods without a second thought. Kubo, a new bounce to his step, goes to a drinking place in the Chonggak area, which they both patronize now and then, but the barmaid who used to serve them is no longer there. From a woman Kubo learns the name of the café in Nagwǒnjǒng where the barmaid has gone and insists that they go there, dragging his ostensibly tired friend by the arm. Kubo doesn't even know the girl's name. In other words, it's his friend who is interested in her. But like a teenage boy Kubo wants the cheap thrill of chasing a girl.

At First

Kubo's friend doesn't want to go. Maybe he's no longer interested in the barmaid. If he still has any feelings for her, presumably these feelings would amount to more than mild interest. They walk to Nagwǒnjǒng, and when they find the café where she works, Kubo discovers that his friend feels neither passion nor indifference. Or it might be that he does not care what he feels. Kubo's friend has grown old, too. Age-wise he is still young but he lacks energy and passion. So what he's constantly seeking is, perhaps, any kind of stimulus at all.

Three hostesses come to their table, and then two more. What attracts so many 'belles' to them is, of course, neither their physique nor their wallets. It is because they are new to the place, and the girls enjoy making the acquaintance  of many men. Kubo's friend asks their names. For some reason all the names end in *ko*.[20] This suffix indicates a certain lack of refinement, which saddens Kubo.

'Are you here to conduct a census?'

A new girl comes to their table. It's her. Seeing both men greet her with apparent familiarity, the two girls sitting next to them move awkwardly to give up their seats. The girl declines – 'No, stay where you are' – and yet she sits down next to Kubo's friend. This girl is no prettier than the other five, but she has a certain grace. While Kubo's friend is exchanging a few words with her, three of the girls leave for other tables. Hostesses never stay interested in a customer who appears to be intimate with one of their colleagues.

'Come on, have a drink,' the girl in charge of the table urges, targeting Kubo's friend. Three beer bottles lie empty on the table, but Kubo's friend seems to have drunk no more than a glass or so. Glass in hand, he pretends to sip and then places the glass back on the table. He is alcohol-intolerant. But of course the girls have never heard of this disease. Their credulous eyes open wide when they learn from Kubo that it is a kind of mental disorder. And again they burst – indiscreetly – into laughter. One girl tells the story of a man, just an occasional drinker, who collapsed after drinking a gallon of Japanese booze, and she asks Kubo whether that, too, could be a case of mental disorder. 'That is dipsomania,' Kubo replies. The twenty-third volume of *The Modern Medical Encyclopedia*, which he has already read with interest, is apparently quite a useful reference book.

Kubo feels a strong impulse to regard all people as mentally ill. Indeed, there are many kinds of mental disorder. Flights of Ideas. Paraphasia. Megalomania. Coprolalia. Nymphomania. Desultory Thoughts. Jealous Delusion. Satyriasis. Pathological Odd Behaviours. Pathological Pseudology. Pathological Immorality. Pathological Lavishness.

Kubo realizes his interest in the subject necessarily qualifies him as one of the above and he laughs cheerfully.

'Then is everyone crazy?' one of the hostesses asks quite naturally – she's been sitting beside Kubo, listening quietly. Kubo turns to face her obliquely. Excusing himself first, he asks her age.

The girl, after a moment's hesitation, says, 'Twenty.'

A woman's age is always an enigma. Yet this girl could not possibly be twenty. Twenty-five, twenty-six. At least twenty-four. Somewhat cruelly,

Kubo tells her that she, too, is a patient. Paralogia. Kubo's friend, intrigued, asks for details of this disease. Kubo opens his notebook on the table and reads out a dialogue between a doctor and a patient:

How many noses do you have? I can't tell whether I have two or more. How many ears do you have? Just one. Three plus two? Seven. How old are you? Twenty-one. (In truth, thirty-eight.) What about your wife? Eighty-one.

Kubo closes the notebook and has a good laugh with his friend. The girls join in, but with the exception of the girl sitting next to Kubo's friend, they obviously don't know what to make of the dialogue. The girl next to Kubo laughs without being aware that the story is intended as a little jab at her transparent pretensions. Every time she laughs or speaks, she affectedly covers her mouth with a handkerchief. She must think her mouth looks ugly. Kubo feels pity and sympathy for her modesty. These sentiments, of course, should be distinguished from affection. Pity and sympathy are quite similar to affection, and yet they never mean quite the same thing. But hatred ... sometimes hatred erupts from true love ... In one of his early works, Kubo thought of using this sentence, which was merely an inference from his narrow experience. It might be true, though. As Kubo mulls over this idle thought, one of the girls asks, 'Then you must be the only person in the world who's not crazy.' Kubo smiles. 'Why, I too am ill. My illness is called Compulsive Talking.'

'What is Compulsive Talking?'

'Oh, constantly prattling on. Senseless small talk is a mental disorder.'

'So that's what Compulsive Talking is.'

Two other girls repeat the name of Kubo's disease. Kubo takes his fountain pen from his inside pocket and scrawls in his notebook. Any observation is useful to a writer. One cannot be lax – not even in a café – in one's preparations for writing. The hostesses seek all kinds of knowledge by talking to a wide variety of customers. Holding his pen up for a moment, Kubo gazes at the table in front of him. Again smiling gently, with a show of satisfaction, he sets his pen in motion. 'Now what vile thing are you writing?' Kubo's friend, half raising himself in his chair, reads aloud as Kubo writes. *The woman sitting in front of him stretched out her legs from*

under the table. Not because she was afraid that his worn-out shoes would trample hers, which were more delicate. Rather, she was at last wearing the ivory-coloured silk stockings that she had so long desired and of which she was so proud.

'Huh,' Kubo's friend sneers. 'One shouldn't make friends with a writer. Whatever you choose to write, please leave out my alcohol intolerance.' And they all laugh wholeheartedly.

Kubo and His Friend

and most of their conversation are beyond the girls' comprehension. Still, they pretend they understand everything. But there's no harm in that, and one shouldn't ridicule their ignorance. Kubo grabs his pen and writes in his notebook:

Isn't ignorance a necessity for these girls? Were they more intelligent, pain, anguish and sorrow . . . all these . . . would make their lives unbearable, and a sudden sense of misery would lay siege to their hearts. The blissful, ephemeral delights they enjoy, no matter how worthless they appear, are made possible only by ignorance.

Kubo writes as if he has uncovered a precious truth. He doesn't refuse the drinks the girls offer him.

It's raining outside. A soft rain, a gentle rain. When it rains this gently so late in the evening, Kubo often becomes sad. The girls are sad as well. Without an umbrella, the girls worry about their only dress and their only shoes and stockings getting wet in the rain.

'Miss Yuki!' a drunken voice calls out. Looking at the darkness beyond the window, Kubo suddenly remembers a woman. *Yuki* – snow in Japanese – may have provoked the memory. In front of a Kwanggyo café, a woman wearing white mourning clothes was calling Kubo in a weak voice. 'May I ask you a question?' she had said, almost in a whisper, and as soon as she saw him stopping, she stretched her hand hesitantly towards the café.

'What are they looking for?'

The flier posted by the café window was written in Chinese and then Korean: *Hostesses Wanted*. Kubo had studied her anew and felt a pang in his heart. She was destitute, that much was clear. But apparently she had been able to keep off the street, not needing to look for a job. Then an unforeseeable misfortune struck, and she was left with no alternative but to take to the streets, her grief still raw. She might have a son, almost grown-up. Maybe it was not a son but a daughter, and that was why the poor woman now had to struggle to make ends meet. Before she was married, she might have lived well, been lovingly cared for. Her pale face had grace, even a sort of dignity. When Kubo cautiously explained the advertisement for hostesses, the woman, who must have been over forty, didn't even wait for him to finish. With an expression of disgust and despair, she bowed to him in silence and calmly left . . .

Kubo turns back to the hostesses and considers them. *Who's more unhappy, that widow or these girls? Whose suffering, whose misery is greater?* He sighs at the thought. But maybe it's not right to dwell on such a thought in a place like this. He puts a fresh cigarette between his lips. The two matchboxes on the table are empty.

A petite hostess scampers to the counter to fetch a match. The girl is almost a child. If she said she was sixteen or seventeen, he would scarcely doubt her. Her clear eyes, the dimples on her cheeks, are yet to be sullied by the grime of this world. It may not only be on account of being drunk that Kubo immediately feels pity and attraction. 'Won't you go somewhere with me tomorrow afternoon?' He makes this spontaneous proposal and thinks that if she were to agree, he'd be happy to spend half a day strolling around outdoors. She smiles gently. The dimples certainly make her look adorable.

Kubo hands her his pocketbook and fountain pen. 'Write O for yes, and X for no, and if it's O, come to the roof of the Hwashin tomorrow at noon, and don't worry, whichever mark you make, I won't open the note until tomorrow morning.' Kubo laughs cheerfully at this new diversion.

Two a.m.

The main Chongno intersection. Though it's raining, there's a constant stream of people here. All these people are perhaps madly in love with the night. Maybe they set out to find some pleasure for the night, maybe they just as easily found it. And, for a brief moment, each of them might have felt himself the happiest of men. But signs of weariness are visibly inscribed on their faces and in their gait. Sorrow and fatigue find no respite, so now they have to go back to their homes, to their rooms, which they had forgotten for a while, or tried to forget.

At this late hour his mother will still be awake, waiting for him. That he didn't take an umbrella may have caused her added worry. Kubo thinks of her small, sad, lonely face. He cannot help feeling sad and lonely himself. Kubo had forced his lonely mother almost entirely out of his mind. But she must have thought about her son, worried about him, in anguish, all day long. *Oh, a mother's love, how infinitely deep and infinitely sad.* A woman's love moves from parents to husband, and then to the son. Is it not motherhood that renders a woman's love so powerful, so sacred?

'See you tomorrow,' Kubo's friend says, but Kubo hardly hears him. *Now I'll have a life. A life. A life for myself, and comfort and rest for my mother.* 'Good night,' his friend says again. Kubo at last turns to him and nods. 'See you tomorrow night.' Kubo, after a slight hesitation, says, 'Tomorrow . . . from tomorrow, I'll stay at home, I'll write . . .'

'Write a good story,' his friend says with real sincerity, and they part company. Kubo finds happiness in the thought that he will write a truly good story. He takes no offence when a policeman on patrol casts a disparaging look at him.

'Kubo!'

His friend suddenly calls him. 'By the way, see what she wrote in your pocketbook.' Kubo pulls the pocketbook out of his inside pocket and sees a big, unequivocal X. He smiles a wry smile for his friend's benefit. I guess I won't be going to the Hwashin tomorrow at noon, he thinks. Yet he hardly feels disappointed. Even if the mark were O, he would feel no joy. Maybe now he wants to think more of his mother's happiness than his own. Maybe he is preoccupied with that alone. Kubo walks along the street in the soft drizzling rain, hastening home.

He may not flatly refuse his mother if she broaches the subject of marriage.

Illustrations by Yi Sang

KIM YUJŎNG

Spicebush Blossoms

Translated by Bruce and Ju-Chan Fulton

Guess what? My rooster got ambushed again. I had finished my lunch and set out for the hills to fetch firewood when I heard wings flapping like crazy. I whipped around and sure enough the two roosters were at it again.

Chŏmsun's rooster was tough as a badger and it had a huge head. But it wasn't just pecking my little one: it would flap its wings and peck at its head, take a short break, then flap its wings again and this time peck at its neck. It was putting on a show and all my wretched rooster could do was lower its beak to the ground and croak. Blood was dripping from the holes in its head, but the big bird kept up the attack.

I watched in silence, feeling as if my own head had burst open and was bleeding and that my eyes were on fire. I thought of whacking the big one with my back-rack stick but instead whacked the ground to separate them.

Chŏmsun must have riled them, trying to get my dander up. Why was that darn girl trying to eat me up these days?

And that business with those measly potatoes four days ago – what did I do wrong? One moment she's heading out with her basket to pick wild greens, fine – but the next she's interfering with my work on the fence. She comes sneaking up behind me and says, 'Well, look at you, working all by yourself!'

What's that *supposed to mean?* Until the previous day she and I were on our best behaviour – scarcely exchanging a word, more or less ignoring each other. What's got her so charged up, a fully grown filly distracting a guy who's hard at work?

'Why, what's wrong with that?' I barked. 'Do I need a work team?'

'So you like working?' And then she said, 'Seems kind of early in the

137

season, why not wait till midsummer?' She followed up the pestering by cackling, then covered her mouth as if she was afraid someone would overhear.

I didn't see much to laugh about and wondered if the heat had got to her. What's more, she kept stealing glances at her house, and all of a sudden her right fist came out from her apron and stopped at my chin. Inside were three chunky little potatoes. My chin felt nice and warm. *Hmm, just steamed?*

'Betcha don't get these at home, do you?' she called out, then she told me to finish them up before anyone found out. 'You *know* how tasty spring potatoes are . . .'

'I don't eat potatoes. You have 'em.' And I pushed her hand away.

But she wasn't about to leave, and instead, her breathing was getting heavy. *What the hell?* Finally I had myself a look at her, and guess what – her dark face was brighter than a carrot, something I'd never seen in the three years my family have been in this village. Her eyes were shooting me such a spiteful look – and that moisture, was it tears? She picked up her basket, bit down on her lip, and flew off so fast towards the paddy that I thought she might tumble over.

The Chŏmsun I knew, if one of the village elders joked to her, 'Hurry up and find yourself a husband,' she wouldn't bat an eyelash and would come back with something like 'You needn't worry, sir, there's a time and a place for everything.' She wasn't a bashful sort. And she wasn't a softie who cried out of vexation. Instead, if she was really angry, she would give me a serious smack on the back with her basket and run off.

Since that godawful spectacle she made of herself, she's been out to get me, she's that desperate.

All right, so maybe I goofed by refusing the potatoes, but does that give her the right to say, 'Betcha don't get these at home, do you?' Her family was in charge of the local tenant farmers and we were always kowtowing to them because they leased us the land we worked. We had no place to live when we landed here, and we were hard up besides, and Chŏmsun's family helped us out by leasing us a site to build on. The harvest always left us short, and Mother and Father wore out a path to their home to borrow grain and then praised them until they were hoarse, saying there could be no nicer family. At the same time, Mother cautioned me – ugly rumours would make the rounds if a couple of sixteen-year-olds were seen hanging out and whispering. She was afraid we would lose our land and get kicked out of our home if I caused trouble over Chŏmsun and got her folks all hot and bothered.

So why does this darn girl have it in for me, it's like she wants my blood to run dry. The evening after that weepy day with the potatoes, I was coming down from the hills with a back-rack of firewood when I heard something croaking like it was fixing to die. Was one of the neighbours slaughtering a chicken? I came alongside the fence behind Chŏmsun's place and my eyes practically popped out. There she was sitting on a straw mat with our brood hen in her lap, hitting it and saying, 'Why don't you drop dead, you damn bird!' I could have forgiven her if she was just giving it a rap on the head, but she was punching it down below, like she wanted it never to lay eggs again.

My eyes were on fire and I was trembling all over. I looked around and made sure she was by herself, and then I took my back-rack stick and whacked the fence right in the mid-section. 'Hey, girl,' I thundered, 'what do you think you're doing – hurting our bird so it won't lay?'

Chŏmsun didn't even flinch, just sat there lady-like, and launched another round of punches and curses. 'Drop dead, you, drop dead!' At first glance you might have thought she was beating their own hen, but it was our hen she'd grabbed. She must have figured out when I'd be coming back, and staged the attack for my benefit. But I couldn't very well go running into someone else's yard to squabble with a girl. All right then, I'd whack their fence every time she smacked our bird! But the more I whacked, the more naked their brushwood fence would be, just bare, bony branches. I wasn't doing myself any favours.

'You bitch!' I roared with the sharpest glare I could manage. 'You're gonna kill our hen?'

That got her to stop. She scurried towards the fence and tossed the hen over my head. 'What a disgusting bird!'

'If it's so disgusting, girl, then why are you cuddling it!' I whirled away, about to blow my stack. And now it was my turn to be disgusted, because the first thing the bird did when it got its wings working was squirt poo onto my forehead. *Oh my god, she really must have popped its egg-sack – now our hen is done for.*

Behind me I heard her mutter 'You're an idiot!' And then 'You were born that way.' That much was tolerable, but then she finished with, 'You idiot! I heard your father can't get it up.'

I felt like my head was wearing a heat dome. I whipped back around, ready to say *What! My father can't get it up?* But her mug had disappeared.

I turned towards home only to hear more of the same, a shitload of abuse. But I couldn't even tell her to piss off. That got me so steamed up that I didn't realize I'd caught my foot on a rock and made it bleed – I almost burst out crying. But that wasn't the end of it.

Chŏmsun liked to sneak over to our place when no one was home and sick her rooster on mine. That nasty rooster was always ready for a scrap, and she knew it would come to that. And so she let it bloody our bird's head, eyes and all. And the times when our rooster wouldn't come out, she lured it with chicken feed to get them fighting.

I had to come up with a plan. I took our rooster to where we kept our sauce crock-pots. They say that *koch'ujang* gets a fighting rooster's spirits up, just like a meal of a poisonous snake energizes a sick cow. I scooped a saucer of *koch'ujang* from its crock and fed it to our bird. It must have found it yummy because it finished half of it.

I figured it would take a while for the stuff to work its magic, and put the bird back in the coop for the time being.

I took two loads of compost out to our dry field, then had a break and fetched the rooster. No one was around except for Chŏmsun. She was hunched up on her mat doing something or other, maybe taking apart old clothing or fluffing up a cotton quilt.

I went to the dry field where Chŏmsun's rooster was strutting around, set my rooster down, and watched. The two birds soon went for each other as usual, but the sauce didn't seem to be working. Her bird pecked and pecked, and it drew blood, until all my bird could do was hop up and down without pecking back. But then, heaven knows how, it went on the attack and raked its claws across the big one's eye and followed up with a good peck to the head. Her rooster flinched and retreated. My little one was quick to charge and gave it another sharp peck, and now it was the big one's ferocious head that couldn't help bleeding. *All right! Koch'ujang does the trick!* Chŏmsun was scowling as she watched from the other side of their fence, surprised that *I* was the one who'd started the fight.

I was high as a kite and kept slapping my bum and sides, yelling, 'Yeah, yeah, keep it up!'

But before long I was standing there like a bump on a log. I felt drained. The big bird had counterattacked, pecking like crazy until my bird froze and made no attempt to resist. Chŏmsun cackled as loud as she could, making sure I heard her. I couldn't bear to watch, so I scooped up my rooster and returned home. Damn – I should have fed it more *koch'ujang* before rushing it into battle. I went back to the crock-pot and shoved its beak into the sauce. It wasn't interested – maybe it was too worked up.

What now? I lay my rooster down and stuck a cigarette holder in its beak. Then diluted the sauce with water and let it run through the opening. It must have stung, because the bird sneezed a few times. But I figured today's pain would take care of tomorrow's bleeding.

After a couple more doses I gave up. The rooster was in good health, but for some reason it had grown listless in my hand and its neck was bent slightly to the side. I took it back to the coop before Father noticed.

This morning my rooster was finally showing some spunk. And then I came back from the field to discover this latest cock fight. That cow must have sneaked over when no one was home and got them going. Assuming she keeps it up, what am I supposed to do? Lock it up and keep an eye on it? I thought this over as I went up into the hills and gathered pine branches. I had a mind to wring her neck. The least I could do was give her a good whipping across the back. So I went whooshing downhill, half running and half walking, with my back-rack full of firewood.

Near home I heard whistling and stopped. Yellow spicebush blossoms were everywhere among the huge rocks on the slopes. And there was Chŏmsun squatting among all those flowers and blowing a reed whistle – it was pathetic. But I was more surprised by the flapping wings that I heard. *Dammit, girl, here you go again, taking my rooster and making it fight your rooster right near my path, and look at you whistling without a care in the world.* I felt the familiar fuming, the fire in my eyes, the surge of tears. I unstrapped my back-rack and tossed it to the ground and took my stick and charged.

Sure enough, closer up I saw my rooster bleeding; it looked practically dead. And there she sat, the darn girl, not flinching. It made me sick the way she kept blowing on that whistle. I used to consider her a cheerful, hard-working girl with a pretty face – the villagers did too – but now she had the eyes of a little fox.

I took in the scene, and before I knew it, I'd whacked her big rooster with my stick. It fell dead without a twitch. I just stood there until she rushed me, glaring, and I ended up flat on my back.

'Damn you, why'd you kill my rooster?'

'What if I did?' I was about to get up, but she pushed me back down. 'You fool, who do you think owns that rooster?'

I was angry and embarrassed, but then I started worrying that we would lose our land and house all on account of me. I hauled myself to my feet, covered my eyes with a sleeve, and just started blubbering.

But when Chŏmsun came up to me and said, 'Now you're not going to do that any more, are you?' I felt I might survive after all.

I was busy wiping my tears, and the next thing I knew, out came 'Nope!'

'Better not or else you won't have a moment's peace!'

'I won't, I promise!'

'Don't worry about the rooster. I'm not going to tattle.' And then she was falling as if something had pushed her, and her hand was on my shoulder and I was falling with her and we came to rest buried among all those ripe yellow spicebush blossoms.

The smell of those blossoms, spicy and fragrant, made me dizzy. I felt like the ground was caving in under me.

'Don't tell anyone,' she said.

'I won't!'

A short while later I heard a voice from below: 'Chŏmsun-*a*, Chŏmsun-*a!* Now where did that girl go off to, leaving all her sewing lying around?' It was Chŏmsun's mother and she sounded furious. She must have just returned home.

Chŏmsun crawled out from beneath the spicebushes and crept down the hill. She looked terrified. And then I crawled around the rocks and bolted back up into the hills.

CH'OE YUN

The Last of Hanak'o

Translated by Bruce and Ju-Chan Fulton

It is forbidden to venture near the canal railing on stormy days. Take precautions in the fog, particularly the winter fog . . . Then enter the labyrinth. And bear in mind, the more frightened you are, the more lost you will be.

He had finished his business in Rome, caught the train, and arrived in Venice after dark. Dreaming an exhausting dream, wandering among fantasies he had yet to confront, he had seen this spectral sign through a window frosted with desultory breath, the words assembled by his unconscious from the travel guides he'd read since arriving in Italy.

He had awakened to find the train crossing the steel bridge that connects Venice with the mainland. Outside was darkness, a darkness not quite ripe. It was barely eight o'clock. And then a real sign rose out of the gloom, 'Venezia, Santa Lucia,' and the train rolled to a stop. He followed the stream of people getting off the train and emerged from the station.

Before him lay the most peculiar city he had visited in his thirty-two years. A floating city full of buildings crowned with weighty ornaments, it swayed on the canals like a gigantic cruise ship on the verge of sinking.

But there was no railing and no fog.

As he boarded the small boat that would take him to his lodgings, he awoke from the odd state of hypnosis that had gradually overtaken him since the start of his journey. The other passengers were silent as ghosts. 'So this is Venice,' he muttered to himself. 'What now?'

At his request a room had been reserved for him by one of the suppliers in Rome at a *pensione* near the Rialto, not far from the centre of the old city, this city of water and fog. A small room that looked down on winding canals and a street lined with worn buildings that time had permeated with moisture, fading their ancient wall paintings. A man at the supplier's said he had stayed at this *pensione*, and if it sounded acceptable, he would go ahead and book a room.

Well, why not?

It seemed so unreal, being in Venice. What was he doing there? Mustering the courage that had been shrinking since his arrival in Italy? Or escaping that which was fanning his courage?

It was all so sudden, so coincidental. It had been four days at best since he had left his daily routine, but the surreal sense of time one experiences while travelling had made the previous day feel like several years ago.

One day – his perception of time was skewed now and he couldn't precisely date it – there had been a call from K. It could easily have been five or six months earlier. K had returned from a distant business trip, he had said. K, a friend from high school. A partner in crime during college, and then a partner in business. The two of them and a few others from high school and college had fallen into a routine of gathering at least a couple of times a month. Not that they had anything special to say, or were anxious to see one another, and most of them were engaged in different lines of work; it was simply that they were friends. Occasionally these friends got together, and if it happened to be the weekend, they all brought a kid or two along with the wife. They were like the model families you see in health food ads. If K had returned from a business trip, he couldn't very well get back to work without calling him first. Of course they had talked about hats – their line of business – and exchanged virtually all the business-related information worth passing on. And a few dirty jokes too.

Chemistry and sociology – their majors in college – had nothing to do with hats, but through sheer coincidence he and K, after stints at one or two other companies, had both settled on the hat business. This was the reason for the special connection between the two, among those others who met regularly. They were serious when they talked about hats. They didn't have much else to talk about now, and so they talked for quite some time about business. But it wasn't he alone who sensed that their conversation was forced and overdrawn. They knew each other better than that. And then K changed the subject. As if something had just occurred to him.

'Do you remember . . . Hanak'o?'

He made no response.

'Someone said she's in Italy.'

'Really? And?'

'I'm just telling you. I thought you might have been wondering about her.'

'Why me?'

'Well, don't you think everyone wonders about her – a little bit, anyway?'

Just as he didn't ask K for particulars – who had seen Hanak'o, when, where, what she was doing – he was sure K avoided asking detailed questions of whomever had passed on the news. Gracefully reserved, these two, they were well versed in the practice of etiquette. There was a brief, awkward silence between them, but he salvaged the conversation with a spicy joke. And a few days later when they were drinking, K mentioned not a word of the phone call to the others or, of course, to him. He too acted as if the call had slipped his mind. Looking back, he felt he actually had forgotten it. And in truth he had.

As always when the discussion turned serious at their drinking parties, they grew animated bringing up examples of the world going to ruin, as if they had decided to change the world just like that. This was a sign that the party was winding down. They were no longer young; their monolithic society had grown slowly more daunting, and they had no proven methods for taking pleasure from life . . . And so they met frequently.

They had their own code word. A code word for a woman. Hanak'o.

There was a woman. This woman had a name, to be sure, a name that did not exactly charm their metropolitan sensibility. But this was not the reason for their code word. And not once had they used that nickname to her face. One evening, after a tedious, pointless day, the usual group were drinking, and the nickname – a spur-of-the-moment joke – became their code word. They were passing through one of life's darker stages, in which they enjoyed creating code words. Most of them were in their early twenties, and all were approaching graduation from college.

One day one of the group had introduced a college student who appeared to be of similar age. A woman of unusually small stature, whose soft voice blended well with theirs in conversation, who would tilt her head to the left and, with utter gravity and an earnest expression, pose questions to them when bravado got the best of their logic.

'Why do you think that way?' she would ask. Or she would say, her eyes slightly melancholy, something like, 'It's because we're all young – I mean, we don't know what to do with our youth.' And so on, embarrassing them all. That was Hanak'o.

So much of it is murky now, he told himself. When was it exactly, which of our gatherings had provided the occasion, and who had introduced her – was it P, or Y, was it K, or me, was it someone else we knew at the time, someone who's since grown distant?

Yes, she had the prettiest nose. Her features in general conveyed no particular atmosphere; they didn't make you sit up and take notice. But that nose of hers: now *that* was charming. Seen from head on or in profile, it was a thing of beauty. And thus her nickname, Hanak'o – the Nose. But this code word had yet to be formalized during that period of their gatherings. And before she was permanently stuck with this nickname, the first thing that came to mind when you thought of her was not necessarily her nose. That she was now called Hanak'o was the result of a mistake they all wanted to hide. A small mistake that hid many truths, that had arisen in drunkenness, that no one wanted to admit or even retrace thoroughly. We all have a secret person we can't deal with comfortably without a nickname, and for them that person was Hanak'o.

Most of them had been classmates since high school, and in their last year of college, with employment tests and job interviews awaiting them, they met almost daily to prepare. And during their company apprenticeships they manufactured any excuse to gather. Once or twice a month one of them would call Hanak'o and she, alone or accompanied by a friend – always the same friend, it seemed she had no other – would join them. He had no memories of this friend, not even her name. His only recollection was that she had never remained to the end of the evening. Just when the gathering seemed to be developing momentum she would excuse herself, saying she lived far away, then whisper a few words into Hanak'o's ear and rush out, Cinderella-like, as if afraid her subway train was about to turn into a pumpkin. None of them made even a pretence of detaining her. For the one who drew their attention was not this silent woman but Hanak'o, she of the occasional witty joke, she whose remarks, even the remarks that brought exclamations, were invariably delivered in a gentle voice.

When a change of atmosphere became necessary for their gatherings, when they tired of psychological warfare with their girlfriends, or when they grew weary of the same old faces but met nonetheless to tilt a glass of beer – those were the times they called Hanak'o. She gladly accepted their invitations, and to the best of his memory she had never turned them down for a reason that was less than plausible; she had menstrual cramps, she would explain, or a friend from back home was visiting. True or not, it didn't matter, for her tone was always serious, enough to make them feel they were entertaining themselves with a museum piece. And contrary to their expectations they found her persuasive. They saw her more frequently after they began their company apprenticeships.

They knew little about her. She was a fine arts major, but whether she painted, sculpted, or both, they weren't sure. No one in their circle was well versed in the arts, and so the occasional particulars she revealed to them sounded quite vague. They knew the word *matière*, but not until after college did they feel compelled to know why it was important to distinguish among stone, earth and wood. Her family life was a blank; all they knew was her telephone number and the address jotted on the occasional letter that reached them. During the few years they knew her, either her address had changed on various occasions or she was using several addresses simultaneously. Once it was a dormitory, often it was in care of So-and-So, once it was a certain studio, and so forth.

For some reason her lifestyle, which could have seemed a bit strange, never stimulated their curiosity. Or might they instead have felt awkward attempting to express their curiosity to her when that lifestyle seemed to befit her so naturally?

Hanak'o was not the first woman to join their gatherings, but there were few women who had lasted as long as she did without upsetting the balance of the meetings. He wondered why that was. Was it the unobtrusive way that she remained beside them, like the air or a comfortable temperature, before disappearing? Until that incident, after which she disappeared once and for all? Yes, until then she was an unobtrusive presence, and none of them expected for a moment that one day she would vanish to some unknown place where she would fail to answer their call.

With the map he had bought near the station he located the hotel that the man in Rome had recommended. 'Take the *vaporetto* and get off at the Rialto; don't cross the bridge, but instead take a left and then another left . . .' He'd spent the entire day on the train and was thoroughly exhausted. There'd been no rest since his arrival in Italy, and the melancholy he'd almost been savouring when he left Seoul had pursued him all along. He stood beside a youth with a handsome profile who skilfully brought in the line and secured it whenever a boat arrived at the dock. As he gazed at the buildings floating on the water, the warm orange glow of the lights inside them deepened the gloom he felt in this chill, moist air of early winter.

What the hell am I supposed to do for two days here? Don't know a damn thing about the city or the country. Maybe I should go on a tour.

'Listen – no matter how busy you are, you've got to see Venice.' That's what K had said after going to Italy and making contact with the suppliers.

Yes, he thought. Everyone wants to come to Venice at least once. A city coveted by newlyweds and lovers. A desolate smile played briefly about his lips. All he could imagine in Venice, this city that made him feel as if everything were slowly sinking into the sea, were dark, dark things. But it wasn't just K's suggestion that had spurred him to come here. His objective wasn't Venice. It was an address in another city very close by.

Don't cross the bridge, but instead take a left, then another left . . . Pensione Albergo Guerrato, where he was booked for two nights, was an old, four-storey building he was sure he would grow tired of seeing over the next two days. A woman with a limp who owned a frighteningly large dog worked there. She had a good command of Italian, English and French.

The room to which she guided him was Number 7 on the third floor. According to the man in Rome, the room looked down on a cosy street that was worth viewing for its colourful daytime array of fruits and vegetables. Somewhat farther off were the Canalazzo and the partly hidden, lamplit Rialto. In the still of the night the street was empty. Infrequently the sound of youthful laughter rang out in the distance and then vanished without an echo. And very near, the peaceful hiss of boats slicing through water aroused in him an odd loneliness. If only there were a face, a person who could caress the tense scales of life as gently as that . . . Why, wherever he went, did he hear something crumbling? He was past thirty, and this sudden visitation of sentiment baffled him.

They knew little about Hanak'o's background. Strangely enough, apart

148

from learning that she had taught children at an art institute with some college classmates before graduation, they had never openly questioned her about herself – what she did for a living, what her blood type was, if she had siblings. And if something remotely similar to such topics came up in conversation, she would be sure to nonchalantly steer the discussion elsewhere. She seemed to do this on purpose, as if she felt time spent talking about herself would be wasted for the others.

But now that he thought about it, he vaguely recalled her saying that she had majored in sculpture. And he remembered her face when she added, smiling, that her sculpting experience actually consisted of working as an assistant for a famous sculptor, wrestling with blocks of stone three or four times taller than she. Hanako really was no larger than a child, and none of them, even in their imagination, could visualize this rare disclosure from her. They had known her for a little over three years, but during their gatherings she had never drawn attention to anything related to herself. Always the same expression. The face lifted up slightly askew at a forty-five-degree angle so that her Natalie Wood nose was prominent. And that was all.

The room was quite small. It had a high ceiling with projecting moulded corners, the kind of ceiling he'd seen several times since arriving in Italy. He lingered briefly in front of the telephone, then lifted the receiver, listened momentarily to the dial tone, and replaced it. Was it daytime on the other side of the globe? That's how far away his life with his wife was. In the space of four years' time the widening of that distance had accelerated shamefully. In the beginning there had been rather sincere conversation. But their seesaw debates couched in such lofty expressions as *existence, value system* and *joint property* quickly became outright arguments. The purchase of the most trivial item or his habit of squeezing the toothpaste tube from the middle or allowing a trace of smoke to continue from a cigarette he had crushed out – these trifling matters produced quarrels that provoked them to deny each other's very being and shook them to their roots.

The final disagreement, caused by the firm silence, the fault-finding vigilance they kept towards each other, as if their vocabularies had evaporated, was violent and long-standing, like a howl followed by complete silence. If not that cause, any other would have sufficed. There were the inevitable periodic disputes they held in order to reject each other. And all along, their play-acting towards the world continued. Together as husband and wife they visited relatives and attended social functions, and when the play was over they returned to their cold war.

Would he have taken this business trip to Italy in such a hurry if there hadn't been that discord, those petty, tiresome disagreements that left their inadequacies exposed in the most degrading manner? Would he have left without telling anyone, as if escaping, dressed as when he went to work, carrying a clumsily packed travel bag? He shook his head without conviction. If there had been no disagreements, would he have recalled what K had said about Hanak'o? Would he have approached with utmost secrecy those of her relatives he knew, and through these and other people, and over the course of several days, obtained her address in Italy?

He thought with a hint of pleasure, like one who possessed a top-secret file, of the hours he had devoted to tracing Hanak'o's address. And he tried to imagine the expression on his wife's face if she were to learn the true intent behind this trip to Italy. But it didn't offer that strong a feeling of compensation. Their malicious insensitivity towards each other was too deep for him to divert his mood through such fancies. Their quarrels were a shabby excuse for the fact that neither of them could deal skilfully with the frequent anxieties and disagreements that had twisted their relationship. If it had been otherwise, regret would have followed their quarrels.

'What in the hell am I doing here? And what am I supposed to do the next two days?' Muttering, he produced one of the guidebooks from his bag and lay down on the bed. The ceiling receded higher towards nothingness. The other side of the globe felt more distant. He gradually fell asleep, thinking he wouldn't be troubled for at least ten hours.

He awoke the next morning to a noisy fog outside the window. Just as the guidebook had said. And just as the man at the supplier's in Rome had said, both sides of the street directly below were packed with the displays of the morning produce market. He left the window open and went down to the dining room. It was early and only a few people were having breakfast. They were young and looked American, and they spoke in undertones, perhaps about the weather, for the woman who operated the *pensione* could be heard reassuring them in her husky voice that the skies would clear later in the day. Two cups of coffee and a slice of toast:

a simple order, and once he was done, he returned to his room, oddly tired. Eight a.m. In the Seoul of his imagination it was the previous night.

He gazed vacantly at the names in large type in the guidebook that lay open before him – Piazza San Marco, Torcello, Salute . . . He decided that he hated travelling by himself. In all of his business trips this was the first time he had a two-day void to fill. It was almost as if he had planned it that way. But hell, this was, after all, the first time he had travelled alone. Before, it was always business, or else he was part of a tour group. A succession of faces surfaced rapidly in his mind – his wife, friends, colleagues at work – but in terms of a hoped-for travelling companion, none lingered in his brain for more than a second. And then the silhouette of Hanako walking away on a riverbank at twilight flashed through his mind like a distant shadow. 'The hours at tourist attractions are quite unpredictable in Venice during the off-season. If you want to squeeze more into your schedule, you have to get an early start. After three o'clock everything closes down.' The voice of K, a passionate consumer of information, echoed faintly in his ear.

He picked up the telephone, then opened his address book to a phone number that had been jotted down almost as an afterthought. Not a number in Seoul, but Hanako's number.

I'll just tell her I'm here on business and her name came up, he told himself. Maybe she's forgotten that little unpleasantness back then.

For the first time he was faintly curious about what Hanako was doing here on the far side of the globe. If memory served him correctly, he had never heard it mentioned that she had family or friends in Italy or that she had studied Italian. But then those weren't the reasons he had come here, either. Obtaining her address and phone number had involved contacting at least four people. True, he could have gone about it more efficiently. But he didn't wish to identify himself during his search, and the unfriendly tone of the man who had finally given him the desired information, who had said he was her classmate, had discouraged direct inquiries about her present situation.

The dialling code was that of a city about an hour by train from Venice. It was supposed to be a tiny city; what could she be doing there? At that moment – and he had no idea why – the thought of a nunnery or a similarly still place came to mind. Maybe it's all the churches, he thought.

Seems like there's one down every alley. Maybe she's not exactly a nun, but something like that. But when her face actually took its place in this mental picture, it didn't sit quite right with him. He'd had the same feeling several times before, and had never been able to pinpoint it. Something vaguely unfamiliar that irritated him and soured his mood.

He obtained an outside line ... then punched in the numbers all at once. A ring ... continued ringing ... He concentrated on the regular, repetitive rhythm as if it offered some sort of message he must decipher. No answer. Was it too early? By his watch it was past eight-thirty. With the light heart of someone putting off homework he wanted to postpone, he gently replaced the receiver.

He considered: From the Rialto I ought to be able to walk to San Marco without asking directions. No, I shouldn't ask directions even if I get lost in that mazelike tangle of alleys. He left, taking a business card with the *pensione*'s address and phone number. He vaguely looked for someone who resembled Hanak'o – looked among the people standing inside the large glass windows of cafés drinking cappucino, the people cleaning the display windows of the high-fashion clothing and leather shops, people scurrying down the narrow shop-lined street, market baskets in hand.

It was strange the way memories of Hanak'o forced themselves upon him like this. Forced? 'Perhaps I should say "stubbornly persist,"' he muttered. Were those memories connected to being in a place not far from where she lived? Or to the foggy labyrinth of alleys and the water that was unfailingly revealed at the end of every one of them he followed? Yes, that was it. Strangely enough, Hanak'o had been associated with water. And maybe that's why it seemed natural that everyone had thought of the riverside for what turned out to be their last trip.

They had all vaguely realized that from time to time Hanak'o saw one of them apart from the group. He himself was one of those she met separately. But no one ever mentioned this. That is, until their contact with her was cut off. He didn't know how it was with the others, but his meetings with her followed a ritualistic sequence. First of all, she would select a café rather than the tearoom where the group met.

'It's got the most comfortable sofas, makes you feel glad you're there – want to try it?' This was how she put it.

Yes. Places that made you feel good. There was probably no one better than Hanak'o at picking places in Seoul that were comfortable and suited to one's mood. Whether she chose a tearoom or a place to drink, it would be an utterly commonplace location on a street they had often used, prompting them to wonder why they had never discovered it before. A place, though, with one special characteristic that was sure to leave an impression. Something memorable – comfortable seat-backs, distinctive decorations, unique teacups ... she never forgot to point them out, and even a person like him, who tended to be obtuse in this respect, found himself responding to such features before long. And so a seemingly ordinary place was transformed into something that left a mark in his recollections. Like someone who kept a list of Seoul's hidden landmarks, she would guide him to a place 'that made you feel good,' wherever it might be, as if secretly inviting him to her own home.

After talking for a short time at this place they would walk the streets. Then have a simple meal. The strange thing was, they all demonstrated an incomprehensible stinginess, which they themselves recognized, when it came to Hanak'o, and not just during their college days, when it would have been quite natural, but after they had found jobs as well. This stinginess remained unchanged even after they had become rather well-to-do. Unlike his dates with other women, he generally selected the most shabby, inexpensive restaurants and he didn't necessarily pay. After the meal, a game or two of table tennis or bowling. Then back they would walk to the original place.

And then ... drawn by a mysterious power to engage in a rite of confession, he had told Hanak'o everything indecent, unspeakable and private about himself. About everything except the girl he was dating. The age at which he'd begun to masturbate, his shameful hidden habits, even secret dissatisfactions with close friends whom Hanak'o knew. She listened to these accounts, head cocked inquisitively, always hearing him out until the end without interruption. The smile that played about her mouth never changed, no matter how shocking the account, and so he sometimes exaggerated these confessions of his hidden vices. He knew of no other woman who would give undivided attention to these trivial accounts. Sometimes he imagined her re-enacting the same scene with a friend of his. This did not make him the least bit jealous.

'I appreciate your opening yourself up to me – it must be hard for you to talk about this.'

On rare occasions she expressed her tiredness in this fashion. It was her way of telling him she wanted to go home.

Instead of waiting with her at the dark bus stop, he would leave for the subway. Again, she never objected, and when he looked back, her expression somehow made it seem that she was elsewhere already. Why had they extended Hanak'o only the bare minimum of patience and consideration?

Suddenly thirsty, he entered a café with unusually transparent windows. Like the other patrons he drank cappucino, the soft fresh cream clinging to the roof of his mouth. He stood like the others, and tried to make himself look as animated. He suppressed his desire to ask directions to San Marco. Back outside, instead of following the signs, he chose crowded streets and wandered about numerous alleys and small plazas. With the self-assurance of someone who refused to be fascinated by the city's attractions, he pulled up his collar and buttoned it, then followed a foggy canal and crossed a small bridge. He was surprised at how fast he was walking.

He wondered if J had been the first of them to try something with her. J, the first of their group to marry. Once, he had received a midnight call from J. He had carefully set the receiver down beside the bed and taken the call in another room. And then, afraid his wife might overhear, he had remembered to replace the bedside phone in its cradle. Because J was drunk, and had brought up Hanak'o. They had been out of touch with her for more than a year by then. To his wife, who had looked up at him wonderingly, he had responded as if the call was unimportant: 'It's just J. Sounds like he's drunk out of his mind.'

J's drunken ramblings had stimulated his curiosity until sleep was banished from his mind. 'This might come as a surprise to you, but there was a time in my life when I really didn't know what to do. I was so stupid. If I'd just pushed a little harder, who knows what would have happened? It's all right, don't worry, the wife's off visiting her family. Hold on, I'll get the letter. Hanak'o wrote back to me. Let's see – I hid it way down there somewhere. Okay, got it. Now listen. I'll just give you the important stuff.' And in a tone exaggerated by his drunkenness he began reading:

'J, you always were a clown when it came to talking about something important. And don't think I'm rejecting you out of hand. I understand you're going through a difficult period, and you simply had to write a letter like this. But think about it, J. Am I really the right person for this letter? You ought to go away for a week or so. After that, if you've found the answer . . . then we can talk some more.'

As he listened to J's drunken drawl, which made the contents of the letter sound ridiculous, he imagined himself in Hanak'o's situation with J before him, and felt irritated enough to punch him. But because his curiosity was greater, the irritation was short-lived.

'You remember how Hanak'o writes, don't you? If you knew the kind of letter I sent her, you'd probably faint. You see, I proposed to her – a very passionate proposal. It was something I had to do. None of you knew a thing. Recently I started thinking about it again. Of course, a week after I proposed, I set the wedding date with the wife. How am I going to get rid of this letter? Oh, Hanak'o is on my mind!'

Had J really indulged in this slurred bout of romantic reminiscence? In any event, he had given the confession a proper hearing. J's case was somewhat unique, but all of them, himself included, had saved up a letter or two from her. Like trophies. After she had disappeared from their gatherings, it was briefly fashionable for them to read aloud to one another the letters they'd occasionally received from her, primarily during the early period of their meetings, when they were in college. It was then, when they gathered over drinks, that they had coined the nickname Hanak'o. She who never failed to answer their letters. She wrote letters that for some unknown reason touched their hearts, making them wonder if she was born to answer all the letters in the world. That there was a woman whose correspondence with them was somehow so profound, so philosophical and elegant, made them arrogant. Hanak'o was the first woman to arouse in him a desire to write letters. During his courtship he had never been taken with an urge to write to his future wife. Once he had embellished a letter to Hanak'o with a line lifted from a poem, and in her reply she had jokingly written, 'You're trying to make me guess the title of that poem, aren't you?' There had been nothing about his relationship with Hanak'o to injure his pride; he had no fear that she would take something the wrong way. And now, despite that incident back then, he was using this business trip as an excuse to look her up. Why was that?

'After all, we're friends.'

Once he had blundered, and this was how she had smoothed it over.

Of course he didn't remember exactly what it was he had said. But the uncomfortable ripples it had caused remained fresh in his mind.

Hanak'o had never been notified about any of their weddings. He couldn't speak for his friends, but in his own case it had been simple carelessness. Needless to say, when he had been preparing the invitations, he had thought of inviting her. But his busy schedule had made him forget. It was the kind of forgetfulness that is unconsciously planned. Those of his friends who had married later couldn't invite Hanak'o because they had lost contact with her, but at least in the case of P and J, who married while they were still seeing her, they had clearly not invited her. After J's wedding he had apologized to her on his behalf.

'You don't really consider weddings that important, do you?' she had responded.

In the distance the steeples of San Marco that he had seen in photos appeared. The wave of humanity that had already surged ashore told him he was approaching the plaza. If it had been only the two gilt lions in the plaza staring resolutely out to sea, he might have been moved. Ordinarily he tended to enjoy throngs of people. But there were simply too many people here, too many vendors, too many flocks of grossly fat pigeons and no room to move about. He purchased an admission ticket for the basilica, but as he was about to enter he realized he had left his camera and binoculars at the *pensione*. And the guidebook he had made a point of purchasing, which described the mosaics inside the basilica. He was crestfallen. But that didn't mean he had any intention of going all the way back to the *pensione*.

Pushed inside by the queue, he was surprised at the scale of the gorgeously coloured mosaics on their golden backgrounds that covered the domes, the walls, even the pillars, with no space left untouched, a sight that drew exclamations from all the sightseers. Otherwise, he felt only the profound boredom of someone ill prepared for his trip. People throughout the world marvelled when they set foot inside this basilica, but the sleepy mixture of thoughts in his head wandered in another time and place.

He sat down at the end of a pew and, recalling what he knew about the Bible, identified a few of the mosaic scenes. And then he let his mind wander as he waited, slothful and bored, for time to pass. Hearing a Korean voice among the many languages flitting past his ear, he focused on it. It was the ringing voice of a young woman explaining to an elderly man the mosaic on the ceiling directly above where he himself sat, a scene from the Book of Exodus. An affectionate father and daughter, he thought.

Again he asked himself what he was doing there. He thought of his daughter at home. She was almost two. Suppressing a sudden surge of frustration, he rose. The young woman offered her father the vacated seat. The exit was more crowded than the entrance.

He walked to the harbour and deeply inhaled the air. Time and again his gaze was drawn to the telephone booths scattered along the waterfront. In Seoul it was probably a gloomy early-winter evening. The fog had lifted from the water. Just then there was a loud cry. A crowd of people flocked the short distance to its source. Instantly a circle formed, and before he knew it, he found himself at its inner edge. There, three men were exchanging punches with the skill of professional boxers, while cursing in Italian. He saw that it was two against one, but everyone looked on wide-eyed with no thought of stopping them. And the single man was putting up a good fight.

The circle gradually widened, and the faces of more onlookers appeared on the balconies of the luxury hotel that stood beside the water. Back and forth they went at each other, three healthy-looking young men in leather jackets, tight-lipped except for an occasional outcry and their rough breathing. Finally the two partners cornered the other, who had fallen, and began kicking him with studied intent. While it seemed that silence ruled the fight itself, the crowd, on the contrary, became more vocal. He did not know the language of this country, and to him the people looked like they were cheering an innocent wrestling match. The spectacle became more violent, and he felt himself making tight fists. No one dared break up the fight. He felt a thrill watching the kicks and punches of the two partners. 'Go on, one more. Finish him off, and get it over with ...' Just then the police waded through the crowd, and in no time they had separated the three men and were leading them away.

The crowd broke up and the pay telephones reappeared, beckoning him. Without hesitation he extracted a telephone number. A number whose location was not on the opposite side of the globe but rather in a small city nearby. After three or four 'hellos' in Italian he heard a gay, high-pitched woman's voice speaking rapidly and at length, saying something he didn't understand. In hurried English he asked for Hanak'o, using her real name, of course. He was put on hold, and then came the gay, raucous blend of several voices speaking in Italian . . . And then a bright voice that he knew. Hanak'o's voice. Speaking not Italian but the Korean that he had longed to hear – '*Yŏboseyo?*' At that very moment the *vaporetto* deposited a group of passengers. Arms around each other's waists, smiling young couples stepped onto a small landing and walked past him. Only then was he released from the caution that had seized him. Suddenly he felt exhilarated.

He gave his name, then produced an awkward, exaggerated laugh. Without waiting for a reply, he launched into a wordy explanation: He was on a business trip. While the contract was being drawn up he had come to Venice. He would have to return to Rome. But first he wanted to see her. He'd gone to a lot of trouble to find out where she lived and to obtain her telephone number. On and on he chattered, frequently repeating the loud, incongruous laugh, giving her no opportunity to speak, as if he were trying to escape something. And then there was an abrupt silence like that of a radio quieted by a power failure. Finally she was able to respond.

'It's good to hear from you. Why don't you come over?' she said in a loud, bright, laughing voice.

And then her voice became the composed, low-pitched tone he remembered so well. Amiably and deliberately, she told him the name of the train station, her work address, the name and appearance of the interior decoration firm where she'd been hired as a designer and other particulars. But there wasn't as much to see in her city as in Venice, she added apologetically.

Although everything about her seemed the same, something had changed. Not her voice. Nor was her tone any less friendly . . . Hadn't she sounded genuinely delighted to hear from him? Suddenly his resolve weakened. To see her he would have to catch a train, wander around looking for the street she'd mentioned, enter her office, wait beside her desk until she'd finished her work, be invited to her living space, eat a home-cooked meal, as the people in this country liked to do and have a pleasant chat – was he really in the mood for all of this? And if she was married, he would have to observe the proprieties and make conversation with her husband . . . He asked her a question, cunningly, he thought.

'How many children do you have?'

She laughed.

He detected something in her voice. 'I hope I won't be disrupting your work,' he said.

After a brief silence she countered with a question of her own: 'Don't you know me any better than that?' Then, at the sound of the tone signalling the end of the allotted time, she added, 'You're not going to be like J, are you, calling but not visiting? Or P, leaving before he even finished his coffee? Come on over. I'm glad to hear from you – really.'

As soon as she had finished, the line went dead. With the click of the telephone something connected in his mind. P had called her? And J?

He recalled the last drinking party they'd had before this trip. He had wanted to keep the trip a secret. The party mellowed him, though, and his plans had popped out of his mouth almost before he realized it. And then someone who hadn't attended the group gatherings for the longest time had unexpectedly brought up Hanak'o's name. 'Who came up with that name, anyway? Makes her sound Japanese. Wouldn't "K'ohana" sound more Korean? Some nickname! She'd be annoyed if she knew.' And then someone else had said, 'She'll never find out.' He recalled that J and P had each chimed in during that conversation. And he recalled very clearly K's phone call several months earlier informing him about Hanak'o. But none of them had said he had actually seen or talked to her; rather they had supposedly heard through a third party that she was living in Italy.

After declaring to Hanak'o that he would leave on the spot, he instead left the harbour and walked down an alley that followed a narrow canal. There he saw houses with a thick layer of moss that looked damper than usual now that it was winter, houses whose walls seemed about to collapse into the water. He saw a small bridge at the end of a wall, and narrow house fronts that had him imagining model families living inside. Occasionally he heard music from the houses, or the everyday bustling noises that come from inside a home, as if these sounds were meant to expose in starker contrast the mossy, sad-looking exteriors that had lost their paint and made the city seem to tilt even farther towards the water.

He allowed his pace to be dictated by the endless variation of the canals, alleys and bridges. A street sign that captured his gaze became a vague guidepost telling him that the Rialto was growing ever more distant. With a gloomy smile he gave himself up to the freedom of the disheartened soul who walks an unfamiliar city without map or destination, to the repose of the person who wanders a maze in silence in a land whose language he neither speaks nor understands. Several times, like an overtone of this city, there sounded lightly in his ears the voice of Hanak'o; no, the voice of Chang Chinja – her real name – an interior designer who worked for a firm called Scobeni: 'Don't you know me any better than that?' No better than that? Like a riddle with many pitfalls, the question drew him deeper and deeper into this city of mazes.

Through the window a train departed for the cities to the north. In the lights of the dusky station he saw once again the white sign reading 'Venezia, Santa Lucia.' His train, the night train for Rome, would leave at any moment. It was too early for sleeping, and only the seats on the upper level had been made into beds. Two passengers were at a window talking with well-wishers. Early though it was, he climbed up to the berth he'd reserved and lay down. The train slowly left the station and began to cross the steel bridge to the mainland. It was about the same hour as when he had arrived. Looking more distant from where he lay, the orange lamps appearing at intervals above the water formed a long curve like a procession of monks. The lamps, which marked the channel for nighttime boat traffic, were each suspended by a black band from a pointed piling, the bands reminding him of a pair of clasped hands. The train accelerated and soon the water had disappeared from his field of vision, leaving him feeling yet again as if something in the far distance was collapsing.

There it went, the city of his momentary stay. Now the train was passing through a dark landscape of fewer and fewer lights and no visible human presence. The passengers below busily reclined their seat-backs to make beds, and suddenly there was quiet. The voices in the corridor became murmurs and the train raced towards thick darkness. Three of the berths in the upper level remained unoccupied. Later that night, when everyone was asleep, people boarding at some station or other would climb up looking for those berths. Maybe Bologna, Florence ...

How could that incident have come about? Could you even call it an incident?

He had no idea how they'd discovered that drinking place in the boggy, marshlike area near the reed grass. It had all started when two of them happened to buy secondhand cars at around the same time. A group of seven had left Seoul during a three-day holiday and driven as far as the Naktong River. Their original goal had been to find a beach that they liked. But they ended up at the river. The group included himself, plus Hanak'o and her woman friend. They had divided up into the two cars, whose owners then took advantage of the journey to practise their driving skills. At the Naktong, a sign advertising fresh raw fish and spicy fish stew had caught their eye, and they had followed a narrow dirt road until the restaurant appeared. Although it was out in the middle of nowhere, they decided to make it their destination for the night. To enter the restaurant they first had to cross a muddy yard that threatened to swallow up their feet. And he seemed to recall a weedlike grass at the side of the yard that gave off a nauseating odour. Was it late autumn? he wondered. Or early winter, like now?

While the meal was being prepared, they walked along the riverbank. No light appeared in any direction, making them feel as if they were at the end of the world. Back at the restaurant they ate and drank unhurriedly, and as the night wore on, the excitement of the trip gave way to a subdued unease. The restaurant seemed to be part of a home, and as soon as they entered the room where they would spend the night, the strange mood, which didn't seem to have originated in any one of them, spread through them all. It was as if this house was cut off from the world and would sink into the marsh at any moment. It was clear that W, one of the drivers, regretted having come such a long way to this place. One of the others kept saying he had to call Seoul, and another complained that he had forgotten an important business meeting the following day and didn't know how to notify the other party. At the time, P was the secret envy of the others because of his upcoming marriage with the daughter of a wealthy family, and although he had insisted at short notice that they take this trip, he had reacted the most irritably when someone raised the delicate question of where they would all sleep. He himself had felt inexplicably hostile towards Hanak'o and her friend, whose expressions hardened as they observed the change in the others.

Perhaps during this trip they had let down their guard to reveal the despondency they all felt after two or three years of life in the real world.

Or maybe the combination of the fatigue of daily life, the alcohol and their long day of travel had triggered a strange chemical reaction that caused irreversible uneasiness.

One of them went outside, then returned with news that the accommodations had been settled, and why not drink some more. This was a friend whose participation in their group had grown infrequent after he started working for a bank. He had given the owner a huge sum, he crowed, in return for a second room.

After that, everything went downhill . . . Seven hours together in the cars had left them with nothing to talk about, and so they sang songs. Well, it was more like screaming than singing. Like the squealing of pigs. Everyone focused on the two women, who were quietly nursing their drinks and attempting to conceal their puzzlement at the deterioration of the group's drunken fellowship, and tried to intimidate them into singing. Any pretence at fun and games was over. They all knew that Hanak'o detested being pressured to sing, and in point of fact her singing was terrible. Knowing this, they demanded, half jokingly, half threateningly, that she sing. Hanak'o's friend stood up instead, prepared to sing in her place. But all of them shouted together for Hanak'o. With an awkward smile her friend sat down. But Hanak'o, for some reason, would not oblige them. And there seemed to be a slight change in her expression.

Then someone bolted up. 'Who wants to bet me whether she'll sing?' he said, gritting his teeth as he approached her. At the same time, someone sitting across from Hanak'o took her by the arms and tried to lift her. Hanak'o's friend rose partly, trying to free her. He himself stood and tried to pull Hanak'o up from behind. Someone threw a bottle against the wall. Someone yelled, just for the sake of yelling. And then someone grabbed the three of them, Hanak'o and the two who were trying to make her stand up, and all three plopped back down to the floor.

He tried to remember how long they had harassed her. No one had tried to put a stop to it. Stop it? You could be sure everyone gladly connived in it. Whether Hanak'o sang wasn't the issue. Her friend's meaningless outcry did nothing to stop them. It wasn't much of a cry anyway, but rather a weak, ridiculous sound that probably didn't carry outside the room. The scene was one of odd frenzy – pushing and shoving, breaking glass, screaming and shouting – as if they were each in their own way observing a strict method to the collective harassment, each playing an assigned role to perfection, all of them now trying to trick one another. It could be said, at that point, at least, that none of them was genuinely drunk. They were faking drunkenness, all of them. Perhaps Hanak'o too.

Hanak'o and her friend were standing now. Their faces were pale. Hanak'o's hair, which she wore pulled back, was dishevelled and unseemly. Her blouse was twisted to the side. Someone pointed out her appearance and burst into laughter. The laugh was instantly infectious, and before long there was a whole-scale frenzy of laughter. It spread even to the two women, who had accepted their punishment, and they laughed in spite of themselves. But their faces were terribly contorted, and they might actually have been crying – it was impossible to tell. Laughing hysterically, they picked up their bags. And then their coats. And then, still laughing, they opened the door, admitting the chill night wind and the stink of the weeds, and walked out into a darkness that was several times thicker now. He had no memory of them laughing after that. The only thing visible beyond the yard was the long, faint line of the riverbank; only an old, dim light bulb illuminated the yard. By that time the dwindling outlines of the women had darkened and then dissolved in the gloom. Nothing was distinguishable save the blades of grass occasionally turned up by the wind so that they reflected the faint light from the bulb.

They gazed towards the dark expanse where the two women had vanished, but no one ran to call them back. They were all well aware that the women would have to walk for a dangerously long time through the darkness before they found another dwelling or came out on the main road. But they continued their frenzied laughing. They were like wind-up toys, unable to stop. Someone closed the door. They all sank into silence, and when they fully realized what had happened, they drank until dawn. The next day they returned to Seoul in leaden quiet.

And this was how Hanak'o had disappeared from their gatherings. It was then, after her name, Chang Chinja, happened to come up in their conversation, that she formally became Hanak'o. This use of her nickname resulted from the subtle interplay of two contradictory desires: to speak of her on the one hand, and to refrain from doing so on the other. Although she would appear by that nickname in their idle talk over drinks, they kept a firm silence about the identity of the shadow that had vanished into the darkness that night when they were all adrift along the Naktong.

And now he was lost, as lost as he had been the night of that trip, which had seemed darker because it was unfamiliar. He turned away from the darkness and curled up towards the wall of his berth. Someone passed by quickly in the corridor, whistling a soft, peaceful tune. Loud snoring rose from the seats below. The three empty berths remained unoccupied.

You'll call home as soon as you get to Rome, he told himself. His feelings hadn't changed a bit. 'I really feel your absence,' you'll tell her. 'We'll have to take a family trip to Venice some time.' You'll say that to her on the phone, even if you can't promise it and your voice lacks conviction. Everything will work out. Just like it has so far. But what if the wife says, 'It won't work this time. Let's talk. Let's be honest with each other for once.' His face wore a sharp scowl as he fell asleep.

Back in Seoul, he arranged a gathering over drinks. As usual, they ended up talking shop, discussing the world situation and talking about business prospects. Like J, P, or whomever, he talked long and loud about the exotic beauty of Italy, the gondolas of Venice (but had that famous attraction ever actually entered his mind?). And then they all got drunk, and as they always did before scattering for the following day's work, they concluded by summarizing the various matters they'd been rambling on about: the world would keep turning; their children were growing so well; they'd get along fine as long as they avoided basic sources of friction with the wives; and maybe the next day they'd be a little bit richer and not quite so tired.

'Don't you know me any better than that?' From time to time Hanako's question echoed in his ear, as if spoken by a ghostly voice. But for a vast number of reasons his life was too busy for him to respond to such a question. His business with the Italian firms that provided raw materials for hats flourished, but he never volunteered for a trip to Rome again. He was never able to satisfy all his desires, but because he received promotions in keeping with his age, it was unnecessary for him to go there on business himself. He had more important matters to decide, matters that kept him busy. So busy that there was no possibility of taking his wife and daughter, who was soon to enter primary school, on a family trip to Venice.

For as long as his business had prospered, his company had received a monthly English-language newsletter in the form of a publicity pamphlet for foreign buyers, issued by the Italian Ministry of Commerce. Several years had passed since his trip to Venice when, one day, the monthly issue arrived with a feature on two Asian women: 'Korean Duo Design Chairs with Asian Charm; Interviewed as They Depart for Home.' Accompanying the interview was a large photo showing Hanak'o's face and the broadly smiling face of the woman who seemed to be her only friend, a woman he could remember nothing about, not even her name. The interview revealed how the pair had become a unique and highly promising design team, beginning with their chance participation in an international interior design contest sponsored by Italy. There was a brief account of Hanak'o's schooldays, all of which was new to him. She had been close to them at the time; how and when had she led a life such as this, unknown to them? The interview conveyed a tone of respect for the pair's single-minded devotion to chair design and to the unique charm of their designs, which aimed simultaneously at bodily comfort and sensuous beauty. The remainder of the feature was taken up with photos and a technical discussion of their designs, along with their plans, and steps they had already taken to open up offices in Korea as well as Italy. The article spoke of the two women alternately as business partners and companions.

Hanak'o's face was angled halfway towards the smiling face of her friend, making her elegant nose even more noticeable.

HONG SŎKCHUNG

A chapter from Hwang Chini

Translated by Bruce and Ju-Chan Fulton

It was a day of cloud and wind, the time of year when summer begins to give way to autumn, and already a few leaves were dropping from branches to be sent whirling into the sky. From South Gate a flock of dusky sparrows took flight, looping about the slate-grey sky before scattering like a shower of dark hail among the paddies and dry fields beyond the city wall to feast upon the nearly ripened grain. Overhead a lone crow uttered an eerie caw, drawing looks of displeasure from passers-by who then answered this ill-omened bird by spitting over their shoulders. There was a desolate feel to the day.

Since early morning would-be spectators had been gathering along the gully between the foot of Chanam Mountain and the wall behind Hwang Chinsa's dwelling in anticipation of the funeral procession for young Ttobok[1] of Granary Row. Word had got out that the pallbearers would probably be passing this way, and the lane that ran along the gully was filled before the morning sun had crested the ridges, and the mountainside as far as Prominence Rock now wore a snowy blanket of onlookers garbed in their traditional white attire.

For days now the dwellings all about – the quarters of the menfolk, the womenfolk and the hired help alike – had been abuzz with talk of Chini and Ttobok of Granary Row. Ears perked up at the story of how this son of a minor official had fallen for the only daughter of a *yangban* family, of how his heart had finally broken when his love went unanswered, of how he was now a wandering ghost, but what really drew the attention of listeners was the news that in a single morning the *yangban*'s daughter's engagement had been broken off by the family of Young Master Yun of Hanyang and that her status had suddenly fallen to the level of a slave girl's. Herein lay the reason for the burst of activity that had swept the area from the first light of dawn, rousting even those sluggards loath to stir from home, once it was known that the young man's bier would pass by the young lady's house.

The previous night Old Granny had lingered outside the paper-panelled sliding door to Chini's room, worry creasing her face, before venturing across the threshold.

'I know I shouldn't be bothering you at a time like this,' she murmured, 'but believe it or not, folks are already staking out a place for themselves to watch tomorrow morning when the body of the Granary Row boy passes by. Well, as they used to say, fight fire with fire, and if you spread your legs to a man, he won't notice your harelip. When those pallbearers come parading by and start in with that damned curse hex, you'd better have the fabric ready for them.'

It was this curse hex that on the one hand accounted for Old Granny's worries, and on the other hand gave the spectators high hopes of feasting their eyes on something thrilling and exciting. For when the pallbearers come to a stop outside a house and the call-and-response begins, the calls from the head pallbearer are like messages from the dead conveyed by a spirit-possessed *mudang* in a *kimil* ritual.[2] When a call-and-response is directed towards a family, it's in their best interest to offer up a bolt of fine cotton fabric to the head pallbearer, who is the speaker for the departed, lest out of his mouth like jumping frogs come all manner of shameful and hidden facts, and if the family is the least bit slow in presenting the fabric, in an instant their good name is dragged through the mud.

It was with indifferent silence that Chini had met Old Granny's worries about the curse hex the previous night. For this reason Old Granny could not bring herself to repeat her concerns that morning, but at the same time she could not conceal her uneasy expression, which seemed to say 'What now?'

Onlookers continued to throng beyond the back wall, while inside the house dead silence reigned. It being early morning, the outer quarters of the home should have been bustling, but the servants in both the inner and outer quarters, buoyed by curiosity, must have joined the spectators outside, for the house was dead-rat still.

What a cold-hearted world! thought Chini. It's one thing to take

pleasure in viewing the celebrations and happy events of others, but if
you have to satisfy your curiosity by witnessing others' pain and sorrow,
then your goodness of heart has left you. Indeed, she asked herself, what
was the use of even thinking in terms of good and bad if people were
heartless and ignorant enough to pack a lunchbox and journey from
distant hamlets to see a prisoner lose his head in the marketplace outside
Ojŏng Gate?

Chini listened attentively to the voices from beyond the back wall –
voices calling out in search of others, foul-mouthed voices saying 'I was
here first!', voices erupting in belly laughter . . . All of them titillated by
the prospect of witnessing her pain and sorrow, her embarrassment and
humiliation.

All right, then, I'd better make sure to show them what they want to see.

And with that, Chini opened her mother-of-pearl chest and retrieved
the wedding finery she had stored deep inside.

It was the *sashi* hour,[3] midmorning, when the funeral procession came
into sight around the corner outside the wall. Appearing first was the
guardian, clad in crimson jacket and black skirt, wearing a gourd mask
draped with bells, brandishing a lance and shield, followed in turn by
the bearers of the red banner inscribed with the name and title of the
deceased, the silk spirit-banner, the elegy banner and the pole-mounted
hempen cloth, and finally the coffin-laden frame itself, the head
pallbearer jingling his handbell as he sang a plaintive dirge, to which the
eight pallbearers, headbands low on their brows, carrying poles across
their shoulders, responded with a dismal refrain.

The time had come for the spectacle all were awaiting. When the head
of the procession arrived at Hwang Chinsa's back gate, the pallbearers
came to a stop and began marching in place, signalling the call-and-
response that precedes the casting of the spirit hex. The call of the head
pallbearer and the response of the other pallbearers were as piteous as the
weeping of a resentful ghost:

> Farewell, mountains and streams; farewell, flowers and trees;
> I begin my journey to the yellow heavens
> Pass over now, oh yes.

But once did I see her, and how lovely she was,
The only daughter of Hwang Chinsa
Pass over now, oh yes.

A goose on the wing without a mate, my love unrequited,
I'm a lonely ghost
Pass over now, oh yes.

The funeral procession resembled a trembling line, the marchers taking one step forward then two steps back, one step back then two steps forward, their dirge blending with the ringing of the bells.

Chini clutched the ring handle of the back gate and steeled herself. She could sense the gazes of the assembled onlookers directed towards the gate. She would have to present herself before these people at just the right time, not too soon and not too late.

Behind her stood Old Granny and the servant girl Igŭmi, tension gripping their fear-blanched faces as they observed their mistress.

The head pallbearer's recitation gradually closed in on its target:

Heartbreaking it is that a body, once gone,
Can never come back
Pass over now, oh yes.

Arrived we are at the home of Hwang Chinsa,
Here we shall stay until . . .
Pass over now, oh yes.

It was then that Chini opened the gate. The instant she appeared, the eyes of all assembled fixed themselves upon her like spear points. The murmuring of the crowd built until finally it muffled the dirge.

The onlookers were in a state of shock. Instead of fleeing to the farthest reaches of the kingdom in fear of being cursed by the deceased, instead of locking herself up and hiding beneath a quilt, Chini had dared to appear before them in the flesh. Who among them could have imagined this in their wildest dreams?

Chini approached the bier as it swayed on its framework of carrying poles. The call-and-response came to a stop. The pallbearers lowered their burden to the ground; the ringing of the bells ceased and the head pallbearer fell silent.

Chini faced the young man's casket. With a flourish she spread wide the folds of her long crimson skirt with its flower pattern and draped it over the casket.

Deathly quiet fell over the lane. It was as if the throng had been doused with cold water.

Chini's lips began to move, as if she were whispering to someone visible before her. And amazingly enough, there arose with unmistakable clarity the face of the young man who had gazed at her in thrall beneath the moon of the *yudu*[4] festival.

'Please hear my words. Though I do not know you, apart from a single glance that night, through your death I have learned of your passion for me. Now that our paths have diverged, it is not possible for me to return your love in all its sincerity. But if by chance we were to meet again in the other world –' and here Chini paused – 'surely would I offer you recompense for your love that went unrequited in this world. As a token of my promise to you, I bestow on this your altar my wedding finery – understand me and accept it. Though human life is entwined with heaven's will, how can the heart not be wrenched by such as this? The living are forever separated from the dead, but with this pledge between us in the next life, may it please you now to depart . . .'

Chini's voice broke and she could not finish. Tears streamed from her eyes.

The assemblage was frozen in place. You could have heard a pin drop.

And then Chini withdrew from the bier. A leaden silence remained in the lane until she had disappeared through the gate.

Chini returned to the detached quarters and went inside and sat down. She had just pledged her love with a dead person's soul, in front of all those people.

Was it the right thing to do?

It was not that Chini feared the inevitable and endless posturing over the rights and wrongs of what she had done, nor was she fazed by the prospect of being bandied about on the tongues of numerous gossips. Rather, it was perfectly clear to her that her action was not a matter of rashness or whim; instead, and most importantly, she had just bestowed upon this dead person's soul every last ounce of love in her possession, and so until her life in this world was spent, she would be like stone or wood, absent this emotion that was love.

Such was Chini's earnest wish at that moment, a desire that infused her entire being, and to this end did she entreat the Seven Star deity.[5]

CH'ŎN UNYŎNG

Needlework

Translated by Na-Young Bae and Bruce Fulton

He wanted the largest spider in the world. He'd brought a picture of it, a creature that looked more like a giant red crab. It was a Goliath spider, and it preyed on birds.

'Look at this symmetry – it's perfect,' the man said, staring at the image. 'Doesn't it look like a, you know, a decalcomania – whatever it's called. I want it just like this, right down to the fuzzy hair.'

What the man wants isn't the spider's hair or the symmetrical spread of its legs. He wants the hard outer shell characteristic of the species *Chelicerata*. It's that exoskeleton that makes spiders, despite their small size, feared by other organisms. And it's that shell that most people want – and that's where I come in. They want it because human skin scars easily – it's more like the skin of a fruit than the shell of a spider. But because of the frailty of skin, it's actually easier than you'd think to tattoo something like a spider's shell on it.

While I lay a towel over the bed the man removes his shirt and positions the spider this way and that, trying to decide where he wants it. Nowhere on his back or front do I see enough room for a foot-long spider to spin a web. On his front is a butterfly with elaborate fluttering wings, its abdomen aligned with his bellybutton. And starting from his wrist is a bamboo stalk that firms the contour of his arm all the way to the shoulder.

I light the alcohol lamp and burn incense. Smoke spreads about the room like a ghost, leaving a scent of pine resin in the air. I need that fragrance; without it I feel like I would go into spasms, needle in hand. I'll have to light a couple more sticks before I finish this job. I take out a number 5 from my needle pack and heat it over the lamp. The needle slowly blackens before turning red-hot.

The man speaks as he watches me disinfect the needle: 'Everybody wants a machine tattoo 'cause they're scared of AIDS. Well, it *is* a lot safer and the colours are way more even. But I like it when you do it with a needle. Getting tattooed by a machine makes me feel like I'm sitting in a dentist chair. You know what it's like when the Novocaine needle goes in? It makes me kind of blah, like I'm biting into a sour persimmon. The thing is, dentists give you that shot and then they go to work on the person in the next chair. And the drilling sound that follows ... it gives me the willies.'

I put the needle down and wipe my hand and the inside of the man's thigh with a ball of cleansing cotton. I keep my mouth shut when I tattoo. I'm not very talkative in the first place. For me, the desire to speak is like a decaying tooth, you might say. A loose tooth at the tip of my tongue that pains me. A tooth that has roots deep inside my gums and constantly reminds me of its existence. If I tried to pull it out and show it to the world it would already be a stinking mess.

He'll probably keep saying things until the job is finished. Things that require an answer from me. He should've learned by now that I don't say much – he's already got two tattoos from me – but like most people who want themselves tattooed with a spider or a scorpion, he's unable to overcome fear with silence. I pour him a glass of strong cognac, no ice. Nobody can use dope when I'm working, and that includes marijuana. You have to be able to endure pain to show me you're worthy of the armour of *Chelicerata*. The man is tensing up. Probably because I'm going right ahead with the needle instead of drawing a rough sketch with a marker. I'm more cautious when I draw the first sketch than when I colour in the tattoo. Because this is when the tattoo's pattern – an inerasable scar – is created. A scar that swells up a tiny bit but doesn't bleed. A scar that lasts forever.

With my needle I start to draw the spider's body about five inches above the man's knee. It'll be shaped like a perfect octagon. It has a brown spot but I only have to outline it. The tail part will be plump, as if an infinite length of transparent thread could be extracted from it. Little by little, the spider begins to show itself beneath the needle tip.

The man, eyes closed, is breathing steadily. The way he lies there – on his back, arms outstretched as if he's cheering, legs splayed awkwardly – it's as if his body knows what *resignation* means. Though a needle wouldn't kill him, he'd be like a butterfly caught in a spider's web if I attacked him – there would be nothing he could do.

I have to concentrate much more when I tattoo the inside of a thigh than a back or a chest, because I have to do it straddling the man's lower leg, and the hair sticking out from under his briefs can be distracting. My even breathing and the warm air streaming out through my nose is enough to heat up a man's crotch. The moment I touch my needle to his skin he gets hard, and by the time I finish the basic pattern I'm afraid he's going to squirt. But never in all my tattooing career has anyone asked me for a lay.

'You can count your lucky stars that you're so unattractive.' Cause when I get a tattoo I have this incredible urge to get it on. But not with you – even though you're first rate when it comes to tattooing. Of course, if every guy you tattooed – and that's a lot of guys – had got into your panties, you'd have to take antibiotics around the clock.'

Bulging cheekbones, fat lumps on my neck, a humpback, a voice that makes people scowl, stubby toes – is it any wonder no one wants to do it with me? As I listen to the man I can almost see the adjective *loathsome* being laid out in front of me and taking on concrete form. And on top of everything else, I stutter. But no one thinks *loathsome* when they see the tattoo that comes out from my needle.

Next I go to my ink cabinet to choose the pigments – Venetian red, India ink and zinc oxide for the maroon colour of the body; chrome green and indigo will probably work for the hairy, fluffy legs. As for the spider's hair – which the man wants to emphasize – titanium will make it look real. Titanium is a metal used for jets and spaceships, but it's also used as a pigment. It has a silver glint that makes it a good choice for tattooing objects like a sword or an archer's bow. This time I'll use it to make the spider's hair look even bushier.

I heat eight needles over the lamp and string a silk thread through the eye of each. Then I wind the thread around the needle until it's about a quarter-inch from the tip. You have to make sure the thread doesn't over-lap, otherwise the ink comes out in a big glob. You also don't want to get dye on the thread near the needle eye, because that's where you pick the needle up. For the first threaded needle I use Venetian red.

The first stitch. I absolutely love this moment. I hold my breath, in goes the needle, and a drop of blood forms in the tiny hole I've made. We call that the first dewdrop. As the dewdrop forms, the ink in the thread slowly runs down the needle. The red ink reaches the tip of the needle and in no time seeps into the tiny hole in the skin. It's really cool to see this; it makes me feel like the words on the tip of my tongue will flow right out. When I tattoo, I no longer stutter.

I dab the blood away with a scrap of gauze and check whether enough colour has run in. Once I'm sure the first stitch is a success my hand speeds up. A steady pace is the key to producing even colours. I add flesh to the spider while making sure I stain just enough ink on each needle. The spider begins to show its bare red flesh. The next step is to cover the flesh with bones. You could say spiders, unlike humans, have bones on the outside – an exoskeleton – but I think of it as a hard shell. I complete the shell with India ink and zinc oxide. With the addition of chrome green, the spider is now furnished with a perfect exoskeleton.

After I dab away the ink and blood on the skin, the tattoo reveals itself. The Goliath spider looks as if it has just finished a rich meal and is enjoying a walk in the jungle. The next moment I myself am a spider, hidden in the jungle. A spider that slides along a clear web reflecting the morning sunlight. I feel a minute movement at the tips of my toes. A careless blue butterfly flutters, caught in my web. I wait silently until the butterfly's beautiful wings become ragged, then wrap my legs with their delicate covering of hair around my prey. Softly, as if caressing a man, as if holding a delicate fruit. And then like a shot from a needle I pierce the butterfly with my fangs.

'The bitches will go ape-shit over this,' the man says, giving me a pat on the shoulder.

I feel like a rag doll whenever I'm done with a tattoo, like I've just had violent sex. It's as if all my energy has been sucked into the spider's fangs. I have a smoke. The man does likewise as he considers his maroon Goliath spider. He now has an outer shell the size of his palm. God only knows if he's that much tougher now.

A man who identifies himself as Detective Mun wants me at the police station; the head priest of Mirŭk Temple has been murdered, and he has some questions. His tone is very cut-and-dried. Mirŭk Temple – the name flutters about in my mind.

'Miss Pak, Pak Yŏngsuk? Kim Hyŏngja is your mother, correct? We have her here. She is a suspect in the murder of the head priest. But there's no evidence, no witnesses – why does it have to be so complicated. Miss Pak, we need you to come in and see Ms Kim. Hello – are you there?'

Detective Mun is digging for answers, any kind of response, but my tongue has hardened to stone.

'Did you know Kim Ponghwan, the Mirŭk Temple head priest? Now what was his Buddhist name – oh yes, Hyŏnp'a, Master Hyŏnp'a.'

The name Kim Ponghwan means nothing. But Hyŏnp'a – the sound of that name is a fierce wave breaking into foam inside my head. I remember a monk with peach-coloured skin. His shaven head gave the impression that he'd trimmed each and every hair, and the grizzled stubble sprouting from that pate twinkled like silvery-grey sand – it was beautiful. Even his old robe had a gleam to it. That monk and *death*?

I yank the phone line from the wall. That long black cord gives me a bad feeling, as if insects are passing through it instead of words. Mum's fingers that used to sew *hanbok* were like a fancy embroidering on a cloth. And the teatime I had with Mum and the monk. Mum's hands – hands straighter yet softer than the bamboo stalks on the teacups, hands through which the jade-coloured tea flowed. Could those hands really have killed the monk? I look down at my brute, calloused hands and imagine them wrapped around old Master Hyonp'a's neck and strangling him. But then, like someone rejected by her parents who's learned to suck it up, I soon regain my cool. I finish the morning clean-up and have my breakfast just like every other day. I make a 'to buy' list of ink dyes and take stock of the bottles of water in the fridge.

I shop at one of those superstores. It resembles a gigantic granary and it's jammed with shoppers pushing their carts. I start with a pack of bottled water and a selection of booze, then move on to the meat section, where I pick out a slab of pork fatback and a hunk of beef shank – fresh, not frozen – and a pork backbone with a lot of meat on it. I'm not crazy about beef but I find some tenderloin and a cut of sirloin with a bit of gristle and add them to my cart.

I eat meat that's not seasoned. I like my beef a little bloody, and cut up in finger-size chunks. And my pork steamed with lots of garlic and onion. But no leafy vegetables. White rice, not vegetables, is what you want with grilled meat – rice in which you can still see the germ. Let the dark, bloody juice sink into that rice and pop a chunk of meat into your mouth along with it – that's when the taste of the meat becomes ecstasy.

As I leave the meat section, the red lumps of flesh on the trays catch my eye. The round chunks remind me of the monk's shaved head. His spot-clean head was like the sun about to rise, but the majesty of its features came with an animalistic odour. And so I sometimes thought of how it would be to tattoo a bloodstain kind of shape, something I'd seen in photos of the Maori people, on the monk's round, hard-looking head. And before long, the bestial feeling from that shaved head would mix with my twisted sexual desire and I'd imagine the monk making love to a woman as she clutched his head with her soft hands.

A chill breeze comes from one of the freezers in the frozen-food section. I feel a tiny buzz in my legs, then a tingle throughout my body, a forgotten sensation – the feeling I had before the epileptic seizures that left my stomach and chest flash-frozen and numb and made me clench my fists and thrash about on the floor. I remember the hill Mum and I walked up hand in hand to get to Mirŭk Temple, where I was supposed to be able to find a cure. And Mum's incessant bowing and the *tock tock* of the clapper on the monk's wood block. And Mum's invocations coiling around me like a spell.

Shaking my head, I hurry outside. My plastic shopping bag is heavy with all the bottled water and packages of meat (plus a toilet brush I picked up from the household section, who knows why). As I approach home my pace quickens. I want to get there and steam the meat in a big pot and feel all that flesh filling my mouth. I can almost taste the warm meat juice oozing out between my teeth.

The lift stays forever on the seventh floor before finally descending to set free a herd of people. The toilet brush is threatening to poke through my shopping bag. I waddle into the lift and press the *Close* button again and again. The double doors take all the time in the world closing. But before they can come together, a hand shoots between them. The doors open just enough to admit a forearm, then a shoulder and then a head. The left leg finishes the sequence and the man is now inside. Uselessly the doors open again, only to gather together once more. The man has his back to me. He's huffing and puffing and his shoulders are heaving.

The lift doesn't move. We're still on the first floor. Neither of us has pressed a floor button. Gathering my bag in one hand, I press 8. The man's finger overlaps mine just as the 8 button turns green. The next moment my bag finally gives up, ripping open and releasing everything onto the floor. The lift lurches into motion and sends me plopping down on top of the meat. Bloody juice oozes from the plastic-wrapped meat. I gather what I can in one arm and strain to get up. The man picks up the rest of my things and places them on top of the pile.

The lift doors clunk open. I exit right, the man exits left and walks away. I dump everything in front of my door and look to see where the man has gone. He's standing at the door at the end of the hallway looking for his keys. Since the apartment at this end is number 806, where the man lives must be 801. This man and I have been getting on that lift, getting off on the same floor, walking the same distance to the ends of the hallway, unlocking our doors, and going inside. If someone could somehow fold the hallway in half with the lift in the middle, the man and I would come together. Like the appendages of the Goliath spider.

All of a sudden a man's face, white and clean like rice, flashes before my eyes. A beautiful face. With my foot I shove my things inside and close the door. Juice still oozes from the meat. I'm starving. I'm ready to plop down right now, rip off the plastic wrap, grab the raw meat and stuff myself with it. I want to feel sated from all the food I'll devour, I want to see blood smeared across the lips of my feral self.

But could Mum really have killed Master Hyŏnp'a?

Two o'clock in the afternoon. I go for a walk along Han River Way. This grand avenue stretches into the centre of the city like a long tendon. From the sky it would look like a flayed human body with tendons and veins spurting everywhere.

I think about the death of the monk, and the death of the monk gets me thinking of the kitten I found at Mirŭk Temple. A pack of cats roved about the temple, wandering the yard and even the dharma hall as if they owned it. I was afraid of those cats but at the same time taken by the beauty I felt was hidden inside them. They were so small and soft, so frail and warm and a little emaciated. The monk would often see them in front of the monks' quarters and throw them a fish head or a chunk of meat that the believers had brought. I glared in envy as the cats with their gleaming eyes savoured the taste of flesh.

On a day when pine dust riled the air, I came across a newborn kitten in a pile of firewood. No sooner had I placed my hand on its warm body than the mother cat appeared from nowhere, back hunched up and ready to attack. I managed to escape with the kitten, but I could almost feel the mother cat's shrill yowl against the back of my head – my hair was standing on end. I felt I was orbiting in another dimension rather than scrambling down a mountain path. There was no reality, only the wind buffeting my ears. I arrived at the village at the foot of the mountain and hid in a public toilet. The kitten in my hand was small, frail and beautiful. But that realization didn't hit me until I threw it into the toilet pit. I stood watching long after it disappeared beneath a desperate swarm of maggots.

I arrive at the War Memorial Museum, buy an admission ticket, and go in. Like most museums and memorials, it's arranged by period, the glass cases in the rooms displaying artefacts variously excavated or preserved. But if you inspect them closely you can tell they're actually intricate replicas made of plastic or wax. Looking at the display, I imagine myself taking out the weapons one at a time and attacking the monk. The arrow leaves the bow with a whoosh and pierces his heart. The seven blades of the Seven-Way Sword slice through his intestines. A staple-shaped caltrop – supposedly used to keep enemy horses from advancing – punctures the monk's foot and releases a great splatter of blood. I fire every weapon there is – including the .45 with which we used to shoot the Commies, a rifle, even a tank gun – but they all leave me unsatisfied. I need a killing mechanism for the monk that's more powerful, and cruel perhaps, but one that doesn't leave any evidence – a method Mum could carry out.

Around the hallway corner I'm brought to a stop by a painting, *Victory at Kwiju*. What captures my attention is the name of the Koryŏ general, Kang Kamch'an, which radiates toughness and tyranny. But the feeling I get from *Victory at Kwiju* is not of violence but rather gentleness – like how I'd feel looking at a landscape of grass swaying in the wind.

Advancing soldiers, spears in hand, charging horses, vapour rushing from their nostrils – all racing in the same direction without a second of hesitation, like grass whistling in the wind. The catchweed swaying in the wind seems so soft, and the soldiers have the liveliness of dancers even as they face death. I can't accept this. War to me isn't some colourful landscape; it's a monochrome portrait shot through with pain and screaming. But blood and killing, which by definition should be present in war, are nowhere to be seen here.

I feel dizzy and sick and my ears are ringing. I need to find the exit. But to do that I have to let the fluorescent directional arrows channel me and the other visitors through all the rooms in the museum – it's the only way out. Like a dwarf snatched by a giant, I struggle through each room, and finally have one last chance at violence – the Experience War Room.

Separate admission required. With my new ticket I squat at the metal door and wait with a group of children, each of them with a notepad. Finally the door opens and an usher comes out to inspect each and every ticket before admitting us. I lag behind as the others rush in, then offer my ticket. The usher reaches for it but doesn't take it. I look up at him. Uniform rigid from ironing, the line of a white neck showing above the sharp crease of his collar – it's the man from Apartment 801. My ticket falls from my hand to the floor. As he stoops to pick it up I flee inside, avoiding his eyes. The room is pitch dark, no illumination whatsoever.

From the darkness comes the boom of a cannon. The acrid smell of gunpowder pierces my nose. I see lights flashing at my feet, hear bullets zing past my head. The yells and screams of soldiers, radio voices requesting back-up, officers shouting orders – in the darkness in which this intense battle is taking place there's a sudden chill breeze, and with it vibrations that feel like the precursors of my epilepsy. I sense a predator lurking in the dark, ready to pounce. I hear someone behind me, his breathing muffled and tense. I feel my hair stand up on the back of my neck, warm breath on my thick ears. The breathing quickens, becomes rougher. The bombardment ceases – as does the breathing. My collar flutters as if in the wind. A red light comes on and the children surge past me as I stand there. I look about the red room before going out.

The man from Apartment 801 is nowhere to be seen. Was it his breathing I felt? The gunpowder smell stings my nose. I pass through the last room with its display of life-size tanks and helicopters and exit the museum. My energy is spent. I lie down next to the tank positioned on the grass. I can almost hear from far off the *tock tock* of the monk's wood block and Mum's invocations. The tingling smell of gunpowder is now a faint scent of incense.

A sword I saw inside flashes through my mind's eye like a ray of light. It's a beautiful sword, long and majestic, its blade swift and keen with a tiger delicately inscribed at its tip. I have dreamed of kneeling down before such beauty and licking the steel edge like a dog. In the dream I couldn't decide if what was stimulating my tongue was the sweaty smell of steel, the scent of incense, or the odour of gunpowder.

'We didn't do an autopsy – the believers were opposed to it – but we've decided nonetheless that he died of old age . . . They *did* say he was practically a living corpse at the end. I don't know why Ms Kim insisted that she killed him, but thanks to her, innocent people have had to suffer.'

Detective Mun is not even looking at me. His indifferent words pierce me to the core, like the smoke from my first cigarette at dawn. It's morning and the station is deserted, but Detective Mun is fussing with his papers and ignores my gaze.

'Then, Mum, didn't, kill, the monk?' I stutter.

'That's what I said. Ms Kim was released yesterday. She must have gone home.'

Saying he's busy with something, Detective Mun scurries off. I go outside, sit down on the steps, and watch the shoes of people passing by. *Home*. Does Mum have a home to go to? Would Mum have returned to Mirŭk Temple? Troublesome questions cascade over me. I feel like a lost child. Like I did that day I stood frozen in front of the *hanbok* shop, looking down the street where Mum had disappeared.

My epilepsy was gone, so Mum and I no longer had a reason to stay at Mirŭk Temple. I had decided to erase all the memories of the temple as I pulled up the metal shutters of our dusty *hanbok* shop – the kitten I'd killed, the teatimes with the monk, even the thick scent of incense and the chanting of the scriptures. From Mum I would learn to weave *hanbok* as beautiful as hers. I would stick by Mum until I could spool thread on the sewing machine and dye the cloth, until I could finally backstitch the turned-in collar of the jacket, which required more delicacy – that was my plan.

But Mum had a different plan. She spent four days sewing a charcoal-dyed cotton outfit, top and bottom, and a yellow ceremonial robe. When she had finished starching these clothes and fulling them with the laundry sticks, she produced a mustard-coloured cloth wrapper containing several rolls of money. Then she took the clothing – which by then I realized she had made for the monk – and left. 'I have to go there' was the last thing she said to me.

So it wasn't Mum who killed the monk. Perhaps her belief that she had killed the monk was a homicidal impulse that, like the weapons displayed at the War Memorial Museum, could not be put into practice. But just as many wars are beautified, someone could have concealed the truth to protect the monk's beauty. I set out for Mirŭk Temple.

Mirŭk Temple, surrounded by woods, is as silent as if the temple itself has turned into forest. It gives no feel of human occupation. The dharma hall and Mirŭk Hall are locked. The pile of dry pine needles in the courtyard gives the impression of an abandoned home. And the gate to the living quarters is bolted. My emotional screws feel rusted and wobbly – I have to tighten them. I climb onto a box that's been left beside the gate and peek inside. The entire hermitage is so quiet it's almost scary. Where did all those cats go? I reach around the gate and draw the bolt.

In the kitchen everything is in its proper place. No scrap of food lingering at the drain. A kitchen knife, long pointy chopsticks, a steel pot, chunks of wood for the firebox, cooking gas that could blow up the living quarters – with such potential murder weapons, where there's a will there's a way. And yet I see no evidence that Mum killed the monk.

I find the room where Mum and I stayed. It's empty except for some items stuffed in the corner that give off a musty smell – old clothes Mum would have worn, along with her bed quilt. No furniture, but only the Buddhist scriptures Mum would have read every day, a straw basket for her sewing materials, some half-empty containers of cheap cosmetics – all resting neatly on a *ramyŏn* box next to the window. I pour the contents of the basket onto the floor. A spool of white thread rolls off, leaving a transparent plastic bag with buttons, chalk and measuring tape, a needle pouch made of fine cloth, a Kirin-brand pack of two dozen gilded needles, a light blue plastic comb and a black hairband.

'The needles won't rust if you put some of your hair in with them,' Mum would say whenever she was putting her needles away. She would roll up a few strands of her long black hair and add them to the pouch. Sometimes she'd do the same with my thick, coarse hair, which came out practically by the handful. I stuff Mum's needle pouch and needle pack into my trouser pocket. Mum wouldn't need them now. I would use them to make beautiful tattoos. I make off with these needles as if they're spoils of war, but for some reason my heart is pounding fiercely.

The man Mr Kim brought is in his late forties and he's supposedly spent his entire life travelling from one gaming table to the next. He has huge cow eyes and his very thick hair is dyed pitch black. Tattooed on the man's shoulder is a blue sail, on his chest a huge square, and on his stomach five rectangles.

'All this me and the other guys got when I was working on the ferry,' and this here rectangle is the letter *miŭm*, see? The tattoo guy was gonna write "Masan Man"[1] but after he did the *miŭm* he got hauled off by the cops. Seriously, with such a huge fucking *miŭm* how the hell was he supposed to write "Masan Man"? Since then my life has been royally screwed. Success? For a guy like me who can't even be a Masan Man? You've got to be kidding . . .'

The man laments as he strokes the bare rough outlines of the tattoos. The five rectangles on his belly are supposed to represent the five *kwang* cards in a *hwat'u* deck, he says. If he had them close to his heart like a charm, he'd be lucky in his gambling – so he thought. But his hopes are now mere lines, bare of any effect.

Two or three people came to see me after I got back from Mirŭk Temple but I couldn't give them a tattoo. If it weren't for Mr Kim I wouldn't have been able to stop this cycle of holing up in my room and living on meat and water for days at a time. Just like today, Mr Kim would sometimes bring a customer in without notice and request a tattoo. The people he brought generally wanted their ugly, vulgar tattoos repaired or else they wanted a tattoo so complicated I'd have to work on it all day to finish it. There was even a man who asked me to tattoo a samurai sword on his penis. Sometimes I just can't say no.

Mr Kim was the one who taught me how to handle a needle. I met him while hanging around the *hanbok* shop after Mum had left. When I saw the bluish stain on Mr Kim's rock-hard arm I felt a peculiar sensation I'd never had before. I caught from him the smell of a welder. A combination of sweat and a fishy metallic odour. The sword tattooed on Mr Kim's arm was beautiful. I had followed Mr Kim to Seoul. If Mum embroidered upon cloth I would embroider upon the frail body of man. Mr Kim was the ray of hope that would help me start anew.

The *miŭm* of the word *Masan* inscribed on the man's chest looks more like a picture frame than a letter. I can tell from this tattooed letter the sense of urgency he must have felt at the time. I have the same reaction to words such as *effort* and *frugality* as well. The will and determination to start over would enable people to bear the excruciating pain of needles penetrating their flesh. On the other hand, a tattoo also implies the upcoming trials of life that one must endure.

There's something that coexists between the flesh and the writing inscribed upon it. Together they make a beautiful scar, or a painful decoration.

I draw a tiger with sharp fangs within the frame of the *miŭm*. The tiger glares at me as if it will burst out of its cage at any moment. I grind charcoal and use it to tattoo prominent stripes on the tiger on his chest. The tiger locked within the square will become not a mere Masan Man, but the insignia embroidered on the robe of a military officer of Chosŏn. Then in the rectangles on his stomach I draw the five *kwang* cards: *il, sam, p'al, pi, ttong*. Now, concealed within his clothes, the man has the set of five *kwang* cards that will allow him to keep calm in any card game. How free and easy would your life be if you had the ultimate set of trump cards hidden within you?

The man looks at himself in the mirror with a smile up to his ears. Soon the repressed pain will come rushing in, but as the man leaves, the set of his shoulders radiates confidence. I light a cigarette and look at the needles and bottles of dye scattered across the floor. The five cards are still where Masan Man slapped them on the floor, the five cards whose exact images I drew on his chest. It wasn't such a hard tattoo to draw, but I feel as if all my energy has been sucked out.

Cigarette between my teeth, I collect the bottle of dye and the gauze I used to wipe off the blood. I hear the doorbell – two lengthy rings. Did Mr Kim leave something behind? I haul myself to my feet and open the door.

It's the man from Apartment 801. He stands stiff and motionless. I open the door in slow motion and move aside so the man can enter. I feel like I've been possessed. Could I have been waiting for him? He takes his time crossing the living room to the sofa, as though he's been coming and going from here forever. He sinks back in the sofa, knees together, eyes on me until I close the door and sit down beside him. Then he looks away and starts in.

'I've always wondered what's on the other side.'

I look at him in profile.

He purses his lips. 'I've always wondered what if I turned right instead of left after getting out of the lift. Or what if I took the bus in the opposite direction instead of going to work in the morning?'

Every time he speaks, his eyes seem to sink deeper in thought. His words glisten like a fish jumping from the ocean depths into the sunlight's compass. When I answer I feel I've caught that flapping fish by the tail.

'I saw, you. At the, War, Memorial Museum.' Compared with his crisp voice, my rigid stutter sounds like the clanging of pots and pans. I say no more and wait for him to speak.

'When I saw you in the lift I smelled something strong, like gunpowder. Well, maybe disinfectant, who knows. I smell gunpowder and hear cannons every day, as you know by now.'

I keep silent.

'Sometimes I go to the control room so I can hear the sound of bombing. When I sit there and close my eyes, I can feel the sound of the wind. It's like the bombs falling from a B-29.'

'Why do you, listen to the, sound of bombs?'

'I like war. War's a strong thing. Strength comes from power. The most beautiful thing in the world is power.'

'There's nothing, like war, here.'

'I know what you do. I know that you only open the door for those men who ring your doorbell twice. You never open it for the paper boy or the Sunday sales guys, because they only ring once.'

'Have you been, watching me? What else, do you know?'

The man puts on a faint smile.

'All the men who come out from your place look much more sure of themselves than when they go in. And I know why. One man who came out of your place last month showed me a long sword on his forearm. He knows – he knows the power weapons have.'

'People beautiful, like you, don't get, tattoos.'

'Beautiful? Look at me. Skin this pale you only find on dead people. I can't even tan it 'cause it's genetically so white. I went to a tanning place but all that happened was my skin got blazing red and the next day went back to the way it was. I always look weak and cowardly. I fucking hate that!' He glares at me with furious eyes.

The faint smile of a moment ago is gone. His light-brown eyes are like those of a cat. Eyes of distrust. The eyes of a girl right before she surrenders her virginity. He continues with an expression both cautious and despairing, as if unveiling what is most shameful and long-festering within him.

'When I was in the army the older guys used to give me a hard time because I looked so girly. I just grit my teeth and put up with it. But then one night the guy next to me started taking my trousers off. I couldn't move . . .'

I wait for him to go on.

'That's when I knew. There were two ways I could survive: cut off my balls or add new ones . . . What do you think I'm choosing? It's obvious – I'm adding. And you can do that for me.'

'Me?'

'Yes, you. You can tattoo my body full of the strongest weapons. A sword, a bow, a missile, an aeroplane, whatever, anything.' He shoots me a look.

'It's like a girl losing her cherry,' I drawl. 'It's not like you can sew it up again. It'll be on you forever. You still want it?'

He reaches out and takes my hand. His hand is warm and soft, like meat just steamed.

I place a thick cut of beef on the grill. When the cold meat touches the hot iron it shrivels up with a sizzle. As I turn it over, I think of cream-filled pastries. Soft, sweet, cream-filled pastries that make you sigh. And then the phone rings.

Detective Mun, the man who informed me of the monk's death, utters my name. He's hesitating, as if he's trying to reach a very important decision. I place a chunk of meat in my mouth and wait for his next words. They come as I bite off a piece of gristle: Mum has killed herself. They found her in the canyon near the foot of Mount Kŭmjŏng. I need to retrieve her body from the morgue. Hearing his faltering voice, I imagine the Grim Reaper reading the roll of the dead.

I hang up and take another bite of meat. I place thin slices of garlic between the meat and the grill. Drops of grease fall into the flames, sending the odour of burning protein everywhere. I try a slice of garlic steeped in meat juice. The half-cooked garlic stings the tip of my tongue. Chewing the garlic, I imagine Mum's body torn open by the rocks in the canyon. But all that comes to mind is a woman's naked white corpse covered in cuts and scars, and not Mum's face.

I look for Mum's needle pouch and needle pack. I had stuffed them in my pocket at Mirŭk Temple and immediately forgotten about them. Maybe I would remember her face if I saw the hair she'd placed in the pouch. I untie the pouch and shake out the contents – short hairs and needles. The hairs are too short and coarse to be Mum's. I lick the tip of my index finger and dab at the hairs on the floor. The hairs belong to the monk.

I picture Mum shaving the monk's head, on her knees, one hand holding the razor and the other pressing down gently on his shoulder. The monk's hair falling from the razor blade, an almost pastoral scene. The devotion with which her delicate hands gather up every last one of the hairs and place them in the pouch. All of this is vivid in my mind, as vivid as my image of Mum and the monk silently drinking tea from a tea table set between them.

Why did Mum say she'd killed the monk? And why had she ended her life? I open the Japanese needle pack Mum had cherished. The needles, sparkling gold, number 1 to number 20. I take one of them and finger its delicate smoothness. Suddenly all my nerves collect at the tip of the needle. I glare at all the needles. All twenty are missing their tips. The needles have lost their sharpness, they're blunt like wire. Mum had deliberately cut off the tips.

'Cut the needles into tiny pieces and mix them into the vegetable purée he drinks every day. Those thin shards will swirl around in his intestines and leave deadly cuts. They'll penetrate his bloodstream, stop his heart and bring on death – but with no external signs.'

Mum's vivid voice is resonating within me.

Every night he turns right after getting out of the lift. Even if he doesn't press my doorbell twice I know he's coming – coming to me. I can feel his tiptoeing steps and hear his deep sigh when he stops at my door.

I tattooed a needle the size of a pinkie on his chest. The needle dyed with titanium looks kind of like a tiny slit. A thin slit like a little girl's vagina. I feel like the whole universe could get sucked in through it.

He now embraces the strongest weapon in the world. A needle – the thinnest, but the strongest and most tender of all things.

PEACE AND WAR

HWANG SUNWŎN

Time for You and Me

Translated by Bruce and Ju-Chan Fulton

And now it was the second day.

The surroundings were the same, a succession of ravines and rounded summits as far as the eye could see. Nothing seemed to move, not even the air.

Captain Chu was supported by a man on each side, held by an arm around the shoulder of each, but still he kept slumping towards the ground. He was more or less being dragged, incapable of walking on his own because of the wound to his thigh. Right off, the men had applied direct pressure and stanched the blood flow. Fortunately the bullet had missed the major artery and there seemed to be no nerve damage, and the men had managed to thread their way through enemy lines. But by morning Chu was experiencing numbness followed by sharp pain – infection?

Chu was well aware of the tremendous boost to the spirit that access to a specific route would offer a party transporting a wounded man. But the men weren't following a route, had no specific destination, were simply walking southward.

Chu knew of a soldier shot in the lower abdomen who had stuffed the entry wound with his fatigue shirt and made it back to base, a thirty-minute-plus trudge, before collapsing. Having a certain destination and knowing how to get there made this possible in spite of the near-fatal wound.

There was no such route for Chu and the two men. But Chu couldn't bring himself to tell Lieutenant Hyŏn and Private First Class Kim that he could no longer walk and that they should leave him and proceed by themselves. For being left behind meant death.

*

When Kim suggested carrying him on his back, Chu silently assented.

Kim had turned nineteen that year and having grown up in a farming village was able to carry Chu a considerable distance.

Then came Hyǒn's turn.

Hyǒn had a quick look at Chu, registered the pistol holstered at the captain's waist. The men had long since rid themselves of knapsack, helmet, rifle and fatigue jacket. Chu's pistol was the only weapon among them.

Chu noticed Hyǒn's glance and read the thought underlying it. Now that he was unable to move unaided his body was a nuisance to the two men carrying it. But there was no way those two men could abandon their superior and continue on alone. Instead they were waiting for him to accept the reality of their situation and use the pistol to do away with himself.

Chu pretended he hadn't noticed Hyǒn's glance. Instead, to lighten the load he discarded his trousers and combat boots before climbing onto the other man's back.

Although Hyǒn couldn't carry Chu as far as Kim had, he was stronger than Chu, who like Hyǒn had been a university student when conscripted, and with his larger build was able to manage the captain's weight well enough.

For two days now the men had survived on edible roots and had barely kept thirst at bay with water from the occasional stream they came across. Worse, the early summer sun was scorching.

Briny sweat streamed down the face of the carrier, leaking into his eyes and mouth. But with his hands holding fast to the load, he could only blink away the moisture or dislodge the drops by blowing them from his lips while shaking his head.

The distance each man could manage gradually dwindled and the handovers became more frequent.

The sweat-soaked fatigue shirt of the man carrying him felt slimy against Chu's chest but reminded the captain all too graphically that he was still alive.

Again it was Hyǒn's turn. As he trudged along, dripping sweat, an image he'd entertained several times resurfaced.

He'd had a dream the night before last, before the clamour of the cymbals and bugles that signalled an attack by the Chinese awakened him. In the dream a jaundiced sun occupied a sallow sky. Beneath it a barren wasteland the colour of the sky extended to the horizon. And he was in the middle of that expanse, dripping sweat and standing calf-deep in the powdery soil of that wasteland.

Those calves of his – he had better be careful. The day before he'd left for the army he and his sweetheart went on an outing. It was a warm day and when he rolled up his trousers she made fun of how long the hair of his calves was. Picking out the longest hair, she laid claim to it and told Hyŏn to take good care of it. And now his calves were about to sink into that dusty earth.

But there was another worry. A hole had appeared in the powdery soil and he was sure it was made by an ant. He had to keep an eye on that hole, he told himself, even though no one had ordered him to do so.

And then a procession of ants the same sallow colour as the soil began to appear from the hole. A huge ant, the same colour as the others, positioned itself just outside the hole and one by one bit off the head of every last ant as it emerged. In no time there was a pile of dead ants. But the next moment the dead ants had turned into soil. Did that mean the barren wasteland that stretched out endlessly before him was composed of dead ants, each with its head bitten off? The jaundiced sun still occupied the sallow sky, and beneath it he had to remain where he was, keeping an eye on that hole.

All Hyŏn could think of now was Chu's weight on his back. There was only one way to be rid of that burden and that was for Chu to give up his attachment to life. Otherwise all three of them would die in this unknown mountain terrain.

His throat burned with thirst.

He thought of the letter from his sweetheart that had arrived five days earlier, the first in some time. In it were these words: *My floral lips will never wither, moistened as they are by the happy memories you provided me.*

Once at the end of a long kiss he had whispered in her ear, 'Your lips have so many layers, layers of countless petals, I'll never be able to taste them all.'

There was something else in that letter, different from previous letters. She no longer addressed him by his given name followed by the somewhat formal *sshi*, but had switched to the much more intimate *tangshin*. This marked a strong sense of union in their relationship. After reading the letter he had looked down at his calves and could almost feel her clear, smiling gaze washing over him.

And now as he carried Chu the sensation of the lips of this person he loved was balm for his burning throat, and her clear, smiling eyes once again washed over him. He staggered on, following her gaze, his own eyes clearing in spite of the perspiration.

They came to a bend in the ridge they were following. Now it was Kim's turn.

A glance at the topography told them they could drop down to the ravine in front of them and go back up the mountain opposite, which would seem to take less time, or they could follow the bends in the ridge and take the long way around.

Hyŏn suggested they go straight down. Practically anybody would have said the same. In their situation even a few steps less could make a difference.

Kim thought otherwise. If they got lost in the woods in the ravine they could expect a delay, in addition to the hard work of going down and then back up again.

When it became evident they weren't about to reach a decision, Chu spoke up. 'Lieutenant Hyŏn, let's do it Private Kim's way.'

Hyŏn's gaze shot to Chu's pistol. And the scene from his dream returned – the jaundiced sun occupying the sallow sky, and beneath it the barren wasteland carpeting the surroundings. And he was in the middle of that expanse, dripping with sweat. Directly before him in the parched soil was a hole, and out from that hole came a procession of small ants, and awaiting them at the opening of the hole was the king of the ants, the same sallow colour, who kept biting off their heads. The ants and their king moved with machine-like precision, the king's jaws opening and closing in time with the ants presenting themselves from the hole. And then the bodies of the ants became the soil. The soil kept building until his calves were almost covered.

Hyŏn couldn't help feeling anxious. But what else could he do other than remain where he stood?

Suddenly he discovered a new hole beside the first one. That new hole hadn't appeared in his dream, he was sure of it, and so he must have conceived it himself just now. But the heedless ants continued to stream from the original hole, losing their heads in the process.

Hyŏn no longer had Chu on his back but continued to perspire.

Around sundown the three men caught a snake, cooked it over a fire, and shared it.

After this meal Hyŏn went off, giving the impression he was responding to nature's call.

A short time later Chu said to Kim, 'You might as well go too.'

Kim observed Chu, trying to read the intention behind these words.

'Lieutenant Hyŏn is gone,' said Chu. 'He couldn't wait any longer.'

'Couldn't wait for what?'

'For me to kill myself.'

And indeed, Hyŏn did not return.

'You should get going yourself,' added Chu, avoiding Kim's gaze.

Kim hesitated a moment, cast a glance at the dark red afterglow receding behind the mountains to the west, and silently offered Chu his back.

With only one man doing the carrying, they didn't make much progress. Go a short distance and rest, go a short distance and rest – that was the routine.

When it was too dark to see they sprawled out where they were.

Each man had visions of the hardtack in his discarded knapsack dancing before his eyes, but by now they had been hungry so long they accepted it as a matter of course.

They thought about Hyŏn. How far had he got? Kim resented the man for abandoning them. Chu, on the other hand, held to the hope that Hyŏn would soon find his way to their home base and have a rescue group sent out for them. Neither man, of course, shared his thoughts with the other.

Kim fell asleep but Chu remained awake. By now he was pretty much used to the pain from his wound. What troubled him, rather, was the thought that if he went to sleep now he would never wake up.

And then for some reason he couldn't have explained, thoughts of the woman came to mind.

A few months earlier his unit had retaken a strategic position high in the mountains and he'd been awarded several days of leave. He'd gone to Pusan and bought the woman's services for a night.

She told him that around the time of the 4 January 1951 Retreat she'd been working at a bar in Seoul when a girl rushed in one evening at sundown, pursued by three foreign soldiers. She'd helped the girl escape out the back door but then in the back room was forced to take the soldiers in her place. She didn't think of them as three individuals, wanted only to turn off her mind and get it over with, and after a seemingly endless night she awoke to the faint light of dawn coming through the window. And then whom should she run into on the street the next day but the very same girl. She didn't recognize her at first but felt incredibly thankful that the girl had come right up to her with a look of obvious delight. And when the girl said she wanted to do something for her, she was overwhelmed.

As Chu listened to this heartwarming story he had an urge to pinpoint the purpose of it. 'So you're saying that in order to relive that feeling of overwhelming gratitude you would put yourself in the same situation, turning off your mind, as you say, until the first light of dawn?'

In the darkness the woman lit a cigarette and Chu heard her say, 'Well, you can't really plan a situation like that. It's just that I found myself there with the girl. And aren't people capable of doing something that seems to make no sense when they think about it afterwards? That was what happened with me and the girl, but if I were in the same situation again I'm not sure what I would do – maybe the same, maybe not.'

And that was the end of their conversation.

Looking back now, Chu realized that over the course of the battles he'd lived through, he too had done things he didn't know he was capable of. Every time he encountered an unanticipated situation, he'd reacted in a way he'd never expected.

No sooner did he realize this than a new thought flashed across his mind. When he had asked the woman sarcastically if, confronted with the same situation, she would again take the place of the other person, wasn't it possible that in a corner of his mind he approved of what she had done – and was hoping deep down inside she would react in the same way the next time?

But now with death facing him as he lay at night on a mountain ridge, he couldn't help feeling he had no right to wish anything of the woman regardless of her situation. What if a third party, knowing of the experiences that had befallen Chu on the battlefield, had presumed to tell him he should have done such-and-so? No way.

Suddenly he felt like picking a fight with someone, it didn't matter who. But there was only the thick darkness with which to contest.

In the end, he too drifted off to sleep.

At first light they were back on their feet and under way. The rest breaks this day were more numerous.

Kim too rid himself of his fatigue trousers and his boots. He was all too aware of what tramping barefoot in the mountains would do to his feet. But he had to get rid of those boots, they were weighing him down.

The soles of his bare feet split open and bled. If only he had the luxury of a nice soft path without jagged rocks to stumble over.

As far as they could see were the rounded summits and the ravines, neither movement nor habitation. And instead of the boom of friendly artillery fire there was only Kim's harsh panting to break the tranquil silence.

Even so, Chu strained to detect any sound out of the ordinary.

At one point Chu pointed off in the distance and suggested they try to find water. Where were they going to find water? Kim asked himself. But he carried Chu to where the captain had pointed and there among the boulders was a spring.

All they managed that day was a distance an able-bodied man could have covered in an hour. For food they had several frogs they ate raw.

With Kim bent forward at the waist, his legs flexed and his head lowered, you might have thought he was crawling. The sharper the angle of the private's body, Chu told himself, the worse his own odds of surviving.

Evening was approaching as they rounded a bend in the ridge and saw a crow launch itself and fly off. In front of them was a sharp drop-off.

As he backed off from the brink Kim looked down and saw a few other crows pecking away at something.

It was a body. Lieutenant Hyŏn's body. He was clad just as he had been the previous day when he abandoned them – undershirt, fatigue trousers and combat boots.

Damned bird, thought Kim. One of the crows was pecking at Hyŏn's face. And then it spotted them, made as if to fly off, but simply cawed a couple of times and resumed feeding.

By now the eyes of the corpse were gone, the sockets empty black hollows.

The two men retreated from the drop-off and sprawled out on the ground, feet facing the bluff. What had remained of their energy was drained by the sight of Hyŏn's body.

A short time later Chu saw Kim rise and totter to the edge of the bluff. The next thing he knew, Kim was hurling rocks into the void. Each rock dispersed the crows, but they simply cawed in displeasure and resettled around the body.

Kim returned and sprawled out again, this time for good.

He turned and looked at Chu. The captain was lying on his back, eyes closed.

Death, which Kim tended to forget in the fierce heat of battle, now felt close. Tomorrow it would be *their* eyes those crows were plucking out. He hoped that instead of Chu dying first and he himself having to watch the captain's eyes plucked out, *he* would be the first to go and thereby oblivious to all that followed.

He had a sudden urge to cry but lacked even the strength to muster tears.

Kim awakened from the depths of sleep to hear Chu muttering. Stars studded the sky above.

'Listen,' said Chu in a lifeless voice. 'Artillery.'

Kim, instantly alert, sat up and strained to listen. Sure enough, the faint boom of artillery, sounding like distant thunder.

'Whose side?'

'Ours – one-fifty-five-calibre howitzers.'

Well, he should know, thought Kim. How far away were they? he asked.

'Far,' said Chu. 'Too far. At the rate we're going it would take us four days to get there.'

Meaning that all the friendly fire in the world would do the two of them no good.

Kim plopped back down.

Chu felt himself dying by the hour. Oddly enough, this realization was crystal clear. And finally, the notion he'd been avoiding until now hit him head on. He had to put that pistol to use. He should have done it in the first place, he was dying for sure, and wouldn't that have solved everything? Maybe Lieutenant Hyŏn wouldn't have hurried off at night and fallen to his death from that bluff. In any event, it wasn't too late to do away with himself. And wouldn't that leave the slim possibility that Private Kim, exhausted though he was, would somehow find his way to home base?

With all the strength at his command he issued Kim an order: 'That artillery fire is coming from the southeast. Go down and around to the left of that drop-off and you'll make it!'

And then carefully and quietly his leaden hand took the pistol from its holster.

At that exact moment a different sound made itself heard among the distant boom of the artillery. Chu was dubious but strained to listen. 'What's that sound?' he asked Kim. He saw Kim lift his head and try to focus, then heard him say, 'What sound?'

'Hmm, can't hear it now.' But then he heard it again, as if it were being carried on the wind. 'There – do you hear it? It's coming from behind us.'

Still Kim heard nothing.

'Sounds like a dog barking.'

At this, Kim's tired body jerked up to a sitting position and he turned and waddled off on his knees. If indeed a dog was barking, there had to be a dwelling not far away.

'Just cross over that ridge!' shouted Chu.

But Kim still heard nothing. Finally he backpedalled towards their resting spot.

There was something Chu wanted to give Kim. Something he himself wanted as well.

Kim lay down muttering. 'By tomorrow there'll be more of those crows; tonight's the last time we'll have our eyes.' He had barely finished when the crack of a gunshot assaulted his ears. Startled, he rolled over to see Chu training his pistol on him in the darkness.

'Get me on your back!' said Chu in a tone surprisingly clear, considering his choked voice.

Not knowing what to make of this, Kim could only rise and do as Chu instructed.

'All right, move!'

Kim felt the muzzle of the pistol against the back of his right ear.

They crossed the ridge and entered a dark forest.

'Hang on a moment!'

Once Kim had stopped, Chu listened carefully, then said, 'Go left!'

A short time later Chu said, 'Hold it!' And then 'Forward!'

Kim went left, went right, went straight ahead, following Chu's orders, knowing his life depended on it, but in all that time he heard nothing. Perhaps the captain, faced with death, was hearing things? And if that was the case, why did this episode have to end with both of them dying? Having toiled to transport Chu by himself since the previous night, he couldn't help feeling a surge of resentment.

But he couldn't stop walking, what with the muzzle of the pistol resting against the back of his ear. That muzzle was keeping his tottering legs in motion.

They reached the foot of a mountain.

'Go right!' And then, 'Straight ahead!'

Only then did Kim hear it – the barking of a dog. It gradually became clearer, but he couldn't tell how far off it was.

From his throat came hot, panting breath. His only thought was that his barely moving legs were sinking, ever sinking, into something bottom-less. He wanted only to plop down where he was. But he was in no position to be resting. The muzzle of the pistol was if anything pushing more forcefully against his ear.

He couldn't see a thing, scarcely realized he was still putting one foot in front of the other. And then off in the darkness there appeared an outline – a thatch-roofed hut? – and before it two more outlines – a man and a barking dog? – and the moment these images registered faintly in his soporific vision he was freed of the muzzle at his ear and Chu's weight on his back.

PAK WANSŎ

Winter Outing

Translated by Marshall R. Pihl

Before slipping into the bath and indulging myself in the pleasant sensation, I began to wonder selfishly whether this hot-spring water was the real thing. The shower and the two taps labelled hot and cold, attached to the ordinary tiled bathtub in this deluxe room at a second-rate inn, weren't the least bit different from what you would find at any cheap bathhouse. Just where, I wondered, is the proof that the hot water pouring from this faucet marked with a red circle is not just heated city water but rather hot-spring water that has gushed up out of the earth?

It wasn't that I had some rare chronic disease that required me to soak in the water; nor had I come here expecting some sort of power in the water, as touted by those who go on about such things. Actually, I was looking for an excuse to feel still more sorry for myself. From the outset, the journey hadn't held portents of pleasure. It was a journey that seemed to have started off wrong, and I was of a mind to let it end up in total disaster.

Though not commercially popular, my husband was an artist of some standing who clung tenaciously to his own rather peculiar artistic outlook, for which he had made his name and gained critical recognition. Owing to preparations for his third one-man show, he had been spending several nights at his studio. Things were at the point where I would occasionally bring him food out of concern for his health or he would drop by the house only to change his clothing. The previous day was one such occasion: I was downtown and had bought some sliced beef and dropped by the studio. Our married daughter was there, modelling for my husband. This was quite a surprise to me since people almost never appear in my husband's paintings. I had thought he enjoyed painting only natural scenes

and animals in highly simplistic or nursery styles. And this painting of a
human figure was utterly different from my husband's usual style. It was
dreadfully detailed, vivid and realistic. But far from questioning this exact
likeness, I was concerned most with the sudden loathing I immediately
felt. It was as though I were looking at a portrait into which he had moved
her soul. Even more sickening was the curious air exuded by model daughter and artist father. A soft, warm and satisfying rapport between a loving
father and daughter – that I can understand. But there was something
more than father and daughter to their secrecy. It was plain to see that
they wanted their intimacy for themselves. Though the two of them welcomed me quite politely, I felt like I was being kept at a distance.

Our daughter, now three years married and her first child just over a
year old, was seated upright on the sofa with a prosperous and elegant
beauty quite unlike that of her maiden years. As I was admiring my daughter in her prime, I was struck with a blinding, shocking realization. Right!
It was just about that very age! My husband's separation from his first
wife in the confusion of the war took place when she was as old as our
daughter was now. Moreover, this daughter was not my own, but had been
born to my husband and his first wife. Daughters always resemble their
mothers and there was no question that my husband recalled through his
daughter the appearance of his wife when he left her behind in the North.
Though I was considerably younger than that woman, I was the one, now
growing old and ugly, at my husband's side, while that woman lived within
my husband's heart, glowing with our daughter's present youth and beauty.
As I realized this, I felt jealousy raising its viper's head. The accommodation of a woman's jealousy generally requires a hank of hair for her to grab.
But, at this moment, whose hair could I grab? I had no choice but to seem
ordinary and restrained – a difficult and painful task. Insistent feelings of
jealousy gave way to a sense of utter disappointment, as if I had lived my
life so far in vain.

I had thrown myself energetically into the task of living, but ... To have
pitied and then loved and then even married this unknown painter of
insecure occupation, twelve years older than me, who had left his parents
and wife behind in the North and come south as a penniless refugee with
a baby daughter on his back; to have smoothed away the distress of this
womanless man and motherless child and to have loved them and waited

upon their needs; these years now seemed, to my chagrined eyes, more like a lost labour. The more I mulled over this feeling of having lived in vain, deceived, the more I felt disgust and let it show in the grimace on my face. My husband and daughter asked solicitously if I were feeling all right. I answered that there were some things distressing me and that I should like to get away and knock around by myself for a while.

'All alone, in the middle of winter!' More than just surprised, my husband was nonplussed. It had been bitterly cold for several days. Through the studio window, I could see the skeletal roadside trees and sparsely peopled, frozen pavements below. I was suddenly overwhelmed with emotion at the sight of winter in this dismal city. Now my talk of a trip, proffered at first only as a complaint, came back to me invested with the feeling of a realistic plan. I made up my mind on the spot that I would get out of town. More than wishing to leave Seoul or to get away from my husband's side, I wanted to cast aside like worn-out shoes this life I had fashioned so perseveringly and to live free and unfettered. As if the bleak winter day outside had taught me that my life had been a complete waste, I suddenly felt an unreasoning yearning for the winter scenery of some distant place. Not caring whether my husband and daughter would be suspicious or surprised, I agitated to leave immediately.

'Well, I guess there's a time for even you to be temperamental!'

With that degree of understanding, my husband gave me a generous amount of spending money, while advising me that I would be best off going to a hot spring since it was winter. I left my husband with the mentality of someone who had just discovered that a cherished treasure was a fake and, as a first reaction, tossed it aside out of disgust.

I went to Onyang by the most convenient means. No sooner had I stepped from the express bus into the unfamiliar street than I was seized by the cold and a feeling of loneliness. The unfamiliarity of the scene before my eyes brought me to the brink of tears. My mood of unfettered freedom was no match for the alien and unwelcoming streets of the hot springs. It seemed most unlikely that I would settle into such a mood. Only my body had ventured forth. In the face of this I smiled grimly as I realized I was tied to patterns of living that had long since permeated my being. With the ample funds from my husband, I headed towards the tourist hotel but then, turning on my heels, found a cheap, second-rate inn. As is my habit when buying sesame oil, I seriously questioned whether their hot-spring water was the real thing. Nevertheless, I took one bath after another despite the inevitable enervation, as if I were saving the cost of a public bath from the charge for the room at the inn. The next morning I was disgusted by their breakfast tray, in spite of its fifteen side dishes, as if I had been bored by such food for days on end. It was actually only my second meal there. I felt like I had been away from home a long time, but in fact I had spent no more than one night away. This realization saddened me to tears.

An errand boy at the inn came to ask whether I was leaving or whether I would stay another day. I felt as if the boy would feel sorry for me if I said I was staying, and so I told him I was leaving right away. Having packed my small overnight bag and emerged onto the street, I felt like I had been driven from the inn by that boy, just as I had been driven from the house by my husband and daughter. The cold here was every bit as severe as it was in Seoul. The lowering sky and harsh wind were well suited to my bitter ruminations on my feeling of fraudulence at having lived wastefully until now.

The streets of this small hot-springs town were not very extensive. Though I made the rounds of the place a dozen times, it didn't take even an hour. I dropped into the tourist hotel and had a cup of coffee. If I was to pretend to my husband that I had stayed at the tourist hotel, then I ought to have some idea of what the interior is like, I thought. Across the street from the hotel, I caught sight of a bus terminal. Antiquated buses, posted with the names of unfamiliar destinations, were turning over their tired motors as the passengers were being called. I saw a way out of my plight. Grabbing anyone I could find, I asked if there weren't some scenic or historical spots worth visiting nearby. The bus girl jumped down from a bus that had just begun to leave and, before I had a chance to say anything, swept me up like so much baggage. I stumbled aboard and found a seat. With less than a dozen passengers, the interior was deserted. The vinyl seat was as cold as a slab of ice.

'Where are we headed?' I asked in an apprehensive voice as the bus gathered speed.

'I'm to let you off at the lake, right?' the bus girl announced, as if I had at some point asked her to take me as far as the lake.

'Lake?'

'Yes, the lake. It's the only place around here that has any good scenery. Except for in the winter, we have all sorts of passengers going there!'

Less than five minutes later, the bus girl demanded my fare and, saying we had arrived at the lake, shoved me off the bus. There was, indeed, a lake there. Solidly frozen, surrounded by a low, bare mountain, it looked gloomy and opaque, as if the sullen sky had simply sat down on the spot. Then, all of a sudden, a jealous wind licked fiercely at the icy surface of the lake and swept up towards me, slapping my cheeks heartlessly like a whip. I hastened to reboard the bus. But it had already left for the next stop, leaving only dust in its wake. Close to tears of utter defeat, I first of all hurried to the lakeside shopping area to escape the harsh wind. A rather large signboard reading *Pleasure Park* hung high above the arched entrance to the shopping area, suggesting the prosperity it enjoyed in any season but winter. But now the shutters on the restaurants, tearooms, variety shops and gift shops were tightly closed and there was no sign of habitation. There were only faded signs rattling dismally with each gust of wind, worsening my feeling of desolation. Several open-air Ping-Pong tables lay coated with frozen snow and layer upon layer of dust; it made a miserable sight, like filthy bedspreads scattered about. There seemed to be not a single occupied building. I felt so helpless I could only wish it was just a dream. I made one tour of the shopping area and again confronted the frozen lake spread out before me. Although it was impossible to launch a boat on a lake that was frozen solid, it was also impossible to throw oneself in to drown. This did not seem the least fortunate; rather, I thought it fearful.

I went searching recklessly into yet another alley. And, indeed, at some distance down this otherwise lifeless alley I could see a house with a tidy front and an open gate with a sign that read *Lodgings*. Spent coal briquettes were stacked by the main gateway and, within the courtyard, white laundry hung frozen to a clothesline, twisted into queer shapes. In a trembling voice I called for the innkeeper. A presentable woman in her fifties emerged from the main building, smiling a warm welcome. Upon seeing her I relaxed as if I had come to my own house and, indeed, wished I were a child for whom she would care. This woman had an intriguing aura. Something about her seemed to wrap me in protection, warm and good and generous, like quilted clothing. I felt as if something I had long forgotten had made its way back to me.

'I was hoping to thaw out a little before moving on. Do you have a warm room available?'

The woman promptly led the way to one of several guest rooms in the front wing of the house and slipped her hand under a taffeta quilt that was spread over the warmest spot on the heated floor. It seemed warm enough, but she was troubled by the chilly drafts. Sorry for the trouble, I asked the woman if I really looked all that cold. I was moved to laughter, but my frozen cheeks would not form into a smile of their own accord.

'Yes, you look just like an icicle. For heaven's sake, let's go into the family room! The floor is all warmed up and we have a heater there too.'

And so, with unreserved sisterly affection, she led me into the main building. In addition to the heater, a curtain had been hung around the inside of the family room, making it as dim and cosy as the interior of a cave. At first I thought there was nobody else in the room, but as my eyes became accustomed to the gloom, I could see an old lady decorously seated at the warm end of the room. The desiccated old lady, looking like a mummy draped with clothing, stared at me without expression and shook her head to the left and right. Since her behaviour signalled disapproval, I hung back, awkwardly. But the woman insisted on drawing me to the warm end of the room and, seating me there, put my hands under the quilt that the old lady had spread out to sit upon. The old lady's lips smiled a little. But she did not stop shaking her head. The woman told me that this was her mother-in-law and then said to the old lady that I was a guest whom she had invited into the family room since I was so cold. And with that, introductions and greetings between me and the old lady were completed. But the old lady continued her head-shaking as before. The woman offered no explanation.

Although gaunt, the erectly seated old lady possessed a singular elegance: her neatly combed white hair was done up in a chignon, and a soft wool sweater was draped over her traditional silk jacket with its crisp white collar. It was, indeed, an extremely unreal elegance. Compared with what I had seen at first, her head-shaking had abated considerably, now looking more like she was swaying in a gentle breeze. I thought perhaps she might stop after a while, but no matter how long I waited she didn't stop. As my body thawed, I became drowsy. Honeyed sleep was overwhelming me – even if someone had proposed to kill me, I would have had to sleep on it.

'I'm pretty well thawed out now. I think I'll have a nap in that room we were just in. Oh, yes, how many minutes between buses back to the hot springs?'

'Minutes? In the winter we have only two in the morning and two in the afternoon. Since the one you came on was the last morning bus, the next one will be about four-thirty. Well, now, how about lunch? I'll be preparing some anyway, so why don't you have something to eat before you go?'

All I could think of was sleep – food was the furthest thing from my mind, but I told her to go ahead. The woman thanked me over and over again. I felt pity, believing that she was fussing so much over the little bit she would make by selling one meal. When I arrived at my room, I stretched out on the nice hot floor, pulled the taffeta quilt over me, and fell into a deep sleep.

The head-shaking old lady was the first thing that came to my mind as I woke up. While it was still unclear to me whether I had seen her in a dream or in reality, the picture of the withered old lady shaking her head floated vividly before me. The curiosity I had deferred because of my sleepiness slowly reasserted itself. I looked at my watch – it wasn't even two o'clock.

'Are you still asleep, ma'am? I expect you're hungry.'

I heard the woman's quiet voice outside the paper door. I stirred a bit and slid it open. The woman, an apron wrapped around her waist, welcomed me out of sleep with the very same show of pleasure as when she had greeted my arrival at her house. She was so pleased to see me up that I even wondered if perhaps she hadn't mistaken me for one of those guests who take some sort of medicine and dispatch themselves to eternal sleep.

The lunch tray soon arrived. Her rather well-made preserves, including marinated sesame leaves, unripened hot peppers and wild carrots, and the other foods – the kimchi, the spicy radish chunks, the steamy radish soup – were not the least bit like what is served in commercial places. They were gratifyingly similar to what you might receive if you dropped in on country relatives. But my mouth was parched and my appetite did not respond. When she saw me gulp down only the bowl of soup, the woman brought me another hot bowl of radish soup. Urging her to join me in the meal, I drew the woman down to sit beside me.

'Oh my, that's not at all necessary! I ate earlier with Mother.'

Since the woman was first to bring up the subject of her mother, I was able to ask naturally about the old lady's head-shaking.

'Your mother doesn't appear to be much pleased with me. Though she didn't say anything, she was shaking her head all the while I was in the room.'

'She's been doing that for some twenty-five years now.'

'Twenty-five years!' I was too startled to close my mouth.

'Yes. Twenty-five years, day in and day out, except for when she sleeps . . .'

I thought I saw the woman's eyes grow moist, but her manner of speaking was composed and tranquil.

To shake her head day in and day out, except when asleep, for twenty-five years was, she explained, her mother-in-law's task in life. When she was healthy and in a good mood, the shaking would be serene, barely visible, as if her head were waving in a gentle breeze; when she was in poor health, the movement would become more pronounced and laborious; and when she was agitated or upset by the household, the movement would grow even stronger and more determined until she would be chaotically shaking her head for dear life as if ranting, 'I don't know! I don't know, I tell you!' They had scraped together whatever money they could lay hands on and tried all kinds of Chinese herbal medicines and even the most highly rated acupuncturist, but all to no avail. She herself was inevitably the first to be worn down; her mother-in-law, on the other hand, though it was distressing, rigorously devoted herself to doing this thing as if it were some fated task she could not set aside until her dying day.

This was a condition that had developed suddenly during the war. My hostess's young husband, who had been a township administrator when the war broke out, was unable to flee in time and had to go into hiding. At first, he hid inside their house, but when the ardour of the new circle that came to power began to turn bloodthirsty, hiding at home became so dangerous that it was out of the question.

Late one night, under cover of darkness, the woman transferred her husband to her family's home village at the foot of Kwangdŏk Mountain, some 5 miles from their house. They did their job so well that only she and her mother-in-law knew of it. Conditions only continued to worsen. Informing became rampant as neighbour turned against neighbour, kin against kin, accusing one another of being 'reactionaries' – the business had so spread that not a day passed without some bloody and ugly incident in one village or another. These were ugly times. Things had reached the point where the woman began to feel she couldn't rely on her own mother-in-law. What would happen if this unsophisticated old lady, honest to a fault and quite incapable of doubting others, were to fall for someone's deception and disclose her husband's whereabouts? It was not a world meant for people like her mother-in-law.

The woman relentlessly drilled her mother-in-law to say 'I don't know,' as if she were teaching multiplication tables to a thick-headed child.

'In any case, Mother, simply say you don't know. Even if the most remarkable person in the world asks, you simply must say you don't know where Daddy is. You must insist that he left the house the day the war broke out and you don't know what's become of him since. Lives are lost these days because of a little loose talk. Even if Daddy's brothers ask, you simply must say you don't know. Even neighbours like Ippŭni's grand-mother or Kaettongi's grandmother, even if they ask, you simply must say you don't know. You can't trust anyone. There, do you understand, Mother?'

The woman helped her mother-in-law energetically, even with the head-shaking, and they practised the 'I don't know' over and over again. Day after day, alone or not, a frightened and lonely expression on her face, the older woman earnestly practised saying 'I don't know, I don't know,' shaking her head at the same time.

Simple villagers, hearing only that war had broken out, were killing and being killed by one another as if possessed by the spirit of the legendary Chinese pillager Tao Zhi. And in this village that had never once heard the sound of a cannon, suddenly planes had come to strafe and bomb without pause, and for days on end gunfire crackled in the surrounding hills like roasting beans. Then came silence, deep as death. One or two of the villagers, who had been cringing in their houses, still as dead rats, cautiously craned their necks outside but then quickly shrank back in again. They still hesitated to talk among themselves. There was no evidence that the Reds had left, yet nothing to indicate that they remained. There was no sign of the gangsters who had joined up with them and taken power, but their flag still fluttered from the pole in the yard of the village headman's house, which had been used by the People's Committee.

At this precarious and uncertain time, the woman's impetuous husband had stolen back to their house in the dead of night. Seoul had already been recovered, it seemed. The Reds had held out here, but how many more days could they last?

It was after the kimchi cabbage had been planted in the kitchen garden and into the season of Cool Winds, when young pumpkins, grown waxy, ripen so well. Mother-in-law, who had pushed through the morning dew out into the back garden to pick the pumpkins, suddenly gave out a rending cry.

'I don't know, I don't know! I really don't know, I tell you!'

It was a ghastly shriek, one that raised gooseflesh and made the blood run cold. The woman ran out and, in a moment of bewilderment, her husband joined her. For a moment, they had lost all discretion. Just around the corner of the outhouse, three or four tired and ragged People's Army soldiers, probably stragglers, had the barrels of their rifles levelled at Mother-in-law. They, too, looked startled. It may well be that they never intended to cause anyone harm but, rather, that they'd met up with Mother-in-law by accident or that, having met her, they were going to ask for food or clothing. But, before they could say a word, Mother-in-law – nailed motionless to the spot – had shaken her head madly and repeated in a high, shrill scream like someone deranged, 'I don't know! I don't know!' In the moment it would take to catch the bloodthirsty glint in one of the stragglers' eyes, his rifle swung towards the woman's husband and sprayed bullets. The woman's husband toppled over, a wretched sight, and they took flight. This event had taken place in only an instant.

Thereafter the mother-in-law had seemed nearly deranged. After long and devoted care, she recovered somewhat. But although the head-shaking, in which she engaged so strenuously upon her son's death at the corner of the outhouse, diminished in intensity, it remained a chronic condition that she couldn't halt. And so she became known to the neighbourhood as Grandmother No-No, a local character.

The woman told this story with distance and detachment, not the least bit garrulous.

'And now, rather than thinking I should find a cure, my only thought is that I must help her.'

'Help her? In what way?'

'As something she is not doing of her own free will, this must be very tiring. I do my best to see that she has three meals a day, that she is physically comfortable, and, well, that sort of thing. Can't I do that little bit until the day she completes her great undertaking and departs from this world?'

I closed my mouth in failure as I tried to laugh at the woman's joke of referring to the endless days of demented head-shaking as a 'great undertaking.' Her attitude was not at all a joking one after all. Indeed, the woman's face even shone dimly with the pride and sense of duty of someone who was actually assisting wholeheartedly in a great undertaking. A shiver passed down my back as I wondered if perhaps this woman was the one accomplishing the great undertaking.

Lunch and the room together came to eight hundred *wŏn*, she said. Giving her a thousand *wŏn*, I asked her to keep it all. The woman fussed and bowed and thanked me so much that I felt uncomfortable. She had done the same when I ordered lunch, but, in all, only a tiny profit would be left from the thousand *wŏn*. For this, she was so obsequious? The reason I found her obsequious attitude so distasteful may well have been that I liked and esteemed the woman so much. Furthermore, the woman's obsequiousness seemed unnatural to her and, being awkward and out of keeping, all the more ugly.

The woman carefully put the thousand *wŏn* into the pocket of her cardigan and, having made a very relieved and grateful face, said something strange.

'With this as my travel money, I shall go to Seoul. Today.'

'Seoul? On such a cold day!'

Having made this remark about the cold weather, I realized with surprise that my response was the same as that of my husband when I had told him I was going on this trip. I suddenly missed my husband, to the point of sadness.

'My son, an only son, attends university in Seoul. The boy was riding on my back that day when he innocently witnessed his father's encounter with those men. That boy, he's already so grown-up! He's done his army service and is now in his third year at university. You know, he's really a good, trustworthy child.'

'But it should be the middle of the winter break now.'

'Yes. But he's tutoring some children to earn extra money and so he couldn't come back home. I'm quite able to earn all he needs for tuition and such, but, well, that's what he says, anyway. It's lonely like this only during the winter, but from spring to autumn business is pretty good here. During the tourist season, especially on Sundays, we were running short of rooms and the place was a madhouse. I made enough to cover tuition and lodging for the new term, and I tucked it away. We have more than enough food stored away to tide us over the winter. If other businesses do as well, the owners close up and go home for a rest during the winter. We're an inn and this is also our family home, but we always keep one or two guest rooms heated and ready for customers. It's not to make money. We simply enjoy offering a warm room to uninformed visitors who, like yourself, sometimes come looking for the lake. Really. On such occasions we honestly give no thought to money. But, of course, if they happen to leave a bit so I can get a little meat or something for Mother, that's always nice. But today, that's not the case. Today, I actually waited for a guest, shamelessly calculating the income in advance; if you hadn't come by, I don't know what would have happened. Thank you, ma'am.'

This time, instead of the servile bowing, she warmly grasped my hand. That put me in a much better mood than the bowing had. But I was still just as ignorant of the situation as before.

'Well, you see, yesterday this strange letter arrived from Seoul.'

'From your son?'

'No. It was from the lady of the house where my son is boarding. She says it's been more than a week since he was last seen there. Ordinarily, in the case of a student with lax morals, she wouldn't tell tales about such a thing, she said, but my son was altogether too conscientious. Wondering if maybe something was up, she was letting me know and suggesting that I might want to visit and make some enquiries. And that was the letter. Couldn't even a conscientious student have stayed at a friend's for a few days, leaving what is not really a home to him but just a boarding house? I suppose as mistress of the house she really shouldn't write letters alarming other people, but I guess I'm even worse, thinking every possible frightful thought. I couldn't sleep a wink last night but ransacked my mind from every crazy angle and finally worked out something kind of, well, superstitious.'

'Superstitious, you say?'

'A silly idea, really. I told myself that if a guest came by our inn today, and I used that money to go to Seoul, then I'd find nothing wrong with my son, but, if I broke open that tightly wrapped packet of tuition money and used some to cover the travel expenses, then I would find something wrong with my son. That's all. I can't tell you what a bad time I had of it, so nervous and anxious, waiting for a guest once I had made up my mind. But you came and made it all come out the right way. I really do thank you.'

The woman thanked me yet again. My heart nearly burst with pity and compassion for this widowed woman who eased her enormous concern for her son's situation by such curious means. The idea that I had brought her good fortune was not the least unpleasant.

'So, I guess you'll be leaving soon.'

'Yes, everything's ready. I asked our neighbour to help with Mother. And now, with the four-thirty bus to the hot springs, I'll be all set.'

'So, we're travelling together!'

'Indeed, so we are. You'd said you'd take the four-thirty to the hot springs . . .'

'No, I mean we'll travel together all the way to Seoul.'

I decided in an instant that I would return to Seoul as well. An inexpressible peace of mind swept over me. I followed the woman into the family room when she went to tell her mother-in-law goodbye. The hands of this mother and daughter, similarly old, held each other tightly.

'Mother, I'm off to Seoul. I have a few things to buy, and I want to see T'aeshik, who's on winter break but says he has to stay there and study. Samsuni from next door is going to keep an eye on you, Mother. Please don't worry about anything and be sure to eat well.'

She might not have actually understood, but the old lady gently waved her head back and forth as always. To me the waving was not 'I don't know, I don't know.' Instead, it seemed more like 'Daughter, there's nothing wrong with T'aeshik, really nothing at all. What sin of ours could be so great that even that boy would have to suffer for it?'

I suddenly wanted to add my hand on top of the still clasped hands of this mother and daughter. There was something flowing freely between those two hands – the intimate hands of strangers, the hands of partners in a great undertaking – something that I wished to measure, to feel and to keep long in my memory. As if this were my first and last opportunity to come into contact with the one thing among all things in this world that was not false, I did it with gratitude. To the two rough but warm hands I added my own weak hand, reverently.

'Peace be with you, Grandmother.'

The old lady's head swayed gently back and forth, but I could feel what she was saying.

'You have not lived your life in vain. Certainly not! By no means have you lived in vain!'

CHO CHŎNGNAE

Land of Exile

Translated by Marshall R. Pihl

'Please, mister . . . I'm old and worthless and my only wish is to close my eyes in peace. I beg you, have pity on me.'

The old man fervently rubbed his palms together. He could scarcely have been more ardent before the Buddha himself. And, as if that were not enough, he knelt on the floor.

'This really isn't necessary, sir,' said the director. 'I fully understand your difficulty. Here, now, won't you have a seat?' He made an awkward attempt to help the old man up.

'Please, mister, promise you'll take him,' the old man pleaded, bending even lower.

'All right. I'll see that he's admitted,' the director managed to answer, distress showing on his face.

'Oh, thank you, mister! I'll never forget your heavenly grace, even when I've passed on to the next world.'

Still kneeling, the old man bowed two or three times, palms pressed tight against his chest. His eyes misted over with tears.

'Sir, please take a seat.'

Why didn't he just leave the boy at the gate and disappear without all this pleading? I'd have taken him in anyway, thought the director.

The old man reseated himself with some reluctance in the chair, then groped in his pocket, sniffing continuously.

'Here, mister – it's all the money I've got. Take it, will you? It's not much but it's a token of my gratitude.'

There in the old man's rough hand were two creased ten-thousand-*wŏn* notes.

'No, no, no. Keep it, sir, and use it for medicine or something. We'll take care of the boy.'

'Take it, I'm begging you. The last expression of the heart of a useless father. If you won't accept it, then how will I be able to turn and leave? Please, mister, take it.'

The old man's tear-filled eyes spoke many times more fervently than his words.

'Well, if you insist.'

The director accepted the money from the old man's trembling hands.

'And here's some underwear for him.'

The old man briefly rubbed his eyes with the back of his hand and then proffered a small bundle.

'Oh, yes.'

As the director took the bundle, he heard a groan of paternal emotion.

'I would have bought an extra change of clothes, but after I got him the underwear I didn't have enough money, you see.'

The old man spoke as if to assuage his guilt, biting back tears that worked the corners of his mouth.

'There's no cause for concern.'

'And please take good care of this.'

The old man carefully produced an old scrap of paper. The director read at a glance the six syllables laboriously drawn on the paper: 'Father is Ch'ŏn Mansŏk.'

'This is my name. "Mansŏk" means "ten thousand bushels." They say my grandfather gave it to me. The life of a poor commoner is nothing but hopes and sorrows, and he wanted me to have this name so I'd become a rich man with ten thousand sacks of rice. But look at me now.'

The old man heaved a deep sigh of despair.

'I know I'm a poor excuse for a father, but I thought he should at least know my name.'

'Yes, of course. Every son must have a father. It's only natural that he should know.'

As he spoke, the director examined the old man anew. Here before him was a man with a pitiful fate, worn out by life and withered like a fallen leaf.

The old man called his son back in from the hallway. Though he had said his son was six, the boy looked thin and scrawny, like a wild melon vine in a drought – he was probably malnourished. The child's wretched appearance prompted new pangs of sorrow in the old man.

It'd be a mistake to stay with him to the bitter end, the old man thought suddenly. A father's remorse, rehearsed countlessly before his visit here.

'No matter how hard your life is, you're not helping yourself by neglecting your health like this. You'll have to be more careful. Don't slack off or you'll be in trouble.'

The doctor's words had shattered Mansŏk's belief that he would be with his son until the end. That ugly picture showing a jumble of bones – what the doctor called an X-ray – seemed to say that his life was like a candle burning low.

Even before the old man had talked himself into visiting the hospital, he suspected how ill he was. Even before he began bleeding from the mouth, there had been other symptoms. His body would shake strangely if he drank, and as the days passed, he had found it increasingly difficult to exert himself. His co-workers, who worked hard and so ate heartily, were aware of the decline in his health even before the doctor.

He began to fear he might breathe his last on the job or on the street. Either way, it would have amounted to abandoning his son as an orphan. Would he live another year? Another two years? He had no way of knowing. Entrusting the child to an orphanage was the only way, he thought, to maintain the family line.

'Ch'ŏlsu, from now on you'll be living here with the director. I want you to do what the man says. Understand?'

As he spoke, the old man bent down and searched the child's small face.

'And you, Daddy?' the child asked briefly, looking into his old father's eyes.

'There you go again. I keep telling you I'll find your mother and bring her back!'

The old man deliberately used a sharp voice.

'When?' countered the child anxiously, all the while staring directly into his father's eyes.

'The moment I find her . . .'

'What if you don't find her?' the child persisted.

The old man was speechless for a moment. Cold sorrow filled his heart.

'I'll be back. I'll find your mum and bring her back . . . honest,' said the old man confidently.

'Daddy, you promise.'

The boy stuck out his little finger. But instead of hooking it with his own to seal the promise, the old man stared intently at his son.

Poor little kid. Why did you have to be born to the likes of me and end up this way? I want you to grow up strong and healthy, well fed . . . Poor little kid.

'Daddy, promise!'

'Okay, okay.'

The old man stuck out his finger, suppressing the massive sobs that surged and tore at his throat.

A small, slender finger linked in midair with a thick, rough finger.

'Daddy, you've got to find Mum and bring her back,' said the boy, squeezing and shaking his father's finger as he spoke.

'Okay, okay.'

'I'm going to pray every night that you find Mum quick.'

'Okay, okay.'

The old man fought back his tears.

My sweet little boy. How are you going to make it all alone? If I had only known, I wouldn't have let you be born. What a useless fuck-up I've been . . . Poor little kid . . .

'Ch'ŏlsu, you be sure to mind the director, now. He won't let you go hungry or make you sleep on straw sacks. It's going to be a lot better here than living with Daddy. Now, you mind what the director says. Understand?'

The boy, perhaps anticipating the impending separation, nodded sullenly.

'Now then, Ch'ŏlsu, come along,' said the director, signalling that the time had come.

The old man unhooked his finger from his son's and straightened up, then nudged the boy towards the director. The boy's thin back resisted the prodding with a pressure that passed through the old man's hand and spread hotly through his body.

'No cause for concern,' said the director, precipitating the farewell.

'I hope . . . you . . .'

The old man bowed deeply several times, but in the end he couldn't get the words out. He seemed to hesitate over his threadbare satchel, but then hurriedly turned and left the office.

'Daddy!'

The old man didn't look back.

He went down the hallway, and as he shuffled out onto the playground the tears finally gushed forth.

'Daddyyy! You've got to find Mummy and bring her back!'

Across the playground, at the main entrance to the orphanage, he could still hear the boy's ringing cries. The old man had intended not to turn around, but that simply was not to be.

He turned. His son, the director's hands on his shoulders, was standing in the vestibule, waving.

'Daddyyy! You'd better come back.'

The old man turned away as tears welled up once again.

'That bitch should be drawn and quartered! Abandoning the poor little kid and running off . . .'

The old man trembled and angrily clenched his teeth.

His wife's face, laughing mindlessly, appeared before his tear-blurred eyes.

'Worthless bitch!'

He hurled insults as if somebody were actually there in front of him. Then he wiped his eyes quickly with the back of his hand. The illusion of his wife disappeared without a trace.

Hatred raged again like fire in his heart. He had spent two years searching the countryside, carrying the little boy on his back, determined to spare neither of them once he caught up with the pair.

'What a stupid fool I was!'

The old man released a despondent sigh. He was tormented as much by the undying hatred he felt for his wife as he was by feelings of remorse.

What notion of glory had possessed him, a homeless common labourer, to set his sights on such a blossom? Though he had been a party to the affair, it still made no sense to him at all. The only thing it had brought was regret. It vexed the old man beyond endurance to know that if he had steered clear back then, he would not now be putting his son into a stranger's hands.

'Why do you still live alone, Mr Ch'ŏn? Aren't you lonely?'

When a woman began to make advances like that he knew he should reject them outright. But he felt agitated, like a cat that had caught the smell of fish.

'Why do you ask such questions when you live alone yourself? Aren't *you* lonely?'

But even as he parried, his nose began to tingle at the woman's smell, which made him feel so odd.

'Since no one will have me, I live by myself, facing this hard life alone. I was born to be lonely – what can I do about it?' she said, suddenly dispirited.

The old man found he was pitying her, but he could feel his heart hammering at the same time.

How stupid can you get? I've spent half my life on the run or else hiding out. How could I be sucked in by the smell of a woman?

He had to steady his throbbing heart. He had to hold out. If he couldn't, he'd have to leave this construction job for another.

This construction project provided plenty of work – unusual for winter. The industrial complex was to begin operating by spring, and before then they had to finish not only the buildings themselves but the workers' apartments too. So, jobs were abundant and the daily pay was not only generous but always on time.

For over thirty years he had wandered from one construction project to another, but he had never come across one as lucrative as this. And it was winter. If a lucrative job can lead to problems, then this one sure had.

'Life is so short, Mr Ch'ŏn. What do you do for fun?'

'What sort of crap is this?'

'Is this your idea of a good time, drinking *soju* every night?'

The woman stared directly at him as she poured him a drink.

'Does anyone drink for fun? If I was having fun, I wouldn't be swilling this stuff.'

'Then we'll have to find some real fun for you.'

'What sort of "real fun"? I just work and eat, one day at a time.'

He tossed down his drink and crunched on some pickled radish.

'Who says you have to "just work and eat, one day at a time" without the pleasures of a wife and kids? What kind of life have you had, Mr Ch'ŏn, living this long without a family? Maybe you think you'll live forever, but you'll get old, and what if you suddenly get ill? Think about it. And who's going to bury you when you die? Who'd offer even a bowl of cold water to your memory after you're dead and gone? You drift through this world following construction jobs. Do you intend to be a wandering ghost in the next world?'

'What is this shit? Why the hell are you running off at the mouth like this?' he shouted, suddenly alarmed.

'Oh, dear! I'm scared to death! Come on, don't get angry and just think for a moment. Am I wrong to say this to a man who still lives by himself?'

'Lay off! Tease a leper for being a leper and he gets angry . . .'

'Then it's not too late – if you'll just give up the leper's life.'

'What are you saying?'

As he studied the florid eyes of this laughing woman, he felt something like an electric shock stinging his groin.

Since this woman Sunim worked at a soup-and-rice house she saw Mansŏk once a day when he came to eat. Vague rumour had it that she had once been married but was driven out, and that the owner of the soup-and-rice house was some distant relative. One thing was clear: she was not one of those barmaids who litter a construction project like rags.

Sunim's words forced Mansŏk to reconsider his circumstances. Sunim had probed, as if with tweezers, at a very painful spot. These ideas had crossed his mind from time to time, but he always tried to forget, to put them out of his mind. On days when these thoughts did come to him, he would get more drunk than ever.

He had experienced countless women while wandering from one construction project to another over the last thirty years. The relation-ships were not based on emotion, but were business transactions. If people looked on manual labourers as the dregs of humanity, then what was to be said of the women who lived off them, spreading their legs to fill their gullets? No matter how long you waited, you'd never hear one of them talk like Sunim just had.

Actually, it had been altogether too long since Mansŏk had heard such words, full of feeling and concern for his future – especially from a woman who was not a barmaid or a prostitute. Mansŏk almost forgot how short of money he was, or that he was forty-nine. Struggling with his surging feelings, he knew he couldn't dismiss these thoughts as easily as in the past.

Why her interest in an old man like him, Mansŏk had asked, when there were so many younger construction workers coming and going at the soup-and-rice house?

'I don't know why. I just felt that way,' she answered, her words trailing off and her face flushing.

'If I'm forty-nine and you're thirty-three, how many years do you think separate us?'

'Deep feelings, like the Great Wall, withstand time,' answered Sunim, quoting history.

'My aching back . . .'

Mansŏk could say no more.

Hearing Sunim's words, Mansŏk began some personal calculations. He wanted to raise kids to follow after him. If he cut way back on his drinking and saved on eating out, he would probably have enough to support a family. If he tightened his belt and lived frugally, then he might be able to sink some roots and be done with the life of a wanderer. She might be the mate he was meant to have and so live a normal life.

This forty-nine-year-old bag of bones, worn out by a life of manual labour, was suddenly revitalized, like a spring tree bursting out in buds. Even his spirits, once always clouded with gloom, now cleared suddenly like the skies in autumn. The booze he used to drink nearly every day barely touched his lips. And he took overtime on the night shift he had once so carefully avoided. Still, he felt no weariness. It was as if he had regained the strength he had known at twenty, when he had worked himself bone-weary in order to bring Chŏmnye home as his bride.

After three months of struggle, he had a tidy sum of money in hand.

'Well, I've saved enough to get us a rented room,' Mansŏk said awkwardly to Sunim.

'Already? I guess I had you pegged right all along! Those younger ones could never have managed this. Oh, how I've waited for this day!'

Sunim was so much more happy and pleased than he had ever expected.

They didn't need a wedding ceremony. They rented a room and set up housekeeping.

Mansŏk's sudden taking of a bride didn't go unnoticed among the loud-mouths at the workplace.

'Better watch out! One whiff of a thirty-year-old woman, and a fifty-year-old man can fall on his face.'

'Sure, sure. At twenty a woman's clam may be soft and fleshy, but at thirty it's tight and sticky. You'll come on to her like a stallion at first but she'll turn you to jelly before you're done!'

Mansŏk gave a broad, indecent grin.

'Eat your hearts out, you shits! I still have what it takes to produce ten sons.'

Actually, Mansŏk couldn't have been happier. His much-too-long life as a wanderer was finally at an end. And now hope began to appear dimly for a future that had once seemed sad and gloomy. He had resigned him-self to the idea that you had to fight your way through life with just your bare fists. But, to some extent, that was an idea that belonged to an earlier time of frustration. The desire to live like a normal person had always lain hidden deep inside his heart.

The evening they moved into their 'bridal chamber,' Mansŏk's heart was alive with the sorrow and pain of times past.

'I can tell from the way you talk that you're from the Chŏlla region, but is this the first time you've been married?' asked Sunim after they had finished their first round of lovemaking to mark the marriage.

'So what if this is the first, or the tenth, or even the twentieth time I've married?' Mansŏk countered brusquely. He was absorbed by other thoughts.

'So what? Well, it's just that I find myself worrying about things, now that we're married.'

'Then worry about the worms you might have cooked into the food! I don't have a wife and kids somewhere else, if that's what's bugging you. Why don't you think about our future instead?'

'But shouldn't I know where your home is, why you turned into a wan-derer, where your parents and brothers and sisters live?'

'Oh, shut up!'

Mansŏk sat bolt upright in bed, his angry eyes bulging with fearsome danger.

'What are you, the town clerk? A policeman? Why are you poking around, digging up useless scraps of the past? You and me, we're just a couple of people whose eyes happened to meet, who rubbed bellies and now we're trying to live together. What's so important about the past? Why the crazy prying? I had so little to show for my life, so of course I ended up drifting like some cloud. Look, I'm just a plain commoner – no home, no family records. If you need to know that kind of stuff, you'd better pack up and get out – now!'

Mansŏk was agitated – enough so to beat her, perhaps.

'No, no. That's not what I meant at all! I only asked out of concern ... I'm sorry. I won't do it again.'

The scolded wife, Sunim, rolled over and sank into a deep sleep. Mansŏk, staring intently at her gaunt shoulders, felt sorry. All she had done was ask her new husband a polite question and he had let himself get worked up. But he couldn't help it. Because of his past he had spent nearly thirty years hiding out or being chased like a criminal. You could call it a life, but how did it differ from death? Granted the times had changed, but still, he couldn't go home again – proof of his continuing guilt. If he were to go back to his home, where the Ch'oe clan lived, they would probably bury him alive, no questions asked. It was a past he'd never told a soul, ever since he had fled his home under cover of the early evening dusk, driven by gunfire of the People's Army, with which he had sided until the day before.

'Dirty slut!'

Mansŏk gave a shudder. Just the thought of it made his body stiffen, sent the blood rushing to his head. And the scenes of that time flashed into his mind unchanged, as if ignoring the passage of time. His memory had never been very sharp, and by the time he was forty he had begun to forget things that had happened only a few days before. But why was that one time implanted so vividly in his mind? Even photographs turn yellow after thirty years, but this memory didn't know how to change. And it wasn't just appearances that hadn't changed. Even the smells of different scenes remained vivid. Why was this?

'They should have cut the head off her dead body!'

Mansŏk closed his eyes tightly and expelled a hot breath.

If that bitch of a wife Chŏmnye hadn't been completely stripped, I probably wouldn't have killed her. If she'd just been naked from the waist down, I could have overlooked it, thinking she was suffering at the hands of that bastard. But that bitch, already pregnant, took off all her clothes and had a roll in the hay with him.

As deputy leader of the People's Committee, Mansŏk had to be away from his house for two days to deliver a report to the Municipal People's Committee. The journey had been a great boost to Mansŏk's spirits.

'Comrade Ch'ŏn, your revolutionary struggle has been glorious. Your appointment as leader, comrade, is only a matter of time. Have a good trip.'

The words of the People's Army commander, spoken as Mansŏk set out on the road, rang in his ears. If only he could become leader. Unseen by the two subordinates walking beside him, Mansŏk curled his hands into fists. The power he had enjoyed as deputy leader was not enough. It wasn't that he needed reasons to avenge the twenty-five years of hunger he had suffered. But, if only he became leader, all of Kamkol, Hangnae and Chukch'on would be his – it was a sure thing.

Actually, there were more than just one or two things wrong with Sugil, the present leader. He might do rather well for a while, but then there would be times of indecision, when fear or hesitation paralysed him. Sugil had been made leader only because he was three years older than Mansŏk.

Even when Elder Ch'oe's oldest grandson, Hyŏnggyu, was about to be executed, Sugil had wavered like an idiot. The grandson, who had studied law in Seoul, was rumoured to have slipped back into the village. Sugil could have brought the entire Ch'oe household into the matter and ruined them, but he had settled for a secret investigation. For the family had already been devastated by the execution of Elder Ch'oe's son, who had served as town administrator some time before. After four days of hiding, Elder Ch'oe's grandson was apprehended in a bamboo grove dugout at his uncle's house.

He had been dragged out back to a pine tree, his fate clearly determined. Gaunt and tight-lipped, he held his captors in a penetrating stare.

'It was Hyŏnggyu who contributed the pig we sacrificed for my mother's mourning,' whispered Sugil in a trembling voice.

'Does that mean we should let him live?' challenged Mansŏk, giving him no leeway.

'Well, I'm not saying we really have to do this . . .'

'Let us be resolute, Comrade Leader, for the good of the revolution . . .' Mansŏk deliberately raised his voice in imitation of the People's Army commander.

Perhaps sensing something strange afoot, the commander came up behind them.

'What are you two doing?'

Sugil's face froze instantly as he gazed, imploringly, at Mansŏk.

'We were saying how we ought to waste no time in dealing with this reactionary,' replied Mansŏk quickly, all the while keeping an eye on Sugil, whose head now drooped with apparent relief.

'Good! Then deal with him at once!'

At the commander's word, Mansŏk winked a signal to his subordinates. The three men hoisted their bamboo spears and lunged at Elder Ch'oe's grandson, who was tied to the trunk of the pine. Screams, long screams, spread forth – screams that seemed to tear through the mountains, rend the skies, rip open the very earth. Sugil stood rigid as a post, eyes tightly closed. *You good-for-nothing, you don't deserve to be leader*, thought Mansŏk, watching him with a mocking sneer.

Quite unlike Sugil, Mansŏk listened to the drawn-out screams with a pleasure that thrilled every joint in his body. The sense of pleasure was, in fact, one of sweet revenge. All the sorrow and pain and mortification they had all known over generations of slavery, and that he himself had endured for his twenty-five years, was slowly, slowly washed away by that thrilling pleasure. For Mansŏk, this feeling amounted to an exhilaration even more intense and passionate than what he felt on top of his wife, Chŏmnye. That sensation was also maddening in its way, but it was too short-lived, and it was followed by a sudden, precipitous hollowness. But the pleasure he took from the screaming lasted as long as the time it took for the unforgettable memories to float up one after the other and then vanish – and, although he was left with a feeling of loss, there was none of the precipitous hollowness.

Buoyed at the thought of soon becoming council leader, he arrived at the Municipal People's Council. He accepted the urgent directives handed down there and retraced his 12-mile route home that same day.

When he got back to the council office the sun was about to set. After walking some 24 miles this long summer's day, Mansŏk was about as tired as he could be. There was no one in the office. He sent his two subordinates home. He would have to meet with the commander personally in order to convey the directives. After resting a while, his feet up on the desk, Mansŏk suddenly became aware of something. There was no reason the office should be empty like this – unless there had been some sort of emergency. He couldn't just sit around like this – he had to check things out.

Mansŏk went out back towards the attached living quarters. He sensed somebody was there.

Closer to the quarters, Mansŏk paused instinctively. A kind of human presence that felt strange to him emanated from the place. He strained to listen. It was clearly the sound of a man and woman making love. Mansŏk tensed, a queer sensation writhing within him. Involuntarily, he shot searching glances left and right. What brazen fool, in broad daylight, in the council's quarters . . . ? By now he had pressed himself close to the window.

Mansŏk almost cried out. He couldn't identify the man, whose buried face was turned away. But the one on her back, moaning, eyes tightly closed, mouth half open, was his very own Chŏmnye.

Mansŏk's head spun and everything seemed to turn dark. The next instant, a rush of heat burst from his stomach, fed as if by flames.

He grabbed the biggest rock he could find. Then he kicked open the door and jumped inside.

'You slut! You filthy slut!'

The man, spread out on top stiffened abruptly and sat up just as the rock thudded against the back of his head. His naked body vomited up an oddly short scream and tumbled to the floor. At almost the same moment, the naked woman jumped up. Arms crossed over her breasts, blanching with fear, she waddled to a corner of the room. Mansŏk, eyes blazing and teeth clenched, stepped closer to her. Cornered, unable to retreat further, the woman trembled, her nude body shrivelling before his eyes. Mansŏk approached her like an animal. He had come to within one step of her.

'Don't – please!'

And then she darted forward, trying to slip away. Mansŏk kicked her hard in the stomach. She gave a short cry, like the man had, and rolled onto the floor.

Mansŏk ground his teeth fiercely and turned back to the man. The fellow moved spasmodically, blood streaming from his head. An arm, stretched into empty space, twitched. The man seemed to be clutching for something. Mansŏk grabbed the prostrate man's head and turned it towards him, then stepped back in shock.

'No! You bastard!'

It was the People's Army commander. Mansŏk had thought all along the man was from the army. But who would have dreamed it was the commander, someone Mansŏk had trusted like heaven itself? His rage at being deceived, worse than his anger at the sight of his wife's face through the window, pulsed through him. The commander, his eyes rolled back and his arm still outstretched, was writhing towards a Russian-made submachine gun nearby. Mansŏk grabbed the weapon, aimed at the man's groin, and pulled the trigger. A staccato burst.

Mansŏk turned to his wife. In the moment that had just passed, she had steadied herself and was crawling on all fours towards the door. His wife's big buttocks loomed before him. The parts exposed between them seemed like those of a pig, filthy and repulsive. Mansŏk aimed at that spot and again pulled the trigger. Another staccato burst.

When the bullets were exhausted, Mansŏk threw down the gun. The room had become a sea of blood where two sprawled corpses spewed forth their intestines.

Mansŏk had to get away. He ran from the building and lit out towards a path into the mountains.

'The world is a place where we must live according to reason. Who are you? Who do you think you are to beat people as if they were dogs? It won't do, it won't do at all. You'll face the wrath of heaven. The wrath of heaven!'

The sound of his father's voice followed him all the way. He could just glimpse his mother's smudged face. And Mansŏk's three-year-old boy was beaming happily as he called, 'Daddy! Daddy!'

His new wife, Sunim, never again asked about the past and went on managing the household as it should be done. Mansŏk must have been thriving on this life, for he felt like a new man – embracing a young wife and able to sleep with a deep warmth unknown to him before.

The heat shimmered and danced on the far side of the construction site. The apartment complex was moving towards completion on schedule.

'I've been feeling a little strange lately,' said his wife, averting her eyes.

'Maybe it's something you ate,' offered Mansŏk, as if to suggest she buy a bottle of tonic.

'That's not it. The flowers haven't bloomed for two months now.'

'Flowers?' Mansŏk asked. But then a light turned on inside his head.

'Oh, you mean you've had news?' asked Mansŏk, excitement in his voice.

'That's what I mean,' responded his wife, mimicking Mansŏk's tone and giving him an embarrassed glance.

'Just pop us out a son. I'll work hard and take good care of him,' said Mansŏk, grabbing his wife's hand.

'That's disgusting! Children don't "pop out" – they're born.'

His wife laughed bashfully.

'If you'd known I'd have to spend my life crushed under the heels of those rich bastards, you probably wouldn't have let me be born in the first place. And then I wouldn't have had this damn luck.'

'Listen to this crap – he says anything he feels like! At your age, what do you know, boy? When you've lived a few more years you'll understand.'

His father had reproached eighteen-year-old Mansŏk no further.

At age twenty-one Mansŏk had taken a wife, though his heart wasn't in it. He cared little for his parents' concerns and, though he regarded wives as an amusement, this one was unusually well turned out. Her face was so pretty as to be wasted on her low-class status. So it was that he married as if it were something unavoidable, and, having slept with her, he became a father. But he still hadn't woken up to the meaning of the word *father* – hadn't even begun to think about it.

But now he was fifty, and his wife was pregnant. And his father's words of thirty-two years before had come back to him, though he didn't know why. Was it because the years had brought understanding with them, as his father had predicted? Mansŏk was dimly aware of something deep and inexpressible in the notion that we live a life only to continue our bloodline.

As his wife's stomach gradually swelled, work at the construction site was coming to an end. Sunim was frightened at the thought that they would soon have to take to the road in search of another construction site, so she went out job-hunting for him.

'Don't be foolish. What have I ever learned to do? All I know is farming and day labour – what the hell use is it to go job-hunting?'

Mansŏk tried to dissuade her from the outset, but she wouldn't listen. Several days later, she finally found an opening for a security guard. But just as Mansŏk had suspected, he was underqualified even for a job like that, one requiring only night work. He fell short in several respects. They required at least a middle-school education, someone aged thirty-five or younger, a financial guarantor and a background investigation. After asking at a few more places, his wife gave up.

'I've been thinking I might as well go back to the soup-and-rice house. We can't live a wandering life.'

At the mention of the soup-and-rice house, Mansŏk went through the roof: 'We what? Can't what? You rub bellies with me and then decide we're going to live here until we die. Is that it? Now open those ears of yours and listen, before I break off those pretty legs: you just park yourself in a corner and stay put! Whether we eat or go hungry, we'll do as I see fit.'

Mansŏk kicked open the door and went out.

But when he thought it over, his wife's feelings made sense. How could he leave her with a baby in her belly, wandering off to who knows where in search of a job? But then, what else could he do? Besides being uneducated and barely able to read, he was an old man of fifty. When he thought of his age, his future seemed black indeed. It was a question of how long he could continue at manual labour. His daily pay at the construction site was already pegged to a rate different from that of the younger labourers.

There was, however, one person he could go to – Mr Pak, the on-site engineer assigned to the construction of the apartment complex. Even though he was a well-educated young man with an important job, he was quite without arrogance or pride. He was warm and sympathetic even towards the unskilled manual labourers. Mansŏk was by now on good terms with him.

After putting it off several times, Mansŏk finally made up his mind and saw Mr Pak. He spelled out his situation in every detail to the engineer.

'I can see you're up against it. Let me ask around, and then why don't we meet again tomorrow,' said Mr Pak with his usual kindness.

The next day, the engineer had a job ready for him.

'Well, it's not much. You'll have to do odd jobs in the apartment super-intendent's office, and the pay isn't very good. I'm not even sure you'd be interested.'

'Much obliged, Mr Pak! If it's really for me, I'll take it – no questions asked. Much obliged.'

Mansŏk bowed over and over. Good humour now shone where black clouds had once engulfed his heart.

And so Mansŏk became a handyman. The monthly pay was barely enough to put food on the table. Even so, Mansŏk was as happy as if he had plucked a star from the heavens. He had pleased his wife, and for the first time in his life he found himself drawing a monthly wage. Finding the job less demanding than construction, he applied himself to his new tasks.

His wife bore him a son, and Mansŏk was happy beyond comprehen-sion. But when he thought of his boy growing up and marrying, his face suddenly froze. Even if the boy married at twenty, Mansŏk would then be seventy. Would he live that long? The thought sent a chill into his heart.

The addition of a baby cost more money than another adult would have. His wife began to complain about his pay. But Mansŏk ignored his wife's grumbling and lavished all his attention on the growing baby. When the New Year arrived without a pay raise, his wife's complaints intensified. Of course the pay wouldn't increase just because they thought it should. A handyman was only a temporary post.

What is meant by living? For all Mansŏk knew, it was taking time by the spoonful and dying little by little as he drank it. The reckoning of his age, those bundled nodes of time, was truly frightening. Forty-eight was different, as was forty-nine, and fifty showed a face more different still. As a tree's leaves change the day after a frost, so did his age seem to rush headlong into oldness. Year by year his body was losing its vigour.

The baby, perhaps inherently immune to childhood in a poor family, grew up in good health. Mansŏk chose the name Ch'ŏlsu for the baby, hoping his son would grow into a worthy man, the sort who appears in primary-school textbooks. In time, their life became more pinched, and his wife's complaining grew more shrill. But Mansŏk, preoccupied with affection for his baby boy, managed to forget such trials.

Several months before the boy's fourth birthday, Mansŏk had to give up his handyman's job because of an administrative cut. It was as if he had walked up to the edge of a cliff on a dark road. He had never felt such dark despair for the future. And his agony was made more pressing by his obligation to a wife and child. His livelihood, from the very next day, was immediately in question. Mansŏk collected his wits and went out to the construction site to ask around. But, aside from possible manual labour, there was nothing he could count on. After wandering about for several days, he learned that there might be work at a construction site opening up more than 50 miles away.

'As long as I have life and breath we'll eat. Take good care of Ch'ŏlsu while I'm gone. I'll send money every couple of days.'

Mansŏk set out for the construction site immediately.

He saved up his daily wages and sent some home every ten days. The vitality remaining in his fifty-three-year-old body was exhausted beyond what even he had believed possible, but Mansŏk gritted his teeth and bore it. He was driven by the conviction that he could not let his little son go hungry, his son with the bright and shiny eyes. To a manual labourer, booze is almost like food. But Mansŏk drew the line – no more than half a pint a day. And there was only *paech'u* kimchi and radish kimchi to go along with it. Finding unique sustenance and joy in saving and sending home his pay, he endured his bone-wearying fatigue day after day for more than two months.

Then one day Mansŏk received a letter. He took one look at the contents, leapt up with a cry, then slumped back down.

He went straight home and found their room coldly vacant and his son, quite unaware, in the care of the soup-and-rice house. His wife had run off with some young guy.

'Just you wait and see, you whore! Until they shovel dirt onto my face, I'll hunt you to the ends of the earth. And, when I've caught you, bitch, I'll tear your crotch into a dozen pieces.'

Mansŏk, grinding his teeth fiercely, grabbed the boy up into his embrace. Before his raging eyes there came a vision of entrails strewn about in a sea of blood and the prostrate, naked corpses of a man and a woman.

'My luck with women was bad from the start. Why should the second time be any better? All I can do now is find her and kill her. Let's just see how far she can run, the stinking bitch!'

A chilly smile formed on Mansŏk's lips and a steely, bloodthirsty glint shone in his eyes.

When he discovered, too late, that she had been careful enough to collect even his modest room deposit, Mansŏk shook with even greater rage. After gathering the few pennies he could from selling off his household effects, Mansŏk hoisted the baby onto his back and set out on a road leading nowhere.

They had probably gone to Seoul, someone said; maybe Pusan, said somebody else – all nothing more than guesswork. He decided to start with Pusan, which was closer, and have a look around. As he and the boy moved from city to city they occasionally went hungry and sometimes even begged. Unlike the days of his youth when he had wandered from one job to another, the world now seemed vast and desolate. At times, on days of endless drizzle or when snow blanketed them, Mansŏk, his little boy gathered in his arms, cried silent and endless tears.

What do people mean by 'living for a lifetime'? Where am I going? What am I doing here in this strange land where I don't know anybody? They call you a human being, but is this how you end up if you never should've been born? You mean to tell me some people are born noble and some people are born low? Where in hell did they get the idea of nobles and commoners anyway? We're just the same – same faces, same minds . . . So, what's the difference? Was it my mistake? Just because you're born low-class, do you have to live like you are? Is the passion in me so different from the others? Is that why I did what I did? Maybe this is what I get for slaughtering so many people like dogs for those three or four months. I probably don't deserve to be alive today. But I didn't ask to be low-born like my father. Was I greedy? Can't you be greedy if you're a commoner? I'll drift like this and then I'll die – it won't be long. But then what happens to the kid? How's the little fellow going to turn out? He's all I'll leave behind. As long as I've got the kid in my arms, I can plug on, in spite of it all. Tomorrow's another day, another place I have to go – but where?

Mansŏk was unable to deal with such agony.

After a while, his wandering brought him close to his childhood home. As in times past, Mansŏk's heart throbbed and his legs tensed.

He thought he might try slipping into the village under cover of darkness, but the next moment he gave up the idea. He couldn't possibly muster up the courage.

Was this what old age did to a man? He was tempted and vexed like never before. Even while he'd been strictly avoiding the place all these years, he had twice approached the outskirts of his home village, on both occasions taking advantage of the night. In the end, though, he had forced himself to leave; his crime was still very much alive.

It was after Mansŏk and his son had wandered for a year and a half that he began to spit up blood. His body seemed withered, desiccated. He knew time was short, but still he sought out a hospital, since his young boy's wellbeing weighed heavily on his mind. The X-ray made it look like he had lived out his term. He headed for Seoul on the last leg of his search for his wife. And so, as his last task on this earth, he wandered around Seoul for six months, looking both for his wife and an orphanage. Unable to keep up his strength, he had decided to entrust his son to an institution. He was spitting up blood more and more frequently. He had come to fear that he would infect and kill his son if he clung to him any longer.

'I was going to raise my kids to be just right ... we'd live as bright as bells and I'd make them into gentlemen,' the old man mumbled to himself as he tottered away, looking as if he were deranged, his back to the orphanage. Tears ran into the sunken hollows of his cheeks.

The images of his two sons' faces, one superimposed on the other, shimmered in the old man's clouded vision. One was his first son, Ch'ilbong, who had died at the hands of the People's Army when he was three; the other, whom he had just left at the orphanage, was Ch'ŏlsu.

The old man knew the time to go home had finally come. This would be his third attempt. Though it might result in his death, he was now determined to set foot on the soil of his home.

It was after the war that he learned that his father, mother and son, Ch'ilbong, had been slaughtered by the People's Army.

'Who's this? It's not Mansŏk, is it?'

When Mansŏk had appeared one night out of the darkness at a drinking house near the ferry, three years after the fighting ended, Old Hwang was as startled as if he had seen a ghost.

'What are you doing here? What are you up to?'

In spite of the impenetrable darkness, Old Hwang looked all around him as he swiftly spoke.

Mansŏk felt himself propelled into the room. At the same time, he stiffened with a chill at the thought that he had actually come to where he shouldn't be.

'Just listen – don't make a sound. The very night you ran away those crazy shits wiped out three members of your family. Who would have thought they'd even go after a three-year-old kid?'

Mansŏk was struck dumb. That was the outcome of three years' unrelenting, anxious fear.

'Since you've come all this way, you might as well spend the night here. You can leave tomorrow morning before dawn.'

Old Hwang added, with an agonized expression, that Mansŏk would probably be buried alive were he ever caught.

'I knew I done something terrible, and that's why – to purge myself – I volunteered for the army as soon as I ran away. For three years straight I ploughed through one battleground after another. I can't count the times I was almost killed. But somehow I've managed to survive so far . . .'

Mansŏk spoke with a pathetic look, seeming to ask for exculpation.

'Did you really do all that?'

Old Hwang stared into Mansŏk's eyes, apparently surprised.

'Would I lie to you, Mr Hwang, just to hear a few nice words?'

'Then you really have done something that counts. But it isn't enough to help the Ch'oe family soften their hatred of you. Those people still bear a deadly grudge, and they'll probably never get over it. You should leave. Go far away and start another life.'

'I'll have to – seeing what I've done . . .'

Even while saying this, Mansŏk was having trouble dealing with it, overwhelmed by a new surge of sorrow and regret. Cloaked by darkness, he had returned to his native soil, but he could never hope to live here again. He had come to ask about his family. But to hear himself bluntly told to go far away caused a strange sorrow to well up within him, a sorrow he couldn't cope with.

'Our world today is just what it was when you people ran around like maniacs. There's only one difference to speak of – it's under new ownership. This world's as treacherous as a seesaw.'

'I must have been out of my mind. Even my mother and father, and they didn't do anything ...'

'Think about it and you'll see it wasn't just your fault. Not that I know anything, but I think it's the times that are at fault – the times. If you're guilty of anything, it's for having a temper like a hot pepper. That and your youth.'

'We thought our day was coming ... We were so angry, so fed up with living like animals ... It was all an awful madness.'

Mansŏk heaved a long sigh, like a mighty wind that sweeps down the hills and valleys before subsiding.

'You know, I still remember. How old were you – about twelve? I mean, when you shoved Elder Ch'oe's grand-nephews into the river. Ever since then, your temper's been as prickly as a fruit thorn. Your father had to put up with a lot of hardship because of that.' Old Hwang, with a pained expression, kept tsk-tsking.

'They dragged Father away and kicked the hell out of him. Not me, but Father. And then, they even ran him out of the village. That's when the hate began to fill my heart like a snake's poison.'

Mansŏk's husky voice had turned hoarse. Though he might forget his birthday from time to time, he was unable to forget those events. All the same, it was also a memory he didn't wish to dwell on.

It was September and a cool wind had been brushing the reeds. Around this time of year the oak leaves were showing signs of changing from their usual deep green and the hairy crabs were starting to fatten up.

Mansŏk was out catching crabs with two of Elder Ch'oe's grand-nephews. The crabs lived in tunnels that they dug between rocks on the reed flats. They were such dim-witted creatures that if you carefully stuck a reed-flower stem into the tunnel and worked it around, pausing a few times, they would bite right into it with one of their big claws. A crab that did that was as good as caught. Those things were so stupid that once they clamped down with a claw they never let go. Even if the claw broke off from the crab, whatever had been grabbed stayed clamped in the claw. Somehow the children got it into their heads that if your finger was bitten you might as well kiss it goodbye. This fear of losing a finger was probably why the children weren't eager to catch crabs – though the animals made a savoury treat when roasted and dipped in soy sauce.

Mansŏk was known among the children for his skill at catching crabs. And it was true. He was quick to spot their tunnels, he lured them out with impressive skill, and he was adroit at handling a hair-covered crab dangling from a reed-flower stem. The other children were full of admiration at Mansŏk's talent.

Mansŏk had come by this accomplishment alone and at a cost in agony quite unknown to the other children. Mansŏk had begun to rummage around the reed flats that stretched wide along the river's edge at the age of six. Unknown to the others, there were lots of tasty things in the reeds to satisfy an appetite. Kingfisher eggs in the spring, their chicks in the summer, crabs in the autumn – all filled Mansŏk's empty stomach. His family could not even feed him plain boiled barley and so his empty stomach always growled. Since he would be out to satisfy his hunger, there was nothing scary to Mansŏk about the crab claws. In the beginning he didn't have a finger that wasn't bitten. Once you're bitten, you have to slam the crab against the ground. When the claw breaks off the crab you grit your teeth and remove the part that's digging into you. But if you try this while the claw is still attached to the crab, you're setting yourself up to get bitten on the other hand by the remaining claw. And if you end up with a finger from each hand caught in each claw, then what?

While he was suffering alone, not a finger without a bite, Mansŏk became pretty skilful at handling the crabs. The pain of a crab bite wasn't something you'd soon forget. Sparks would flash inside his eyes and even the tip of his penis would burn. And the finger would hurt as if it were falling off. But he never lost a finger. *That much pain was no big deal*, Mansŏk thought, if he could rid himself of the hunger that coloured his vision yellow and made his knees buckle.

But the pain so scared the other children that they had no heart for catching crabs, and the children of the Ch'oe family, in particular, would back away at the mere sight of a crab flourishing its ten hairy legs. Mansŏk inwardly scorned and dismissed such children: 'You kids think just because you're from some rich man's family that I'm not as good as you. Well, if I was going to take you out, I could do it with one punch!' he would mutter to himself.

On that day, Elder Ch'oe's two grand-nephews had offered him three sweet potatoes if he would catch them five crabs. It wasn't a bad piece of business and so Mansŏk set out to provide. Murmuring to himself about well-boiled sweet potatoes, he threw himself into the task. He was twitching a reed-flower stem at what was to be the fourth crab when a scream pierced the air. Mansŏk sat bolt upright.

The younger of the two Ch'oe children, a nine-year-old, had been crouching beside a small crock that held the catch. Now he was gasping for breath, jumping up and down, and screaming madly. And there, attached to a finger on the hand of the arm that was flailing the air was a crab. The older brother, who was Mansŏk's age, not knowing what else to do, was calling out 'Mother! Mother!' It was obvious that the younger boy had been playing with the crabs as they crawled around the inner sides of the crock, and had got himself bitten squarely on the finger.

Mansŏk dashed over, grabbed the boy's waving arm, and swung it downwards with all his might. But still the crab dangled from the finger. He pressed the boy's palm against the ground and drove his heel down on the crab. Its body was crushed and the claw fell off. As usual, the claw still held fast to the finger. The kid was still letting loose his gasping cries, but Mansŏk quickly managed to open the claw and release the finger. It began at that moment.

'You little shit!'

Mansŏk saw stars. The older boy had just punched Mansŏk in the cheek.

'What'd you do that for?'

It was so sudden that Mansŏk was in a daze.

'Don't play dumb.'

Again the fist came flying.

Mansŏk had no time to duck, and as he absorbed the blow it began to dawn on him that he was being blamed for something he hadn't done. Perplexed, he retreated several steps.

'I know what you're up to. Lay off the rough stuff,' yelled Mansŏk, confronting them and poised for a fight.

He set his teeth and his eyes took on a threatening glint. Surprised by Mansŏk's nerve, the older boy hesitated.

'It's all your fault that my brother got bitten, so now I'm telling you to stick your hands down in there.'

The bigger boy pointed towards the crock full of crabs while the little one studied his hand and cried mournfully.

'What?'

Mansŏk felt his stomach turning over. Yet again he was up against the unfairness he had to face because he was a commoner. The prejudice wasn't something expressed in words. Since it was unreasoning, words were unnecessary, completely useless. It all came down to doing as he was told.

But he couldn't stick his hands inside a crock full of crabs. It wasn't a question of being at fault or not. The other kid was his own age, not an adult. He couldn't let that kid order him around. He'd sooner drop dead on the spot.

'Well, are you going to stick them in or not?' the big kid yelled.

'You'd have to kill me first!'

Mansŏk confronted him with a scornful laugh.

'How's that? Someone of your sort defying me? Maybe we'd better take you up on that. Sure, why not? Hey, Tongjin, let's half kill this asshole!' said the big one to his brother and the two raised their clenched fists.

'Hey, boy! Don't make trouble, no matter what you think. Remember your origins. He who endures is the better man.'

Every time there was trouble, big or little, his meek and gentle father would repeat these words. Even in the midst of this attack by the two ganged up against him, his father's words popped into his mind. But they couldn't ward off this beating.

Mansŏk ducked the fists that came flying at him. Though he didn't live or eat very well, he had a body that started hauling firewood before he was ten and, since he turned ten, carried a back-rack. And he was skilled enough in fighting to make quick work of the two Ch'oe boys, who had been brought up eating meat.

Mansŏk knew how to win a fight in a single round. The big boy, whose punch had missed, sprang at Mansŏk, panting. Mansŏk took aim at his groin and let his foot fly. The boy, unable even to cry out, fell flat on his back, writhing.

'Get up! Come on, get up!' cried the younger one, shaking his older brother, who lay pale and twisting on the ground.

'Your turn to get punched, you little bastard.'

Mansŏk pulled the younger one up by his collar and gave him a ruthless thrashing. By now, Mansŏk was beside himself. He had a sharp and fiery temper that, once aroused, he could not control, so much so that his mother would curse him as 'tiger bait.'

Mansŏk had the fearsome thought that he could kill these two and no one would be any the wiser. It crossed his mind that he could pummel them some more and then throw them in the river. So he beat them unconscious and dragged them one by one to the edge of the river, and it was then he was discovered by grown-ups from the village.

His father was dragged to the Ch'oe house, beaten half to death and carried back home. Before long, the Ch'oe men turned up at their door. Mansŏk's father, still barely able to move, fell to the ground, crying and pleading for mercy, but the men loaded all their household effects onto a cart and dumped them by the river. His father had to build a dugout for them to live in on a mountain slope across the river. Having lost their tenancy with the Ch'oes, they were reduced to going hungry as often as they ate. But his father neither punished nor rebuked Mansŏk.

'You're just like your grandfather. Your blood's too hot for a commoner!'

His father, bedridden with pain, mumbled half to himself as tears ran down his face.

It was not until four years later that his father was forgiven by the Ch'oes and allowed to move back into the old house.

Mansŏk finally let out the words he had so hesitated to say and then dropped his head.

'Would you know, by any chance, how my parents' graves ... ?'

'I'm ashamed to have to say this. But who do you think would have come forward to bury them in the face of all that bloodthirsty terror? We all had our tails tucked between our legs, afraid we'd get into serious trouble, including me.'

Old Hwang spoke very directly. Mansŏk, his head lowered, gave no response.

Mansŏk had never hoped that his parents might possibly have a grave. All he wanted was to know their final resting place.

When it came to reactionaries, could anyone have been more reactionary than him? His mother, father and three-year-old kid suffered a harsher death than anyone else. Who would have dared to step forward and offer to care for their bodies? In what pit were they buried together?

'Mr Hwang, thank you. I'll have to leave you now.'

Mansŏk rose.

'What are you talking about? Have yourself a nap and leave before cockcrow.'

'No, that won't do. If they catch sight of me moving around at dawn, you'll be in a prickly situation, Mr Hwang. It'd be best to slip away right now.'

'Had I known you'd leave like this, I would have made you a rice ball or something.'

'Mr Hwang, as long as I live, I'll never forget the time you saved me.'

'No, no. Neither you nor I have done anything wrong, except for being born with the wrong blood in our veins. I understand what's going on inside you. When you really look at it, a man like me has nothing to boast of. People like me who seek an easy life, laughing in spite of this and laughing in spite of that, are no better than spineless idiots. Compared with people like me, how much of a man you are! You are really what a man is. So, for you to thank me is to insult me. To have kept your whereabouts secret was the proper duty of a small man like me who'll never live so boldly as you.'

Moisture was forming in Old Hwang's eyes.

'Mr Hwang, I wish you a long, long life,' said Mansŏk in a choking voice, his head lowered in contrition.

'Forget it – every bit of it! Go and live your own life fully. That's your way out.'

Mansŏk parted from Old Hwang in the darkness.

As soon as Mansŏk's eyes grew accustomed to the dark he could faintly make out the river's course. Looking out at that river, he could no longer move. A ferry across the river could have taken him to his home.

Mansŏk had made his way past the village shrine when gunfire broke out behind him like beans popping on a skillet. In between the shots he could hear shouts of agitation. Mansŏk was unable to run as fast as his burning heart urged. He had already walked 24 miles that day, coming and going, and was thoroughly exhausted. The sound of gunfire came gradually closer. When Mansŏk reached the ferry, Old Hwang was just tying up his boat.

'Mr Hwang. You've got to help me!'

'What happened?'

'I've just killed the People's Army commander. Please, take me in your boat.'

'Are you crazy? If we go out in that boat, we'll get shot dead in the middle of the river. Quick, run to the reeds! To the reeds. The fog's just started to rise and it'll be dark soon. Run quickly! Now!'

Old Hwang stamped his foot and Mansǒk made a dash for the reed flats.

Sure enough, the evening fog was rising slowly along the shores. The afterglow on the river's surface was as ardent as the call of a scops owl. The wind soughing in the reeds sounded like a baby's whimper and left the stalks undulating. Mansǒk felt relieved and turned all his strength to crawling through the flats. With this much wind blowing against the reeds, the ripple caused by a single man does not stand out. This he had learned from experience, having been in and out of these reeds since he was a child.

By the time he made it to the middle of the wide and even stand of reeds, Mansǒk had heard three or four gunshots at the riverbank. He waited until it grew pitch dark and then leapt into the river. Avoiding the main roads, he went up into the mountains.

At that time his very life had rested in the hands of Old Hwang.

Early July through to early September had been like a dream for Mansǒk. For those two months, Mansǒk really believed the world was his.

They said they would liberate the farmer-labourers. They said rich men and landlords would be eliminated and all power would go to the commoners. Mansǒk had no need to think or mull it over. He was in his element, like a fish in water. He waved a freshly sharpened sickle and a bloodthirsty glint shot from his eyes.

The first thing Mansǒk did was burn down the Ch'oes' ancestral shrine hall.

'Starting now, I'm going to rip the Ch'oe family up by its roots!' he shouted as he stared at the flaming building. 'I'll wipe them all out! There'll be nothing left with a cock hanging from it.'

Nobody dared get in the way of Mansǒk and the deadly sickle he brandished. Anyone who challenged him would have lost his head to the flying sickle. Some who were fast on their feet managed to escape him, but not the Ch'oe men, who were all caught and dragged in. They were beaten until half dead, and each day one of them died, tied to the pine out back.

Even though the Ch'oe family was in constant mourning, not a single bier was to be seen; they hadn't been able to retrieve the corpses.

Among the entire Ch'oe family there was no food to eat, not in any of their houses. All their grain had been looted, so thoroughly that they could not even make gruel.

'It's not right. You wouldn't treat animals like that – how can you do it to humans? They have little children there – you've got to at least let them cook gruel. Mansŏk, boy, change your mind and let them at least cook gruel. These things simply aren't done, not even if you were avenging your own father's murder.'

His father clung to Mansŏk as he pleaded.

'You've got to stop this reactionary talk. You've suffered this all your life and you're still not disgusted? Is that it?'

Mansŏk shook himself loose from his father and shot a look skyward.

'You've got to get rid of this bullheadedness. Whether you like them or not, those people have given us our daily bread.'

'Father, is that all you can say? If you don't change your attitude, and soon, do you know what will happen? You'll end up just like those damn Ch'oes.'

A cold look had come over Mansŏk's face.

'Yes, you will. I think you exaggerate, Father. When have those people ever fed us? We worked our fingers to the bone so the likes of them could get big and fat, and all we eat is chaff and sweepings – it's barely enough to live on.'

His daughter-in-law showed with her eyes that she took her husband's side.

Old Mr Ch'ŏn kept his mouth shut after that. They had all changed so completely, even his daughter-in-law. People who change their minds face death, they said. The two of them were like different people. His son could butcher people without blinking an eye, and overnight his daughter-in-law had cast off her modest manner and turned into a genuine adulteress. His daughter-in-law, as head of the Alliance of Democratic

Women, was wielding power just like his son. For this beautiful daughter-in-law, whose eyes had always been demurely lowered, to have changed so much grieved the old man deeply. No, it's that Communist Party that makes people change so. The more he thought about it, the more frightened and fearful he became.

Mansŏk was so intent on being the eagle who, wings full out, soared as he wished that he was totally unaware of the fires that smouldered beneath his feet. He had no inkling that his wife had fallen madly for the pistol-packing People's Army commander, who with just a few words, ran everything so briskly. Even when she would turn down Mansŏk's bedtime requests because she was 'tired', rather than growing suspicious he would feel sorry for burdening his wife, who had struggled to accomplish revolutionary tasks during the day.

Mansŏk stuck to out-of-the-way villages to avoid being picked up by the People's Volunteer Army.[1] All the while he was tormented by that ugly dream every night – the dream of a man and woman writhing naked, then collapsing, their guts spewn out on the floor in a sea of blood.

If the thought came to him while he was eating, he would become nauseous and unable to eat any more. After about one month on the run, he heard that the People's Army had lost the battle and were, for the most part, withdrawing to the mountains. Mansŏk thought deeply on what would have become of him if none of this had happened and he had remained in his native village. The world would have turned inside out again. Obviously, members of the Ch'oe family who had managed to escape would have descended on him. He then would have had no course but to run off with the People's Army.

The war had ended. But the mopping up was not yet finished, just as sweeping remains when the threshing's done. There were the Red guerrillas who had escaped into the mountains, only to descend to the villages to prowl at night, as well as those who had sided with the rebels still to be ferreted out.

'It's obvious, don't you think? Some went to the mountains, but those who didn't see the writing on the wall were overthrown. They were rounded up and faced an ugly fate.'

Old Hwang had shaken his head as if loath to draw his story out any further.

Mansŏk released a sigh as long as the river's course. And he slowly stepped through the darkness. Just as Mr Hwang had said, he had no choice but to go and live somewhere far away. And now he had nothing – nothing gained, nothing saved, nothing whatsoever. Just emptiness and absurdity.

He really had wanted to go to school. But they told him learning wasn't for just anyone. They told him that commoners had their own tasks that were different – gathering wood, packing a back-rack and grazing cattle. While the Ch'oe kids sat in the shade of a tree eating watermelons until their stomachs burst, he had to be out leaping around the sun-baked paddy paths, shouting himself hoarse to shoo the birds away. In winter, of course, he had to gather up the children's book bags and carry them to school. While dressed in clothing padded several times thicker than his and wearing mittens as well, those children complained they couldn't carry book bags because their hands were cold.

To get two sticky-rice cakes to eat, he had to show them his cock and peel back the foreskin, in spite of the pain it caused. To have a single persimmon, he spent half a day as their mount in a horse-riding game. He was willing to do almost anything if it meant putting something in a stomach that knew only constant hunger. But that was only until he was thirteen or fourteen. After he turned fifteen, he began to grit his teeth until the roots ached.

'Mansŏk, Mansŏk! You've got to let me go! I'll give you all my fields and paddies if you'll just let me go.'

When they breathed their last some of the Ch'oes had rubbed their palms in supplication hard enough to start a fire.

'Mansŏk. I mean, Deputy Leader, sir. Your esteemed father and I were friends for thirty years. Won't you spare me? Please ...'

Some gushed tears as they writhed on the floor.

'Comrade Deputy Leader ... comrade ... Deputy Leader ...'

Some, lips trembling, couldn't manage to speak.

Some emptied their bowels, some pissed themselves sloppily, some trembled from head to foot but then went as stiff as boards.

Not one of them still trumpeted the grandeur, the arrogance, the self-importance or the authority they had shown a few days earlier. 'You ill-bred trash! You could learn manners from a dog! How dare you act like this before your betters?' Had even one among them responded in such a way, he might well have been allowed to live.

As if guarded by their departed souls, this land was not something he could return to, thought Mansŏk, as he turned his back to the river and began to step quickly into the darkness.

Old Mansŏk, constantly wiping away his tears, took three or four hours to walk from the suburban orphanage to the business district in the centre of town. Without a single coin to his name, he had no choice but to walk.

He found the pedestrian overpass that had caught his eye earlier. The old man barely managed the strength to grasp the handrail and climb the steps. He took off one of his black rubber shoes and squatted down at the near end of the bridge where the two flights of steps from the sidewalk met. The single black shoe rested in front of him.

He had to get a meal each day and he had to get the bus fare home.

He could no longer do manual labour. Whatever job site he inquired at, they had no work to give him. His wrinkled and desiccated face was still a face, but his drooping shoulders revealed at a glance that this was no longer the body of a labouring man. Even if a sympathetic or green foreman were to assign him some task he wouldn't have had the strength to carry it out. Not only had his body grown loose and slack, but he was apt to spit up blood if he taxed himself.

The old man's eyes were closed, his head hung low. In his shabby appearance he was every bit the beggar.

The old man was not at all interested in how many coins had collected in the rubber shoe, for his heart was already home. With the day of his death drawing near, the old man was more inclined that way. At some point, his heart had started to focus increasingly on that place.

Home was a land where nothing whatsoever was left for him, a land with not a single face to welcome him. If there were something there, it would be just an ugly past. For what reason could his heart, in spite of it all, be drawn to that place at the risk of his very life? For all the thought he gave to it, he couldn't understand his own feelings.

He had wandered some two years, following the construction sites. One reclamation project where he worked for a while was no more than 25 miles from his birthplace. At first, afraid he might run into some familiar face, he thought about finding some other place to work. But the conditions there were too good to turn his back on easily. Reclamation projects were always long-term, and since they were mostly government operations, they had the advantage of regular pay. And so after wavering a bit, he decided to accept the risks and then settled in.

Two months passed, then three, without his encountering any familiar face. During that time a hankering stole into his heart. He was taken with a wish to see Mr Hwang, if only once. Once he got that idea into his head, he began to find himself disconcerted often. Countless people worked at the site. Many shared the same life, each day exerting themselves and putting away three meals. But they lacked the human-heartedness suggested by a well-baked sweet potato or a warm, snug room on a snowy night. They worked together easily like a team when they were on the job, but when the work was done, they would go their separate ways and quite forget their working life. The life of the wanderer has always been like this.

And they were not without women. But, compared with the men, these women were even more like vacant shadows. Selling their bodies for a few coins, they would turn into inert lumps of flesh as soon as their task was over. Doing it with them, no matter how many times he tried, always left Mansŏk feeling he had just bathed in a tub filled only to his ankles with tepid water. How he longed to be immersed up to his neck in a steaming hot tub of water! Suddenly the thought of Chŏmnye's body came to mind. How he longed to be drenched with sweat and get that faint and listless feeling, like all his body's strength had been drained away! But then came the memory that flooded in and instantly destroyed his longing. In broad daylight, in the council's quarters, writhing . . .

Perhaps it was this rootlessness that made him want to see Old Hwang again.

The men had one day off a week. That day was boring and frustrating for him. He wasn't particularly drawn to drinking or gambling. But his heart did brim with thoughts of buying a bottle of *chŏngjong* and visiting Old Hwang.

Mansŏk held out as long as he could and then, some time after lunch, he ended up on a bus.

He got off the bus at the town of P, about 10 miles before his home village. It wasn't long before the sun was about to set. At a roadside shop,

Mansŏk bought two bottles of *chŏngjong*. Then he found a place to eat. He ordered a double portion of soup and rice and a glass of *soju*. With 10 miles to walk in the dark, he had to stoke up well.

'You mean they're still not done with the burying?'

'That's what I said.'

'No kidding! How long has it been since the war ended? You mean they've been burying their people for two years now?'

'Hey, look. You can't see anything but your rose-coloured view of things. Are you telling me you don't know how many of them were killed?'

'I know. If the People's Army had kicked them around for another six months back then, the Ch'oe clan would have been wiped out.'

Mansŏk, his glass of *soju* moving to his lips, froze in place. A shock, at which his body seemed to stiffen, hit the back of his head. With a flick of his eyes Mansŏk examined the faces of the two men. There was nothing familiar about them. He unconsciously heaved a great sigh.

'So true. It's a good thing for the Ch'oe family that the national army won when they did.'

'Yeah, but were they able to get their dead reburied properly then?'

'What? With so many people just buried like dried fish on a string in this pit or that, how could they tell whose bones were whose?'

'It was insane! What must the children have thought as they tried to rebury what they hoped were the bones of their parents?'

'God knows! I say devotion like that ought to be rewarded.'

'Well, while the Ch'oes care for their departed like that, what about the people who took up the rebel cause or the scattered souls of their families?'

'That's not your worry. At this point the Ch'oe family is blind with rage. What would they care about the souls of dead traitors?'

Mansŏk, emptying one glass of *soju* after another, felt a tension that chilled him. Unlike his heart, which told him to clear out of the place, his body, growing heavier, was sinking down into his seat.

'No, that's not what I'm saying. I mean, as long as the revengeful spirits of the dead, for whatever reason, are out and moving around, that village will never settle down in peace.'

'So the Ch'oe clan will bury the commoners who they see as their enemies?'

'It's a crazy business. When you think how they buried that silly Chŏmbagu alive – and he was nobody – then you know these Ch'oes aren't normal people.'

Chŏmbagu, that dimwit with the coin-sized mole on the left of his forehead. He would dance for joy, grab a spear and, as if his day had come, carry out whatever was asked of him. And, when he had run a spear through someone's chest, he would show his yellow teeth and make a gaping laugh. That face was not a laughing face as much as the look of an angry, growling dog. It was an expression that came from fear, and people called it his 'dog laugh.' Chŏmbagu, buried alive. Somewhat deficient mentally, doubtless he was unable to sense that the situation around him had worsened. Would Chŏmbagu have been laughing his dog laugh even while being buried alive?

Mansŏk's arm trembled with anger as he raised the glass of *soju*.

'In any event, the Reds aren't coming down from the hills any more, so we can breathe easy. No more sleepless nights.'

'Right, they seem pretty well rounded up. After Sugil, the leader, was killed last October, not one has come down, even to his village.'

'Then the one who died with Sugil – his face bashed beyond recognition – that must have been the Mansŏk who was deputy leader?'

'Could be. That would explain why no one's seen a trace of him. Imagine if only Sugil had died and Mansŏk had survived – wouldn't that mean another round of terror for the Ch'oe family? That Mansŏk was something else, venomous as ten poison snakes.'

'Oh, yeah. He was a nasty sort, eating roasted snakes before he was ten.'

'I heard the same thing!'

'But, Mansŏk kills a People's Army commander and his own wife and then runs away. And this was nearly two weeks before the People's Army pulled out. Wouldn't Mansŏk have been a candidate for their firing squad? So how could he have joined up with them again?'

'You're really testing my patience! Whoever else may have been involved, who did the most wrong? The guy who fucked somebody's wife or the husband who killed the guy? And since they'd have their own baggage, too, wouldn't old wounds – long forgotten – get opened up again? And so when the People's Army are running for their lives, why not let bygones be bygones and take him back in? One fierce specimen like Mansŏk would've been better than ten ordinary people.'

'True. For sure.'

Mansŏk, his face ashen, quickly got up and left. He set out in the direction opposite to where Old Hwang lived. There should be buses headed towards the construction site, he was thinking.

Back at the construction site, Mansŏk drank the two bottles of clear rice brew he had bought to give Old Hwang. And for four days he was sick in bed, unable to budge.

He had never gone catching and roasting snakes to eat before he was ten. True, he had often thought about what it would be like to eat roasted snake. People eat cows, pigs, dogs and chickens. They eat grasshoppers and frogs. Yet there seems to be something about snakes that keeps people from eating them. Come summer, snakes were common in riverside reed patches and thickets in the foothills. Children, when they caught sight of a snake, would turn tail and run away. But then, all it took was for somebody to catch one, then they would all grab stones and go on the attack. They would always make sure that the snake died in a welter of wounds. But, even then, the children would not retreat. If they didn't chop it into pieces, the snake would drink the dew overnight, come back to life at dawn and surely return for revenge. The revived snake would go around to the house of each boy who had tried to kill it and kill him by biting off his dink. So the children were only satisfied if they could stone a snake to death and chop it into pieces. A child would grab hold of his crotch with one hand while throwing rocks with all his might. But Mansŏk didn't throw any rocks. He was hungry and weak and had no need to exert himself to kill the snake; he was most concerned with what he might do to roast and eat its flesh. The eels caught in the river were incredibly tasty. Since snakes and eels were cousins, so to speak, he would be lost in thoughts of how sweet and nutlike the taste of river eel was when he put it hot and sizzling into his mouth.

It looked like Sugil had turned partisan, attacked the village, and then got himself killed. He was, indeed, a miserable wretch. It had seemed to Mansŏk that Sugil, living with a widowed mother, somehow scraped along even closer to starvation than he did.

'With luck like this, what's the point of living? I'm just living for my mother. Once she's dead and gone I'm going to give up this shithole world.'

He would talk like this, Sugil, who had more spirit than muscle.

Becoming Leader of the People's Committee, though, seemed to energize him. Still, he had been somewhat troubled by all the random killing. In the end, he had died on his home turf.

It seemed that Mansŏk had already been taken for dead by the people of his home village, particularly those in the Ch'oe clan. In that case, only Old Hwang and his wife knew of his existence. There was no way that that fact would slip out of tight-lipped Old Hwang. Mansŏk's life had already ended. Now no trace of him remained in his native place.

Mansŏk, sick in bed for four days, thought seriously about his lot in life. It was true emptiness, meaninglessness. If anything had changed, it was just that he went from tenant farmer to migrant labourer.

Mansŏk made up his mind never to go near the land of his home again. He had stuck to that decision for nearly thirty years now. No matter how good the job at the site, he always avoided it if it was close to home.

Evening fog was spreading thickly along the riverbank, like the aftermath of some sadness. The old man had been standing there a long time, shoulders drooped as if weighted and staring vacantly at the swirling of the fog as it spread into a stand of reeds.

Would there still be, even now, so many hairy crabs in those reeds? He had roasted them to eat when he was young and, after he grew, they made the best of snacks to go with booze. After knocking back a glass of *soju* the taste you could get chewing on a crab leg soaked in mellow soy sauce . . .

The old man swallowed and wiped his mouth with the palm of his hand. The rough surface of his palm on the skin around his mouth felt deeply incised, like the scar of a wound. The old man looked down at the palm of his hand with a wasted feeling: a palm that had calloused all it could, and then heaved up many little cracks. Perhaps it was the hardened scar tissue, but he could feel no pain even when stabbed by something sizable.

The old man gave a long, thin sigh. In the eyes that looked down into the palm there rose a melancholy the colour of the fog.

Long years. Years that have flown by so fast. Empty, meaningless years . . .

The old man set his teeth so firmly that the corners of his mouth began to droop as he turned his gaze towards the riverbank once more. The fog, like some living thing, was devouring both the rambling patches of reeds and the wide body of the river itself.

If it weren't for those reeds . . .

The old man's body trembled. Now that he finally stood face to face with the river, the memory of that day approached, tearing away at the intervening years so that it seemed to have happened yesterday.

The fog stopped spreading. Thin darkness was being laid out, one furrow after another. The old man felt a chill run down his back as he looked around. It was dark enough now to blur the outline of the mountain ridge. He felt the pang of hunger and a heavy fatigue that made him want to lie down. Now he just wanted to get to the tavern.

The old man turned heavy feet towards the tavern, which stood unchanged from the old days, except that the roof had turned to slate. What's the worst that could happen, he wondered in his miserable state, but still he waited until it was a bit darker. He was invaded to the marrow of his bones by a helpless sense of guilt.

Could Old Hwang still be alive? If so, he would be over seventy. He had left the running of the tavern to his wife while he operated the ferry by himself. This Old Hwang would launch his ferry even for one person, whether late at night or early dawn, winter or summer. This man who always had a smile didn't seem to hate or be hated by anyone in the world. Everyone in any of the surrounding villages – Kamkol, Hangnae, Chukch'on – all felt warmly protective of Old Hwang and his wife. It was Old Hwang who had glanced up at him for the first time and bellowed, 'Why are you doing this? Are you crazy? The world may change and the times can be unpredictable but if you can't rely on a man, he's useless!'

'Be careful what you say, Mr Hwang! Please. As someone who should take the lead, how can you talk like that?'

'Well, now, listen to what I say. Haven't you thought about what happened to the pro-Japanese collaborators after Liberation?'

'What are you talking about? Oh, do you think things today are just like they were back then? Well, I have just one last thing to tell you and

I want you to open your ears wide and listen carefully. Since it was you who said it, Mr Hwang, I'll pretend I didn't hear it. But if you ever talk like that again, I'll report you on the spot – no questions asked! Don't forget that!'

Old Hwang, mouth agape, could make no answer.

He doubted whether his father and Old Hwang clearly understood what it was like to live in the world at that time or where the purpose of living a life lay. They both said one had to live by reason. Though he might once have known what reason was all about, he didn't know now.

Old Hwang was probably so old now that even if they collided on some street corner they probably wouldn't recognize each other. The times had rounded a long bend and flowed on.

The old man entered the twilight with a bit of a groping gait, as if he were making his way across stepping stones. He had a dilapidated bag strapped to his bent shoulders. After a few steps towards the tavern, he stopped and began to cough. He covered his mouth with one hand and clutched at the clothing covering his chest with the other. The feeble coughing spun inside his throat. He was unable to stop the coughing, and his body began to curl up.

The old man was nearly in a squat when the coughing stopped. When a fit of coughing racked him like this, his chest seethed with a nearly unendurable fever and seemed to flutter like shredded rice-paper. And there came the sweat that drenched his body as it was being swept by a chill.

No good. It's all over.

He shook his head as he had that thought again. Each time the coughing racked his chest, the old man felt death come another step closer.

Legs shaking, the old man placed his palms on his knees and slowly rose. A stinking dizziness invaded him dimly like the fog spreading across the riverbank.

He paused in front of the tavern gate. *Should I say something to make myself known?* But no words came to mind; there was only the amiable face of a young Mr Hwang flickering before him.

'Hello, anyone home?'

The old man shouted with what strength he had. But his voice, though he could hear it, was so weak and trembling.

Cho Chŏngnae

'Is someone there?'

A man emerged from a shed and looked around.

The old man strained to see. Although the gloom of evening had already settled in, he could sense that the man in the distance was not an old one.

Mr Hwang's son? the old man thought suddenly. That powerful youth, though a poor substitute for his father, had taken over the oars of the ferry. 'A big help to me. But that kid came into the world three years too early, I think. Ended up getting yanked around – first by this side, then by that side. How it troubled me when that happened . . .'

He could hear Mr Hwang's voice vividly.

'Who is it?' a sturdy man in his forties was asking quietly.

'I, uh . . . are you still running a tavern here?' the old man began, pushing aside a tangle of questions.

'How? When the bridge fell in and the ferry was wiped out the tavern dried up too.'

Answering slowly and deliberately, he took in the old man's shabby appearance with a look of dissatisfaction.

'They put a bridge over this river?' asked the old man, unable to hide his surprise.

'That was some time back. You haven't been around here for a while, have you?'

He slowly studied the old man with a different look in his eyes. The old man instinctively assumed a defensive posture. It was a dark refraction of the feelings experienced over the thirty years since that day. But, as a matter of habit, he did not reveal the hard mass of those feelings in the least when he opened his mouth to speak.

'I took up peddling as a young man when I got sick of farming.'

'Really? Well, were you able to make some money?' the younger man asked with a sarcastic tone. The old man's shabbiness seemed very far removed from money.

'Could Old Hwang still live here?' the old man asked casually, suppressing his unquiet heart.

'Who is Old Hwang?'

The man shook his head, emphasizing that he knew nothing at all. Instantly, the old man felt abandoned. This man, clearly the owner of the tavern, didn't know of Old Hwang. Had Mr Hwang died? Had he moved away?

'You know, Hwang Sundol . . . ran the ferry . . .'

'Ah, the former owner here! He died more than ten years ago. His son sold us the place and moved off to the city.'

Nothing registered in the old man's ears. He hadn't come here to see his native turf. He had come to find Mr Hwang. His heart was drawn to his birthplace while he wandered rootlessly, not just out of heartache for the troubled spirits of his dead parents but also because Mr Hwang was there. Even that bottle of rice brew he had bought with money barely scraped together from begging – that was for Mr Hwang. But Mr Hwang had already died some ten years before.

'So, where are you headed, mister?'

At the tavern owner's question, the old man came out of his reverie.

'You wouldn't happen to know, would you, where Mr Hwang's grave is?' the old man asked as he narrowly opened his watery eyes.

'Well, I really don't,' the owner answered bluntly.

All the old man could do was nod feebly.

'Well, safe travels.'

With that the tavern owner turned away.

'I wonder if I could get a little something to eat?' the old man ventured to the tavern owner's back.

'Well . . .'

'Don't worry, I'm not asking for a free meal.'

'No, that's not it. It's just that we don't have much to go with the rice. Let's go in first,' said the tavern owner, again turning to go.

The darkness had closed in all around them. The old man looked down towards the riverbank. In the thick grey darkness he could no longer make out the outlines of the fog that had risen up in solid billows like a living thing. *If only Mr Hwang were here . . .* A desolate sorrow spread through his heart like the fog that covered the riverbank.

'What are you doing, mister? Let's go in,' the tavern owner called.

'I had to relieve myself,' said the old man by way of excuse, before going through the brushwood gate.

Since it was around dinnertime, the rice was brought right out.

'Could I have a glass of *soju*?'

Even before he gave thought to lifting a spoon, the old man first wanted a drink. As he spoke, he thought of the bottle of *chŏngjong* he had kept so carefully in his bag. He had meant to drink it, sitting together with Mr Hwang. He had bought it to soothe away, cup by cup, the weakness and weariness that had overwhelmed his flesh and his feelings. This was only the third bottle of expensive rice brew that he had bought in all his life. He hadn't been able to offer the first two bottles to Mr Hwang and now, once more, it was the same thing.

The old man poured a glass of *soju* almost to overflowing and drank it in a gulp. 'Ahh . . .' He closed his eyes softly as he felt the prickling force of the spirits ride down his throat. Throughout the wasted years he'd spent floating aimlessly about – pushed by the wind, clouds for a roof – the one thing that had stood by him, unchanged, was the taste of *soju*.

'Here, won't you have a glass?'

He offered his emptied glass to the owner.

'Oh, no. If I want to drink, I'll serve myself. How can I take a drink from a customer?' said the owner, declining with a wave of his hand.

'Come, now. Don't be so cold-hearted, undermining the good feelings that come from sharing a glass. You can tell from the sight of me that I'm not the type who can often buy a second round. Please have one!' The old man looked forlorn but spoke emphatically.

'If that's the case . . .'

The owner accepted the glass.

The hand with which the old man poured the spirits trembled slightly but righted the bottle neatly, just when the glass filled up.

'If you were looking for the ferry, mister, you must be on your way to the Chukch'on area?' the owner asked as he returned the glass.

The old man merely nodded, his eyes narrowed, as if collecting many thoughts.

'I learned when I came here that everything on from Chukch'on belongs to the Ch'oe family.'

As before, the old man only nodded.

'I'm told the Ch'oe family came forward to build the bridge. And it seems they're going to put up a middle school and high school, too, after a while.'

The old man nodded as he pulled out a cigarette.

'Actually, with one of them a national assembly man, can't they do anything they want? There may be other families around, but they're all like beggars living off the Ch'oes.'

'Well . . .' The old man was about to say something, but then made as if to empty his glass.

'You were going to say . . . ?' The owner gazed at the old man.

'Well . . . I was wondering who the Ch'oe clan leaders are.'

'Well, the ones about my age, the ones who are educated. Not that there aren't any elders, but they all seem to stay in the background. All the same, I've heard talk. They say those elders aren't very well received.'

'How come?'

'Not so bright, I hear. The brainy ones were all killed off in the war, they say.'

The old man fixed his eyes on the wall, his face hardened.

'I understand that the Ch'oes dropped like flies during the war. Except for the Harvest Festival and New Year's, they say the largest observance in the Ch'oe households is their joint memorial service in late July. A spectacle worth watching.'

The old man, eyes tightly closed, took one deep drag after another on his cigarette.

'Those Ch'oes had wielded such power, but then the war broke out and they fell into the hands of the rabble and their lives weren't worth shit. How could they ever be avenged? There wasn't a place where that rabble didn't go wild. The Ch'oes got the worst of it here, they say. Maybe you witnessed some of that creepy stuff, mister?'

'Oh no, no . . .'

The old man stubbed out his cigarette and shook his head vehemently.

'Where were you living back then?' the owner asked, looking more gently into the old man's face.

'I left before the war – just in time, I guess. So I don't know a thing about what went on here during the fighting,' the old man asserted.

'Well, they say those ceremonies are something to behold. You've missed quite the spectacle, mister.'

The owner seemed to be quietly anticipating some reaction to his story of those days, but when his expectation was frustrated a look of failure showed in his eyes.

'Spectacle? What could have been good about it? People killing and getting killed. Have the poor luck to see something like that and you feel sick for life!'

'Well, it wasn't your ordinary spectacle. What an event that must have been, the rabble going wild. Really must have been worth seeing.'

The old man did not wish to reply further. It grated badly on his nerves to hear the man talk of 'the rabble this' and 'the rabble that,' but he told himself not to find fault. What could this man have known? If he's now about forty, then it happened when he was around ten; and if he's thirty-five now, he was five then. The man takes the horrific killing and being killed of that time as simply another entertaining tale of long, long ago. That's what thirty years adds up to.

'I've enjoyed the meal but I'd better be on my way.'

The old man struggled to his feet.

'It's pitch black out there. Will you be all right?'

'I know these roads . . .'

Maybe it was the drink, maybe fatigue, but the old man was staggering as he cut across the yard.

'It's dark. Please take care!' the owner shouted.

The staggering old man receded into the darkness, his battered bag clutched tightly to his side.

The old man's corpse was discovered beneath the bridge the following morning, the battered bag still clutched to his side. No one recognized his drawn face. In order to establish his identity, the police went through his personal effects. But all that came out of his bag were a few coins and a half-empty bottle of rice brew.

Instead of disposing of the corpse right away, the police left it beside the road all day long, visible to anyone passing by. But no one turned up who recognized the old man.

Quite a few people were attracted by talk that a man had fallen into the river and drowned. Among them was the owner of the tavern. It gave him a fright, but the next moment he had cooled down. Why would he want to report that he had seen the man and then suffer the nuisance of a summons to the police station?

'If we assume that he threw himself into the river last night, then he probably did it upstream, near the old ferry crossing. Then overnight he would have floated down here. Make out the incident report that way.'

A man in civilian clothing was giving the orders.

'I understand, sir.'

The uniformed policeman saluted him. With that, they unrolled a straw mat and covered the corpse from the head down.

HELL CHOSŎN

YI SANG

Wings

Translated by Kevin O'Rourke

Have you ever met a stuffed genius?

Look no farther – I feel good about being one.

Makes me feel good about romance too.

It's only when my body creaks with fatigue that my mind begins to glint like a silver coin. Nicotine takes over my wormy tummy, and a clean page opens in my mind where I can plop down my *paduk* stones of wit and paradox. It's known as the awful disease of common sense.

I'm drawing up plans to live with a woman again. I'm a bit of a schizophrenic, inadequate in the arts of love but aware of the acme of intellectualism. I plan a life where I have half the woman – that's half of everything. I plan to dip one foot in, sort of like two giggling suns staring at each other. Maybe life is so boring I've opted out. Goodbye.

Goodbye. It might be good occasionally to practise the ultimate irony: wolf down the dishes you dislike most. Wit and paradox and . . .

Maybe construct an artificial self, not a novel ready-made product, but something convenient and saleable.

Block out the nineteenth century – if you can – from your consciousness. The Dostoevsky spirit is garbage. And I don't know who called Hugo a chunk of French bread, but the comment is apt. You can't afford to let life or the personality quirk of a life model deceive you. And don't seek out calamity. Do you understand what I'm saying . . . When the Band-Aid bursts you get blood. You just have to believe the wound will heal soon. Goodbye.

Emotion is pose (maybe more accurately an indicator of a small element in pose). Emotion cuts off its supply when pose intensifies to immobility.

My view of the world comes from reflection on my unusual development.

Queen bee and widow. Is there a woman in the world who isn't a widow in her heart? I see all women as widow-natured. Is this insulting to women? Goodbye.

No. 33 is set up a bit like a brothel. Eighteen households shoulder to shoulder, one roof; identical papered doors, identical fire holes in the kitchen; and the residents are all young flowers. The sun doesn't come in here. The girls pretend to be unaware of the rising sun. They stop the sun getting in by running a clothesline across their sliding doors and hanging stained bedding up to dry. They nap in the dark interiors. Don't they sleep at night? How would I know? I sleep day and night myself. The eighteen households in No. 33 spend quiet days.

But only the days are quiet. At dusk when the girls bring in the bedding and light the lamps, the houses take on a much more exotic appearance. And as the night progresses, doors slide open and shut more frequently. No. 33 becomes busy, busy. And it exudes all sorts of smells: grilling mackerel, foundation cream, rice water, soap . . .

But it's the nameplates that really put the heads nodding in comprehension. No. 33 has a sort of collective main gate – at a bit of a remove and never closed, a continuation of the street, really. Peddlers stream in and out all day long. The girls don't go to the gate to buy bean curd; they buy in their rooms. Obviously then, there's little point in having eighteen nameplates on the main gate. Instead the girls have signs over their sliding doors – Hall of Great Patience, Hall of Good Fortune and so on; each girl inserts her card in a corner of the sign.

In our place – well, it's really my wife's place – we follow the house custom: my wife's card – about the size of four cigarette packs – sits above the sliding door.

I don't mix with the residents. I don't even greet them. I don't want to greet anyone except my wife because it seems to me that greeting people or mixing with people would not be good for my wife's reputation. That's how important she is to me. Why do I prize her so? I prize her because she is a flower among flowers. Like her name card, she is the smallest and the most beautiful of the flowers in the eighteen houses. She lights up a sunless area under the galvanized roof. The way I cling to this beautiful flower makes me indescribably ashamed to be who I am.

I love my room – it's not really a house; we don't have a house. The temperature is right for my body temperature and the degree of dimness is appropriate for good sight. I never aspired to a cooler or warmer room; I don't want a room that's brighter or more comfortable. This room fulfils my needs, and I reciprocate with feelings of gratitude. I am delighted by the thought that perhaps I came into the world with this room in mind.

I don't calculate happiness or unhappiness. In other words, when I'm happy, I don't need to think, and by the same token, when I'm unhappy, I find it unnecessary to think. To spend each day as it comes in utter unthinking idleness, for me that is the ultimate perfection – no more to be said. I'm most content, most at ease, idling my time away in a room that matches my mind and body. In other words, I have reached an absolute state of being that forswears worldly considerations such as happiness and unhappiness. And I like this.

If you count from the main gate inwards, my room – my absolute space – is room seven. A bit of Lucky Seven, I suppose. I love the number 7; to me it's like a government decoration. Who'd guess that this room, actually two rooms divided by a paper partition, is a symbol of my karma?

The sun comes into the outer room – a book-jacket-sized chunk of early morning sunlight; by afternoon when it leaves, it's reduced to the size of a handkerchief. The sun never gets into the inner room, which, needless to say, is my room. I can't remember whether it was me or my wife who decided she should have the room with the sunlight and I should have the room with no sunlight. But I have no complaints.

When my wife goes out for the day, I slip quickly into her room and open the window on the east side. When I open the window, streaming sunlight plays across her dressing table until all the tiny bottles glitter sumptuously. Looking at this glittering array is a joy beyond words. I take out a tiny magnifying glass and drag it across the *chirigami* my wife uses and I play the fire game, refracting the parallel sun-rays and concentrating them into a focal point until the tissue scorches and a slender thread of smoke appears. The savour of impatient anxiety I experience during those few seconds while waiting for the inevitable hole to burn in the paper brings a thrill of exquisite pleasure so acute I think I'll die.

When I tire of the fire game, I take out my wife's hand mirror and play all sorts of games with it. The only practical use a mirror has is to show your face; otherwise it's a toy.

I soon tire of this game too. The focus of my amusement moves from physical things to the things of the mind. I toss the hand mirror aside and move to my wife's dressing table, to the wide variety of cosmetics bottles lined up on display there. These bottles are the most glamorous things in the world. I choose one, pull out the stopper, put the bottle to my nose and take a gentle breathless sniff. An exotic sensual fragrance seeps into my lungs and I can't help closing my eyes. It's clearly a splash of my wife's body smell. I put the stopper back in the bottle. From what part of my wife's body do I get this smell? I'm not sure. Why? Because the smell is the accumulation of all my wife's body smells.

My wife's room always glitters. In contrast with my room, which hasn't a single nail in the wall, my wife's room has nails all around the base of the ceiling, on each of which is hung one of her splendid skirts or blouses. The variegated array of patterns is lovely to look at. I always imagine my wife naked under these skirts and I think of her assuming various poses – I'm afraid I'm not very gentlemanly in my imaginings.

Of course, I don't have clothes. My wife doesn't give me clothes. The corduroy suit I wear serves as sleep wear, everyday wear and special wear. And I have a high-necked sweater that I use as an undershirt throughout the year. All my clothes are dark-coloured. I guess this is so they won't look too bad until they can be washed. I wear soft *sarumada* with elastic in the waist and legs, and I play to my heart's content without making a sound.

Before I know it, the sunlight handkerchief has left the room; my wife isn't back yet. Already I'm a bit fatigued from my activities and I figure I should be in my own room when she gets here, so I cross over to my own room. It's dark. I pull the quilt over my head and take a nap. I never fold away my bedding, so it has a very welcoming intimacy, like an extension of my body. Sometimes sleep comes easily. Other times I ache all over and I can't get to sleep. That's when I pick a study topic. I've made a lot of discoveries under my damp quilt. I've written a lot of dissertations, composed a lot of poems. But when I fall asleep, all my discoveries dissolve like soap in the moist air that fills the room. And when I waken again, my insides are like a pillow stuffed with cotton rags or buckwheat husks; I'm a nerve bundle in clothes.

I hate bedbugs most of all. Even in winter there are always a few in my room, and if there's anything that bothers me in this world, it's those damn bedbugs. When they bite, I scratch the itchy spot till it bleeds. The bite smarts. It's a profoundly pleasurable sensation. I fall into a deep, satisfying sleep.

My intellectual life under the quilt brings no positive outcomes. There is no necessity for them. Were there positive outcomes, I would have to discuss them with my wife, which means I would certainly get an earful from her. It's not so much that I'm afraid of being reproved by my wife as that I find the process irritating. I'd rather be the laziest animal rather than have to work as an integral member of society or be lectured by my wife. I wish I could cast off this meaningless human mask.

I'm discomfited by human society; I'm discomfited by life. It's all so alienating.

My wife washes twice a day. I don't even wash once. I go to the loo during the night, usually around four or five o'clock. On bright moonlit nights, I like to stand, just stand, in the courtyard before coming back in. So, you see, I rarely come face to face with any of the occupants of our eighteen domiciles, and yet I remember the faces of almost half the young women who live here. None of them is as pretty as my wife.

Around 11 a.m. my wife washes herself for the first time; a rather basic affair. The second wash, about 7 p.m., is much more demanding. She wears better, cleaner clothes at night than during the day. She goes out in the daytime and she also goes out at night.

Has my wife a job? I have no way of knowing what her job is. If she hadn't a job, she could stay at home like me – there'd be no need to go out. But she goes out. Not only does she go out, she also has a lot of visitors. On days when she has a lot of visitors I have to stay in my room under the quilt. I can't play the fire game; I can't sniff her cosmetics. That's when I get consciously depressed. And then she gives me money. A fifty-*chŏn* silver coin. I like that. Of course, I have no idea what to use the silver coins for, so I toss them onto the head of the bed. Eventually there's quite a pile. One day my wife noticed the pile of coins and bought me a dummy piggy bank. I put the coins in the piggy bank one at a time. My wife took away the key. After that I remember occasionally putting money in the piggy bank. I am lazy. I remember seeing a new bauble in my wife's hair – a pimple-like eruption – and wondering if that meant the piggy bank was lighter. But I never touched the piggy bank at the head of the bed. My innate laziness didn't allow me to excite myself about such things.

On days when my wife has a lot of callers, I can't sleep like I sleep on rainy days, no matter how I snuggle into the quilt. So that's when I study why my wife always has money, why she always has lots of money.

Visitors don't seem to be aware that I'm at the other side of the partition. They joke freely with her, things I wouldn't dream of saying. Three or four of the regulars are relatively gentlemanly in their behaviour in that they usually go home right after midnight, but there's the odd one who seems lacking in refinement, the kind that brings in food and eats it here. The boorish type has his snack and is satisfied.

I've begun to study what my wife's occupation might be, but my viewpoint is narrow and my knowledge is poor so that I find it difficult to reach a satisfactory conclusion.

My wife always wears new *pŏsŏn* socks. And she cooks. I've never actually seen her cooking, but she serves me breakfast and dinner in my room every day, and there's no one here except her and me. Clearly she does the cooking herself. But she never calls me into her room.

I eat and sleep alone in the inner room – always. The food tastes terrible and the side dishes are very meagre. I eat my feed without comment, like a pup or a hen, but I can't say I never have resentful feelings. I'm getting inexorably paler and thinner. My strength is failing day by day. My bones are beginning to jut out from malnutrition. I toss and turn all night because I ache all over.

And so, buried under the quilt, I speculate on the source of my wife's money, and I try to figure out what the food might be that's served in the other room, basing my analysis on the smells that seep through the paper partition. I don't sleep very well.

I know now. I know that my wife's money – though I can't imagine why – comes from the visitors, whom I've always considered to be silly fools. But why do they leave money when they're going? Why does my wife take the money? The etiquette of all this escapes me.

Is it just a matter of etiquette? Or is it payment for something? A wage? Does my wife appear to them to be an object of charity?

The more I think of it the more muddled my head becomes. The only conclusion I reach before falling asleep is that it's not nice. Of course, it never occurs to me to ask my wife about it. I figure it would be tiresome to do this, and I want to wake up in a few hours as a new man with a clean slate.

When the guests leave or when my wife gets back home from a late outing, she puts on something comfortable and comes into my room. She pulls back the quilt and whispers a few encouraging words in my ear in an effort to comfort me. I look at her beautiful face and laugh in a way that is neither derisive, nor wry, nor loud. She responds with a serene laugh. But make no mistake: I don't miss the slightest tint of sadness in her face.

My wife knows when I'm hungry. Yet she never offers me leftovers from the outer room. This, I believe, is a mark of respect for me. And even though I'm hungry, I like this feeling of emotional strength. I never remember what my wife chatters about; all I know is the silver coin she leaves on the pillow, which shines faintly in the lamplight as she takes her leave.

How many silver coins are in the dummy piggy bank? I don't lift it to see. I have neither desire nor aspiration: I simply drop the silver coins through the button-shaped slot.

Why my wife's guests give her money when they are leaving is as unsolvable a mystery to me as why she gives me money when she's leaving my room. And though I'm not averse to her leaving money on her way out, there's no great pleasure involved. I just like the brief – hardly worth mentioning – sensation of money in my hand disappearing down the slot of the piggy bank.

One day I threw the piggy bank in the loo. I don't know how much was in it, but there were a lot of silver coins. I reflect that planet Earth where I live is hurtling at an unbelievable speed through boundless space and I am filled with feelings of futility. I figure our bustling world will make me dizzy and I want to get off right now. After such thoughts under the quilt, it's tiresome to continue putting silver coins in the piggy bank. I hoped my wife would use the piggy bank herself; she needed the money. From the outset money was useless to me, so I waited in hope that she would take the piggy bank to her own room and keep it there. But she didn't. I thought about putting it in her room myself, but she had so many callers I never got a chance. That's why I threw it in the loo.

With a heavy heart I waited for my wife to give me a good telling-off. But she said nothing, asked nothing. Furthermore, she continued to leave money by my pillow when she was going. Soon there were a lot of silver coins there.

I began a new round of under-the-quilt research on whether the impulse of the callers to give my wife money and her impulse to give me money had any motivation other than pleasure. And if pleasure was the motivating factor, I wondered what kind of pleasure. Of course, under-the-quilt research is not going to produce an answer to this question. Pleasure, pleasure . . . I'm surprised to find this is the only subject that interests me at the moment.

My wife invariably keeps me more or less confined, and while I have no reason to complain about this, I want to experience the presence or absence of this pleasure thing.

I took advantage of my wife going out for the evening to have an outing myself. I didn't forget to bring the silver coins with me. I changed them for paper money on the street. It came to five *wŏn*. I put the money in my pocket and proceeded to comb the streets, trying to forget the object of the outing. Seeing the streets again after such a long interval filled me with wonder and excitement. And though I tired quickly, I put up with the tiredness. I drifted until it was late through one street after another: I had no sense of purpose. Of course I didn't spend a copper. There was no reason to spend anything. I seemed to have lost the facility to spend money.

It became more and more difficult to put up with the fatigue, and in the end I only got home with difficulty. I knew I had to go through my wife's room to get to my room, but I was worried that she might have a visitor, so I hesitated outside the sliding door and coughed diffidently. The door whammed open to reveal my wife's face and the face of a stranger behind her. I hesitated for a moment, dazzled by the light.

It wasn't that I didn't see the anger in my wife's eyes. I saw it all right, but I had to ignore it. What else could I do? One way or another I had to go through her room to get to mine.

I pulled the quilt over my head. My legs were aching so badly it was unbearable. I thought I would pass out from the palpitations I was having under the quilt. I was short of breath, though I hadn't noticed it while I was walking. Cold sweat drenched my spine. I regretted the outing. I wished I could forget the fatigue and get to sleep. I needed a good sleep.

For a long time, I lay there at an angle; gradually the palpitations subsided. At least I'll live, I thought. I turned over, lay on my back facing the ceiling, and stretched my legs.

Then the palpitations took over again. The partition carried the whispers of my wife and her visitor, their voices so low I couldn't understand. I opened my eyes wide in an effort to hear more clearly. By this stage my wife and the man were on their feet, arranging coats and hats. The door slid open. I heard the scratch of heels, followed by the plop of the man stepping down into the courtyard, then walking a few steps, and my wife's rubber shoes sliding after him. Their footsteps faded towards the main gate.

I had never seen my wife do this before. She never whispered with her visitors. There might be times when I was wrapped in the quilt and missed what a caller said, usually because he was tongue-tied and drunk, but I never missed a word my wife said in that voice of hers that was neither low nor loud. I mightn't like what she said, but I took comfort in the calm way she said it. I surmised that there was some not insignificant reason for my wife's behaviour, and that saddened me, but because I was tired, I resolved not to do further under-the-quilt research tonight. I waited for sleep to come; it wasn't easy but eventually I fell asleep. My dreams wandered through a jumble of topsy-turvy street scenes.

I was shaken violently. My wife had come back after seeing off her visitor; she found me asleep and shook me. I opened my eyes wide and examined her face. She was not smiling. Anger lit her eyes, and her thin lips were trembling. Her anger would not be appeased easily. I closed my eyes and waited for the thunderbolt to strike. She took a few angry breaths, her skirt gave a swish, the connecting door opened and closed, and she disappeared into her own room. I turned over, pulled the quilt over my head and lay on my belly like a toad. I was hungry. Again I regretted tonight's outing.

I lay there under the quilt and told my wife I was sorry. *You misunderstood . . . I thought it was very late; I had no idea it wasn't midnight.* I was so tired. After being confined for so long, it was a mistake to walk so far. A mistake all right, but just a mistake. Why did I go out?

I wanted to give the money at the head of my bed to someone . . . anyone. That's all. And if that was wrong, I admit it; it was wrong. I'm sorry, I really am.

Had I been able to spend the five *wŏn*, I don't think I'd have got back before midnight. But the streets were very busy; there were people everywhere, and I had no idea who to give the five *wŏn* to. And in the search process I ran out of energy.

Most of all, I wanted to rest; I wanted to lie down. I had no choice but to return home. It was unfortunate that all this happened before midnight. I felt bad about it. I had no problem saying I was sorry. But if I couldn't clear up my wife's misunderstanding, what was the point in saying I was sorry? It was so frustrating.

I fretted for an hour. Then I threw off the quilt, got up and staggered into my wife's room. I hardly knew what I was doing. I just about remember throwing myself down on my wife's bedding, reaching into my trousers pocket, taking out the five *wŏn* and thrusting it into her hand.

When I woke up next day, I was in bed in my wife's room. This was the first time I had slept in my wife's room since we moved into No. 33.

The sun was high in the window: my wife had gone out; she was no longer by my side. No, that's not correct. For all I knew she had gone out last night when I lost consciousness. But I don't want to go into that. I felt unwell all over; I hadn't the strength to move a finger. A patch of sunlight, smaller than a *pojagi* book wrapper, dazzled my eyes. Dust particles – like microbes – ran riot through the light. My nose was blocked. I closed my eyes again, pulled the quilt over my head and tried to sleep. My wife's fragrance was a provocative fire in my nose. I twisted and turned; I was contorted. Sleep wouldn't come; the effort to sleep was frustrated by the scent of the cosmetics, caps off, arrayed on my wife's dressing table.

It was a terrible feeling. I kicked off the quilt, jumped out of bed and went back to my room. My breakfast, cold now, lay where my wife had put it before she went out. I was hungry. The spoon in my mouth was as cold as chilled raw fish. I put the spoon down and crept under the quilt. My bedding, empty all night, extended its customary warm welcome for me. I pulled the quilt over my head, stretched out and slept.

The lights were on when I awoke. My wife was not back yet. Well, maybe she'd been back and gone out again. Not much point in going into that.

My head was clearer now. I thought about last night's happenings. I couldn't explain the pleasure it gave me when I fell into my wife's bed and put the five *wŏn* in her hand. I had discovered why callers gave her money when they were leaving and her secret psychology in giving me money; I was overjoyed, laughing inside. What a fool I was not to have known this. My shoulders lifted dance-like.

As a result of all this, I felt the urge to go out again tonight. But I had no money. Damn, why did I give that five *wŏn* to my wife last night? And I regretted sticking the piggy bank in the loo. I was silly enough to put my hand in my trouser pocket, where the five *wŏn* had been – force of habit, I suppose. I rummaged around and was surprised by what I found: two *wŏn*. I didn't need a lot. Anything was good. Thank heaven for little favours.

Newly energized, I threw on my old corduroy suit, flapped my wings and headed for the street, oblivious of the hunger in my tummy and my impoverished appearance. Once on the street I was consumed with anxiety: I wanted time's arrow to shoot straight past midnight. Giving money to my wife and sleeping in her room was all very fine, but the look in her eyes if I got it wrong and arrived back before midnight was a cause of no little worry. I stopped to peer at every clock in the street and kept on wandering aimlessly. Today I didn't tire quickly. My big concern was how slowly time was passing.

Finally, when the clock at Seoul Station assured me it was past midnight, I headed for home. My wife was talking to a gentleman visitor at the two-pillar gate. I ignored them, walked past and went into my room. My wife came back a little later. Once back in her room, she did something she never did at night: she swept the floor. Afterwards I heard her lying down. I opened the connecting door, went into her room and pressed the two *wǒn* firmly into her hand. She looked in my face several times as if she thought it strange that I had come back again tonight without spending the money. She said nothing, but she let me sleep beside her. I wouldn't exchange the joy of this for anything in the world. I slept peacefully and well.

Next morning when I woke up, there was no sign of her. I went back to my own room and laid my tired body down for some more sleep.

The lights were on when my wife shook me awake. She told me to come into her room. This was also something she had never done before. She took me by the arm, a smile ever present on her face. I couldn't help feeling a bit anxious. Did that smiling exterior conceal some untoward plot?

I went along with my wife's wishes and allowed her to lead me into her room. A dinner table was nicely arrayed there. Come to think of it, I hadn't eaten for two days. With all my messing around, I had been unaware that I was hungry.

Should a thunderbolt strike after this last supper, I thought, I'd have no regrets. For me, the world was unbearably tedious. Everything was irksome and annoying. I might even enjoy a sudden calamity. I put these thoughts out of my mind, sat down opposite my wife, and ate this strange supper. My wife and I never talked much. When I finished, I got up quietly and crossed into my room. My wife didn't stop me. I leaned back against the wall, smoked a cigarette and waited. If the thunderbolt is going to strike, let it strike now.

Five minutes, ten minutes.

There was no thunderbolt. Gradually the tension eased. Suddenly it was in my head to go out again tonight and I wished I had some money.

But I had no money. That was clear. Suppose I went out tonight, could I look forward to joy later? The road ahead was dark, dark. Angry, I pulled the quilt over my head; I tossed and turned. Dinner kept coming back up my throat. I felt sick.

Anything that fell from heaven would be appreciated; *why not a sudden money shower?* It was incredibly unfair and sad. I knew no other way to get money. I think I must have cried in bed. Why have I no money?

At that moment my wife came into the room again. I started in surprise. *The thunderbolt will strike now.* I curled up toad style, hardly daring to breathe. But the words that slid from her lips were gentle, affectionate. 'I know why you're crying,' she said. 'It's because you have no money, isn't it?' I was startled. Her ability to see into me like that was not without its disturbing aspects, but the good side was that I felt she was going to give me money. If she does, I thought, that will be wonderful! Wrapped in the bedding like a dried fish, I didn't dare lift my head as I waited for her next move. Right, she said, and she dropped something on my pillow, so light and easy, I knew from the sound it had to be paper money.

'It's okay to come home a bit later tonight,' she whispered in my ear.

That wouldn't be a problem. My first reaction was to be happy and grateful to get the money.

So I set out. Being prone to night blindness, I decided to restrict my wanderings to the brighter streets. I dropped into the tearoom in the corner of Seoul Station's first- and second-class waiting room. What a discovery! First of all, no one I knew frequented the place. And even if they did, they left immediately. I decided to spend some time here every day.

In the first place, it had the most accurate clock in the city. I didn't want to put my trust in an inferior clock and maybe end up going home early and getting a bloody nose.

I sat in an empty booth – no one opposite me – and sipped well-brewed coffee. Hurrying passengers seemed to enjoy a cup of coffee. They drank quickly, stared at the wall as if they had something on their minds, and left in a hurry. Sad. But I preferred this sad atmosphere to the dull atmosphere of the tearooms in the streets; it was more real. From time to time I heard train whistles, sometimes sharp, sometimes sonorous, more intimate than Mozart. I read the names of the few dishes on the menu; I read them over and over; I read them up, down and sideways. They were fuzzy like the names of childhood friends.

I don't know how long I sat there: I was a bit confused. Customers were scarce and the cleanup had begun, so I concluded it must be near closing time. Had to be after eleven, I thought. Can't stay here. So where will I go until midnight? I took my worries outside with me. It was raining; pretty heavy rain, obviously bad news for someone with neither rainwear nor umbrella. But I couldn't hang around here all night, not looking as weird as I did. So I said, *What the hell, it's only rain*, and off I went.

The cold was difficult to bear. My corduroys were soon wet. The wet seeped inside until I was soaked. I put up with it as long as I could. Traipsing through the streets was a struggle, and eventually I was so cold I couldn't take it any longer. Bouts of shivering and chattering teeth. I increased the pace. Surely, I thought, my wife won't have a visitor on a terrible night like this. I have to go home. If, unfortunately, she has a visitor, I'll explain the situation. When I explain the situation and she sees the rain, she'll understand.

I flew home. My wife had a visitor. I was so cold and wet that in my confusion I forgot to knock and I saw something my wife wouldn't want me to see. I splashed across the floor of her room and into my own room, leaving big footprints in my wake; I threw off my soaked clothes and wrapped myself in the quilt. I began to shiver; the chills increased in intensity. The earth seemed about to collapse under me. I lost consciousness.

The next day when I woke, my wife was sitting by my pillow wearing a worried expression. I had caught a chill. I was still cold; my head was aching; I was drooling and miserable; my legs and arms were stretched with fatigue. My wife felt my forehead and said I'd have to take medicine. From the cold of her hand on my forehead I knew I had quite a temperature. If I have to take something, I thought, it'll be an antipyretic. My wife handed me four white pills and a cup of warm water. 'Take these,' she said. 'Have a good sleep and you'll be fine.' I popped the pills into my mouth. From the acrid taste I figured they were aspirin. I pulled up the quilt and fell into the sleep of the dead.

I had a runny nose and was sick for several days. I kept taking the pills all the while. My cold got better, but I still had the taste of sumac in my mouth.

I began getting the urge to go out again. But my wife advised me not to. She told me to take my pills and rest in bed. It was on a foolish outing, she said, that I had caught the cold and caused her so much bother.

This was true. So I promised not to go out. I would keep taking my pills and build myself up.

I pulled the quilt over my head and slept. For some strange reason I couldn't keep my eyes open night or day. I believed firmly that my constant sleepiness was a sign I was getting physically stronger.

I spent most of a month like this. My hair and beard were so unbearably scruffy I thought I'd have a look in the mirror. So when my wife went out, I took the opportunity to slip into her room and sit at her dressing table. I was a sight to behold: hair and beard were a mess. I'll have to get a haircut today, I thought, as I took the caps off the cosmetics and sniffed. Among the fragrances I had forgotten for the past while was that body smell that always knotted me into a ball. I whispered her name in my heart. *Yŏnshimi!*

And I played my game of setting the bugs on fire with a magnifying glass – it had been such a long time. And the mirror game. The sunlight streaming in the window was uncommonly warm. It's May, I thought, isn't it?

I had a big stretch, threw my wife's pillow on the floor, and pillowed on it. I wanted to boast to God about the lovely peaceful times I was enjoying. I made no compromise with the world. God would neither praise nor punish me.

Next moment something really shocking caught my eye. A box of Adalin sleeping pills. I found them under my wife's dressing table. They looked just like aspirin. I opened the box. Four gone.

I remember taking four aspirin this morning. And I slept. I had been so unbearably sleepy yesterday, the day before and the day before that. Even after my cold cleared up, my wife kept giving me aspirin. There was a fire one day in one of the other places, and I slept though it – dead to the world. That's how deeply I'd slept. I'd been taking Adalin for a month and thought I was taking aspirin. This was very serious indeed.

I was suddenly dizzy; I thought I might faint. I put the box of pills in my pocket and left. I started up the mountain; I didn't want to look at anyone or anything in this world. I tried not to think of my wife and me as I walked, because I knew I could easily faint on the road. I wanted to find a sunny place, to sit there and slowly examine my relationship with my wife. All I could think of was the newly blossomed forsythia – I hadn't seen it so far this year – the larks in the air, and stories of stones hatching chicks. Fortunately, I didn't pass out by the roadside.

There was a bench. I sat down and began to consider the aspirin and Adalin question. I was so confused I couldn't think straight. It took less than five minutes for the irritating questions that filled my head to put me in a rotten humour. I took the Adalin out of my pocket and chewed the remaining six tablets. They tasted funny. Then I stretched out longways on the bench. Why did I do this? I have no idea. I suppose I just wanted to do it. I fell into a deep sleep. As I slept I could hear the water trickling between the stones.

I didn't wake up until early the following morning. I had slept through the night. The landscape was totally yellow. Thoughts of aspirin and Adalin flashed like lightning through the yellowing light.

Aspirin, Adalin, aspirin, Adalin, Marx, Malthus, *matroos*, aspirin, Adalin . . .

For a month my wife had fed me Adalin, tricking me into thinking they were aspirin. The box of Adalin I found in her room was clear proof.

Why did she want me to sleep night and day?

While she had me asleep night and day, what was she doing?

Was she trying to kill me little by little?

On further consideration, maybe it was aspirin I had been taking for the last month. Maybe she was taking the Adalin herself because something was bothering her and she couldn't sleep. That put me in a very bad light. How awful to entertain terrible doubts about my wife!

So I lurched off the bench. My legs were unstable and I felt dizzy. With great difficulty I began to walk home. It was nearly 8 a.m.

I wanted to confess all my misconceived thoughts and ask my wife's forgiveness. I was in such a hurry I forgot what I had to say.

What happened next was simply awful. I saw something I should never – ever – see. I closed the sliding door quickly and stood there for a moment, head down, eyes closed. I held on to the pillar, trying to control a fit of dizziness. Suddenly the sliding door whammed open, and my wife, her dress in disarray, reached out and grabbed me by the throat. I was dizzy and tumbled down. She fell on top of me and began to shred me with her teeth. It was so painful I thought I'd die. But I hadn't the strength of mind or body to resist. I just lay on my belly wondering what would happen next. Then the man came out, swept my wife into his arms, and carried her inside. My wife said nothing. I was shocked by her submissiveness when the man carried her in his arms. I hated it.

My wife was very abusive: she accused me of being out all night robbing people and whoring. This was too much! I was so shocked I couldn't say anything.

I wanted to shout, 'You're the one who tried to kill me,' but if I spluttered out something so rash – perhaps even baseless – there was no knowing what awful mischief might result. Common sense said I'd better stomach my pain.

I'll never know why I did what I did, but I dusted myself off, got up, took out whatever change was left in my pocket, eased open the sliding door, left the money on the door's sill and took off at a run.

Several times I was almost hit by a car, but I managed to get to Seoul Station. I sat down in a place with no one facing me and wondered what I might get to take the bitter taste out of my mouth.

Coffee! Yes, that would be good. Here I was in the station hall and I realized I'd forgotten that I hadn't a copper in my pocket. The rest is a bit vague. I hesitated – lifeless – I didn't know what to do. I went back and forth, back and forth, like a man in a daze.

I have no idea where I went. All I know is that several hours later when I realized I was on the roof of the Mitsukoshi Department Store, it was nearly midday.

I hunkered down and reflected on the twenty-six years of my life. The hazy recesses of memory produced nothing noteworthy.

I asked myself again, *Do you have any desire in life?* I didn't want to answer yes or no. I had difficulty coming to grips with the fact of my existence.

I bent down to look at a bowl of goldfish. They were beautiful. Big and small – all fresh and lovely to behold. In the beaming May sunlight the goldfish cast a shadow on the bottom of the bowl. Their fins rippled as if imitating a waving handkerchief. I was so intent on counting the fins that I didn't straighten up for a long time. My back was warm.

I looked down at the grimy street. Weary lives floundered there, oscillating like the fins of the goldfish, lives that couldn't get free, tangled around an invisible sticky cord. Fatigue and hunger are dragging me down, I thought, sucking me inexorably into the grime of the street.

Where to now? My wife's face came at me like a thunderbolt. Aspirin and Adalin.

It was a mutual misunderstanding. Surely my wife didn't give me Adalin instead of aspirin? I couldn't believe she would do that. She had no reason. So was I out robbing and whoring that night? Believe me, no way.

As a couple we were fated to limp through life fundamentally out of step. There was no need to look for logic in what either of us did. There was no need to change anything. All we had to do was limp on through the world wherever fact and misunderstanding took us. Isn't that right? But should my steps lead back to my wife? That was hard to determine. Should I go back? Where should I go?

The midday siren wailed. A moment when everyone spread wings and flapped like chickens while glass, steel, marble, paper and ink seethed to a crescendo. Midday dramatizing the exotic!

Suddenly my armpits were itchy. Ah, yes, that's where my artificial wings once sprouted. They weren't there today. Erased pages of hope and desire flashed through my head – like a flip through the dictionary. I stopped. I wanted to cry out:

Sprout again, wings!
Let me fly, fly, fly; one more time let me fly.
One more time, let me try to fly!

KIM SŬNGOK

Seoul: Winter 1964

Translated by Marshall R. Pihl

Anyone who spent the winter of 1964 in Seoul would probably remember those stalls that appeared on the streets once it got dark – selling hotchpotch, roasted sparrows and three kinds of booze; made so that to step inside you had to lift a curtain being whipped by a bitter wind that swept the frozen streets; where the long flame of a carbide lamp inside fluttered with the gusts; and where a middle-aged man in a dyed army jacket poured drinks and roasted snacks for you. Well, it was in one of those stalls that the three of us happened to meet that night. By the three of us, I mean myself, a graduate student named An who wore thick glasses and a man in his mid-thirties of whom I knew nothing except that he was obviously poor – a man whose particulars, actually, I hadn't the least desire to know.

The chitchat started off between me and the graduate student, and when the small talk and self-introductions were over I knew he was a 25-year-old flower of Korean youth, a graduate student with a major that I (who hadn't even got close to a college) had never even dreamed of and the oldest son of a rich family; and he probably knew I was a 25-year-old country boy, that I had volunteered for the Military Academy when I got out of high school only to fail and then enter the army, where I caught the clap once, and that I was now working in the military affairs section of a local government office.

We had introduced ourselves and now there was nothing to talk about. For a while we just drank quietly and then, when I picked up a charred sparrow, something occurred to me to say and so, after thanking the sparrow, I began to talk.

'An, do you love flies?'

'No, until now, I . . . do you, Kim?'

'Yes,' I replied. 'Because they can fly. No, because even while they can fly, they can be caught in my hand. Have you ever caught something in your hand that can fly?'

'Just a moment now. Let me see.' For a while he looked at me blankly from behind his glasses as he screwed up his face. Then he said, 'No, I haven't. Except for flies, of course.'

The weather that day had been unusually warm, and the ice had melted and filled the streets with mud, but as the temperature dropped again by evening, the mud had begun to freeze once more beneath our feet. My leather shoes were not solid enough to block the chill that crept up from the freezing ground. Actually, a booze stall like this was meant just for people who thought they might stop for a glass on the way home; it wasn't the place to be drinking and chatting with the man standing next to you. This thought had just occurred to me when Four-Eyes asked me quite a question. *This guy's all right*, I thought. So I made my cold and numb feet hold on a little longer.

'Kim, do you love things that wiggle?' is what he asked me.

'Sure do,' I answered abruptly, with an air of triumph. Recollection can give you this sense of satisfaction, whether you're thinking of something sad or pleasant. When the recollection is sad, your feelings of satisfaction are quiet and lonely, but when the recollection is pleasant, you feel a sense of triumph. 'After I flunked the Military Academy exams, I stayed on at a boarding house in Miari with a friend who had also failed his college entrance exams. That was the first time in Seoul for me, you know. My dreams of becoming an officer were shattered, and I was really depressed. I felt as if I would never get over my disappointment. You probably know, but the bigger the dream, the more powerful is the sense of despair that failure gives you. The thing I took interest in at that time was the inside of a full bus in the morning. My friend and I would get through breakfast as quickly as possible and then trot up to the bus stop at the top of the Miari ridge. I mean, panting like dogs. Do you know what are the most enviable and the most marvellous things in the eyes of a young man from the country who's in Seoul for the first time? The most enviable thing is the lights that come on in the windows of the buildings at night – no, rather, the people who are moving back and forth in that light. And the most marvellous thing is a pretty girl standing beside you in a bus, not one inch away. Sometimes it's possible to stand so that you're not only touching the flesh of her wrist but even rubbing against her thigh. For this, I once spent a whole day riding around town, transferring from one city bus to another. Of course, I was so exhausted that night I puked, but—'

'Just a minute. What are you leading up to?'

'I was getting ready to tell you a story about loving things that wiggle. Listen for a moment. My friend and I would work our way deep into a full morning-rush-hour bus like a couple of pickpockets. Then we'd stand in front of a pretty young girl who had found herself a seat. I would take hold of a strap and lean my head against my raised arm, a little dazed from running for the bus. Then I would slowly ease my eyes down towards the girl's tummy. I wouldn't be able to see it right off, but after a while, when my vision had cleared, I could make out the girl's tummy quietly moving up and down.'

'That up-and-down movement . . . that'd be her breathing, right?'

'Yes, of course. The tummy of a corpse doesn't move, does it? At any rate, I have no idea why it soothed and lifted my spirits so very much to watch that quiet movement inside a full morning bus. Really, I love that movement with a passion.'

'That's quite a lewd story,' said An in a strange voice.

That made me angry. I had remembered that story on purpose, just in case I got on some kind of quiz program on the radio and was asked, 'What is the freshest thing in the world?' The others might say lettuce or daybreak in May or an angel's forehead, but I would say that that movement was the freshest thing.

'No, it isn't a lewd story, at all.' I spoke with an unyielding tone. 'It's a true story.'

'Why should there be a connection between being true and not being lewd?'

'I don't know. I don't know anything about connections. Actually, though . . .'

'But still, that motion – a "movement up and down," wasn't it? That certainly isn't wiggling. It seems you still don't love things that wiggle!'

We fell into another silence and were just fingering our drinks. *Bastard.*

If he doesn't think that's wiggling, it's okay by me, I was thinking. But then, a moment later, he spoke.

'I've just been thinking it over, Kim, and I've come to the conclusion that your movement up and down is, after all, one kind of wiggling.'

'It is, isn't it?' I was pleased. 'No question about it, that's wiggling. What I love more than anything is a girl's tummy. What kind of wiggling do you love, An?'

'It's not a kind of wiggling. Just wiggling itself. All alone. For instance . . . a demonstration . . .'

'Demonstration? A demonstration? Then . . .'

'Seoul is a concentration of every sort of desire. Do you understand?'

'No, I don't,' I replied in my clearest possible voice.

Then our conversation broke off again. This time, though, the silence lasted a long time. I lifted my shot glass to my mouth. When I had emptied it, I could see him holding his to his mouth and drinking with his eyes closed. I thought to myself, with some regret, that the time had come for me to get up and go. So that was that. I was thinking that all of this just confirmed what I had expected to begin with, and I was considering whether to say, 'Until next time, then . . .' or 'It's been enjoyable,' when An, who had finished his drink, caught me by the hand.

'Don't you think we've been telling lies?'

'No.' I was a little annoyed. 'I don't know whether you've been lying, An, but everything I've said is the truth.'

'Well, I have the feeling that we have been lying to each other.' He spoke after blinking his reddened eyes once or twice behind his glasses. 'Whenever I meet a new friend of about our age, I always want to tell a story about wiggling. So I tell the story, but it doesn't take even five minutes.'

For a moment I'd thought I might understand what he was talking about, but now I wasn't sure.

'Now let's talk about something else,' he began again.

But I thought it might be fun to give this lover of serious stories a hard time, and, what's more, I wanted to enjoy the drunk's privilege of listening to the sound of his own voice. So I started talking before he could.

'Of the streetlights that are lined up in front of the P'yŏnghwa Market, the eighth one from the east end is not lit . . .' As soon as I saw him getting confused, I continued with renewed inspiration. 'And of the windows on the sixth floor of the Hwashin Department Store, light was visible only in the three middle ones.'

But now, it was I who was thrown into confusion.

Reason was, a startled look of delight began to light up An's face.

He started to speak rapidly. 'There were thirty-two people at the West Gate bus stop; seventeen were women, five were children, twenty-one were youths and six were elders.'

'When was that?'

'That's as of seven-fifteen this evening.'

'Ah,' I said and began to feel discouraged for a moment. But then I bounced back in great humour and really began to lay it on.

'There are two chocolate wrappers in the first rubbish bin in the alley next to the Tansŏngsa Theatre.'

'When was this?'

'As of 9 p.m. on the fourteenth.'

'One of the branches is broken on the walnut tree in front of the main entrance to the Red Cross Hospital.'

'At a bar in the third block of Ŭlchiro that has no sign there are five girls named Mija, and they are known in the order they came to work there: Big Mija, Second Mija, Third Mija, Fourth Mija and Last Mija.'

'But that's something other people would know too. I don't think you're the only one who has visited that place, Kim.'

'Ah, you're right! I never thought of that. Well, one night I slept with Big Mija, and the next morning she bought me a pair of shorts from a woman who came around selling things on a daily instalment plan. Now, there was one hundred and ten *wŏn* in the empty bottle she used for keeping her money in.'

'That's more like it. That fact is entirely your property alone, Kim *hyŏng*.'

He called me 'older brother' as our speech conveyed our growing familiarity with each other.

'I –' We both began to speak at the same time. And then each yielded to the other.

'I, ah . . .' This time it was his turn. 'I saw the trolley on a tram bound from West Gate to Seoul Station kick out bright blue sparks exactly five times while within my field of vision. The tram was passing by there at seven twenty-five this evening.'

'You were staying in the West Gate area this evening, weren't you, An *hyŏng*?'

'Yes, only in the West Gate area.'

'I'm a couple of blocks up Chongno. There's a fingernail scratch about two centimetres long a little below the handle of the door to the toilet in the Yŏngbo Building.'

He laughed loudly. 'You left that scratch yourself, didn't you, Kim *hyŏng*?'

I was embarrassed, but I had to nod. It was true.

'How did you know?' I asked him.

'Well, I've had that experience too,' he answered. 'But it's not a particularly pleasant memory. It'd be better, after all, for us to stick to things that we happen to have discovered and kept as our own secrets. That other sort of thing leaves a bad taste with you.'

'But I've done that sort of thing lots of times and I must say I rather enj–' I was about to say I enjoyed it, but I suddenly felt a sense of disgust for the whole thing and broke off with a nod of agreement with his opinion.

But about that time something struck me as strange. If this fellow in the shiny glasses sitting next to me really was the son of a rich family and was highly educated to boot, why did he seem so undignified?

'An *hyŏng*. It's true that you're from a rich family, isn't it? And that you're a graduate student too?' I asked.

'With about thirty million *wŏn* in property alone. That would be rich, wouldn't it? But, of course, that's my father's. As for being a graduate student, I've got a student ID card right here . . .' As he spoke, he rummaged through his pockets and pulled out a wallet.

'An ID isn't necessary. It's just that there's something a bit odd. It just struck me as strange that a person like you would be sitting in a cheap booze stall talking with a guy like me about things worth keeping to yourself.'

'Well, that, all . . . that's,' he began in a voice tinged with excitement. 'That's . . . but first, there's something I'd like to ask you, Kim *hyŏng*. Why are you roaming the streets on such a cold night?'

'It's not my usual practice. I've got to have some money in my pocket before I can come out at night, you know.'

'Well, yes. But why do you come out?'

'It's better than sitting in a boarding house and staring at the wall.'

'When you come out at night, don't you feel something – a kind of fullness and abundance?'

'A what?'

'A something. I suppose we could call it "life." I do think I understand why you asked me your question, Kim *hyŏng*. My answer would be something like this. It's night. I come out into the streets from my house. I feel that I've been liberated, untied from any place in particular. It may not be so, but that's what I feel. Don't you feel that, Kim *hyŏng*?'

'Well . . .'

'I'm no longer involved, caught up with all sorts of things – they're left at a distance for me to survey. Isn't that it?'

'Well, that's a little . . .'

'No, don't say it's difficult. In other words, all the things that just went grazing by me during the day stand stripped bare, frozen and helpless, before my gaze at night. Now, wouldn't that have some significance – looking at things and enjoying them like that, I mean.'

'Significance? What significance does that have? I don't count the bricks in buildings in the second block of Chongno because there's some significance in it. I just . . .'

'Right. It's meaningless. No, there may be significance there, but I don't understand it yet. You probably don't either, Kim *hyŏng*. Why don't we just go and find out together some time? And not fake it, either.'

'I'm a little confused. Is that your answer, An *hyŏng*? I'm lost. All of a sudden this "significance" and all . . .'

'Oh, I'm sorry! Well, this would be my answer. That I come out on the streets at night simply because I feel a sense of fullness and closeness.' Then he lowered his voice.

'Kim *hyŏng*, it seems you and I came by different ways to get to the same point. Even supposing this might be the wrong point, the fault isn't ours.' Now he spoke in a bright and cheery voice. 'Say, this isn't the place for us. Let's go somewhere warm, have a proper drink and call it a night. I'm going to take a walk around and then go to an inn. When I happen to go roaming the streets at night, I always stay over at an inn and then go home. It's my favourite plan of action.'

Each of us reached into his pocket, about to pay the bill. At that point, a man addressed us. It was a man beside us who had set his glass down and was warming his hands over the coal briquette fire. He hadn't come in so much to drink as to warm himself at the fire, it seemed. He had on a fairly clean coat and his hair, slicked down in modest fashion, glistened here and there with highlights whenever the flame of the carbide lamp fluttered. Though his background wasn't clear, he was a man of about thirty-five who had the look of poverty about him. Maybe it was his weak chin, or maybe it was because the edges of his eyelids were unusually red. He just spoke in our direction, not addressing himself to me or to An in particular.

'Excuse me. But would it be all right if I joined you? I've got some money on me,' he said in a listless voice.

From the sound of that listless voice it seemed that, while he wasn't necessarily pleading to go along, he dearly wanted to. An and I looked at each other for a moment, and then I said, 'Well, friend, if you've got money for the booze ...'

'Let's all go together,' An added.

'Thank you,' the man said in the same listless voice, and followed after us.

An's expression indicated that this wasn't what he'd planned on, and I, too, didn't have pleasant premonitions. There had been a number of occasions when I had enjoyed myself in the company of people I'd met over a drink, but they usually didn't ask to join the group in a listless voice like that. To make a go of it, you've got to come on lustily, wearing a face that bubbles over with good cheer.

We moseyed along the street, looking here and peering there, like people who had suddenly forgotten their destination. From a medicine ad pasted on a telephone pole a pretty girl looked down at us with a desolate smile that seemed to say, *It's cold up here, but what can I do about it?* A neon sign advertising *soju* on the roof of a building flashed enthusiastically; beside it, a neon sign for medicine would go on for long stretches and then, as if it had nearly forgotten, would hurriedly flash off and back on again; beggars crouched here and there like hunks of rock on the now hard-frozen pavements; and people, hunched over intently, quickly passed them by. A wind-whipped piece of paper skittered over from the other side of the street and landed at my feet. I picked it up and saw it was a handbill pushing some beer hall's 'Service by Beauties – Special Low Prices.'

'What time has it got to?' the listless man asked An.

'It's ten to nine,' An answered after a moment.

'Have you two eaten supper? I haven't eaten yet, so why don't I treat?' the listless man said as he looked at each of us in turn.

'I've eaten,' An and I replied simultaneously.

'You can eat by yourself,' I suggested.

'I guess I'll skip it,' the listless man answered.

'Please. We'll go along with you,' said An.

'Thank you. Then . . .'

We went into a nearby Chinese restaurant. After we'd sat down in a room, he kindly asked us again to have something. And again we refused. But he offered once more.

'Is it all right even if I order something very expensive?' I asked in an effort to make him withdraw the offer.

'Yes, anything you want,' he said in a voice that was now strong for the first time. 'I've decided to use this money up, you see.'

I felt sure the man had some scheme in mind, but still, I asked for a whole chicken and some booze to wash it down with. He gave the waiter my order along with his own. An stared at me in disbelief.

It was just about then that I heard the low moans of a woman coming from the next room.

'Won't you have something too?' the man said to An.

'No.' An refused curtly in a voice that seemed sober.

We turned our ears to the moans in the next room, which were quiet but growing more frequent. From a distance came the faint click-clack of trams and the sound, like flooding water, of rushing automobiles. And from somewhere nearby we could hear the occasional sound of a buzzer. But we in our room were wrapped in an awkward silence.

'There is something I would like to explain to you,' the good-hearted man began. 'I would be grateful if you would listen a while . . . During the day today, my wife died. She had been admitted to Severance Hospital.' He looked searchingly at us but without sadness in his face as he spoke.

'Oh, that's too bad.' 'I'm sorry to hear that.' An and I offered condolences.

'We were very happy together, my wife and I. Since my wife couldn't have children, we had all our time to ourselves. We didn't have a lot of money, but whenever we came by a little, we'd enjoy travelling around together. We'd visit Suwŏn when the strawberries were in season and take in Anyang for the grapes. In the summer, we'd go to Taech'ŏn and then visit Kyŏngju in the autumn. We'd see films and shows in the evenings whenever we could.'

'What illness did she have?' An asked cautiously.

'The doctor said it was acute meningitis. Though she had had acute appendicitis once and also acute pneumonia, she got over them all right. But this acute attack killed her ... now she's dead.'

The man dropped his head and mumbled to himself for a while. An poked my knee with his finger and gave me a look that said, *What do you think? Shouldn't we get out?* I felt the same way, but just then the man raised his head and resumed his story. So we had to stay put.

'My wife and I were married the year before last. I had met her by accident. She once said her family lived somewhere in the Taegu area, but we never had any contact with them. I don't even know where her family home is. So I had no choice in the matter.' He lowered his head and mumbled again.

'You had no choice in what?' I asked.

It looked as if he hadn't heard me. But after a moment he looked up again and continued with eyes that seemed to beg our pardon.

'I sold my wife's body to the hospital. I had no choice. I'm only a salesman, selling books on instalment. I had no idea what to do. They gave me four thousand *wŏn*. I was standing by the fence in front of Severance Hospital until just before I met you two gentlemen. I had been trying to figure out which building had the morgue with my wife's body in it, but I couldn't. So I just stood there and watched the dirty white smoke coming out of the chimneys. What will become of her? Is it true that the students will practise their dissection on her, splitting her head apart with a saw and cutting her stomach open with a knife?'

We could only keep our mouths shut. The waiter brought dishes of sliced pickled radishes and onions.

'I'm sorry to have told you such an unpleasant story. It's just that I couldn't keep it inside me. There's one thing, though, I'd like to discuss – what should I do with this money? I'd like to get rid of it tonight.'

'Spend it, then,' An quickly replied.

'Will you two stay with me until it's all gone?' he asked. We didn't answer right away. 'Please stay with me,' he said. We agreed.

'Let's blow it in good style,' he said, smiling for the first time. But his voice was as lifeless as before.

By the time we left the Chinese restaurant we were all drunk, one thousand *wŏn* of the money was gone, and he looked as if he were crying with one eye while laughing with the other. An was telling me that he was tired of figuring out a way to escape, and I was mumbling, *I got the accents all wrong, damn accents!* The street was cold and empty, like a ghost town you might see in a movie, but the sign was still flashing diligently and the medicine sign had shaken off its lethargy. The girl on the telephone pole was smiling, telling us, *Same old me.*

'Where shall we go now?' the man said.

'Where shall we go?' An said.

'Where shall we go?' I echoed.

But we hadn't any place to go. Beside the Chinese restaurant we had just left was the display window of a men's clothing shop. The man pointed towards it and then dragged us inside the shop.

'Let's see some neckties. My wife is buying them for us,' he bellowed.

Each of us picked out a mottled-looking one, and six hundred *wŏn* was eliminated. We left the shop.

'Where shall we go?' the man said.

We still had nowhere to go. There was an orange peddler outside the shop.

'My wife liked oranges,' the man cried and bounded over to the peddler's cart where the oranges were laid out for sale. Another three hundred *wŏn* was gone. While we were peeling the skins off the oranges with our teeth, we paced restlessly up and down.

'Taxi!' the man shouted.

A taxi stopped in front of us. As soon as we had got in, the man said, 'Severance Hospital!'

'No. That's useless,' An quickly exclaimed.

'Useless?' the man muttered. 'Where, then?' There was no answer.

'Where are you going?' asked the driver in a sullen voice. 'If you haven't any place to go, then get out.'

We got out of the taxi. We still hadn't gone more than twenty paces from the Chinese restaurant. The scream of a siren rose from the far end of the street and came closer and closer. Two fire engines roared past us.

'Taxi!' the man screamed.

Another taxi stopped in front of us. No sooner had we got in than the man said, 'Follow those fire engines!'

I was peeling my third orange.

'Are we on our way to see a fire now?' An asked the man. 'We can't. There isn't enough time before curfew.[1] It's already ten-thirty. We should find something more amusing. How much money is left now?'

The man rummaged through his pockets and pulled out all the money. Then he handed it over to An. An and I counted it together. There was nineteen hundred *wŏn* in large bills, a few coins and several ten-*wŏn* notes.

'Good,' said An as he handed back the money.

'Fortunately, there are women in this world who concentrate on showing off what it is in particular that makes them women.'

'Are you speaking of my wife?' the man asked in sad tones. 'My wife's characteristic was that she laughed too much.'

'Oh, no. I was suggesting that we go up to see the girls in the third block of Chongno,' An said.

The man gave a smile that seemed to show contempt for An and turned his head away. By then we had arrived at the scene of the fire. Thirty *wŏn* more was gone. The fire had broken out in a ground-floor paint shop, and the flames were now billowing out the windows of a hairdressing school on the second floor. We heard police whistles, fire sirens, the crackling of flames and streams of water crashing against the walls of the building, but there was no sound of people. The people stood as if in a still-life painting, reflecting the blaze with faces as red as if overcome by shame.

Each of us took one of the paint cans rolling around at our feet, set it up and squatted on it to watch the fire. I was hoping it would burn a little longer. The *School of Hairdressing* sign had caught fire, and flames began to lick at the *dressing*.

'Kim *hyŏng*, let's go on with our conversation,' An said.

'Fires and such are nothing at all, not worth the bother. The only thing is that tonight we have seen ahead of time what we would have seen in tomorrow morning's newspapers. That fire isn't yours, Kim *hyŏng*, it's not mine and it's not this man's. It's just our common property now. But a fire doesn't go on for ever. Therefore, I find no interest in fires. What do you think, Kim *hyŏng*?'

'I feel the same way.' I gave him the first answer that came to mind. I was watching the *Hair* catch fire.

'No. I was in error just now. The fire is not ours; the fire belongs wholly to the fire itself. We are nothing at all to the fire. Therefore I find no interest in fires. What do you think, Kim *hyŏng*?'

'I feel the same way.'

A stream of water struck the burning *Hair*. Grey smoke billowed out where the water landed. Our listless friend suddenly leaped to his feet.

'It's my wife!' he shrieked, eyes bulging, as he gestured towards the glowing flames. 'She's tossing her head back and forth. She's tossing her head, crying that it'll crack with the pain. Darling!'

'The pain was caused by meningitis. Those are just flames carried in the wind. Sit down. How could your wife possibly be in the fire?' An said as he pulled the man back down. Then he turned to me and whispered quietly, 'This guy's giving us quite a show.'

I noticed the *Hair* flickering where I thought the fire had gone out. The stream of water splashed it again. But their aim was off, and the stream wavered back and forth. The flames licked nimbly at *of*. I was hoping they would catch on to *School* as well and that I would be the only one among all the spectators to have seen the sign burn all the way through. But then, just as the fire was becoming a living thing to me, I suddenly withdrew my wish to be the only one.

From where we were squatting, I had seen something white flying towards the burning building. A pigeon that fell into the flames.

'Didn't something just fly into the fire?' I turned and asked An.

'Yes, something did,' An answered and then turned to the man. 'Did you see it?' he asked.

The man was sitting, speechless. At that point, a policeman sprinted over towards us.

'You're the one!' the policeman said, grabbing the man with one hand. 'Did you just throw something into the fire?'

'I didn't throw anything.'

'How's that?' he shouted at the man, making as if to strike him. 'I saw you throw something. What did you throw into the fire?'

'Money.'

'Money?'

'I wrapped some money and a rock in a handkerchief and threw it into the fire.'

'Is that the truth?' the policeman asked us.

'Yes, it was money. This man has the strange belief that he'll be lucky in business if he comes to a fire and throws some money in it. Perhaps you could say he's a little odd, but he's just a small-time businessman who wouldn't do any harm,' An answered.

'How much money was it?'

'A one-*wŏn* coin,' An answered again.

After the policeman had left, An asked the man, 'Did you really throw money into the fire?'

'Yes.'

'All of it?'

'Yes.'

For quite a while we just sat there listening to the crackling of the leaping flames. After a time, An spoke to the man.

'It looks as if we finally used the money up, after all. Well, I guess we've carried out our promise to you, so we'll be going now.'

'Good night, sir,' I added in parting.

An and I turned and started to walk away. The man came after us and grabbed each of us by an arm.

'I'm afraid to be left alone,' he said, trembling.

'It's almost curfew. I'm going to go find an inn,' An said.

'I'm headed home,' I said.

'Can't we all go together? Just stay with me for tonight. I beg of you. Please come along with me,' the man said, grabbing and tugging at my arm as if it were a fan. He was probably doing the same to An.

'Where do you want to go?' I asked him.

'I'm going to get some money at a place near here, and then I was hoping we would all go to an inn together.'

'To an inn?' I said as I counted the money in my pocket with my fingers.

'If it's the cost of the room you're worried about, I'll pay for all three. Shall we go together, then?' An said, addressing himself to the man and me.

'No, no. I don't want to cause you any trouble. Just follow me a moment.'

'Are you going to go borrow money?'

'No, this money is owed to me.'

'Somewhere nearby?'

'Yes, if this is the Namyŏng-dong area.'

'It certainly looks like Namyŏng-dong to me,' I said.

With the man in the lead and the two of us following, we walked away from the fire.

'It's much too late to go collecting debts,' An said to him.

'Yes, but I've got to collect it.'

We entered a dark back alley. After turning several corners, the man stopped in front of a house where the front-gate light was lit. An and I stopped some ten paces behind him. He rang the bell. After a while the gate opened, and we could hear the man talking with someone standing inside.

'I'd like to see the man of the house.'

'He's sleeping now.'

'The lady, then?'

'She's sleeping too.'

'I really must see someone.'

'Wait a moment, please.'

The gate closed again. An hurried over to the man and pulled at his arm.

'Forget about it. Let's go.'

'That's all right. I've got to collect this money.'

An walked back again to where he had stood before. The gate opened.

'Sorry to trouble you so late at night,' the man bowed and said, facing the gate.

'Who are you, sir?' came a woman's sleep-filled voice from the gate.

'I'm sorry to have come so late, but it's just that . . .'

'Who are you, please? You seem to have been drinking, sir.'

'I've come to collect an instalment on a book you've bought.' Then he suddenly broke into a near scream, 'I've come for a book payment.' Now he rested his hands against the gatepost and, burying his face in his arms, burst into sobs. 'I've come for a book payment. I've come for . . .,' he continued in tears.

'Come back tomorrow, please.' The gate slammed shut.

The man continued to cry for quite a while, mumbling 'Darling' now and then. We waited, still about ten paces away, for the crying to end. After some time, he came stumbling towards us.

The three of us, heads lowered, walked through the dark alleys and back out onto the main street. A strong, cold wind was blowing through the deserted streets.

'It's terribly cold,' the man said, sounding concerned for us.

'It is, rather. Let's go find an inn right now,' An said.

'Shall we get one room for each of us?' An asked as we went into the first inn we saw. 'That'd be a good idea, wouldn't it?'

'I think it'd be better for us to share the same room,' I said, thinking of the man.

The man stood vacantly, looking as if he wanted solely for us to arrange things. He also looked as if he had no idea where he was. Inside the inn, we felt the same awkward confusion of not knowing what to do next that strikes you when you leave a theatre after the show. The streets seemed narrower and closer than the interior of the inn. All those rooms, one after the other, that's where we had to go.

'How would it be for us all to take the same room?' I repeated.

'I'm exhausted,' said An. 'Let's each take a single room and get some sleep.'

'I don't want to be alone,' the man muttered.

'It'd be more comfortable for you to sleep by yourself,' An said.

Each of us headed for one of the three adjoining rooms indicated by the errand boy. Before we separated, I said, 'Let's buy a pack of cards and play a hand.'

But An said, 'I'm completely exhausted. If you want, why don't you two play?' and went into his room.

'I'm dead tired too. Good night,' I said to the man and went into my room. After filling in a false name, address, age and occupation in the register, I drank the water the bellboy had left and pulled the quilt up over my head. I slept a sound, dreamless sleep.

The next morning An woke me early.

'That man is dead,' An whispered in my ear.

'Huh?' I was wide awake.

'I just took a look into his room, and sure enough, he was dead.'

'Sure enough?' I said. 'Does anyone else know?'

'It doesn't look as if anyone else knows about it yet. I think we'd better get out of here right away – no noisy complications.'

'Suicide?'

'No doubt about it.'

I dressed quickly. An ant was crawling along the floor towards my feet. I had a feeling the ant was going to climb up my foot, so I quickly stepped aside.

Outside, hail was falling in the early dawn. We moved away from the inn, walking as quickly as possible.

'I knew he was going to kill himself sooner or later,' An said.

'I hadn't the least suspicion,' I said, telling the truth.

'I was expecting it,' An said, turning up the collar of his coat. 'But what could we do?'

'Nothing. We had no choice. I had no idea,' I said.

'If we had expected it, what should we have done?' An asked me.

'Fuck! What could we do? How were we to know what he wanted us to do?'

'That's it. I thought he wouldn't die on us if we just left him alone. I thought that was the best way to handle it.'

'I had no idea that man was going to die. Fuck! He must have been carrying poison around in his pocket all night!'

An stopped beneath a scrawny roadside tree that was gathering snow. I stopped with him. With an odd look on his face, he asked me, 'You and I are definitely twenty-five, aren't we, Kim *hyŏng*?'

'I definitely am!'

'I definitely am too.' He nodded once. 'It frightens me.'

'What does?' I asked.

'That "something". That . . .' His voice was like a sigh. 'Doesn't it seem as if we've become old?'

'We're barely twenty-five,' I said.

'At any rate,' he said, putting out his hand, 'let's say goodbye here. Enjoy yourself,' he said as I took his hand.

We separated. I dashed across the street where a bus was just stopping for passengers. When I got on and looked out the window, I could see, through the branches of the scrawny tree, An standing in the falling snow, pondering something or other.

O CHŎNGHŬI

Wayfarer

Translated by Bruce and Ju-Chan Fulton

The snow had started that morning. Hyeja opened the window, sat on the sill, and watched the carefree flakes turn the world giddy. The neighbourhood was still, the snow muffling every tiny, squirming noise. There were no calls for the baseballs that came flying into her yard several times a day, no sound of children sneaking over the wall after them. When the girl who rented the room near the front gate worked the day shift, the neighbourhood children had taken advantage of the house being left empty and climbed over the wall. Hyeja would have her hands full; old habits die hard. The day she'd returned, a boy nonchalantly climbed over the wall, glancing at her where she leaned against the door to the veranda watching him. When finally she shouted 'Hey!' the boy protested: 'We do this all the time, me and the other kids. What else can we do if no one's home?' Strangely, the boy's grumbling had reassured her. It had helped her dismiss the notion that the house was haunted, that the cursed, unkempt garden was being watched over by a wicked ogre.

Now and then a layer of snow weighing down the bare branches plummeted to the ground and the sparrows searching for food took wing. There were no footprints in the snow between the rented room and the gate; the young woman must not have left for work yet.

Hyeja went out to the yard and gathered a handful of snow. The white blanket came up to her ankles. If it kept coming down like this, it would easily be knee-deep by nightfall. She ought to sweep it away, she told herself, but she didn't move. The sound of a piano, an unadorned, inelegant melody, had caught her attention. Hyeja sang along in a soft voice:

> *Hills, fields, trees*
> *Under white, white snow.*
> *We grow up pure of heart, you know.*

She had sung this ditty as a child, and so had her own children. Probably some young mum, alone at home with time on her hands after sending her children off to school, had been watching the snowflakes fall when the melody had come to mind and she had tapped it out on the keyboard.

The music abruptly stopped, leaving Hyeja standing blankly, mouth open. In the profound silence, her dream of the night before came back to her.

She had first dreamed this dream as a child, but the last time had been long enough ago that she had almost forgotten it. In this dream she was on a street, always the same street, following an endless stone wall, a mossy, crumbling structure that resembled an ancient fortress wall suffering from neglect. 'Where am I? I've been here before,' she would murmur happily enough, taken with the familiar ambience of the place. She followed that wall seemingly for ever, because she had a hunch, which became a conviction, that if she reached into one of the crevices where the wall was worn and crumbling, she would surely find a token of something that had been promised her – a small, pretty button, a secret mark, a tiny, folded piece of paper. But then she would awaken. She couldn't identify the street, not at the beginning of the dream, not at the end; all she did was wander along it. Awakening from the dream meant the loss of this street she had constantly followed yet again, and the return of that helpless sensation of being deserted. She felt like a lost child. Where could that street be leading? And why did it all seem so familiar? Her old, wraithlike mother, who was still alive, would have answered right away in her lucid, precise manner: it was the road to the other world, or else a road travelled in a former life. That Hyeja was having this dream again after almost two years offered a hint, no, an assurance, that she was actually back home.

Her hands were growing numb. The snow she clutched was melting. She wiped her wet hands on her clothes, stamped the snow from her feet, and returned inside. Her room and the veranda were utter chaos, and it seemed she was always stepping on a water glass, a rag, the transistor radio, her pyjamas, you name it. It was only natural. She had returned home a week earlier and hadn't tended to the house since. Of course she cooked to satisfy her malignant hunger, but the dirty dishes would be shoved aside. She would fill the bathtub and soak for hours, until the hot water cooled, chilling her, and then, unclothed, she would pace the darkened veranda. She had spent much of the day before yesterday gazing at her daughter's yellow, flower-shaped hairpin, which she had found in a crack in the concrete patio out at the back. The girl, now in her last year of middle school, was long past the age of using such hairpins.

Her mother-in-law had lived here until the month before, looking after Hyeja's husband and the two children. But now the house was empty except for Hyeja's belongings. What to do with Hyeja when she comes home from the hospital? There must have been a lot of discussion and thought. And finally her husband had made a clean break, removing her name from the family register and turning the house over to her – a rather unusual display of concern on his part. 'I'll be moving out before too long,' he had told her after the doctor said she was ready for discharge. 'One option, if you don't want to go back to the house, is to sell it and get yourself a small apartment. Coming from me, maybe that idea doesn't appeal to you, but an apartment would have its advantages. And you could stay with your family till the house is sold ...' Hyeja hadn't seen him since. In any event, for an ex-husband, he had sounded considerate. Technically she had initiated the divorce, and he tended to agree it was unavoidable. But while she was in the hospital? That seemed to have pained him.

Hyeja had returned to this house, though, as soon as she was discharged. Humans are forgetful creatures, the doctor had said. She was returned to full health, mentally and physically. She could live a normal life, as she had before. And she shouldn't be afraid, that was the most important thing. She felt lethargic, as if resting up after a long journey. Occasionally she was startled into a sense of reality by the ring of the telephone and the voices of people seeking her departed husband and children. 'No, they're not here, they moved ... I don't know.' Curt, blunt responses and the conversation was over, after which she would frantically rummage through the house for some trace of them. It was as if she wanted to obliterate all the time she had been away. The stickers on the wall, the long, black strands of glossy hair in the hairbrush, the handkerchief with the embroidered corner – she discovered these and other traces, but all they did was make her powerfully, vividly aware of the enormous gap that now separated her from them. They wouldn't be coming back, and she could never recover the hours she'd been away from them. Hadn't they been capable of the stronger ties that a deeper love offered? Even if they couldn't conceal from each other the shame and fear that lurked persistently in the depths of their hearts? After scouring the house one last time she had clasped her arms about her upraised knees and silently sobbed. After she had cried herself to exhaustion, she felt a gentle gnawing in her empty stomach. That familiar hunger was like an old friend who had come to comfort her.

The doorbell jarred Hyeja awake. Her late lunch of cold rice mixed with *koch'ujang* had been followed by a short nap. Who could it be? Confused and startled, she opened the door to the veranda just as the bell rang again. 'Registered mail! Your seal, please!'[1] The postman's cap was visible above the iron gate. Flustered by the postman's insistence – why would anyone have sent her a registered letter? – she opened the dressing-table drawers in succession from force of habit. Most were empty and, sure enough, her seal wasn't there. 'I don't have it!' Hyeja shouted in agitation towards the gate. 'Then forget it and just give me your thumbprint!' came the response.

The letter was for Hyeja's tenant. There was no sign of life from across the yard, and the girl's kitchen door, which gave access to her room, was padlocked. Hyeja pushed the kitchen window open, deposited the letter, and went back inside. As she steadied her pounding heart, her hand stopped in the act of closing the yawning drawers of her dressing table. There it was, her little appointment book, long forgotten but certainly hers, smudged by her own hands. She fished it out and hastily turned the pages. '29th: Tŏksu Palace'; 'dry-clean winter suit'; '16th: 3 p.m., Araya'; 'Shinsegye, Bargain Sale, 15th–21st, woollen shirt & vest' – among these notes were items faintly remembered but many she couldn't recall. '3rd: Umi Florist, flower basket, mixed carnations X 60' – a gift for a teacher's sixtieth-birthday celebration? Sometimes smiling, sometimes frowning as she searched her memory, Hyeja read each of the entries. And then at the back, a column of telephone numbers, those of her college classmates. They were members of a circle, friends who met once a month, women with whom she felt somewhat close. Why hadn't she thought of them? Finally, something to do. She began quickly to dial. First the editorial offices at the women's magazine where Sukcha worked. But Sukcha had long since left, she was informed. Then Aegyŏng's house. 'The number you have dialled is out of service; please check the number and try again.' She examined the Arabic numerals and redialled. Same result. It was strange. She felt bewitched. Myŏnghwa's telephone rang incessantly – no answer. Patiently she dialled Ch'unja at home. 'Not at this number any more,' came a curt voice, followed by a click. Hyeja replaced the receiver and let her mind go blank, oppressed for the first time by the enormous reality of the two years she had lost. She felt bitter and betrayed.

This'll be the last one, she swore to herself, and like a gambler staking her destiny on her last card, she dialled the fifth number with grim determination. She heard the ring and then a 'Hello,' and Chŏngok's face rose before her. She forced herself to speak slowly: 'Chŏngok? It's me, Hyeja.' 'Oh, my goodness! My goodness!' This ambiguous exclamation was followed by silence. Hyeja imagined a terrified look on Chŏngok's face, the look of someone who had received a call from the dead. 'It's been a long time.' 'It really has,' said Chŏngok. 'How is your health?' And then, still sounding flustered, she added, 'Where are you?' 'I'm home now. How are the others doing? I haven't been able to reach anybody.' 'Well, that's understandable – a lot of us have moved.'

Hyeja told her friend she would like to see her. There was a brief pause. 'Well, as it turns out, we're throwing a farewell party for Pongsŏn. She's going overseas with her husband. Remember the Sky Lounge on the thirteenth floor of the Kolon Building, in Kwanggyo? We're meeting there at seven o'clock. Everyone'll be happy to see you.'

Next, Hyeja telephoned the puppet centre. Min, her teacher, made puppets but he also played an important role in puppet theatre. He had produced puppet shows on television – *Little Red Riding Hood* and *Master Sun and Mistress Moon* – using puppets Hyeja had made. Back then Min had praised the originality of her conceptions and the puppets' lifelike expressions. He had piqued her interest by suggesting she hold an exhibition. But now Hyeja discovered that in Min's case, as well, the two years had made a difference. Though she gave her full name when he answered – Kim Hyeja – Min failed to make the connection. She had to explain she was the creator of the puppets in *Little Red Riding Hood* and *Master Sun and Mistress Moon*, and finally Min uttered a faint exclamation. Only then did he slip into his usual tone: 'It's been a while, hasn't it? How have you been?' He must have known all about it too. Among the people who knew 'how she had been,' she had no doubt been fodder for dozens of stale conversations. 'How is your health?' he asked. 'Couldn't be better. Are you still doing puppet shows?' She wished to talk at great length. He'd been kind to her; he'd liked her puppets. 'Why don't you come around some time,' he suggested. She wanted to say she could visit right then, that she had three or four hours till her dinner engagement, but she reluctantly set down the receiver, tempering her regret with the realization that he was perpetually busy. He was so taken up with his work that he was still single in his forties, writing books about puppet shows and rushing from little theatres to primary school auditoriums to television stations. Even so, he wouldn't have forgotten his interest in displaying her puppets. He wouldn't have forgotten his suggestion that she hold an exhibition, complete with a puppet show. She had to see him, the following day if possible. She could get back to making her puppets. With her puppet shows she could tour schools on remote islands and other out-of-the-way places. And if she supplied each of the schools with a set of puppets from the show at a discount, then the children could set up little theatres at home and have their own puppet shows. Wouldn't that be fun? This was exactly the meaningful work she wanted, and she could earn a bit of money doing it. It would be a wonderful thing to do, and it made perfect sense. If she could live on her own earnings, she would for the first time be independent, would have an existence genuinely her own. Determined to begin creating puppets again, she felt a burst of energy. And then she scolded herself relentlessly for the disgraceful life she had led, a life that had been parasitic, pure and simple. That evening she would tell her friends what she was doing now. She would tell them her rosy plans for the future. After all, did any of them know as much about puppets and puppet shows as she did? It wouldn't be stretching the truth to talk about the exhibition she'd do with Min, her teacher, and about the touring performances. True, they hadn't been arranged yet, but they would be sooner or later, she was sure of it. Hadn't Min always shown an interest in her puppets? Maybe it was all in her mind, that business about herself being the focus of repeated conversations among her friends. And Min's initial failure to recognize her on the phone, the electric shock of recognition, the evasiveness she had read into his vague invitation to visit – wasn't she acting out some sort of victimization complex? Other people don't have as much interest in us as we think they do, her doctor had said. And they don't remember us for as long as we think they should. To Min and her friends, the story about her was merely a single short column buried in the evening newspaper one summer day two years before. Had they spent the last two years making sure they remembered this unfortunate incident involving an acquaintance of theirs? Of course not. While they were raising children, building up their assets, and clutching greedily for a ray of joy in their lives, she'd been killing time with endlessly tedious games of cat's-cradle, sitting in the sun from one to three in the afternoon, enduring those stupid question-and-answer sessions with her doctor, and all the while cherishing a desire to put that incident out of her mind. Instead of following her husband's suggestion to change her surroundings she had returned home. And a very good thing it was. If not for the solitude of the empty house, if not for the despair of being alone, would she have thought of resuming her work with puppets? Would she have turned up that little address book?

Up to the attic she went, to the corner where she had moved the huge trunk in which she had packed her work things. Odds and ends now took up her former basement workshop.

Thick dust coated the trunk. The ornamental lock had rusted, but it was open. And there, under a single sheet of newspaper, were her things, just as she had left them. Sections of wire mesh of various thicknesses, tubes of hardened adhesive, dyed feathers, a handful of sparkle, the faces of the weaver girl and the herder boy and the unfinished winged clothes of the fairy. Strangely, she felt pangs of sorrow as, one by one, she uncovered these items lying silently like ash in the trunk she herself had closed and no one had opened. And when she had brought them all into view, the heads, arms and legs, the remnants of fabric for the various costumes – all of it swept haphazardly into the trunk – another layer of newspaper appeared. She closed her eyes and took a deep breath. She knew all too well what lay hidden there at the bottom, entrenched like a rock in the depths of her bosom. It was her last creation, the lovely princess, sunk deep in a century-long slumber from which she couldn't awaken. Hyeja had dressed her, was ironing her gorgeous dress one last time – and then it had happened. With trembling hands she removed the newspaper, and there was the face of the princess, lush hair streaming proudly through her coronet. There was her body. And there in her gorgeous costume, like so many severed links of a chain, were the glittering, golden remains of moths.

The snow had dwindled to flurries and the distant skies were clearing in spite of the approaching dusk. It was four o'clock. Ample time until Hyeja's meeting with her friends, but she began to prepare. She couldn't deny the joy and excitement she felt at the prospect of leaving this house where loneliness settled along with the night. She washed her face and took her time over her makeup. An extra touch here and there wouldn't be noticed at night. Besides, she'd finally be back with her girlfriends tonight, and what would they care? She flung open her wardrobe and inspected the clothes on their hangers, but found nothing she cared to go out in. She hadn't tried on those clothes for two years, and she'd gained an enormous amount of weight. She would have been the first to admit that their shapes and colours weren't suitable, but what really depressed her, after she had tried on practically all of them, was not being able to button up a single one. Finally she came across something that fitted, a sack dress that was fashionable a decade earlier. It had been made just for her, a loose black velvet dress with a great white collar, a dress that fell like a cape from her shoulders. The times she wore it outside the house to meet her husband after work, he had said she looked like quite the little girl – implying that she was too old for it. He was particular about what she wore. And Hyeja, who followed new fashions closely, had tucked it away in the wardrobe for good. She realized now how much heavier she was, for the dress confined her as if she actually were inside a sack. She gathered her long hair in a clasp and looked in the mirror. The person she saw resembled a silent-movie actress.

The glass door to the veranda rattled open and in came the voice of Hyeja's tenant: 'Auntie, I'm going out. Could you please close my coal duct a little later?' She must have returned while Hyeja had been rummaging through the trunk. Hyeja scowled towards the front gate as she heard it open and shut. The girl had said she worked at a factory where she had a day shift one day and a night shift the next, but as far as Hyeja could tell, she'd brought a man home three times in the past week. 'That's no good – I should get rid of her,' she muttered decisively. 'I have better things to do than tend to coal for that slut. Ought to tell her I'm selling the house and ask her to vacate, ought to do it right away, tomorrow.'

Hyeja waited until five o'clock, then donned her coat and left. Even with the snow slowing down traffic, she could get downtown in thirty or forty minutes. Still, she left hurriedly, ushered out of her empty house by the gathering darkness.

Deposited by the bus on the broad avenue of Chongno with plenty of time to spare, Hyeja descended into the pedestrian underpass that crossed to the other side. The poorly ventilated passage stank, and was slushy with tracked-in snow. The subway rumbled underfoot. To the busy stream of people beneath the pale lights Hyeja gave unguarded looks as she slowly walked along.

The snow had stopped for good, and the darkening streets were windy. At the underpass exit Hyeja took a deep breath and gained her bearings. She hadn't been to the city centre in a long while, but her mental map was clear. As she set off, she glimpsed the frozen fountain near the clock tower, which read five-forty, and next to the fountain the giant Christmas tree whose tiny lights were just starting to twinkle. And then, floating hazily in the distance beyond the tree with its coat of pure white, were the lights of the Sky Lounge on the thirteenth floor of the Kolon Building. There were no crossings, which meant three more underpasses to negotiate. She had more than enough time, though. Should she arrive early and sit there all by herself? No, that wouldn't look good. As she scanned the surroundings for a place to thaw out over coffee, her gaze settled on a brown building across the street and to the left. At that very instant, the Kolon Building, the large tree with its blinking lights and all the rest, were swept from her field of vision. She saw nothing but that fifteen-storey building in which every window was lit up. Why hadn't she thought of that? It had never occurred to her, when Chŏngok had mentioned the Kolon Building, that her own husband worked right across the street. Chiding herself, she quickly reentered the underpass. Most likely he was still in his office; he always worked late. And hadn't he always encouraged her to come to him with any problems? For two people who had been closer to each other than anyone else for such a long period of their lives, what could be so troublesome or complicated about sharing a hot cup of coffee on a cold day? If people begrudged each other such simple contacts, what would that say about their lives, and how could they possibly get along with others? What's more, wasn't she off to a fresh start, full of marvellous plans? If she could resume her work right away, perhaps with her mentor, Min, a man unrivalled in the world of puppet shows, it would make even her husband a believer.

Her monologue came to an end when the lift reached the fifth floor and the Yŏng'u Trading Company, which also occupied the sixth and seventh floors. The security guard intercepted her. 'What can I do for you, ma'am?' Hyeja hesitated at this unanticipated obstacle, but quickly gathered herself. 'I'm here to see the head of the Planning Office.' The security guard picked up the intercom. 'Who did you say you were?' he asked while waiting to be connected. 'Tell him it's his wife.' The young security guard cocked his head sceptically and scrutinized Hyeja, then handed her the receiver. 'Planning – this is the manager speaking.' The resounding voice filled the handset, as if the man were right beside her. 'Is that . . . you? It's me, Yŏngsŏn's mum,' Hyeja stammered, suddenly intimidated by the placid, oddly unfamiliar voice.

'Who's calling? This is the manager of the Planning Office, but . . . I wonder if it's Mr Yi Kidŏk you're looking for.' 'Yes, could I have Yi Kidŏk, please? This is his wife.' Hyeja's flustered response brought a low exclamation from the other end. 'This is Yi Kunho. One moment, please, and I'll be right out.' Presently, from the hallway to the left there appeared a tall, slender man. He'd lost a lot of hair and now wore glasses, but Hyeja recognized him at once: Yi Kunho, who'd joined the company at the same time as her husband and was quite close to him. He'd married late, and until then he could always count on a bed at their house if he was too drunk to go home. Hyeja was guided to a small reception room where two people were talking. They left at once, and the room fell quiet except for the hiss of the radiator. Sensing in her counterpart an extreme discomfort that perplexed her, Hyeja glanced about the stark room, which contained a table and a few chairs. After requesting coffee over the intercom Yi Kunho finally said, 'You look a lot better. How is your health?' Everyone asked about her health. 'Is the gunpowder in a safe place?' was how it sounded to her. Hyeja smiled but said nothing. 'How are you getting along?' 'I've started work.' 'Well, that's good to hear. May I ask what kind of work?' 'Sure. It involves puppet shows. Also, I'm thinking about moving. I remembered what he told me – you know, about how a change of scenery might be a good thing? But I guess he's not at his desk?' Hyeja ventured a smile. A look of surprise creased Yi's brow. 'You didn't know?' A young woman in a short-sleeved sweater arrived with the coffee and set it on the table. Silently Yi added sugar to his cup and began slowly to stir. 'Didn't know what?' 'He's at the New York office. It's been a month now.' Hyeja found her gaze riveted on the scarlet imprint of her lips on the cup from which she had just drank. The room was so hot! Her undergarments were sweaty. And her tight-fitting clothes constricted her, made her feel choked. She unbuttoned her coat and her flesh spilled over the collar of the cramped velvet dress. She produced her handkerchief and dabbed at her face and neck, leaving thick smudges of powder, rouge and eyeshadow on the white cloth. She was embarrassed to admit it, but her makeup was too thick. 'He took the children, reckons to be there about three years. I'm not quite sure, but maybe he didn't tell you out of concern for opening old wounds.' 'It's all right. I was on my way somewhere and just … stopped by. He said I was always welcome to drop in and talk things over … I'd better be on my way,' she said in a dull tone, distracted by the suffocating sensation, the perspiration streaming inside her clothes and the air in the room, which felt dirty and stuffy. She rose heavily. 'Are you all right? You don't look well,' Yi said solicitously, noticing her pale, sweaty face. 'I feel kind of hot. Thank you for your time – I know you're busy. And I appreciate your kindness.' The lift door closed on Yi's politely bowing form and she began silently to weep.

The electronic display on the clock tower read seven-twenty. Twenty minutes past the appointed hour and not one familiar face had appeared. From her window seat Hyeja could track the flow of time, second by second, for the clock tower was directly across from her. The Christmas tree lights were pellucid and the city had lit up in profound splendour. Seven-thirty came and went. The lounge, quiet at first, was now almost full, and with every opening and closing of the door Hyeja shot an anxious look towards the entrance. Was it possible they hadn't recognized her? She really did look different from before. So different she scarcely recognized the face with its dark background imprinted like a negative on the window. Desperate for people and the world to forget what she had done, she had worked hard to change her appearance. She had gained weight with the help of the hunger and the hellish sleep that was regularly induced through a regimen of medication and injections, and she had let her hair grow out. Her hair had turned light grey, something Hyeja didn't realize until the woman who shared her sickroom accused her of stealing a hairpin, attacked her, and plucked out a handful of it. Hyeja moved nearer to the entrance, where she could be seen more easily, and ordered a gin and tonic. An hour had passed. The lounge felt toasty in its tight glass envelope. Hyeja removed her coat and placed it over a chair, and discreetly undid the buttons at her throat and chest so she could breathe more easily.

A thin slice of lemon and a scarlet cherry floated in the transparent, ice-filled glass in front of her. The drink tasted like sour water and it made her want to pucker up and spit. The Western saying 'Looks good, tastes good' wasn't very apt, she thought, as she forlornly watched the floating ice cubes shrink. Presently they melted away and the lemon taste grew suspiciously weak. Her hopes grew fainter that the others would appear. Nine o'clock passed, and as she ordered another gin and tonic she was seized by a doubt that seemed all too real: had she misunderstood the time and place of the gathering? In her desperation, had she somehow convinced herself that today was the date when in fact it was tomorrow or the day after? It was a lonely business staring at the ice cubes clinking against the glass before disappearing. Staring and waiting. And when ten o'clock arrived and she ordered yet another gin and tonic, the young waiter looked askance at her, as if she were a phantom, this obese woman with long, wiry, grey hair tumbling over a broad, white collar that resembled the ribbed semicircle of a folding fan. They weren't coming, she was sure of it. An intense rage came over her. Knowing she would appear at their gathering, they had changed the meeting place – no doubt about it. They were sitting somewhere nearby, pointing at her, whispering about her as she sat, all too visible through the window, sick and tired of waiting. 'God, she actually called me. She said she tried the rest of you too. Consider yourselves lucky you missed her.' 'That man died, and she's running free? But what for? I mean, she's practically an *invalid*.' Hyeja covered her ears, as if actually hearing these voices. 'Self-defence, huh? Well, whatever she wants to call it, it happened.' 'Is it true he divorced her? Well, I can believe it. How could a person live with someone like that? I'd be scared.' 'Is *that* what you call being faithful to your husband?' 'Maybe she lost her head – I'll bet she was terrified.' 'That's probably why she ended up in a mental hospital.' When Hyeja recalled what others had said and then read between the lines, it was always a *man* that was killed, not a burglar. Even her husband. He'd kept trying to find out if the man really was a burglar. Maybe the man didn't have a relationship with her, but wasn't he at least a casual acquaintance? Her husband had been skilfully circuitous but wouldn't give up. 'I never saw him before,' she had said. 'Do you want to know what I was doing? *This* is what I was doing, just like you see here. Now will you please leave me alone? What do you want, anyway?' These thoughts, thousands of times recalled, she repeated to herself, and as she did so she clamped her mouth shut and cried. The fact that she had been wearing only a slip and the man was unarmed had left lingering doubts.

Hyeja suddenly realized all was quiet. She looked about. The lounge was deserted except for a couple sitting at a window table, foreheads touching. The waiter produced a great yawn as he leaned against the bar watching Hyeja. The clock on the tower read eleven.

The subway rumbled beneath Hyeja's feet before rolling into the deep of the night. Not much sign of life in the underpasses, just the slush under-foot, and everywhere the stink. The same three underpasses to negotiate, and when Hyeja rose to the surface she gazed up at the wind-swept heav-ens. An uncertain number of stars twinkled dimly in the misty air.

She had just climbed the last step out of the underpass when she bumped her knee against something and lost her balance. Coins clinked and scattered at her feet. The fluorescent light was off and the opening to the underpass was dark. Instinctively she stooped over and looked down. She had tripped over someone hunched up in a blanket and had kicked over a tin bowl. 'I'm sorry,' she hastened to say. 'I've got something on my mind and I just –' Then she realized that the woman beneath the blanket with the sleeping child in her arms was blind. Eyes downcast, chin lifted, the woman extended a hand, groped for the scattered coins, gathered them in. Hyeja bent over to help and managed in the dim light to pick up the coins that had fallen to the steps. She was about to place them in the bowl when the woman's hand shot out and seized her wrist. The strength and tenacity of her grip startled Hyeja. The hand didn't release its painful, lurching hold until the woman was sure every last coin had been shaken free from Hyeja's palm. Hyeja gazed at the woman as she massaged her stinging wrist. The woman curled back into a ball beneath the blanket, perhaps to sleep, perhaps to doze. You thought I was going to take your money? Well, it's mostly my fault, for being spaced out and walking right into you. The wind buffeted the opening to the underpass with a chill ferocity. Hyeja hunkered down beside the woman. The Christmas tree next to the frozen fountain continued its lonely blinking. The clock tower read eleven-thirty. 'Aren't you cold? Have you eaten? Look how sound asleep your baby is! Don't you want to go home now? It's supposed to get colder.' The woman gave no reply. 'Where are you staying? Why don't I help you across the street? You don't want to go to sleep out here and freeze to death. Especially with your baby . . .' But as Hyeja gently lifted the quilt her hand was slapped. The woman's eyes glared. 'Fucking leech – don't you have anything better to do than bother me! Go home, wash your feet and go to bed, you busybody!' Bloodshot eyes gazing furiously at Hyeja, the woman clutched her child, took up her bowl, stomped a few steps lower, and plopped herself down. Frightened, Hyeja hurried off.

The wind blew stronger. Passersby raised their collars and scurried along or else chased down taxis. On which side of the street was that taxi stand where she used to catch cabs to her neighbourhood? Hyeja had walked scarcely a block when she noticed that the pedestrians, most of them, weren't there any more. Vehicles sped past. No taxis waited, headlights off, even at the taxi stands. How to get home? She didn't have a clue. But what troubled her the most was the hunger tearing at her stomach. Only those three watery gin and tonics since lunch, and it was vexing to think that their sourish, puckery taste was stimulating her appetite. As always when she was hungry, Hyeja's mouth watered for a heaping bowl of white rice; fish swabbed in oil and grilled; piping-hot fried scallion cakes; and all the rest. It had been the same at the hospital: perpetual hunger. Once her daughter had brought her a container of chicken still warm from the grill. How the girl in her dazzling white summer hat had cried as she watched Hyeja devour the food. 'Mummy, forgive us. What we did was a crime,' she said before offering a short goodbye and leaving. Hyeja hadn't seen her since. But now, if she could just eat something, it didn't matter what . . . If she could just put it in her mouth, just a bite . . . There would be plenty of time later to think about getting home.

Clutching her belly and looking about, Hyeja finally spied a street-side *p'ojang mach'a*, its canvas curtains brightly lit from inside. She entered. A woman was putting away knives, cutting boards, saucepans.

'Could I have something to eat? Anything you've got – I'm really hungry.'

Startled by Hyeja's abruptness, the woman observed her before silently serving up two skewers of fish cakes along with soup.

'That's all there is. I'm out of everything else. I was just about to go home . . .'

The fish cakes were gone in an instant. The woman ladled out more soup and Hyeja took it in a gulp, then held out her bowl again while wiping her mouth. The woman apologetically waved her hand no. She obviously pitied Hyeja. 'All that's left is *soju* – really.' The woman uncapped a bottle with her teeth, and Hyeja accepted it, paid and left.

She kept to the stone wall of the old palace, the wall angling away from the street. It was like walking in a dream, quiet except for the slow fall of her feet. The alcohol gently warmed her stomach. Unbelievably, her hunger had vanished. With every gust of wind, the ancient trees inside the mossy stone wall threw back their manes and wailed. Hyeja stopped every few steps to let more *soju* trickle into her mouth. She had once tried on glasses with thick lenses, and now, as then, the ground seemed to fall away under her feet. 'You broke your promise,' Hyeja said aloud. These were the heart-felt words she had shouted tearfully in her childhood when she was left all alone by playmates who abandoned her and went home without a word of explanation other than saying they were tired of playing house; or when they played hide-and-seek and she was 'it' and they hid in a place where she couldn't possibly find them and never came out, or else called off the game without telling her.

She cursed her liar of a daughter, who had bloomed more lovely with each new day, even when she cried and said, 'I can't believe we put you in this place; I can't believe we have to live like this; I wish I were dead.' Yes, her husband and children had left her all alone in an empty house and gone their merry way. Just like those faithless little creatures of her childhood.

Where would this street beside the stone wall lead? Her dream of the previous evening returned to her. Was *this* the street she walked in her dreams? Although she knew there would be a token for her in a crevice among the crumbling stones, the memory of waking in distress from those dreams made her anxious. She tilted the bottle of *soju* and the liquid gurgled down her throat. She drank it all at once, a wonder drug in a dream from which she would never awaken. 'You all think I'm a murderer, you're on red alert in case I show up, you're avoiding me . . .' Having announced this, with a grand gesture she hurled the empty bottle into the night. 'Anyone else would have done the same thing. What was I supposed to do?' On that day she'd been making dolls in her basement workshop as she always did after the children left for school. It was a sweltering summer day, she had turned on the hotplate to melt some oxhide glue, and the basement felt like a steam bath. The front gate was locked, she wasn't expecting visitors, and she was working in her slip. She had finished the details of attaching the sleeping princess's hair and accessories and was intent on adding the finishing touches when she saw the man standing in the doorway. There had been no sound of his entry. What she had seen then was not the man's face but her own nearly naked body. It was pure terror, though, that had caused her to plunge the hot soldering iron into the man's eyes as he approached.

The alcohol made Hyeja feel something was blooming from everywhere inside her as she swayed down the street. Looking straight ahead, she passed her hand along the stone wall, searching the crevices of the crumbling stones for a token of that pledge of love, that hidden, secret promise of her dream. But then she heard a murmuring in her ear: 'They've all forgotten you and there's nothing you can do, is there? And even if you hadn't stabbed him with that soldering iron, you wouldn't be any better off than you are now.' She vaguely realized that the place where this street ended, this street along the stone wall that she had visited in her dreams, was merely the desolate present of wakefulness. But still she moved, one step at a time, deeper into the darkness, her blossoming body telling her the street would never end.

KYUNG-SOOK SHIN

House on the Prairie

Translated by Bruce and Ju-Chan Fulton

It sits ivy-covered in the middle of a prairie.

People passing by regard it with curiosity, unable to fathom the reason for its existence. Wouldn't you wonder what a vacant house is doing on a lonely prairie bounded only by paddy after dry field after paddy? For a long time it's given no indication of a human presence, and no one appears to live there now. It presents a dreary scene except for the homey white-lace curtain, whose intricate weave gives the impression that you can feel the movement of the weaver's hands. Considering the house is vacant, you might think someone would make off with the curtain, but it's still there. The house seems never to have had a gate, and the steps leading straight up to the front entry look steep. One, two, three, four . . . nine steps in all. Empty though the house is, the seasons haven't forsaken it. By summer the structure is newly wrapped in ivy. No one appears to be tending the house and yet the vividly green ivy embraces it as if partaking of an emerald feast, luring people to the entrance. But then the visitors sense the eeriness lurking in that green colour and they turn back without entering. When the winds sweep across the prairie, the gleaming leaves shooting out from the tenacious vines resemble turquoise tongues. Those vines seem ready to coil themselves around the neck of anyone who dares enter. Only the steps extending up to the entrance have escaped the clutches of the vines and their gleaming leaves. Steep and seemingly long-untrodden, today they are a bleached-out path into the eerie, turquoise-coloured ivy.

Who would believe this empty house was once filled with happiness and song? And with joy the likes of which you might encounter only in a legend? The winds on the prairie, that's who. They know that this house on the prairie used to be filled with joy. To this day, when they have nothing else to do, they talk among themselves about the man and the woman. About their wretched appearance when they first arrived at the prairie, and about their love.

One day a man and a woman came upon the prairie. Lacking a house of their own, they could not become husband and wife. In the city they were too poor to be able to love each other. They walked and they walked, step after sorrowful step, fetching up in front of the house on the prairie. The empty house tugged at their heartstrings. They cracked open the door and went into the living room and then ventured into the other rooms. No one stopped them. They spent the night there. Nothing happened. They brought in the bare necessities and lived there. All seemed well. The woman wiped the living-room floor and changed the rusty tap in the bathroom. The man climbed onto the roof and sealed the leaks, then had himself a look around. He saw only dry field after paddy after dry field and far in the distance a ridgeline. The scenery seemed to look back at him calmly as if understanding that he and the woman wanted to live there in the house. The man and the woman cried, believing their love had finally found a nest. Over and over they felt each other's face: how in creation had such luck come to them? The man worked at a construction site some distance away. The woman delivered his lunch, wrapped in a cloth. They had wanted to be together, and now that they lived in the empty house on the prairie they wished for nothing more. In the afternoon she prepared dinner and sang as she awaited his return. The man would arrive home happy from listening to her songs resonating across the prairie. This was their life. From time to time she would hold his hands and tremble in fear that something would come between them and the next moment carry their trouble-free days off on the wind. The man would bring his wrinkled face to hers and whisper that they had nothing more to lose, that if this prairie was dream-like, then all they had to do was dream on. Please don't worry, he told her.

And she no longer worried.

For a baby girl was born to them. The girl became five years of age and during those five years the three of them were left alone in the house on the prairie. The man worked hard, the woman mothered the girl and the once desolate house now wore a radiant gleam. There was a vase with flowers, and the woman wove a white-lace curtain and draped it over the window. The man was now a foreman and no longer had to lug rocks or sand on his back to earn his pay. And their girl was healthy, her red cheeks cute and fleshy and her bottom nice and plump. The girl took every opportunity to ask, 'Mummy, am I pretty? Daddy, am I pretty?' Responding to her coquetry was one of the joys of their life. They were grateful for the happiness bestowed on them by the empty house on the prairie. But it seemed that the house wanted to bestow on them only that much happiness and no more.

One day the woman took the girl to the city. She bought all the items on her shopping list and returned to the house. The wind blew more than you would think for early summer. Each of the woman's hands held a heavy load and the girl toddled along ahead of her. They arrived at the steep steps leading to the entrance, and that's when it happened. The girl climbed the first step and turned back towards the woman. Her cheeks were pale, as if the outing had tired her. But still she asked playfully, 'Mummy, am I pretty?'

'Yes, you are,' the woman answered.

The girl climbed another step and asked, 'Mummy, am I pretty?'

'You sure are,' said the woman.

From the third step the girl asked again, 'Mummy, am I pretty?'

Feeling weighed down by what she carried but fearful of disappointing the girl, the woman managed a cheery reply: 'I've never seen a girl as pretty as you!'

The girl jumped up and down in delight whenever the woman answered. At the fourth step, the fifth, the sixth, the seventh and the eighth – with each steep step she climbed she never failed to turn her pale face towards the woman and ask,

'Mummy, am I pretty?'

And the woman never failed to answer, 'You're the prettiest girl in the whole wide world,' feeling all the while that what she carried was about to pull her arms loose from her shoulders. Silently she pleaded, *Oh I wish the girl would stop asking that question and just open the door.*

But when the girl had climbed the ninth and last step she turned back to the woman and asked,

'Mummy, am I pretty?'

The items carried by the woman plopped onto the ground. *Whoo* went the ivy leaves in the wind. 'Yes, I *said* you're pretty!' the woman shouted. The next instant something felt wrong: she sensed an uncontrollable force penetrating her. She never meant to push the girl, simply reached out to give her a slap on the bottom, but the moment her hand made contact the girl, as if sucked into a whirling funnel, went tumbling down the steps she had climbed so laboriously.

'Noooo!' The woman ran down the steps, but the house on the prairie would bestow no more happiness. No drop of blood could be seen, but the girl lay pale and dying. With her last breath she asked, 'Mummy, am I pretty?'

Time passed quietly.

Sorrow never recovered, and time remained desolate. The man tried to console the woman but she had lost her smile. He tried to love her more but she was forever gazing off into the distance. What was it, the unknowable, unstoppable force that had penetrated her like a tongue that day – what? The woman aged. Each day made her look a year older, her face more haggard and weathered and her cheekbones more prominent. She could have been the man's mother or his older sister. But then another opportunity for happiness arrived. In the desolation of their lives another baby was born to them. With the new baby their love began to recover, if only barely. The woman put flowers in the vase for the first time in a long while. The newborn was another girl. The man comforted the woman, saying the baby looked just like the older girl – she must have been reborn! Only then did the woman smile; no longer did she gaze off into the distance. She gradually recovered her youth and again looked like the woman the man had always known. She loved the baby. Perhaps more than the man did. The man worried now and then that her love for the baby was obsessive, but his concern was outweighed by relief that she had returned to her old self. The baby grew strong and healthy and already she was five years old. The woman and the man wondered if they should return to the city for the girl's sake. They couldn't decide: their situation was slightly improved but still they were needy. The man suggested staying a little longer, saying the day would come for them to live with the girl in the city. The woman believed him and his 'day that would come.' That day gave them hope. Perhaps the empty house on the prairie was jealous of their hope.

At first the woman was unaware. She simply held the girl's hand and boarded the bus to the city to buy household items just like before. It was a monthly shopping trip and she always had too much to carry. The wind blew more than you would think for early summer. The woman still had no clue: she had forgotten that today was the day her firstborn had died. The realization that that day five years ago was recurring came at the bottom of the steps to the house on the prairie. The girl, who had been following the woman until then, suddenly toddled in front of her, arrived at the first step, climbed it, and asked,

'Mummy, am I pretty?'

The woman wanted to drop what she was holding and embrace the girl, saying, *Baby, stop that.* The girl had never asked such a question. The girl, her manner frosty, recoiled from the woman, then asked again,

'Mummy, am I pretty?'

The woman couldn't help answering, 'Mmm, yes, you're pretty.' She broke out in a cold sweat. *What is happening?*

From the second step the girl asked again,

'Mummy, am I pretty?'

The woman felt her knees buckle. The nightmare of five years ago had returned. Desperately she answered, 'You sure are.'

From the third step the girl asked again,

'Mummy, am I pretty?'

With all her strength the woman pressed down with the soles of her feet. 'Yes, you are.'

Help me, honey! the woman silently pleaded to the man. And now they were at the ninth step. She tried to focus: *I absolutely* mustn't *make the same mistake.* The girl climbed the ninth and last step, as on that day five years ago, and turned her pale face towards the woman.

'Mummy, am I pretty?'

As much as she tried to steel herself, the woman was shuddering. 'Yes, you are,' she answered, 'the prettiest girl in the whole wide world.' The girl stared at the trembling woman with a dubious expression and said, 'Then why did you push me, Mummy?'

When the man returned from work, the house on the prairie was empty. There was no sight of the woman and the girl, only the shopping items scattered about the steep steps. The man waited for them for the longest time. He stopped eating, he didn't go to work, and he waited, more for the woman than for the girl. But the woman didn't come. Every night the ivy coiled itself about him and then released him. Each passing night left him more wasted. And then one gusty night he heard the ivy leaves calling out and he squatted down to listen: *Mummy, am I pretty?* He shut his ears but still heard the woman's feeble voice: *Yes, you are.* At daybreak, his face devoid of colour, he slipped out of the house on the prairie and left, never to return.

The empty house is still there on the prairie. Oddly enough, the turquoise hue of the ivy leaves gleams more with each passing day. Even if you're a poor wayfarer who happens upon the house as you pass by the prairie, you mustn't stop. Once upon a time happiness and song lived in that house. But even if the homey, white-lace curtain woven by the woman entices you to enter and settle in, you must back off. Unless you wish every night to hear the *whoo* of the gleaming, turquoise-coloured ivy leaves and the nine steep steps whispering on the wind: *Then why did you push me, Mummy?*

P'YŎN HYEYŎNG

The First Anniversary

Translated by Cindy Chen with Bruce and Ju-Chan Fulton

Clutching the large, long box to his chest, he made his way into the apartment building. It was as dark as it was during the air-raid blackout drills: all the lights were off except for the lift display, whose red flicker reflected from the bank of mailboxes. A flood of brochures, unclaimed post, empty cans and such foretold the building's imminent renovation.

The man steered himself towards the stairway. Best to avoid the lift, given the increasingly capricious state of the power supply. He had once found himself trapped inside it during a power cut. He had jabbed at the emergency button, hoping the caretaker would come to his rescue. No such luck. He had begun to wonder if the demolition crew would get to him first. Eventually he had fallen asleep even as he willed the lift not to plunge to the bottom of the shaft. Not until the next morning was the power restored and he was liberated along with his parcels.

As he climbed the dark stairs, his upper body seemed magically to disjoin from his lower body and take the lead. While his eyes searched for the outlines of the steps, his legs bore him upwards in synchronized strides. He knew by heart the number of steps between each floor, the rise between each step and the next, and the location of each bicycle-obstructed emergency exit. What he didn't know was that mounds of rubbish and garbage had been accumulating in front of the emergency exits by the day, and several times he had tripped over these mounds.

He perched himself on a step leading to the fifth-floor stairwell. It was just as dark there as elsewhere in the building. This box was his last delivery of the day. He gave it a shake. No unusual noises or smells. No signs of leaks. There were times that kimchi juice had leaked out, leaving a trail of red splatters on the stairs behind him as well as pungent blotches on his khaki trousers. The splatters on the concrete had faded a bit each time he returned to these unlit flights of stairs – which meant several times a week, and always a delivery to the same woman. Sometimes it was kimchi he delivered, at other times it was crab pickled in soy sauce. Sometimes it was hot pepper paste, and sometimes the *ramyŏn* that the woman could have purchased at any supermarket. He had delivered sandals, he had delivered Western-style leather boots, he had delivered platform trainers. As well as airy underwear, a polka-dot dress, an upright steam cleaner – the list went on. His employer offered the only home delivery service in the region, so when the woman ordered something through the home shopping channels or the online shopping outlets, he delivered it. He was getting to know her pretty well – at least this was how he felt when he pictured the woman wearing the bra and underwear he had delivered, eating rice topped with the pickled crab he had delivered and going out afterward in the polka-dot dress he had delivered.

He felt a puff of air, breathed in its burden of concrete dust. Dust-laden air had been circulating stubbornly through the city ever since the construction of the new amusement park had got under way four years earlier. The park grounds and the building where the woman lived were separated only by the river bisecting the city. From a distance the amusement park was a jumbled mess, resembling demolition as much as construction. But closer up the array of construction cranes announced the arrival of the new park. A temporary office trailer sat like a huge waste container in a secluded corner of the construction site. Workers in yellow hard hats streamed in and out of the site, while debris-loaded trucks barrelled up and down the adjoining streets.

Construction was the obvious source of the city's unrelenting noise and dust, but the amusement park project was not the sole culprit. In fact, the entire city was being rebuilt. For every new building that took a month to erect, an old building was torn down in mere hours. The hodgepodge of residential areas was gradually being replaced by apartment jungles. The noise, the temporary perimeter walls, the truckloads of debris and the yellow hard hats – these sights and sounds of construction were as familiar to the residents as the alleys they navigated daily. But the more the city changed, the more it remained the same. Buildings would age until the owners had them razed and built right back up again for better profits. The opening of the amusement park would not alter this cycle.

He inadvertently kicked something made of glass and heard fragments ricochet off the floor. The sharp *crack* sent a cat darting out from an apartment and scurrying down to the far end of the hallway. The hallway was heaped with garbage where stray cats foraged. He plunked down the box and tried to catch his breath. The numbers outside the apartment units had peeled off – was this Number 4 or Number 5? He peeked through an open door and saw only a dusty gloom mottled with garbage and abandoned furniture.

The building was to be renovated. Even without the renovation notice the man would have assumed, and correctly too, that renovation in this case meant more than just replastering the exterior walls and repainting the building. With the exception of the structural skeleton and the number of units, everything about the building – the facilities and even the wiring – was to be replaced. When it had been completed, this building where the woman lived, along with its telephone poles, was one of the tallest structures in the area. But that was nineteen years before, and with construction on the surrounding apartment blocks soon to be finished, this building might end up looking no grander than the chimney of a rubbish incinerator. His deliveries to the woman's apartment had given him firsthand knowledge of the mass evacuation of the residents, who had been rushed into signing off on the renovation. After putting up with three years of bare-bones accommodation elsewhere, they would finally be allowed back into their facelifted apartments.

He tried the doorbell for Number 607 – dead. He was certain the lift display had been flickering down in the lobby. The power to the lift must have gone off while he was trudging up to the sixth floor. After thanking God that he hadn't taken the lift he banged on the steel door to the apartment. Nothing stirred. He pressed his face to the door and shouted. 'Hello! Anyone home?' Not once during the past year or so that he had been making deliveries to the woman had she failed to answer. He fished out his cellphone and punched in the number on the packing list. He heard a faint ringing inside. He let it continue, then checked the packing list by the glow of the phone. A rubber plant. The pot had probably been smashed as a result of his pratfall just now. He had once refunded the woman for the cost of a jar of makeup that had arrived broken. Even though the manufacturer was entirely at fault for the shoddy packaging, he had to shoulder the blame, and a day's pay was blown.

Leaving the woman's parcel in the hallway would not be a problem. After all, she was the sole remaining resident on the sixth floor. How likely were the occupants of the other floors to steal from outside her door? Only rubbish was ever left out. And no one would be able to distinguish the box if he camouflaged it with a pile of garbage. The very idea brought life back to his arms. The woman would be expecting more items. He would return then and deliver everything together. If the rubber plant should die in the meantime, well, too bad. Back down the stairs he went. The gloomy recesses of the stairway had the musty stink of a rubbish incinerator's ash pit.

Instead of going home, the man drove to the photo shop. A stop at the warehouse earlier in the day had pushed him further behind on his schedule than usual. He had wanted to arrive in the woman's neighbourhood by the afternoon, but his day hadn't gone as planned. Her building was the only occupied one left in the neighbourhood. It and the apartment complexes under construction everywhere in the surrounding area would become a massive new residential suburb, a 'new city.' Almost all the items he delivered here were the woman's. Her building was too far from the other neighbourhoods on his route. This, along with the return trip to the warehouse, had translated into a lot of wasted energy. Several attempts at replotting the route had proved futile. His delivery zone extended over nine localities and was compounded with detours to the warehouse and the sorting centre – no wonder he often found himself still working at 10 p.m.

At the *ding* of the shopkeeper's bell, the photographer emerged from the back room of the shop. Their eyes met in greeting and the man positioned himself in front of the camera. The two men had been born and raised in the area, attending the same primary school. The majority of their schoolmates had moved away after growing up. The handful of those who could not leave made peace with their lives, and either went to work for someone or opened a shop of their own. But all of them, including the photographer, had high hopes for life in the new city. As did the man. Once people began to settle in this new city, the demand for deliveries would soar – that would be a good thing, he reckoned. But it also meant that his daily load would increase, a thought that made his heart sink. His truck was perpetually loaded with heavy boxes. If only he could retrieve the deposit he had paid the company when he was hired, he would quit the delivery job on the spot. But he knew this was impossible unless someone could be lured to this urban fringe to replace him. And so he rested his hopes on the new city.

'Still up and at it?' the man said as he retrieved a stool from the corner and perched himself on it. 'I thought you might have hit the sack early.' But the truth was, the photographer, who was always complaining about his lack of business, would welcome a customer at any time of the day.

The photographer gently shook his head. 'Don't worry, happens all the time.' He put his eye to the camera lens.

The man looked into the camera as if it was a mirror and adjusted his shirt, slid his glasses to the very tip of his nose and squared his shoulders. It had been pointed out to him at the previous head-shot session that he tended to slouch to the left.

'Relax your shoulders a little.'

The man let his squared shoulders drop. But not too much – that might imply cowardice.

'So that's today's pose?'

'Yes,' the man answered, afraid of nodding lest his glasses slide off the end of his nose.

The photographer counted to three. Off went the flash.

The man flipped through a weekly tabloid magazine while waiting for the photos to be developed. He could hear a child fussing in the living quarters at the back of the shop.

The photographer craned his head towards the back, then asked, 'How's work?'

The question was unexpected. Though the two men had gone to the same primary school, their acquaintance was skin-deep and they had never bothered much with conversation. It was routine for the man to leaf through lowbrow magazines while the photographer was in the darkroom.

'Good enough to keep myself fed,' the man answered with a chuckle. *What a boring answer*, he told himself. To hide the awkwardness he felt, he forced a louder laugh.

'You know, I'm thinking of looking for another line of work,' said the photographer. 'I'll let my wife run the shop. Business has dried up so much, she can handle it.'

'Anything special in mind?'

'Well, I'm looking.'

The man gave it a brief think and then offered, 'How about home delivery?'

'Could I start right away? If so, yes, that would work.'

'No, not right away.' The man paused for effect. '*But*, if you're interested, I can look into it for you.'

'Would you? That'd be great!'

The man returned to his magazine, practically burying his face in it. *Maybe it's the photographer who will make it possible for me to get back my deposit! Hey, don't let him see you smiling. Not so fast with the promises – haste makes waste. Talk up the job too much and you'll lose your credibility.* And then he feigned nonchalance as he flipped through the magazine.

'What are all these head shots for?' the photographer asked as he handed over the developed prints. The man had been coming in for head shots every week or so.

'Well, not much, just mementos.'

'Mementos?'

The man nodded emphatically.

'You have that many occasions to mark with these mementos?' The photographer gave a brief snort as he pocketed the man's payment.

Jotting down the date on the back of each print, the man replied philosophically, 'Every day needs something to remember it by.' He sounded as though he had given long thought to his answer. But the words jerked him back to reality – his life was, in fact, devoid of all meaningful anniversaries. Except for the death of his parents. They had passed away only hours apart, from injuries sustained in a freak accident – their car had broken down, and as they were looking beneath it on the highway shoulder they were struck by another vehicle. He was barely out of his teens. He didn't think of their deaths as an occasion to memorialize. He had no close relatives who would take his parents' place in celebrating his birthday. Nor did he have a girlfriend with whom he could count down to their hundredth-day anniversary or relive their first kiss. No employers or jobs had felt worthy of commemorating. And he despised national holidays and Christmas, because the deliveries always mushroomed on such days.

'Anniversary,' he repeated under his breath. His voice was weary.

The truth was, he needed the head shots for the dozen or so résumés that he liked to busy himself with on his days off. In black ink he would tediously fill in the blank spaces with the details of his high-school-level education and the odd jobs he had worked, all the while asking himself, *How the hell have I managed to lead such a shitty life?* The question was cast like a fishing line into the deepest corner of his soul, and what he reeled back in was self-pity. Rolling a glue stick over the back of the photos, he pasted one onto each résumé. All the head shots were by intent as comical as possible. Better than looking pathetic. He sent the completed résumés to all the companies in the big city.

Whether it was his lack of qualifications or his photo, none of the companies responded. Perhaps handwritten résumés were too primitive by current standards to be taken seriously. Nevertheless, he filled out the résumés as he might have a journal. Some days he would neatly record weekly lists of items he'd delivered, or the names of the localities he'd delivered to. On other days he would record the names of apartment buildings sprouting up in the new city, or he would list and group by manufacturer all the cup-*ramyŏn* shelved in his neighbourhood supermarkets. Once he even included his by now useless dual certification in English- and Korean-language typewriting, as well as his abacus-mathematics certification. On the day of his typing test, his nerves made his fingers slip off the keys, and yet he passed with flying colours. He enjoyed the clicking and tapping made by the keyboard. The sounds reminded him of the drumming of raindrops. And on the day of his abacus-mathematics test he was stumped by a mental arithmetic problem involving a two-digit number and a three-digit number. But instead of doing it in his head he had copied the problem down on his answer sheet and used an abacus. Both tests had been taken long ago, and neither certification was of any use now. He was fully aware that his qualifications alone would never land him a job with a company in the city, and that sending out more résumés was not a solution. He was doomed to remain an applicant from the suburbs. There were times when he found solace in the potential of the new city to transform even his neighbourhood into something recognizably metropolitan. But he also found it humiliating not to be able to improve on his life of hopping from one rented half-basement room to another. Be it humiliation or solace, nothing could enhance his life at this point.

As he climbed the stairs, he compared the dust dislodged from the steps to gentle sighs from the ageing walls. In the hallway he retrieved the large box with the woman's potted rubber plant from beneath the rubbish pile, placed a smaller box atop it and picked up the boxes. They obstructed his view, but it made no difference because it was nighttime and dark inside the building.

'Hello! Anyone home?' he called to the woman's closed door. His voice echoed along the empty hallway. He tried the woman on his cellphone. No answer. He peered through the door crack into the pitch-dark apartment. Maybe the woman had moved. He recalled the renovation notice in the building lobby, which mentioned a start date for the interior demolition. That day was approaching, and the residents had been taking their leave of the decrepit building.

Puzzled, he set down the boxes. *Why would she want a rubber plant at a time like this? Is she planning to hang around for a while?* Inside the smaller box was a bottle of grapeseed oil. He tried to imagine the woman tidying up the living room with its new rubber plant, and cooking with the oil. He could picture how the woman's clothes, the oil and the potted plant might look though he had never actually seen them. Her face, however, was always obscure. He pounded on the door. From the far end of the hallway he heard, against the hush of the building, the wind rustling among some plastic bags.

He considered leaving, but instead gave the doorknob a twist. The door swung open silently. He stepped in and called out cautiously, 'Hello?'

Nothing in the inky darkness suggested the woman was there. Boxes in his arms, he scanned the apartment. Everything looked to be in its proper place, as though the woman had left mere moments ago. Was she coming right back, or was she gone for good? He couldn't tell. Just as he was about to leave, light spilled into the apartment through the balcony off the living room. Like a searchlight, it brought every detail into glaring view – a grease-stained frying pan on the kitchen stove, a pair of women's sandals in the doorway. *Did I deliver those sandals?* They seemed to be telling him that the woman wouldn't be back any time soon, but this was only a vague hunch – after all, he knew nothing of the woman aside from the items he had delivered to her. Drawn by the light, he drifted towards the balcony, and through the window he traced the light to a huge wheel radiating a rainbow of primary colours. The wheel slowly turned, all the while surveying the woman's apartment. Its light illuminated the river, the water glimmering in a spinning kaleidoscope of colours. The wheel, he saw, was sitting on the other side of the river, awaiting the grand opening.

He stared blankly at the wheel. It was a while before it dawned on him that the lights were coming from a Ferris wheel and that the maintenance crew was probably testing the ride. The man had never been on a Ferris wheel. When his parents were alive, they were always overextended, trying to make ends meet. Even if they had had the wherewithal, there was no Ferris wheel where they lived on the outskirts of the city. And his was not the happy family that would have gone on a Sunday outing to an amusement park miles away. Not until he was older did he realize that these parks were no longer rare finds, nor were they difficult to access, and on occasion he visited them with his friends. He had ridden roller-coasters at 70 miles an hour or faster. He had zipped along upside-down on rides. In comparison, the Ferris wheel was a bore. It was not a ride that attracted droves of boys. It offered no speed, no adrenaline rush from watching the world go topsy-turvy. It left people with no trembles and no thrills. The Ferris wheel moved as sluggishly as his life, and only high enough to offer a view of the nearby clusters of squat multi-family blocks. He knew that couples sought the close confines of the Ferris wheel gondola to make out or engage in steamier frolics. If only he had known a woman intimately enough to do that . . .

The man had brought home the two boxes and opened them – in spite of company regulations requiring him to return all undelivered parcels to the sender by a certain time. The more he looked at the woman's name on the packing list, the more it became his own name. The woman still wasn't answering the phone. A few days after his second attempt to deliver the woman's parcels he had attempted another delivery, but it seemed that demolition was under way. Not only was the building littered with debris, he was stopped by the construction crew. He flattered himself thinking that the woman had disappeared so she could leave him with the packages to make up for all the gifts of which his life had deprived him. And with the curious anticipation of people opening presents he now opened the woman's packages. On a wall calendar he itemized every parcel – the potted rubber plant, the grapeseed oil, a lace nightgown, a kitchenware set won in a lottery commemorating the manufacturer's 10-million sales milestone, a seven-piece knife set complete with wooden block, a bamboo floor mat and a pillow embroidered with chrysanthemums.

He enjoyed guessing at the function of an object, and so he delighted in unexpected gifts more than thoughtful ones tailor-made for the recipient. He put the rubber plant outside where it would shield the window of his half-basement room. Subsequently he would rub the grapeseed oil all over himself after showering, and he used the oil to cook eggs and stir-fried potatoes. He wondered why the woman preferred such bland oil, and decided she was either health-conscious or susceptible to trends. Even a culinary ignoramus like himself understood that cooking had its own vogue. From the kitchenware set he picked out the wide cooking pot; he would use it as a basin. Coincidentally, his own plastic basin had cracked and he was considering buying a new one. He spread out the bamboo mat on the floor, found it too chilly to sit on, and layered a quilt over it. He wondered why the woman had bought a bamboo mat now that summer was all but over. Perhaps she was overly sensitive to heat. He remembered from his school days a boy nicknamed Hotpants because he was the first to change into his summer uniform and the last to change out of it. He felt as though the parcels were full of clues that would allow him to piece together the puzzle that was this woman.

There were times when he had to deliver identical items to the woman. The wide-brimmed hat was one such item. A few days after he had attempted delivery of a pink hat, he was given the exact same hat to deliver, except this one was blue. *It's the same hat! Is she that vain?* He ended up giving the hats to his landlady. 'You expect *me* to wear *these*?' the landlady had muttered, only to become so enamoured with how they looked that they soon became an extension of her. He had beamed with pride, as if

he were the one who had gone to the trouble of finding them. The landlady always wore one of the hats while supervising the expansion of the
building in which he lived. The plan was to add a third and a fourth floor
to the multi-family building as well as to repair the exterior walls. The
construction forced him to shut his window to keep out the clouds of
cement dust. Even then, an immaculate white veil of dust managed to
steal into his room and settle on his black television. The house trembled
with the drilling. If he was in bed, the shriek and the rumble made him
nauseous. Sometimes he hurled his pillow at the ceiling, rattling the fluorescent light fixture. And then he would retch, a long thread of saliva
hanging from his chin. The clamour bombarded him until late at night.
He kept the seven-piece knife set in its original packaging. It would be a
gift for the photographer's wife. One day the photographer had shown up
at the sorting centre and ever since had accompanied him on his deliveries.
The man would make it appear that he finished around seven. This
delighted the photographer, who would ask if work always finished so
early. The man equivocated, saying not always. He neglected to mention
that after the photographer had left, he would deliver his remaining parcels. He didn't feel guilty. Once he left, the photographer would learn he'd
been deceived but of course would also realize the man had no choice.

From his drawer the man produced all the head shots he had had taken
for his résumés. Aside from the subtle differences in the length of his hair
and the style of his clothes, his comical face had remained unchanged. He
tried to arrange the photos chronologically on the floor without looking
at the date written on the back. The oldest and the most recent of the
bunch could be easily distinguished; not so with the rest. He pored over
his many inscrutable faces from the past. They betrayed no thoughts, no
emotions.

He selected a photo from the previous winter. In it he wore a black
turtleneck and looked emaciated, though in reality he was just tired. He
had never worked a shift when he was not plagued by migraine and fatigue.
His hair was longer then – out went the hair; he cropped it from the picture. Next, he cut his eyes out of a photo taken the previous summer. They
were guilty of being bloodshot. The day that photo was taken, he had
caught conjunctivitis from a woman in the sorting centre office. Tears were
oozing from his festering eyes. The gelled mucus looked like pus. His eyes

stung and the world looked blurry and disconnected. The photographer had asked if he really wanted a photo taken with his eyes in such a state. Instead of answering, he had reached out, intending to shoo a fly away, causing the startled photographer to step back out of his reach. In a dejected voice he had tried to explain himself: 'There was a fly on your shirt.'

And here was that photo from two years earlier. His short hair had served to exaggerate his sagging, nearly lobeless ears – out went the ears. The cropped hair, the cut-out eyes and the excised ears looked grossly misshapen because the photos were small to begin with and his scissoring was clumsy. He pasted these cropped features onto his most recent photo, the one in which he had slid his glasses down to the tip of his nose. And suddenly the hair was bushy and the bloodshot eyes ghoulish and the elfin ears protruded from the hair like a goblin's horns. He glued the mutilated photo onto a résumé. Beneath the name of his high school he listed every last item he had received by way of the woman.

The woman suggested that they meet at the amusement park. Until she mentioned her name the man hadn't recognized her voice on the phone. Her name had come to be synonymous with his own. While the woman retold her ordeal in tracking him down, his eyes surveyed every corner of his room for her items. The rubber plant was wilting under dense construction dust, its shrivelled, yellowing leaves fluttering to the floor like the dust. To revive its parched, barren roots would take a miracle. As for the pink and the blue wide-brimmed hats, his landlady continued to alternate between them as she supervised the construction work. The dusty hats had been bleached out by the sun so that the colours were almost indistinguishable. The construction had dragged on for a whole season, and still no end in sight. The cooking pot-turned-basin was scratched from the tiled bathroom floor. More than half the bottle of grapeseed oil had been used on his body and for cooking. The dust-saturated bamboo mat was plastered to the floor like oiled floor paper beneath the quilt. He liked to fold the quilt and sit on it while he ate *ramyŏn* and trimmed his nails. He had donned the woman's lacy nightgown and masturbated to indiscernible images of her face, his scattershot ejaculate leaving the gown mottled with yellow. At night he slept with his head on the woman's chrysanthemum-embroidered pillow, leaving a depression in its centre. Only then did he realize that these items had never been presents to him. He would need to apologize to the woman and refund her money if he wanted to avoid legal problems.

The amusement park rides were undergoing safety tests. A blazing red roller-coaster was tearing up and down its track along the river, following a choreographed sequence of loops and dives. Travelling at over 70 miles an hour, it could induce vertigo in mere onlookers. The chance of derailment was slim to none, but the man's heart remained in his throat until the roller-coaster finally pulled into the station. Adjacent to it a pirate ship was oscillating like a pendulum and wailing with each swing.

The Ferris wheel sat in the farthest corner of the park. The woman was waiting in front of it. 'There's no place to sit here – let's go for a ride.' He trotted after the woman and followed her into the first gondola to arrive. As soon as the woman had taken her seat, she started a stopwatch. 'I'm timing the ride,' she explained, adding that she was in charge of test-riding the Ferris wheel. 'The wheel revolves at the same speed, but for some reason each ride is timed a little differently.'

He looked out the gondola window and saw another gondola teetering at the end of each bicycle-spoke-like steel arm. He relished the gondola's subtle sway in the breeze. They ascended so slowly he could scarcely feel the movement.

'I just want to say I'm sorry.' He hung his head.

'What's done is done, yes?' Her tone was mild. Gone were the haughty demands over the phone to have the packages returned to her at once. He offered to refund the entire cost. The woman nodded with a matter-of-fact expression and resumed staring at her stopwatch.

'You seem to like hats,' he ventured.

'I do?' The woman looked puzzled.

He reminded her that she had bought two identical hats, in different colours.

'Did I really?' The woman giggled, exposing her teeth. He countered with a fleeting smile, for lack of anything to say. He wondered if his teeth looked as dark as the woman's. Her bland countenance offered no answer. He studied her. Until now he had never seen her head on. It was as though he was meeting her for the very first time when in fact he had made deliveries to her almost weekly. He had only ever seen her face through the crack in her apartment door, and the impassiveness of her face had blinded him to the harmony of her features, leaving him with only an impression of unfriendliness.

'Where do you stay these days?'

'Here.' She didn't bother to look up from the stopwatch. He wasn't sure if *here* meant the gondola, the amusement park, or the city itself. He began to feel uneasy and his hand kept reaching for the résumé in his breast pocket. That résumé was urging him to work up his nerve. But for what he didn't know.

He heaved a sigh and looked out the gondola window. They were slowly rising high above the world of construction below. He could see the empty frames of the park's mammoth rides spinning and spiralling tirelessly, could hear their motors moan. And then the woman's apartment building came into sight across the river. It gleamed in the light from the nighttime construction work. That light made it difficult to see that the building had been disembowelled and was now an empty shell. The surrounding buildings with their overwhelmingly grey cement looked like so many dying trees. A bit higher and he might be able to see the multi-family housing development where he lived. The sprawl of the development was encircled by apartment blocks; from above it would probably look like the sunken pit of a trap. He wanted to see even farther – if possible, out to the scar-like chaos of roads that led into other cities. He stood up but in doing so banged his head against the ceiling. Defeated, he perched himself on the seat, head bent over.

The woman was across from him. Their knees sometimes brushed against each other when he shifted in his seat. The sensation tempted him to steal glances at her. Her face remained blank. He wanted to ask her what else she liked besides hats, whether she was sensitive to the heat, if she hated being so petite that she needed platform trainers. He wanted to tell her that she actually didn't look very small at all. He wanted to tease her – 'You can't seem to cook!' – and he wanted her to laugh with him afterwards. He was curious as to why she had left behind her sandals – they were still new – and indeed why she had abandoned everything in her apartment. Did she know that the Ferris-wheel lights illuminated her apartment every night? But he clamped his mouth shut as his mind mulled over the restless deluge of questions that he was afraid he might unwittingly blurt out.

The ground was a dazzling orb of light. In it the man saw himself driving a truck, taking packages to an endless list of strangers, his face hard like cardboard from hauling boxes all day. He also saw the photographer taking head shots for customers who, if not stoic, had an elusive curl to the corners of their mouth. The stiff prints of their head shots were being cut to standard size. He saw his landlady in her hat, dozing off in a chair overlooking the construction work. Then there was the woman, latching a gondola door shut and fixating on her stopwatch. He waved at them all.

Cheerful staccato music entered the gondola, as though in acknowledgement of his wave. A mellifluous prerecorded voice announced that at 500 feet off the ground, they had reached the apex of the ride. He had never expected the ground to look so fantastic from this height. It would have been a romantic spot for a kiss, and the mischievous music lingered knowingly. He suddenly felt bashful and pretended to be oblivious to the music. The woman was unmoved. Was she even listening? The globe-like wheel began to descend gradually. He rubbed stupidly at his parched lips.

'I gave your hats to my landlady,' he blurted as the woman stared out the window.

'I see.' After a brief pause, she asked, 'What did they look like?'

'They have a wide brim that's turned down a little in front, and a small bow at the back.' Her eyes followed his fingers in the air as they outlined the shape of the hat. He thought there was a hint of a smile in the woman's face, then decided he was mistaken.

By now the photographer should have paid his deposit for the job, but he had yet to hear from him. He was growing fretful, but resisted phoning the photographer. The more desperate he sounded, the more complacent the photographer might become. For the time being, he would skip the weekly head-shot session. He might have to buttonhole the photographer and implore him to pay the deposit. The longer he waited, the more difficult it would be to get his deposit back, which meant he could never leave his suburban district and would have to roam the under-construction city by day to make his deliveries. Unnerved by the thought, he pulled out the résumé from his breast pocket.

'What do you think of this photo?'

'The red eyes look kind of funny.'

He ran his hand over the bloodshot eyes and elfin ears. He had an idea. He offered the woman his résumé.

'Would you like to have it?'

The woman stared incredulously at him and shook her head. Of course – whatever would she want with it, especially from a stranger? So, what now? In the end he stuck it in the narrow slit between the seat and its frame. A corner of the bleached paper stuck out like a flag. The rest of the page would ride the Ferris wheel in a perpetual circle. On most days, wherever those bloodshot eyes looked they would see cities under construction, but on a cloudless day they would see a city in the distance.

The Ferris wheel continued to revolve after they had touched down. The feeling of solid ground beneath his feet was dizzying. He steadied himself enough for a polite bow to the woman and bade her goodbye. She handed him a piece of paper with a list of the packages she hadn't received, and the cost of each. He slid the paper into his pocket and asked, 'How long did it take?'

The woman glanced at her stopwatch. 'Less time than usual.'

He left the woman and walked towards the amusement park entrance. In his truck were some parcels for her. He didn't know the contents of those parcels, because he hadn't had a chance to look over the packing list. Perhaps it wasn't the woman who had placed those orders. But the parcels might keep coming after he reimbursed her. And when those packages arrived, he could continue to visit her at the amusement park and to ride the Ferris wheel with her in order to deliver them. He toyed with the thought of ordering something under the woman's name.

He started the engine and looked back at the Ferris wheel and its empty gondolas, the wheel's glistening lights flowing over the night-cloaked city. The wheel dawdled on its axis, as if to say the world would come to a grinding halt if it stopped. His eyes searched for his résumé-waving gondola, a far from easy task amid the neon glow. He set the truck in motion and thought he heard the parcels pushing and shoving one another among the crowded cargo. He drove off into the night towards the city. Those parcels needed delivering.

CHOI SUCHOL

River Dark

Translated by Bruce and Ju-Chan Fulton

Early last summer he took a solitary holiday on Ullŭng Island. Instead of the fancier and faster charter boat he went by ferry, arriving after several hours of pitching and rolling on the East Sea. Dumping his bag in the hotel room he'd reserved, he went out onto the balcony. *Free at last!* Off to his right was Sŏngin Peak, the high point on the island. His eye followed the ridgeline down to the indigo-blue water lapping at its base like a dragon thirsting for the mountain's vital energy.

He had long wanted to set out on his own on an off-season trip. Several opportunities had arisen, but each time, the exigencies of day-to-day living had tripped him up and he'd had to reschedule. His family were well aware of these false starts, and at the revelation of his latest plan they had sent him off with expressions that were equal parts *Good for you* and *Be my guest*. But neither his family nor he himself could have explained why Ullŭng was his destination – why *there*? Simply put, he'd been quite the romantic when he was much younger, and although that facet of his temperament had pretty much eroded in the whirl of daily life, he'd become blindly attached to his youthful dream.

He was at his absolute leisure, even to the point of monotony, on Ullŭng. Not for him the hike up Sŏngin Peak or the pleasure-boat cruise around the island. What mattered was that he had finally made the trip here, alone. He desired only a lack of desire for anything; all he wanted was to be as lazy and lethargic as possible.

A typical humdrum day started with a late breakfast at the hotel, after which he'd mosey about the island, returning around sundown to the dock in front of the hotel for a bottle of *soju* and a bite of the local seafood. He learned from the proprietor of the eatery that the deep blue

337

colour of the sea was owing to the abundant seaweed, which the strong sunlight made squishy and kept afloat. The man also related a tapestry of legends about the island as well as tales of the islets nearby.

Dusk found him back at the hotel, in the bar off the lobby. He sometimes drank coffee, but mostly beer or highballs. The bar had the ambience of a countryside tearoom – when the waitress brought him his beverage, whether soft or hard, she would park herself next to him and strike up a conversation, ultimately dropping hints that he should buy her a drink. At first he was fazed – how could a self-respecting hotel countenance blatant wheedling by the waitresses? But then his lethargic game plan kicked in again and he decided it didn't matter. If it was tea she wanted, fine; if a drink, he'd buy that for her too. But because he wasn't interested in her, he answered her sporadic questions half-heartedly and didn't initiate conversation. Inevitably she'd grow bored, dutifully toss down her drink and move to another table.

She looked to be in her mid-thirties. She had a broad, swarthy face, lustreless skin and hair, and fleshy forearms and legs and a flabby midriff – so much for keeping herself up. And she always wore a blank, seemingly unwary expression or, more frequently, a frown of mild irritation that might have been a ploy to entice the guys.

But sometimes he found himself staring at her, and the next thing he knew he'd be hankering to ask her questions. He convinced himself she'd drifted in on the tide after leaving her ancestral village on the mainland at a young age and shuttling from place to place. What ferry of fate had brought her here, and which vessel of destiny would deliver her? If at some point the locals tired of her, she'd have to leave. He imagined her on some old rust-bucket riding the currents to islands even smaller than Ullŭng.

None of these questions escaped his lips. What could the curiosity or compassion of others, their favour or disdain, add to the fabric of her life beyond a few stray threads? But on his last night he found himself wavering as she sat there across from him. Not because of her. Rather he felt he'd come face to face with an expanse of sea grass that shimmied back and forth with the movement of the water, and he imagined that grass beckoning him closer and himself responding by forging his way through it and past the woman.

For as long as he could remember, water and rivers had been a familiar presence. He'd grown up in a city where the two streams of a great river came together; nearby were lakes. Many were the hours he spent by the river with friends and family during the summer and winter school breaks. He lived with the river and it became part of him. But when after many years he returned home for a visit and sought out the river that had been flowing all that time in his memory, invested with recollections from his youth, he found it ailing.

It was a late spring day when he drove out to the riverside. The river stank to high heaven. A new dam upstream had lowered the water level, and the surface was coated with black scum. The foul water barely moved, flowing in fits and starts, like a long-bedridden man struggling to turn over.

Witnessing the river he'd neglected, already polluted beyond hope, he felt a storm surge of regret and pent-up anger spill into a stream of sorrow as all at once his recollections of the past, his hope that children would come to enjoy the big-hearted flow as he had, decomposed along with the river.

When primary school was out for the summer his family had liked to go down to the river for picnics. The water was clear and cool, the sand soft and clean. The only lack, if one could call it that, was of shady trees. Back then anyway, beach parasols weren't common, so once settled at the riverside you were at the mercy of the sun. Some tried to make do with an umbrella or a sunshade; others took refuge in the pine groves some distance off.

Then one summer day his father fashioned an awning of sorts, or more precisely a canopy, out of four posts and a blue tarpaulin, and it became a fixture at the riverside outings. It wasn't much to look at, but it offered pleasant shade the summer through. Before long, similar shelters were being erected here and there.

Late in the season, after one last frolic at the riverside, his family decided to bury the canopy and retrieve it the following summer. They chose an abandoned sesame patch for the purpose. No worries about the vinyl tarp, but would the wooden posts rot? Thankfully the soil was dry and sandy.

When next summer came around, he found himself fixating on the canopy. When he could wait no longer he went to look for the sesame patch. All he found were windswept mounds of sand with a straggling of weeds. Where was the canopy? Here he dug, there he dug, and finally he found it! The blue tarp was crumpled, ripped and faded, the posts a bit soft and wasted, but the boy's sense of wonder, the pleasant surprise of it all, was undiminished. Young as he was, he felt blessed that there was that in this world which awaited discovery while embedded in nature and undergoing transformation along with it.

But all too soon those same people had polluted the river beyond redemption.

Now that he thought about it, hadn't he been traipsing around this island with the image of the decaying river lodged in his mind? He understood now why he had wanted to come here: he had to, before it was too late! If there were a place of unspoiled nature, not yet polluted by human hand, perhaps it would be Ullŭng. And if he were to pass the time here doing nothing and desiring nothing, then perhaps the living river, now moribund, that used to flow inside him might come back to life and carry him in its flow.

But here too the situation was iffy. With feverish voices the islanders were wont to proclaim that their lives would improve with all the development projects soon to begin. Hearing such talk, he imagined the river about to revive inside him suddenly polluted for ever and gasping for dear life, an aortic vessel obstructed by a vile growth. He understood people's fretfulness over the irony of living evanescent lives in steadfast nature, but didn't that fretfulness block the passage of time within them, bringing their lives to a standstill?

The woman across from him sprang to her feet, wrenching him from his reveries. She eyed the door, perhaps checking for footloose would-be customers. Observing her, he realized why a sound night's sleep was proving as elusive here as at home: during his time here, the river of his childhood was repeating a painful cycle, resurrecting to clarity but the next moment reverting to a decaying trickle.

Turn by turn the river wended its way towards the woman across from him. Where would it empty out – into radiant purity once it reached her, or into dark decay once it enveloped her? While he was wondering, the river and her life merged in a single flow.

Late the previous night he'd seen her emerging from a second-floor guest room. Who knows, maybe deep down inside she was waiting for him to invite her to his room tonight.

Without a word he rose and left. He found open-air seating at the humble eatery at the dock and had a bottle of *soju* with fresh raw squid on the side. Add this to the bottle of *soju* with which he'd washed down his dinner, and by the time he paid the bill he was pleasantly drunk.

Back at the hotel, he found the bar closed for the night. Gazing at the dark window, he felt an urge to talk to the woman. But she was nowhere to be seen. Like the polluted river that had disappeared into the gloom of his darkened memories, she had vanished into the deep of the night.

Step by ponderous step he climbed the stairs to the third floor and, listing towards the wall, was nearing his room when the door to the VIP suite at the far end of the hall banged open and a throng of people burst into the corridor. 'Come on, hurry, we can't miss this opportunity, we don't want to keep him waiting!' someone called out. The group rushed past him, a mix of middle-aged men and women – the hotel staff, with the woman from the bar bringing up the rear while attempting to work her arms into her jacket. Spotting him, she slowed down enough to babble, with a twinkle in her boozy eyes, 'You look like you're feeling no pain, sir. It's party time for us – we've got ourselves a big spender!'

Barely finishing, she chased down the group. It took a moment for it all to register. But by then she'd disappeared to the lower level. Standing askew, he looked back at the dim light at the near end of the hall, where the stairs disappeared down and around the corner. The river was following in her course, decaying as it went, and he never did learn her name.

INTO THE NEW WORLD

CH'OE INHO

The Poplar Tree

Translated by Bruce and Ju-Chan Fulton

He was an unusual man.

For a time he was a high-jumper. At his best he routinely cleared 2.3 metres. He was more than a match for anyone in the village.

His personal best was 2.4 metres. No matter how tall you were, he could leap over you. As he could any wall, without ruffling a shirtsleeve – he made it look effortless. He was a splendid man, the sort you rarely see.

It was only a matter of time until he set a new world record, everyone thought at one point. But he wasn't a professional athlete. He was a black-smith, a maker of sickles, axes and such.

People liked to watch him high-jump.

We used to ask him to jump for us. But since he wasn't a professional, we didn't make a high-jump bar for him, the kind that wobbles and falls if you brush it on the way over, and we didn't prepare a sand pit to soften his landing. Instead, we'd ask him to jump over a tall bush-clover fence, or else a couple of the tallest of us kids would make like a horse and rider and dare him to jump over our heads.

He didn't often give in to a straightforward request to jump. At the same time, he didn't want people to think his talent for high-jumping had gone to his head, so if we phrased our request in the form of a dare it always worked. He'd strip to the waist, crouch down before the object to be jumped, and then, whoosh, he was a mad whirl of motion, riding on the wind, slicing clean over whoever stood on the 'horse.' Not once did he fall short. Quite a man, he was.

And because we thought him quite a man, we convinced ourselves that one day he would clear the flagpole at the school playground.

As for me, I believed he would one day jump a great mountain at a single bound. At a single bound he would clear the clouds floating in the sky, grab the stars that twinkled beyond and drop them at our feet. And if only he wanted, at a single bound he would clear not only the crimson twilight painting a distant peak but the rainbow that follows a shower in the western sky, the rainbow resplendent as the striped sleeves of a girl's *saektong* jacket.

'Uncle, can you jump over that rainbow?'

'Of course I can,' he confidently replied. 'As long as I have a runway that stretches out nice and wide all the way to the horizon.'

But he couldn't jump higher than 2.4 metres. That was as far up as he went. It was also the height of the highest chin-up bar at our school playground. There wasn't one of us who could even reach that bar from the ground.

Great as he was, though, he was not a happy man. One summer all three of his children drowned while playing in a stream, first one going under and then the older ones lost in their turn while attempting a rescue. The news drove his wife mad, and eventually she disappeared. And then the peddler of women's items who came around to the village once a month reported having seen her – once at the seashore, once beside a grave and some time or other at the riverside. And to us she reported that the woman had sprouted scales all over – but not a word of it did we believe.

After losing his children and his wife the man turned a bit strange. He still made horseshoes, sickles and hammers, but his sickles couldn't cut grass and his hammers couldn't drive a nail. He didn't high-jump. People mocked him: he couldn't even clear a brook that us children could jump across.

It got to the point where he'd spend all day in his shop working the bellows but never producing anything, not even a horseshoe.

He was crazy, all the villagers scoffed, but we remained true to him as always – he was our hero. I continued to believe he could jump the flagpole if only he wanted, continued to believe he would one day clear the lovely colours of the rainbow unscathed. Whenever the opportunity presented itself, we asked him to jump over the highest chin-up bar for us. But he would shake his head.

'Little ones, I can't jump high any more – my legs are rusty.'

But we didn't believe him. You see, he was our hope.

'Yes, you can, Uncle. You can jump over it. You're a great man.'

Finally, not wanting to disappoint us, he gave in. A mad dash down the playground, and he soared into the air. But his jump was ridiculously short. His leg hooked the bar and he fell to the ground with a scream, breaking the limb.

His leg was never the same again. He hobbled when he walked. He couldn't jump 30 centimetres high. A frog could have outjumped him. He couldn't even hop from one stepping stone to the next across the stream – you could bet he would fall in.

One day he planted a poplar sapling in his yard. I helped him. But why was he doing this? The reason escaped me. He'd planted tomatoes and *paech'u*, peppers and squashes there, and had lived a hand-to-mouth exist-ence on these foods. So the idea of planting a poplar tree instead of a fruit tree whose produce he could readily consume was incomprehensible.

Finally I asked him.

'Because a poplar grows tall faster than any other tree.'

'But ... a poplar doesn't produce any fruit, Uncle. Why not plant an apple tree or a peach tree?'

'No, little one,' he said with a smile. 'I don't go hungry any more. I've got all the tomatoes and potatoes I want.'

'Then what are you planting a poplar for?'

'So I can jump higher.'

And with that he hobbled to the freshly planted tree and jumped over the single shoot.

'See, I jumped over that tree – I jumped it.'

'But Uncle, I can jump over it too.' So saying, I proudly demonstrated.

'But every day that tree will grow a little taller. A year from now it'll be as tall as you are. In two years it'll be as tall as that chin-up bar, in three years it'll be up to the flagpole, in four years up to the electric pole and in five years it'll grow to the sky. Every day I'm going to jump over that tree. If I can keep it up, then one day I'll be able to jump as high as the sky.'

Every day he watered the tree; every day he put his heart into making it grow. True to his word, the tree did grow, but it wasn't noticeably larger every morning like, say, a morning glory, which seems to spurt up over-night when it blooms. Its growth seemed retarded – just like the hour hand of a clock, which doesn't appear to move at all.

And every day he jumped over the tree, hobble and all.

A year later, the poplar tree was as tall as I. Its verdant leaves trembled in the wind like the bracken-fern hands of schoolchildren cheering in the playground.

'Look,' he said proudly. 'I'm jumping over the tree.'

And right before my eyes he half-ran, half-hobbled up to the poplar and cleared it.

Before we knew it, we were growing too. Some of us were already sneaking cigarettes out in the wheat fields and no longer paid him much attention. We were gradually learning new pleasures, finding more interesting things to do. Along with our curiosity about pleasures we'd never tasted – alcohol, tobacco, girls and such – black hair was growing by the day in our nether regions. I alone continued to visit him, and it was for me alone that he half-hobbled, half-ran to the poplar tree and jumped over it.

After two years the poplar had outgrown me and was tall as the lower chin-up bar. At the time, I was in love with a girl. Her beauty dazzled me, and on the raised paths among the rice paddies she would whisper to me.

'I don't love you, and I don't want you. There's nobody I like except him.' She indicated a scarecrow standing amid the golden ears of rice. 'I'm going to marry him. I'm going to have his baby.'

Poking out of the rice paddies in autumn were countless scarecrows, each one a trunk of straw beneath a tattered farmer's hat. The flocks of sparrows weren't the least bit daunted. It was beyond me why the girl had said she loved a scarecrow.

For several days I went alone to the rice paddies and stood with my arms out like a scarecrow. And on one of those days I saw the girl and a man take off their clothes and roll around among the abundant stalks of rice. The girl then carried the child of the man, not of the scarecrow. The girl was a liar.

After I'd got over my sorrow, I went to see the blacksmith.

'Now just you watch, I'm going to jump over that tree,' he proclaimed. 'I can do it.'

He hobbled up to the tree and cleared it.

'What'd I tell you? I'll jump over that tree as high as it grows. Yes I will.'

But he was older now and bent-over. An old man, really, and that was the extent of it. All but two of his teeth were gone. His three children had long since perished, and his wife still hadn't returned.

'I saw his wife,' the peddler of women's things reported. 'She makes rice cakes out of sand at the seashore and sells them at the market. I tried one – scrumptious! "Your husband's waiting for you," I told her. "Why not go back with me?" And this is what she said – "You tell him he can wait. He can wait till I've made rice cakes out of all that sand and sold every last one of them."'

After three years the poplar was tall as the flagpole. It was a very handsome tree. Its roots were planted firmly in the ground and the vibrant young limbs stretched out as wide as you please. Its leaves were as lush as the hair growing from a man's broad chest. Compared with the tree, the blacksmith was an old man approaching death. The mouth that spoke to me now held only one tooth.

'Good to see you, little one. Watch closely, because I'm going to jump over that tree.'

He still called me 'little one.' Unfortunately, I was no longer little – I was a young man.

He started running, a slow-motion hobble. And then he was up like the wind, a bird in flight, gently brushing the air like the needles of a silver fir. Over the poplar he went.

'There, you saw it! I jumped it! I jumped that poplar tree!'

After four years the poplar had grown to the sky. You should have seen it – the top was no longer visible. Birds built nests of twigs and straw in its branches and laid their eggs. Low-lying clouds draped the midsection of the tree. In summer the whole village turned out to nap at the foot of the poplar; there was so much shade, you didn't have to fight for it.

'I saw the blacksmith's wife up above the clouds. She lives in a shelter she made on the top branches. She has three children. Honest. If you don't believe me, climb up there and see for yourself.'

So said one of the more mischievous youngsters after climbing the tree all the way above the clouds.

Of course, since I wasn't a little boy any more, I didn't have the lightness of body to climb the tree and see whether things above the clouds were as this boy had said.

When next I saw the blacksmith he had aged completely. His last remaining tooth was gone.

'Well, well, little one,' he said with a smile of delight. 'From the time you were young you asked if I could jump over the clouds – remember?'

'Indeed I do, Grandfather.'

'Well, here's your chance. I want you to watch me jump over that tree.'

He made a long approach, hobbling as best he could. Then suddenly he was aloft, sucked into the sky. I gazed reverently towards the top of the tree he had soared over. He couldn't be seen. I waited for him to return to earth. But he never came down. At first I thought it was because the poplar was so high – high enough that its top couldn't be spotted. So I waited till the sun set, but still he didn't land. And then after the longest time something fell to the ground with a thunk. I picked it up – a worn-out shoe.

Recently I visited the village. Brought the wife and our two children. The village had changed, but the poplar still stood. Strange thing was, it now looked very small to me, stunted even. Its leaves were withered, its branches broken. It was painfully contorted, like the body of a drowning victim.

When would he reappear before our eyes, landing on the ground, the form of this unusual man who had jumped higher than anyone on earth?

This morning I'm going to plant an apple tree in our yard, a tree that grows very, very slowly. Every morning I'll jump over that tree. And one day I'll jump over the clouds and at long last meet up with him in that other world, that unusual place he disappeared to.

You see, I've finally learned. Learned that the world we live in is actually a stopping point, a place to which we leaped from the distant place we once inhabited; that we'll move on to an earth that will receive our tired souls for all time. Yes, we are hanging in the balance, all of us. We are all going around upside-down.

HWANG CHŎNGŬN

The Bone Thief

Translated by Bruce and Ju-Chan Fulton

You'll likely find this in the snow.

Along with me, however far I got.

Call me what you will – the man, this evidence of the man, that S.O.B., that thing, it – but from this point on, I'll be *he*.

By the time he arrived at the house he'd lost many faces. And those that remained? He had trouble calling them up, his own included. It was winter, and at the turnoff to the house the car got stuck in the mud, the right front wheel hollowing out a rut. From the passenger seat he heard the whine of spinning metal and rubber. The estate agent jerked the steering wheel back and forth, then shifted down and stomped on the petrol pedal, spraying mud in all directions. Dogs were howling. The estate agent left him in the car and tramped 30 yards ahead to a house sitting all by itself, where he scrounged an armful of spent coal-briquettes tossed out in the snow. He got out to help, grabbing a handful of desiccated weeds and mashing them into the coal-briquette husks with his foot. Crushing more briquettes into the mud and layering the ash about the tyre, they finally managed to free the vehicle. They drove to safe ground, left the car, and went the rest of the way on foot. But the estate agent couldn't find the key to the house, and back to the car he went, unleashing obscenities along the way.

His back to the front gate, he looked about. A few steps ahead of him the land fell away in an arid field that stretched out in all directions. Unlimited visibility. Half a mile off was a dwelling, its roof a flat, thick-blue presence, whether tin or tile he couldn't tell. It made a sharp contrast with the drab field.

The wind stung his face and he turned back to the gate, sticking his hands in his coat pockets. Except for the gentle wooded incline behind the house there was just the bare land. Next door was the only other dwelling in the immediate vicinity. It had no gate or wall, and across the exposed yard he could see a tap sticking out of the ground, the pipe bundled up against the cold, and behind it an old-fashioned kitchen and the veranda. Where the front gate would have been was a pen – the source of the vicious frenzy of barking. He counted five huge dogs, murky steam billowing from their mouths. They didn't seem to be pets or watchdogs; maybe they were sold for meat? He was still regarding them when the estate agent returned. In through the gate they went, and the dogs in the pen stopped barking. Inside, not bothering to remove their shoes, they stepped up from the entrance to the living room, and he followed the estate agent through two bedrooms and then to the kitchen. The kitchen was a paltry affair, with a tap sticking waist-high out of the wall. It was originally a cowshed, explained the estate agent, and to him that's still what it looked like, the floor, walls and ceiling plastered with cement and lacking the tiles you would expect in a space with running water. And there was something peculiar about the floor beneath the tap. There had to be a drain, but when he bent over to check, he saw no opening, only some cabbage leaves stuck to the floor, and only their fringes dried up, suggesting that the tap had been used not so long ago. When he asked if someone was living there now, the estate agent considered him with an expression he read as *What a weird question*. He turned the tap to a trickle, and when he turned it off it squeaked. Rusty water pooled and grew still, a few speckles of something or other rising to the surface.

I'll take it, he said, and the estate agent's face lit up in a smile. A ten-minute drive in the mud-caked vehicle took them back to the city boundary and a succession of closely packed buildings. Three bus lines served this route, explained the estate agent, so commuting in from the province shouldn't be an issue. The man had perked up the moment he knew he had a renter, and from then on it was a nonstop spiel – the house was close to the city, no different, really, from *living* in the city, but off the beaten track, quiet and out in the open. Back at his office, the estate agent pounced on the phone.

Hunched over on the sofa, hands clasped between upraised knees, he gazed at the vermillion stamp pad and the newspaper on the coffee table. The headline announced that a city on the East Coast was cut off by heavy snow accompanied by bitter cold. Below was a photo of an old man gazing at the camera with a forlorn expression as he stood beneath the eaves of a home half collapsed from snow weighing down the roof. He caught the estate agent saying they had a possible tenant and he was with him in the office. The estate agent ended the call and turned towards him, saying the honourable landlord was on his way.

Hmm. What if he asked the estate agent, *If he's the honourable landlord, does that make me the bastard tenant?* He tried to imagine the embarrassed look on the man's face if he followed up with a laugh or a stinging remark. If it were Chang, definitely the stinging remark – this was an opportunity Chang wouldn't have missed. The estate agent who'd secured their former place was an older fellow who was also in the habit of referring to the owner as 'honourable landlord.' When Chang had cruelly called him out on that, the estate agent had responded with a nervous chuckle and the look of someone chomping into a live frog. *Fuck me, why can't I be like him!* And there he sat, wondering how a person can speak his mind and leave nothing unsaid. Until a man bundled in a parka on top of a Gore-Tex jacket popped in. His cheeks were bright red, as if he'd walked some distance into a headwind. The estate agent made the introductions. The man gave him a blasé glance, then turned back to the estate agent and launched into a diatribe: he'd taken a hosing on the last sale – and where did the estate agent get off calling him *after* the deal had closed to report that a prospective buyer with a higher offer had just shown up? Why not hook him up in the first place with people who would pay top dollar for his properties? He could almost see the man frothing at the mouth. In the mirror, he watched as the estate agent's face contorted in displeasure only to transform into a coy smile – *not bad*. And then the man jerked back around and popped the question: So, when can you move in?

The following Saturday afternoon he packed his television and a few boxes of books and odds and ends, loaded them in his car, and drove to the house. He stacked the boxes in the room he would use for storage and in the other room he plugged in the TV. Only one channel came on, and there was too much static to identify it. The screen was a mosaic of faded colours jumping every which way, and all he could make out was a figure he took for a man, speaking in a sibilant voice. So much for the TV. He returned to the other room and began unpacking. Out of the boxes came shirts, several pairs of trousers, jackets and a chess set and a few other items he was still trying to figure out why he'd brought here. He laid it all out on the floor and considered. Most of the items he'd used right up until he'd packed. And then he noticed his hands were dirty from handling them just now – how odd. He went to the kitchen-cum-bathroom-cum-just-right-for-a-cowshed space and gazed down at the floor at the drainage basin that lacked a drain. He turned on the water and inspected it – rust-coloured like before, probably undrinkable. He let it fill his cupped palms and took a sip. Sure enough, it had a bitter, metallic taste. He'd need bottled water.

As he headed for his car, keys in hand, a woman emerged from the house next door, a plastic bowl in hand. Spotting him, she stopped short of the dog pen. She had a round face with narrow eyes and sparse eyebrows. Behind her on the veranda stood an older woman, thin grey hair gathered in a tight bun at the back of her head. From inside the car he observed the women staring at him, stock-still, like prairie dogs on red alert. He stomped on the petrol pedal and felt frozen mud splatter against the underside of the car.

There was a long queue of cars at the entrance to the familiar shopping mart. He tried a neighbouring mart, but the traffic there was even worse, so back to the first one he went. Enveloped by the exhaust from the car ahead, he inched his way towards the car park. And that's when he heard the weather report on the radio. Into the mart he went, pushing a shopping cart containing a crumpled receipt and an ice-pop wrapper. Passing the usual array of merchandise, he wheeled over to the bottled-water display and loaded up with nine 5-litre bottles, the weight bringing the cart down on its haunches. Next came brown rice and barley, dried foods and finally instant meals, which he layered on top of the bottles. Everywhere were cardboard signs limiting sales of fuel and water and alcohol to personal consumption only – no wholesale purchases allowed. The supermarket was a mess, the shelves not restocked or tidied and the normally clean floors tracked with spillage and footprints. He wormed his way among the edgy throng. Going down the aisles, navigating around corners, waiting for checkout, extricating himself from the car park – by the time he was back on the road, the sun had gone down.

It was blustery. Five minutes past the bus stop was the turnoff to the house. He groped his way up the winding dirt road, tinted yellow by his headlights, until he spotted the lights of the neighbouring home. As he fixed them in his sights, he heard barking from the darkness.

Inside, he turned off the TV and spread out a blanket where he would sleep on the floor. Off went the room light and all was dark. The wind came whistling across the field, the gusts thudding against the walls. Was that his cellphone ringing in one of the boxes – no, couldn't be, he'd snapped the damned thing in half the day before. After one last round of barking at the wind, the dogs fell silent. Before he knew it, he was dreaming. He and Chang were on a bus, sitting in the back, watching the sharp outlines of the passengers in front of them. *Bang!* There was an impact, and then sand was showering through the windows and the roof. So much sand. He was swept, rolling and tumbling, from the bus, and there before him was the sallow face of the one he loved, which, just like his own, was sinking into the sand. Chang's eyes were shut, his mouth open. The next moment the sand had buried Chang's ears and was advancing towards his mouth. *Chang,* he cried out. *Hey, Chang, you can't breathe if your mouth gets covered!* But it was too late. Sobbing, he kept trying to clear the sand that kept covering his lover's face.

It was Chang in the dream, that was for sure, but was it really Chang's face? Was the face in the dream the same as Chang's face in real life, down to the last detail? No – the more he thought about it, the more convinced he was they were different. First of all, that wasn't how Chang had died. If in the dream there'd been a motorcycle, a truck, an incline, a guardrail, or maybe something wintry, then perhaps he could connect it with Chang's death. He knew nothing about Chang's final moment. He'd been notified the afternoon of Chang's death, had gone to the hospital, but not until the third day of the vigil – after two days of shock and confusion – was he able to see him. Behind the glass partition was Chang and a coffin. A coffin and Chang in death. A man and woman in hospital gowns entered and bowed to those who, like him, were attending the transfer of the body to the casket. His wary eyes followed as they tidied and secured Chang.

As far as he could tell, the woman was the undertaker and the man her assistant. The plump lady and the skinny man looked peculiarly familiar and yet unfamiliar, the peculiarity being their strange familiarity. They were respectful and professional in their handling of the body. He felt the arm of the person next to him but didn't move.

Chang's skull, caved in at the rear, had been packed with cotton, and the edges of the cavity were dark and shrivelled. The skull and face were held together by careless black stitching that began at the back of the ear and ended at the jaw in a small knot whose ends stuck out. He couldn't remove his gaze from the knot. Why did they have to do *that*? He wondered what would happen if he pulled out the knot – would something sprout? And what next, would the intensity of his gaze cause him to see yellow and would his eyeballs then burst?

The mourners moved behind the glass partition to pay their last respects, carrying him in their wake. From where Chang lay came the pungent smell of vinegar. A prayer commenced. He felt something sticky and spongy underfoot. It took a series of awkward, one-legged inspections of his shoe soles before he identified it – hair, lots of it, curly, short, long, yellow, red, the tangled hair of the dead. It was all over the floor. Among the mourners, Chang's sister wailed the most. She touched Chang's cheek then jerked her hand away, muttering, *It's so cold*.

A year later he'd learned that the place where he'd lived with Chang had been leased under Chang's name. Chang's sister informed him of this and asked him to move.

What could he do in his drained state? Stand up to her and make an earnest claim for his share of the deposit and all the rest? That would involve starting out with a *Yes, but*, accompanied by the appropriate facial expression, and then a second exchange, and his attitude would have to be just right, and a next round and a next . . . But he didn't have the energy to marshal all the right words and expressions and attitudes. Which left him with the inevitable decision to move – to this place with the cowshed with the drainage basin with no drain. To put it kindly, his volition was depleted.

The next morning he went to the cowshed, turned on the tap and watched it drip, insubstantial as fine fishbones. He needed to wash and leave for work, but as he looked at the water gathering in the drainless drainage basin he tried in vain to call up a distinct image of Chang's face. Sure, it's human nature to forget. *But hell, it's only been a year!* He washed his face with the hard, freezing water, layered himself in thick garments and wedged himself into his frost-covered car, already as tired as he felt after a day's work. He took a deep breath and fired the ignition. The car wouldn't start. He tried again.

And then a third time. And a fourth.

And after a considerable interval, a fifth.

So much for the car. Back inside he went, and that was the end of his life in human society.

He looked down at the tap above the drainage basin that lacked a drain.

Feels like it's been a hundred years.

It wouldn't have surprised him. It was only three months since he'd moved to this house with the cowshed with the drainless drain, but for all he knew, a century had come and gone. Not a drop of the rust-coloured water was to be seen from the tap. Nor could he hear water moving through the pipes. Which meant the deep freeze had arrived. And the temperature was still plummeting. There had been strong winds followed by a bout of sleet; water had frozen and the air was frigid. The weather pattern was unusual and temporary, according to the TV, but to him the unusual was now usual and temporary had become permanent. The last news report before the power went off had the temperature in the metropolitan area pegged at minus 37 degrees Celsius. A month ago he'd removed the floor covering and made a fire of scrap wood on the bare cement floor. He'd kept it going ever since. So what if the landlord raised hell about the blackened floor and the sooty wall? He spent his days gazing at the soot formation and the steady fire and eating what he'd cooked over its flames. In the afternoon, tucking his head deep inside the furry hood of his parka, he went out to gather firewood.

As soon as he set foot outside the gate the dogs would start barking. Even though they'd seen him numerous times by now. The barking dogs were three in number, the other two having frozen to death. The mother and daughter – if that's what they were, it was merely a convenient assumption on his part – were rarely to be seen. The old mother looked like the daughter, and the daughter looked like the old mother, which made them both look ancient. He'd seen the younger one dragging a dead dog from the pen. Forelegs in one hand and hind legs in the other, she swung the carcass back and forth for momentum before tossing it towards the field. It flew through the air, a stiff leather sack, and landed with a thud. After she had gone inside, he ventured to the drop-off and discovered a boneyard below. Some of the bones looked to be from puppies, some from full-grown dogs. Which confirmed his hunch that the women raised the animals for meat, and the ones that happened to die before they were slaughtered got dumped here. But the second of the dead dogs had been hauled inside. Which meant the women had either eaten it or cut it up and stashed it away.

He slid down the shallow embankment to the lumpy ground with its desiccated tangle of vegetation, landing with a *crack* on the skull of a dog whose hide hadn't yet rotted away. A jet fighter flew overhead, south to north, followed by a helicopter struggling mightily to keep up. Leaflets were dropping like fish scales from the tail of the helicopter, warning residents to evacuate to the shelters. Gathering the leaflets, he went inside and added them to the fire. They burned with an acrid smell.

He lavished attention on the fire.

The room he and Chang had shared in their old place had a bed, a desk and a few other pieces of furniture – items he presumed had passed into the hands of Chang's sister and the rest of his family. Apart from those belongings, Chang had had quite a few books, some of which he'd brought here in the boxes. Maybe if the temperature kept going down and he ran out of firewood he'd have to burn those books, box and all. He still couldn't visualize Chang's face clearly; more vivid were his memories of him. Memories centred in his sense of touch. Memories of touch through feel. Memories of the bumps and ridges of Chang's body, memories of feeling him again and again, memories stored in the palm of his hand. Memories that had worked their way into his cells, never to be forgotten. Chang was small and thin and his body temperature was unusually warm. He was beautiful, sensitive, talented and, when angry, pertinacious. This one's bound for an early death, he'd always thought. Either that or, surprise, he'd outlive everyone else. How could he have known Chang would be gone so soon.

It's a sunny day, Cho! Go out and get some sun! His last words, spoken a few days before his death, when he'd paused, somehow distracted, in the living room just before heading out the door for work. Strictly speaking, they weren't his last words – Chang had lived a few days more – but they were the last words he remembered. *It's a sunny day, Cho! Go out and get some sun!*

The memorial observance at the hospital was a religious ceremony, Chang and his siblings having been born into a Christian family. He remembered Chang saying that for him, going to church was like a habit. The Lord's Prayer at the beginning of the service appealed to him, as did the Credo at the end, and he tolerated what came between. But he didn't trust or much like the God that was spoken of there. Once when he was young, Chang said, a beggar drifted into the church in the midst of a prayer in a Christmas Eve service. Christmas – the word had always conjured up images of sugar cookies to Chang. The beggar loitered in the back of the sanctuary asking for food until the parishioners shoved him out the door. Of all nights the beggar had chosen Christmas Eve, and of all places a church. So, sure, he must have had ulterior motives, but in any event the service continued without interruption. Afterward the parishioners, their cheeks rosy red in their nice warm church, exchanged presents. That experience couldn't help but leave Chang dubious. They all said they loved their neighbours. They didn't say they didn't love their neighbours when they didn't; they did say they *did* love them when they didn't – which was worse than not loving them at all. Worse than not saying it in the first place. The song they sang so fervently, especially during Christmas or Thanksgiving, was 'You Were Born to Be Loved.' If there were a you that was born to be loved, did that mean there was also a you that was born not to be loved? And who would constitute the one type, and who the other?

Doesn't fucking matter, Chang had said. *The point is, loving others never enters their mind*. But that didn't stop Chang from going to church.

It must have been spring.

He got off work early and went with Chang to watch a film about an old man who received a telegram from his brother and set off across the continent riding on a John Deere lawnmower to see him. Chang looked content afterwards. On their way home they stopped at a convenience shop and had a can of beer each, then set off towards their place, hand in hand. A middle-aged man came staggering down the street and fixed them with a stare. Once past them, he reversed direction and hollered, *Chang! Brother Chang, is that you!* Bringing them to a stop. Head cocked dubiously, reeking of alcohol, the man staggered up to them and stood there, slouching, then affected a series of great nods. *Brother Chang*, what *are you doing, holding a guy's hand? That's just plain weird. What's the meaning of this? You disgusting little faggots!* He tried to steer the man away. *Move along, sir. Please. Just leave us alone.* And then Chang spoke. *Disgusting? Me, disgusting? I think* you're *disgusting!* Fists flew. The awning of the fruit stand was ripped, and the man fell and cracked his head – truth be told, not so much from Chang's punches as from his inability to stand up straight. Chang was deemed to have started it, and was taken into custody. Who would have thought it?

Chang, whom he'd assumed would skip church the following Sunday, rose early and readied himself to leave. He accompanied him out of concern. During the service the older folks kept looking back at him with undisguised curiosity, while the victim and his family, faces prim and proper, kept their backs to him. Others remained stern and tight-lipped, and others sent him *Look-how-friendly-I-am* nods of greeting. Chang sat with a twinkle in his eye, seemingly amused by it all. After the service, everyone gathered in the church dining hall for lunch. With a rattle of chopsticks and spoons, sets of eating utensils were passed around and the parishioners set to. There came a whisper, *Those . . . you know*, and then a brief hush. And again the rattle of utensils. Very deliberately Chang finished chewing what was in his mouth, then turned towards a couple who had been gawking at them. *You really want to know, don't you. All right – he sticks his in me and I stick mine in him. Now, don't be alarmed. I do have my preferences, but I have no desire to stick mine in either of you.*

Chang attended a few weeks more, until the minister telephoned him to say he was no longer welcome. *No problem!* said Chang, and he ended the call.

*

He opened his eyes and checked the fire. Burning just fine before he went to sleep, it was dying now. He nursed it back to life. Night was approaching. He heard the squeak of the ice expanding where it had worked its way into the chinks in the walls. With every gust of wind, the roof creaked like a wrecked ship coming apart. His stomach was empty. He'd managed to slake his thirst by licking at frost or gathering snow after the occasional meagre snowfall, but he hadn't eaten solid food for the last five days. He'd been rationing his salt and his few remaining handfuls of grain, the soupy mixture he cooked more water than stock.

Maybe he should go to one of the shelters before it was too late? There'd been a call to evacuate, after all. And at the shelter, who knows, he'd probably be fed. Add it all up and he'd have a nice comfy place for the time being. Maybe he'd see a rerun of that scene in the church dining hall, complete with the rattling of spoons and chopsticks. He broke into a laugh, and the laugh turned into a coughing fit. *Hey.* How about grabbing one of the dogs? A dog meant meat. And it would soon be night. Tonight, then. He gazed at the fire and awaited nightfall. And when the time came, he added another jacket to the parka he hadn't taken off for months, bundled his mouth and chin inside a towel, pulled the hood down snug over his head and went out.

The moon was front and centre in the night sky. The icy air felt like screws tightening about his eyes and cheeks. Dizzy from hunger, he took measured breaths and felt his way towards the pen, only a few yards away. A muted light shone in the window of the neighbouring home. The dogs, only two of them now, started barking. Near the pen he groped along the ground until he found a rock; it was bigger than his fist. Even metal, if frozen solid, breaks easily. There, that blue ring, that had to be the padlock. He smashed down on it with the rock, the first few times wary of the noise, but then he no longer cared and he heard the *clang! bang!* of the impact echoing from the field. The towel around his mouth grew moist. With every breath he took, the towel clung more tightly to his skin, numbing his chin. Maybe his chin would be better unprotected, the towel was so cold. The vicious barking had turned to whimpers and the dogs were slinking towards the back of the pen. *And I'm eating that?* Suddenly he felt nauseous. Back at his place there'd been no second thoughts about eating dog, but now that the moment was nigh, no way could he go through with it. But he could still use the beast to keep himself warm. Actually, they could keep each other warm. He eyed the rock and brought it down on the ring one last time. And felt a hard object hit him in the back, knocking him to the ground. And then kicks directed at his squirming body. He rolled over and got up. Arms and legs moving robotically, he advanced towards his counterpart, who was rushing at him.

He felt as if he'd been dropped into an alien world of darkness and chill, and there the two of them silently exchanged punches and kicks. He reached for the unyielding attacker and grabbed a handful of hair that felt strangely clinging. Beneath the stringy hair was a small head. A person, an old person. With a shiver up his spine, he shoved the head aside and fled. Back at his place, he tasted blood from his lip. Unwinding the ice-encrusted towel from his chin, he sprawled out next to the fire. He felt heavy, as though weighed down by a load of gravel, and soon he was fast asleep. When he awoke, his drowsy eyes spotted someone looking at him through the window. It had to be his neighbour. Whether she was making sure he stayed put, stealing something of his to get back at him, merely checking out the situation, or whatever, her face was impassive and inscrutable. He silently observed her watching him and was asleep again before he knew it.

He heard snow falling.

How long had he slept? The fire was almost out, and for a while he couldn't move, stiff from the cold and the brawl with the woman and the depth of his sleep. It took deep abdominal breathing before his back and chest began to unlock. As air filled his paper-thin lungs, he was able to sit up. The frozen air made breathing painful. He stuck his hand into the ash to feel what was left of the fire, then removed some of the spent ash, added paper and twigs, got the fire going again, and sat there watching it. It was calm and quiet. He sat practically motionless on the blanket, but still could hear every tiny rustle he made, until it started getting on his nerves. He saw whitish speckles, heard tiny pellets *tap-tapping* against the window. He went outside and saw snow accumulating in the yard. From the edge of the veranda he stuck a leg into the white mass; it came up to his knee. Marvelling at the virgin snow, he gazed down, scooped a handful, and tasted it – cold and dry. Looking up and seeing the snowfall easing, he went out through the gate.

All was still.

He felt as if he'd awakened from a 10,000-year slumber.

The silence was eerie. Why weren't the dogs barking? He turned towards the pen. The ground inside was covered with snow, the dogs nowhere to be seen. Were they buried in a drift? Ploughing through the snow, he entered the neighbours' yard. The doors were unlocked, the women gone. Gone before he'd known it, and maybe the dogs along with them.

He stood in the desolate interior, which felt abandoned ever so long ago, then stepped down to the kitchen. He rummaged through the drawers, groped the shelves, looked into every nook and cranny, and finally found a porcelain jar bearing a crude drawing of a thistle; in it was rock salt. He put it in his pocket.

During the vigil Chang's family were cordial enough, but it was clear they wanted him gone. Dithering like a boy who knows he's got himself into trouble, he ended up attending the entire three days. Most of the mourners didn't know who he was, but the relatives who had any inkling of his relationship with Chang kept a furtive watch over him. Chang's sister and brothers greeted the new arrivals, sometimes choking up in the process, but after sharing an anecdote about Chang's childhood they would end up chuckling. From time to time he went out to the back of the building to stare at the wall and sigh. Returning, he was met with looks of disappointment from the family, who, if not for fear of making a scene, would probably have asked him to leave. And when the other mourners left in their cars for the long drive to the crematorium, he followed suit. The family checked in at the waiting room and in due course were summoned to the crematorium chamber. In his crumpled suit he kept himself apart, reeling at this the end of the three-day vigil. From behind the others he saw the coffin bearing Chang sucked along the belt towards the incinerator. And when the family left for the mausoleum nearby with the funerary urn, he followed them. With the formalities concluded, the mourners were visibly weary from their ordeal, but in their expressions he detected a tinge of *Finally*. And when they had all left the mausoleum, he remained. There was something he couldn't say. But wanted to say. There was something he desired. A fragment of bone.

Bone.

Of Chang.

And now as he stared into his fire he wondered about the mausoleum. Was it buried in snow? Had the staff gone off to a shelter? Would only the urns be left there now? Just once he'd gone back. It was summer, and at 90 kilometrers an hour it had taken him two and a half hours. The road was well paved and he hadn't got lost. The turnoff was thick with tall grass and drooping, faded trumpet vines. Chang's urn was on a shelf where he could view it at eye level from where he sat. He spent half an hour gazing at the urn and the items all around it – a cloth peony, the book containing the words of the God Chang had no longer believed in or liked, a statuette topped with a crown of thorns, a photo of Chang from before he had known him – and then he left. He'd been in agony on the return home, and hadn't gone back since. And now he worked out the distance to the city boundary, and then, if he were to take the road he had driven before, from there to the mausoleum.

At 90 kilometres an hour, two and a half hours.

On foot, four kilometres an hour max, walking ten hours a day, so six days. In the snow, a little longer.

He kept thinking as snow slid from the roof and plopped down to the ground. The wind blew all through the night. He rummaged through the boxes and found his rucksack, which he stuffed with socks and his blanket. He added matches, a lighter, a spare pair of gloves and a pouch containing his remaining grain and salt – the last he took special care with. Might as well take the lantern too. He used a shoelace to tie the lightest of his pots to the outside of the rucksack. It was now or never. He probably could have rigged up a pair of snowshoes, but he had far to go and no time to dally. He had to leave before his food ran out. He could live and he could go on, there was no doubt in his mind.

The morning star drew him out and on his way.

He drank in the air and could almost feel frost coating the lining of his lungs. He lifted a leg high, rested his foot on the snow, and brought his full weight onto it, burying it deep. The texture was dry, the walking wouldn't be that bad. He lifted the other leg, then brought it down. Took another step, and another. Through his hat he could hear himself breathing – *huh-hoo, huh-hoo*.

His imagination went to work.

He visualized a door opening, the mausoleum with not a soul in sight, a man entering, a snow-covered giant, his back and head heaped with snow, heat and odour radiating from his body. With every step he took, he dreamed about *him*. And through his dream about *him* he was nearing fullness and with that fullness he could live and he could go on.

Huh-hoo.

Huh . . .

You'll likely find this in the snow.

JUNG YOUNG MOON

Home on the Range

Translated by Bruce and Ju-Chan Fulton

I was staying with a friend back then. Not my Friend of All Friends. Just someone I'd gotten to know, and we'd hit it off. That was my perception anyway. He wasn't a fussy sort. I wasn't either. Everything was fine with him. And with me too. The house he lived in was smack dab in the middle of a livestock range. And the range was a perfectly natural surrounding. The range and the house were his. That range was home to a herd of sheep. There were no other livestock, no milk cows or domesticated deer. There were rabbits, but the sheep were the priority.

There was a hill on the range, a gentle slope. Walking up that hill wasn't a chore as long as I didn't overdo it. But I didn't take much pleasure from the walk unless I was herding the sheep. Which for the most part involved lying on the grass at a distance as they grazed. My favourite place was a crater-like hollow midway up the hill, where I would lie still and gaze at the sky. From there the sky was confined by the near outlines of the hill. But from higher up it was vast.

I liked to refer to this range of ours as a free range. Granted it was fenced, but the term *free range* made me feel that all life within it ranged freely. To be sure, the free-ranging sheep had to turn back at the fence, knowing they shouldn't go outside it. They could have if they'd wanted – the fence was old and broken-down – but they didn't. Whether this was a matter of learned behaviour or inborn timidity I couldn't tell.

I wasn't sure how many sheep were in the herd. And my friend never told me. If I were curious, I could have asked. But it didn't matter to me. And there weren't that many of them. I could have counted them easily enough – even if they were on the move.

But I viewed them as a herd and they moved as a herd. One of the main characteristics I discovered about sheep is that they like forming themselves into a herd. From time to time I found one or two strays, but they soon came to their senses and made their way back to where they belonged. And when the sheep were on the move, they made sure the herd didn't leave them behind. By nature, sheep are not loners.

At the times when sheep are usually sheared, our sheep weren't. Their fleece didn't look attractive, because we neglected grooming them. In any event, we had little use for their wool; they were being raised for their meat instead. But prospective buyers of mature sheep for their meat were few. Considering the lack of demand, it was a blessing that the herd wasn't large. The main consumers of their meat were those who shepherded them – namely my friend and me and two helping hands. These two men lived in the nearby village and came by once every few days to help with chores. They put in their time, then took a break or, if they'd slaughtered a sheep, ate some of the mutton before taking the leftovers home to their family. They both hit the bottle hard and were always a bit tipsy.

Our range was in a remote area and difficult to find, but there were occasional visitors in the form of stragglers who had missed the turnoff to the large cattle ranch nearby, which catered to tourists. Hanging from our gatepost was a welcome sign, but you might not have felt welcome at the sight of the post leaning so far that the sign almost touched the ground. Next to the sign was the kind of small stone pagoda you would see on the path to a temple up in the hills. I never did figure out why it was there. Nor could my friend enlighten me. There was no temple adjoining our pasture.

I functioned as a guide to the lost souls who showed up at our gate. But I didn't go on at length about the sheep and I only answered those questions that struck my fancy. Once these accidental tourists realized I wasn't their friendly neighbourhood guide, they shut up. Mainly I wanted to prevent them from getting up close and personal with our sheep or squealing and startling them. Whenever kids were present I had to be on constant alert lest a miscreant throw something at them. Despite my best efforts a kid occasionally succeeded at this nefarious deed, earning an instant ejection. That created discord with the parents, but I stood firm. I was not unaware that I was an imperfect guide, but I didn't mind.

The serene range never seemed to change, but it wore a different aspect from one season to the next. During the long, snow-packed winter the sheep stayed quietly in their pen. Nibbling at the hay tossed to them at feeding time, they waited for winter to end so they could go back out on the range. They liked summer best, when the pasture was covered with new grass that they could graze to their heart's content, to the accompaniment of a mad chorus of screaming insects.

The range was absolute heaven for a butterfly collector. Butterflies were plentiful and some of their patterns were absolutely beautiful. But there were no tiger swallowtails, my favourite. In my humble opinion they are incomparable. And so I felt no attachment to the butterflies fluttering over our range. But that didn't stop them from passing overhead, dancing enticingly for one another, never for me, moving sometimes in a line and sometimes front to back or back to front. For all I knew, their dancing was meant to impart detailed information about honey to their comrades, in the way honeybees do – how far away the honey-infused flowers are, how to get there, how yummy the honey is. Whatever the case, there seemed to be meaning to their dancing.

For me the most affecting time on the range was when no sheep were to be seen. In the morning, when the range was frequently shrouded in mist, or on a midsummer day when the skies clouded over and thick fog curtained the pasture, the sheep were concealed, their existence known only through their bleating, sometimes from afar and sometimes nearby. Never did the range feel as eerie and yet cosy as it did then. Such moments were almost surreal. Unless you experienced them at that time and place it would be difficult to really feel yourself seized by that surreal eeriness.

My position at the range was ambiguous. I had arrived as a guest but there was no way I could remain a guest there forever. My friend the owner had hoped I would be a help but learned right off I wasn't of much use in that capacity and gave up on the idea. Even so, I became a caretaker, or something resembling a caretaker. In my mind, that is; no one bestowed that title on me. But I did nothing in the way of caretaking, or in any specific role for that matter. I did, though, volunteer in a few different ways for my friend. As long as it wasn't physically demanding. I didn't do what I wasn't cut out for. What I mainly did was watch the herd in the way I thought they wanted to be watched, and to listen to their bleating in the way I thought they wished to be heard. And I didn't let them stray beyond the fence – but I didn't consider that task absolutely necessary, because they had never done that before. But I performed that task anyway. If something wasn't absolutely necessary I tended not to do it, but who wants to get hung up on tendencies?

Day in and day out I kept an eye on the sheep but never did I develop great affection for each and every one of them. My friend knew each of them, but I didn't. To me the sheep existed as a herd, and I dealt with them as a herd. If I picked one out of the crowd, I wasn't left with a good impression. The individual somehow came across to me as irritable and nervous, and indeed it was not that those sheep lacked such traits. They were distrusting and in no way sheepish – totally different from docile, trusting cows. And different as well from goats, which, though cantankerous, are also adorable. I could have spent time in close proximity to any of the sheep, but I felt there was something ominous about that. They were all right as a herd, though, and the ominous feeling I experienced with a single sheep was absent. Needless to say, this was all a matter of my own feelings.

What I liked about the sheep was their appearance. They looked like they were chewing their thoughts the way a ruminant chews its cud. They chewed and they chewed, all day long. Their day was spent chewing. With their four-compartment stomach they chewed and swallowed and regurgitated and chewed all over again. All the while they looked to be lost in thought but I didn't think they actually were. Rather than thought-lost they appeared thought-less, what with the endless movement of their chin in time with their chewing. But they could also resemble deep thinkers – though I had no idea whatever it was they might have been thinking. Anyway, their enigmatic look was food for my own thought.

I had hoped in a vague sort of way to spend a year there. A vague sort of year. But that didn't mean I wanted to see the range in spring, summer, autumn, and winter. There was no reason it had to be a year. But a year had passed and I hadn't left. How could I leave before I found a reason to leave? Where I happened to be was no longer important for me.

For a time I didn't venture outside my home on the range. I had come to feel that the world beyond was off limits. But then I broadened my radius, like livestock sneaking through a gap in the fence to sniff the outside world.

My first discovery during my strolls beyond the range was a nearby quarry. And there, my intrigue camouflaged by a tedious expression, I watched the sweaty stonemason industriously chiselling a gravestone or some such object. He didn't seem to mind being observed. Not that my watchful eye made him more industrious. He worked at the same industrious rate, to the point that I wanted to tell him not to overdo it. I was absorbed in watching him absorbed in his work. Once in a while I dozed off, only to be awakened by the ring of chisel against rock, a sound that brought me to my feet. How would I like to help him? he once asked me. I had to chuckle, it was such a preposterous notion.

There was also a river nearby, and one day I tagged along with my friend to a potter's studio there. My friend and the potter made a big production out of greeting each other. The potter's lifestyle was a bit too intense for my taste. That intensity could be detected in his every word, indeed was reflected in his every word. But the intensity of his life didn't seem in any way positive. I have to say I find the intense approach to life somewhat laughable. I myself have taken the opposite approach and have no complaints about my rather insipid life.

And for a lark, I went to a temple. I was sure I had never gone there before, but somehow I felt as if I had. As I grew older everything began to feel like a rerun, either exactly the same or only slightly changed, and while this seemed natural, the moment a rerun began I couldn't help feeling that something was peculiar. I got to chatting with the old monk at the temple. When I mentioned that he came across to me as a sort of fraud, he didn't exactly deny it. Not that his speech was laced with obscenities, mind you, but now and then a vulgarity was mixed in. It was fun shooting the breeze with him. He liked to talk about women. And suddenly he would launch himself towards the dharma hall to chant a sutra while beating on his wooden fish. I followed him there, sat nearby, and gawked at his shenanigans. When he was finished, he would give me a deadpan look and we went back to our bantering.

I enjoyed listening to his chanting, which filled the cool dharma hall with a tone that was more languid than clear and ringing. For fun I followed along, and even memorized a few lines: 'When Bodhisattva Avalokiteshvara was practising the profound Prajna Paramita, he illuminated the Five Skandhas and saw that they are all empty, and he crossed beyond all suffering and difficulty. Shariputra, form, does not differ from emptiness; emptiness does not differ from form. Form itself is emptiness; emptiness itself is form. So too are feeling, cognition, formation and consciousness.' The Heart Sutra[1] was the only sutra he liked to chant; I wondered if he knew any others.

When he was done, we each had a cup of tea. Not bad, the monk kept saying – his subtle way of emphasizing its quality. I gently shook my cup so the tea leaves would sink, but they kept floating. 'Come on, just drink it,' said the monk. And to show me, he drank his tea, leaves and all. Again I gave my cup a gentle shake, but the leaves stayed afloat. What the heck – I went ahead and drank it as was. Between sips of tea the monk told me in so many words to chill out, not be a stick in the mud and open my heart – there was no set way of doing things. I responded with a shrug. Which brought another prescription. Staring at me, he said, 'Live the way you are!' Enjoying the delicate taste of the tea, I told him I already was. The monk chuckled, and we diverted our attention to the shrilling of the cicadas, which rose in a blood-curdling crescendo before levelling off. And so it was that I went almost daily to the temple for a gabfest with the old monk.

One of my days on the range left me with long-lasting memories, though there was nothing earth-shaking about it. On that day I went to market for my friend to sell a pair of rabbits. He had given me a choice: one of the sheep or two of the rabbits. He said he could do it himself but wanted me to have the opportunity. I tried to imagine myself taking a sheep to market. Me, a shepherd? No thanks. So I put the two rabbits in a sack with a hole they could breathe through. They wriggled around inside. 'I'll bet it's stuffy in there,' I told them.

Off we went to the bus stop. Nobody was there. A field stretched out along the near side of the road, and along the far side ran a stream. A bridge crossed the stream and led to a village. *Village*, though, was somewhat of an extravagance, considering there was only a scattering of houses in sight. Suddenly it struck me that the pole bearing the beaten-up sign for the bus stop was leaning. Thinking I'd like to see it lean more, I gave the pole a subtle shove but it didn't budge.

Beneath the sign I waited patiently for the bus. Suddenly I felt abandoned, but I managed to block out the feeling. I didn't like watching myself when my feelings were out of control. Instead I told myself, *Here I am, behaving myself at a country bus stop.*

I was feeling kind of bored and contemplated raising a cloud of dust with my shoe and watching it while feeling the energy drain from me in the presence of the powerless, silently rising cloud of dust – but I didn't actually do it. The thought alone was sufficient; it wasn't necessary to carry it out. For me, execution was less important than unexecuted thought.

Hmm, maybe if I looked in the direction from which the bus was coming, I would see it coming in no time. So I went ahead and looked, but all I saw was the empty road stretching into the distance. Then I looked at myself and discovered I had stuck my hands in my pockets. This was something I often did when I was standing around with nothing to do. It was as though my pockets were for my hands to stick into, and my hands were for sticking into my pockets. I thought about taking them out but left them in.

Just then I saw someone coming across the bridge – it was a woman and she had a bundle on her head. She looked like she was toddling, which I found quite unusual. She kept her head turned away from me as if there were something about me to be avoided, and looked instead in the direction from which the bus would come. I did the opposite, observing her, curious about the bundle. What was inside? I tried to convince myself I didn't care. But I couldn't hide my curiosity. And then she turned and looked at me. And then at my sack. She said something, but I understood only half of it. She had a strong accent – probably not native to this region.

Even so, I was able to figure out what she wanted to say, and I answered her. She likewise seemed to understand only half of what I said but figured out what I wanted to say. We both made ourselves understood through our half-understood conversation, she learning there were rabbits in my sack and I learning there were mushrooms in her bundle.

Finally the bus came into sight. We climbed aboard and soon arrived in town. Without a goodbye the woman disappeared. I found the market, which like all markets since the old days was active every five days, and ended up with a spot between two old women. I wasn't looking for a spot between two old women, it just happened that way. Deep down inside I was worried some guy would tell me I was on his turf, but no such person showed up. There wasn't much activity and already by noon the purveyors looked ready to pack up their goods and leave.

I nodded in greeting to the old women. They observed the newcomer with curious eyes and I observed them with nonchalant eyes, though I likewise had never seen them before. *I should have brought a sheep, darn it, then I could draw more curiosity from them.* One woman had spinach, bracken fern and other greens for sale, the other had three chickens that I assumed she wanted to get rid of. The chickens, tied to one another so they couldn't fly off, rested quietly, stomachs to the ground.

The novelty of my unexpected appearance didn't last long. With me in the middle, the vegetable vendor blurted something out to the chicken vendor. Something off-putting, to say the least. She was *really* plugged up: every morning was hell, the agony indescribable. I didn't want to hear it but couldn't help listening. Why did they have to engage in verbal Ping-Pong with me as the net?

Well, perhaps they had started in on constipation before I arrived. Still, why didn't they stop it when they saw me? But then the chicken woman saw the bet and raised it. She had *haemorrhoids*, and the suffering was indescribable. I happened to be afflicted with the same malady and had a mind to say, *I hear your pain, ladies*, but thought better of it.

The vegetable woman let loose again, maybe thinking her constipation was more severe than the chicken woman's haemorrhoids. I couldn't hold my silence any longer. 'How bad is it?' I guess I fancied myself a consti-pation expert and a know-it-all for easing the pain. The two women gaped at me. 'What, you got a cure?' the chicken woman asked.

I put on my absorbed-in-thought expression. The two old women eyed me. I looked back and forth at them, the one with constipation and the other with haemorrhoids. What came out from my mouth was, 'Well, bad habits lead to constipation and also to haemorrhoids. There are more people than you might think who are constipated and haemorrhoidal.' They stared at me as if it was the most ludicrous thing they'd ever heard. I stared at them as if their reaction was the most ludicrous thing I'd ever seen.

Just then one of the chickens shot up as if someone had lit a fire under it, and went *cluckcluckcluck!* What a clever bird, I told myself, it clucks whenever it wants. And what do you know, there on the ground were two white eggs. 'What a clever bird,' I marvelled, 'it not only clucks at any old time, it *lays eggs* in any old place.' The chicken woman gathered the eggs

and looked back and forth at me and the other woman, apparently counting the eggs and the mouths to feed and finding herself in a fix because
of the mismatch.

No way she'll ignore me, country folks aren't that hard-boiled. Well guess
what, they *were* that hard-boiled. The chicken woman reached out right
in front of me to give the vegetable woman one of the eggs, then ate the
other one herself. The vegetable vendor eyed me, and now she was the
one in a fix, and the next thing I knew, she gave me her egg. *Wow, they're
not so hard-boiled after all.*

Holding the still warm egg, I carefully made an aperture in the top and
slurped the white and then the yoke. Never had I tasted such a fresh,
delicious egg. I expressed my gratitude to the vegetable woman and the
hen. And the chicken woman? No need, and so I didn't. The vegetable
woman looked like she had a heart, but not the chicken woman. And the
vegetable woman spoke tenderly to me. I didn't ask her about herself, but
she told me anyway. And then she asked about me. I said only that I
worked at the sheep range. She said she knew the owner well and that her
dear departed husband used to work there.

Just then a young woman appeared and bought some greens, and a short
time later a middle-aged woman purchased two of the chickens. I tried
to talk her into buying my rabbits but she didn't go for it. Not long after,
an old man bought one of the rabbits, but declined my offer of a discount
if he were to buy both of them.

Noon had passed and the flow of market-goers seemed to have dried
up. My stomach started growling. But I remained between the two old
women, listening to the rumbling that signalled chow time. What to do
with the remaining rabbit? The chicken woman had a clever idea – her
chicken for my rabbit. I weighed the offer but it was a no-brainer. The
remaining chicken was the two-for-one egg-laying hen.

Done for the day, I got up. The vegetable woman said she would stick
around with her unsold greens, and the chicken woman said she would
keep her company. And then I realized that when I had got up, something
else had got up with me. And that something was hanging from my rear
end. Gum. Deposited where I sat by someone before I had arrived. I didn't
figure either woman for the culprit.

Flustered, I removed the gum, but not all of it came off. And what did come off was stuck to my fingers. I removed the gum from my fingers, but again not all of it came off. One of the characteristics of gum is that it's difficult to remove, and the gum attached to me was offering a model demonstration. The two oldsters were getting a kick out of it. I laughed as well but I wasn't getting a kick out of it. This kind of mishap was fun as long as you were the spectator. But I was always on the receiving end, and the mishap was more than just slightly unwelcome. I guess I should have been thankful it was merely gum on bum. I wanted to blame my misfortune on the gum but the gum was blameless and so I blamed it on my sorry butt instead.

I pulled the hen up by the string around its legs and, as if venting my sticky misfortune, gave the string a little yank. The dazed hen sprang to its feet and followed its new master not knowing it had a new master. But then it displayed the inborn recalcitrance of chickens and I had to practically drag it. The hen went along, as if it preferred not to move under its own power, seemingly oblivious to how tiring the dragging was for both it and me. Or more precisely, it seemed to pretend to go along. Finally I had to put it in the rabbit sack. After a brief stir it poked its head through the breathing hole. It didn't look thrilled, its expression telling me something like *Don't you think you're overdoing it?*

The chicken and I went down the road through this godforsaken town. I spotted a banner – it was Sports Day at the primary school dead ahead. But there were no sporting events – no paper gourd cracking open to shower the kids with confetti, no kids sprinting and tripping over their feet and falling. I rechecked the banner, saw the date, and realized the festivities had already taken place and were for the townspeople and not the schoolkids. I looked across the school's empty playground, and through a classroom window in the one-storey building saw kids all looking in the same direction – towards the teacher, a woman, as she industriously jotted down something on the blackboard. The kids kept looking up in unison and looking down in unison. For some reason this saddened me deeply. Actually this was all in my imagination – the classroom was in fact empty. The school was doubtless on summer holiday.

I went into a restaurant, found a table and placed the sack on the floor next to it, and ordered a meal along with a bottle of *soju*. Drinking with a meal was for me an inexpensive and long-cherished luxury. The *soju* came out first and I started in. The first shot on an empty stomach was the best, and I enjoyed the taste spreading throughout my mouth as I scanned the surroundings. The guy at the next table looked already loaded and was mumbling something or other. His head was lowered as if he were meditating. He was moving back and forth and from side to side as if he couldn't keep his balance. Still looking at him out of the corner of my eye, I had another silent sip.

Suddenly he jerked his head up and glared at me through hazy eyes. 'What're you lookin' at?' he growled. As if I were the one who was glowering at him. Next he tried to pick a fight. Should I give him the real me? I decided not to. The real me would probably have left by now. But I couldn't leave, there was still some *soju* left. And just then my meal arrived.

By now the drunk was ugly. It was a challenge to enjoy my meal in peace, but I quietly put up with him. The lush decided to make an issue of my lack of a response. Still I didn't respond. You don't want to get started with a drunk. But that doesn't always work. And it didn't work now.

He lurched to his feet, staggered over, and looked down at me. I pretended to be nonchalant and kept my eyes on the shot glass in front of me. The outlook wasn't rosy. If I just sat there, I might get slugged in the mug before I knew it. Even if I kept up my guard, I was too much of a slug to avoid a flying fist. In the meantime, the woman who ran the place periodically stuck her head out from the kitchen with a so-what's-new look, which she punctuated by rattling the dishes she was washing until I thought they would break.

What if I made the first move? Maybe that would get me out of this mess. As it turned out, he was too loaded to stand up straight. And I wasn't born to cause trouble. I had a hunch he would tire himself out. And I was right. Before long he seemed to run out of steam, or maybe something else had crossed his mind, but in any event he was having trouble keeping his eyes open and he slumped down in his chair and started gibbering. I didn't understand a word of it. And then his head came down on the table and he started snoring, but the gibbering continued – and then he was talking in his sleep.

Listening to his sleep-talking, I took my time eating my meal and finishing my *soju*. As his babbling died down, his snoring cranked up. I finished my meal and hit the road again. I took the hen out from the sack and tried again to make it walk, but it still didn't want to do things my way, so back in the sack it went. Hardly a soul was to be seen on the road. A guy was leaning against a back-rack, butt parked on the ground, eyes closed. It must have been a sweet nap. I wanted to conk out then and there myself but I continued on my way. Tipsy from the *soju*, I thought that everything around me was moving along with me. Now I was out of town and still there was no one to be seen. I took my time. I felt sleepy and told myself that if this kept up, maybe I could walk in my sleep. Just then an oxcart came by. Sitting at an angle in the cart was an old man. I was hoping for a lift but he pretty much ignored me. From the way his head drooped, maybe he had nodded off too. It was nap time for everyone. It looked like the ox was taking its somnolent master home. And it seemed to know the way. Maybe that's all it knew.

As I watched the receding cart I sang a short song, the kind that once you start in, you sing it over and over. And I thought some murky thoughts, the kind you end up forgetting after you've walked for a while even though you remember you were thinking while you walked, thinking thoughts about how useless it is to make an effort to sort out your thoughts.

Before I knew it, I was almost back to our free range. I arrived at the bus stop nearby but didn't go straight home. Not that I no longer considered myself to be home on the range. I merely stood there without reason, or more precisely I stood there for no particular reason. The road stretched out into the distance. 'The long, stretched-out road is played out,' I murmured. Me and my wordplay. I liked to play with words. Words are good to play with.

In this case *played out* meant lying dead with your four limbs stretched out. 'The long, stretched-out road is played out,' I murmured again. And here *stretched-out* reminded me of a dead animal. Again I observed the scene that lay ahead. I didn't want to see it just as it appeared, I wanted to tweak it, but I couldn't think of a good tweak and so I left the scene alone.

Mindlessly I paced about the bus stop – meaningless thought expressed in meaningless behaviour. I felt my thoughts were gradually losing themselves in behaviour that had no outcome. This confused me. So I went back to where I had started pacing and stayed there. When I had stood there pointlessly for a sufficient length of time, I began to pointlessly enjoy it.

A short while later the bus arrived and an old woman got off. The woman selling greens at the market. It was like we had arranged to meet here. She said hello. I did likewise – what did I have to lose? She said she lived in the village across the bridge. I had a look at it. It was a miserable-looking village in a miserable location. And then out of the blue she blurted an invitation: How about some potatoes at her place? They were yummy, she said. I was in no position to decline and so I said sure.

She took the lead, and the chicken and I followed. From the bridge I looked down at the stream. The water wasn't deep, and I saw a school of minnows. Instead of hurrying me along, the old woman waited calmly for me at the far end.

We entered the village. The houses were flimsy and one of them seemed about to collapse. Another one looked abandoned, what with all the weeds in the yard. A narrow path led between low walls. I caught a whiff of cow dung. All that this scene needed was pumpkin vines draping the walls, and the moment this thought came to mind some pumpkin vines came into sight. I stopped beside the pumpkin vines and stood there for a brief time thinking that standing beside a wall draped in pumpkin vines was enough to make a person smile. Again the old woman stopped to wait for me.

Her home was at the far end of the village. You could hardly call it a human habitation. A huff and a puff would blow it right down. I wondered if goblins popped out of it at night. The wretched dwelling was coming apart at the seams but it struck me as almost holy.

She went to the potato patch in her kitchen garden. I kept an eye on her as she unearthed the potatoes. Then something got into me and I began digging along with her. The digging was fun and just for fun I dug a few potatoes. Those potatoes I dug for fun were nice and fleshy.

The old woman went into her kitchen to steam the potatoes. Smoke was soon rising from the chimney at the side of the house. 'Nice little puffs, that's the best way to describe it,' I murmured. Faint traces of a bush-clover broom were visible on the bare ground – it must have been several days ago that the old woman had swept it. The kitchen garden also contained peppers, cucumbers and aubergines, all of them ripening nicely. The aubergines looked luscious with their lustrous skin. A few stalks of corn that looked fully ripe stood to the side of the garden.

Off to another side was a small pool of water. I couldn't figure out why it was there – it didn't look drinkable, so maybe it was used for the vegetables. Had it always been there? Or was it dug after the woman's house was built?

The pool didn't look deep but the water was inky. My face was reflected on the glassy surface and for a brief time I watched it. And then a leaf fell onto the water, causing a faint shimmer, and my face broke apart. And then the shimmering stopped and my face reappeared.

Suddenly I remembered once having been fixated on water like I was now. I couldn't remember if it was a pool of water like this one, a well, or a pond. But I was almost sure it was a place where water had pooled. As I was watching I thought I saw something on the surface sinking slowly, ever so slowly, as if in a display of mastery by a trickster. I couldn't remember what the slowly sinking object was. It could have been a leaf; it could have been something else.

In any event, what I remembered was that the object, whatever it was, that object I couldn't remember, that object that was able to sink ever so slowly, was sinking slowly before my eyes. The memory was suddenly so fresh in my mind it saddened me a bit. But soon I felt better knowing I was capable of feeling a brief moment of sadness. I knew it was difficult for such a memory to last long, and felt good that such a difficult-to-last memory had resurfaced.

A short time later, out came the steamed potatoes. Corn too? Nope. Potatoes would be better with corn. Finally I had to remind myself this was potato time, not corn time. *C'mon, stupid!* And so we dug in. Yikes – I burned the roof of my mouth and made a fuss. She cackled. And the next moment I let loose with a racy joke that left her howling in laughter, potato in hand rather than mouth. Here was an unspoiled woman. I lacked the proclivity for saying something people found funny, but now and then I said something that people found hilarious and that I myself believed was funny.

I didn't find it odd that I was eating potatoes at the home of a woman I had just met that day. Eating potatoes together made me feel that she and I now knew each other. We talked about this and we talked about that. This and that. Nothing special. And then she said she came from a family of slash-and-burn farmers, and when she was young, that's what her family did. I looked at her in a new light, this descendant of itinerant people who were over the rainbow and gone.

I tried to picture the woman before me as a girl who with her parents set fire to the woods and tilled the fields of ash. It wasn't easy. I could, though, imagine a girl with a sooty face. It must have been a marvellous experience. The old woman pointed off in the distance, showing me where the fire fields used to be. I looked towards the hills she indicated. 'Well, you can't see it from here,' she said. Once again I tried to picture the girl who with her parents had tilled those fields that couldn't be seen from here.

Suddenly we were hit with a rain shower. Lightning flashed and thunder boomed. At first the thunder was far away and suddenly it was close by. *You always hear thunder far away and suddenly it's close by.* The thunder sounded so good I had myself another potato.

As we ate we watched the rain streak from the sky and stream from the eaves. Faint billows of steam rose from the heap of decomposing grass at the side of the yard; the compost smelled good. I pointed out the steam. 'That's compost for you,' said the old woman. For her it was just compost but for me it was fodder for my delight.

Watching the rain at a humble dwelling in this hillside hamlet, the home of an old woman I didn't know very well, for some strange reason warmed my heart, but on the other hand saddened me. But the warmth outweighed the sadness. That warmth reminded me of the heat inside the potatoes I was eating.

And that was all. And the fact that that was all was good, there was no more to it than that. The rain stopped and I got to my feet. She looked like she wanted me to stay longer. I said I would come again when I had the time. She said I was always welcome.

After I left I paused where the pumpkin vines draped the wall and I paused again on the bridge over the stream. I looked down from the bridge, expecting to see something. The shallow stream flowed over a bed composed of rocks of various sizes. Maybe that school of minnows was cutting through the water and swimming upstream. But I couldn't see them. I felt dispirited.

But soon I was in-spirited by a thought: *What would it be like to live in the water like a minnow? Or to live in the sky like a bird? Or to live in the ground like a mole or a mole cricket?* It would feel different for sure. But apart from that, how could I know?

I lifted my gaze to the sky. As I had expected, not a bird was in sight. I lowered my gaze to the stream and heard something. Running water. I closed my eyes and listened to it. It still sounded like running water. The sound grew clearer. I guess that was what I needed, and I left.

It was evening when I got home on the range. The rain shower made the sodden sheep look like they'd jumped in a lake. My friend watched silently as I headed for my room. I stopped and offered him the hen. He silently accepted it, or rather he took the string tied around its ankle. He didn't ask about his rabbits. He studied me as if the two-rabbits-turned-one-hen was a mystery, but left it at that. He never asked me why I acted as I did, tended merely to look at me uncomprehendingly.

Sleep was long in coming that night, and I tossed and turned thinking about all that had happened that day. When finally I got to sleep I had a dream. My friend and I were arguing. I said I was going to move in with the sheep but my friend said no way, that wouldn't be good for them. I was cross when I woke up.

Out on the range I went. Whenever I had an urge to get a handle on all my unclaimed baggage, I would take a stroll around the range to calm myself. In the dead of night, when sleep wouldn't come and my head was somehow the clearer for it, I would walk the pasture gazing at the star-studded sky. Sometimes I took a tumble and bruised my knee and would have to rub it before going back.

It was delightful wandering the range late at night when the sheep too must have been sleeping and all was quiet. It was especially delightful when the moon was full and bright and sky and earth met at the crest of the hills. I couldn't tell if the illusion of sky meeting earth arose from a natural phenomenon, but in any event I liked the unreality of it. Strolling the range at such times I indulged myself in fanciful speculation. In my imagination the sheep might die in an epidemic or from having their throats cut, their remains strewn about the range, a scene bizarre yet lyrical. Or they might be absent from the range, and in their place a great beast or two, perhaps elephants or giraffes, casting huge shadows. The incongruity of such animals that were not home on the range made me appreciate the range in a new way.

As it happened, there was no moon that night, full or otherwise, only a few stars. All was dark. It was a chore to put one foot in front of the other. I ended up stumbling and falling, and god knows why, instead of getting back on my feet I moved on all fours. I felt I was a sheep. And for a short time I sheepishly walked the range. Back in my room I saw that my knees were red.

Time passed and a new season arrived. I didn't know what I wanted, or even if I had something I wanted. My past faded into my memory, and some of my memories were erased. All I could focus on were meaningless things, and I was happy to do so. On one such day I went to a prehistoric archaeological site not far from the range. My friend had told me about it, suggesting I go there if I were bored. I went there not from a desire to learn more about the locale where I'd been staying, but probably because I was drawn to it as a prehistoric site.

All that was left at the site were vestiges of a dwelling – hollows in the ground that might have been rooms; the artefacts must have been removed to a museum. The site was pretty much neglected, whether because its significance as a historic site was minimal or else not properly recognized I didn't know. There was no Access Restricted sign.

'It's a ruin all right,' I said to myself. The word *ruin* didn't adequately convey the emotional impact I expected here. I focused intently on this prehistoric place that had been buried in time and had now reappeared in time, but it didn't arouse much in the way of feelings. Was this because no words were adequate to convey my impression of the place? Whatever the reason, I remained there for some time before I was able to come up with an impression: 'The people who lived here must have lived simple lives, using simple tools to make the simplest of objects.' Sure enough, it was a lame impression. And the site itself struck me as unremarkable. My impressions of things, whether I found them significant or insignificant, depended on my ability to express those impressions.

I had myself a wide-angle view of the prehistoric archaeological site and its setting. Gradually it lost all meaning for me. To anything that I observed long enough a moment arrived in which it all became meaningless. That moment had come sooner this time than at others.

It wasn't that I wanted to sing on the spur of the moment, but a song suitable for singing at such a place came to mind, and I launched in on it. But then I broke off, feeling as if something was forcing me to break off singing, but there was no such something. Suddenly I recalled having heard that there was a limestone cave nearby. Fortunately I spied a rusty sign indicating its location.

I left the archeological site and started up a narrow path into the hills. Visible far below were railroad tracks for the trains that used to transport coal and limestone from the local mines. Those mines must have been shut down and abandoned, because the tracks were overgrown with undergrowth. I guessed the mines were scattered among the rugged mountains. This locality where slash-and-burn farmers had lived not so long ago was growing on me.

I wouldn't have called the scenery exquisite, but there was a nice harmony among the steep mountains near and far, the narrow fields squeezed between them and the stream flowing through it all. 'Mother Nature's composition always approaches the ideal,' I murmured. *Wow, nice thought!* I told myself.

The trail grew rugged and was covered with lush growth. I was being tripped up enough to get me thinking of turning back. But I didn't give up. And after a while the cave appeared. A 'Cave Unsafe – Do Not Enter' sign was posted at the entrance. After a furtive look about, I went in anyway. The cave had a wide mouth, allowing sunlight to penetrate deep inside. A complex array of passages led in from the entrance. I remained where I was, thinking the cave was not what I had imagined – did a cave have to be this complicated? Then again, I'd never been at the entrance to this cave wondering what lay inside.

Gingerly I went down the man-made steps, thinking I might find the faint outlines of cave paintings from long ago. No such luck. I went to the middle of a chamber thinking I was in a large room, and tried to imagine all the effort that cave had devoted to becoming a cave, but I came up short. But not so short that I couldn't think that it mustn't have been easy for the cave. Which told me that my knowledge of caves was basic, nothing more.

I shouted into several of the passages, listening to the differences in the echoes. The shouts rang inside the cave, some of the echoes spilling outside while others fell far into the dark depths. I ventured farther into the chamber. I felt I was toting a certain thought on my back – or at least that it was possible for me to express it in that way. It was getting darker and finally a world of utter darkness appeared. And like a person entering a dark world, I groped the wall and slowly advanced. But suddenly the way ahead was blocked. I stood still in the darkness like a person who's lost his way. And indeed that is how I felt. I wasn't one to think that everything depends on how one thinks. I was, though, a tad frightened.

In reality, finding my way back to the entrance to the cave didn't seem all that difficult. Even so, I stood there like a person trapped in a cave who can't find the entrance. And then I heard a sound, or at least I thought I heard a sound, but I didn't know what it might be or where it might have been coming from. Bats? I imagined countless bats hanging from the ceiling of the cave watching me with their atrophied eyes. I didn't think it was right for me to make my own noise, so I kept silent. And then the surroundings became silent.

In darkness so deep I couldn't distinguish myself, I felt my body was gone and only my thoughts remained. The least I could do was retain those thoughts, and so I didn't attempt to dispense with them.

All of a sudden the events of that day at the market came to mind: meeting the two old women, watching the hen unexpectedly laying, contending with the menacing, slobbering drunk, eating potatoes at the vegetable woman's home, observing the pool of water in her yard and at that moment remembering from long ago a time I thought I saw something on the surface of the water sinking slowly, ever so slowly, as if in a display of mastery by a trickster – all of these events were still fresh in my memory.

Before I knew it, I felt myself smiling. And then all those thoughts submerged like the sound I thought I had heard going silent. And then among those submerged thoughts there flashed an image of none other than the herd of sheep that were home on the range. They couldn't be seen because of the fog but I knew they were somewhere in that fog because of their bleating, which I found so peculiar. And that's the way in which the sheep range comes to mind – a fog-shrouded scene in which nothing can be seen, not the sheep grazing on the green, hilly pasture, not the free range in the light of the moon, not the range absent the sheep who have returned to their pen. And then the fog slowly dissipates and there on the range is an elephant. I imagine it not as a real live elephant but as a gigantic stuffed specimen, similar to the imitation elephant you might see in a celebration of the Buddha's birthday.

KIM CHUNGHYŎK

The Glass Shield

Translated by Kevin O'Rourke

We sat in the subway unravelling tangled balls of yarn. The work was simple. All we had to do was catch one end of the yarn and carefully loosen the kinks; look for the tangled bit, pass the yarn through and the kink untangled easily. We each had a ball of yarn in our hands. We concentrated all sensation in our fingertips, working in rhythm with the rattling subway car.

There were very few people on the subway, so our yarn operation went ahead smoothly. One or two stole suspicious glances at us, but there really was no need for suspicion. You couldn't blow up the subway with yarn, nor could you set a fire or kill someone with it. Yarn was just yarn. If the crowd did the *wave* in support of our efforts to unravel the kinks, that would be great, but there was no reason to stop us doing what we were doing. We stretched the unravelled yarn along the subway seats. As the yarn grew in length, the distance between us increased. Blue and red yarn heaped up on the green seats.

'This is too easy,' M said. 'Why didn't it work earlier?'

M's ball of blue yarn was reduced to half its original size.

'That's us,' I answered weakly as I unravelled the red yarn. 'Screwing things up is what we do best.'

Two hours ago M and I had taken our thirtieth job interview. At the end of it the panel gave us the standard 'That's all right, you can go now.'

'Screwing everything up,' M repeated. 'Why didn't you put that in our CVs? Under special skills maybe? They might take pity on us and give us the jobs.'

'Did you list slagging off your friends under hobbies?'

As we talked we kept our eyes trained on the balls of yarn. It was a miserable morning and our situation was grim. We shut up and concentrated on unravelling the yarn.

'Is this the circle line?'

'I think so.'

'Maybe that's why I'm a bit dizzy.'

'It's not the circle line that has you dizzy, it's looking at the ball of yarn for too long. We need a rest.'

I looked out the window and saw that we were above ground again. It was almost as if the subway had waited for us to take our eyes off the yarn before clanking its way above ground. Bright lights and small buildings and myriad signboards opened out like a collage in front of us. Not so much a landscape as a series of paintings stuck together. We looked out the window as we waited for the train to go below ground again. Tightly stretched electric lines showed the way. The subway stayed above ground. We were in the last car, so if we stuck our noses to the glass and contorted our bodies, we could see the curve the front of the train was making. This made the circle line idea come to life. Two stations later, the front of the train dipped and disappeared underground. The scene on top went with it. The window became a mirror, reflecting the two of us instead of the scene above. We began to unravel the yarn again.

I flushed when I thought of the laughter of the interview panel two hours ago. M and I always took company recruitment exams together. We wanted to work in the same company. That was part of it. But the heart of the matter was that M and I couldn't take an exam on our own. We were inseparable, two sides of a coin, the front and back of a single person. Without M, I was a page of paper so thin I couldn't stand on my own. And I believe I meant the same to M. We took thirty company entrance exams together. A hundred games, a hundred losses. Our win ratio was zero, but we never once entertained the thought of taking an exam each on our own.

We also took the interviews together. We even went into the interview room together. We were once asked if we were homosexual. Some companies said they only wanted one new recruit. Still, we were obdurate. We insisted we had to do the interview together so that we could show our true worth, and we drove the personnel managers crazy in the process. Some companies refused our demands, but more often than not the personnel man just said, 'As you wish.'

We tried out new approaches, in the belief that we could rewrite the history of interviewing, but we found the interview panels rather cool to us. We tried to impress them with our repertory of tandem jokes, but very often they threw us out before our time was up. We couldn't understand why. Once, when we were being thrown out, we asked the personnel manager why we were being failed. He looked at each of us in turn. 'Try a gagman exam,' he said and pushed us out. 'Well, at least it's fun,' M said with a laugh.

We did a gag routine in an interview for an internet management company – we didn't even raise a laugh from the panel. In an interview for an animation production company, we tried a clumsy magic show. M set off the sprinkler system in the ceiling while he was trying to light a handkerchief he had prepared as a prop. We did a parody of peddlers selling their goods in the subway in an interview for management personnel in a company that publishes English-language textbooks. The peddler piece got the best response. We used outrageous English back and forth between us to advertise one of their books. One man on the interview panel laughed so hard he fell off his chair. When the personnel manager was explaining why we failed, he said, 'You know, our book is not the kind of bogus text that's sold on the subway.' We had forgotten the first rule of interview preparation. You've got to research the company. We prepared diligently, but all we knew about the company was that it sold English textbooks. We never gave a thought to the quality of the texts the company was selling.

Our preparation for yesterday's interview was thorough by our standards. Over supper, we read and reread the company materials we had downloaded. It was a computer game company, and they were looking for recruits in concept planning and testing. In addition to having the basics of programming, applicants needed to be bursting with ideas, to have outstanding imagination, confidence in all game situations and the grit to finish any game they started. We didn't have any of these qualifications, but we sent in our applications anyway in the belief that we could always play games.

'Don't you think we have some imagination?' M asked.

'Of course we do,' I said, 'and lots of ideas too.'

We didn't know if our imaginations were the kind the company was looking for, but we felt that this company best suited our sensibilities.

'But how will we show our imaginations? Should we try the magic show again?'

'No, not that again. Do you want to set the company on fire? We'll hit their weak spot. We'll prepare an interview totally unrelated to imagination. That'll get them thinking. We'll get better scores that way. Our approach will be the direct opposite of all the other applicants'.'

'How do you mean?'

'What do applicants lack most?'

'We just studied that. Patience and loyalty.'

'Right. We'll show them patience. There's nothing more important for computer game testers.'

'So how do we do it? You mean we should do a trial of strength – stand on hot stones for ten minutes, or something like that?'

That was the genesis of our yarn-unravelling routine, which we duly performed in front of the interview board. No practice was necessary. You don't need practice to unravel a tangled ball of yarn; you need patience and determination. We prepared a few introductory remarks and went to bed early.

Next day.

'Gentlemen, instead of introducing ourselves, we'd like to make a little presentation. We believe that testing computer games is like unravelling a tangled ball of yarn. We'll show you how to unravel the kinks by patiently loosening the yarn step by step.'

I thought we had a terrific concept. And the reaction from the interviewing panel was good. As we pulled the blue and red yarn from the paper bag, I thought I detected a stir of interest from the panel. But we had a problem. We had tangled the yarn too much in the waiting room. Beads of sweat dotted our foreheads by the end of the first minute. Three minutes later the situation was no better. After five minutes our bodies were drenched in sweat. The sweat on our hands made the yarn even more knotted. All we managed to unravel in five minutes was about a foot of yarn. M began to pull instead of unravel. I sighed. Finally, M muttered 'Ah shit' in an undertone. That finished it.

'Okay, that's enough. Very good idea. But you both seem lacking in patience. Practice unravelling the yarn and apply again.'

The panel laughed. I felt like throwing the balls of yarn at them, but they had done nothing wrong. Outside the interview room, one of the applicants waiting his turn saw our pickled appearance and said, 'What sort of questions did they ask to produce a sweat like that?' I wanted to hit him too, but it wasn't his fault. We were the problem.

'If you hadn't sighed back there . . .'

'So it's my fault?'

'No, no, if you hadn't sighed, I'd have sighed first.'

'If you'd sighed first, I'd have said "Ah shit".'

A hundred games, a hundred losses. That was us. We got on a subway with good air-conditioning. We had sweated so much, and it was so hot! When I had cooled down a bit, I thought I'd like to complete the unravelling.

It took thirty minutes to unravel the yarn completely. The volume of blue and red yarn on the subway seat seemed enormous. The sight of so much red and blue against the background of the green seat overwhelmed the onlookers. It was like an artist's painting, like the landscape of my heart. It was beautiful, I thought.

'It's pretty long.'

'Fifty yards maybe. What do you think? Longer maybe. A hundred yards? More?'

'We'll measure it. Each carriage is twenty yards long. If we keep going back and forward with the yarn, we'll get the length.'

'How do you know the carriage is twenty yards?'

'It's written over there, stupid!'

I pointed at the notice over the door. The length and width of the carriage and the carriage's number were written there. When I rode the subway on my own and had nothing particular to think about, I used to read that notice. Sometimes I remembered the carriage number. It would be nice to get on the same carriage on the same train. People going to work at the same time every day probably get on the same train every day, but none of them could tell you the number of the carriage.

There were only four other passengers in the carriage. No one would think it strange if we went back and forth with the yarn. M took the end of the blue yarn and got up. He took a firm grip on the yarn, moving slowly like a man walking an invisible dog. The yarn on the seat uncoiled like a snake and followed him. M got to the end of the car and twisted the yarn.

But he had nothing to fix it to, so it just followed him when he began to walk back. We wouldn't get an accurate measurement this way.

'The yarn keeps following me. Will you stand at the other end and hold it?'

'Who'll hold it at this end, then? Do you want me to hire someone part-time? Come on, just keep walking to the end of the train.'

'Fine. Why didn't you say so at the beginning, you clown?'

M began walking the yarn again. He was afraid it would get caught in the doors between carriages, but there was no problem. M kept walking, matching his movement to the rhythm of the carriage. I let the yarn out a little at a time so that it wouldn't tangle. It was like flying a kite. M was already out of sight, but I could feel him on the yarn. The blue yarn kept following him. After five minutes, I was at the end of the blue yarn. I wrapped the end of the yarn around my finger so as not to lose my grip on it. Would M know I was at the end of the ball? Suddenly the yarn tightened. More force would break it. I could feel M on the other end. Then the yarn fell to the floor.

A few minutes later the connecting door opened and M's smiling face was revealed.

'This is really fun. Everyone stared at me. Go and see for yourself. The expression on the faces is priceless.'

'Did you get the measurement? How far did you go?'

'At first I counted the carriages, but with everyone looking at me I forgot the count. The length doesn't matter anyway. If you don't want to go, I'll go again?'

Before I had time to reply M had the yarn in his hand again. I couldn't figure out where all the fun was, but if it was enough to get M this excited, then I couldn't afford to miss it. I took the end of the yarn from him. Disappointment was written across his face, but for my sake he was willing to let the yarn go. Just as I took the red yarn in my hand the connecting door opened and the guard came in.

'Is this your yarn?' he asked. He had the ball of blue yarn in his hand. What had taken us thirty minutes to unravel, the guard had returned to its original tangled state in one sweep. I had the red yarn in my hand, and red yarn was coiled on the seat. There was no way out of it.

'Yes, it's mine. Is there a problem?'

'There's been a report of a suspicious man in a suit setting a bomb.'
'A bomb?'

I didn't realize my voice had risen. Someone thought the blue yarn was a bomb fuse. Clearly someone somewhere was using colourful bomb fuses.

'What's the yarn doing on the ground? Have you set a bomb?'

'Ah please, sir, you're not accusing me of setting a bomb. Would I set a bomb?'

'And why isn't it going off?' M interjected. 'Isn't it about time it exploded?'

The guard looked at each of us in turn. Two men dressed in suits with a ball of red yarn and a ball of blue yarn was not a common sight. M kept giggling.

'I'm afraid you'll have to come with me.'

The guard grabbed the red yarn on the seat, went through all the newspapers on the luggage rack and examined every corner of the seat. He knew there couldn't be a bomb. Anyone could see we didn't have bomb faces. I don't mean that a bomber is a separate entity, it's just that someone who's going to blow up the world would have a different light in his eyes. Our eyes said firecracker rather than bomb. The passengers moved to the next carriage when they heard the bomb talk.

'I'm sorry,' I said quietly to the guard. 'The truth is we're in the art business.' He turned and looked at me. It was as if he were hearing the word *art* for the first time in his life. And I felt as if I were saying that word for the first time in my life.

'What do you mean, *art*?' The guard and M looked at me at the same time.

'Don't you know what art is?' I asked.

'Is setting a bomb art?' he said.

'There's no bomb,' I said. 'My friend there has an acute sense of fun. It's obvious if you look at the yarn. It's not a fuse or anything like that, it's just an ordinary length of yarn. We're just ordinary people stuck in the daily grind, creating a special experience; you could call it a performance, or an event. We're into art.'

'You're telling me that laying yarn on the floor is art?'

'You could call it an event that links the splintered heart of humankind to the yarn image. What better space than the subway to represent modern life?'

M kept giggling, but the guard listened attentively to what I was saying. He hesitated, unsure what he ought to say. His attitude had softened considerably, perhaps because of the impact of the art word or perhaps because I was so respectful in my bearing.

'I understand what you're saying,' the guard said, 'but you can't do that on the subway.'

'Can't do what?' I asked.

'Art things,' he said.

'Ah art! I said. 'Okay, I understand.'

'This is a public space. You'll appreciate that you can never tell what's going to happen next in a public space.'

'Ah yes, I'm sorry. We'll find somewhere else.'

'I'll have to confiscate the yarn. Will you show me your identity cards? I need to record some details.'

He checked our ID cards and moved to another carriage. We got off at the next station. We had never seen the station before, and we had no idea what part of the city it was in, but that didn't matter. We were afraid the guard would return and say he'd changed his mind and we'd have to go with him.

'Art, my arse!' M cried. 'You didn't get to do any art. I was the only one who got to do the art. What a pity!' M was giggling again.

And truth to tell, I did have a sense of missed opportunity. This may be seen as a casual remark, but I was genuinely curious about the reaction of passengers when they saw me taking the yarn through the cars. For folks stuck in humdrum daily routines, it could be a special experience.

'One man told me he thought my trousers were unravelling. Maybe I should have bared my bum? There was a guy taking photographs too. It was fantastic fun. Such a special experience for me ...'

We rode the bus until we were nearly home. We got off the bus and went into a beer hall. Our suits stank, we had sweated so much. As we drank beer, a yarnlike liquid infused itself throughout our bodies. Eyes closed and feeling the beer, I figured I could calculate the length of my body.

We discussed our next interview. It was the day after tomorrow with a company making electrical kitchen appliances. The more I talked with M and the more interviews we did, the more it seemed that we were evaluating the companies rather than the companies evaluating us. We had developed a basic principle: we would not take a job in a company that didn't accept our unique interviewing style. We were the losers, of course, but the loss seemed inevitable. We had started this way and we had to see it through.

'Why don't we cook something for the interview?' M suggested, his face already red from the beer. He must have swallowed some red yarn.

'Feed the interview panel some shitty dish and then say, "Now we see the necessity of kitchen scales!" Is that what you mean?'

'What a brain! What insight!'

'We'll fail anyway. Maybe we should throw in some diarrhoea pills?'

'And if they say thank you for helping us lose weight and give us the jobs, what then?'

'It will mean a life selling kitchen scales.'

'I wouldn't like that.'

'So why apply for the job?'

'I thought we could use the scales for a fun interview.'

'That's what I thought. The bottom line is we'll never get a job. We're twenty-seven already.'

'Twenty-seven? Is that all we are? We'll get something eventually.'

'What'll we get? Is there anything we do well?'

M grew sullen. We drank in silence. Every beer we drank, we put the price of it on the left-hand side of the table. The money on the right kept moving to the left. We hoped to get drunk before the money was all gone, but we couldn't get drunk as long as we kept watching the money. We were still clear-headed.

'Four beers left.'

'Why can't we get drunk?'

'Let's put the next one down the hatch.'

We took the beers in our hands and gulped them down. We belched, we were dizzy, we were drunk. When the money was spent, we went home.

When I woke the next day, I had a ring of pain wrapped like Saturn's rings around the general area of my head. The ring turned in a circle, pressing down relentlessly on my head. M seemed in a similar state. We had a bowl of *tchamppong* but just ate the soup with the Chinese vegetables and left the noodles. Looking at what was left, I recalled yesterday's interview. The noodles, like the yarn, offended the eye. We put the bowl outside the door, lay down again, and looked at the ceiling. We had nothing to say. We had to prepare for tomorrow's interview, but we were not in the mood.

The cellphone rang at about three in the afternoon. It was a friend of ours who had found a job a couple of months ago at an internet newspaper company. He had been drinking with us when he got the news, and he was so happy he smacked a big kiss on my cheek. M had sweet-talked him into staying out with us until four in the morning. Our newly employed friend, of course, paid the bill. He lost his cellphone and wallet that day, and he was left with a cut on his chin that he couldn't account for.

'You fellows were so jealous of me getting the job you hit me, right?' he grumbled, but we weren't the kind of guys who were jealous of such things. The company that had taken him on was pretty prominent, but it was also well known for long hours and poor wages. Next day he had us meet him at a department store and bought us a tie each. Good luck in your interview, he was saying. He treated himself to a new suit, the latest model of cellphone, and a leather wallet.

As we left the department store he said, 'Now I'm going to begin the exotic second half of my life.'

'He figures he'll score a lot of goals in the second half since he used so much energy in the first half. Twenty-nil maybe?' M said. The sarcastic tone may have been because our friend's 'exotic second half' remark had stung. Anyway, we had had no contact with him for a while. Age twenty-seven and the second half, I figure, aren't concepts that belong together. As far as we're concerned, we still haven't finished the first quarter.

'Is M there by any chance?' My friend on the cellphone lowered his voice as if he wanted to say something to me privately.

'He's lying here beside me. We've taken pills, we're doing a double suicide . . . We've no jobs, no money and our heads are splitting from beer.'

I was so hoarse I suppose I could have been taken seriously. I hawked up the mucus in my throat and swallowed it again.

'Don't be going on like that . . . So you're together. Ask M if he was on the subway yesterday.'

'Here, I'll put him on. Ask him yourself. I think he's still alive.'

'Come on, you know I rub him the wrong way. Just ask him, was he on the subway?'

M was asleep. That or he knew we were talking about him and was pretending to be asleep.

'He was on the subway. We both were.'

'You were on it together. Did you go around the carriages carrying blue yarn?'

'How do you know about that?'

'Ah, I'm right. It was M, wasn't it? It's hard to make him out in the suit.'

'How do you know about the suit?'

'He's on the internet. Take down this address.'

I typed in the address he gave me. It was a private blog called 'Street Scene.' Sure enough, photos of M were there. Dressed in a suit, eyes cast down, M was walking towards the camera. You could barely see the blue yarn behind him. Actually it looked more like a line superimposed on the photograph than a length of yarn. There were five photos in all. The last one, a rear view, gave a clearer view of the yarn.

The photos had been uploaded five hours ago, and already there were 200 comments. The comments reflected a wide variety of opinion. Someone who had lost a sweetheart in an accident thought the unravelling yarn was a symbol of an unforgettable love. Someone else thought the yarn symbolized a trip around the country. A third party thought the blue line had been superimposed on the photo. I woke M. He laughed when he saw the photos. The more he read of the comments, the more he laughed. When he finished the last comment, he fell on the floor laughing.

'*Ya*,' he exclaimed, 'what incredible imaginations! How do they do it? Imagine thinking it was a picture of someone pulling a lily-livered lover's rotten tooth!'

M rolled across the floor. I didn't think the comments were funny enough to warrant rolling on the floor, but M obviously did. Such a variety of comment was unbelievable. And to think that I could have been the hero!

'My paper is going crazy trying to make contact. M obviously considers himself some kind of street artist. What the hell was he doing with the blue yarn?'

Our friend sounded annoyed. Perhaps he had heard M's laughter and thought it a bit ridiculous. He had never liked M's tricks and jokes. 'I can't understand why you stick to him like glue,' he often said. And for every such remark I liked him that much less. It was the word *understand* that irked. You can never understand human relations, I thought. When he made such comments, I wanted to say something back, but I was afraid I'd lose a friend. I liked his earnestness and I liked those big eyes full of curiosity.

I wanted to tell him the long, complex story of the interview room, but I was afraid M would be demeaned in the telling. And I'd be demeaned too.

'Actually, we were doing art.'

'Art? What do you mean, art? What art are you two into?'

'Subway performance art. Joining the splintered heart of modern man with yarn. That sort of thing.'

'How long have you been at that sort of thing? You two and art don't mix.'

M was now at the computer, writing something. Another joke. I was curious what he might write under the pictures.

'We've been at it for a long time. You just didn't know about it. Recently we did a performance on the bus.'

'What did you do on the bus?'

I imagined a bus. What could you do on a bus? Let's see . . . a driver, seats, a bell to get off, straps to hold on to . . .

'We heaped blue yarn on an ad on the back of the seat.'

'Why did you do that?'

'It was an experiment to see what people could do with yarn.'

'And what did they do with it?'

I wondered what you could do with a piece of blue yarn while sitting in a bus. I couldn't think of anything. I covered the speaker on the phone with my hand and asked M, who was still working the keyboard.

'You could strangle the person in front,' he said.

'People have very poor imaginations,' I said. 'Most of them just knit.'

'I'm surprised to hear you two are at that kind of thing. I'll call you again later.'

After the call, I saw what M had written: *Maybe it was an attempt to tie up the subway with blue yarn?*

'That's a bit weak,' I said.

'Weak, you say. Okay, I'll think about it some more. Not much imagination, I'm afraid.'

We lay down again and thought about what you could do with the blue yarn, but we got sleepy. It was seven o'clock when we woke and it was dark outside. Time, we felt, was being stolen from us. Everything was too fast. Maybe we thought the first quarter wasn't over yet, but what if our friend was right and the second half had already begun? Maybe we were asleep in the changing room while everyone else was running around in the stadium.

M got up abruptly and spilled the coins from the piggy bank onto the desk. He separated them by denomination, very carefully, like a dealer in a casino. He counted the coins in stacks of ten. The operation didn't take very long because we regularly took money from the piggy bank.

'How much is left?' I asked, looking at the ceiling. More to know how bad our situation was than to know how much was actually left.

'Maybe enough to buy a box of *ramyŏn*.'

'Let's buy the *ramyŏn* before the money runs out.'

M divided the coins between his two side pockets and went out. I lay there quietly, imagining life without M. I couldn't visualize it very well, but I figured the time had come for each of us to make his own life. The room I was lying in was like a sinking ship. We were living in that sinking ship with our arms tightly wound around each other. Life had become a sort of three-legged race. Running with one leg tied, trying to match the breathing of the other, was bound to be slower than running with two free legs. It was fun, but inevitably it was slow. I figured we were too far behind now. We would have to loosen the ties that bound our legs before it was too late. I wondered what M's reaction would be. Maybe he was just waiting for me to loosen the ties first. The phone rang while I was wondering how I'd say my bit to M.

'I told the editor about you two. He wants me to interview you. Do you have time tomorrow?'

'We have a job interview tomorrow.'

'Won't you be free in the afternoon? We'll meet at five.'

'But what sort of interview do you have in mind? We don't do interviews.'

'The editor has already written the captions. "Blue Yarn Imagination, Street Artists." It'll be okay. Come on, do it.'

'I'll ask M.'

'What's there to ask? You two are like an old married couple. Come to the office at five. We'll take some photos in the subway nearby. Wear your suits. You'll have suits on for the job interview anyway.'

I put down the phone and stared at the ceiling again. Blue Yarn Imagination, Street Artists. Art. Art be damned! It was all a pain in the neck. I didn't want to do anything. I didn't want to do the interview, and I didn't want to go to the office. I wanted someone to grab me by the scruff of the neck and drag me somewhere.

'What do you think I bought,' M shouted as he opened the door. Such an innocent face. He produced a sword from behind his back. A plastic sword but rather finely made.

'Lovely, isn't it?'

'Lovely indeed. Where did you get the money?'

'It makes a sound too.'

He struck the sword on the floor. There was a sharp ringing sound, the ring of steel on steel. M went around the room striking various items. The desk rang out, the tiny wardrobe rang out, the computer keyboard rang out. It was like listening to the sound track of a war film. He struck me and I rang out.

'Did you buy the *ramyŏn*?'

'Oh, I forgot. I went to buy *ramyŏn*, didn't I? Anyway, there's money left over.'

'You need two swords for a sword fight.'

'They're selling them at the intersection outside. Shall I buy another?'

'Forget it. Sword fights at our age? The rest of the money is for *ramyŏn*.'

'What's wrong with our age?'

I told M about the newspaper interview. He thought it was great. This was a bit unexpected. I had thought he mightn't want to do an interview. M was excited. We need identical suits – uniforms!' he shouted. But we both were well aware that we didn't have that kind of money.

We went out to the intersection. Under the lurid lights there was a large display of toys: cars and trains; guns and arrows; and shields. Most were crudely made. I could see why M chose the sword. We bought another plastic sword. And we bought a transparent plastic shield. I thought at first it was made from glass – that it would break if you let it fall. You could see through it, but it wouldn't block an attack; and you'd have to clean it every day . . . That's what I thought. It was fun. But when I touched it, I knew it wasn't glass; it was transparent plastic. A shield that you could see through would have many advantages in a fight. Having bought the sword and shield, we had enough money left to buy about ten packets of *ramyŏn*. For a proper sword fight we really needed two shields, but we had to leave some money for *ramyŏn*.

The shield gave off a ringing sound too. A ringing sword seemed fair enough, but the idea of a ringing shield was strange. If you bopped your head on the shield, it rang out; if you hit the shield with your fist, it rang out. And the sound of sword on shield was a double ring. A strange novelty item set.

'I don't want to do the job interview tomorrow,' M said, banging his sword off the railing at the side of the road.

'Why?' I asked, likewise striking the railing with my sword.

'I don't like the idea of a company that sells scales. How about you?'

'I don't like it much either.'

'Let's give it a miss.'

'Fine.'

We banged our swords off the railing as we walked. Passersby stared at us. Still, we kept striking the railing. Street noise tended to drown out the ringing of the swords on the railing. M struck the shield I was carrying.

'Why not try to be artists?' he said. 'We seem to have what it takes. Let the interview tomorrow be our formal introduction into the world of art.'

'Art isn't for everyone, is it? What do we know about art? Of course, if acting the fool can be construed as art, we're Number One . . . I don't really want to do the interview. Interviewing us for acting the fool is a bit of a joke, isn't it?'

'But fun, surely?'

I couldn't see where the fun was. I hit the shield in my left hand with the sword in my right hand. I hit it hard, but the sound wasn't any louder. Traffic sounds and the radio in the cosmetics shop drowned out the sound of our swords. We went home.

There were now 500 comments tagged onto the photos. M sat in front of the monitor and absorbed himself in reading them. I was too tired. My mouth had a sandy taste: I was still feeling the effects of the beer.

Next day we slept in. We skipped the scales interview, had a late lunch, then put on our suits and headed for the internet newspaper office. The prospect of the interview was a bit scary, but we were determined to enjoy ourselves. We took a deep breath and went into the office.

Our friend greeted us. 'I know nothing about art,' he said, 'so I've arranged for an art professional to do the interview.'

The art professional extended each of us his card. *Professional Art Reporter* was written on it. It was amazing that such a job existed, but since we were artists too, we made an effort to be very composed when we greeted him. We headed for the subway in the company of the professional art reporter and a photographer. 'Today's photo concept is freedom,' the photographer said. 'Do you understand?' Of course, we had no idea what a free photo was.

We walked through the subway carriage carrying the blue yarn the art professional had given us. It was more like rope than yarn. He said it would have to be this thick to get it to come out clearly in a photo.

'There's nothing free about this. We're not exactly slaves in chains,' M muttered. I felt the same way.

'Well then, feel free to do your own thing,' the photographer said with a sigh. M took out the swords and shield and showed them to the professional art reporter. M had spent an hour shoving all sorts of things into his bag before we left home. You never know, he said, what they might need for the photographs.

'Why don't you photograph these?' M suggested. 'Could be fun.'

'What are you going to do with them?'

'Have a sword fight.'

'That sounds a bit childish. Why not stick with the string?'

We ignored the professional and launched into a sword fight. I had shield and sword. M just had the sword. M rushed at me with a shout: 'Fool, do you think you can block my sword with that silly shield?'

'Don't make me laugh,' I roared. 'Do you think you can break my glass shield with a plastic sword? I can see every move you make through the shield.'

Our swords clashed. The ring of steel echoed through the carriage. The sound was much louder than I expected. The professional art reporter gaped at us with an expression that said this isn't fun, it's ridiculously childish. But we continued the sword fight, each of us seemingly intent on killing his opponent. The cameraman clicked the camera shutter industriously, but he didn't look too happy.

Two small kids who had been sitting at a distance approached. The sight of two men in suits in a sword fight was special. The kids followed the fight closely. Two women who appeared to be the kids' mothers moved close. Two grandfathers intrigued by the clanging of the swords came up to us and two lovers also came up to us. The crowd gradually grew. We were sweating bricks in our attempts to exploit each other's defensive weaknesses, but our movements were so ridiculously slow that we didn't seem to be fighting at all. It was more like a dance. The two kids were pulling their mums' hands. 'Buy me a sword, buy me a sword,' each cried insistently. In the space of five minutes thirty people had gathered around. Their delight in the performance was written on their faces. The art professional brightened, the photographer's finger on the shutter speeded up. I tied M up with the blue yarn. Well, it was more like draping the yarn across him than tying him up. The train arrived at a station. We left the swords and shield in the carriage and exited onto the platform. The swords and shield were presents for the two kids.

'That was fun, wasn't it?' M said proudly. The art professional laughed. We went to a coffee shop for the interview. As soon as we sat down, the art professional began to shower us with questions. We weren't able to answer very many. The questions were much too difficult.

'Bruce Nauman recorded his body language in picture form, the expression of an art concept. Have you been influenced by such art forms?'

'Bruce who?'

'Bruce Nauman. He said that the committed artist helps the world by illuminating the mystery of the real. What do you think is the meaning of what you do as artists?'

'We believe we're helping the world by illuminating everyday reality.'

'And what is everyday reality?'

'Having fun, I suppose.'

It was that kind of interview.

We made a joke of every answer. When asked how he intended to solve economic problems M answered 'Economically'. When asked why we use yarn for our performance, I said we made a ball of mistakes in our lives and they were all unravelling. The art professional found the interview increasingly tough going. He was primarily interested in our novelty performances at job interviews. We had so little to say that we had to sublimate what we did into art.

'We loved the fun of performing in the job interview space. We had no interest in getting jobs ourselves, but we did interviews regularly. We'd do a magic show for the interview panel or we'd put on a yarn event for them. Now that was fun.'

'What was the yarn event?'

'We'd sit down the members of the interview panel and unravel tangled yarn. We were trying to see how long they'd put up with it, a kind of experiment in company patience.'

'How did it work out?'

'Didn't last five minutes; they had no patience. If you're going to pick the right person for the job, you ought to be able to wait five minutes. Trying to evaluate someone in five minutes in an interview room is a bit of a joke, don't you think?'

'That's true. So you're actually making fun artistically of the rigidity of formal societal structures? How often have you done your job interview performance routine?'

'About thirty times, different routine every time, of course.'

We were very happy to talk about the interviews. About interviews we had plenty to say. Having begun with the lie that we had no intention of taking a job anyway, we had the feeling that we really had been doing art.

Next day the article appeared in the internet paper under the headline 'Internet Pranksters Captivate a Society Without Imagination.' There was a photo of us sword fighting, one of me tying M up with the blue yarn and one of the big crowd watching the sword fight. Most of the article was about our interviews.

'It's fair enough, isn't it?'

'Yeah, the professional touch is there. The article really makes us look like artists.'

The article made us famous. Someone suggested that we make a documentary, *Street Artists*. There was a query from a university – could we teach a course titled Revolutionary Concepts? There were lots of requests for interviews. We rejected all offers except one, to join the panel of interviewers for an advertising company. Interviews were an area in which we felt we had competence. Of course, we weren't allowed to decide which candidates got the jobs. There were ten people on the panel. We were just excited to be interviewing someone.

We discussed the interview over dinner the evening before. This was a new situation for us; the examinees were now the examiners. And yet nothing had changed. Our primary preoccupation was the same: how to make the interview fun. That was all we thought about.

'There's been another phone call asking us to take on job interviews.'

'How many is that? We'll soon be professionals.'

'Sounds good. Professional interviewers. That's for us.'

There were lots of companies out there and companies regularly needed recruits. With a little more effort we'd be pros. At our preparatory meeting for the advertising company interview, we decided to make a firecracker. We let the firecracker off in the middle of the interview. *Poom!* With the explosion, coloured thread showered the applicants. The others on the interview panel were equally shocked because we hadn't told them in advance what we planned to do. The applicants provided varied responses. One applicant shouted, another broke out in a cold sweat, a third fell backwards over his chair. We had set the firecracker off to test their tension levels. We gave the highest marks to the fellow who burst out laughing when the firecracker went off. You can't do anything when you're tense.

'What's the next company on our list?'

'A securities company. What sort of event do you think would be appropriate?'

'Do you know anything about securities?'

'No, not a thing.'

'Why not get the applicants to question the members of the board. They ask the questions; we give the answers. We know from experience that framing a good question is a skill.'

'That sounds like fun.'

The interviews were fun. And discussing the interviews beforehand was fun. True to our usual form, we staged a lot of novelty events. We let off firecrackers as in the advertising interview; we filled a box with odd items, got the applicant to pick one, and challenged him to make us laugh with the item selected; we asked the applicants to compose cheerleader songs in support of their cause. M and I, of course, sang our own cheerleader song. Many of the applicants liked our questions and our novelty event approach. We were more like people charged with making the interview a fun experience than actual members of the interview panel. If interviews had been conducted like this, I thought, we'd have got jobs too.

This, we thought, was our first experience of doing something meaningful. If you were to ask us what exactly we meant by *meaningful*, we wouldn't be able to answer. All we knew was that it was now the second half; we felt we were no longer on our own, asleep in the changing room. Fail-aholics ourselves for a time, we were now charged with giving encouragement to other fail-aholics. We were delighted to be someone's shield. Even if the shield was only plastic or glass.

We had just completed our twentieth or twenty-first interview assignment. The interview had been for web designers. There had been so many applicants we were exhausted. We didn't feel like talking on the way home. We had to ask different questions of each applicant, based on the individual's personality and answers already given. And not everyone was able to adapt to the novelty event we had prepared. Bit by bit we reached the stage of exhaustion. We were running out of ideas and the process was becoming less and less fun. No fun after only twenty assignments. That was strange. We sat side by side in the back of the bus and looked out the window.

'Nothing's easy, is it?' M said. The question seemed directed at himself rather than me.

'We'll have to go back to the beginning again,' I said. Like M, I was still looking out of the window. 'This is not for us.'

We were viewing the same scene.

'To the beginning? You mean back to doing interviews every day? That was fun all right, but this is better.'

'No. Further back.'

'Go to college again?'

'No, further.'

M turned his head and smiled at me.

'You don't mean a suicide pact and meet again in our new life? Not that, surely?'

'No.'

'I'm not sure what you mean by "the beginning." We must have got here from some fork in the road.'

'What was your dream?'

'Dream? Why suddenly ask about dreams? That's childish . . .' M turned back to the window. He said nothing more. He wasn't looking at the scene outside, he was trying to remember his dream. Once M told me he wanted to be a head gardener. He also said he'd like to travel and he'd like to be a zookeeper. M stuck his head out the window. We said nothing. I looked at M's profile. It occurred to me that this might be our last time in a bus together. We'd been sitting vacantly on a bus, we'd had a brief conversation and now we'd passed a specific point. We had passed a fork in the road. He chose the left and I chose the right. I felt as if the ties that bound our ankles had been loosened without us even being aware of it. Tightly stretched electric wires showed where we had come from. I couldn't put a name on it, I couldn't date it precisely, but I felt that a phase of my life was ending.

HAN YUJOO

Black-and-White Photographer

Translated by Janet Hong

Betty's name is Betty and her last name is unknown. Betty leads an ordinary life in a small house with her husband and son. Her son's name is Alan and the dog's name is Toy. Her husband's name is Jim. Betty loves her husband, Jim. Jim loves Betty and their son, Alan, and on the weekends he walks their dog, Toy, around the neighbourhood.

One day, Jim comes home from work a little earlier than usual. His face is flushed. He asks Betty for a glass of water. As Betty picks up the water jug from the kitchen table, she senses at this very moment what people commonly refer to as *the future* starting, that its start is starting. Betty casts off her slippers without thinking and goes to Jim. Jim wipes his sweaty forehead with his sleeve. As he receives the glass of water, he drops it. Alan hasn't come home from school yet. A large puddle of water collects on the floor. The broken glass scatters in a mysterious formation. Water splatters Betty's bare feet. It's difficult to distinguish the water droplets from the glass shards. As Betty turns towards the cupboard to take out the vacuum cleaner, she asks Jim what's wrong.

Jim says that he has found his brother. It is his younger twin, who had occupied the same womb but was separated from him four months after birth. Jim senses that his past, frozen like a lifeless black-and-white photograph until now, will come alive. As Jim brings his sleeve to his face to wipe the tears that start to flow, Betty walks towards him with her arms outstretched in joy. Betty cleans up the broken glass only after Alan comes home. When Alan walks in, Toy springs out. The boy and dog watch Betty and Jim, who are still locked in an embrace. Betty is happy: Jim's birth will become whole and Jim will be happy.

Jim's brother's name was Jim. The older Jim and the younger Jim have different last names, but they don't come to mind now. When Jim went to Jim's house, knocked on the front door, and was greeted by Jim, both Jims saw themselves in each other's face, and saw each other in their own face. And out from the doorway sprang a dog, a child, a smaller child and a woman. The dog's name was Toy, the child's name was Alan, the smaller child's name was John and the woman's name was Betty. The two Jims embraced each other and became the most famous twins in the whole world. Requests for newspaper and magazine interviews never ended. The two Jims had the same face, voice, height, weight and job. Jim was a police-man. The names of their wives, ex-wives, children and dogs were also the same.

Jim's family invites Jim's family to their home. Betty looks lovely. Com-pliments are exchanged over the turkey resting on two tables that have been put together. Betty and Betty eat without talking. A withered stain on the floor, seven pairs of overlapping legs beneath the table, the trans-parency of a single small shard of glass left undetected. The two Bettys think about Jim and Jim's ex-wives, Linda and Linda. Betty has never met Linda before and Betty has once written to Linda. Betty wonders if the feelings she had when she and Jim first fell in love, met each other's family, exchanged vows and rings, were really her own. The children's names are Alan and Alan. The two Alans resemble each other. John's name and photo didn't appear in the newspaper. Because there is only one John and he is without a counterpart. While Alan, John and Alan, who resemble one another by a third, run out to the yard, and while Jim and Jim sit side by side on the living-room sofa, Betty clears the table, and Betty goes to the bathroom. As Betty piles up the dirty dishes with their food scraps, and as Betty sits on the edge of the bathtub and lights a cigarette, Betty cries and Betty weeps. For decades while an invisible force pulled the two Jims together, where were Linda and Betty, and Betty and Linda, and what were they doing? Who was I?

The clock in the kitchen is pointing to eight. The refrigerator stops refrigerating. In the sink, the kitchen knife slips down between the china. It makes a clunking noise. The person Jim fell in love with, was it me or was it Jim? Blood from the meat has soaked into the cutting board. The small glass shard that has gone undetected lies in wait for someone's bare foot. Betty pats her face dry and arranges some cookies on a plate. She takes off her apron. When Betty steps out of the bathroom into the living room as if she is slipping, the black clock hanging above the TV points to eight. In the years that follow, whenever Betty recalls this moment, she cannot be sure whether it had been eight in the morning or eight at night.

It's raining. Seven days and seven nights passed. It thundered from time to time and I woke up from the noise. While I was half asleep, I heard Betty's story in my dream. I had no idea who told me. It was a story I already knew. There are times when lightning flashes through the tiny window that's cracked open. Then the walls grow pale, like they're about to say something. No, it's an illusion. Or maybe a vain hope. Poor Betty . . . However, no one should pity Betty.

The rain falls in a steady rhythm. From time to time I hear the faint sound of distant cars sweeping through puddles. When I lie still and gaze up at the ceiling, I can't see anything. What time was it now? Was it early morning? Because I could still hear the occasional passing car, maybe it wasn't yet past midnight. The sound comforted me. I won't be able to fall asleep until a few rays creep in through the cracks in the boards that cover the window, barely enough for a couple of fingers to fit through. Right now, the only name I can remember is the proper noun Betty. *Tap, tap-tap-tap, tap, tap-tap.* The dark raindrops falling on the roof sound like Morse code. But I can't decipher them. The sounds slip past meaninglessly like the first time I heard a foreign language. When lightning strikes, they are wiped clean. There is no feeling in my bound hands. A thin rope is wound tightly around my wrists so that the backs of my hands are touching – so tight it digs into my skin every time I try to move my hands. On the first night my wrists hurt, on the second night my whole body ached and today nothing hurts. My dulled nerves block the pain. I didn't shout during the past seven days. Because when a person decides to lock up a person, everything – even the soundproofing of the room – is planned from start to finish. No one would hear anything.

And I count the remaining days. One, two, three, four. The days that haven't come slip past helplessly. When lightning flashes and darkness paints the walls, there are faces I remember. Faces of family, friends and people who have slipped past. Faces with no clear contours. Now even their names are hazy in my memory. It's a sad thing. But the tears don't come. There's a reason for everything. However, this principle operates according to chance. This person with bound hands and feet who is staring up at the ceiling, locked up in an unknown place, could easily be someone else with a different name. If I think this, I get angry. So angry I can't stand it. There's a fire inside me. This fire will burn my body.

Inside my pocket is a crumpled-up letter. The words in the letter are so clear in my mind that I don't need to take out the letter and read it again. It smells like dust. The smell is grey like ash. Typed neatly in black in the centre of a white square are the words: *If one million* wŏn *isn't deposited in three days, your only son's finger will be cut off.* It was the first letter. The account number was fake, and *three days* and *one million* wŏn were very ambiguous figures. More than anything, one million *wŏn* became the problem. Three days pass. The finger is safe. The police dismiss the case as a prank. A few months pass. The finger is safe. People have almost forgotten the incident, but I sometimes wondered which finger he would have started with. Mum's room gets the most sun in the whole house. The top of her dresser is cluttered with glass bottles containing liquids and solids. At the very back of her worn, shallow drawer is the first letter. When I start to read it word by word, phantom pains start from my left pinky and travel to the ring finger, then to the middle finger.

The second letter sails in. This time, the name of each family member is written on the letter. It says that the son's finger will be cut off if one hundred million *wŏn* isn't ready in three days. Every night a piece of white paper with jumbled-up inky words slips in through the crack under the door. The letter is kept secret. But it doesn't contain instructions on how to deliver the money. Investigators come and go. From their clothes and the air they give off, it's easy to tell they are the police. When one hundred million *wŏn* is compared to the pinky finger of a child who has just turned ten, there is no way of knowing which is more important. I want to hear what my parents and the investigators are saying quietly to each other in the living room. The corners of their words are pared away, as if I'm listening to static on the radio. The television is switched on. A soap opera is playing. Now, buried under the noise of characters shouting, their words are even more difficult to pick up. I want to ask them. I want to ask them if one finger is worth one hundred million *wŏn* or if ten fingers are worth one hundred million *wŏn*. There is no clock in the room. There is no one who will tell you the truth. Perhaps there is no truth we can call the truth. The letter is written on ordinary white paper and the words are typed in a common font. There probably won't be a single fingerprint. The age when people could be tracked through their handwriting or the kind of paper they used has passed. There is no stamp on the envelope. It was inside the mailbox with the electricity bill. The mailbox cost ten thousand *wŏn*. Some people want addresses just to receive letters. But more than anything, people need houses. They pay their phone, water and electricity bills, and the term *payment* is used rather than *pay*, and a house is needed to receive bank brochures, advertisements and gift catalogues. A house is also needed to receive things like Christmas and New Year's cards. A house makes one think of home and home makes one think of family. It isn't clear whether the word *family* can conjure up the words *love, warmth,* or *relationship*. According to certain stories, such homes do exist. The people who live upstairs have been out of the country for a long time. Post that couldn't fit into the mailbox is heaped up on the ground. Magazines wrapped in plastic with names such as *Our Nation 21, The Green Review, Geo* and *American Traveler* create layers of red, yellow, blue and black. I think about stealing a few of them, but in the end, I don't. It's also unclear where the people downstairs have gone. Their mailbox is stuffed with payment notices from banks and credit-card companies. It pains me to see the red print on the envelopes. Another family moves in downstairs. From time to time, people from an undisclosed administration or debt collection agency knock on the door downstairs, and the head of the new household doesn't open the door, and from behind the steel front door, tiny children claim they have no ties with the person in question, that he is a complete stranger, that they have never even seen him. Once, a chain letter went around. The letters were scattered all over a mountain where I went on a field trip. They said that whoever read them would go blind. All the payment notices are meant for just one person. That person's last name is Kim. The first name was so common that I can't remember it now.

I gradually lose the feeling in my fingers. I can't grip a pencil and chopsticks slip out of my hand. Three days pass this way, and nothing happens. I think it would be nice to go to a foreign country. America, China, France, Thailand, it doesn't matter. Not as many countries come to mind as I expected. I want to be in the midst of a foreign language that would naturally infiltrate my ears, then my mind, then my veins. If I can put two oceans between myself and this place, safety can be guaranteed by a time difference of twelve hours. The anxiety that resided in just a few fingers gradually spreads through my whole body and nervous system. Soon, the third letter will arrive, and then everyone will feel the danger. An incident that hasn't started also doesn't end. I look at my pinky, valued at one hundred million *wŏn*. It's an outrageously expensive object.

Finally, the third letter arrives. For this story to start, three characters are needed. This time, there is only one name written on the envelope. It's my name. The day before, my family and I had gone out to eat grilled cow's intestines. Cow's stomach, cow's liver and cow's intestines travel down the throat. They say that a cow has four or even six stomachs. A cow's protein-rich innards will soon transform into my flesh and bones. I can't tell if I'm the one that has swallowed grease or if the grease has swallowed me. I reek of barbecued meat. My entire being is slipping into something unknown. My parents barely speak while we're eating. I get the feeling that I will be safe tonight. The garlic is burning. However, feelings shouldn't be trusted. Father eats a piece of grilled onion. The multi-layered onion reminds me of a Babushka doll. A lizard cuts off its tail and escapes when danger strikes, but because my finger is different from a lizard's tail, it won't grow back once it's cut off. They say that a cat has nine lives, so even in life-threatening situations, they do not back down. Back down, beat down. Beat down, bow down. Bow down, break down. Break down, burn down. I concentrate on making endless word-play. I, who am not a cat, suspect that these stories were made up by those afraid of dying. Mum orders some beer. Companies that make alcoholic drinks should package them in paper cartons, not glass bottles. Even juice bottles should be made of plastic. I'm scared of the hours that are approaching. My parents are in a good mood today. It's because the letter will arrive tomorrow, and nothing should happen today.

The next morning, I head to school. An ordinary white sedan follows me. The horn honks softly. A man with ordinary features steps out of the car. In an ordinary tone, he tells me that my father has had an accident. There is a kind of insistence in the way he speaks, but I'm not suspicious of him. It's already been several months since the second letter arrived, and my mind is filled with all sorts of worries of my own. I'm wearing black sneakers, grey trousers and a black T-shirt. My mum fills my closet with achromatic colours. After I've been in the car for five minutes, I begin to wonder if she knows what I'm wearing today. For a missing person report to be filed, a description is needed, and she probably won't be able to remember anything about my physical appearance. It's June 1991. It's an ordinary time when some are being born and some are going to their grave. When I ask if Father is badly injured, the man replies that it's not too serious. When I ask if the hospital is close by, he says it's not too far. I've been in the car for five minutes. The man starts to whistle. When I ask him who he is, he says he works with my father. And who are you supposed to be? he asks me. My whole body freezes up in terror.

He stops on the side of a quiet street and blindfolds me. No more talking, he says. I follow his order not to attract any attention and crawl down to the back-seat floor. He binds my hands. The car makes left turns, right turns and U-turns again and again. They are perfectly ordinary driving actions. Tears flow from my eyes. I sniffle as I cry. Shut up, he says, don't make a sound. I swallow my tears. It feels as though I've heard those words for a long time. Once at school, I was asked if I knew the difference between time and the hour of the day. It was maths class and we were learning how to tell time. I answered that time is in constant motion and each hour of the day is a fixed point. I never found out if I was right or wrong. Suddenly, the term *non-partisan representative* comes to mind. In the dark I try to guess the time. I force myself to remember that the situation I'm in is happening right now. Time brims over. 8:03, 8:04, 8:09. The hour is festering with sores. I've never seen a sore. Suddenly, I'm unbelievably sleepy. There is nothing I can do.

He writes the letter after he has locked me in the storage room. It says that if he doesn't get five hundred million *wŏn* in three days, he'll cut off my finger. He treats the letter with care. While I doze off, he goes to what had been my home until just a few hours before and sticks the letter in our mailbox. In the mailbox is a car brochure advertising the latest model. And glued to the back of the brochure is a free packet of lettuce seeds. He puts the seeds in his pocket and comes back to the storage room. The morning passes this way. There is no one home and no one learns I missed school that day. At three o'clock in the afternoon, school is dismissed. Troublemakers sometimes toss the milk cartons they were given at lunch onto the two-lane street in front of the school. The cars drive over them and the cartons explode in a white spray. The milk leaves a long, pointed stain on the asphalt. The children shout. It doesn't matter if it's white, a stain is still a stain. The stain's expiration date is 8 April 2001. But the stain will follow the tire tracks, travel to other places and soon grow dirty. Suddenly, the term *black-and-white photographer* comes to mind. There are children who throw up right after they take a sip. Children suspect that milk, commonly referred to as nature's perfect food, is fed to students either because the Ministry of Education is in league with the dairy industry or because the Ministry of Health and Welfare aims to raise the entire nation's average height, making us the tallest race in Asia. Where I live, there aren't extremely poor kids or they're not noticed, and most children can probably afford to buy a carton of milk every day. Milk, which is no longer special around here, is mashed into a white smear on the road, fed to dogs and cats, or used as an instrument of violence. There is more than enough milk. If we took all the milk in the whole country and dumped it into the Han River at the same time, what would happen to Seoul? Once he has returned to the storage room, he checks on me, toppled over asleep, and brings a small plastic flower pot from the corner. The pot is half filled with dried dirt. When he cuts off the corner of the packet, the seeds spill out like grains of sand. Lettuce seeds, a flower pot, soil, water and sunlight are needed to grow lettuce. Just as three characters are needed to start this story. He takes out a 500-ml water bottle, unscrews the cap and pours some water into the pot. Barely any light comes into the room. No one has read the third letter yet. Seeds and a flower pot, and soil and sunlight and water are needed to grow lettuce, but time is needed more than anything. Sunlight and water are needed every day, and the frail stem needs to be reinforced with a thin support so that it won't topple over. But more than anything, one needs to wait to grow lettuce. One needs to wait for the new bud that's smaller than a seed to push its way through the dirt, for the thread-like stem to rise up, for the small curve of the leaf to spread out, for each small seed to calmly defy gravity. The man puts down the pot and straightens up, and I wake to the sound of his hands slapping against his trousers to brush off the dirt. My hands are tied. I raise myself from the sofa. Slowly he approaches me. I start to cry again.

The very first person to find the letter is Father. On his way home from work, he stops by the convenience shop to buy two cans of tuna and a pack of cigarettes. It hasn't been that long since the convenience shop with its familiar blue sign that's the same all over the world came into our neighbourhood. I felt a sense of relief when the shop first opened its doors. They said that for 24 hours, 52 weeks and 365 days, the sign that lights up the shop would never be turned off. That fact comforted me. Whether it was late at night or early in the morning, its doors remained open, and inside was a person who wasn't yet asleep, and the display shelves were filled with merchandise that wasn't opened yet. Snack bags inflated with nitrogen. Drinks in every colour behind the glass doors of the refrigerator. Processed foods. Occasionally I picture the convenience shop that lights up the empty street at night. I seek refuge in that place I'd hardly stepped inside. First-aid kits, security personnel, cargo trans-portation vehicles, plastic bags, bills, coins, telephones, plastic, glass, vinyl, plastic. Father takes out the familiar envelope from the mailbox. At the same time, a heap of magazines, catalogues and bills spill from the mail-box above. Father's footsteps on the stairs are anxious. There is no one home. He sticks in his key and opens the door. He puts the letter on the table. He waits.

The very first person to read the letter is my mum. She snips off the end of the envelope with the kitchen scissors. Father looks for me. Mother's face turns pale.

They call the police. My mum can't remember what I was last wearing. Father opens and closes my bedroom door several times. There is dirt on the shoes that the investigators have removed. They drink a glass of water and then start to talk. They ask my parents the standard questions. Mum is half out of her mind. Father tries to act calm. For this story to start, five characters are needed. One of the investigators also has a son. I don't know his name or age. The investigator thinks about his son. My parents read the letter again and again. It's a neat letter printed in the same block letters as the first and second letters. Mum's face is stained black with mascara. I've seen that face before. My aunt is a painter, and on a shelf in her room I once found a face like that in a Picasso book. It was a crying woman. At the time, I thought it was monstrous. I don't remember the other paintings. My parents and the investigators wait for the phone to ring. The small living room fills with tension. Father lights a cigarette. The investigators, too, take out their cigarettes from their trouser pockets and smoke. Just then the phone rings. It's my teacher from school.

What puts Father to the test is the five hundred million *wŏn*. To hand over a bundle of fifty thousand paper bills in three days seems impossible. Friends and relatives gradually find out that I've been kidnapped. My grandmother wails. There is no time. Like the old saying that time is money, the property of time that never waits for anything also applies to money. Of all the countless figures in the world, why five hundred million *wŏn*? If he had demanded a billion *wŏn* or more, an amount so astronomical that anybody would be forced to give up in defeat, how would this story go on? Time is slipping by. The sun has already set. Two of the investigators leave. As they walk down the steps, they whisper to each other. One of the investigators' sons is working on a school project. He's making a decahedral out of cardboard. The finished decahedral looks like a ball. One of the properties of a ball is that it can roll. The investigator's wife is removing the stitching from an old quilt. The investigator drinks a cup of coffee while he watches a soap opera. The decahedral, each side covered in different-coloured paper, rolls by. Soon, it comes to a stop.

My father is thinking. He isn't sure if one finger is worth five hundred million *wŏn* or if ten fingers are worth five hundred million *wŏn*. If the item to be exchanged is my life, the story would change. That's the problem. Father wonders if chopping off a finger is a metaphor for taking my life. Father is a law-abiding citizen, obeying almost every law except a few trivial ones, and he never missed a day of work except on special occasions, like funerals and weddings. In a word, he was a true family man. So it's only natural that he would lose his temper. Why is this happening to our family?

My father is thinking. According to the National Statistics Office, there are close to twenty child kidnappings each year. This means that twenty families out of all the families in the country must undergo such incidents every year. The chances are approximately five hundred thousand to one. Chances always betray us. The more ordinary a family is, the more tragic the situation seems. What puts Mum to the test is simply love. For this story to start, two characters are needed. I had turned upside down in my mother's belly. The obstetrician, who was a devout Catholic, permitted a Caesarean section only at the very last moment. I started talking earlier than others my age. Mum, Dad, I would call out with a lisp. Mum even faints for a moment. Father slaps her cheek. The inexplicable feelings she has had towards me until now start to come alive, one by one. She had truly believed they were feelings of love. She was wrong. She frequently feared her child was a monster or a mutant. There's nothing she can do. That's why she must, at times, demonstrate her love in strange ways. Mum cries.

And I cry too. He slaps my cheeks. I'm used to it. It doesn't hurt that much. I catch a whiff of dirt. I know instinctively that I mustn't provoke him. I think I've seen him before. I'm probably wrong. I'm just trying to find comfort by assuming that I know him. I decide that I don't know him. I want to live. I take a breath and ask.

He tells me to be quiet. His response doesn't stray an inch from what I expected. I close my mouth. A lot of time remains. The finger's expiration date is two-and-a-quarter days from now. He turns on the television. The picture is sharp. I'm momentarily awed that there is reception here. He watches a football match. It's taking place in a foreign country. The ball rolls on the grass. One of the properties of a ball is that it can roll. To have a football match, one needs a grass field, two goalposts, key players, a referee, linesmen, flags, coaches, substitutes and a ball. To watch an entire match, one needs to wait. A match lasts more than ninety minutes. And gravity is needed most of all. One of the properties of gravity is that it makes a ball roll. Skilled players know how to handle gravity. Maybe it's gravity that has brought me to this place. A dog barks in the distance. I'm hungry. One player is awarded a penalty kick. It's just him against the goalie. I get nervous for a second. It's a strange moment. The ball misses the net. This is to be expected, since there is a higher chance of missing a penalty kick. But the crowd jeers. A replay shows the ball sailing into the stands. The game resumes. There's never been a time that I wasn't me. That truth haunts everyone. The first half ends after three minutes of stoppage time. He turns to look at me. Aren't you hungry? The storage room is dark and I'm hungry. I don't know if it's hunger or pain. He removes the plastic wrapper and takes out the food. Cold dumplings are set in front of me. I'm relieved as soon as I see the food. I want to ask, why did you choose me, why me? He takes a water bottle from a plastic bag and pours water into a paper cup. To eat dumplings, one needs to buy dumplings. To drink water, one needs to buy drinking water. For this story to start, I'm needed. People are driven by their desires. For this story to continue, desire is needed. The desire for a bag filled with green paper bills, the desire to live, the desire to get your child back, the desire to reverse time, the desire for someone else's child. Don't do anything stupid, he mumbles in a low voice as he unties my hands. My wrists burn. Doing something stupid is also a desire. The dry air inside the storage room causes a rash. My skin, my whole body, no, my whole being is so itchy I can't stand it. He puts a pair of chopsticks in my hands. He places a paper cup of water in front of me. Hang on for just three more days, he says. I need to go to the bathroom. There is no bathroom in the storage room. He takes out a pocket knife and slowly cuts away the top of a 1.5-litre plastic bottle. The movement of the knife is chilling. I think he purposely took out the knife to scare me. If that's the case, he succeeded. I'm so scared I can't think straight. The knife goes back into his pocket. One player scores a goal. The commentator says that the dull match is coming alive again. The second half is almost over. Suddenly, the words *Ouagadougou, Panama Canal* flash across my mind. Is it the name of a place?

The one who answers the phone is Father. To avoid being traced, the man uses a pay phone in the middle of a busy city-centre street. It's a classic method. I'm still tied up in the storage room and I'm hungry. Because I can't use my hands, I pick up a dumpling with my mouth. It's ice cold. I cry as I chew. I'm thirsty. The phone rings ominously. As soon as Father picks up the receiver, the machine starts to record. He asks if the money is ready. Father wants to listen to my voice, but the man won't give an inch. He tells Father not to contact the police. But he probably knows that the police are recording the entire conversation. He says he will call again tomorrow. He says that if five hundred million *wŏn* isn't ready, the kid won't have a finger.

I'm just a paper doll. I can't do anything.

According to statistics, 90 percent of kidnappers are arrested in the end. The football match has ended. The referee gave the whistle a long blow. A team has won. One of the properties of all ball games is that at the end of every game, one team wins and another loses, or both teams tie. The reason so many people are obsessed with football or baseball is that such games race towards the end from the second they start. Every game must end and every game must have progression. I'm anxious. Perhaps my life will end here. I make an effort to use the future tense. There's no use. At dawn he comes back to the storage room. My parents sat awake all night. Father is listing everything that can be exchanged for cash. He will have to withdraw all his savings, file a personal accident claim and get help from friends and relatives. But who will help out with that kind of money all of a sudden? He can only come up with five hundred million *wŏn* if he sells the house. Could he sell the house in three days? Father shakes his head. A house, more than anything, is needed to sustain a family. Time passes even in a dilemma. A weekly magazine is spread open on the table and an article describes a battle taking place on the West African coast. It's no longer shocking news. Father drinks a cup of coffee, urinates in the bathroom, and while squeezing toothpaste onto his toothbrush, he cries. His tears are sucked down the drain. Mum spills hot coffee on her knee. The morning light makes its way through the cracks of her scream. The fluorescent light in the living room is still on. According to statistics, 90 percent of kidnapped children are murdered.

Light seeps into the storage room. It's time for school. My form teacher has two young children. Before going to work, he looks down at the peaceful faces of his sleeping children and is comforted. On the bus, he is troubled by thoughts of me. My desk is still empty. The kids start to wonder why. Someone called yesterday, looking for me. It was Inshik. He has a sibling three years younger than him, and Inshik's mother is pregnant with her third child. As the due date grows closer, Inshik's father buys a new car. The interior of the new car is spacious and comfortable. He spent a lot of money to install a stereo and get leather seats. I've seen that car. It was a rainy day. Inshik's mother had come to pick him up in the new car. He waved goodbye to me. I opened my umbrella. Stuck to the back window was a small sticker with the words *Baby on Board*. As I watched the car slowly disappear, I repeated the words to myself: baby on board. The teacher tells the other students that I've caught a cold. They don't think much about it. Someone from the office calls for Father. He makes up an excuse. The investigators come. The ash that they carelessly dropped from their cigarettes leaves a grey mark on the floor.

There's no time. He wakes me up and gives me a bun. Inside the wrapper is a monster sticker. I put the sticker in my pocket. He turns on the

Black-and-White Photographer

television. A middle-aged couple is talking about their problems. They have two daughters in their late teens. Before all their problems can be revealed, he changes the channel. A weather forecast is on. A storm is approaching. The forecaster is wearing a raincoat. To prevent damage to infrastructure ... As soon as I hear the word *damage*, I shiver. Before he ties up my hands again, I pee into the plastic bottle. He waters the lettuce seeds. In a burst of courage, I ask him why me. I ask him when and where he found me. Peering into the pot, he says lazily, It couldn't be a girl. I don't understand what he means. He tells me he'll leave my hands untied if I promise to behave. I nod. He avoids my eyes. A shadow falls across his face. It's an ordinary face. It wasn't far-fetched to have thought that I'd seen him before. Suddenly, the word *sinkhole* comes to mind.

At noon, he ties me up again. After he has shut the window with care and made a thorough inspection of the room, he leaves. I don't know where he's going. Probably to make a phone call. It's not even the weekend, but the city-centre streets are overflowing with people. He walks for a long time with his hands shoved in his pockets. Heat rises from the pavement. Pay phones are hard to find these days. He stops for a moment in front of a medical supplies shop. He purchases a blood-pressure cuff. From the convenience shop next door, he purchases buns. The buns expire in twelve days. With a plastic bag in each hand, he forces his way through the crowd, his arms swinging. There's a pay phone near the steps of the subway entrance. He enters the booth.

Again, the one who answers is Father. As soon as he picks up the receiver, the machine starts to record. The man detects the sound. He asks if the money is ready. Father says yes. The man has no way of knowing if that's true. Father asks if he can speak to me. The man says that I'm safe and that I had bread for breakfast and dumplings for lunch. What he's saying isn't a complete lie. Father starts to sob. Mum, sitting beside him, weeps silently. The man tells Father to put the money in a plastic bag and place it under the streetlight in front of a fast-food restaurant near the Shinch'on overpass, making it look like it's rubbish. Father says all right. According to their conversation, I will be left by the back gate of Shinch'on Church as soon as the money is delivered. The story could have ended this way.

In a daze Mum slumps down onto the cold kitchen floor and thinks

419

about me. Mugs with sticky coffee stains at the bottom are piled precariously in the sink. Fruit flies swarm. Fire ants gather as well. When the
block of wood that has fallen to the floor is moved accidentally, thousands
of red ants scatter in all directions. The block of wood is actually a package
of imitation crab meat. What thoughts my mum is having about me, I
have no idea.

On the third morning, the lettuce seeds start to sprout. Transparent
leaves unfurl like insect wings. There are about twenty new leaves in the
little pot. The man marvels. After he waters them, he cracks open the
window and places the pot on the sill in the sliver of sunlight. I can't
remember last night's dream. I barely slept. After he shakes me awake, he
gives me a bun. It's a red-bean bun. It will expire in twelve days. Inside
the plastic wrapper is a monster sticker. I put the sticker in my pocket. I'm
anxious. I chew and swallow. Flour, sugar and lumpy red-bean paste travel
down my throat. It feels like I'm swallowing stones. It seems he barely
sleeps. He feeds me and wakes me and feeds me and watches me. Since I
have never met any other kidnappers, I don't know what type of kidnapper
he is. He doesn't hit me or swear at me. He turns on the television. The
morning news is on. There was a big accident the night before on the
Honam Expressway. A bus tipped over. There are ten dead and seventeen in critical condition. The injured have been taken to the hospital and
are being treated. He changes the channel. The National Assembly building fills the screen. The newscaster says there have been unforeseen
difficulties in the passing of a certain bill. The man changes the channel.
A news update reports that a battle has broken out on the West African
coast. But Africa is too far away. Some people say we have now reached
the end of civilization, but in another country, what we call civilization
has not yet started. He changes the channel. Commercials flash on the
screen. He turns off the television.

The exchange is set for 8:00 p.m. It's right after sunset. Father takes a
deep breath and walks down the narrow street. Policemen in civilian
clothes are hiding everywhere. The story could end this way. Shinch'on at
eight o'clock on a Friday night is filled with people. Whether it's people
or objects, nothing exists in reasonable proportions – there's always an
abundance or a shortage. It's the same with emotions. To hide his nervous-
ness, Father purposely takes big strides. People bump into him. People go

out for different reasons. Some meet others, some buy things and some
dine out. They must satisfy their desires, whether it's for food, sex, or
wealth, and to do so, they need time, money and people. Father passes
yellow, red and blue cosmetic shops and stops beneath the pedestrian
crossing sign in front of a white bakery. Hundreds of people are waiting
for the light to turn green. Right then, someone grabs Father's arm. The
buses and taxis on the four-lane street haven't moved. Lights blink. He
whispers into Father's ear. Be quiet and listen to me carefully. Father stares
straight ahead as if frozen. With his left hand, the man feels for the small
knife in his pocket. Pass the bag behind you, he says. And don't attract
any attention. Slowly Father passes the black plastic bag filled with a hundred ten-thousand-*wŏn* bills behind him and receives a black plastic bag
of the same size and shape in return. Father is sweating. The light changes.
All at once, hundreds of people are released – fire ants, all of them. There's
nothing they can do about it either. The man disappears into the crowd.
People push past Father, who stands glued to the same spot. His legs give
way. The investigators lose the man. Father dashes to Shinch'on Church.
He runs up and down along the stone wall several times, but I'm not there.
Inside the plastic bag Father received was a neatly folded newspaper. It
was the scarlet-coloured *Munhwa ilbo*. Except for the creases where the
paper was folded, the man left behind no fingerprints or other traces. My
parents despair.

It's past midnight when he returns to the storage room. I'm lying face
down on the sofa with my hands tied behind me. Tired foam shows
through the torn vinyl of the sofa. I smell dirt. It's going to rain soon.
I'm anxious. In my dream I'm inside a dry bathtub. Fire ants parade by.
He wakes me up and gives me dumplings. The swollen dumplings have
no flavour. The skin is white and the filling is black. His hands are white
and his hair is black. These are simple facts. They're no longer
shocking.

He turns on the television. There's nothing on. He uses the plastic bag
filled with a hundred million *wŏn* as a pillow and lies down on the floor
where a mat is spread. The storage room is small. Hardly anything is stored
in it. It occurs to me that all storage rooms in the world should be inves-
tigated. They would reveal people and bones and soggy memories. As
I strain my ears to listen to the vibrations coming up through the floor,

I await his decision. In the distance, people are moving. The floor seems to bulge. It feels like it is.

It's my fourth morning in the storage room. After he wakes me and unties my hands, he gives me a bun. It's the same kind. Inside the plastic wrapper is the same monster sticker. The sprouts in the pot have grown even more. I get a strange feeling. There are three stickers in my pocket. He turns on the television. He doesn't watch it. He's thinking. I watch him from behind. He's a thin person. His square shoulders are tense. They are cutting sharp 90-degree angles into the television screen. He doesn't hit me. All he did was slap me a few times the first night. I remember reading an article in the newspaper about a Chinese boy who gnawed off all his fingers. He couldn't feel pain because he didn't have any pain receptors. They say animals have pain receptors in order to prevent greater damage to the body. My pain receptors were fully alive, so rather than chewing my fingers off, I sucked them constantly. Both my thumbs were always swollen. My parents rubbed disinfectant or ointment on my thumbs, and sometimes wrapped gauze around them. Because those methods didn't work, they even scratched the sides of my thumbs with a razor blade. All things take time. The shape of my mouth changed. I was as helpless as a plant. I grew older in a kind of stupor. When night comes, day comes. It's been five days. He disappears and comes back. It rains. I concentrate on wordplay. Village and pillage. Creation and cremation. Winter and splinter. Attic and static. Ammunition and premonition. I think up these words, then forget them. Six days pass. Father takes a necktie from the closet. Mother breaks a teacup. She turns on the stove to boil water. A blue flame appears. Without thinking, she puts her hand close to the flame.

It's warm. I know that all pain disappears in a second. But I'm scared. So scared I can't stand it. Every morning, he waters the lettuce. The sprouts have grown considerably. I look down at my wristwatch. It's an old watch that has to be wound once a day. I secretly took it from the small wooden box where Father keeps his things. The hands of the watch have stopped at 4:24. Even now, I can't remember if it was 4:24 in the afternoon or 4:24 in the morning.

The next morning, he loads me into the car and takes me somewhere. Eyes covered, I sit in the backseat like a piece of luggage. My black shirt and black trainers absorb the sun. It's warm. The car rattles with every bump in the road. I hear coins fall. I really need to go to the bathroom. I wet my trousers. After driving for a long time, he stops the car. The engine turns off and everything is silent. He puts something in my shirt pocket. I flinch. He uncovers my eyes. Both of my hands are soon freed. I'm dizzy. I stand leaning to one side and look up at his face. He avoids my gaze. So long, he says. I sink to the ground. The car pulls farther away. The licence plate is cleverly covered up. Everything grows hazy. I cover myself in sunlight and fall asleep. There is nothing I can do.

Someone wakes me. When I open my eyes, I see an elderly man's face. To begin this story . . . I sit up slowly. There's a two-lane road in front of me. It's a country road. There are signs for lodgings and seafood restaurants. I push aside the elderly man's outstretched hand and start walking. He calls out to me.

I turn and look at his face. It's a worried face. But I can't trust him. I ask him which way it is to the bus terminal. He answers that it doesn't matter which way I go.

This is an island connected to the mainland and either way will lead me to a terminal. He offers me a ride, but I can't trust anyone. I wave him off and set off blindly. My lips are parched. Trucks and buses go both ways on the perimeter road. Although he said this was an island, I cannot see the sea. As if in a trance, I keep walking. There is a fire inside me. The rash I'd forgotten about suddenly grows unbearable. There is moisture left on the leaves, and once I step into the shade, it's cool. It's always the senses that cause problems. I look at my watch. It's 4:24. A van pulls up beside me. The driver rolls down his window and offers me a ride. I shake my head stupidly. A long time passes. I learn from a sign that this is Kanghwa Island. I've lost all sensation in my legs. When I realize that having no sensation is also a problem, I'm standing in front of a small police station.

There is a ten-thousand-*wŏn* bill in my shirt pocket. I keep it safe. I go back home. My parents hug me until I'm numb and refuse to let me go. My pain receptors come alive again, but I don't feel good. I was still young. There were still an absurd number of days left ahead of me. They said it was a miracle that I had returned alive. But I realize the word *miracle* is no more than a figure of speech. School hasn't changed. I tell the other kids that I was ill with a bad cold. The kids don't think much about it. After school, Inshik takes me to the house of another friend, whose father works for an airline. Inside a desk drawer are neat rows of black-and-white film canisters filled with foreign coins. I don't remember the kid's name. Two years pass. Ever since that day, my parents haven't laid a finger on me. I realize how appropriate the expression *not lay a finger on* is. I nearly forget that I have pain receptors. When I have dreams, I'm always in a bathtub. The water comes up only halfway or I'm barely able to soak my feet.

I move on to middle school. My fingers survive. Because of my height, I'm assigned the second seat in the first row on the first day. I haven't grown an inch since that day. I still look like a kid. The stinging wind cuts through my baggy uniform. The school playground is still frozen. On the way to school, I run into kids dressed in the same uniform. They threaten me. For this story to start, many characters are needed. An incident never ends. The next day, and the next, they wait for me in the same alley. I'm sick of it all. It's no longer shocking. I don't avoid it. It's because there is too much time. I frequently get punched. Now I know it was in order to avoid accidental rape that he doesn't kidnap girls. Uncomfortable desires grow each day. One day, a kid chokes me for fun. Instantly the past comes rushing back.

Is one hundred million *wŏn* too much or too little? There's no such thing as an appropriate sum. I now have seven monster stickers. I use them to count the days. Even when I nod off, I keep them clenched tight in my fists. In the evenings, it's easier to move my hands. I pick up the dumplings with chopsticks. The water bottle smells bad. The rain lashes down. Even the rain smells bad. It's been a week. It's a long time, long enough for someone to create the world. I'm so scared and anxious I can't stand it. I start to sing. The song starts out low and anxious and then grows louder and louder until it pushes the darkness out of the storage room. He gets angry. He flings down the television remote and comes towards me. I don't stop singing. I run from him. Blue, red, purple, yellow, black, light, darkness, photo, veto, hollow, shallow, echo, depot, delay, deflate, decay, deflate, cremate, castrate, mutate, stalemate. I sing and run around the storage room. But I trip over the potted plant and fall. Dirt and lettuce sprouts scatter. To kill the plant, I need to wait. The underdeveloped leaves will soon rot and become dirt again. Return, retreat, reject, reverse, remember, dismember, disfigure, dislocate, dominate, fornicate, subjugate, subdue, submit, subtract, subpar, subvert, submerge. I keep singing. He slaps me a few times. It doesn't hurt that much. There is nothing I can do. Navy, crimson, violet, amber, black, green, white, light, shadow, grass, wind, mother, father, light, darkness, flowers, trees and the sea. I sing. He threatens me. To end this incident, I need to wait. This story could have ended this way. His voice grows louder and louder with anger. He swings his arms like a crazy person. At last he grabs me by the collar and starts to choke me. My song fades lifelessly. Now it has ended.

KIM AERAN

The Future of Silence

Translated by Bruce and Ju-Chan Fulton

I have an old name. A very long name. To utter that name would require a lifetime. But even a lifetime might be too short – you could try for hundreds, even thousands of years, and even if you were successful, you might discover that my name has become twice as long in the process. Which is why I myself have never been able to remember it. When I get to wondering about my name, I try to grab hold of a memory of what it was or what it might have been part of, and a few clues glimmer.

I wonder who I am. And how old I am.

The first cry at birth, maybe that was my name. An inarticulate rant of despair directed towards the void, just before death, that might have been my name. Simple love couched in complicated syntax, maybe that was my name. Words swelling with grief like a dam about to be breached, that might have been my name. I cannot memorize my name. But I can tell you who I am. And whoever you are, you will probably hear my language as your own.

I was born today. And soon I will disappear. We all have our one day to live, each of us. We're born old, we age a day and we die old. That one day is as long as the history of a species, but as short as a yawn. The moment we're born, we're breathing our background and history. We are born in a previous life and we die in that life. When we utter the distinctive words of our language, temporality and space surge towards us, the far reaches of time catapulting towards us, great stones skipping across water. Perhaps that's true of your language as well, assuming it's an old one.

I wonder who I am. And how many of us there are.

I am the spirit of the breath and energy released from a language at the moment of its extinction. I am a gigantic eye, a huge mouth. I am given life for a day, a brief span in which I look back over my previous life. I am both singular and plural, a collective and its parts, a fog bank and its separate wisps. I am the synthesis of all that helps me to be me, and the weight of the silence that makes such syntheses erase themselves. I am the volume of absence, the density of loss, the force generated when a light flickers on only to be snuffed out. I am the heat from decomposing animals and rotting food.

I wonder who I am. And where I live.

I'm light as a cloud, free as the wind, and constantly on the move. I readily embrace those who are similar to me. Did you know that spirits make love? And when we uncouple, I enlarge until I blanket the ground with the shade in which I shroud words. I am the beginning and the end, the unknown and the known, a song for virtually everything and at the same time nothing. This is the only way in which I can explain myself – I suppose I could try the syntax from one of the other tribes, but it wouldn't help. We lack a tangible body, we are faceless. But we know who we are and what we are.

Today I left at death's doorstep the lone speaker of a lone language. He was an old man with late-stage cancer of the larynx. For a man with a complexion so dark, his bushy eyebrows were a startling white. He had a small hole in his throat, through which he spoke. That small, round device in his throat was my last domicile. To be sure, I dwelled in his chest and his head and his eyes as well. But it was only by roaming outside of him thanks to his breath, his musculature and his will that I was able to move in my accustomed manner. And it was only through occasional contamination and frequent failure in relationships with others that I became healthier. And this is what he had wanted. As a boy, he had been a good runner. His boyhood dream was to go as far as he could with only his two legs to sustain him, and much later he realized that dream, a dream he had harboured for precisely twenty years. But that place he reached, after days of running, days of walking, more running and walking, the place that was farthest away, was, lo and behold, his family home. His life span drew to a close when he was aged ninety. Before closing his eyes for the last time, he looked out into the void and spewed out a gasp, perhaps the last words he would ever speak. But no one understood him. Because the old man was the sole surviving speaker, and listener, of that language. The odd, unsettling, mechanical voice continued to issue from the prosthesis in his throat. Even if you had spoken the same language, you would have had to be hyper-focused to make out what he was trying to say. He sounded like static from a radio that's in between stations. Even so, *he* knew what he was saying. How he wished someone else were there who understood. The age of the listener wouldn't have mattered, nor the gender, profession, or temperament, or whether the person was a saint or a ruthless criminal. He longed for someone to lend an ear, to look at him, offer a nod and respond to him in his mother tongue with, 'It's been so long since I had a chat with someone' or 'It's such a friendly, natural feeling it brings tears to my eyes.' Or just a simple 'Yeah' or 'Sure.'

Many of the people here have disabilities. The majority, after all, are elderly. Among them are an old woman who though blind possesses a superlative memory, and an old man with dementia whom you'll hear every day gibbering in the six different tribal languages he learned as a boy. There's a former shaman with a chronic middle-ear infection who no longer commands respect, and a warrior who once dreamed of moving to the city and becoming a consumer but who no longer dreams and who awaits only the soda he has for dessert. Each is the last fluent speaker of his or her language. As are the majority of the people here. They realized long ago they existed in a universe where their mother tongue could be aired loud and clear. But they were, each of them, like a wailing child separated from its mother in the cacophony of a marketplace. Because in the end all was dead except oneself and a language that was immensely beautiful, colossally exquisite and yet unbearable to a lone person. They tried to understand what had happened to them in the depths of an incomprehensible darkness and silence. They spent their days trying to cheer themselves up with the thought that anyone could have been left all alone in the world as the sole surviving speaker, and it was just their luck that they were those individuals. They had to convince themselves that this was the status quo and it would never, ever change. It took some of them all their life to accept this simple truth. Some remained optimistic till the day they died, hoping for a miracle – that one day someone would come calling with a 'Good morning' in the tribal language and prattle on about this, that, or the other thing, face devoid of pity, contempt, or curiosity. Sad to say, it didn't happen. The people here have taken hold of the word *alone* and they won't let it go till it wastes away. Every day they try a dose of despondence, as if it's a venomous tonic. In their suffering and stoicism, their isolation and fear, their hope and expectation, they felt their loneliness crystallize into a bitter salt. And now they don't even consider explaining what it's like to taste these one-of-a-kind crystals of loneliness. Because if one of them slips from their mouth they very well might drown in the surge of their feeling and the flood of their words. Before proceeding with the stories of these people, perhaps I should explain where they live.

This place belongs to a special district; access to and from the outside is limited. It's a grand-scale complex of exhibition halls boasting a superb setting, each hall serving as a learning centre, research lab and folk village. Its official name is the Museum of Moribund Languages, and it was established with the goal of preserving dying languages and educating the world about their importance. Even the people at the Centre had to scratch their heads at the choice of the remote site for the museum – parched, ochre wasteland that stretches out endlessly in every direction. The Centre announced its plans for the museum and practically overnight the heavy equipment arrived, the transporters raising clouds of dust. After a spasmodic flurry of nailing, the construction was done and the workers were gone.

As of now a thousand-plus speakers maintaining a thousand-plus languages occupy the complex. They work in the museum by day and return to their dormitory at night. Each exhibition hall preserves the distinctive heritage maintained for generations by the tribe. Each language has its own hall with its own speaker, dressed in traditional attire. Very rarely is a hall occupied by two or more speakers. The handful of speakers who have a partner are the objects of great envy by the sole occupants – even if those partners are of the same sex or are total strangers to each other. On the other hand, those with partners worry themselves sick that the partner might die first, and then what? This is true even if they are not fond of each other, for they all have witnessed others going mad from loneliness.

The thousand-plus exhibition halls were built with natural materials and traditional methods, and in accordance with the characteristic climate and scenery of each tribe. But there's something not quite right about the majority of the halls, a certain lack of substance – rocks made of Styrofoam and coated with standard-issue paint, plastic palm trees, look-out platforms with cement poking through spaces where the posts are connected to the flooring, the Caucasian mannequins appearing at random in obvious disregard of the characteristics peculiar to each tribe. The various halls are loosely connected by paths winding among man-made ponds, low hills and bamboo groves. Placed conveniently among them are snack bars, maintenance rooms, dormitories and public toilets. Each building is numbered on the map distributed free of charge at the ticket booth. Most of the tourists stick to one area, since it would take days to cover the entire site at their leisure. Those who designed the complex believed that each tribe should have ample space to itself. Think of a nation whose present population is not even three: even there the survivors need at least that much breathing room for the history and culture that have accumulated over the millennia. That way visitors will have the impression that something is being 'preserved.' For even if they understand that what they see are models rather than real-life objects, it won't do if they come away feeling that the halls are basically artificial.

The centrepiece of the complex is the fountain. But it's words rather than water that issue from this particular fountain. It consists of a metal column that supports a gigantic glass sphere in which the six continents are etched. Inside the transparent sphere letters and characters from all the languages float freely, glittering, the product of holograms. People love to watch the cheery dance of the spotlit letters, which never stops during visiting hours, except at twelve noon, when the movement briefly freezes, the sphere opens up like a blossoming flower and the words cascade down among the petals.

It proved costly to keep up the museum. The Centre expected tourists to generate enough revenue to offset expenses and debt. But not many visitors travelled to this distant place, arriving coated in dust. If it were a museum for automobiles or dinosaur fossils, then maybe. But a museum for languages at risk of vanishing? Wouldn't a zoo, a robot museum, or even a worm museum have better prospects? And so the museum laboured under the weight of chronic red ink, the revenue insufficient for basic maintenance and for housing and feeding the thousand-plus residents. In the end, the Centre decided to double the ticket price, which resulted in even fewer visitors, until now there are only a few dozen a day at most. Even so, the thousand-plus residents turn out every day for those few visitors, waiting, just waiting in their shabby exhibition rooms, silently keeping to one spot all day long, their expressions like those of the personages on postage stamps. And when the visitors arrive, they come to life, offering a greeting in their native tongue and performing a song and dance: Off to the side is a display of the native script along with books and folk artefacts – a knife with geometric designs on the handle, a headpiece with colourful tassels, baskets woven of plant stalks. CD compilations of tribal songs, chants and history are available at a special discount.

The Centre established this complex to protect and raise awareness of languages that face extinction throughout the world. However, the outcome proved to be the opposite, and perhaps that was the Centre's covert wish – they mourned in order to forget, praised in order to disdain, commemorated in order to kill off. Maybe it was all planned from the start. Again today a long-lived language, that of my last speaker, vanished in the blink of an eye. It's been happening every couple of weeks, and no one gets alarmed any more. So here I am in the heavens above, having departed from my last speaker. As bits and pieces of my past come to mind, I look down and see a discarded admission ticket blown by the wind. On the cheap paper I see an image of several speakers in their colourful traditional garb; they're all waving and smiling. I smile back at them. That was our job, after all – to smile and smile again, no matter what, to smile absolutely and forever, as if we would never die.

The museum hours are 8 a.m. to 6 p.m. As the doors close for the night, the lights in the complex are extinguished and all grows still and black, like mud flats submerged at high tide in the dead of night. Bordered by the low hills, the dormitories are in the far reaches of the complex. They aren't indicated on the pamphlet given to visitors. Maybe the Museum of Moribund Languages doesn't appear on any of the Centre's maps, maybe it doesn't formally exist on Planet Earth.

Kim Aeran

In the dormitories everyone abides by the rules, which include lights-out and bedtime. And except for their daily appearance in the exhibition halls, they're always in the dorms. When the sun goes down, they go to sleep Centre-style in Centre-style rooms. They eat Centre-style from uniform food trays, and attend to their business Centre-style in regulation toilets. But in case you're wondering, this doesn't make them people of the Centre. Theirs is a peculiar existence, like that of people in a group image who turn ghostly as the photo fades. The Centre does not force them to learn its language. Although there would be several advantages to stand-ardizing communications with the residents, the Centre fears they will take the standard language and create their own patois from it. Under the pretext of safeguarding the distinct characteristics of each language, the administrators prohibit the mixing of one tribal tongue with another.

The majority of those here are orphans, in the sense that they are alone not only in the museum but wherever they might go in the outside world. To be accepted in the museum, one must meet several qualifications. Minori-ties and their languages are scattered about the globe, but that in itself doesn't guarantee acceptance. For a language to be accepted by the Centre, it must have fewer than ten speakers. The media carry on about how the Centre seeks agreement with the qualifications from all the residents. The problem is, many of the residents don't have a clear understanding of the term *agree-ment*. Some say that in the confusion of the moment they were pressured to relocate here, others say, 'Consent form – what the hell *for*?' Still others say, 'They rounded us up all right, but if they want to say they put out a "call for applications," who cares?' Or 'They drafted us.' Or 'They hunted us.' But now these once hot-blooded grumblers have also got on in years and are locked in silence, the last surviving speaker of their language. The policy of the Centre is to maintain every exhibition room even after the last speaker dies. Every couple of weeks a room in the dormitories and the exhibition halls becomes vacant. Where the last speaker used to be there is now a mannequin, dressed in the same traditional outfit, which looks one size larger on its arti-ficial frame. And if you can believe it, the exhibition room is labelled with a red sticker reading *Extinct* in the language of the Centre.

For those who still live, the routine in the exhibition rooms they occupy is similar. They sit woodenly off to the side, rising instantly at the arrival of tourists to gather themselves and speak a few words in their language – a hello and perhaps their name and who named them. There are slight variations from room to room. One tribe might phrase the greeting, 'Our earth spirit consents to welcome you,' another might say, 'You must speak our ancestral language if you wish to pass through.' Through the ear buds of a small audio device the visitors hear these greetings rendered in the language of the Centre, after which they continue their tour of the complex, tagging along after their guide and occasionally raising a rude or silly question before departing. Quite a few dispense with the listening device altogether, engrossed in 'appreciation' – for example, at exhibition halls where, instead of an explanatory plaque about the designated language, there is only a sign reading 'Untranslatable' or 'Under Reconstruction'. In such halls the speaker crouches like an animal in a cage, his or her face decidedly gloomier than those of other speakers, eyes regarding the visitors with an otherworldly gleam. Because the speakers have survived so long, they've taken on a shrivelled look, like rice grains from the Bronze Age stoppered in test tubes – *yuck*. These speakers are especially popular as background for selfies for the tourists.

The different tribes perform various greetings. A speaker might touch his cheek to the visitor's or kiss the visitor's foot or the crown of his or her head. But such contact, indeed any direct contact between speaker and visitor, has been prohibited by the Centre ever since a speaker slashed a visitor across the neck on impulse – a speaker who for a decade had conformed to Centre guidelines by greeting tourists with a smile and saying, 'What a nice day!' 'What splendid weather!' or some such thing. I know the story because this man was my last speaker. Something blade-sharp was in his fist. It turned out that, several days before the attack, the man had broken in half one of his tribe's CDs and hidden the jagged piece inside his shirt. The victim clutched his neck and collapsed, and the CD fragment fell to the floor, blood running from its shiny plastic surface.

If you can imagine teeming bugs exposed to daylight when the rock covering them is lifted, if you can imagine them scuttling off, that's what the Babel of languages is like here. The syntax, the tenses, the melody that only the gods can decipher and delight in – if on the five lines of a musical score you were to notate masculine and feminine, singular and plural, active and passive, low speech and honorifics, for each of the languages, you would have a majestic orchestral performance of the heptatonic scale of human vocal sounds: the velar, the lingual, the bilabial, the dental, the semi-dental, the nasal and the guttural. To these we must of course add intonation, gesture and facial expression. In the resulting chromatic chords, we can see that the gods detest tediousness and humans cannot tolerate sameness. I could offer endless examples but will settle for a few, all of them related to me by my neighbours among the spirits. One tribe has several dozen tones. When they sing, they sound like the exotic tropical bird with the shrivelled scarlet throat. How the resulting sounds, which to a stranger would simply sound guttural, can be expanded into tens of thousands of sentences is a mystery even to me. Another tribe has a tense for past life and a tense for reincarnated life. It's anyone's guess how these tenses were established. Another language includes a verb that conjugates in more than 150 ways. That one word is like a beam of light reflected and refracted by a prism. It reflects the sound and casts a rainbow onto the language's spirit. For another people, *love* is a conjunction and *neighbourliness* an adverb. But for other tribes, such qualities as love have no name tag; there is no word for them. For one tribe, a single syllable suffices for 'I miss you'; for another, a dozen sentences are necessary. And for one of the Arctic peoples, puffs of steam from the mouth can function as words.

Life goes on here, the speakers, their faces and their stories as various as the languages they speak. An illiterate old singer recites eons-old verses without skipping a line, as painstakingly as if her body were a Braille text of the saga. She's destined to disappear, just like the long, straight horns of the Arabian oryx, sought after because they're so beautiful.

One of the oldest men here was in his youth a porter for a group of foreign linguists. Across rivers and up through mountain canyons he packed their huge recorder. When from time to time he heard the voices of his people coming from the device, he realized his daily burden was something special. Back then scholars transported half a ton of aluminum disks to record the tribal sagas, and these were what the boy toted to the most remote areas in the backcountry. He had little inkling how quickly the words and songs would be lost. And how could he have ever anticipated that one day he would be on display as a living tape recording?

There once was a baby born in the complex, the first after the museum opened. The young parents belonged to different language groups. How could it have happened, considering the surveillance and control that characterized life in the complex? In their wisdom the older residents simply nodded; such was human nature, any day and everywhere. The delivery was smooth and we all cherished the new life, so soft and warm – how could we not, considering most of us were getting on in years? The Centre wished to observe the baby's development, and all considered it most likely that the baby would live with the parents as long as the Centre didn't impose massive restrictions. It would grow up under the care of at least one of the parents, and would learn the tribal language. But the young parents worried about the baby being left all alone in the museum after their deaths. They knew all too well the weight of the suffering their child would endure. And it wasn't only their baby – they thought no one should have to live like that. In the end they gave up the baby, leaving it, unbeknownst to others, in the vehicle of one of the Centre people. They wanted the baby to grow up with the Centre people, to be a person of the Centre. It agonized them to do this, but they believed their pain was nothing compared with the despair and loneliness the baby would face in the years to come if left alone in the museum.

And now, back to my speaker. So good at running in his youth, and afflicted with cancer of the larynx in his old age, he had been a brave young man who once escaped the museum. He came here at the age of fifteen. He'd been plied with alcohol by a stranger and fallen asleep, and he awoke to find himself in the museum. For several days he pleaded his case to anyone he saw, but no one was receptive, for no one understood his language. After several bouts of rage, resistance, imploring and discouragement, he soon adapted to life here. Needless to say, for the first several months he was listless and seemed a bit distracted. And then one day he jumped to his feet at the arrival of the tourists, and managed to surprise even himself by offering a jovial hello. Followed by a 'Nice to meet you' and 'What a great day!'

On his thirty-fifth birthday he found himself in the cafeteria spooning out the remainder of a can of fish. He had no idea what kind of fish it was, only that it bore the Centre's traditional seasoning and was artificially flavoured. He was nauseated by the smell – which reminded him of what he imagined to be the smell of flowers boiled in a pot – and in the beginning he wouldn't have touched it. But now he was sucking the oily fish juice from his fingers as he scanned the surroundings. He intended to leave the museum that night, it was a plan he had long harboured, and he carried out the escape calmly and carefully. Slipping out of the queue of residents filing back to the dormitories, he changed his clothes in the artificial bamboo grove, blended in with the tourists and blithely walked out. It was simpler than he had thought, no big deal, really. Crossing the border from a simulation of life to a real life was such a simple affair – why had it taken him so long to carry out? Relying on the few Centre words he had picked up, he started to navigate his way home. Following the stars, he ran, walked and ran some more. His heels were chapped and cracked and his toes bled, but he didn't care. Imagining a new life back home, he endured. Of course he couldn't be sure his people were still there. The Centre had designated him the sole surviving speaker of his tribal language, but what if that was only a stratagem? When he had left twenty years earlier, there had been six adults and three children. Perhaps in the meantime the village had grown to a respectable size. And yet he was dogged by an ominous feeling. He began to notice that the nearer he drew to home, the more ugly charred remains of trees he saw. On he walked, sustained by the thought that once he arrived, he would stay up the whole night chatting with the villagers. When he grew delusional from fatigue, he recalled the fruit with the oh so sweet and refreshing nectar that he had eaten growing up. When at last he arrived after his months-long ordeal, clearing a path across deep valleys and high ridges, there was only an endless, dust-swept plain. All the trees had been cut down, the trunks sticking out of the ground a ghastly reminder of what once had been.

He returned to the Museum of Moribund Languages as uneventfully as when he had escaped. The staff observed the beggar-like man with blank and yet knowing expressions. After some routine questions they issued him a few simple reminders and sent him off to scrub himself down with disinfectant in the shower. After taking medication from the medical team, he returned to his dormitory. For days he slept deeply, perspiring the whole time, his body feverish, occasionally calling out in his sleep. And when he awoke, he felt that something about him was different. Whenever he swallowed, he felt a foreign substance that left his throat sore; the pain extended to his ears. When he talked, he sounded like the static from a broken radio. Long years passed and when the transistor finally went dead, no further sound came from him.

In addition to the inner-ear inflammation, cancer of the larynx and dementia that afflict the speakers here, they suffer from a potent and lifelong nostalgia for and about words. The simplest, most harmless words, words they had taken in their stride when hearing them in the past, now sent them reeling. Someone might unwittingly blurt out 'heavenly peach' in his language and break down in tears; another might come out with 'palm tree' and feel heartbroken. Baby babble and gesturing will leave one man choked up, while 'spring green' or 'smooch' makes another man sigh. My speaker wanted to bid farewell to all those words and for a long time he kept his mouth shut. Even so, various fleeting thoughts managed to communicate with him, like a tacit assertion, or the decomposing corpse of a murder victim that floats to the surface after several days. For him the mother tongue was like the air he breathed, the thoughts he contemplated, it was imprinted in him; it wasn't something he could erase or stop simply by saying he didn't want to speak any more. And so he failed in his attempt to part from his language. But that didn't mean he reconciled himself to it. Day after day he felt lonely when he didn't speak and lonelier when he did speak. And so he spent most of his life longing for his language – a language two could speak and not just him alone, or why not three, or even five, that would be terrific, language boisterous and nonsensical, the words alluring, deceiving, joking, angering, soothing, criticizing, making excuses, pleading a cause. He wanted to have his way with me, free and easy. He wanted to linger among the patterned cascade of echoes generated when he spoke my name. That humble wish often left him with a heart-rending feeling. As he lay dying, he told himself he would never forget the wealth of words in his vocabulary for expressing sounds, describing tastes and depicting feelings. By then he was reduced to the bestial utterances I've mentioned, but I knew instantly that the name he was trying to call was mine.

I remember how he looked before he breathed his last – the shivering body and the face emitting mechanical sounds like a robot with feelings. As he continued to murmur and mutter, *oo-uh-uh* and *huh-uh-uh*, his face looked like a river of ice coming apart. Imagine a glacier that's existed for millions of years, steadfast and imperturbable, suddenly showing cracks and shedding ice. That's what his expression was like, serene and majestic, and although it was unfortunate, he seemed almost indifferent to what was happening. I felt I was witnessing something unnatural, a struggling downfall that would leave no reverberation in the outside world. And then he was gone, without having managed a complete sentence. When he closed his eyes, the world became shrouded in an inexplicable tranquillity – tranquil, at least, to me. At the same time, I felt a peculiar longing, an unexpected desire, which, it turned out, was to visit the place I was born.

I once heard of a planet too cold for even the gods to inhabit. That planet is ringed with concentric bands of echoes of the last dreams and final outcries of the people below. The wide, colourful bands are dyed with the patterned spirits of the tribal languages – we become yellow dust and ice chips after we die. Such are our superstitions and legends. How could I become cold as ice? It's strange to contemplate, but I am fine with the notion that I'll live on, somewhere. But I learned when I left my last speaker that there's a crucial problem with the story of that planet. Our final stop is not that planet where the cold freezes even the breath of the gods. Rather, our final resting place, after our speaker's death, is not the next world, is not the cosmos; it's a smelter, a place as hot as Hades.

Far away I see a few enormous spirits riding off on the wind, moving in a stubborn, one-way flow. On and on they flow, and suddenly they're being sucked into a huge funnel. The next moment they begin to vanish in a whirlwind, like iron filings collected by a magnet. I don't want to go there and I turn away, but the magnet is pulling me, and before long I'm looking down, captivated by the scene unfolding below. Beyond the low hills cradling the museum, roads radiate endlessly in all directions. Crammed among those roads are factories identical in size and shape. And surprise, the museum is right in the middle, nestled within the hills and the disk-shaped plot of land, and beyond stretch the interminable factories. For the first time, from this lofty vantage point, I see the lie of the land.

Who am I? And what's going to happen to me?

I was born in a drawing on a tree, a carving on a rock. My first name was Misunderstanding. But over time and by necessity people changed my name to Understanding. I liked my name, or whatever it might have been part of. I was a song of simple love couched in complicated syntax, singular and plural, origin and end, everything and nothing. I had my one day to live, and yet during that day I looked down on an entire life. I expanded and my name lengthened. It became so long that in the long flow of time no one could ever utter it in its entirety. But at this moment I realize that in another world it could be summarized in a single word. For some that word might be *energy*, for others *fuel* and still others might think of *natural resources*. I may have been what made this world go around, I may have been that which is worth dying for. As I'm sucked into this huge, mysterious funnel I recall my final dwelling, the Museum of Moribund Languages, and its prized fountain – the unique glass globe with the hologram of the free-floating letters and characters of the various tribal languages. The cheery dance of the spotlit letters continues until twelve noon, when the movement briefly freezes, the sphere opens up like a blossoming flower, and the words cascade down among the petals. I always thought it was beautiful. But now I see it's a nightmarish beauty. I see that the glass globe will not bring this pretty dream to an end any time soon, and as I repeat yet another cycle of death, I can't bring myself to look away.

I am indebted to Nicholas Evans's *Dying Words* for the references to the old saga-reciting woman and for information on recording devices – Kim Aeran.

Glossary

chirigami   old-style Japanese tissue.

chŏn   Korean monetary unit: 100 *chŏn* equal one *wŏn*.

chŏngjong   a traditional Korean rice brew, similar to sake.

chusa   informal title for a man.

hanbok   'Korean clothing': traditional attire, designed for ease of movement and consisting of an upper garment (*chŏgori*) for both men and women and either a full, wraparound skirt (*ch'ima*) for women or loose trousers (*paji*) for men.

Hangŭl   Korean alphabet.

hwat'u   'flower cards'; Korean card game.

hyŏng   designation for a male's older brother or a friend or colleague older than oneself; occasionally used among women.

kendo   Japanese martial art involving poles used as weapons.

kisaeng   'skilled student': a young woman of outcast status trained in the arts of singing, musical performance, dancing, poetry and occasionally martial arts and medicine; a companion for a *yangban* man.

koch'ujang   red pepper paste.

kwang   valued card in the game of *hwat'u*.

makkŏlli   rice brew.

mium   the *Hangŭl* letter ㅁ.

mudang   a practitioner, by definition female, of native Korean spirituality.

paduk   board game also known as *go*.

paech'u   Korean cabbage used for making kimchi; napa cabbage; bok choy cabbage.

pojagi   traditional Korean cloth wrapper.

p'ojang mach'a   a portable stall, originally drawn by a hand cart or horse cart and covered with a canopy, serving street food and alcoholic beverages.

pŏsŏn   traditional Korean quilted socks.

p'yŏng   unit of area for an indoor space, especially an apartment.

ramyŏn   instant noodles; ramen.

saektong   a clothing pattern of stripes of various colours, originally five in number, signifying happiness, good health and longevity.

saengwŏn   informal title for a man.

sarumada   Japanese underwear.

sŏdang   Korean traditional, private village school, open to boys aged seven to fourteen and offering initial training in the Chinese classics.

soju   distilled alcoholic beverage.

sŏllŏngt'ang   a soup of ox bone and brisket, seasoned with black pepper, red pepper, minced garlic and shallots.

sŏndal   informal title for a man.

sŏwŏn   a memorial hall in which distinguished scholars of the past are honoured in Buddhist ceremonies.

wŏn   Korean monetary unit.

yangban   elite literati class in Chosŏn society.

Notes

Tradition

CH'AE MANSHIK
A Man Called Hŭngbo

1 *southeast quadrant*: A reference to Korean geomancy (*p'ungsu*), according to which one's fortune may be influenced by considerations of topography and geographical direction. (See also Note 9 for 'The Old Hatter'.)

2 *The Romance of the Three Kingdoms*: One of the four great classical novels of Chinese literature, written down in the fourteenth century and attributed to Luo Guanzhong. It tells the epic story of warring factions from the end of the Han Dynasty to the unification of the Three Kingdoms.

YI MUNYŎL
The Old Hatter

1 *topknot*: During the Chosŏn period, *yangban* men grew their hair long, tied it into a topknot and wore a headband. They then wore a horsehair hat or crown over the headband. A *yangban* never undid his topknot even when he went to bed. In folklore, the topknot was also a phallic symbol.

2 *A horsehair hat was an emblem of adulthood and authority*: Horsehair hats were worn only by married *yangban* men. Unmarried men, commoners and slaves were treated as minors regardless of their age. A *yangban* took much greater care of his hat than the rest of his apparel.

3 *Zilu*: A disciple of Confucius and a man of absolute loyalty to his ideals. While being pursued, he stopped to straighten his apparel, as befitting a gentleman, and was killed on the spot.

4 *Three Han Kingdoms*: Tribal nations (Mahan, Chinhan, Pyŏnhan) that existed from several centuries BC to the first or second century AD. Here, a reference to the dawn of civilization on the Korean Peninsula.

5 *break our spirits*: Children of the same clan tended to be one another's playmates, and parents readily compensated for any damage their children caused while at play.

6 *headcloths*: Yangban women were supposed to stay indoors and not be seen by any male except the men of their family. If a *yangban* woman had to leave the house, she took utmost care to expose as little of herself as possible, wrapping herself in a cape-like headcloth.

7 *major families*: Each clan has one head family, descended in a line of first sons from the clan's founder. Besides the head family there are several major families, descended from the first sons of other prominent ancestors.

8 *ceramic stakes*: East Asian peoples believed in geomancy, the flow of auspicious force along invisible veins in the earth, according to which one had to carefully choose 'good' spots for constructing houses, shops and graves. Not only the Chinese but later the Japanese too drove ceramic or iron stakes into Korea's earth to 'cut' the veins of auspicious force, in the hope of preventing the birth of formidable national heroes.

9 *mortuary plank*: A plank with seven holes representing the Big Dipper, used by geomancers in selecting a propitious burial site for one's parents.

10 *Children paint each other's sleeping faces for fun*: A taboo based on the belief that a man's soul leaves him when he falls asleep and returns to him when he wakes up. Therefore, if someone painted a sleeping man's face, his soul could not return to him because it could not recognize its host.

11 *ordinance prohibiting topknots*: Decreed in 1895 by King Kojong in an attempt to alter the heavily Confucian frame of people's minds by eliminating this Confucian symbol of masculine dignity. A number of scholars responded by committing suicide rather than cutting off their topknot and thereby 'defacing one's body,' a cardinal impiety to

the parents who had given birth to the child and raised him with loving care.

12 *fire in the stove to heat the cold floor*: Traditional Korean houses have heating flues underneath the stone or cement floor, which carry heat from the ground-level stove.

Women and Men

PAK T' AEWŎN
A Day in the Life of Kubo the Novelist

Translator's note: I have made two major adjustments in translating Pak T'aewŏn's experimental novella into English. First, the writer uses a peculiar mixture of verb tenses: he habitually starts a paragraph in the past tense and then, as if staging a scene, narrates the rest in the present. Also, he tends to assign the past tense to external actions, while everything that is filtered through Kubo's perception is described in the present tense. Pak, however, is not consistent on these points. To avoid confusion in English, I have simplified the tenses in some parts. Second, the writer often uses a comma to split the subject from the predicate. In translation, these commas do not produce the same effects as in the original Korean. I have omitted most of the commas between subject and predicate, in some cases replacing them with other forms of punctuation, such as the dash.

1 *B*su: B stands for bromide and *su* is the Korean pronunciation of the Chinese character for water. The nurse's pronunciation reflects a Japanese accent.

2 *Hwashin*: Korea's first department store; opened in Seoul in 1931.

3 *Kyŏngsŏng Stadium*: Kyŏngsŏng, or Keijō in Japanese, was the name of Seoul during the colonial period.

4 *Taishō*: 'Great righteousness', the designation for the period 1912–26 in Japan, corresponding to the reign of the Japanese emperor known posthumously as the Taishō emperor.

5 *picture cards* (ttakchi): Cards used by children in a game called slap-match.

6 *Ishikawa Takuboku*: A Japanese poet (1886–1912) best known for reviving the traditional *tanka* form of poetry.

7 *Tzu Lu*: (542–480 BC) A well-known disciple of Confucius.

8 *Kong Jung*: (AD 153–208) A Confucian scholar and a minister of state during the Later Han Dynasty.

9 *old palace*: Tŏksu Palace, one of the major royal palaces of Chosŏn. Originally called Kyŏngun Palace, it acquired its present name in 1907 after King Kojong was forced to concede the throne. When the palace was opened to the public in 1933, a children's park was built inside the walls. The Taehan Gate is the front gate of the palace.

10 *modernology*: A neologism coined by Kon Wajirō (1888–1973), a renowned Japanese professor of architecture and a pioneer of cultural anthropology. Kon formed the term by combining the Chinese characters for 'modern' and 'archaeology' and used it to refer to a new discipline that would scientifically analyse contemporary social phenomena, especially changing trends in modern culture.

11 The Tale of Ch'unhyang: A classic Korean fictional narrative from the eighteenth century, a love story involving the crossing of class boundaries and featuring Ch'unhyang, daughter of a *kisaeng*, and Mongnyong, son of the local magistrate.

12 *Sŏhae's horse laugh* . . . Scarlet Flames: Ch'oe Sŏhae (born Ch'oe Haksong, 1901–1932), an iconic figure in Korean proletarian literature; author of 'Scarlet Flames' (Hongyŏm; trans. Jin-kyung Lee, 'Bloody Flames'), pp. 42–64 in Theodore Hughes, Jae-Yong Kim, Jin-kyung Lee and Sang-Kyung Lee (eds.), *Rat Fire: Korean Stories from the Japanese Empire* (Ithaca, NY: Cornell University East Asia Program, 2013).

13 *Schipa's 'Ahi Ahi Ahi'*: Tito Schipa (1888–1965), Italian tenor. 'Ahi Ahi Ahi' is an aria Falstaff sings in Verdi's opera *Falstaff*.

14 *ŭndan pillbox and Roto eyewash*: Popular Japanese goods. Ŭndan is the Korean term for a small, round, silver-coloured pill commonly used as a breath mint or digestive aid. Roto is a famous eyewash brand.

15 *Stendhal's* De l'amour . . . All Quiet on the Western Front . . . *Yoshiiya Nobuko, Akutagawa Ryunosuke*: *De l'amour* is an 1822 philosophical treatise on love by French writer Stendhal. *All Quiet on the Western*

Front is German author Erich Maria Remarque's 1929 novel set during the First World War. Akutagawa Ryunosuke (1892–1927) is regarded as the father of the Japanese short story. Yoshiiya Nobuko (1896–1973) was an author of Japanese fiction whose works on women's friendship and same-sex love, such as *Onna no yūjō* (*Friendship between Women*, 1933–34), were especially popular among women students.

16 A Love Parade: A 1929 musical-comedy film directed by Ernst Lubitsch and starring Maurice Chevalier and Jeannette MacDonald.

17 *Ginza*: Tokyo's most fashionable shopping and entertainment district.

18 '*Song of Sorrow*': 'Sushimga', a folk song originating in northwestern Korea, where, it is said, capable men were rarely tapped for positions in the Chosŏn bureaucracy.

19 *Tokkyŏn's* Tragic Melody of a Buddhist Temple *and Yun Paengnam's* Tale of a Great Robber: Tokkyŏn is the pen name of Ch'oe Sangdŏk (1901–70), a writer and journalist. *The Tragic Melody of a Buddhist Temple* (*Sŭngbang pi'gok*) was serialized in the *Chosŏn ilbo*, a daily newspaper, in 1927. Yun Paengnam (1888–1954) was a writer, playwright and film director. *Tale of a Great Robber* (*Taedojŏn*) was serialized in the *Tonga ilbo*, also a Seoul daily, in 1930–31.

20 *For some reason all the names end in* ko: Given names ending with *ko* are typical of Japanese women. This suggests that the Korean hostesses used Japanese nicknames in their work at the café.

HONG SŎKCHUNG
A chapter from Hwang Chini

1 *the funeral procession for young Ttobok*: Transporting the coffin to the gravesite is a crucial step among the preparations for burial. The leader of the funeral procession sings a mournful song, while family members, relatives and friends follow the bier. A gourd mask, the central accoutrement in traditional Korean mask dance (*t'alchum*), is regarded as a protective god and represents spiritual guidance for the deceased.

2 kimil *ritual*: A native Korean ritual, originating in P'yŏngan Province, in which a *mudang* channels the spirit of the deceased while guiding it from this world to the other world.

3 sashi *hour*: 'Watch of the snake'; in traditional chronological termin-
ology, the eleventh of the twenty-four hours, 9:30–10:30 a.m.
4 yudu: The fifteenth day of the sixth lunar month, traditionally celebrated
by bathing in a stream to wash away malign spirits and consuming
ginseng-chicken soup to fortify oneself against the summer heat.
5 *Seven Star deity*: In native Korean spirituality, the spirit associated
with the seven stars that constitute the Ursa Major constellation; this
spirit is thought to have agency over an individual's fate.

CH'ŎN UNYŎNG
Needlework

1 *Masan Man*: Masan is a city in South Kyŏngsang Province, on the
south coast of the Korean Peninsula, and presumably the home of the
man requesting a tattoo thus written.

Peace and War

CHO CHŎNGNAE
Land of Exile

1 *People's Volunteer Army:* Irregular forces consisting of those in North
Korean-occupied areas of South Korea who volunteered or were conscripted to support the regular North Korean People's Army during
the Korean War.

Hell Chosŏn

KIM SŬNGOK
Seoul: Winter 1964

1 *curfew:* During the Park Chung Hee regime (1961–79), when this story
takes place, the people of South Korea were subject to a curfew

extending from midnight to 4 a.m. The curfew, instituted by the US military government in the southern sector of the Korean Peninsula at the end of the Second World War, was subsequently maintained by the South Korean authorities and was not lifted until 4 January 1982.

O CHŎNGHŬI
Wayfarer

1 *Your seal, please!*: A person's name, engraved in stone or wood, was stamped on official documents.

Into the New World

JUNG YOUNG MOON
Home on the Range

1 The Heart Sutra: a Buddhist scripture. The translation is by the Buddhist Text Translation Society.

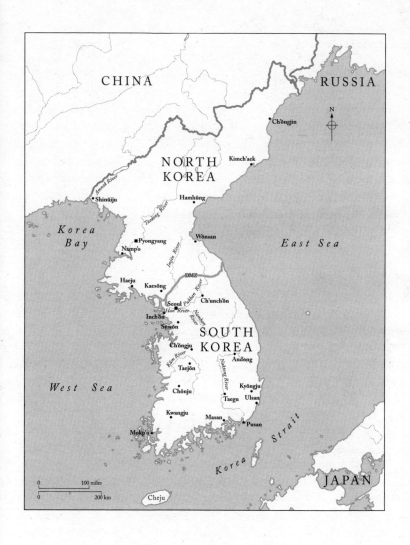

CHINA

RUSSIA

N

Chŏngjin

NORTH
KOREA

Kimch'aek

Amnak River

Shinŭiju

Hamhŭng

Korea
Bay

Taedong River

Wŏnsan

East Sea

Pyongyang

Imjin River

Namp'o

Haeju

Kaesŏng

DMZ

Pukhan River

Seoul

Ch'unch'ŏn

Inch'ŏn

Han River

Namhan River

Suwŏn

SOUTH
KOREA

Chŏngju

Kŭm River

Andong

Taejŏn

Nakdong River

Kyŏngju

West Sea

Chŏnju

Taegu

Ulsan

Kwangju

Masan

Mokp'o

Pusan

Korea Strait

0   100 miles

0   200 km

JAPAN

Cheju

Permissions

12. Pak Wansŏ, 'Winter Outing'. Text copyright © 박완서, courtesy of Wonsook Ho. First published in 배반의 여름 (2006). Translation copyright © Marshall R. Pihl. Previously published in *Land of Exile: Contemporary Korean Fiction*, trans. and ed. Marshall R. Pihl and Bruce & Ju-Chan Fulton. Armonk, NY: M. E. Sharpe, 1993; expanded edn, 2007.

13. Cho Chŏngnae, 'Land of Exile'. Text copyright © 조정래. First published in 유형의 땅 (1981). Translation copyright © Marshall R. Pihl. Previously published in *Land of Exile: Contemporary Korean Fiction*, trans. and ed. Marshall R. Pihl and Bruce & Ju-Chan Fulton. Armonk, NY: M. E. Sharpe, 1993; expanded edn, 2007.

14. Yi Sang, 'Wings'. Translation copyright © Kevin O'Rourke. Previously published as *Wings*, trans. Kevin O'Rourke, Bi-lingual Edition, Modern Korean Literature 091. Seoul: ASIA Publishers, 2015.

15. Kim Sŭngok, 'Seoul: Winter 1964'. Text copyright © 김승옥. First published in 서울, 1964 년 겨울 (1965). Translation copyright © Marshall R. Pihl. Previously published in *Listening to Korea: A Korean Anthology*, ed. Marshall R. Pihl. New York: Praeger, 1973. Published also in *Land of Exile: Contemporary Korean Fiction*, trans. and ed. Marshall R. Pihl and Bruce and Ju-Chan Fulton. Armonk, NY: M. E. Sharpe, 1993; expanded edn, 2007. Published also in *Modern Korean Fiction: An Anthology*, ed. Bruce Fulton and Youngmin Kwon. New York: Columbia University Press, 2005. Published also in *Reading Korea: 12 Contemporary Stories*. Manila: Anvil Publishing, 2008.

16. O Chŏnghŭi, 'Wayfarer.' Text copyright © 오정희, courtesy of Moonji Publishing Co., Ltd. Seoul, Korea. First published in 바람의 넋 (1986). Translation copyright © Bruce and Ju-Chan Fulton. Previously published in *Wayfarer: New Fiction by Korean Women*, ed. and trans. Bruce and Ju-Chan Fulton. Seattle: Women in Translation, 1997. Published also in *Modern Korean Fiction: An Anthology*, ed. Bruce Fulton and Youngmin Kwon. New York: Columbia University Press, 2005. Published also in *The Future of Silence: Fiction by Korean Women*, trans. and ed. Bruce and Ju-Chan Fulton. Brookline, MA: Zephyr Press, 2016.

published in *The Future of Silence: Fiction by Korean Women*, trans. and ed. Bruce and Ju-Chan Fulton. Brookline, MA: Zephyr Press, 2016.